# GATEWAY
## OF THE
# SAVIOURS

## A J DALTON

GOLLANCZ

LONDON

Copyright © A J Dalton 2013
*All rights reserved*

The right of A J Dalton to be identified as the author
of this work has been asserted by him in accordance
with the Copyright, Designs and Patents Act 1988.

First published in Great Britain in 2013 by Gollancz
An imprint of the Orion Publishing Group
Orion House, 5 Upper St Martin's Lane,
London WC2H 9EA
An Hachette UK Company

A CIP catalogue record for this book
is available from the British Library

ISBN 978 0 575 12317 5 (Cased)
ISBN 978 0 575 12318 2 (Trade Paperback)

1 3 5 7 9 10 8 6 4 2

Typeset at The Spartan Press Ltd,
Lymington, Hants

Printed in Great Britain by Clays Ltd,
St Ives plc

The Orion Publishing Group's policy is to use papers that
are natural, renewable and recyclable products and made
from wood grown in sustainable forests. The logging and
manufacturing processes are expected to conform to the
environmental regulations of the country of origin.

www.ajdalton.eu
www.orionbooks.co.uk

To Siouxsie, Mum, Dad, Chris, David, Galen,
Caspar, Lachlan and Katarina with love.

# Acknowledgements

With a salute to my vigilant reading group: Paul Leeming (stalwart), eagle-eyed Mike Ranson, the as-yet-unmet Sandi Wakefield, the commentating Becky Unicorn, the dragon-minded Phil Sharrock and the particular Beatriz Ogeia.

With thanks to Matt White, Nick White and Oliver Flude, for their unstinting and beery support.

Beware those who do not read fantasy,
for they must find their fantasy elsewhere.

## CHAPTER 1:

# The sixth time

D ust. As strong as the seals on his father's chambers were, the dust of the realm still found its way inside to cover everything. It was in the air, invisible but there, like so many things. It coated the inside of his throat and made his eyes run constantly. It was a permanent taste in the back of his mouth and he could feel it causing damage down in his lungs. When he moved, it caused irritation between his robes and his body, and sores at his joints. There was no escaping the dust, for it was pretty much all that was left of his realm. Certainly, there was still enough rock below ground to shelter his kind, the Declension, but the surface was a lifeless wasteland continuously scoured by the solar winds of their erratic and failing sun. Some said that there was less and less rock each year; as the dust storms blew, they exposed that which lay beneath and tore hungrily at it.

Some said that it was time for the Declension to leave their home-realm once and for all, before they were ground down to nothing along with the Geas of the realm. Another faction, led by his father, insisted that to abandon the Geas – that which had given the Declension life in time before remembering – would be to commit suicide as a people anyway. His father's faction was in no doubt that the Geas could be saved with the blood tribute supplied from all the lesser realms ruled by the Declension. This faction even claimed that, despite the failing sun, life could be restored to the surface once the volume of tribute became sufficient to both sustain the Geas and feed the ground properly. It was imperative, therefore, that the Declension continue to spread through the cosmos in search of new realms to conquer and from which to draw resource. To do otherwise, most believed, would be to see an end to their kind one way or another.

Ba'zel swept the dust from the smooth surfaces of his father's chambers for the sixth time that day and then used his limited magic to push the dust out through the seals. Why he bothered he was not entirely sure, for there would only be more dust to remove as soon as he had finished the current sweep. His father said the chambers would become uninhabitable if they were not constantly cleaned, but Ba'zel suspected his father actually just wanted to keep his *unstable* son occupied and out of trouble. After all, many other lines of the Declension used retainers for such menial labour. Besides that, the repetitive nature of the work also reminded Ba'zel of the sort of drill Mentor Ho'zen put him through each day in order to discipline his *unstable* mind and fitful magicks.

Those who were *unstable*, of course, were a threat to the future unity and common goal of the Declension. Such individuals were therefore confined and closely watched. All young were naturally *unstable* and most of the time kept within the chambers of their line, in part to protect them from less influential – and thus more desperate and predatory – elders of other lines. But an *unstable* youth would only be tolerated for so long, even within their own line. If they did not quickly show signs of developing some discipline, then all their blood and life energy would be fed back into the Geas, in the hope that they would be reborn with a greater willingness to mould themselves to the wider and long-term needs of the Declension. It was the only way their kind could survive, Ba'zel's father had explained . . . and had also begun to mention with increasing frequency of late.

Ba'zel knew he was running out of time. If his lessons with Mentor Ho'zen didn't soon start showing more success, then there wouldn't be any more lessons. There wouldn't be any more anything.

And his skin wasn't thickening and hardening the way it should, either. He was as pale and soft as one freshly reborn. Whenever he was permitted to come close to the realm's surface, even relatively diffuse light from above would sear him and cause him agony. Ba'zel's father had used the power and position of their line and faction to secure Ba'zel *extra* time in the realm's sun-metal chamber, to which some lines were not permitted access for generations at a time. Yet the privilege had only succeeded in partially blinding Ba'zel and covering his body in large, weeping blisters. The last time he'd been forced into the sun-metal chamber, he'd felt the blood boiling in his veins as if he were being cooked alive. He'd screamed for days after.

Time was running out. If he could not form the stone-like skin that was normal in his kind as they matured, then he'd be of no value to the Declension, either in the home-realm or any other realm. Now, whenever his father returned to their chambers, his eyes would only regard Ba'zel briefly before turning away. The very sight Ba'zel presented spoke of wrongness and being *unstable*. His father's disappointment and disgust were increasingly palpable. His father would mutter about how Ba'zel's mother had also been *unstable* – the only thing Ba'zel had ever heard mentioned about his mother – and would then question Mentor Ho'zen intently about how the lessons had gone that day. Then no more would be said until Ba'zel's father went from their chambers the next morning.

Yes, time was running out. The cleaning now forgotten, Ba'zel agitatedly paced backwards and forwards. It wasn't his fault his skin wouldn't harden. For all Mentor Ho'zen spoke of how mental discipline could overcome any pain, it wasn't Ba'zel's fault that both the sun's cursed light and sun-metal threatened to kill him, was it? He told himself he did all he could to master Mentor Ho'zen's impatient lessons. Yet what could he do? Would his father be proud of him if he meekly submitted to his blood and life energy being fed to the Geas? Or be even more ashamed? Or would he be just relieved, perhaps?

Feeling eyes on him, Ba'zel turned to look at the small and pathetic creature crouched in the cage in the corner of the room. It was from some lesser realm or other and served as a supply of blood and life energy for him and his father. When younger, Ba'zel had fancied that the chitterings and doleful eyes of the creature had denoted intelligence – a thought that had made Ba'zel more than a little queasy when drinking its blood at first – but his father had been adamant that the creature was nothing more than the lowest type of animal, and that Ba'zel should never think to do anything as stupid as naming it. It was *not* a pet. It was unworthy of affection of any sort.

'What should I do, creature?' Ba'zel asked.

The creature did not reply, of course; just continued staring vacantly at him.

Ba'zel reached out and lifted the latch, letting the door of the cage slowly swing open. The creature now always displayed the lassitude of one drained too many times over the years: the frenzy of its early days had long since disappeared. It could not pose any real danger. Its muscles were wasted and it seemed old and spent. All it had eaten for the length of its captivity was the thin and negligible waste he and his father produced – and that diet only seemed to have contributed further to the creature's gradual decline. The creature trembled and crammed itself into the far corner of its home.

'Yes, it is frightening, is it not? Are you worried you will get into trouble by leaving? Do you think I have opened the door so you can be drained for the second time today, perhaps for the last time in your life?'

Ba'zel sighed. 'Do you even understand I have offered you freedom? Perhaps you are right to fear freedom, creature. Beyond these chambers you would not last more than the blink of an eye. Perhaps it is safer to stay in your prison, then. Yet to remain can only mean a slow death for you. I do not know, but perhaps you have come to desire it, to be finally left alone.'

The creature whimpered plaintively.

'I know. Perhaps then there is no true freedom and therefore no escape. Only the choice of a slow or quick death. I understand why you would want to remain – so that you might cling on for as long as possible. Me, I think I would prefer it to be quick.'

Ba'zel hesitated. 'You see, the Mentor is late coming today. It is the first time that has happened. He has not sent me a thought saying he is ill or has been appropriated by a more influential line. I do not think he will come at all, creature. And I find I cannot even endure waiting for him, or waiting for my father to return. If I can get past the seals, I will leave, and allow the sun, some elder or the Geas to consume me. Goodbye, creature. I hope . . .' *What should one say at such a time, to such a primitive animal?* '. . . I hope you achieve the manner of death you most desire.'

So saying, Ba'zel shook the dust from his grey out-of-chamber robes and put them on. He also retrieved his ceremonial mask from where it

4

lay near the tomes of his line, since it might offer him some protection from the light. Moreover, given that the mask was usually worn by those wishing to conceal both the shame of their hunger and their identity when on their way to the feeding pools, it might encourage others to give him something of a wide berth. Small though he might be, his kind were at their most unpredictable and dangerous when desperate with hunger.

Ba'zel tried to calm his mind, trotting through the trope with which Mentor Ho'zen started every lesson. Now, what was the mental phrasing with which his father sealed and unsealed their chambers? Ba'zel knew its signature, but had never attempted to frame anything so complex himself. For an inexperienced or *unstable* practitioner of magic, there was considerable risk in attempting such a weave. If he could not keep the threads separate throughout, they might form a loop in which his mind was caught for the rest of eternity. He would become disconnected from his body but be trapped within it, fully aware but powerless to command it. Or he might spin the threads into an *unstable* pattern that would unravel just as he was passing out of the chamber. The damage done to him by the dust of this realm would be as nothing compared to a stone wall becoming solid right as he was in the middle of it. Or, then again, his father might have set deadly traps and triggers to snare anyone who attempted the seals except himself.

*Best not to think about it*, Ba'zel told himself. *Calm. Say the trope again. That's it. Calm.*

'You must act with confidence!' Mentor Ho'zen had always instructed him sternly. 'A weave begun with doubt and uncertainty will never be stable enough to succeed. Don't look at me like that, young Ba'zel! You know confidence is not some character trait – it is merely a behaviour to be learned and used with discipline. Discipline, leading to confidence, leading to a stable weave. Otherwise, the first weave you attempt in earnest will likely fail and that will be the end of you. Without discipline, there is only death. Are you confident, young Ba'zel?'

'Yes, Mentor Ho'zen!' Ba'zel always replied as confidently as he was able, but always with a slight hitch and tremor in his voice to betray him.

'You are the scion of a powerful line and must be proud of that. Our kind looks to you for leadership. It wishes you to be strong so that our people can be strong, so that we will succeed in every realm we touch, so that we will be *saved* as a people. You must become a Saviour. Anything else would be a betrayal of your kind. Now tell me again. Are you confident, young Ba'zel?'

He understood the words and ideas behind them, but as hard as he tried, he never quite seemed able to embody them. He wondered if there was a weave to help him with embodiment, but that was just circular daydreaming. Without the confidence to cast the weave, he would never be capable of the magic to capture the confidence he needed.

*Calm. A clear assertion of will. There is nothing to lose. If it goes wrong, that will be that and you'll never know any different. It will be a relief of sorts.*

His breathing stopped and his heart stilled. He was as still as the stone. He asserted his will so that his essence became contiguous with the barrier. Again he asserted himself, to create separation on the other side. His robes and mask snagged within the rock and he felt panic begin to well within. His heart was about to flutter back into life! *Calm, calm!* His every instinct screamed that he should try and force the material through, but he knew that would be to give in to the panic. *Calm, calm! Just stop! Become part of the stone again. Now ease into the separation once more. That's it, that's it. Calm.*

With a cry he fell into the corridor beyond his father's chambers, dust pluming up from the floor and temporarily blinding him. He coughed, his heart beating so hard that it felt as if it would punch its way out of him through his back. He felt broken inside, but he'd made it.

He'd made it! Perversely, he wondered if his father would be proud that Ba'zel had found the discipline to achieve such a weave. But no, any such pride would be as nothing compared to the outrage his father would feel upon learning that Ba'zel had, without permission, wilfully left their chambers. His father would be disgusted by such an act of disobedience, for it was yet further evidence of his son being so *unstable*. This act alone would warrant Ba'zel's immediate sacrifice to the Geas.

Was it too late to go back? He was trembling now, the weave having drained him. He was probably too weak to return to the chambers, as further attested by his sudden thirst and hunger. In any event, he could not bear the thought of becoming a caged and cowering creature once more, always waiting to be drained to the point of death. Besides, Mentor Ho'zen would not be coming again: there were no more lessons to be had back in the chambers, no more chances to show his discipline. And even if Ba'zel did return, his father would no doubt sense he'd tampered with the seals and exact immediate and final retribution.

He no longer had a home. Where to go? He couldn't think clearly though, so desperate was he for sustenance. Instinct told him he must seek out the feeding pools. He could almost smell and taste the blood from here, despite its distance. He salivated and had to wipe his chin.

He rearranged his robes, settled his mask back into place and strode quickly through the warren of corridors his people inhabited beneath their realm's surface. As he reached the main tunnels, he lifted his chin so that he would not display anything but confidence to an observer. So intent was he on reaching the pools, so fixated was he on feeding to renew himself, so concentrated was he on his purpose, he hardly had to feign any sort of confidence of will.

Suddenly, coming towards him out of the gloom was a large, prowling elder. The elder's nasal aperture widened, either in hunger or in order to identify this approaching stranger. Unable to control his response, Ba'zel found a growl issuing from his throat. Displaying such indiscipline in front of another was shameful, but it succeeded in startling the elder; and they passed each other holding close to opposing walls of the corridor. Fantasies of attacking the elder crowded Ba'zel's mind. It took some effort to dispel them: if he started giving in to such impulses, he wouldn't survive very long at all.

He'd only been to the feeding pools once before. When he'd been very young, his father had brought him before the members of his faction to be ritually anointed in the blood that fed the Geas of their realm and people. It had been a deliberate and public display, for his father was ever the politician, even within his own faction. But Ba'zel had ruined everything by slipping and falling into the deepest and thickest of the pools. He'd been at the point of drowning when his father, after considerable deliberation, had finally submitted himself to the indignity of diving in to save his son. The ancient robes of their line had of course been ruined, and rumours about Ba'zel being ill-omened had been whispered ever since. His father had never been able to forgive him. How could he?

The corridors of the warren all looked much the same, but Ba'zel had no trouble sensing the direction of the feeding pools. Both the blood and Geas called to him, promising him life from death. It was all he could do not to break into a run, but to do so would be to show such a loss of control that it could not be tolerated in the presence of others. He would be attacked en masse by every elder in the area, and torn apart so that not one scrap of him remained.

The closer he came to the pools, the more elders he sensed around him, some standing like statues, some secreted in the walls and others lurking in the shadows. Their thoughts hummed just beyond the range of his hearing and limited magic.

They would know him for one that was young. He sensed eyes turn towards him. Minds probed him. His nerves jangled – would they sense that too? He could not bear the scrutiny. They would find cracks in him and force them wide, exposing the soft and vulnerable flesh and being below.

He ground his jaws together in fear, praying the mask would hide the telltale reflex. The edges of his jaws crumbled and became dust in his mouth. Dust. Suddenly, he dragged his feet to make long trenches in the dust; and kicked the stuff up into the air. He turned his thoughts to dust and crouched lower. They were already coming for him, long limbs slashing through the air.

He kicked more and more up, tumbling to stay within the fog and away from the extended, scything forearms and legs. He kept his thoughts drifting and billowing and escaped into a small tunnel off the side of the main space. The larger elders would be unable to pursue him here unless they decided to use valuable energy coming through the stone. He stumbled further away, knowing that every stride he took would make him less and less worth the effort of a chase.

His body shaking with exhaustion, he went to hands and knees and crawled on. If he were to meet an oncoming elder now, it would all be over. Yet he sensed the tunnel led away from the feeding pools and up towards the surface, so it was likely to be little frequented. The deep drifts of dust certainly suggested it was rarely used.

Gasping, he allowed himself a moment's rest, sitting back against the parched and crumbling wall. It sucked at him, as if trying to leech the last of his life energy. He struggled to breathe, his body wheezing worse than it ever had before. He pulled the mask away, thinking that would help, but it only allowed more choking grit and heat to get at him. *So thirsty! Calm, calm. Just wait for those below to settle, then try for the pools again. Perhaps at night, when it will be quieter.*

But foreign thoughts of surprise, shock, betrayal and then outrage came seeking him out. His father had now discovered his absence from their chambers.

*Ba'zel!* thundered the thoughts. *Where are you? Yes, you hear me. What have you done? You will return here at once! I will not repeat myself.*

Ba'zel whimpered and cringed lower against the wall, putting his arms around his head, as if that might somehow keep his father's anger at bay.

*How dare you? You are no son of mine!*

Pain stabbed at Ba'zel's temples and he came close to passing out. *Calm*, he prayed. *Calm!*

There were long moments of terrible and threatening silence. If Ba'zel had had the will and energy to answer his father, he would not have known what to say. What could ever be said that would excuse the shame he was bringing on his father's line?

When his father's mind spoke again, it was with more control. He sounded conciliatory now, almost patient as he said, *Ba'zel, there is no need for this. It is not too late. Come, let us talk, you and I, before you are discovered by others. Like you, I am afraid. Afraid that the other lines will discover you are alone outside our chambers. Afraid that they will mean you harm, particularly the enemies of our faction. They will seek to use you against me. I am afraid that they will declare you* unstable *and a risk to our kind that can no longer be sustained. After all, what sort of young would be outside the chambers of their line without escort? Come to me quickly then, before you are discovered, and we will talk.*

He almost believed his father, so desperately wanted to believe him. Imagined talking together as if they were both elders. But Ba'zel was no elder. He was an *unstable* son who was unworthy of any exchange of words each night his father returned to their chambers. No, he was less than that – for had his father not just said Ba'zel was no son of his? He was . . . the creature in the corner. Less than a pet. He was unworthy of affection of any sort. He could believe his father was afraid for himself, afraid for his position and faction, perhaps even afraid for his people. Beyond that, however, Ba'zel knew his father lied. If he were able to return to his father's chambers, there would be no conversation. Just as there would be no more lessons, there would be no more talk, and no more mercy.

*Will you defy me then by not answering?* his father whispered in disbelief, anger beginning to tinge his words once more. *Truly you are beyond help. Any discipline you may once have displayed has either completely foundered or has always been the sort of mimicry mere animals adopt. How dare you risk my line like this? I knew I should have let you drown all that time ago. As it is, I must now suffer the shame of putting out a clarion call to all our kind about your escape. I must beg them to kill you on sight. Were I not to do so, and it were discovered I knowingly put our entire kind at risk with one so* unstable, *then my life would also be forfeit.* A moment's hesitation. *So be it.*

And the call went out, first as a keening whirl of thought, and then, as it was taken up by others, as the howl of a hunt. Ba'zel pushed himself away from the wall and frantically scrambled up the small tunnel. They would not hesitate to come for him through the stone, now that he'd been declared a threat to all his kind. How long did he have left? Seconds?

There was no hope of ever getting close to the feeding pools, but he furiously focused his mind on the place so as to mislead those searching for him. The tunnel began to narrow as he forged up and he feared he would become stuck, but the walls were becoming softer, reluctantly allowing him to keep moving forward. The soft edge would make separation for those coming through the stone more difficult. He deliberately kicked dust up into the tunnel behind him – not that it required much effort in the desiccated surroundings of this realm.

Panting and coughing hard, he kept his head down and pushed on. The top of his head and his hands began to burn and he knew he must be close. He could not see anything but a blinding whiteness. He pulled the hood of his robe over his head and wrapped his hands in its voluminous sleeves. It helped a little, but he could feel his skin start to bubble and crack. He gagged as he smelt the sweet iron of charring flesh and burning blood.

With a final surge, he pushed through an avalanche of sliding sand and suffocating dust and out onto the barren surface of the realm. He knew better than to open his eyes immediately, having come close to being blinded permanently by the realm's cruel and ancient sun on a number of occasions. Winds tore at his robes, seeking to pull back the material and sacrifice him to the angry and ailing eye of the heavens. Ba'zel wrapped himself as tightly as he could and tottered away from where he had emerged.

He was fortunate that he seemed to have come out into the tail end of a storm, for its energies would make him hard to follow for a while. On the other hand, it kept him deaf to pursuit and disorientated when it came to direction. And he needed to find his way off the surface as soon as possible, for he would not be able to survive here for more than a handful of minutes. His entire skin felt aflame and the agony was only increasing. How long before he passed out or lost all feeling and sense of self?

His lungs felt like they were shrivelling up, all the moisture drawn out of them. He staggered in the direction of the storm, casting his mind out as far as he could. Eddies and currents burned across his internal vision. He stumbled on the shifting, sinking surface, barely keeping his feet. A hacking cough racked his body and there was blood at the back of his throat. Shadows loomed through his mind now, filling him with darkness. Was he entering the void already?

He risked opening his eyes a crack and fancied he could see dark shapes among the swirling dust devils. He sloughed closer, all but at the end of his strength.

*Sifters, hear me!* he begged. *I have nothing to offer you but the last of my life.*

The narrow besailed giants stood with long limbs rooted deep in the surface. Every so often a leg would ponderously rise and anchor itself elsewhere, as a sifter repositioned itself with the changing wind. Ridged and textured flares of skin stretched between their thin bodies and upper limbs. The skin gently glowed as it absorbed particles of energy from the storm and filtered any remaining sustenance from the fine dust of the air. The sifters always travelled in the wake of the storms, feeding as best they could.

Some said that the sifters had once been close cousins of the

Declension, but had chosen to adapt themselves to the realm's surface rather than hide below. Others said the strange and unsightly creatures could never have been related to the Declension and must have been a lesser race, cast off by the unknowable Chi'a in the time before remembering, when the Chi'a had apparently passed through this realm – as they had so many other realms – on their Great Voyage. Still others claimed that the sifters were a simple indigenous life form of this realm, of extremely limited intelligence and entirely reactive, just like the plant-forms of other realms. What all agreed on, however, was that the sifters were completely harmless and possessing of so little life energy of their own that it was not worth the effort of bleeding or consuming them.

To Ba'zel, who had nowhere left to go and no other hope, the sifters were worth his every last effort. He slumped to his knees, which quickly began to become buried. He would be pulled down or covered over soon, for he did not have it within him to rise again. This would be his dusty grave. As the last of the energy and moisture was whisked from him, the dry husk of his body would begin to collapse. It would be blown to the winds in the next storm and the last of his essence would be sifted from the air by the silent giants. He would be nothing but a few motes of dust lost in the endless storm.

*The last of my life is yours to do with as you will. Command or use it as you wish. Or spurn it if it is of no worth to you. I am sorry. I have and am nothing else. Should you be able to, tell Mentor Ho'zen and my father that I tried my best and that I am sorry for their shame. I did not wish to be so* unstable. *I wish it could have been otherwise.* He smiled grimly. *For see where being* unstable *has brought me. See what it has won me. See what it will make of me. See how I am nothing but dust.*

The final eddies, currents and patterns of energy faded from before his mind's eye. He could feel nothing but a sort of weightlessness. Frenziedly, he tried to find his body and its pain, but there was nothing there. He couldn't even hear the storm. Or taste the sapping heat or the blood from the ruptures and lesions inside him. Or smell anything of substance. Here it was, then. A last few moments of floating. Or a disembodied floating forever.

*We will command, use and spurn you then!* came the whisper.

'What?' he croaked. 'Who are you?'

*We have taken you up in the fold of our wings. You will be protected for a while, perhaps replenished. We will take you to the Gate.*

'The Gate? Why? What would you have of me?'

*You agree to being commanded, used and spurned by us?*

'Yes.'

*Then leave this place.*

He felt fear. 'Can I not stay here with you?'

There was a pause. *No.*

'But . . .' But what? He had no right to ask anything of them. No right to ask anything of anyone. No right to ask anything of any realm, or of the cosmos. No right to existence. 'You would not have me become dust?'

*One day. One day you will become dust and return to us. All the cosmos comes to us as dust eventually. In this way, we know of realms in the furthest reaches of the cosmos. It is inevitable that you will return to us.*

'But you have spared me from that now, in your mercy. Why?'

*So that you may leave this place and find the other realms of the Declension.*

'You want that?'

*Yes and no. It grieves us. Look at what has become of we sifters – as you call us – and our realm, because of the Declension. You will see what is being done to other realms by them. This end may be inevitable, we do not know. It is enough for us that the Declension reject you – because of that we shall spare you, for now, and allow you moments in other realms.*

'What purpose will I have to give me discipline and meaning there? I must have discipline and meaning or the existence will be terrible beyond enduring. I would rather be dust.'

*You must find discipline and meaning in enduring, then, as we do. You must search for new purpose even if you cannot discover it before becoming dust. It is all we know and can tell you. But we are here now. We command you to leave and to remember your promise to us.*

Ba'zel was gently lowered back to the ground before he could even ask exactly what it was he had promised. He shielded his eyes as he watched the sifter lever itself away. Although its movements were slow and measured, it was soon lost in the white and grey storm once more. Ba'zel's skin began to pain him again and he knew he had to get moving. He'd been brought to a slope where the ground was firmer than elsewhere. There had to be rock just below. He ascended the slope and looked into the gaping mouth of a wide tunnel. He wasted no time hurrying down, out of the light.

He did not know this entrance but sensed great energies at play not far away. He navigated his way through long well-maintained corridors, peering anxiously in all directions at intersections, expecting to see the flicker of rapid movement at any moment; but all remained deserted. It was through these corridors that the lesser races were marched from the Gate of the Waking Dream to the place of bloodletting at the feeding pools. For their own protection, these races were kept under close guard at all times, and lurking elders were regularly swept from the corridors. That meant that even if his people had now established where he was, they would have to come some distance before he was in sight. For the first time since leaving his father's chambers, he genuinely began to believe there might be some chance of escape.

With a measure of renewed energy, he ran for the Gate's chamber. Although he possibly had a good lead, the elders could move with frightening speed, and some possessed arcane magicks far beyond his understanding. Mentor Ho'zen had made mention several times of great magicks that could potentially alter space and time. What if Ba'zel's pursuers were to slow time down so much in this corridor that he never reached the chamber? He prayed such a spell would require more preparation and energy than was immediately available to those coming after him. Yes, he sensed them now! They'd entered the corridors and were swarming after him in massive numbers.

Panicking now, he flew round the next corner and saw the doors to the chamber ahead. As he raced forward, an enormous guard stepped out of the shadows of an alcove to the side of the doors and levelled a trident of rarest sun-metal at him. The glare of the weapon hurt Ba'zel's eyes as much as the sun itself, and he slid to a halt with a cry of shock and pain. The guard was an elder of prodigious size. The scars criss-crossing his hard skull marked him as one of the most experienced of the warrior lines. There would be no defeating or eluding him.

'So small?' the elder observed with a mixture of disgust and amusement. He sniffed. 'Young, too. I would not usually deign to notice one such as you, let alone do you the honour of raising my weapon. I can only wonder at the oddity of your being able to cause so much trouble and disorder. There is no power of significance within you, so what lack is there in our kind that has allowed you to come so far? Has your instability somehow already affected us? Surely it is not some sort of infection that has weakened us?'

Ba'zel's mouth had never felt so dry. 'I-I . . .'

'See how you waver,' the warrior sneered. 'There is no confidence of will about you, no discipline of being. You are not even worthy to sully the points of this trident. You should be dispatched like the lowest animal, and never fed back into the Geas. Your existence cannot be permitted an instant longer!'

The elder took a deliberate step forward, the movement breaking the spell of paralysis in which Ba'zel had been caught. Words tumbled from his lips so quickly that they had barely formed in his mind before he spoke them out loud. 'The Eldest sent me! *She* bids you stand aside and allow me entrance to the chamber. Further, you are to render me whatever assistance I might require, even falling on your own weapon should I command it. But I will not command that, for you are un-worthy of such mercy. Instead, you will guard these doors against those coming on behind me, do you understand?' He finished with a gasp, hardly believing what he had said. None would dare mention the Eldest, let alone invoke *her* authority, lest they wanted to attract that unforgiving and eternal being's attention.

The guard growled but had no choice but to fall back. Even if he suspected Ba'zel of lying, failure to obey instantly the very idea of the Eldest's authority was enough to warrant death. It would be for the Eldest – not a mere guard – to punish any using *her* name in vain. And the punishment would be more terrible than could be imagined. There were various stories of members of the Declension immediately committing suicide upon fearing they had used the Eldest's name inappropriately – death was preferable to the alternative, and if their bodies were then fed to the Geas they would be reborn with wiser wills and tongues.

The guard's eyes were impossibly wide as Ba'zel came forward. 'Surely you are insane. Your mind is gone rabid. Your line must have mixed with another race, for you are not of the Declension,' the elder hissed. Yet he opened the doors and let Ba'zel pass.

There was a *boom* as the doors closed behind Ba'zel and he was sealed inside the chamber. His eyes went straight to the shimmering portal atop the dais in the middle of the wide circular space. The light coming from the Gate of the Waking Dream was the first Ba'zel had seen of the other linked realms of the Geas. Watchers both in the home-realm and the other realms held the Gate always open by keeping the same shared images of place in their minds. It seemed that just as thoughts could be shared between realms, so the realms could be materially connected. Mentor Ho'zen had spoken about the different realms actually being different levels of existence and consciousness – the Declension naturally being the highest, with their superior magic and elevated consciousness – but Ba'zel had only been able to follow the explanation in a general sense. He'd understood that it was only right a tribute of life energy was drawn from the Geas of every other realm in order to feed the Geas of the Declension's home-realm. The faction of Ba'zel's father claimed that, since all the Geas across the realms were linked, the potential fall of the Geas of the home-realm represented the potential collapse of all the other realms as well, the end of all life!

The lesser races were fortunate, then, the Mentor had carefully elucidated, that the Declension had discovered the means to travel between the realms and to sustain the Geas of their own realm. The Declension were indeed the Saviours of every realm. They were the intellectual and spiritual leaders of the known cosmos. They were light and hope in what would otherwise be just an empty and eternal void.

And of all the races in the realms of the Geas, it was only the Declension who could steer the realms towards the truly divine and eternal, who could lead others on the Great Voyage. For was it not the Watchers of the Declension who had first searched the cosmos with their minds for trace of the ancient Chi'a who had gone before them? Was it not these selfsame Watchers who had finally sensed and shared in ancient memories of the Chi'a elsewhere in the cosmos? Had they not thereby discovered other realms of the cosmos through which the Chi'a had passed on their own Great Voyage before travelling beyond? Had those Watchers not then influenced the dreams of, and whispered new ideas into, the minds of the races of those other realms, until the same thoughts and images were synchronised and shared between the realms and material travel between them was possible? Indeed, was it not the Watchers of the Declension who, with each new realm occupied, were able to probe further into the cosmos and deeper into the shared consciousness, in order to discover yet more realms and levels of existence? Yes, it was the Watchers of the Declension who would ultimately lead them all to divinity and eternity.

The Gate of the Waking Dream was therefore a holy place of sorts to Ba'zel's kind. He went to his knees, so awed was he by its beauty and meaning. Although it was radiant, it did not hurt his eyes like most other light did. He saw images from different realms drifting and twisting before him. Perhaps they were more than images, for they looked entirely real, if extremely distant. He didn't understand much of what he saw, and that only served to overwhelm him more. He had never seen such vibrant colours. The Gate made his own realm seem muted and drab by comparison. *He* felt muted and drab, utterly inadequate before it. How could he presume to approach such wonder? He would only begrime it, cover it with dust.

A figure slowly came around the Gate and placed itself between Ba'zel and the portal.

'F-Father! You h-have found me!' He would have grovelled and writhed on the floor in an abject display, but his father's glittering black eyes held him in place.

His father's voice was like stone cracking. 'Did you think I would not know the mind of the least of my line? How is it you have not ended this already, you wretch? Are you so *unstable* that you are utterly insensible to the horror of what you are? Quickly, end this before others come and I am further shamed! Or must I lower myself further still by doing it for you?'

Something told Ba'zel not to reveal that the sifters had told him to leave the realm. 'Father, the Declension say I am no part of them. Can I not just go elsewhere, disavowing any claims to line, name, race or realm? I will be a different race of my own, a lesser race if you will. I will work in the deepest mine in some other realm. Can the Declension not simply forget I exist? Can they not just leave me be?'

'Fool!' his father replied with an impatient stamp. 'You will always be a part of the Geas of this realm. The Geas is old and occasionally sick. The creation of those who are *unstable* like you is but a symptom of its illness. Left unchecked, those symptoms can become devastating in their own right. You must be destroyed! Even were you to attempt the

Gate to travel elsewhere, you would not have the strength and discipline of mind and magic to survive it. And were you to survive, the Declension would have no choice but to send one of the . . .' and here his voice unconsciously dropped to a whisper as he pronounced the word '. . . Virtues after you. Better you kill yourself here and now. Do so at once! I insist!'

'Father, spare me! Please!'

'You have the temerity to ask yet more of me? You are despicable and shameless in every way. I see I must end you myself!'

His father bared his stone fangs and raised clawed hands. Ba'zel responded with a snarl and a yell and leapt forward. His father had not expected this of his son, just as no elder would expect it of a younger one. It could only be a futile gesture, after all, and none of the Declension would ever indulge themselves in such a waste of time and energy. So why would Ba'zel attack? What could it mean? Was there something the elder still did not know about his *unstable* son?

Ba'zel's father swayed back in momentary confusion, then he blinked. Of course. The futile attack was precisely the sort of non-sensical behaviour one might expect of the *unstable*. With a roar he lunged forward again, with deadly eviscerating intent.

But the moment's hesitation proved enough. It decided whether Ba'zel would live or die. Landing just short of his oncoming father, Ba'zel dropped through the stone floor. As his father flew over the top of him, Ba'zel swooped back up into the chamber behind and past his father. Ba'zel leapt for the Gate.

'Son! I beg you!' his father shouted in appeal.

Never had he heard his father's voice break so. Never had he heard him use such words. Ba'zel hesitated and looked back round at his parent.

'Kill yourself! Please!'

And Ba'zel stepped into the Gate and the maelstrom of the cosmos.

Mentor Ho'zen fidgeted as he sat in the chambers and presence of Elder Starus, the head of the Faction of Departure. The scrutiny of one so large was of course terrifying, but the blood lamps that burned around the chamber also made it difficult for the Mentor to control himself. The lamps were an outrageous display of wealth and power, of course, for every other member of the Declension – save perhaps the Eldest herself – made do with lamps of tallow rendered from the bodies of those fed to the Geas, or lamps of the black oil from decomposing bodies. But Elder Starus was no fool – he also knew that the cloying heady scent of burning blood and the frisson of life energy released into the air kept most of those with whom he dealt completely distracted and at a disadvantage. Despite his best efforts, Mentor Ho'zen's nasal aperture flared hungrily and he shamed himself.

Elder Starus smiled knowingly. 'I heard Elder Faal's pathetic call about his *unstable* son having fled his chambers. All went as we intended, I take it?'

Mentor Ho'zen smiled weakly and whined, 'Yes, Great One. Ba'zel escaped entirely on his own. There is nothing to suggest any other parties were involved. Elder Faal may ask why I was not with his son for lessons that day but I will simply inform him I was ill. He will not suspect me. He has always believed Ba'zel actually was *unstable*. I made sure of that.'

The elder nodded. 'And Ba'zel is dead?'

The Mentor hesitated. 'No, but he went through the Gate. Surely one of the Virtues will be sent after him.'

'Hmm. He is worse than dead then. Faal is shamed and the influence of his faction must become diminished. If we are fortunate, he will become distracted with grief, although I suspect he is not so weak. I wonder if there is a way, however, that we can start a rumour that he is properly grief-stricken yet hiding it. If so, we might see him entirely dropped by his faction. Wouldn't that be something! Perhaps if we point out he seems to have been keeping to his chambers much more of late . . . I will give it some thought. In the meantime, Mentor, I am well pleased.'

So saying, the elder waved forward a retainer who had been waiting with two goblets from a tray. The elder took one goblet and then gestured for the other to be taken to the Mentor.

The Mentor gave the unworthy retainer but a passing glance and eagerly took the proffered blood, for his nasal aperture had already caught an exotic and intoxicating scent from the goblet. Yet he caught himself and sensibly waited for the other to drink first. Elder Starus was apparently in no mood to rush, and so the Mentor was forced to wait in agony as the other first shifted his bulk so that he was more comfortable and then chose to speak expansively. 'I saw you notice my new retainer, Mentor. It has of course had its ears put out and its tongue removed. It represents a lesser race from the fifth realm, you know. I have been promised that it will last longer than the races of the other realms, which is just as well, for the blood of its race isn't much to savour. Retainers just don't seem to last as long as they used to. It's quite an inconvenience.'

Mentor Ho'zen made a polite desperate noise.

'Now, this blood,' the elder continued, 'is from the *sixth* realm. It is quite a rarity, for the race that donated it seems particularly short-lived when coming into our proximity. Apparently, there is a great problem with supply, even for the Saviours in that realm. But I am assured it is worth all the effort of collection.' The elder sipped at his goblet experimentally and pulled a face. 'Not as fresh as it could be.' He put the goblet aside. 'But tell me what you think of it, Mentor. I'd be interested in the opinion of one as learned as yourself.'

Mentor Ho'zen wasted no time in finally trying the blood. It was so imbued with life energy that he found it utterly addictive. He guzzled it and could not lower the goblet until he'd completely drained it. Immediately, he was giddy. He burped and grinned apologetically. 'Potent, Great One, quite potent. Indeed, that is my most potent opinion.' He giggled. 'My most *learned* opinion, I should shay . . . say!' Light-headed and suddenly brave, he blurted, 'And it ish alsho my learned opinion, Great One, that we should now shpeak of the poshition of influence within your faction that I wash promished.'

'Indeed?' the elder responded mildly. 'You would presume to make demands of me within my own chambers then?'

'Cshertainly not, Great One!' the Mentor slurred. 'But I cshertainly think it'sh time we dishcussed the poshition.'

'That is demand enough.' Elder Starus sighed. 'Very well, you may approach and receive the mark of my line.'

Mentor Ho'zen rose to swaying feet, stumbled forward and then knelt. Elder Starus extended his huge hand, placed it on the Mentor's head and then squeezed until the learned skull broke open.

'Ahhh. Now this is far fresher. Forgive me, Mentor, but I have always found the blood of our own kind more to my taste. Even in death, you serve your new faction well, for now it is certain that there is nothing linking Ba'zel's escape to us. I will see to it that you are properly fed to the Geas and prayers are said so that you will be reborn into the position of influence that was promised you.'

# CHAPTER 2:

# And a bad hunter

In his dreams Jillan was always happy. Or at least he always started out as happy. He would find himself waking in his parents' small house, his mother already moving around in the main room as she prepared bread and honey for his breakfast, a small fire dancing in the hearth. He would splash cold water on his face from the ewer and bowl in his room, dress, choose one of the lucky stones from his collection to put in the pocket of his trews and then come out to the heavy oak table where they had their meals as a family.

His mother Maria would always smile and ask him how he had slept and about his dreams. She would listen carefully, even if the dreams sounded silly when described out loud. Jillan would tell her that he often dreamed about waking up in his room and then coming out to the main room to have precisely this sort of conversation. Jed, his father, would laugh and shake his head, until Maria frowned at her husband and told him not to make light of things he did not properly understand. Jed would school his expression and nod repentantly until Maria turned round to attend to the bread toasting on the hearth, at which point Jed would wink conspiratorially at his son, poke his tongue out at his wife and make Jillan giggle. Maria would whirl back round, a scowl of amused fury on her face, and declare that men were the bane of any good woman's life and that she would be keeping all the breakfast for herself. Then a loud argument would start, in which Jed complained of a broken heart and Maria's cruelty, Jillan would declare all innocence and blame his father for getting them into trouble, and

Maria would bewail her generous nature that made her forgiving of two such devils.

At last they would sit to have breakfast and they would anticipate the day ahead. It was then that the dream would always begin to change, for Jillan's stomach would pain him and he'd ask to stay at home rather than go to the school he dreaded so much. Jed would ask if Jillan was scared of going to school; whether he was being bullied by Haal, Elder Corin's son.

'N-No!' Jillan would protest. 'He's just an idiot! I'm not scared of him.'

'Then what is it? You know you can tell us anything.'

Jillan shifted uncomfortably. He glanced at his mother for help, but she only watched him with a mix of apprehension and curiosity. Finally, he blurted, 'Minister Praxis hates me! He always picks on me! And I haven't done anything wrong, not really! But don't say anything, pleeease, because that'll only make things worse.'

There was a terrible anger in his father's eyes, a dangerous anger. 'I knew that snake couldn't be trusted to leave well enough alone!'

'Jillan!' Maria snapped, demanding his attention. 'Get your things and go! I need to talk to your father. Don't worry: all will be well!' Her eyes then blazed as she turned on his father.

But Jillan didn't want to go. The Minister was out there. The arguments and detention. Coming home late and being attacked. Lashing out. Poor Karl. It had been an accident! Becoming a fugitive who was hunted by Heroes, the Saint and the strange creature who might be a Saviour. And then the terrible, terrible thing that happened to his parents, the thing he refused to think about, he refused to believe, the thing he told himself was just a bad dream.

It was all out there, just beyond the door to their small home. Waiting and hungry . . . trying to get in.

There was a heavy and demanding knock on the front door and Jillan gasped. 'No! Don't let them in!'

It was the Minister and the elders coming for Karl's killer, to torture the Chaos out of Jillan. It was Heroes coming for his parents. It was the townsfolk of Godsend come to tear them apart. It was the whole Empire trying to force its way in so that they might be saved from themselves. It was the blessed Saviours coming to exorcise their souls.

'Who's there?' Jed would begin to reach for the latch, too far away for Jillan to stop him in time.

Heart pounding and blood roaring in his ears, Jillan would flee to his parents' room and the small window there, but he knew there were things crouched in the darkness just beyond the frame. His mother screamed . . .

And Jillan sat bolt upright in his bed, suddenly awake. He wiped a shaking hand across his sweaty forehead. The vest in which he'd slept was soaked. He blinked and, as he did most mornings, worked to shake off the lingering terror of his dreams. He blanked his mind as best he could, shutting out the haunting impressions.

*How long can you keep this up for?* whispered the taint, whose voice had started to become stronger of late.

Exhausted, he crawled from his bed and splashed cold water on his face from the ewer and bowl in his room. Then he rinsed himself down. He began to shiver and his teeth rattled in the cool temperature of the dawn.

*Small price to pay to be free of such dreams and to be sure you're out and about before everyone else, eh? Can't stand their stares and whispering, can you?*

He didn't have the energy to argue. Hurriedly, he dressed and chose a red stone from his collection to put in one of his pockets. He fancied that it warmed his hands slightly, and he felt a little better. Just as his father had always done, every time he came home without having successfully hunted anything, he brought a new stone for the collection instead. The collection was becoming quite large now, for there seemed to be a scarcity of game about, even given that spring was only just beginning to arrive.

*You're just a bad hunter, is more like it,* the taint admonished. *That's what most of them think, you know. The other hunters manage well enough, which is just as well with all these extra mouths about, eh?*

When Jillan had overcome the mad Saint Azual, the army of Heroes that had descended on Godsend had lost all momentum. Weapons hanging loose in their hands, soldiers had stood stupidly looking upon the world as if for the first time, or as if waking from a bad dream. They had been freed but had nowhere to go. The majority had therefore remained in Godsend and helped to rebuild the fortified town. Yet they represented a size of population which the town's food stores could ill sustain.

*Taking on a Saint is one thing, but once all the dust settles what real use is your magic if it can't even catch you a couple of rabbits, eh? Still, maybe the rabbits are just smarter than you.*

'I probably just need a bit more luck is all,' Jillan said to himself, sweeping the entire stone collection into his pockets.

Gold gleamed at him from the dark corner of the room where he'd abandoned his rune-inscribed leather armour after the battle with the Saint. He retrieved it now and buckled it on, still amazed at how little it weighed him down. If anything, it made him feel lighter.

Now feeling ready to leave his room, he stepped into the kitchen. The hearth was cold. Neither was there anyone preparing breakfast for him. But Samnir slept soundlessly – almost like one of the dead – in Jed's armchair. The soldier had apparently come home long after Jillan had turned in for the night, gnawed on some of the hard bread and cheese Jillan had left out for him and then fallen asleep where he sat, without even removing his sword belt or boots. The old man's skin looked grey and there were deep hollows around his eyes – he was working too hard training the men, settling disputes and dealing with all the trivial details involved in commanding a large standing force. Jillan hardly ever saw his friend any more – awake, at any rate.

*The least you could do is catch a decent bit of meat for him, so he can keep his strength up. Thinking about it, you could do with putting a bit on those bones of yours too. Get too scrawny and Hella's eyes might start drifting towards those who cut a finer and more manly figure, someone like Haal perhaps?*

Jillan ignored the taint and managed to put its voice out of his mind for a while. He knew that in its own perverse and roundabout fashion it sought to look out for him, but all too often it seemed to want to goad or provoke him with half-truths and suspicions, so that he might give it a measure of free rein over both himself and his magic. He feared that if he let it have too much leeway, he'd never be able to wrestle it back.

He was tempted to wake Samnir. It would be good to tell him about his dreams. But the old soldier got too little sleep as it was, and he wouldn't want to listen to a boy's silly dreams anyway. Not for the first time Jillan sighed over the fact that Aspin had had to return to the mountains with his people to bury their dead chief and help choose a new one. Aspin had always been good at listening, and seemed to have some ability when it came to reading people and events.

And Jillan's other friends never seemed to be around either. Freda had disappeared months ago, no one knew where. The rock blight that gave her stone-like skin and was rumoured to be contagious meant very few individuals desired her company, and a good number knew she had been a hanger-on to the generally despised Miserath, the Lord of Mayhem and likely betrayer of the other pagan gods. No matter where she had visited in Godsend, there had always been those who made the cross sign against evil upon seeing her. In the end she had just stopped being around.

The woodsman Ash was only ever to be found in the town's inn, and although he would be eager to offer Jillan a welcome it would always involve one rapid toast after another, and one tankard after another – until they no longer knew each other's names and an angry Samnir was there, forbidding Jillan to enter the inn again.

Then there was Thomas the blacksmith, who went at his forge and clanged metal on his anvil day and night. Some whispered that he fought a demon or dragon in his mind's eye, that he still wrestled with the grief of having lost his family. Yet he would grin at Jillan's arrival – while still continuing to work – and nod periodically as Jillan spoke. Whether the blacksmith really heard him, Jillan wasn't sure. If Jillan stopped speaking, there might be some brief monosyllable from the huge man, but it was anyone's guess if it was prompt, question, mere acknowledgement or a grunt of physical effort. Thomas seemed to want to rebuild Godsend single-handedly, and so Jillan left him to the rhythm of his hammer and nodding.

Yet none of it really mattered, for there was still his beloved Hella. She was as busy as everyone else – what with running her father's stall when he was away trading with other towns, and being one of the few left with a good enough grasp of numbers for keeping a tally book to be trusted with overseeing the daily distribution from the town's storage barns – but she still found precious moments for them to share. He stole kisses from her every morning before others were about and they talked about their plans for the future. Her brow would furrow slightly, she would tug absently on a lock of her wheat-gold hair and her usually clear sky-blue eyes would cloud over whenever they spoke of such things. He knew she had waking dreams of the passing seasons, the growth of life and their possible happiness – he held his breath at such times, for her visions were powerful and he feared to interrupt them lest it cause her some shock or pain. When she came back to herself, she would blink, smile gently at him and make him believe there would never be another winter.

Deciding he would tell Hella about his dreams instead, if they found the time, he left Samnir to his sleep. Jillan took a heel of stale bread, dipped it in water and began to chew as he shouldered his longbow and stepped out into the grey light of Godsend.

He wove his way through the higgledy-piggledy maze of stone cottages, huts, hovels and lean-tos that constituted the southern quarter of Godsend, and approached the wide Gathering Place at the centre of town. At all but the same moment, a mule-drawn wagon emerged from a side street and a woman stifled a scream.

'Saviours preserve us! The devil himself! I told you he would know. Oh, what is to become of us?'

Jillan looked up to see a young mother clutching a babe to her chest and her husband raising a stave to protect them. What appeared to be all the family's possessions were in the back of the wagon. The mule stopped with a sigh.

Realising they were waiting for him to speak, Jillan quietly commented, 'You're leaving then?'

Neither of them answered, but the man's expression became slightly guilty and he shifted uncomfortably in his seat.

Jillan cleared his throat. 'It's all right. No one will try and stop you.'

'Y-You're not gonna hurt us?' the husband said.

'Don't you trust him or lower that weapon, Franklyn!' hissed his life mate.

'Peace, woman! If he wanted to hurt us, there's little I could do against his witchery.' Yet Franklyn was careful to keep his eyes on Jillan as he spoke.

'Nay, husband! Remain wary, for he seeks to ensnare us with his lies. Keep your faith fixed on the blessed Saviours and we may yet win free of the Chaos creature and this cursed place. Its powers will be unable to touch us if you keep your mind clear.' She began to mumble a prayer.

'Look,' Jillan said tiredly. 'There's nothing I want of you. Be on your way as you wish. Do you have enough food to at least see you as far as the next town?'

'It's the want of food that sees us leaving,' the husband replied unhappily. 'What with the young one and all . . .'

'I understand. Godspeed!' Jillan nodded.

'The pagan gods!' the woman breathed. 'He curses us!' She made the sign of the cross over herself and her child, then over Franklyn.

'And the Empire will be coming. I have to think of my family,' Franklyn confessed.

'Don't explain yourself and your heart to him! He will seize upon it, feed upon it!' the wife squealed, setting off her babe.

'I understand.' Jillan smiled and waved them on before the child could wake all the houses around and bring out the curious and any interested in making trouble.

Franklyn nodded gratefully and flicked his reins. The mule leaned forward and the wagon began to trundle away.

*Good riddance! The place will be better off without that sort. You don't need such traitors on the inside. And it's fewer mouths to feed*, the taint said with some satisfaction.

'They're not traitors really. They're just scared, is all. How can I blame them? I'd do the same if I could, if Hella and I had a child and somewhere that would take us in, somewhere safe.'

*But Franklyn's lot aren't heading somewhere safe, are they? They're back off to the Empire. No more freedom of thought and so on. They'll be Drawn again. They'll be mindless slaves again.*

'Maybe. Willing slaves, though. Happy slaves. In a safe community. With enough food to eat.'

*Idiot! There's just no talking to you sometimes. What have we been through for, otherwise? Why did your parents sacrifice themselves? Why did you even bother standing against Azual? Why do you think thousands of people in Godsend have chosen to follow you? What's wrong with you lately, Jillan? Have you completely forgotten yourself?*

He didn't know how to answer. He just didn't know what Godsend had to offer the likes of Franklyn's family. No, that wasn't true. He knew exactly what Godsend offered – the terrible prospect of the full force of the Empire descending upon them. *The Empire will be coming.*

29

He had to face it. He'd spent the winter in some sort of dream of contentment and denial, as his relationship with Hella had blossomed. The Empire was coming. It would descend on the town and kill or capture them all. It was why Samnir worked all the hours he could remain on his feet, why Thomas hammered on and on in his forge, and why Ash drank himself to the point of oblivion. It could never be enough. The Empire was coming. Did they follow him? There was no way he could defend Godsend against the entire Empire. He'd doomed them all! Rather than him being there to defend them, they'd probably be better off if he left them. Then they'd be able to blame him and make a show of welcoming the Empire, so that they might be shown some mercy.

Shaken to the core, he wandered distractedly through the Gathering Place and entered the northern quarter on the way to Hella's home. He passed the inn, where orange eyes watched him from the darkness beneath the stairs up to the porch.

*Off hunting, I see. Bring me back some squirrels!* the large black wolf that was Ash's companion said silently to Jillan.

Jillan stopped. He answered by rote: 'Ash doesn't like it when you have squirrel meat. He says it gives you terrible wind.'

The wolf's large tongue lolled out and his white teeth showed. *Ha! The human will never know. He's unconscious most of the time.*

Jillan frowned. 'Why doesn't he do something other than drink?'

The wolf shifted as if shrugging. *He seems to enjoy it, even though it makes him incapable of hunting and causes him to urinate where he sleeps, as if he were sick or feeble with age. Why do you humans do anything you do? You are a species often lacking in sense. I do not know how it is you manage to survive sometimes. The woodsman only still lives because the Geas has seen to bless him with good timing – he always passes out before he can seriously injure himself. As for you others . . .*

'Perhaps we will not survive,' Jillan murmured.

*Perhaps not. The only real loss, though, would be that I would have no one to get squirrels on my behalf.*

'Maybe. But it is likely to be the Saviours who undo us while they are in the process of seizing the Geas. Then there will be no more squirrels either.'

*There is that. Unless you can convince all the humans to destroy themselves before the Saviours seize the Geas. Or you destroy all the Saviours, but I don't think your kind is strong enough for that. You don't eat enough squirrels, after all.*

'It can't just be that we don't eat enough squirrels. Why aren't we strong enough?'

The wolf yawned. *Listen, there are two types of animals. There are those like wolves, and even squirrels, who live without apology or permission from others. And then there are those like cattle, who are content to be herded around and kept in relative comfort until they're slaughtered. Sheep and cows tend to like their farmers, fences and warm barns. It makes them feel secure. Remove the farmer and so on and the cattle are unable to cope with their freedom. They lose all sense of self and direction. They go getting stuck in ditches, falling down rocks and tangled in bushes, making them even easier prey for any passing wolf. Stupid creatures get what they deserve, really.*

*It's just a matter of will though. Once you decide which of the two types of animal you are, that'll decide how you live, how you behave, and pretty much how you'll end up. Cattle rarely change, you see. Give them freedom and they have no idea what to do with it. When they're without clear direction, they panic and run scared, straight into trouble, usually, or low so loudly that every wolf in the area knows exactly where they are. Some just die of fright on the spot.*

*That is why your kind isn't strong enough, human. Now, all this chat has made me hungry, so why don't you run along and get me some squirrels – if you're up to it?*

Numbly, Jillan nodded and went on his way, trying to make sense of what the wolf had said. He certainly didn't want to be a sheep or a cow. He didn't really fancy being a squirrel either. Neither could he convince himself he was much like a wolf.

*Why on earth are you preoccupying yourself with fantasies about animals?* the taint asked in bafflement.

'Didn't you hear the wolf?'

*What wolf? I heard no howling save for your madness. You must be daydreaming. It's the lack of sleep.*

So the taint hadn't heard anything the wolf had said. He hadn't imagined it all, had he? Maybe the taint wasn't meant to have heard it.

Jillan deliberately turned his thoughts back to Hella and found his pace increasing as he neared her home.

*A far more suitable fantasy, if I may say?* the taint snickered.

'You may not!' Jillan replied hotly and banished the voice for a while.

As he rounded the last corner and the house came into view, he saw her waiting on the bottom step, which was unusual. She was wearing the same clothes as the day before – a long ochre dress and a white apron. They were rumpled and creased. Her hair was slightly unkempt and her expression was careworn. Something was wrong!

Jillan hurried forward and she ran into his arms. She hugged him hard.

'What's wrong?'

Hella pulled him down onto the step next to her and held his hand tightly. 'It's Pa! He got back late last night from Heroes' Brook. Jillan, he was attacked! A group of wild men or bandits took everything he had, including the wagon and the horse! How could such a thing happen?'

'Is he hurt? I should see to him!' Jillan declared and started to rise.

Hella shook her head, pulled him back down and took a calming breath. 'It's all right. He has a deep cut over his eye and several lumps on his head. And he was shaking terribly, so I called the physicker-woman during the night. She's tended to him. She said he should be kept warm and allowed to rest undisturbed through the morning but that I should be sure to wake him around midday. If I have trouble rousing him, I should fetch her at once b-because . . .' her eyes watered '. . . because . . . sometimes p-people never wake up when they've hit . . .' she hiccupped '. . . their head!'

Feeling utterly helpless he put an arm around her and held her tight.

'Oh, Jillan! They took all our supplies! We have nothing left. And no horse or wagon for trade!' she sobbed.

'It's all right,' he said soothingly. 'We'll work something out.'

'But the town has too little to eat already! You don't know just how little there is in the storage barns. I haven't told anyone because it would cause panic. Samnir told me it's getting harder and harder to keep discipline because the men are hungry. And some have begun to desert. Oh, Jillan, what are we going to *do*?'

She stared into his eyes pleadingly. He swallowed hard, thinking desperately. 'I . . . I will talk to Samnir and maybe we can go after these robbers.' Yet the doubt was plain in his voice.

'Jillan, how will we find them?' Her voice became raised. She'd never shouted at him before. 'Father says that it's becoming dangerous everywhere! Heroes' Brook and Saviours' Paradise have their gates locked all the time and their fields and cattle are always heavily guarded. They're not just scared of gangs either, for there is the plague as well. They're turning away most travellers, sometimes with bloodshed. Jillan, Pa's ruined and it's all turning crazy! It's . . . Chaos! The Chaos has come!'

He flinched as if slapped, and let her go. Her hands fluttered over her mouth and she watched him fearfully. Did she blame him for all the trouble? How could she? She didn't think he had been used by the Chaos, did she? She couldn't! She wouldn't kiss someone she believed to be like that. She wouldn't say she loved such a person.

Hella was speaking again, her voice trembling. 'I'm scared is all. I want you to give me answers, but I know that's not fair. Godsend still has some cattle it can afford to slaughter. And spring is here now.' She tried to smile but failed. 'There will be more food from the forest. I'm scared. Scared for the town. Scared for my pa. Scared we won't be able to marry . . .'

'Hella! What are you saying?' he cried, coming to his feet.

'Jillan, don't!' she begged him. There were fresh tears in her eyes. 'I don't know *what* I'm saying! It's all too much. We'll talk later. There are things I should tell you.'

'I don't understand.' What was happening? 'What things?'

'Tonight, I promise. I must see to Pa,' she croaked, wiping her face and avoiding his eyes. She quickly got up and went up the stairs.

He reached after her but she was already closing the door behind her.

Minister Praxis lay with his nose and forehead pressed against the cold stone floor of the holy audience chamber of the Great Temple at the heart of the Empire. He'd been prostrate like this for over a week, but he'd never been so happy in his miserable life. To be in this place, so close to the blessed Saviours . . . He'd never dared hope he was worthy even to touch the floor they may once have walked across. He would wait for all eternity for them to appear if necessary. And if they never

33

appeared, then that was their divine will and their judgement upon his own wretchedness.

Elite temple guards came and went as they finished their shifts or refreshed the candles, but he no longer noticed them. He no longer noticed the drops of rain that dripped from the ceiling, ran along the joins in the flagstones of the floor and found their way onto his tongue. He no longer felt the pain and stiffness of his limbs. He must shed himself of selfishness, of all sense of self-obsessed need, if he was ever to be a suitable vessel for the will of the blessed Saviours, surely his only reason for being. He was aware only of his sin, the sin of failing his Saint and, through that failing, the blessed Saviours. How imperfect and lowly he was! Never could his suffering be enough. Ah, the pain of that knowledge! His existence was a torment and punishment to him, and therefore must not be allowed to end until the blessed Saviours willed it. Death would be their divine mercy and he knew he was not deserving of such mercy.

There was only his sin and failure. He had not done enough to prepare against the Chaos. He had underestimated its dark and sneaking ways, just as he had underestimated the boy who was the bane of the Empire. Jillan! The Minister stared at the flagstones so hard his eyes almost fell from their sockets at mere thought of the name. His heart hesitated, his bowels turned to ice, his teeth clenched so hard his jaw came close to dislocating. The evil in that boy was so distilled, so pure, that it could only be a miracle wrought by the blessed Saviours themselves that kept the world sufficiently ordered to remain intact.

All the signs had been there from the beginning. The Minister knew he should have acted when he'd had the chance, when Jillan had been within his power as one of the pupils in his class back in Godsend. He should have throttled that boy during that last detention, or taken him out and pitched him into the town's well. The creature had caused him no end of trouble in the lessons, with his sly questions and professions of innocence. No one could be entirely innocent, not even the most faithful of the Empire's Ministers. No one!

Saint Azual was right to have exiled the failed Minister of Godsend, he saw that now. It was his own fault that Jillan had left detention, foully murdered a classmate and then fled the town unpunished. It was right that the failed Minister had had to suffer among the pagans of the mountains. Yet even then he'd failed, for in his arrogance he'd believed that he had redeemed himself and was therefore free to return to Godsend. Instead he'd led the pagans and the Chaos itself into the town and ultimately brought about the demise of the holy Saint and the triumph of the boy. The perfidious boy had been using the Minister all along! He, Minister Praxis, in his own vanity, had terribly underestimated just how dark and sneaking were the ways of the Chaos. He had allowed the very Chaos itself to use him!

Full of so much loathing he could no longer contain it, the Minister retched on the floor. His empty stomach heaved up its digestive juices and he pressed his face into a pool of bile. Let the liquid burn away all that he was. Let the venom of the taint within eat him alive. Let him drown in it, here, right now. He was anathema to the Empire of the blessed Saviours and should not be tolerated by it for an instant longer.

Yet when he had thrown himself upon the ground and prayed for that very thing before – having learned that the Saint had fallen, and having fled in horror into the forests beyond Godsend – Captain Skathis had emerged from the trees as if in answer to his prayer and dragged him up by the scruff of the neck. The Captain had even cuffed him around the back of the head, as if to knock sense into him, remind him of his faith and teach him a lesson.

'Be a man!' the Captain had grated. '*Sacrifice and duty safeguard the People against the Chaos*, isn't that what you Ministers like to tell us? Well, enough of your womanly wailing! Pick your feet up. We've got a long walk ahead of us to the Great Temple.'

'W-We're going to the Great Temple?' he'd asked in wonder.

'Of course, you idiot!' had come the sneered answer. 'If you think I'm going to let you weep yourself to death out here in the wilds, leaving me to face the displeasure of the Empire on my own, then you've got another think coming. And if you start flagging, believe me, I will take great joy in bullying and kicking your arse all the way there. Now, wipe your nose and stop snivelling. You make me sick.'

The scarred Captain had been like some sort of angel or holy messenger, come to prevent the Minister's death and provide divine instruction. How could the Minister have dared to think of blasphemously ending the life that had been gifted to him by the blessed Saviours? It was yet another sin and failing on his part. Thus he'd humbly made the pilgrimage with the good but impatient Captain Skathis across the southern and central regions, all the way to the Great Temple itself. As soon as the Great Temple had come into sight, the Minister had wanted to complete the rest of his journey on his knees, but, good as his word, the Captain had savagely begun to kick the Minister up the behind, making it all but impossible.

Upon arrival, there had been temple retainers waiting for them, for were not the blessed Saviours all-knowing? One had taken the Captain to report to his army superiors, while another had led the Minister to this audience chamber and commanded him to lie prone while awaiting the pleasure of the blessed Saviours.

And so here he lay, with his face in his own thin vomit. His treacherous thoughts and self-pity had led him back to another sinful contemplation of suicide. This time, without the need for the angelic Captain to drag him up by the scruff of the neck, he moved his mouth and nose up so that he would neither wallow nor drown in his own cesspit of self. There could be no selfish suicide. There was only the will of the blessed Saviours. Only them. Nothing else. Here surely was the revelation of the People's existence.

'Praxis!' came the quietest of whispers, a whisper that he heard as much in his mind as he did in the chamber without. It came again, louder this time and more dreadful. 'Praxis!'

'I am here, divine one!' he squeaked, losing control of his bladder and nearly passing out.

'Be calm, Praxis. See, I speak through another, for you would be undone by my presence. See!'

The Minister pulled his head up a few inches and blearily made out a glassy-eyed infant girl seated on the simple but large stone throne across the gloomy chamber.

'Praxis, you may approach,' the terrible voice commanded, channelled incongruously by the youngster.

The Minister tried to drag his limbs under him, to lever himself forward, but they hardly obeyed, so stiff and rigid had they become. He squirmed forward across the flagstones, whimpering in agony and terror that he might not be able to obey the divine instruction. He bent his ankles and pushed with his toes, shoving himself a few more inches forward. Slowly, slowly, he made his way across the floor, heedlessly scraping cloth and then skin from his knees and elbows, until at last he grovelled before the throne.

In the age it had taken to cover the dozen or so yards, the girl-child seemed to have become years older, her hair and nails growing to an unnatural length. She was taller now, her frame more filled out. Her clothes no longer fitted. If she continued to age at this speed, she would be a bent old woman within a handful of minutes.

'Hear me, Praxis!' the alien voice resonated powerfully around the chamber. 'You will now take the place of my son Azual. You will become Saint of the southern region in his place. Yet you will first need to restore order to that region by Drawing them back to us. You will also seize the youth Jillan, so that he may reveal to us the dark lair of the Geas, that which you know as the Chaos. Once we find this lair, the Chaos will be ended once and for all and this world will be made a paradise. Do you understand?'

Praxis thrashed about in a paroxysm of joy as he replied to the middle-aged woman, who displayed a tracery of lines and wrinkles on her face where a few moments before there had only been fair, unblemished skin. 'Praise be, most blessed and divine Saviour!' He sobbed. 'You have gifted me with a vision of such beauty, may your will be done! I am transported by it and utterly yours. How must the Drawing be done, beneficent one?'

'Through the holy communion, Praxis, through the holy communion. I have allowed this woman before you to drink of my essence so that she might be my vessel and body. Her flesh is my flesh, and her blood is my blood. It is the divine power of that blood which purges and burns the imperfection from her and rushes her towards an eternity with us, that which you call death. Come, take this tapping tube and partake of my blood, so that you may commune fully with us. It will complete you. Rise, Saint Praxis!' the unearthly voice directed him.

Insensible with religious fervour, Praxis found himself crouching before the woman and pushing a thin tube of sun-metal into a vein in one of her arms. Scarlet blood arced from the end of the tube into his mouth. He swallowed greedily and within moments could miraculously stand straight once more, his limbs suffused with such power and energy that he felt as if he was born anew. An ecstasy came upon him as he transcended the pathetic being he had been before. He became intoxicated with it and swayed slightly, blood missing his mouth and pouring down his chin and clothes.

*Enough!* pulsed the voice in his mind, the white-haired woman too old and frail to speak clearly to him any more. *No more of my blood, lest you end up sharing the same fate as this other vessel. You have had sufficient that we may now commune mind to mind and spirit to spirit. Enough, I say!*

With an effort of will Saint Praxis ceased drinking, removed the tapping tube and placed it carefully inside his long black coat. The shrunken woman sighed her final breath and moved no more. 'As you will it, divine one!' Saint Praxis said, in some sort of blessing over the dead one.

*And so you will Draw the People back to us, Praxis. Through you, drops of my blood will be shared with them, and then you will Draw the essence of their own tainted blood from them. They will be cleansed through this holy communion. It will bind them to you so that you may better guide them in their faith. It will restore order, peace and prosperity to the region. It will confound the influence of the Chaos and force it back into the darkness. Truly, you will bring Salvation to the People in our name!*

'Praise be, divine one!' the Saint replied fervently. 'Yet there are so many of them. It will take a long time to Draw them all. And they have allowed themselves to become corrupted. Will they not resist?'

*Fear not, Praxis. Be of good faith, for we will be with you.*

He was about to cast himself back upon the ground as he realised his doubt was all but sinful and that he should beg for forgiveness, but the Saviour was merciful and continued without further castigation.

*The People of the southern region were naturally Drawn when young, and still something of that remains with them. Through Azual, they received some small part of my essence such that I will be able to call on them, when you present yourself to them, and remind them of the right path and their duty to the Empire. The majority will be compliant. There will be more blood than you can consume alone, so it should be sent to the Great Temple for the magic of the Chaos within it to be properly cleansed and expunged. It will be a tithe of sorts.*

*But pay special attention to the young among your flock. As children enter puberty, they become more tempted by sins of the flesh and spirit and far more vulnerable to the influence of the Chaos. Therefore, you should be sure to visit the towns in the region regularly, in order to Draw the children just before they can reach that age.*

'Yes, divine one!' the Saint moaned, all but overcome by the divine knowledge. 'And what of those who do resist?' An edge came into his voice. 'What of *Godsend*, that benighted town that has given itself entirely over to the Chaos, that town which first fostered and nurtured the foul corruption and plague of the Chaos, that town which is a living blasphemy to the true faith, that town which even now provides succour to the bane of the Empire?'

A feeling of righteous malevolence communicated itself to his mind. *Sweet Praxis, it is good you anticipate the need to punish such resistance. Yet do you really think the all-knowing Saviours had not foreseen all that has come to pass? Beyond this chamber, General Thormodius and our eastern army await you. With him at your side, there will be none in the south to stand against you. You will be the instrument of our divine retribution! Those who attempt to resist will have been so corrupted by the Chaos that they must be beyond saving. Only keep alive those who may give us advantage over the bane.*

'Yes! The girl Hella, divine one! She has been the familiar of the bane from the start and worked to seduce others so that the Chaos has influence over them. She must be made an example of, divine one, to serve as warning to the People and punishment for the bane! Ah, but evil always wears the comeliest mask.'

*Then go tear off her face, so that all may see the horror and decay beneath, sweet Praxis!*

'As you will it, blessed one, as you will it!'

Once the presence of the Saviour had faded away, Saint Praxis strode purposefully out of the holy audience chamber. No longer was there anything nervous or twitchy about him, for his faith, suffering and self-denial had at last seen him beatified and raised up. He now had a greater sense of self and conviction than he had ever known. He was clear of eye and unflinching of purpose. And that entire purpose was bent on bringing down the boy Jillan and his witch of a paramour Hella.

He found General Thormodius with the angelic Captain Skathis at his side. Standing tall, the Saint stared down at the two large men. The Captain shifted uncomfortably and looked down and away. The

General held the gaze for a few long moments, and then was forced to blink and nod his head slightly in welcome and acknowledgement.

'What is your will, holy one?'

Saint Praxis allowed himself a satisfied grin and thought of all the different horrors he would visit on Godsend and the evil creatures that dwelt within.


Jillan stumbled through the forests beyond the walls of Godsend. He needed to think, to make sense of it all.

*Jillan, slow down. You're tired. Look at how disturbed your sleep has been in recent weeks. It's no wonder your mind's in a muddle*, the taint calmly told him.

Jillan stopped and looked around, not exactly sure where he was. It seemed his feet had led him into the gloomier parts of the forest that few of Godsend's hunters ever frequented because of a fear of pagans, old superstitions and mere fancies about what lurked in the dark and bottomless pools hereabouts. The giant pine trees stood relatively close together and had such thick branches that it was impossible to tell if it was full daylight above the canopy or not. There was an eerie silence everywhere. No rustling of mice and burrowing creatures beneath the thick carpet of pine needles covering the ground. No scampering squirrels among the branches. No whir of insects. No birdsong even. The air was warm and close, giving the place a brooding feel, the sort of feeling that would scare the usual forest creatures away.

Although the ground was fairly even, it sloped down slightly and he fancied he glimpsed the surface of water ahead of him between the trees. If he couldn't shoot anything with his bow here, then maybe he could use the fishing line in his tunic to hook a few fish or eels for the pot. And it would be good to sit thinking quietly for a while.

He moved forward noiselessly and came to the edge of a flat dark pool that looked to be a hundred paces across. There were purplish fleshy water-plants along the edges, so he decided the water couldn't be entirely acidic or poisonous. It didn't seem stagnant either. He threw out his line and lure and sat on a conveniently wide and level rock to contemplate his reflection.

The water was a perfectly still mirror, one that showed him a gaunt and limp-haired youth, a troubled youth. He hardly recognised himself.

Hella had panicked him when she had said they might not be able to get married. If they couldn't have each other, then what else was there? What had it all been for? He'd already lost his parents to the cursed Empire, and he'd be damned if he'd let it take Hella from him as well. Yet Hella's father Jacob had been attacked and they'd lost everything they had. And now, just as Franklyn had pointed out, the Empire would be coming for Godsend itself.

He mustn't let the panic, the sick feeling in his gut, that feeling he had when his dreams turned bad, get the better of him. It messed with his thoughts and paralysed him. If it gained control then he'd never be able to do anything to stop them from taking Hella or Godsend. What to do?

His reflection looked back at him, watching and waiting. The dark youth in the water could provide no answers, however. The pool was empty and mournful. How could he end it or ever be free of it? The question threatened to drown him. It was the sort of question he'd asked in the Minister's classroom, which seemed a lifetime ago, the sort of question that had effectively ended his childhood, seen Karl killed and his parents sacrifice themselves. Would it now murder all of Godsend?

He should never have asked it of the Minister. No wonder he had provoked his ire. Oh, why hadn't Jillan's parents let him stay at home that day when he said his stomach hurt? It was a sickness, a taint, a corruption in him that had then affected everything around him. After all, hadn't he caused the plague? He knew that was what they all whispered behind his back. Had he corrupted all of Godsend, then? He was surely the cause, and that was why the Empire was coming, before he could corrupt the entire region and perhaps the whole Empire itself.

The dark youth in the water continued to stare at him, its eyes devouring light and mesmerising Jillan.

His was the blame. Should he leave Godsend, freeing it of its corruption? The Empire would perhaps pursue him instead of destroying the town, his friends and his beloved Hella. If he truly loved them, maybe he should leave. Yet where would he go? He dared not lead the Empire to Aspin's home in the mountains. There was nowhere, no escape. The Empire would capture and use him, which would then endanger the Geas. He could never allow that to happen! Those he

41

loved – and the Geas – could only be saved if he were to end his life before he fell into the hands of the Empire.

Jillan's reflection was still staring at him. Was it larger than before? It seemed to have come closer to the surface somehow. Its hand reached out towards his own and he fancied that he might actually be able to touch the barrier between its world and his, the barrier between his world of torment and its world of peace, between his world of ill-starred light and its world of eternal darkness. He could just let go of his place in the world and find release and rest in the tender embrace of the deep. It could draw him down gently and soothe away his fears and troubles forever.

His fishing line drifted between his gaze and the other's. Jillan blinked, and in that briefest of moments heard the taint screaming insanely at him. His hand was touching the surface of the water and was about to intertwine its fingers with the dark youth's. What was he doing? Jillan and the dark youth gasped in horror and Jillan struggled to lean back and away from the water without overbalancing. He grimaced in panic and the dark youth snarled back at him, anger turning it into something ugly. It was far more than just a reflection and it was coming for him! Jillan instinctively called on magic from his core.

*No!*

But it was too late. Bright energy spewed from his hands, lighting up the glade red for an instant before being absorbed by the murky pool. The dark youth seemed to become more solid and began to push through the surface of the water.

*Idiot! You're only giving it more of yourself! It's a phagus!*

'A-A what?'

*Never mind! Run! Move, you dolt!*

Jillan lurched back and fell heavily onto the flat rock. He turned clumsily, the fatigue caused by his use of magic robbing him of co-ordination and balance. He sprawled onto his front as the phagus hauled itself up and out of the pool and onto the rock behind him. A wet hand clamped around Jillan's ankle in a vice-like grip. He cried out in fear and kicked back.

Where the phagus touched him, his skin burned like ice and his foot became numb. The cold began to spread up his leg. The taint was screaming incoherently now and fled in agony, abandoning him.

'You will betray the Geas!' gurgled the phagus in outrage. 'It must not be allowed!'

'Never!' Jillan cried. 'I won't. I swear it! I will do anything you want.'

The phagus hardly hesitated in its answer. 'The risk is too great. Better you be returned to the earth from which you came, so that you may nourish other growth in the land.'

An image of old bones sunk in the silt at the bottom of the pool came into Jillan's mind. The flesh had long since rotted away, but had fed fish as it did so, and helped make the water a healthy soup to feed the surrounding plants. The plants had been picked by a physicker-woman in times gone past and been made into a broth to feed the sick and bring them new life. The life the bones had once been a part of had been passed on to others, to enrich them.

'See,' the phagus croaked, 'you need not grieve. Death is simply a change of state. You will live on through other lives. Such life is eternal. Do not struggle against it. Look into my eyes and tell me you do not know and want such release. You want to be free of the struggle, do you not? My eyes, Jillan!

Yet Jillan knew better than to look back at the doppelgänger, to allow its gaze to overwhelm him. He kicked with his free leg and connected with something that squelched. The phagus simply grunted and dragged Jillan towards it with the hand around his ankle.

Desperately, Jillan threw his arms out and curled his fingers over the edge of the rock where he lay. He hung on for dear life. The phagus stretched him, its strength beyond anything human. The killing cold crept up over the thigh of Jillan's trapped leg.

He knew he could not hold on. The deadening touch came higher but, as it reached Jillan's torso, the pagan runes on his armour flared into life and filled the glade with a blinding white-gold light. The phagus screeched and had to let go to shield its eyes.

Jillan squirmed forward, pulling himself to the end of the flat rock, and then let his weight bring him down to the forest floor a few feet below. He scrabbled, grabbed his bow for a crutch, got his good leg under him and pushed away. His other leg had absolutely no feeling in it and he barely avoided ending up back on the ground.

'Jillan, you know there is nowhere to escape!' the phagus belched behind him. He could hear it coming for him again. 'Think of those who you love. You know they can only be saved when this is ended. Come, let me free you of this.'

Its words sucked hungrily at his will. He shouted back at it. 'I have always fought to protect the People and the Geas. You must believe me!'

'Lies!' the phagus hissed as it slithered after him. 'It has always been the same with your selfish kind. Once before you humans pleaded with us and offered us passionate promises, so that we would share our sacred groves and pools with you. Then you set to felling our ancient trees and contaminating our waters, driving even holy Akwar from this place.'

'That wasn't me!' Jillan protested, trying to block out the visions the phagus shared with him.

'You seized the land as your own, undid the gods and gifted everything to the all-consuming incomers. Betraying and jealous humans! You will destroy the Geas itself.'

'Never!'

'Never? You humans lie even to yourselves. I know your mind. I am but your reflection. There is something impossibly self-obsessed about your kind. You want everything, even if it is far beyond you, and that makes you self-destructive. You cannot deny it. You have already shared your thoughts with me. I know you have considered ending your life, even if fleetingly. You know it is the surest way to safeguard the Geas. You know the risk is too great otherwise. Stop running, Jillan.'

He was frozen in place. The words of the phagus sounded like his own. The demand he end his life was his own. 'No!' he said softly. 'My parents have already died to protect the Geas. Surely that is enough.'

'If you would sacrifice anything to protect the Geas, then you must be prepared to return the life and magic that the Geas first gifted you.'

'Please, there must be another way!' In his mind's eye Jillan saw the hands of the phagus stretching out for him again.

Numbing and implacable words. 'Try to be better than the rest of your kind. Submit to it. Let go. There will be no pain.'

Long damp fingers slid around his throat. He had nothing left. There was no more magic. There were no more arguments. There was only the regret he would not see Hella again, that there were still things unresolved between them, that he wouldn't see her summer smile again, smell her wheat-ripened hair, lie under a tree with her . . . He couldn't let her image go, *would* not let it go. 'I cannot deny her!' Jillan swore, pulling his head forward, yanking his hunting knife from his belt and slashing back at the phagus all in one motion.

'Betrayer!' the phagus accused him in a cold fury. 'See how your selfish desire comes before protecting the Geas. You speak the same lies to me as all your kind. Now you will die!'

Jillan cast his knife behind him and heard it thud into the phagus, but he could sense it was not seriously hurt. He took a panicky hop forward, wrestling with his quiver as it swung away from him by its strap. He failed to put the foot of his dead leg down squarely and the traitorous limb began to twist him around. He knew he was going to fall, so gave into it as he grabbed an arrow, let the quiver fall and raised his bow. He hit the ground sitting down and facing back towards the pool, but ready to shoot.

The phagus was crouched like a toad on the rock and preparing to leap at him, a horrific and slimy version of himself. Instantly, its eyes fixed him where he was and he was unable to release his arrow. It had him. All he saw were the dark pools of its eyes.

The dark youth came to Jillan and took him in its icy clutches. It pulled him to the pool and then into the freezing depths.

*Hella, I'm so sorry!* he thought as he drifted down and down.

He hardly felt his body any more. The pain of the cold was gone. It was darkest night. He was so tired. It was like going to sleep. He saw the last bubbles of air escape from his lips and lift away.

His armour dragged him to the bottom of the pool, to lie among the other bones there. Strong hands gripped him and he thought that the phagus had come to pull him apart and feast on him, but instead he was pulled further down still, through muck and detritus, silt and sediment, through loose stones and then rock.

Down still.

'Hold on, friend Jillan!' came a gritted voice.

Did he know it?

'There is air here. It's a cavern. Breathe, friend Jillan!'

Wasn't he breathing? He had no way of telling. Surely he was dead. Was this one of the tests the eternal Saviours set the dead before allowing them to join them in paradise, or one of the tricks that pagan ghosts were known to play on the newly departed?

'I am sorry, friend Jillan.'

Something hard hit him in the back. And again. He vomited violently, evil-smelling fluid pouring out of his nose and mouth. Fire ignited in his chest. His mind screamed for mercy, but his body did not have enough strength for more than a sigh and then a groan. Yes, this was life: he recognised the agony of it. Death was far less painful, far more alluring. Ah, but how it burned! He was sick again and wiped a shaking hand across his mouth.

'S-S-So c-cold!' His teeth chattered. His body convulsed weakly a few times as it tried and failed to shiver some warmth back into itself.

'Fear not. Friend Anupal knew you would need the thing called fire. But I must take you quickly, he said.'

'F-Freda, is that you?' Jillan whispered, his eyes becoming too heavy to stay open.

'Here, let me do it! You're spilling most of it down his front, dear heart! I didn't spend an hour making this soup just for you to go bathing him in it. It might be good for his complexion, you never know, but that's not our primary concern right now, now is it? Those big hands of yours can't handle the spoon properly, dear Freda. You'd be best employed drying yourself down, you know. Do you not remember what I told you about water expanding when it freezes? The nights still get very cold. Tough though that stony skin of yours may look, if water gets between your joints and seams and you leave it till the morning, then it'll be me having to pick up the pieces, pick up *your* pieces in point of fact. So show some sense and consideration, dear one, hmm?'

Jillan felt heat pouring down his throat. There was the crackle of a nearby fire.

'Then we stroke his neck down the front like this and it triggers the swallowing reflex in him. See, these people are very basic and reactive creatures really. Like plants turning towards the light and all that. Moths to a flame, blah, blah.'

The soup began to spread warmth through Jillan's body. He tasted onions and celery, herbs and hearty root vegetables. It had been a long time since he'd tasted decent cooking. It reminded him of good things

– his mother and father, evenings playing dice games in their snug kitchen – and he began to feel better. He greedily swallowed the next spoonful.

'And now he wakes up. You can cease your fretting and nervous crunching of your fingers now, dear Freda. Besides, you know how it puts my teeth on edge.'

'Sorry, sorry, friend Anupal,' came a contrite but happy mumble.

Jillan opened his eyes and made out a blurred beatific face looking back at him. It wore a halo that dazzled the eye. As things finally came into focus, Jillan realised he was looking upon one of the many visages of Miserath, the Lord of Mayhem, whom Freda always called *friend Anupal* and the Empire called something like *the Peculiar*. Jillan frowned. Hadn't Miserath been thrown down by Torpeth during the battle and then killed by the mad Saint Azual?

'Surprise!' smiled the Peculiar delightedly, with a flourish of his hands as if he were a travelling performer of tricks who had come to entertain the simple folk of a remote town and relieve them of their hard-earned coin. 'Yes, I am here to save you once again, young Jillan. And a good job too, eh, or that water phagus would have been the end of you, hmm?'

'B-But . . .' Jillan coughed and wheezed.

'I know, I know. You don't know whether to express your joy or gratitude first. It's all a bit overwhelming, so take a moment. There'll be time enough for celebration later. You didn't really think I'd succumb to a silly old Saint and his Saviours, now did you? I *am* something of a god, after all. Really, Jillan, you ought to know better. And while we're at it, what on earth did you think you were trying to achieve with that phagus? Did you really think I'd let you go and kill yourself when there's still the matter of our bargain to be settled, hmm? I really must insist that you do *not* try and kill yourself again . . . or not until you've fulfilled your promise to me, at least. A promise to a god is no small thing, you know. It's a holy vow, young Jillan! It's sinful not to observe that vow, you know.'

'I-I didn't—'

'Oh, come along, we both know better than that. A phagus reflects more than just your pretty face back at you. It mirrors your thoughts and desires as well, to lure and ensnare you. It wouldn't have been able to touch you or offer you death unless you were already considering it.'

Jillan shook his head in denial, but found it painful and quickly thought better of it. He looked around. They were in a natural bowl in a lighter part of the forest. They sheltered beneath a twisted hawthorn tree, but otherwise there were the usual scented pines spaced all around. Shafts of sunlight created a cage of spears around them and their fire. The Peculiar, with hands on hips and a sword of shining sun-metal bent around his head, ostensibly to keep the thoughts of others out, stood over Jillan, while a grinning Freda hunkered in an area of shadow, the coloured stones he'd once gifted her winking around the base of her neck.

Jillan returned her smile and – needing no further encouragement – the large woman lumbered forward, unintentionally knocking the Peculiar aside and eliciting a yelp of protest. Freda eagerly pushed a bowl of soup and a spoon into Jillan's hands. 'More dead trees to eat, friend Jillan!'

'Dear one, we are trying to have a conversation here!' the Peculiar reprimanded her, but then gave up with a noise of disgust as he saw Jillan gratefully receive the bowl and fill his mouth. The pagan god stepped away a small distance to allow them a few moments together and paced impatiently.

Jillan could not help eating quickly and, all too soon, the bowl was empty. Now he realised he was uncomfortably warm. His damp armour was beginning to steam, so close was he to the fire. He struggled with the leather buckles and Freda helped him shrug the armour off.

'Phew! Thank you, Freda! Thank you for everything. F-For saving me, and everything.'

Her brown-grey face split with another grin and her small obsidian eyes glittered. 'Friend Jillan has done many things for Freda. I wanted to do something for Jillan.'

'But where have you been all this while? I stopped seeing you in Godsend. I missed you, Freda,' Jillan said in a kindly fashion.

Freda looked uncomfortable. 'I looked for someone called Jan in Godsend, son of a friend, but he was not there. I frightened people instead. Best to keep friend Anupal company, here among the trees, so he did not become lonely and angry.'

The Peculiar snorted at this but did not otherwise argue.

Freda brightened. 'But I have always been near when friend Jillan came into the forest, in case bad animals came near. Animals do not come near Freda.'

Jillan laughed. Now he knew why he'd had so little luck hunting. 'And what else have you been up to out here?'

'Er . . . well, waiting, I think.' She looked towards the Peculiar, who was now coming close. 'Friend Anupal . . .'

'. . . has been waiting for the season to turn, for the right moment to ask that you deliver on your end of our bargain, young Jillan. Time is a place, in many ways, and we had to wait until we arrived at our destination, you see. Now is the coming together of the necessary people in the right place. If we had not come to you when and where we did, when payment was due, you would have been dead at the hands of the phagus, would you not, Jillan? It was more than good fortune. Similarly, if we did not now demand you deliver on our bargain, then you and Godsend would be lost. And if we had come asking too soon, you would not have understood or accepted the genuine need, and would have fought against it. *Now* is the time and place where understanding, meaning and action become one. You must leave with us and help us find Haven. You must claim the entire power of the Geas as your own, Jillan, so that you may drive out the elseworlders, those you once termed your blessed Saviours. You cannot refuse, for to remain here would see the moment lost and every chance ended. You know that you are now plagued by thoughts of self-destruction because the Empire is closing in on you. They already stalk you in your dreams, do they not? Your mind is hardly your own any more, is it, hmm?'

Jillan gasped. In quiet shock he asked, 'How did you know?'

The Peculiar gave him a sad smile. 'How could it be otherwise? How else would the phagus have come so close to making you its own? The elseworlders use every means at their disposal to see you harassed, cornered, used and ultimately undone. You must have once been forced to drink of their blood-driven magic, yes? The Saint?'

Jillan shuddered at the memory and nodded.

'And you were then bound together. It is through him that the elseworlders have discovered some access to you . . .'

He dimly remembered meeting a fearsome and impossible creature in some dream-cave. What had they spoken about?

'. . . and must have found some hold on your mind. You will never be free unless you come with us now and help us find Haven. You cannot refuse.'

'I . . . cannot leave without . . . without at least saying goodbye.'

'No!' the Peculiar replied firmly. 'There is no going back in time and place, not even for one such as me. Were you to attempt it, those in Godsend would beg that you stay, or then demand they accompany you on your noble quest, or some such nonsense. You would more than likely be unable to deny them. You would linger in your goodbyes until too much time had passed. You would bring others with you who would divide our energies and slow us down. Jillan, if you truly love any in Godsend, you will leave with us now and not look back.'

'I . . . I . . .' He couldn't just leave. How could he do that to her? The Peculiar said there was no choice, but wasn't there *always* a choice? Surely there was a choice, some way. Was the god lying? Wasn't one of the Peculiar's pagan names the King of Lies, and another Miserath, the Traitor God?

'I could always insist?' the Peculiar murmured, suddenly close in front of him and his eyes becoming bewitching rainbows. 'A vow made to a god is as binding—'

Jillan gave him a grim little smile and hooded his gaze. 'You could, *friend* Anupal, and I would fight you every step of the way. If that is what you want, then so be it, but I would doubt our chances of future success. There are words I must share with those I most care about before I will agree to go anywhere with you! I still remember the disingenuous nature of our bargain, Anupal. How could I not? Yes, as agreed, you saw my parents freed and to the walls of Hyvan's Cross. But then what became of them? What will become of me, Anupal, when you see me to the walls of Haven, eh? Tell me that!'

Hella had promised they would talk that evening. There were things she needed to tell him. She was his heart. He could not deny her.

The Peculiar sat back on his heels and glared balefully at Jillan for a second or two. Then the pagan god calmed his features and was a handsome open-faced individual of indeterminate age once more. 'Very well, good Jillan, go say your goodbyes. Understand that I simply sought to spare you the pain of them, but perhaps it was no kindness on my part.' The Peculiar rose gracefully as Jillan pulled his armour back towards him. 'We will await you here, then. You will find Godsend that way. Stay away from any pools you pass, eh? And do not tarry overlong, my brave warrior, for unlike us the Empire never rests idle or sleeps.'

As Jillan marched off between the trees with the bow Freda had somehow retrieved for him over his shoulder, the Peculiar hurried to pull a long midnight-blue cape with attached bonnet from beneath the hawthorn tree.

'Friend Anupal, what are you doing?' Freda asked nervously. She realised he was about to leave and became scared. 'And where are you going? Oh, I fear what it is you will do, friend Anupal!'

For a moment the Peculiar looked back at her. 'I do what I must, dear one, as I have ever done – you know that. Offer a man dying of thirst a poison chalice and will he not drink? Trust me, dear one. All will be well.'

She blinked as he began to shift into a female form. Then he was gone.

As Jillan neared Godsend, his steps began to slow, reluctant to arrive. What would he say to her? How could he ever explain? And to Samnir? Ash, Thomas, Haal, Jacob, all of the people who had decided to remain despite the threat of the Empire? He was the one who had turned Godsend into this outpost of defiance and asked the inhabitants to fight alongside the pagans against the Saint and his Heroes. How could he now abandon them like this? They would never understand. Should he plead with them to flee for the mountains? No, the elderly would never survive. Perhaps the Peculiar had been right. Perhaps there was just no explaining.

*What's happening?* the taint asked from afar.

Jillan stepped onto the main road leading to Godsend's north gate. The sky had turned the sort of leaden grey that promised a filthy storm ahead. His temples itched.

*You survived the phagus, then?*

'No thanks to you!' he bit back.

The taint hesitated. *It nearly finished me, you know. The magic in you is much diminished. I'm not sure if it will ever return.* A pause. *How did you survive?*

'Freda and Miserath.'

*What? Nothing good ever comes of—*

'Nothing good?' Jillan shouted. 'They saved me from a watery grave! Where were you, eh?'

*All I'm saying is that when it comes to Miserath you need to be cautious. You didn't promise him anything, did you?*

Jillan walked on in a tight silence, refusing to be drawn further. He didn't owe the taint any sort of explanation, as far as he was concerned. He felt betrayed somehow.

The town appeared in the distance, between the swaying trees on either side of the road. The gates stood open, but they were well manned by guards. Not that more than a single trader had approached the town all through the winter. Word about the plague having started in Godsend had clearly spread across the region faster even than the plague itself. And those who had fled during the aftermath of the battle would have carried news of the unconscionable acts committed by the inhabitants of that town. A more fallen and forsaken place was not to be found. Perhaps it was no surprise Jacob had been attacked. He was lucky they'd allowed him his life.

He heard wolfwhistles and catcalls from the guards, carried to him on the rising wind. He wondered at the commotion, which sounded good-natured. He came closer with a smile on his lips, for the ready banter of the soldiers usually raised his spirits even when he'd failed to bring back any game from the forest.

Just outside the gates a large youth was in some sort of clinch with a young maid. He was bent over her and kissing her. Was that Haal? Jillan frowned. He hadn't realised Haal had been courting anyone, let alone stepping out with them. Clearly, they'd been heading into the forest for some privacy but had been overcome by eager passion before moving beyond sight of the guards. Jillan's smile broadened. He was pleased for Haal.

The smile froze on Jillan's lips. It burned like ice, even colder than the touch of the phagus. Surely he recognised that midnight-blue cape she was wearing. And the halo of gold hair framing the face within the bonnet. A beautiful face that displayed rapture. A betraying face. This was not the chaste and diffident kiss of friends; it was the lusty embrace of two people very much in love.

*What is this?* the taint asked queasily. *I—*

'You told me so?' Jillan replied moltenly.

He felt sick to his stomach. And worse. A blade of sun-metal had been thrust into his guts and they had spilled onto the ground. Thunder rolled in the distance, and he could believe the sky had fallen and flattened the world.

*I don't understand it. It makes no sense!*

But Jillan did understand it. This was what she'd wanted to talk to him about. This was why they'd never get married. It made so much sense whole empires could be founded on it, the passage of the sun and the phases of the moon could be predicted by it. It was *he* who made no sense. His self-delusion and stupidity were where there was a lack of sense. No wonder she didn't want to know him any more, someone whose mind knew only crazed dreams when asleep and heard voices when awake, a voice he spoke to out loud. Someone who hadn't been able to do anything useful or say anything sensible when he'd been told her father had been attacked.

He'd murdered all reason when he'd killed the Saint, he now knew. There was no order left, only betrayal and chaos. No wonder his mind was constantly beset and fragmenting. Far from saving anyone, including himself, he'd damned them all! Samnir, Ash and Thomas suffered in silent desperation and avoided him because of it. Hella . . . sweet Hella . . . smart Hella wanted no part of him, wanted to be free of him.

He had not freed Godsend; he had doomed it. He could not save it; he could only damn it. It all made sense. What had he been thinking? At last it all made sense.

The storm rose around him and rain lashed down his cheeks. He turned on his heel and strode back into the forest, back towards Miserath and Freda. Pain and rage were all that remained to him, and all he deserved. And they were all he'd have until he'd put things right or died trying.

# CHAPTER 3:

# Caused by the unstable element

He was nothing but dust within the maelstrom of the cosmos. Its near-infinite forces had instantly pulled him inside out, torn him apart and annihilated him. Only dust, randomly drifting, chaotically swirled and blown every which way. At least there was no pain or searing sun. It was almost a release. For an infinitesimal moment his troubled and *unstable* nature sensed what it was to find a sort of peace. But then it was gone, all but before it had arrived. Yet it was enough for him to conceive of purpose, to conceive what his own Great Voyage might be. It began to pull him out of the random and chaotic. He had purpose, and thus the assertion of self. He knew direction. His will drew him through the Waking Dream towards other realms, faster and faster. As he came closer to them, dust coalesced around him, giving form and a sense of gravity and the grave.

He hurtled through a shining gateway and slammed violently into a stone floor. He lay as if broken for long moments, and then the momentum of the blood and magic within him jolted him off the ground and into the agony of an animated state. His body convulsed once, twice and then let go a tortured groan.

'Do not try to rise too quickly,' ground a voice around him. 'You might put weight onto your limbs before they have rediscovered their proper strength. They will then snap and you will become a less effective servant to the Declension.'

Ba'zel looked up and around. He was in a roughly hewn red-stoned chamber. The stone stained his hands and clothes and there was a strong smell of sulphur about it. The iridescent Gateway of the Waking Dream was behind him, the shining and watery surface between the posts providing enough light by which to see. Across the chamber from him, and as high as the roof, was a hulking elder bearing the skull scars of the warrior line. Ba'zel had never seen one so old. The elder's skull had the pronounced ridges and horn-like growths of an ancient, where Ba'zel's own skull was still shamefully smooth. The elder's limbs were anything but thin and refined; rather, they served as thick and heavy pillars to support his size.

Ba'zel knew he could not afford to waste any time. They could be coming after him through the Gate at any moment. Creaking and wobbling alarmingly, he levered himself up.

'You are in the third realm,' the warrior said matter-of-factly. 'Who are you and what is your intended destination? We have no need of another here.'

Ba'zel drew himself up and looked the warrior in the eye. Back in the home-realm there would be no question of the elder's higher standing, but here in one of the other realms of the Geas the elder was just a simple guardian, while Ba'zel would be expected to be a Watcher or organising intellect. Yet he hesitated weakly as he began to answer: 'I am . . .' he could not give his true name, for it denoted too lowly a rank '. . . Ma'zel, scion of the house, line and faction of Faal.'

As the elder's eyes narrowed in suspicion, Ba'zel exaggerated his unsteadiness and went back to the floor. 'I have not . . . travelled through the Gate before. It is quite . . . an interruption. I had intended to make it to the seventh realm, which always has a need for more Watchers to help search for an eighth realm, and take us further on the Great Voyage. I must have failed to construct the correct Waking Dream image in my mind's eye to find the seventh realm safely.'

The elder snorted, but not so contemptuously as to cause a degree of offence that would demand violence in response. 'It is not unknown in one so young, Ma'zel, scion of Faal. If you are not fully familiar with the location image, you will inevitably struggle to construct it accurately. You must either return through this Gate to the home-realm and try again, although the result will likely be the same, or you must pass through our Gate that connects this realm to the fourth and find your way on from there. Watchers in both this realm and the fourth keep the Gate between them stable and you will be able to see the correct Waking Dream image before entering. Then you must find the Gate to the fifth, hence the Gate to the sixth, and finally the Gate to the seventh.'

'Very well. You will lead me to the Gate to the fourth.'

'Of course, replenishing your strength with the beings of this realm as we go,' the elder assented. Then a cunning look came into his eye. 'The house of Faal heads the Faction of Origin, does it not? Curious that one of its line should be at the forefront of leading us in the footsteps of the Chi'a, entities who never returned to their origin.'

The warrior was testing him. It was naturally his duty as a guardian of the Gate, but it was also something his kind did to each other whenever they could. It weeded out weakness and ensured only the very strongest had the highest standing. It ensured the Declension remained strong and capable of meeting the extreme demands of the Great Voyage. From the first day of his existence onwards, Ba'zel had been tested. Mentor Ho'zen had tested him daily in their lessons, and then his father had returned home in the evenings to test him yet more. To the Declension existence was a test, a test at which they intended to be more than successful. The Chi'a would not find them wanting. No, rather, it was the beings of all other realms that the Declension would test and inevitably find wanting.

Ba'zel was half inclined not to respond to the elder's clumsy attempts to find some advantage over him, but failure to respond in kind might be construed as an insult as to the other's significance, so Ba'zel smiled indulgently and observed with the sort of remark he'd heard his father say many times before: 'Unless the Chi'a *were* actually seeking to return to their own origin on their Great Voyage? Their path could well have been circular, no? Indeed, there would be a self-affirming logic to that. They were the answer to their own question. Surely the discovery of such unity and self-determination is the purpose of our own Great Voyage, rather than any desire to be stretched thin and ultimately broken apart across the cosmos.'

'An interesting notion,' the elder conceded as he led Ba'zel from the chamber and into a labyrinth of corridors. 'You intend to return to the home-realm one day?'

'Oh, yes,' Ba'zel replied blithely, 'whether as dust or something else.'

Elder Thraal passed out of his chamber and entered the long winding corridors up towards the inner sanctum of the Great Saviour himself. The elder had only walked these levels once before, when his kind had first arrived in this realm millennia ago and all the elders had come to kneel in order to receive the sacrament from their all-seeing leader. The Great Saviour had then removed himself from them, entombing himself so that he might devote all his energies to an ages-long contemplation of this part of the cosmos and a search for sign of the Chi'a and an eighth realm. He'd left the more trivial concerns of the seventh realm and the search for its Geas to the elders he'd brought with him, upon whom he'd bestowed the blessing of his sacrament.

The sacrament bound them all to the Great Saviour and meant that the major purpose and intentions of the Declension in the seventh realm could hardly be thwarted by the actions – intentional or otherwise – of any of its elders or, through them, any of its other members or Drawn races. If it weren't for those few pagans and aberrants who still eluded them, the Declension's goals in the seventh realm would surely have been achieved already. Yet there had ever been the problem of the *unstable*. *Unstable* elements were both inevitable and required if reality and existence were to continue. It was the nature of things, or so it was believed. Without an *unstable* element, all would already be decided; there would be no freedom or movement of will; individual existence would cease; individual races and realms would be no more. It was precisely why small quantities of sun-metal were found in every realm, the inert but sometimes reactive element that prevented the assertive nature and will of various pagan gods and forces from ever becoming truly omniscient or omnipotent. It was precisely why most realms had a quixotic character like the Peculiar, which both helped and hindered all parties involved.

Yet with the *unstable*, Elder Thraal knew, came opportunity. Look how carefully ensuring the southern region of this realm had become *unstable* had served to undo many of the more ambitious opponents among his kind, had taken him a step closer to securing the Geas and helped advance his personal ambition. Look how the agreement he'd made with the Peculiar now brought him further possible advantage.

He scaled higher, leaving deep tracks in the dust of ages and tearing rents through thick walls of cobweb. The arachnids of this place had become outlandish in size, as they had learned to catch the moths, mice, rats and cats – and even human retainers? – that had strayed up here from the levels below. Had they even learned to mimic the sort of light and scent that would attract their prey? With an occasional squeak, huge spiders crashed heavily to the floor as Elder Thraal passed, their life energy Drawn inexorably out of them and their empty bodies joining the general litter of bones and fur in the corridor.

He passed the chambers of the elders who had chosen and agreed to be the sleeping Watchers of the Gate, those who kept the Gate to the home-realm and the greatly distant Gate to the sixth properly open. Then the still chambers of the remaining elders of his kind, some of whom helped the Great Saviour in his endeavour, but the majority of whom watched the seventh realm through its Waking Dream, searching ruthlessly through its mythology and memory, considering its present and working to decide its future. Their decisions came through him, as the ever-wakeful Watcher of the Elders, and it was his task to instigate the necessary action through the organising intellects and their Saints. His was a position of direct influence, albeit that the cost was high, for he aged faster than the other elders.

At last he came to the corridor-like outerchamber of the Great Saviour's tomb, the place where the twelve Disciples stood their vigil. Six giant suits of dull and dusty armour stood with visors lowered along one side of the long and narrow chamber, and six along the other. Any-one seeking to approach the Great Saviour's resting place was invited to pass between the six pairs of guards before reaching the sealed door at the end of the chamber, a door that bore the terrifying sigil of the Eldest's line. The Null Dragon served as warning, threat and, ultim-ately, weapon. Its mouth swallowed sound, its eyes devoured light. Its nostrils stole the air and its icy scales drew all heat and energy from its surroundings. It was a living death. Elder Thraal felt weakened by it, even at this distance.

And this chamber was the approach by which those seeking audience were *invited*. Elder Thraal shuddered to think what awaited those who sought to pass through the stone walls or floor illicitly. No doubt there were ensnaring wards and sun-metal webs to trap and punish even the strongest transgressor forever. Any misstep now and all he had worked for so long to achieve would be lost before he knew it. Perhaps choosing to leave his chamber to come here had been the misstep. Maybe he'd already lost everything. Even before leaving his chamber, he may have misstepped in making the agreement with the Peculiar. But it had been sanctioned by all the elders, and even by the Great Saviour himself. Had the Great Saviour designed things all along then, so that Elder Thraal's own ambitions would ultimately bring him here, ensnare and destroy him? Had the Great Saviour always *known*? Had the Great Saviour deliberately allowed Elder Thraal to raise the inexperienced D'Shaa to the rank of organising intellect, let him put the mad Saint in place, destabilise the southern region and undo D'Selle? All to deliver the means of securing the Geas and the ambitious Elder Thraal into the Great Saviour's hands? Elder Thraal suddenly knew fear. He should never have dared. How could he ever have allowed himself to think he was somehow better than others, that he deserved to be raised above them?

He wanted to go creeping back down to his chamber and pretend he had never come here. But he could not, for he had put the Peculiar in play, and it was becoming ever more dangerous. If steps were not taken now, the Geas might become entirely lost to them. He had no choice. He was trapped. Perhaps he always had been. Trapped by the purpose and intentions of the Declension in this realm, bound by its sacrament. After all, was he not just one small part of the Declension, one small aspect of its all-defining will and purpose? His reason was not his own.

The all-defining will and purpose of the Declension . . . except for the uncertainty caused by the *unstable* element. His reason *must* be his own in some measure. Perhaps it had been temporarily stolen from him instead, stolen by the terrible Null Dragon, just as it tried to rob him of his other proper senses.

Elder Thraal gathered himself. He must play this part or forfeit himself. He must hold to his ambition, for it was all that would see him through. Why hadn't he seen it before? Perhaps the Great Saviour was as trapped as he was by the passing of time and events. Yes, the Great Saviour, even if he did know of Elder Thraal's ambitions, probably dared not see his rival removed for fear it would lose them the Geas. Maybe it was the Great Saviour who was the one afraid of undoing himself. After all, which of the two of them was it who actually hid in his chamber behind guards, wards and a sigil? Which of the two of them was it who would now make demand of the Disciples and be in no doubt that he would be obeyed? Yes, Elder Thraal was now in no doubt as to which of the two of them would ultimately triumph in this realm.

He looked at the first of the suits of ancient armour and addressed it. He could see nothing except darkness behind the visor. None knew exactly what the Disciples were, whether they were Saviours bent and folded up inside the metal carapaces, a little-known race from one of the other realms or something else. They had simply always been there. Some speculated that the suits of armour were actually empty and some sort of magical vehicle for the Great Saviour's will. All Elder Thraal knew and cared about, however, was that they were powerful, and he intended to use that power for his own ends. 'I come to speak, eternal one! The agreement was made with the Peculiar, as per your command. He retrieved the rock woman. He also found the boy and used him to halt something of the plague. As you will have anticipated in your wisdom, eternal one, the Peculiar did not bring the two beings to us. He broke the agreement, as I am sure you had foreseen would happen. Instead of placing the beings within our power, of course, he used the boy to rally the pagans, defeat the Saint named Azual, and bring chaos to the whole southern region.

'There have been two principal consequences to these events, eternal one, consequences I am sure you intended. No doubt there are others to which I am blind, given my lesser rank and nature. The first consequence is that the Geas is now more tightly bound to the boy than ever before. I, like all of our kind, rejoice at this, for it gives us a clear direction for seizing that Geas which is rightfully ours. We have reason to pause, however, for just as the Geas is bound to the boy, so the boy is bound to the Peculiar, through oath and deed. The Peculiar has broken his agreement with us, eternal one, so surely will use the boy for ends that do not coincide with our own. He is loose and now threatens to destabilise the entire Empire. And here is the second consequence, eternal one: the instability of the southern region is likely to spread to the other regions, unless we intervene to bend events back to our will. I already fear for the western region, since its organising intellect, D'Selle, was undone by his own conspiracies, leaving the Saint named Izat of that region with more freedom than is prudent. I can exercise some manner of control, for the sacrament of my own blood was passed on through D'Selle to that Saint, but it is a secondary and limited control, particularly with a Saint who is one of the eldest of the humans. Further, we have had to withdraw our army from the eastern region to settle the south, but the eastern region was ever rife with resistance, barbarians and pagans of some power. We must consider how long the organising intellect of the east can maintain stability there.

'With instability spreading, eternal one, the Peculiar will find it ever easier to pass undetected, until he has passed entirely beyond our means to limit him in any degree. I therefore humbly come to you now, eternal one, to ask for your guidance and all-seeing word, that I may make them manifest as action. Never have we been closer to revealing and seizing the Geas, to establishing the absolute will of the Declension in this realm, but by the same inevitable token never has the force of the *unstable* been greater. Now are the moments when we must meet all that is *unstable* with an equal or greater force if we are to secure the eternal glory of the Declension. Are these not now the moments of unity, when purpose, action and consequence become one, when past, present and future are decided? Are these not the moments of our pre-destination? Eternal one, guide us!'

The last appeal was shouted, but echoed not at all in the chamber. It sounded oddly false to the ear. The Disciples stared emptily back at Elder Thraal.

He realised he was standing tensely so he deliberately relaxed, as if submitting to the will, word and wisdom of the Great Saviour that was to come. He lowered his head to wait, knowing that it might be anything from days to years before any sign was forthcoming that he had even been heard. He tried to still his mind, but could not help wondering what would happen in just a few more months if he did not instigate some action. Those who slept would often lose track of the passing of time in the realm, which was partly why the ever-wakeful Watcher of the Elders was always required. In the past, when he'd received no timely response from the other elders, he'd been forced to decide on actions himself, but that had always been where minor matters were concerned. Dare he do the same now at such a crucial moment? The alternative was unthinkable: attempting to wake the Great Saviour fully. Even if he survived the approach into the Great Saviour's resting place and had enough strength remaining to endure proximity to the eternal one, seeking to awake him would be considered an attempted assassination and Elder Thraal would be undone by the eternal one in the instant.

Dare he decide on actions himself? Even without the power of the Disciples to aid him, there was much he could do through the Saints, Heroes and People alone to slow and waylay the Peculiar and the boy, particularly if Elder Thraal were to wrest the girl from Godsend and find the way to access the boy's sacred heart.

Why would his mind not still? His thoughts were as jumbled and fantastical as one of the younger and lesser ranks. Perhaps the increasing instability had affected them, and through them influenced him. He forced it all to slow and reasserted his control. Had the helmet of the armour to the right shifted to look straight at him? Could it hear his thoughts even now? He brutally quietened himself.

The silence shifted. The air became heavy and pressed in on Elder Thraal's exterior, threatening to break it. The elder softened himself, both to ease his discomfort and so that he could not be seen as offering challenge to the other presence. Cold flame billowed from the Null Dragon and discordant sound rang through the armoured figures.

'We see you, Watcher! Six of these will go to assert our will across the regions of the Empire, strengthen even more the faith of the People and thus answer any encroaching chaos. The Saint of the western region will welcome the sacrament carried there by one of our Disciples, else a greater tithe be exacted from that region. We name D'Syr the organising intellect for the western region, and she shall provide that sacrament. The others will go to every region and part also to watch for sign of the Peculiar's passing. The boy will lead us to the Geas and it will be ours. Then the Great Cull can finally begin.'

Elder Thraal bowed. 'As is your will, eternal one.'

'As is our will, Watcher. Remember that we see you always.'

Elder Thraal bowed again, already tasting his victory.

Aspin watched the struggling flames in the fireplace as a bitterly cold wind found its way round the shutters and the door of his small hut. Wind even managed to find its way down the chimney, which shouldn't have been possible, unless the flue was stuck. The roof creaked ominously, as if it were about to lift off, and everything else rattled hard, as when the headwoman prepared to cast her foretelling bones. There seemed to be more rushing air in the dwelling than it could hold. Was it about to be blown apart? In any event, it seemed that Wayfar of the Warring Winds did not want him here.

He blew on his hands and his breath came out in clouds. He would probably be warmer outside, in some patch of sunlight, than in here. What sort of mountain man was he that he could not stand the cold? Yet ever since he'd returned from the lowlands, he'd found the mountains a hard and inhospitable place to live. He dared not mention it out loud, though, for the other warriors would only sneer that he had become soft in his time away.

Besides, being allowed a hut of his own was a sign that he was now considered a warrior grown, no longer in need of the immediate protection of his father's roof and fire. He was expected to fend for himself and was entitled to take a life mate too, if he could satisfy her parents that he could provide well for a family of his own. How would it look to the mountain people then if he completely abandoned his hut and went creeping back to his father's fireside? The shame to his father would be so great that he would be likely to turn Aspin away anyway.

His feet becoming numb, he stamped, which caused him pain more than anything else. He put his hands beneath his armpits and paced backwards and forwards for a while. He was tempted to go and pay his general respects to his father, just to get warm, but quickly shied away from that. Aspin couldn't help using his unusual ability to *read* others, and was becoming increasingly uncomfortable in his father's presence, because it was clear to Aspin that his father had designs on becoming the next chief of the different mountain communities. Whenever Aspin approached snow-haired Slavin's fire, talk would quickly turn to the matter of which daughters of the mountain would be suitable for Aspin as a life mate; whether their fathers could call on a good number of warriors; whether their mothers advised their husbands well and traded advantageously between clans and communities; whether strong sons and canny daughters might be sired; and so on. Aspin was in no doubt that his father cared not at all for his son's desires in the matter. No,

Slavin's ever-growing preoccupation was to gain those alliances that would not only see him recognised as first among the mountain men, but would also see him secure as chief for generations to come.

Aspin knew better than to tell his father that his spirit often guided his thoughts, eyes and steps towards the home of the coal-haired and leaf-eyed Veena from the waterfall peak. Her community worked a mine but was small and far from wealthy. The clans of the waterfall peak tended to keep themselves to themselves, which was to Aspin's liking and also meant word was unlikely to reach Slavin's ear too quickly about the paths his son's feet found for themselves. Veena's father had been crippled in a cave-in some years before, so he had turned potter in order to scrape a living and see his family fed. When Aspin had first come calling, Veena's mother had made a point of taking him aside, her hands wringing, to confess that her family was too poor to offer any sort of dowry beyond its best pots, and Aspin had spoken for hours to persuade her finally that it was he who should make gift to them.

Aspin could *read* well that it would be a disaster to tell his father. He saw it in his mind's eye as if it had already happened: Slavin forbidding him to go near the waterfall peak again, gently explaining that Aspin showing attention to the girl was bound to keep other possible suitors away, was bound to rob her of the sort of suitable pairing she would normally dream of. It would be selfishness and cruelty on Aspin's part to see Veena any more. After all, how would they live, when Veena's family had nothing to speak of and Aspin had little more than a draughty hovel to his name? Aspin declaring proudly that there was none to match his skill as a hunter. Slavin becoming angry and calling Veena a doe-eyed temptress who had filled Aspin's head with selfish and childish fantasies – when Aspin could be so much more than a savage surrounded by the stinking skins of goats! Aspin becoming angry at the insult to Veena. And then the accusation . . . Aspin condemning his father for becoming obsessed with power and putting his own rise before his duty to the gods. Slavin's eyes blazing at the slight to his honour and giving Aspin but one chance to remember his lowly place and to beg his father's forgiveness.

There were several potential outcomes to the confrontation, none of them good. An honour challenge to combat, almost unheard of between two members of the same clan, let alone between father and son. One or both of them being mortally wounded. Or Aspin avoiding combat by begging his father's forgiveness and continuing to see Veena in secret, only for Slavin's warriors to spy on Aspin and finally confine him to his hut until Veena had been paired with another. Or Aspin pairing with the mountain daughter of Slavin's choice, only for Slavin to become an unchallenged tyrant to his people.

Aspin blinked hard, as if a film of ice had covered his eyes while the vision possessed him. The cold air had become a blade in his chest that cut at his heart. He saw the fire in the hearth had utterly died. Did Sinisar of the Shining Path, He Who Gave the Heat and Light of Life, also forsake him while he remained here? Surely this hut held only doom for Aspin if he lingered too long. Slavin would eventually find out about Veena. It was only a matter of time before Slavin paired his son with a mountain daughter of his own choice. One way or another, Slavin would become chief.

Taking his bow and spears, Aspin fled his hut. Where could he go? How could he halt his father's obsession? He refused to think of killing the man who had raised him with love and who even now probably believed he would claim the position of chief in part for his beloved son. To see hurt and incomprehension replace that love in his father's dying eyes would be beyond Aspin's ability to endure.

With no clear destination in mind, he climbed to the lower village and followed its twisted paths between the stone cottages and goat pens. Perhaps the gods would guide him.

Two children of six or seven years old jumped into his path, brandishing toy spears. He barely noticed and absently stepped around them. They looked disappointed for a moment or two, then ran off to ambush someone more rewarding. Gladhand the Stubborn rose from where he was raking his stony garden, a garden that returned little to him except edible mosses and a few mean herbs every year, and waited to catch the warrior's eye. But Aspin didn't see him. Gladhand the Stubborn shrugged and, without concern, went back to his lifelong battle with the earth, muttering the occasional prayer to Gar of the Still Stone.

Rain began to spit from the piled sky as Aspin climbed higher, but it could not break his reverie. For once, the sweeping slopes, magnificent boulders and broken ridges that became visible above and below did nothing to help him forget his troubles. The distant green of the low-lands and the purple-blue bruises within and behind the clouds could not make him wonder about peoples and sights elsewhere.

In his distraction he took the meandering path to the pool where the women washed their clothes. There were screams and shrieks of outrage as he came round the small crag that hid the col from the view of any except those who came along the path. Fortunately, none of the dozen or so were bathing, but a fair few had their small-clothes laid out on rocks to drain and dry. There was a splashing and scramble to remove these garments from Aspin's sight. Blushing and keeping his eyes carefully averted, Aspin mumbled an apology and hurried away down another jagged path.

Moments later there was laughter and a cackle or two behind him. One of the older women even shouted after him that she could wash his clothes for him if that was what he wanted, although her stiff hands were not as quick as they had once been and he would need to bear with him. 'Be not shy or afeared, young warrior! We will not hurt you!' another called. 'Come, the son of Slavin should be vigorous and able to stand proud!' More knowing laughter.

Hardly seeing where he was going, he stumbled along rarely frequented paths, some that turned back on themselves, some that led him to impassable walls of rock and others that ended in dizzying drops. How could he become so lost here, a place he'd spent pretty much all his life? Outcroppings and silhouettes that had once been the familiar landscape of his youth now seemed disorientating and threatening. What was happening to him? Was he becoming mad? Had Gar of the Still Stone now forsaken him also? How had he offended against the gods? Close to panic, he fell to his knees, cracking them painfully on sharp pieces of shale, and raised his hands in supplication.

'Forgive me, you gods! I do not know how I have erred, but will offer restitution however I may. Guide me, I beseech you! Do not turn your faces from me or your creation against me, I beg. No man can live longer with such horror and punishment, and his final moments would be terrible moments of torment as he realised his transgression against the divine. Have mercy!' Yet the gods were not known for their mercy.

'Show me your will! Guide me so that I may be an instrument to that will!'

Cold wind drove into his face. Hail pelted him, stinging, blinding and choking him. Akwar of the Wandering Waters now combined with Wayfar to lash him. He dared not use his hands to protect himself. Thunder rolled in the distance. He could not keep the tears from his eyes, although they were immediately whisked away.

He could not keep his balance in the sudden gusts and toppled backwards. His spears and bow were almost snapped by the force with which he was thrown. He gathered up his weapons and fled in fear, leaping haphazardly from rock to path to rock again. One slip or moment of bad judgement now and it would spell his doom. Or if the gods chose to loosen a rock, make a stone more slippery, hide the light from him or blow him off course mid-leap, then that would be their final judgement.

He jumped and slid his way across a scree slope, caromed off several giant stones and then careered straight into the side wall of a dwelling place which had appeared as if from nowhere, as if rising up out of the ground to halt his flight. He lay stunned on the ground for long moments. Dark clouds gathered above him and then unleashed their deluge.

Aspin crawled around the corner of the building, head bowed low. To his consternation, he found that he had come to the door of the headwoman's home, the wide building that served as gateway between lower and upper village, between the wider community and the seat of the chief and his chosen warriors, between the people and the holy site of the highest peak in the mountains, and between mortals and the gods. This place was the gateway and crossroads of past, present and future, of wisdom, knowledge and dreams, of ancestral spirits, ominous shades and tantalising phantasms. It was the place Aspin had unconsciously been trying to avoid since his return to the mountains, but the place to which he had ultimately been brought by his own steps, desperate prayer and promise to the gods. None could avoid the future. None could hide from their own dreams forever. Otherwise, he might as well deny all self-knowledge, fear his own existence and knowingly dishonour the gods to whom he owed his life.

'What kept you?' called Torpeth's voice from inside. 'You should know better than to keep your elders waiting, young warrior. Must I come help you as if you were naught but a crawling child attempting its first steps?'

The naked holy man of the mountains jumped over the door sill and helped the shivering Aspin into the smoky interior. 'Come. Some pine nuts will see you restored.'

'Pine nuts may suit old goats and other thoughtless creatures,' croaked the headwoman's voice from somewhere in the gloom, 'but a bowl of my tea will do more to warm and calm him.'

Torpeth cackled and slapped his thighs as if he'd never heard anything funnier. In the process he dropped the unprepared Aspin to the compacted floor by the fire. The ancient holy man then sprang to remove a pot of gently roiling tea from the hot stones around the flames. As he poured out a bowl, the hairs of his lower limbs and nether regions began to singe and fill the shadowy dwelling with an un-pleasant, acrid smell. Having passed the tea to Aspin, Torpeth suddenly realised he was smouldering, and capered around as he attempted to extinguish himself with judicious smacks to the sensitive parts of his body. He yelped louder and louder.

'You leap and cry like a young maiden seeking attention at a wedding dance,' the headwoman creaked with humour.

Aspin watched in bemusement, struggling to understand what he witnessed. He realised there must be herbs in the fire affecting his faculties. And the tea was probably some perception-altering con-coction as well. At least he was no longer shivering; instead, a numbing and soporific torpor had already come over him. One moment he was stiflingly hot, and cold to the marrow the next. A lassitude in his limbs meant he couldn't even lift the bowl out of his lap and to his lips any more.

'Settle down, old goat!' the darkness boomed, and Torpeth subsided at once.

Out of a face as lined and dark as old oak, child-clear eyes of startling blue gazed at Aspin. 'Youth! Have you spent every day drunk for grief or in celebration? Did you take some succubus into your bed, so that it could steal your wits while you slept? Did you come too close to a bucking mule and have it stave in your head, so that you could no longer think straight?'

'I d-don't understand,' Aspin answered thickly, only just managing to coordinate lips and tongue.

'Dolt! Perhaps you are still in the thrall of the dark one, for did you not freely speak with Miserath himself while in the lowlands? You were not so backward before! What must the gods do, personally deliver the invitation before you come to pay your respects to your own head-woman? Or is it your father's pride that now has the better of you? Yes, you know of what I speak – do not pretend otherwise.'

'I-I . . .' Aspin began miserably, and then gave up.

'Beloved Sal, he has been caught in the fork of showing his father suitable respect and of knowing fear of the future,' Torpeth whispered. 'Perhaps a moment's pity?'

'Pity, old goat?' she all but shouted. 'You would speak such a word when your actions in ages past show you do not understand its mean-ing? And you do not know it now!'

Spittle flew from the wizened old woman's mouth as she spoke. It hit Torpeth and he grovelled in the dirt before her. 'Forgive me, beloved, forgive me!' he wailed.

She sneered down at him. 'It is not my place to forgive you, old goat. You know that. Only the gods can offer you forgiveness, but in their wisdom they have judged that, as punishment, you should live on and on with the reality of all that you have caused and all that you have done to our people. You are the naked warrior, in and of your own making. It is only my place to deny you any comfort or happiness. And I deny you that utterly, Torpeth *the Great*. I will *never* be yours.'

'Beloved!' The holy man squirmed, tears streaming down his face. 'Beloved, it is a kindness that you but allow me into your company, that you but let me hear your words, even when they are words of scorn.'

'Silence, old goat! You remind me that perhaps I should ignore you more than I already do. I will think on it further. You will keep your peace until I have done so, else I will not believe you love me in any way. Besides, my attention is better spent on this mooncalf warrior here. Where there is no hope for you, old goat, there may yet be hope for this child and our people.'

The headwoman's angry gaze turned back to Aspin. She clearly did not like what she saw. 'Ah, but he is a dolt! If only you had taught him better, old goat! See, he has dallied and dawdled for far too long. He must think the world waits upon his wonder and whim. See, he has now caused all sorts of dilemma and troubles for himself and others. He has wantonly delayed so that he might indulge his fancy and fantasy with the winsome woman of the waterfall peak. Meanwhile, the seasons and the world turn. The others know better than to remain idle. Already, they have spun new stratagems to ensnare us, already they pull the threads tightly around us in a cinch. Even now, it is not entirely this dolt's homemade troubles and volition that bring him here – it is the concatenation of events elsewhere forcing his feet and hands. Must I now cast the foretelling bones to tell the mooncalf what he already knows? Well, mooncalf, must I rattle the remains of your ancestors before you come to the realisation your friends in the lowlands are beset by enemies on all sides? Must I disturb that which is best left undisturbed? Will that help you understand? The youth Jillan will start to act out of desperation, and struggle like a rabbit whose foot is caught in such a snare that all movement only pulls the trap tighter. Must I weaken myself before you see that rabbit must either chew its leg off, if it has the courage, or wait quietly for the hunter to come and claim its life? Must I make promises to the dead before you see you are also that rabbit and the snare of these mountains is about to pull tighter around you? Well, dolt, must I?'

'I must leave,' Aspin said leadenly. 'My father will never forgive me.'

Torpeth nodded quietly.

Aspin blinked. 'Will my leaving prevent him finding the alliances he seeks? Will it prevent him becoming chief? Will it . . . will it . . . prevent him dooming us all?'

The headwoman rocked backwards and forwards for a moment as she thought on his questions. At last she gave him a toothless grin. 'Not entirely witless, then? Will your leaving prevent our doom? If only something so small could do so, eh, young warrior? If only it could undo the selfish deeds committed by Torpeth the so-called Great so long ago . . .'

The holy man hid his eyes and lowered his head in shame. He folded in on himself, hugging and wrapping his arms around his torso, so that he would be as small as possible, beneath their very notice.

'For the doom of our people may have been decided for us in times long gone. Much as you might wish it otherwise, young warrior, the present and future can do little to change the past. Your father may simply help to decide how quickly our inevitable doom comes upon us. Surely you can *read* what your leaving will mean.'

Aspin nodded. 'My leaving will deny my father certain alliances and make him less secure, but he will become chief nevertheless. He will not be able to become a tyrant quickly. In fact, he will perhaps be a good chief for a while.' Aspin smiled momentarily at that, before adding, 'Something goes wrong later on but I cannot read what or why.'

From beneath the begrimed soles of his feet, one of Torpeth's eyes looked quizzically at Aspin, but the holy man otherwise kept himself bound up.

The headwoman grunted. 'So. You will leave us now, right away. And the meddling and mischievous old goat must go with you.'

Now Torpeth's head came free. The look of horror stretching his features made him all but unrecognisable. 'Beloved, do not send me away!'

She turned a terrible eye towards him. 'Do not, old goat? Do not! You, who brought the preacher from the lowlands here? You, who argued to let him be taken to the upper village, that moment helping to cause the death of Chief Blackwing and allowing his son to take his place at too young an age? Braggar was all raging fire when he became our chieftain, the brightly burning energy of youth that is careless of the precious fuel it burns even in summer, unwary of the perishing winter to come and the need to hoard fuel to stave off the killing cold when it comes. Neither did he have the experience to bank his fire so that it would last through the night and into the morning of the next day. Too quickly and brightly he burned. He did not hesitate to leave the mountains to face the others, taking all our warriors, youth and strength with him. All the while he was flattered and tempted by the smiles and promises of the preacher, so that Braggar did not hear the words of caution spoken by wiser heads, or see the ill omens with which nature and the gods demanded his attention. Would the age-wily Blackwing have acted at all like this, had he been alive? You need not answer.'

The headwoman's eyes rolled back and her voice took on a fearsome tone and cadence that was completely different to anything she had uttered before, as if other spirits, and perhaps even the gods, spoke through her. 'And what came of your meddling, Torpeth, he who was once the favoured servant of the gods? And what will come of it, cursed Torpeth? Brave Braggar and the strength of his people were lost, inevitably betrayed by the preacher. Azual, he who was the instrument of the others, was undone, leaving the way clear for the preacher. For, just as you raised Praxis up among our people, and allowed him to learn some of our secrets, wretched Torpeth, so he has risen up among the others. Praxis is now risen and marches in strength! You have made Praxis a far greater evil to us than ever Azual could have been, damned Torpeth! For Praxis knows us well, foul Torpeth, knows our strength and where we lie. His eyes and intent will soon turn to these mountains and he will bring us our doom. You, crazed Torpeth, have brought disaster to our people more surely than snow-haired Slavin or even our dark brother Miserath ever can. And it is not just our people you will ruin, for, with the doom of our people, so the gods will be ended and the Geas itself raped until it is no more. The entire world has been and will be undone by you, as it ever was, misbegotten Torpeth.'

The naked man thrashed on the ground as if his entrails were being pulled out. He tried to scream, but only silence came from the rictus mask of his face and throat. Involuntarily, his hands raked up dust and dirt, nails tearing, and crammed the earth into his mouth, nose and eyes.

Yet the detonating voice and judgement did not relent. 'And still you plead this *Do not!* of us. Still you think only of yourself and your wants and desires. Miserable and mischievous Torpeth! Your crimes, sins and blasphemies are beyond all compass and penitence. Nothing you do can repay what you have done, yet payment will ever be due while we keep you animated enough that you may be tortured and tormented by all that you have brought to pass. No longer will the people of these mountains suffer your presence. All will turn their face from you, be they person or animal. Should you seek to milk a goat, her udders will be dry. Should you seek out birds, they will stop laying eggs and smash any in the nest or roost. Should you find any pine nuts, they will rot and wither in your hands. These mountains are now denied you. You are the lowest creature that ever existed, and will only find response now from the annihilating others. You will accompany our servant here into the lowlands and do whatever he commands and whatever you may. Only when the impossible is made possible will you ever be permitted the death and rebirth of the Geas. Otherwise, the eternal annihilation of the others is all you will have. Our servant Sal will live, like you, as witness to the doom of our world, and only she will understand what you suffer, the closest thing to compassion or love that you will ever know, but it will remain impossible for you ever to see her again. That is our judgement and will, sweet Torpeth, and now you are banished forever more from our notice!'

The silence that followed was as awful as the speaking of the curse had been. Rigid with fear, Aspin realised he had messed his breeches. Torpeth lay stricken and stretched out, as if dead. The headwoman gasped and her eyes became her own once more. She shuddered and leaned forward, panting to get her breath. In a normal voice, and as if she was not entirely aware of what had just passed, she said, 'The old goat will go with you now. You will leave right away. Do not attempt to take your leave of your father, for you know he will not understand and will only seek to confine you. I will tell him you have gone, and with that he must be satisfied, although he will never be contented.'

Yet there was someone Aspin cared about just as much – perhaps more – someone for whom he could find the power of his voice, albeit strangled and strained. 'A-And Veena?' She of the leaf-green eyes, night-spun hair and deliberate gentleness. 'What of her? May I exchange oaths with her before . . . before . . . May I ask her to . . . wait, at least?' He feared the answer as much as he anticipated it, as much as he already knew it.

The headwoman looked genuinely sad and heart-weary for him. She answered quietly, like a leaf falling from a tree, or a snowflake touching the ground, or a blade of grass trembling in a breeze. 'Should she wait for one who might never return? Should she see out her days always hating to look to the horizon for fear of the lack of any sign you are coming back to her? Should she never bear children or know the comfort of a warm body next to hers? Should wrinkles appear on her face and streaks of white appear in her hair without her ever knowing passion? Will she ever know happiness in such a life? Perhaps the answer is yes, young warrior, perhaps it is. For once, I do not know. In this, I am no wise woman. In this, even the gods would be silent. I believe there are mysteries and matters that no power can ever dictate, young warrior, and this is one of them. The human heart is as terrible as it is wonderful and sometimes miraculous. I am sorry I have no simple answer for you, but probably the only person who can ever give an answer is you yourself.'

The headwoman shifted. 'Now, lean closer, for I will whisper the secret of the Broken Path to you, to speed you on your way, although one day you may wish you had never heard it. Then you will haul this rubbish of skin and bones out of here for me, this poor thing called Torpeth, and I will wish you godspeed, luck and pity, young warrior. Be not down of heart at what you leave behind, for it is your past. Look forward with joy to helping your friends in the lowlands, and you may yet delay the doom of your people, and save her upon whom you've fixed your heart. Be brave, young warrior, and you may yet know happiness, short though it may be. Whole lifetimes can be lived in such moments, dear Aspin, whole lifetimes.'

Ba'zel broke open another of the beings of the third realm and drank down its purple blood before the magic could dissipate and the fluid thicken and harden. He felt sick to his every extremity – he'd long since taken in enough to sustain him, and the excess now gurgled in his stomach and came back up his throat uncomfortably. He saw it as somehow greedy and wasteful to keep having more, but knew his kind generally considered it only wise for an individual to build their personal reserves whenever the opportunity presented itself. Not to do so was to allow the escape of prey that a rival might then claim. It was therefore stupidity and weakness not to gorge when faced with the chance.

He casually discarded the retainer's body and made a point of looking round as if for further sustenance. He let his sight miss a few of the beings cowering in the shadows – if he consumed more, he knew he would become observably ill, and the large warrior leading him would be unlikely to tolerate such obvious signs of weakness. Ba'zel also subtly muted the power of his presence so that he would not incidentally draw energy from his surroundings and any nearby retainers. There was little chance the elder would notice Ba'zel's reduced draw anyway, since the elder drew so strongly himself from all around, just his proximity ageing the beings of the third realm with devastating effect.

'What is this place?' Ba'zel asked, mostly to distract the warrior.

'Why do you ask?' came back the suspicious response.

'One never knows what may come in useful,' he extemporised. 'Perhaps I can learn something from this place to help us when we find the eighth realm. And it might amuse me.'

'*Amuse?*' the warrior sneered, contempt obvious in his voice. 'This is no concept of the Declension!'

'Then perhaps we have been influenced unduly by our contact with – and consumption of – the beings of other realms. But do not misunderstand me, for I do not talk of anything frivolous or wasteful. Instead, I talk of testing the reality here, in order to find its principal lack. I use the term *amuse* as a functional exponent for a larger complex of meaning and intent, be assured. Answer my question.'

The warrior brooded on the young Saviour's words for several moments and then, with a grudging look, began to explain the strangeness of the realm's particular labyrinth. 'We are passing through the Chamber of Infinite Echoes. Throughout the aeons that we have been here, this place has never been silent. We do not believe it was ever silent before our arrival either. The sound of all life in this realm somehow ends up here, even if much of it is fainter than the fading memory of a youthful dream. Some postulate that all the sound of the past is here also, including the sound of this realm's moment of creation, whatever that was. Whether that is the case or not, all agree that all this is the very sound of the realm's Geas, which will also be the key to our at last finding and claiming that Geas. We are very close now. Since our arrival, our Watchers have waited here, in the Waking Dream of this realm. Our Great Saviour has spoken that all that can be heard will soon have been heard. The Geas, in its entirety, will finally be revealed to us. We will seize it and then the Great Cull will begin, so that the Geas of the home-realm may be fed properly and restored for aeons to come, until we have found more realms to conquer and use as stepping stones on our Great Voyage.'

Ba'zel nearly swooned with nausea. What was wrong with him? 'What are these constructions here?' he blurted and gestured randomly as more of the angular objects that littered the dark materialised around them. 'They are made of base metals, are they not? To what end?'

'Meaningless artefacts of this realm,' the warrior snorted. 'Before our arrival, the beings of this realm seemed to preoccupy themselves primarily with building these . . . *engines*, I think they call them. Yes, building more and more engines, some of them truly vast, and procreating, of course. You see, Ma'zel, scion of Faal, the beings here have only ever had a vague notion of their Geas, which is partly why we have found it so hard to uncover its hiding place. At the same time, it was that very same vagueness that made it so easy for our organising intellects to conquer and cow the beings of this realm in the first place. For the beings here had only a passing interest in gods and spirits with which to resist us. They much preferred their engines, as if they were shrines of a sort, shrines to artifice and artistry. They seemed to think that *amusement* and inspiration could make them greater than they already were, could allow them to create . . . create what? Who knows? A new Geas? Life? New realms of artifice? Perhaps they would have ultimately succeeded, but it is of no consequence now. Here, then, is what amusement brings, Ma'zel.'

Ba'zel knew that he was being baited by the untiring warrior. The elder would keep testing, nudging, prompting, jostling, picking and nagging at him until they parted ways or until Ba'zel succumbed and a fatal confrontation ensued. Ba'zel knew he was slowly being worn down and that the elder would finally triumph. *My energies and skin are too thin to withstand him for that much longer.*

His only chance was if they came to the Gate of the fourth realm quickly. How, though? The warrior would be unlikely to allow that. Perhaps the warrior had been deliberately walking them in circles since they'd entered the labyrinth, to ensure that they never actually arrived at the Gate. *I should have studied these engines more closely from the beginning, so that I would know if we had passed any of them more than once.*

'Perhaps we should take this opportunity to study some of these engines,' Ba'zel ventured with a shrug. 'Who knows what they might reveal? Perhaps the inspiration of the original artists came from their Geas and they sought to represent its essence.'

'*Artists!*' the warrior scornfully echoed. 'What is becoming of our kind? There is only one true art, and that is the art of the Declension and our superior expression of being. Our every word and action is our art, as we make progress on our Great Voyage. Do not speak to me of other beings as true artists! Come!'

In answer, Ba'zel deliberately lingered by the next engine to which they came. It was rusted through and teetering on the point of collapse. 'I do not know that the Eldest shares your mind. But perhaps you're right, I should not delay in my service to the intent that is the Great Voyage.' With that, Ba'zel picked up his feet and began to overtake the warrior.

There had been an audible and sharp intake of breath from the elder at Ba'zel's mention of the Eldest. To name her was always to risk attracting her attention. Somehow, she always *knew* what had been said and been thought. There could be no hiding or deception whatsoever. And all too frequently death came to those who were not totally unambiguous and self-erasing in their loyalty to her. A stray word or speculative thought could be fatal. The warrior now hurried to lead Ba'zel as quickly as the young Saviour wanted to go. 'Tell on, Ma'zel, scion of Faal. I have shared information with you and lead you still, so it would only be in accord if you reciprocated. Out here in the third realm we are sometimes slow to learn of the latest thought of the home-realm, so you will forgive us if the norms we follow are . . . are . . .'

'As old as these engines?'

The warrior swallowed hard, accepting the insult. 'Perhaps. And perhaps what you tell might also win followers to the Faction of Origin.'

The elder was almost begging, a quite unseemly display in one so large. Ba'zel waved the other onto greater speed and then condescended to say, 'Well, it is said that the thinking of the Eldest is so expanded beyond our own that we can never successfully know it. In fact, that which we don't know and instinctively dismiss will be completely known and incorporated by her. Where our own examination of the art of other realms reveals nothing, she can glean secrets of the various Geas, and perhaps even the cosmos itself. Her greatness, therefore, continues to increase while we remain the same. How else could she guide us further and further through the different realms and levels of consciousness and being? In their proximity to her, those in the home-realm perhaps see and accept this more quickly than those in the other realms. Terms like *amusement* and *art* are used more often by our kind in the home-realm. Therefore, perhaps those in the home-realm are closer to her will. I do hope that those in the other realms do not drift so far from that will that a *purge* becomes necessary. Yet perhaps it is inevitable.'

'A purge!' the warrior yelped with despicable cowardice, and raced ahead. 'The gate is not far, Watcher. We have travelled more quickly than I could have hoped. See, its light shimmers just ahead there.'

Abruptly, the Chamber of Infinite Echoes took on a strange pitch. The engines and the space itself began to resonate. The thin membranes of Ba'zel's skull buzzed painfully. What was happening?

'Members of the Declension!' thundered a hideous voice from all around. 'OBEDIENCE is come! All in this realm will make themselves known to me.'

'A Virtue? Here!' squealed the warrior, staring at Ba'zel. 'What have you done? What have you brought among us? Why Obedience, of all the Virtues? None here has disobeyed, I swear it!'

'I-It is the purge!' Ba'zel choked. 'It has come sooner than I anticipated. Quickly! See me into the next realm and the Virtue may consider your alacrity of service as a sign of loyalty and obedience!'

They dashed forward and Ba'zel hurled himself into the shining portal as the entire third realm roared with anger and its light was extinguished.

# CHAPTER 4:

# Undoing means and ends

'**A** nice day though it is for a walk,' the Peculiar opined as he looked up at the clean spring sky, 'we dare not amble along like this for too long. Jillan, you'll need to pick up those plodding feet of yours if we're ever going to make it as far as the western region in order to find the temple of Akwar and the route on to Haven. Creation will get bored and entirely give up if we carry on at this pace. Meanwhile, our enemies close in around us. Do you not think you might run for a stretch? Come, it will make you fit, no?'

Jillan glared at the diaphanous young man the Peculiar had chosen to represent himself as that morning. The sword of sun-metal bent around the god's brow was an artful crown that only augmented his beauty. The toga that robed the vision did nothing to hide the holy avatar's lean muscles and perfect physique either. It was all intended to persuade the onlooker of the divine majesty of Miserath, and to cause them to seek his favour by accession to his will. Jillan was not swayed one jot by the spectacle, nor would he have been if the Lord of Mayhem had transformed and bedecked himself as an exquisite female. Even with his magic much diminished, Jillan's state of mind meant he was far beyond such influence. *She* had done this to him. Crushed the heart within his chest and burned all the love out of him. The depiction before him now left him cold and provoked only a dull resentment at the obvious attempt to manipulate him.

'I have an idea,' Jillan said flatly. 'You will change yourself into a horse and I will ride you all the way, whipping your behind when you dare to flag.'

'What?' the Peculiar seethed, his beauty slipping for a moment. 'How dare you? That is a blasphemy!'

Freda, who rolled along the road just behind Jillan, made a rumbling noise in her chest, which all knew to be her sign of amusement. The stony skin at the corners of her mouth cracked as she struggled not to grin too conspicuously. She only succeeded in increasing the Peculiar's outrage.

'Need I remind you I am a *god*? You should be worshipping me, if anything. I am not some beast of burden, to be used as you see fit! Besides, if I were to increase my size, I would become more disparate and insubstantial. My back would not be solid enough to support you. You will desist from having any such ideas again!'

'All right, keep your hair on,' Jillan replied disinterestedly. Then his eyes narrowed. 'We'll have to get a horse from elsewhere, and I think I know just the place and people. We need to take the road for Heroes' Brook.'

'Are you mad?' the Peculiar asked, rolling his eyes in opposite directions. 'We'll get no welcome there. Minister Stixis has ever had a tight grip on that town. Even I would struggle to pass unnoticed or affect their affairs. And it can be no coincidence that the plague has yet to find its way into the community. There is no place for any such as us.'

'Am I mad?' Jillan shouted back at the god. 'You should know, shouldn't you? Are you not the god of such things? Many would certainly question the wisdom of even speaking to you, let alone making an agreement with you and accompanying you the length and breadth of the Empire! All this *is* madness!'

'Friend Jillan, it's all right,' Freda said tentatively. 'I do not think you are mad. You are brave. And kind.'

'And what has it ever got me, eh?' he snarled savagely. 'What has it ever done for my friends except see them dead of plague, dead in battle or imprisoned within the walls of Godsend?'

'And what did it do for your parents?' The Peculiar nodded.

'Yes!' Jillan screamed, silencing the birds in the trees. He swallowed. More quietly, he repeated, 'Yes. What did it do for them?'

'They died saving the son they loved above all else,' the Peculiar reminded him. 'They willingly gave themselves so that you could survive, freely be yourself and thus challenge the tyranny of the Empire. Do not make a mockery of their love and sacrifice, Jillan. They would not want to see you like this. They would want you to accept your responsibility and claim the power of the Geas.'

'*Me* make a mockery of them?' Jillan hissed. 'It was *you* who saw them to the gates of Hyvan's Cross and then abandoned them! It was your half-promises and falseness that betrayed their lives! It was *you* who mocked them, just as you have always mocked humankind. And did not Torpeth once say you had even betrayed your fellow gods?'

'Was it me who betrayed your parents, Jillan? Was it really? Or was it your wilfulness right from the start that brought all this about? Was it not your defiance of the Minister and your murder of Karl? Or would you blame me for that? Was it not *your* magic that brought the plague and death to so many?'

'People only died of my magic because the Saint had Drawn their own magic out of them when they were young, a magic that otherwise would have saved them. Once I discovered that, I healed as many as I could. Did you do the same, or were you too busy spinning new schemes and devising new deceits, you who are called the King of Lies?'

Freda put her hands over her ears, unable to cope with her only friends arguing. She made a crooning noise to block out their voices and squeezed her eyes tight.

'You speak of what you do not understand.' The Peculiar sniffed. 'If it were not for what you term my *schemes*, Freda here would have been boiled alive and eaten by Goza, the greedy Saint of the north. Azual would never have been defeated either. And you would be dead at the bottom of a phagus pool. Think on that before you choose to get pious and sanctimonious with me, boy! Even now, I'm having to drag you along as if you were a surly child not wanting to go to school.'

'And you would have me believe you are acting selflessly in all this, I suppose? Ridiculous! Your empty schemes are self-justifying and ultimately useless, Miserath, are they not? They only create mayhem, I suspect. Whenever you plan for a different goal, I expect it's just a roll of the dice as to whether you actually achieve it. You could not even reliably obtain me a horse in advance, could you?'

The Peculiar pulled a gargoyle face at Jillan and stuck out his tongue. 'So provide us with a horse, he who would presume to know the gods better than they do themselves! Before you put me to sleep with your self-pitying carping.'

Knowing better than to answer further, Jillan clenched his jaw and turned on his heel. He tugged on Freda's arm, to signal to her that they were leaving, and started the march towards Heroes' Brook. Freda and the Peculiar trailed along in silence behind him.

As they went, the Peculiar suddenly glanced back over his shoulder, as if to catch something following them. The road was empty. He frowned at the trees along each side of the road. Nothing stirred. With an irritated growl to himself, he turned back to catch up with his charges.

Samnir heard her voice calling to him seductively. He tried to resist, but something in him responded to it and dragged him towards her. Why could he never deny her?

*Because we share a wonderful love, sweet Samnir,* Saint Izat whispered. *You feel it as much as I do. Your body feels it and yearns to be with me again. Why would you resist me? Our union is a blessed sacrament. We are wedded by love, blood and mind, my dearest.*

'No!' he insisted in his sleep, and fought his way to wakefulness.

He was exhausted. He could not train and fight with the men during the day, only then to fight his Saint during the night.

'Too old, too old,' he muttered as he rubbed at his gritty eyes. 'And she knows me too well.'

He'd fallen asleep in the chair again, and knew his limbs would be stiff and his joints sore all day as a consequence. Even worse, Jillan had apparently failed to light any sort of fire to warm their cottage the night before, or to leave out any cold supper for when Samnir returned home late. It was quite unlike the boy.

'Jillan!' he shouted a bit testily, never at his best when he hadn't eaten. He cleared his throat a bit so that his voice wouldn't be quite so gruff. 'Where are ye, lad? Come on, up ye get! The hunting so bad that we didn't even have enough to trade for bread?' The soldier winced even as the words left his mouth. His humour was too rough. Jillan had become sensitive about his recent run of bad luck with the bow. 'Sorry, lad – meant nothing by it. Come out here and we'll swap our news. I heard that one of the younger Heroes – Halson, I think his name is – intends to ask the carpenter's daughter to step out with him. Help me out, lad, what's her name, now?'

There was only silence from Jillan's room.

'Jillan!' he shouted more loudly. 'Now where's that lad got to?'

Jillan's bow was gone from its usual place by the door. Had he already left for the woods? Thinking on it, perhaps the bow hadn't been there last night either. Maybe the boy had been so hungry he'd gone to spend the night at Jacob the trader's. That would explain the lack of a fire and cold supper here. Still, Samnir was surprised Jacob would have allowed Jillan to spend the night through. Or was Jacob still away from Godsend?

'Why, you young rogue, Jillan Hunterson.' Samnir smiled. 'Hella's pa won't be best pleased if he finds out you've been helping yourself to more than just his stores while he's away! Still, it's probably past due that Jacob and I had that chat about getting the two of you settled. By all that's right and holy, you should have your happiness while you can.'

The soldier heaved himself to his feet and hobbled over to the curtain that divided Jillan's bedchamber from the main room. There was indeed no sign of the boy, so Samnir collected his sword belt off the floor and slowly straightened up, his back cracking in several places.

'Ah! That's got it. Can't expect the men to stand to attention if I'm bent double myself, now can I?'

There was more to it than that, of course. If he didn't look the part of a strong leader, then he wouldn't be able to instil confidence in the men, and then even more would try to desert. The town couldn't afford to lose them, since the food stores running low had already seen a spate of men disappearing each night. Godsend partly struggled to support so many fighting men because it was a small town, but the main problem was that trade between the towns of the region had gone into bad decline. In the normal way and order of things, as the town closest to the wilds, Godsend would have been able to offer the rich furs its hunters brought in, the semi-precious stones found close to the mountains and its much renowned spring-fresh ales in exchange for extra foodstuffs. But the normal way and order of things had been completely destroyed during the battle with the Saint. Now, none of the other towns seemed eager for Godsend's goods. Whether it was because they represented unnecessary luxury or were somehow seen as tainted, he wasn't entirely sure. It was probably a bit of both. After all, Godsend was reputed to be the origin of the plague. Jacob had made a point of telling traders from other towns that Jillan had ended the sickness in Godsend, only for a number of them to ask in all earnestness whether that was sign the town's entire population had pledged itself to the Chaos.

Samnir had hoped that, with the death of the Saint, everyone in the south would have been able to see the world differently and understand the Empire for what it was. He had hoped the people of the south would have come together as one, to stand against the Empire's tyranny. They had been freed of the Saint's controlling mind and magic, and now had the chance to fight for the freedom of all the People. He now realised he'd been a fool to think such things. Not only did the other towns seem to want nothing to do with Godsend, but its own Heroes seemed less and less sure there was anything worth staying and fighting for.

He'd done everything he could think of to keep morale high and the men distracted, but discipline was an increasing problem. He'd organised competitions among the men to find champions in the use of different weapons and skills. He'd prevailed upon some of the mountain warriors to teach their style of combat before they'd had to return home. He'd drafted in some of Godsend's hunters to teach the men tracking and an ambush-and-retreat sort of warfare suited to the woods. He'd tasked those soldiers with a feel for stone and wood to help with rebuilding, so that they would take pride in their town. He'd even encouraged his Heroes to think of starting the families that they'd always been forbidden in the Empire. Still things had not improved, and finally, to reduce the number of desertions, he'd been forced to seal all the town's gates at night, increase the numbers of guards, double the number of patrols, promote some of the harder men to officer positions and institute a tougher system of punishment. In short, he'd just ended up turning Godsend into exactly the sort of prison it had always been under the Empire. The thought sickened him and made him feel he had failed somehow.

It wasn't enough to fight the Empire. The men – and the townsfolk themselves – also needed a sense of meaning to replace the idea of the Empire. Very few had turned to a worship of the old pagan gods, for were not those gods fallen? What use could the gods be against the Empire? Besides, every Hero and citizen of Godsend had been raised to mistrust those gods, to think habitually of them as selfish and conniving aspects of the Chaos, aspects that had no real interest in the well-being of the People – quite the opposite, in fact. Samnir himself had no real interest in bending his knee to some non-manifest decrepit supernatural being. *I may as well start praying like some superstitious peasant to stones, trees, water, the sun and chickens*, he chuckled to himself. But that still left the question of what could possibly replace the faith and natural order of the Empire, not to mention – and it could not be denied – the peace, prosperity and moments of fulfilment it offered.

'Why have I fought so hard myself?' he pondered out loud. 'The boy, of course. And his magic, a magic he once told me is the People's birthright, a birthright that has been stolen from the People by the Empire. I have known Saints well enough to know they are more than capable of crimes of such enormity. I know in my gut, heart and mind that the Saviours have done anything but *save* the People. My very soul chimes with the truth in Jillan's words when he says they ensure we are less than we should be, but do others hear it as I do? Do they *want* to hear it? The truth is too hard to bear. Most are terrified of even beginning to believe it. It would mean they'd lived a lie. It would mean the Book of Saviours, which they had learned all their lives, was nothing but falseness. It would mean an end to their devotion to Saviours, Saints, Ministers and even Heroes. It would mean . . . chaos. They would knowingly have to allow the world to be turned over to the Chaos, and their every instinct would resist such a thing. Even I am not sure it can ever be wise. Look at the region – already town is turning against town, mistrustful, and probably frightened, of the selfish nature of others now that we are no longer united in working towards the greater good of the Empire. How long before neighbour turns against neighbour in the same town, or in Godsend itself? Will we ultimately destroy ourselves by following this course, even without the Empire coming to reclaim this region? Yes, unless we can recreate a unity be-tween the towns.'

Godsend had to lead the region towards a new type of unity, or there could be no hope whatsoever. And it needed to do it soon, before those in the south began to tear themselves apart and all the People fled back to the Empire. It was high time Godsend sent representations with offers of healing, trade and protection to the other towns. Samnir was slightly angry with himself that he hadn't seen the need sooner, but there had been more than enough to do inside Godsend during the winter, just seeing to it that everyone had shelter, provisions and enough wood to stay warm.

And it was also high time Jillan became a more visible figurehead around which the People could rally. The young lad could cure the plague, had a message to share, whether he fully realised it or not, and could represent some new sort of hope. If the boy could just be persuaded to step forward a little more, then the region might have some chance of mounting a credible resistance against the wider Empire. Thus far, however, Jillan had fought shy of being too visible, and Samnir had indulged it, thinking the boy too young for such responsibilities and pressure. But now he wondered if he'd mollycoddled him, too sensitive to the loss of his parents. How well had Samnir really served Jillan in seeking to protect him from the realities of Godsend's situation? How well had he served Godsend itself?

'What were you really trying to achieve, you old fool? To restore a childhood to the lad that was already lost? To give him something you never had yourself? Fool! It's simple – if the lad's old enough to be stepping out with Hella and staying away from home for the night, then he's more than old enough to take on all the duties of adulthood.'

Growling at himself, Samnir now knew he hadn't done enough. It was never enough. He just prayed he hadn't left it too late. First, to find the boy and tell him what was now expected. Then to organise a new town council that could oversee the embassies to other towns. Jacob the trader would need to be a member, if not the head, of course. Jillan himself, probably. Thomas, if he could be wrestled away from his smithy. Ash, if only to give the inebriate something to do other than drink the town dry. Samnir or one of his senior officers. Halson the carpenter. Maybe they should find someone who could teach the children of the town, now that there would never be another Minister. And the town could decide on the other members.

Before leaving the small dwelling place, Samnir made sure to wet his face and quickly use his lethal blade of sun-metal to shave. He'd taken up again this ritual of his early years as a Hero, in order to test the steadiness of his hand and reassure himself of his own mettle. He raked his hand through his coarse salt-and-pepper hair a few times and then stepped out into the early morning light of Godsend.

He marched through the southern quarter of the town, nodding to the animal tenders who were already up and on their way to take the town's remaining cattle and sheep to the grazing pastures beyond the west gate. Samnir noted the squad of Heroes already waiting at the gate to accompany and guard the workers for the day. The soldiers saluted smartly as he passed, which he acknowledged approvingly before taking the turning to Jacob's house.

He heard Hella's raised voice from a street away, angry and clearly telling someone off. A low voice in reply, by turns conciliatory and defiant. Samnir couldn't help smiling to himself as he assumed Jillan was receiving an early lesson in married life. The smile froze on his face as he rounded a corner to find Hella shouting from the top of her stairs down at Haal Corinson. What was this? The way the young woman was brandishing a besom broom and the way the youth was holding the side of his face made it clear she'd just fetched him a hefty clout.

'. . . you kissing me, Hella!'

'Haal Corinson, I don't know what you've been drinking, but I did no such thing. I was here tending my sick father all day. I didn't even go to our stall yesterday. You'd better not have been spreading your lies around the town, you hear, or you'll be sorry! I don't know what Jillan will say when he finds out.'

'You didn't seem worried about that yesterday!' Haal protested. 'And so what if he should find out? It's not like you're life mates or anything. And there's no Minister to say the words neither!'

Hella's cheeks flamed as red as Haal's own. 'That's none of your concern, Haal Corinson! Those are private matters, not for the likes of you. You've always been jealous of us, and you're just trying to ruin it all. Why must you always be so cursed mean?' She stamped her foot. 'Just you remember what happened to Reba the Gossip some years back!'

'Jealous?' Haal snorted. 'Of that devil-friend? No honest man would be jealous of that—'

'That's enough!' snapped Samnir, who had approached without them noticing. 'Before one of you says something you'll really regret. The middle of the street is no place for this. In fact, there's *no* place for such talk. The pair of you should be ashamed of yourselves.'

Haal looked down at his feet, but mumbled, 'Hen't done nothing wrong. Plenty saw her come kiss me outside the north gate!'

Hella opened her mouth to retort, but Samnir pre-empted her in tones that would have made one of his own veterans quail. 'I said that's *enough*! Hella, look at me! Where's Jillan? And how is it your father's sick? No one even informed me he'd returned.'

Hella blinked. 'Jillan said he was going to tell you my father was attacked. Robbers on the road from Heroes' Brook. They took everything, even our horses!'

'What?' Samnir exclaimed. 'I haven't seen Jillan. He wasn't home last night. I assumed he was here with you.'

Hella shook her head, worry creasing her brow. 'I last saw him yesterday morning. He was supposed to come to see me last evening so we could have a talk. When he didn't come knocking, I imagined he was angry. We'd had words, you see, but I think he misunderstood me.' Now her voice took on a frightened note. 'Samnir, where can he be?'

Haal had looked up at Hella's mention of her argument with Jillan. He nodded slightly, as if it came as no surprise. It all made sense to him, and his jaw stuck out as if he'd been vindicated.

Samnir was in no doubt Haal believed the claims he was making to be true. Yet none of it sounded like the young woman Jillan cared about so much. He thought furiously for some seconds before speaking again, looking at each of them in turn to be sure he had their attention.

'There is too much here for me not to believe some great mischief has gone on. No, Haal, I cannot accept that mischief is down to Hella. Think, lad! Hella cannot have had any part in the robbery, and yet it has somehow coincided both with what you yourself have experienced and Jillan's disappearance. I cannot fathom it entirely, but my every instinct tells me something has moved with deliberateness against us.

There is some shape to all this that feels familiar, if I could but grasp it. You will trust me in this, both of you. Do you understand? Without Jillan, this town will not be able to stand against the Empire for long. I fear we have allowed him to be taken from us far too easily. We have not been vigilant. We have been remiss, the three of us. We have become caught up in our own daily concerns and struggles, looking at what is immediately before us rather than watching the season and sky for what lies ahead. Can you see that?'

Wide-eyed, they nodded back at him. 'Has the Empire already taken him then?' Hella ventured. 'Is it already over for us?'

'I pray not!' Samnir replied fiercely. 'While I still have the strength to raise my sword, I will not be stayed. While I still breathe the air, I cannot give up this fight. While my will survives, I cannot rest. Jillan has given us this freedom, and for that we all owe him. We must do whatever we can. To do otherwise would be to let him down. Worse, it would be to let each other down, to let ourselves down. We must put aside any division between us before it can undo us. It would only otherwise allow our enemies in among us all the sooner. I fear the Empire will look to march in strength against us now. We must be ready. It is time Godsend finally awoke from its winter slumber and prepared itself properly. We must watch closely for the Empire's coming. We must do whatever we may to marshal the region. And we must do what we can to see if we can wrest Jillan back to us.'

Haal drew his heavy brows down, a new determination about him. 'What should I do?'

'You must organise the search of the town, Haal Corinson. Rouse Thomas, Ash and whomever you may. I will send out parties of my Heroes to scour the woods. I will also lead a sizeable contingent to hunt down these thieves. We need those supplies they have taken, the exercise will usefully direct the restlessness of some of the men, and it will communicate a positive message to the towns of the region.'

'More than that,' Hella insisted. 'Jillan's quite capable of having gone off after the thieves on his own. You must question them, Samnir.' Sternly, she warned him, 'You mustn't just go killing them.'

Samnir inclined his head. 'As you command, milady.' Then he turned serious again. 'How well is your father? For a difficult task yet remains, one that is perhaps as important to the survival of this town as any other. Perhaps you can work in his stead for a while, Hella.'

'The physicker-woman said he should be allowed on his feet for a few hours today. We will do whatever we can, but he is weak. What would you have of us?'

'Hella, we need to win support from the other towns. I have never known how to negotiate, barter and dicker well, and do not know where to begin. I do not know anyone on the councils of the other towns either. Jacob has many acquaintances through his trade, how-ever. I wish to give him full authority to represent all the resources of Godsend. If we cannot win support, then we will at least need to be able to gather useful information about what goes on elsewhere in the Empire.'

'So, if not agreements, then spies,' Hella said after a moment, beginning to think out loud. 'If you have men who are discreet and trustworthy, then we can instruct them. They must know how to watch, listen, subtly question, influence and bribe where necessary. If we act quickly, then no trace of Jillan should escape us. We'll have him hauled back, and then he can have a good piece of my mind! I'll never let him out of my sight again.'

Jillan smiled and drew on his diminished magic, fully prepared to kill the dozen or so people ranged around them with bows drawn. After all, in stealing from Godsend the thieves had endangered the lives of the townsfolk, so it seemed only right that the thieves should pay with their own lives in turn.

'Oh, how droll!' The Peculiar laughed. 'They have come to us! And here I was thinking it would be a right old bother getting a horse. Looks like it will be far more fun than I had imagined.'

'Silence!' barked a large man standing on a low rock. His clothes looked oft-patched and his beard was slightly matted, but his aim was steady and his eye unblinking. 'Take off that crown and throw it over here, pretty boy, or my arrow will make a mess of you!'

The Peculiar drew himself up. 'Perhaps you've heard of me? Miser-ath? Anupal, friend to every man? Ring any bells?'

The large man moved his jaw sideways and spat on the ground. 'Nope! You can take off those fancy clothes too.'

'You are as foolish as you are impertinent,' the Peculiar said in a low thrum. 'You are as backward as you are large.' The eyelids of a few of the younger thieves seemed to be getting heavy. 'You are as ill-mannered as you are Unclean.' A few bowstrings slackened.

'That's as maybe,' the large man replied, apparently unaffected by the Peculiar's words, 'but if you don't step to it then, on my child's life, I'll put a hole straight through you.'

The thieves who had been losing concentration came back to them-selves with a start, glared suspiciously at the Peculiar and pulled their bowstrings to their limits, ready to let fly. The Peculiar looked around the group, distaste marring his perfect features, before replying, 'Some of you *are* Unclean then. Nonetheless, I will take this child that you offer. I'm not sure what I'll do with it, but I'll no doubt think of something. Where is it? Ah, yes, I see the woman holding the babe over there, deep in the shadows beneath those trees.'

The mother cried out in dismay as she realised that she was not safe from the bedevilling stranger's scrutiny, and that he had designs on her child. Anger and outrage quickly possessed the large man and he did not hesitate to release his arrow. It flashed across the small glade faster than Jillan could turn his head.

A blink. Then the Peculiar was stifling a yawn with one hand and waving the arrow admonishingly with the other. He shook his head and tutted. 'You see, you really should be more careful when making an oath in front of a god. It can get you into all sorts of trouble. And thieves should ever be wary from whom they steal, hmm? On top of all that, you then think to attack me. Imagine! Just where does your blasphemy end?'

'What have we done?' groaned a thin man half concealed behind the trunk of a tree.

A gaunt youth wailed, and Jillan realised that it was a woman dressed in a man's old clothes. 'We have damned ourselves!'

A haggard-looking fellow dropped his bow and went to his knees in prayer.

The other thieves fidgeted, twitched and shifted nervously, looking to the large man for a lead.

'Tebrus, what are we to do?' called a querulous voice.

The large man refused to be panicked. With slow calm he took another arrow from his quiver and nocked it to his bow. 'A nice enough trick!' he said loudly. 'But we have all seen much the same at fairs, have we not? And I have never seen anyone catch more than one arrow at a time. On my mark! Do you hear me? Get a grip of yourselves! On my mark, you scoundrels! Be masters of yourselves, or masters of none!'

As the thieves began to rally, Jillan thought he detected a hint of misgiving about the Peculiar, who hissed in quick response to the man Tebrus, 'I have indulged you thus far, but now I tire of this!' The god's voice turned into something more powerful and compelling. 'I have already warned you and given you sign. You exhaust my patience. You will give me the child or your defiance will force me to take your miserable lives.'

Freda whined in distress and hunkered low to the ground. She began to sink down, making the earth tremble around her.

The magic in Jillan suddenly began to fight free, impatient, frustrated, but most of all enraged. It responded to the awful tension in the air – demanding that the storm break violently. Jillan's ears whistled and his temples ached. Damn them all. 'I will undo you all!' he roared, amplifying the vibrations Freda had started so that the whole glade shook.

The child screamed and the mother sobbed hysterically. The praying man fell backwards. The gaunt young woman and several others staggered. A stripling not much older than Jillan cowered in fear. Even Tebrus himself flinched, his face becoming pale.

'Give us the child!' the Peculiar demanded.

Jillan rounded on him, eyes blazing and red sparks dancing between his fingers. '*Shut up!* We are not here for any child!'

'It's him! The devil himself!' the mother wept as she desperately came forward for the closeness of her husband. 'The slayer of the Saint! See, Tebrus, what you have brought down upon us! I told you what we did was wrong. Our sin has won his notice and now he has come to claim us!'

'Enough!' Jillan keened, the fury of his magic distorting his normal voice. 'You have stolen from Godsend. You have taken our food and two of our horses. You will return them at once. We will take one of the horses ourselves and you will see the rest taken to the very gates of Godsend. At once!'

Part of him wanted the large man to refuse. He wanted to hear reviling words, see sneering disdain, feel his hatred. He wanted Tebrus to try and kill him. He wanted a reason to annihilate all of them, annihilate everything.

'I . . . cannot return that food,' Tebrus averred with determination.

Annihilate everything – so that there would be no more wanting, no more heartache, or tragedy, or mourning. No more desire, ambition or delusion. No more misleading ambition and false dreaming. No more lost parents or their children.

Jillan raised hands that glowed with murderous intent. The Peculiar grinned like a loon, shadows elongating his features so that they appeared malign.

'Tebrus, please!' his wife begged.

The magic within Jillan howled in painful delight. It would not be kept in check.

He gathered his will and unleashed it.

A stone fist crunched against Jillan's jaw, starring his vision. He lurched and stumbled into a spin, throwing energy every which way, destroying trees and shattering several of the flagstones of the road which passed through the glade. The detonation was deafening, pieces of wood and stone raining down around them.

'Look at them, friend Jillan!' Freda yelled. 'They are starving! What other choice do they have?'

'What other choice do *I* have? Should I let those I care about die so that these wrongdoers might live?' he spat.

Noise came rushing back in. He drew the last of his energy from his core, not caring if it killed him, and began to raise his hands again.

From behind him she caught his wrists in her giant fists and clamped them down at his sides. He struggled but, even if he had not already drained himself through use of magic, could never have resisted her strength.

'Freda, let go! You don't understand. They took everything she had, everything *I* had.'

'You are right, friend Jillan. I do not understand this realm of the Overlords. I never have. I did not understand the Underlords either.

I was forced to flee them. I do not understand how this phagus got the better of you. Nor do I really know what happened to make you leave those whom you say you care about. But I do know and understand something of you, friend Jillan. It is too easy for you to kill these people. They cannot stand against you. Is this not what you call murder? Is this not the sort of thing for which you fought against the Saint?'

No! She was taking away his reason. His magic began to fade. No. The Peculiar's face fell, disgusted. Damn them all.

Tebrus had fallen awkwardly off the rock on which he'd been standing. He clambered back up now, looking to see how his band was arrayed. Most were crouched with hands over their ears or arms covering their heads, weapons forgotten. Two looked up and ran into the trees before he could stop them. He found his bow intact, but had landed on his quiver and either snapped most of his arrows or flattened the fletchings on them. His physique subtly taking on more muscle, the Peculiar came forward to meet the bandit leader. Freda released Jillan, now that he no longer burned with power, and went to the Peculiar's side. She tightened her fists so that her knuckles cracked ominously.

Tebrus's shoulders slumped. He knew the fight was lost. Defeatedly, he waved the Peculiar and Freda back. 'Take your damned food then. We will willingly hand over what remains, which is the larger part, if you but leave us one bag of grain.'

The Peculiar's eyes drifted towards the woman and child, and Tebrus moved to stand in front of them, not fearing to meet and challenge the god's eye. The deity finally sighed, shrugged and replied, 'The horses are our main concern for now. You haven't eaten them, hmm?'

'Of course not.' Tebrus frowned, not realising the Peculiar was playing with him.

'Then hand them over like a good fellow and we can afford to be generous with some of the supplies.'

'No,' Jillan interjected tiredly, stepping closer. 'That food is not ours to gift. It belongs to Godsend. And I will not provision this group so that it can continue to waylay every traveller that comes down the road.'

'We hang them then?' the Peculiar asked brightly.

There was angry murmuring and the thieves came to their feet, drawing knives and swords. Tebrus quickly raised his hand, ordering them to hold, and raised an enquiring eyebrow at Jillan.

'What are you doing out here like this, anyway?' Jillan asked. 'Where are you from? You do not look like forest people.'

'We have been cast out by Heroes' Brook. Because of the plague.'

'I didn't think the plague had reached Heroes' Brook.'

'It hasn't,' Tebrus replied sourly. He made the sign against evil, and the Peculiar twitched. 'But Minister Stixis wanted to make doubly sure it never did. He convinced the town council to cleanse the town of everything that was *Unclean*.'

'And you are Unclean.' The Peculiar smiled. 'You were born with some evil in you that meant you could never be successfully Drawn towards the Saviours, never truly be members of the Minister's flock.'

Tebrus couldn't keep the anger from his face. 'Yes! That is what the Minister declared when I was but thirteen years of age.'

'What happened then?' Jillan asked.

'What need is there for me to speak of such things?'

Jillan looked back at him intently.

'Very well then, if that at least will satisfy you! My parents were advised by the Minister to turn me out, of course, but they were good people and refused to do that to their own. It saw them shunned by the town. My father could no longer find work and we ended up living on the charity of others.'

'Not that there's much of the sort in that place,' spat a thickset bald member of the band.

'Aye,' Tebrus agreed. 'My folks lost their home and ended up dying in a hovel by the town's slurry pits. And now the town has turned us all out, a few of us Unclean, and a few unfortunate enough to be related to us. Stixis thinks all the trouble in the region is because the People have allowed themselves to become corrupted without their even realising it, through generations of small compromises and, or so he says, *a gradual attrition*. He preaches that just a single step off the right path can see the People lost. It is time to return to the right path without delay, excuse or compromise.'

'Got 'em all stirred up and praying harder than ever,' the thickset man confirmed. 'We were probably lucky to escape with our lives. And now we live how best we may!' He said the last with some defiance.

'But now I will have a question of you, lad,' Tebrus returned. 'Is it true what they say? About the Saint? That he is . . .'

'Yes,' Jillan replied evenly. 'He's dead.'

The woman with the child stifled a sob and members of the group exchanged worried glances. The thickset man looked unperturbed, however, as he said, 'It's just as I told you. I was Drawn by the Saint himself, so I knew it to be true. My mind feels freer than it ever was before, and I am glad of it. Yet it is that feeling that has scared 'em all so bad in Heroes' Brook, you know. Them folk cannot bear the loneliness that's come on them all of a sudden. They're not used to it, see, whereas I was always kept at arm's length by the rest for marrying one of those they call Unclean.'

The Peculiar yawned. 'Interesting though you may find all this, Jillan, it's not really moving us along any, now is it? We have places to be.'

Jillan ignored him and directed his speech to Tebrus again. 'It will not be long before the townsfolk decide they can no longer have you robbing traders on their way to Heroes' Brook, you know that. They will all too soon hunt you down. But Godsend can offer you sanctuary. Return the supplies to them, and they will take you in.'

Suspicion clouded Tebrus's face, but the rest of his band betrayed desperate looks of hope. 'Why would they?'

'Godsend accepts the Unclean as ordinary citizens. We have one called Ash among us, and he always finds a welcome at the inn. That which you took from us belonged to our main trader, Jacob. If he suffers, all of Godsend suffers, for it is not as big a town as either Saviours' Paradise or Heroes' Brook. Godsend will be grateful if you can restore their trader. Beyond all that, you can tell the commander, Samnir, that Jillan offered the town's protection to you.'

Tebrus hesitated, clearly wanting to believe him, but at the same time knowing he needed to be wary on behalf of those he led. He chewed his bottom lip. The babe behind him began to grizzle weakly. The mother jigged her child up and down and made comforting noises before stepping close to her man's ear. 'Husband, they could have killed us and simply taken whatever they wanted. Think of our child. He does not do well out here in these strange woods.'

The Peculiar sighed impatiently. 'Listen to your woman, Tebrus.

Jillan largely speaks the truth. And if it makes it easier for you, I will renounce my claim on the child for a dozen years. If it is sickly, then I do not wish to be burdened with it right now. I will even provide it with my divine blessing and mark to see it protected for—'

'No, demon!' Tebrus snarled. 'You will renounce your unholy claim on my son and then we will agree to join Godsend and serve its interests!'

'Now look here. You spoke your oath of your own free will. And you should be happy that your son will grow as one favoured by a god! You should be thanking me and sacrificing a sacred bull in my honour, or whatever it is they do these days. Why, how quickly your lowly kind forgets those gods that first moulded you from mud and gave you life. How quickly you forget those who provided you light, warmth, sustenance and shelter when you could not fend for yourselves. Arrogant mortals!'

'None of us forgets!' the thickset man gnashed back. 'We do not forget how our faces were pushed back into the mud under the heel of the old gods! We do not forget how, in their arrogance, those gods fell before the Saviours and abandoned us to the Empire. We do not forget the dark ages during which many had nothing to eat but for that mud from which they came. *I* know of you, Miserath, even if no one else here does. *I* know that you are only here now – when a Saint has been overcome – because you hope to be restored to the power and strength you once had over us. *I* know that you are just a conniving and long-lived shape-shifter who fits himself to every pattern and nuance in order to find selfish opportunity. Yes, even one as *lowly* as myself sees you for what you are. Why would you want creatures as *lowly* as ourselves to bow in devotion to you? It is because you are unable to command any but the *lowly*, is it not? It is because you yourself are *lowly*. And low you are! There is none lower, none more base, none more bent on pulling us back into the mud, than you. You have ever been the jealous enemy of humanity. You seek constantly to frustrate, prostrate and undo us. The life of this one child is a far greater prize than you have come close to in ages, is it not? A wondrous, beautiful prize. What would you not do to rule such an innocent absolutely, to mould it entirely by your will while innocence yet remains essential to it? What a terrible weapon would you then have to use against us.'

For once the Peculiar was at a loss. His jaw hung open and his eyes stopped moving.

'Friend Anupal, is it really true? Say it's not true,' Freda said softly.

Jillan turned unforgiving eyes on the Peculiar. 'You will renounce all claim on the child in an attempt to prove this man does not tell the truth. Do so, and I will not argue our own agreement again.'

The Peculiar's face flickered back to life and he managed a weak and sickly grin. 'It is of course untrue. You may have heard the chime of truth in his words, but it was a mere echo of a true story and belief that has changed greatly through the ages. With each telling, something small has changed in it, be the change ever so small that it is not even realised by the teller. Yet the story has been told so many times, and there have been so many changes, that it is now utterly distorted. It may still be recognisable to some, just as some believe they can see ghosts, but the belief to which it gives rise is most certainly not a real one, not a true one.' His grin became firmer, more believable. 'Of course I will renounce my claim on the child, friend Jillan, if it is so important to you. Consider it a sign of my good faith, friend Tebrus, although it was your band, in seeking to rob us, who committed the first wrong here.'

'Very good of you, I'm sure,' Tebrus said without any trace of politeness. 'We will bring one of the horses for you and, as I anticipate, part ways. Good Jillan, we will join Godsend and do whatever is asked of us by its commander, this Samnir. We thank you for what you have done here and will not forget it. Wherever it is you travel, go safely.'

The thickset member of the band glowered at Miserath even while he addressed Jillan, 'Aye, lad, sleep with one eye open and a weapon in your hand. If he says turn left, then you turn right. You understand my meaning.' He looked to Freda and dipped his head. 'Good day, milady.' Then he turned on his heel and stalked off into the trees, followed by many of the others.

They waited a short time, not exchanging many words, until one of the band returned leading a grey horse. 'She's been well treated. There's some feed for her in the bags on her back.'

'It's Floss!' Jillan smiled.

The horse snuffed the air and tossed its head as it recognised Jillan. It came forward eagerly and he stroked its nose. Then he took hold of its mane and vaulted up into the makeshift saddle. He was no experienced rider, but Hella had shown him the basics a few times, for which he was very grateful. Floss obediently stepped where he nudged and pulled, except when he went near Freda, for then the horse shied. Freda looked disappointed but not surprised.

Tebrus motioned his wife and the others to leave, and waved at Jillan. As if in blessing, the bearded leader made the sign against evil over the horse and rider, causing the Peculiar to flinch hard, and then melted away into the forest.

'Phew! What a rigmarole!' announced the Peculiar.

'Not as much fun as you'd hoped, I imagine,' Jillan observed.

The Peculiar scowled for a moment and then shrugged. 'Got you the horse in the end though, didn't I?'

'Not really,' Freda rumbled.

'Don't you start!' the Peculiar complained. 'I really am feeling a bit outnumbered and unappreciated today. And I still need to help you two orphans get some distance before the sun sets.'

'Any particular reason?' Jillan asked, a new suspicion in his voice.

'Yeeees! Mortals like you always seem to need to eat, don't you? Every five minutes or so, from what I can judge. We haven't really got enough provisions with us and we don't want to waste time hunting, now do we, especially when you're such a bad hunter? So we need to get close to Thorndell, where we can get a meal and stuff to take with us, before it's too dark to find our way. I would have suggested asking Tebrus for some supplies, but you were getting all holier than thou about Jacob's food being gifted away, Jillan. Besides, Thorndell's on our way. It'll take us through the forests towards the west far faster than retracing our route back towards Godsend and then taking the route off towards Saviours' Paradise.'

Jillan frowned. 'Where is this Thorndell? How come I've never heard of it, if it's so close?'

'Of course you've heard of it. It's that back o' the woods place towards Heroes' Brook. The main road doesn't actually pass through Thorndell, so towns don't trade with it all that much. Maybe Godsend hasn't had anything to do with it in a fair few years – I don't know – but I'm sure it's still there. Maybe it's been hiding from the Empire.

Come on, this way! They're usually pleased to see me there, which will be a refreshing change.'

The Peculiar began to lead them out, but then his head whipped back at impossible speed to regard the road behind them. He made a strangled noise in his throat.

'What is it, friend Anupal?' Freda asked.

'There's been something following us since Godsend. I catch stray half-thoughts but can't quite pinpoint them. They ghost away as soon as I focus on them. It shouldn't be possible for anything to evade me.'

'Maybe you're imagining it, or it's your guilty conscience,' Jillan suggested helpfully.

'You two go on without me and I'll catch you up,' the Peculiar replied irritably. 'A handful of miles from here you'll come to a dip in the road. Leave the road to the left and follow the hollow down until you come to a springhead. Then stay between the arms of water coming off the spring, as they quickly get deeper and it's perilous to try and cross them further on. As long as you're between the arms, you're going the right way. But don't dawdle, understand? Don't stop to smell any flowers, don't let anything catch your eye, don't look at your pretty reflection in any pool, Jillan, and don't rest your weary feet for too long anywhere. These woods are dangerous for the innocent, the unwary and the downright-deserve-it.'

Jillan didn't waste any time moving off on Floss, calling over his shoulder, 'Come on, Freda. See you, Miserath! Take care. Stay out of trouble if you can. Wouldn't want anything too nasty happening to you. Not yet anyway.'

In a foul mood, and cursing all creation under his breath, the Peculiar went back the other way.

Saint Praxis marched into Hyvan's Cross, waving benignly at the citizens crowding the route up the mount. The People threw themselves to the ground in prayer or in supplication for a blessing as he passed. Young children were held towards him by parents so that his holy touch could be bestowed upon them; the sick were carried forward so that he might choose to save them, and the lame crawled towards him so that he might mend them. How he despised them all! All they did was wail, howl and plead for their selfish needs, desires and wants to be fulfilled, rather than praise the glory of the blessed Saviours and ask that the divine will be made known to them. This was a corrupt People. They only protested their faith and fawned over him like this because they hoped to gain personal and individual advantage from him. This was a wanton People. They only smiled, sang and cried in ecstasy because they were afraid of the ten thousand Heroes marching at his back – otherwise, he knew, they would claw, fight and murder to come close to him and his possible favour. This was a craven People.

Where had these thousands been when Godsend had been beset and so tested by the Chaos? Where had they been when Saint Azual – the blessed Saviours enshrine his soul – had fought to save the tormented and the lost? They had been at their rich tables, filling their guts to the point of bursting; in their beds, rutting like beasts on heat; and in hostelries, drinking, speaking profanities and swearing themselves to unholy powers. This was a fallen People.

He eyed them with contempt as he went up into the crooked city. They were bloated and ill-looking through self-abuse. They stank worse than the excrement of any demon, their eyes clouded and their faces like open sores. They belched and croaked as if they were already dead and the gases of putrefaction were escaping their bodies. There was a miasma about them that tasted so bitter on the back of his throat that he thought it must be a poison to the weak.

'Plague!' hissed General Thormodius from just behind Saint Praxis. 'You men, keep them back from the holy one. Use your weapons without hesitation.'

Hardened veterans of campaigns in the eastern deserts moved past the Saint and quickly had the People falling back in terror. All it took was one citizen losing a limb and the rest were cowering back and begging for mercy.

*And just as easily does the Chaos cow you. How little the sickening and mindless masses are prepared to sacrifice for the holy Empire.* 'Do not worry on my account, General. I have walked unharmed among the pagans themselves and been protected by our blessed Saviours. It is right that your men guard themselves, however, from those that have brought affliction on themselves through loose behaviour, abandoned morals and a dereliction of worship. Looking at the People here, in the Saint's own city, is it any wonder the Chaos found a hold in this wild region? Fair Saint Azual was beset by dark agencies and whispering demons on all sides. They must have crept out of the long shadows and evil bogs of the ancient forests and found entrance here via the sewers and a noisome fog. They will have insinuated promises and temptations into the ears of the gluttonous, avaricious and lustful People of this place, to be invited in by them. Thus, I see that it was sweet Saint Azual's own People that destroyed him, just as it was always written in the holy Book of Saviours. General Thormodius, we have much work ahead of us if we are to see these People saved from the Chaos and returned to the good care of the Empire. I fear much of that work will be bloody, for do not the physickers say ill humours must be bled from their patients? So we will purge the People of this plague and their corruption.'

The General's expression did not flicker. 'As is your will, holy one. My men do not fear blood.'

'That is good, General. And I will bestow my blessing on your men in the days ahead so that they need not fear the plague or the dark and sneaking ways of the Chaos.'

The lines of the General's face tightened for a moment and he glared at a young girl in the crowd who looked like she might run forward to beseech the Saint for some boon. 'My men are as humble before you, holy one, as they are sworn to Saint Dionan. They are servants of the Empire and think only of their duty and sacrifice. We are yours to command.'

The host wound its way up through the city until it came to the open space before the Saint's temple at the summit of the mount. Like many of the dwellings of Hyvan's Cross, the temple had been carved out of the soft red rock of the place. There were no straight lines, for the will of the swirling winds had moulded and hollowed the pinnacle as it saw fit. Smooth curves and undulations made the rock seem like a sleeping giant or a curled slumbering dragon. A moaning breath issued from the round caves and arches, rising, falling and leaving none in any doubt that the rock was live. Natural cracks, seams and veins in the rock combined with areas of paler colour to form layers of runes over the edifice. Sand and dust drifted to form others, the script of the gods still in the process of being written.

'What blasphemy is this?' the Saint rasped. 'Do you not see the pagan runes, General?'

'No, holy one, but I do not have your holy sight and wisdom.'

'Holy one.' Captain Skathis bowed as he approached. 'May I speak?'

'Rise, angelic Skathis, and say on.'

'It pleased Saint Azual to make this his home, where once it had been a place dedicated to the pagan god Wayfar.'

'I will have none of it! General Thormodius, tear this abomination down and have it turned to dust. I do not care that it will take some days. Co-opt as many citizens as you need. This place must be remade and properly sanctified in the name of the Saviours. Just the sight of it mortifies my flesh. Have a humbler temple built using a hard stone from elsewhere.'

'As is your will, holy one,' the General said softly.

'In the meantime, Captain Skathis, I will take the house of the city's richest burgher as my place of rest and contemplation. Have the burgher's family put out on the street so that they might properly learn the humility, duty and sacrifice required of them. Come, angelic Skathis, attend me, for it is time your men reformed the personal retinue and guard of the Saint.'

Saint Praxis stalked away, accompanied by Captain Skathis. The Captain signalled a particular squad of Heroes to follow them, several dozen men who had remained as guard in Hyvan's Cross when Saint Azual had marched on Godsend months before. These Heroes had always been commanded by Captain Skathis, and always been loyal to the Saint of the southern region and no other.

General Thormodius watched them go and then turned his eyes back to the ancient temple he had been ordered to destroy. He made his face more unreadable than ever before.

A rictus grin of pleasure permanently transformed the face of Saint Praxis. So much power was his to command now that he had shared the sacrament of holy communion with the Heroes commanded by the angelic Captain! He knew their minds; so that his own mind and being were expanded and greater. He could see the world through them; so that he now had a minute understanding of all things and events. Nothing would escape him again. No *one* would escape him again. He would hold all the People in his mind, eye and hand. No longer would they be permitted their corrupting self-indulgences and irreligious perversions. Yes, the People were imperfect, and would always be lesser and unworthy, but Saint Praxis could not bear to have them sullying the sanctity of the Saviours any more than was absolutely necessary. The People had been given leeway for far too long – the tragic fall and lesson of Saint Azual was proof positive of that. Where were the People's displays of grief? Where were their self-blame and self-flagellation? Too long had the misguided and misdirecting concepts of *kindness* and *understanding* allowed transgressors to escape punishment; too long had they allowed the Chaos to work its suborning evil. Even he, when Minister of Godsend, had been guilty of allowing too much leeway and showing too much kindness to the bane of the Empire, the soul-destroying Jillan. But never again! Never again would he be prevailed upon to demonstrate kindness or mercy, lest it encourage the People in their wrongdoing. Never again would he show tolerance, lest it waste an opportunity for the People to learn and improve themselves. The region must be purged of all comfort. He would not allow it to rest until at the point of death, for the only purpose of their lives was to build a pure and shining civilisation as glorious shrine to the Saviours, as inspiration to other less fortunate regions, and as a light so powerful it would burn the pagans from existence. Every part of this miserable world would be so illuminated that there would be no shadow or hiding place left to the Chaos. Then, and only then, would the world be made a holy paradise of the Saviours.

Overwhelmed by the holy magic of the sacrament and the power of the holy vision it had given him, Saint Praxis fell back in the ornate armchair he now occupied in the burgher's house. The main room on the ground floor was slightly ostentatious, with its wooden floorboards, white-plastered walls and glass-filled windows, but it was large enough to perform as an audience chamber and contain the solid cabinets, shelves and tables required to accommodate all the ledgers and scrolls for keeping track of and running a successful enterprise. The table in front of the armchair even had upon it all the paraphernalia – an inkwell, quills, blotter and seal – a scribe or man of letters would need to keep records or draw up instructions. The burgher who had once owned all this had clearly been vain and conceited, but had also understood the essential importance of function and practicality. All this Saint Praxis saw in an instant, and his holy mind immediately knew how it could all be turned to the service and greater good of the Empire.

The other occupant of the room, who had quite rightly been beneath the Saint's notice up until that point, cleared his throat. 'Holy one, are you well?'

Saint Praxis looked up, his gaze blazing, and spoke in a reverberating voice: 'Why, my angelic Captain, I am well now that my great work has begun. Come, you are the last of my retinue to share the holy sacrament, for you have ever been the most humble and true. You have selflessly watched over your men to see them properly blessed, with no thought for yourself. Come now, do not hesitate. Take up the holy wafer from the table and place it on your tongue.'

The Captain's scarred and skin-melted face twisted as he eyed the piece of bread that had been anointed with a single drop of the holy Saint's blood. 'I fear I am not worthy of it, holy one.'

'Do not be fearful, my angelic Captain, for I have judged you worthy,' the Saint replied powerfully, the glass in the windows beginning to sing. He drew on the holy magic gifted to him in the Great Temple and made it resonate with the far smaller amount that still existed in the Captain's blood from the time when he had been Drawn to the Saviours as a youth by Saint Azual. 'It is my will, good Captain.' The magic took hold of the Captain, so that he could not resist, and began to bend him to its command. 'And I shall help my faithful servant as you in turn help me.'

Saint Praxis rose and brought the wafer to the Captain's mouth. He pulled the man's jaw down and placed the sliver inside. 'Body of my body, blood of my blood,' he said in benediction and closed the soldier's mouth. 'Body of your body, blood of your blood,' he intoned as he jabbed the tapping tube of sun-metal into the Captain's arm, released a bright jet of blood and magic and began to drink it.

The Saint did not stop until he could properly hear the Captain's thoughts and the man had visibly become paler. Then he removed the tube and gently caressed the soldier's face. 'There, my angelic Captain, now you will never have to be alone again. I will always be watching over you, will always be there to protect you whenever the Chaos seeks to enter in.'

'Th-ank you, ho-ly one,' the Captain replied through gritted teeth, a tear trickling from one eye.

Saint Praxis returned to his armchair, steepled his fingers and relaxed his hold on the Captain. 'Now, my angelic Captain, the hard work truly begins. We must expedite the purging of the People with all speed, for the longer we delay, the longer the Chaos has to spread its evil. I will prepare the sacrament of holy communion for all the citizens of Hyvan's Cross, and you will see it distributed. Your men must be sure to see each citizen consume the holy wafer. Except for the children who have never been Drawn, for they should be brought to me so that I may deal with them personally. Then you must ensure that each citizen is bled, collecting it in barrels. Find the burgher we put out of this place and have him assist you with the barrels and organisation. Each barrel must be brought to me for my blessing before it is sealed and sent on in the burgher's wagons to the Great Temple. Ask the General for help as you need it, but keep all main concerns in your own care. I want the whole of Hyvan's Cross Drawn back to the Saviours within a handful of days. Do you understand?'

'A-as is your will, holy one.'

'Very good. And now that we can speak more freely, tell me, how far do you trust General Thormodius? Do not demur because of his rank or seek to be polite, for I will know that as a lie of sorts.'

'H-Holy one . . .' the Captain struggled. 'His first loyalty can only ever be to Saint Dionan, he that Drew the General to the Saviours. Through the General, Saint Dionan will know all that goes on here, though it be of little use to him. Yet surely the holy Saint's only interest will be the good of the Empire.'

'Ah, my Captain, I pray that it is true and cannot question the wisdom of our blessed Saviours. Nonetheless, please keep a careful watch, so that through you and your men I will know his every word and deed. That is all, good Captain. Come, do not look so dull of eye and heavy of limb, for then the Chaos will tempt you towards sluggishness and slow your actions. That risks the Chaos quickly overtaking you, for it is never idle and never rests in its enmity. Rejoice, good Captain, that we will save the People in their time of greatest peril. Be of good faith and let it sustain you, for all too soon we will have purged the Chaos from the very midst of the People. Once more they will be clear of eye, quick of wit and firm of purpose. The region will rise as one, and the People will move as one, to smite the unholy Jillan and raze Godsend to the ground. Then nothing will stand between us and the scheming pagans in the mountains. The will of the Saviours shall be done, and we will make of this mortal hell a holy paradise!'

# CHAPTER 5:

# Will see all turn to chaos

Elder Faal, head of the Faction of Origin, began to put his affairs in order. He knew his time as a member of the Declension was at an end. *She* had summoned him.

Using a nail, he scratched a final entry in the book of his bloodline. It detailed the shame of Ba'zel's departure, without excuse. He read back through the events he had recorded in a last attempt to find an explanation for what had happened, but there was no coherent or underlying pattern that he could see. With only a brief hesitation, he wrote his final word concerning his offspring: *unstable*. Then he added a brief statement confirming that the bloodline of the House of Faal was no more, and that the bloodline of Elder Skarla now had precedence and could be declared the House of Skarla.

He closed the book and laid it aside. It was right that his line should end, for it had not delivered enough to the Declension to warrant the resources used to sustain him and his son. It was right that his life energy and blood be fed back to the Geas so that it could be used to nurture those more worthy. Through them, he would both be reborn and bettered . . . Unless *she* decided he was somehow tainted and should not even be fed to the Geas, needy though it might be. Then he would meet his final ending, and it would be as if his bloodline had never even existed. The book of his bloodline would be reduced to dust; *she* would remove all memory of him from the minds of the Declension and his name would never be mentioned anywhere in the cosmos again.

If *she* determined his final ending was for the good of the Declension, then it was right that it should so transpire.

He brushed the thick dust off the table where he sat and pulled the larger book of the Faction of Origin towards him. The dust clouded into the air and he was forced to close his eyes for some moments before it settled. Without Ba'zel around to clean the chambers constantly, everything had become buried in thick drifts and layers of silt, sand and grit. And it was right that it should, for in the same way civilisations and their ruins were interred by the dust of ages. In just this way his bloodline was passing and would also disappear.

Death was a dust that they all breathed, he saw that now. The skin that they shed over millennia and the dried-out powder that they all became once dead would mix with the air and substance of their realm, so that it was then consumed by those who called themselves *the living*, although they might more accurately term themselves *the dying*. There was no escaping it, for it permeated all matter in this realm, even the Geas. Had his faction been wrong then to think that the Geas of the home-realm could be sustained forever as the origin? Surely not, if the realm could but be cleansed of the dust of death. He giggled to himself as he imagined Ba'zel and his broom set to sweeping the entire realm as punishment for his misdeeds. Elder Faal shook his head in self-reproof. Such whimsical and giddy thoughts were said to be a sign of mental fragmentation, a loss of sanity. It only tended to happen to the most ancient of his kind when they could no longer support and contain the vast and ever-increasing knowledge and experience of their own exist-ence, when they could no longer bear the strain of the Great Voyage or even apprehend its reality. Apparently, it could also happen to those who knew death was close.

He returned to the book of the Faction of Origin, knowing that its simple truths would restore him. It was the archive of the entire line of thinking of which he was a part. It was as old as the Declension itself, and therefore a fundamental aspect and pillar of his kind. Some of the earliest entries by the Great Belloraine were entirely erased with read-ing, and in a form of language almost incomprehensible to most, but the faint marks remained as evidence of the beginning of the faction's line of thinking, and all that followed came from that origin, so nothing was lost. It would have been a sacrilege of sorts to have the book copied, of course, for nothing in the cosmos could exist *twice*. It was one of the few principles upon which all the factions agreed. There was always difference. A copy might *appear* to be exactly the same as the original, but beyond the appearance there would always be difference.

For these last moments the book was his. It always remained in the possession of the head of the faction, for in many ways it *was* the faction. When he was gone, it would pass to a new head and bloodline, as it had done many times in the past. He had already made sure that the second member of the faction knew the magical signature required to access these chambers, so that they would be able to retrieve the book without difficulty. The last thing he would want was another of the factions gaining advantage because of delay or disarray among his own.

He gently turned the translucent and membraned pages of skin, letting his eyes drift over the commentaries and principles put down by previous heads of the faction. He paused at a page where he'd lingered many times before, and read lines from the *Interpretations of Innar*, lines which had always inspired musing and meditation in him, and even given him a strange sort of comfort.

*None should fear being fed to the Geas, for it is a return to the origin and a return to ourselves. In feeding the Geas, we feed ourselves with immortality. There is no living and dying in it, only eternity.*

He preferred the *Interpretations of Innar* over the various *Implications* and *Inferences* written by other heads, even though all *Interpretations* – because they too often dealt with the present rather than the future – were generally considered of less value by most of his faction. Perhaps if, from the beginning, he'd dwelt on other entries in the book more . . . He briefly worried over the worth of the entry he'd added to the book himself – a fairly unexceptional *Iteration* of the principles of origin – and then closed the tome. It was enough. It would be for the next head of the faction to take forward his words as inspiration or instruction as they saw fit. He rose from the table and readied himself to leave his chambers for the last time.

A movement in the corner of the room caught his attention. It was the caged creature from the second realm. Even as lesser realms went, the second realm had not been much to speak of. Its Geas had been quickly found and the Great Cull instituted without much trouble, for the beings of the realm had been extremely weak and gentle, so weak that their entire kind and Geas had made little appreciable difference to the strength of the Geas of the home-realm. This insipid creature was likely to be the last of its kind and realm in the cosmos, and it would eventually find its death in a small soiled cage. It revolted him. For all that, though, he could not help remembering how fascinated Ba'zel had been with it and how much time his son had spent talking to it. He could not help wondering whether Ba'zel would chance to come across the devoid remains of the second realm during his flight and realise he'd wasted his time and existence with this creature; whether he would become repentant and somehow find a way to make amends. He could not help hoping for his son.

Elder Faal sighed. Everything reminded him of Ba'zel, even something as pathetic and tawdry as this lesser being. Try as he might to discipline his thoughts, Ba'zel was always there in his mind. It was unbecoming of an elder of his standing, and a sure sign of his own imperfection and the necessity of his undoing. He tried to shut out all thoughts of his son, the *unstable* element, but it seemed the instability had infected and disrupted his mind, as was the inevitable way with the *unstable* element. *She* was right to summon him to his end.

On a strange impulse, the elder opened the cage and pulled the being out. It squeaked and looked up at him imploringly, not with adoration but with a final plea, a plea for an ending. *I will not identify with this lesser being, this vermin, but I almost understand it, now, at this moment when I face my own end.* He paused, and a look of *gratitude?* came into the lesser being's eyes. Then he ended the creature in an instant, so that there would be no unseemly struggle or pain. It was the same quick ending that he would want for himself, and for his son, wherever he might be. For there were far worse endings possible, such as at the hands of a Virtue.

With a shudder, he dusted off his hands, glanced around his chambers and then stepped out through his wards into the corridor beyond. He straightened his robes and moved purposefully towards the intersection that would allow him to make his way to the lowest levels of the Declension's catacombs. It was seen as a sign of weakness to travel too far on foot instead of passing directly through walls and floors, but he knew he needed to conserve all his energy for the difficult task ahead, the task of coming into *her* presence. Besides, any member or members of the Declension foolish enough to attack the head of a faction, even one going to his end, would not exist long enough to regret their action.

The corridors wound down and down, becoming low and narrow, so that he had to bend double to continue. He extended his digits into claws, hooked them into the rock and dragged himself further along the tunnels, the hard ridges of his back cutting deep grooves and gashes in the opposing rock face. For long hours he pushed, shunted and scraped through the darkness, until he eventually came to an unyielding and metallic rock, the first of the adamantine layers close to the heart of their realm, where *she* rested with the Geas. The Eldest waited for him.

Now he altered his state and sank downwards, the density of the metallic rock slowing him and stretching him thin. He was so dispersed by it he thought he would never be able to reassemble himself, his limits at breaking point. Even if he came through, he knew he would be left plastic, forevermore damaged. Here was the Eldest's main defence, if defence *she* truly needed, for none would be able to come before *her* in their full power.

And a second layer, this one crystalline. It fractured and fragmented him. It shattered and sheered him. No being of light could come through here unharmed. He struggled to keep himself on a single plane and crept agonisingly closer.

The third layer was the worst, for it seemed alive in the way it attacked and ate at him. It was a hungry and acidic poison that sought to dissolve him to nothing. It ravaged him, easily stripping him of the exoskeleton he'd always thought impenetrable. He was left as soft and trembling as the very youngest of his kind. It bit into his centre and visited pain so acute on him that all thought was wiped away.

At the very last, when he was about to lose touch with his own existence, he slid down into a void, where he spun and dropped a thousand feet before hammering into an obsidian floor. The magic of his life flickered fitfully, but the thick red light suffusing the place soothed and restored him, until his life was a strong flame once more. He raised himself to his knees, before wondering if he dared rise any further. Meekly he whispered, 'I am summoned.'

*Her* presence was all around, like a pressure on his sore body and soul. *She* was everywhere and in everything, for the Eldest was said to have long since transcended to total disembodiment.

*Her* voice was felt, heard, smelt, tasted and seen all at once. It was soft and thrilling, but full of such power, he knew that if it should be raised in anger, he would be obliterated in the instant. 'Faal, do not abandon our son.'

He whimpered. *She* was so far beyond his understanding, how could he answer? 'As is your will, most holy!'

'You have questions. Speak them.'

'You are the holy of holies and the bloodline of us all. Yet Ba'zel has shown himself unworthy of your care, unworthy to call himself a member of the Declension, or Saviour. How can he not be abandoned?'

'He is our son. The memory you have of that female you think of as his mother is a false memory I placed in your mind. Ba'zel is the result of a union between you and me, Faal. Always in the past I have immediately destroyed those with whom I have coupled, but that has left me to raise the issue myself, and I have only succeeded in creating those monsters you call the Virtues, beings who are useful to me but ultimately insufficient for our true intention and ambition. With Ba'zel, I chose to have him raised by another, by you, Faal. You were different to those others with whom I coupled, for you gave completely of yourself, asked for nothing in return and did not plead for your life.'

'I . . .' But he could not imagine it. 'Why . . .' But he could not ask such a question.

'Would you think to know our true intention and ambition?' the Eldest asked with a subtle note of warning.

'Never!' He cringed. 'Have I erred in not protecting him better?'

'No. All has happened as I knew and willed it would.'

'B-But is Ba'zel not *unstable*? Is he not a danger to us all?'

He sensed *her* amusement. 'Faal, how long does it take us to find and claim each new realm?'

He hesitated, unsure. He wasn't old enough to be able to answer with any real confidence. 'Millennia?'

'It takes longer with each new realm, with each step further and deeper into the cosmos. The first and second realms fell quickly and with such ease, but the sixth has had us mired for an aeon and the seventh is causing us unexpected trouble. If we are not careful, we will come to an entire standstill, perhaps even have to take a step back-wards, which would be potentially fatal for our kind, for we might then lack the resources to recover the ground lost. Our progress through the cosmos would halt and we would go into a slow and terrible decline, finally forced to consume ourselves.'

The enormity of what *she* described, and the horror of *her* apoca-lyptic vision, all but undid him. He could not respond as *she* continued. 'We have begun to atrophy, Faal. We come to occupy a new realm and, with our untiring will, bend everything to our fixed scheme. Yet that fixity also entraps us. Some of our kind reside permanently in the Waking Dream, forever asleep. I believe they can never be awoken. Others have not moved for so long that they have likely lost all ability to do so. Our increasing omnipotence also threatens to be our absolute impotence, unless we can also Draw all the *unstable* elements of the cosmos to us. I created Ba'zel so that he could become the means to that end.'

Faal groaned. 'And I let him escape us.'

'As he was meant to do. I created him so that he would ever seek to escape and cause instability, even though his internal state would remain stable. So he will be able to find those others in each realm who are also *unstable*, and they will be drawn to him. Through him, they will ultimately be Drawn to us.'

'But what of the danger? Might he not unite them against us and gainsay the Declension?'

More amusement. 'Just as I created him, so I can uncreate him, Faal. No, he will bring them all to us and deliver them into our power.'

'What if he should fail? Was not a Virtue sent after him? Surely he cannot stand against such.'

'The Virtue will test him. If Ba'zel fails, then little of consequence is lost and I will simply create a new means for my intention. Should Ba'zel succeed against the Virtue, however, then he will be further moulded to the task assigned him and it will be deeply written and confirmed in his mind and nature. After that, there will be little to prevent him suborning those that are *unstable* in the seventh realm, so that we are no longer atrophied and are freed to seize the life energy and Geas that we need. We will leap further across the cosmos than ever before, in our new greatness surely travelling as far on the Great Voyage as the Chi'a before us.'

'As is your will, mother of us all. Just tell me what you would have of me.'

'Simply this, Faal. Should Ba'zel ever return, welcome him in. Do not turn him away or abandon him. Enfold him in your arms and power, and all will be delivered to us.'

'Eldest, I am ever humbled before the glory of the Declension.' Did he dare? 'May I ask but one question for myself? One moment of selfishness?'

'Would you test my patience, Faal? I will allow you that choice and nothing more.'

'The Origin. I would know if my faction is in error. Surely it cannot be that the Great Belloraine was ever . . . misunderstood by the line of thinking that followed her, can it?'

The Eldest was silent for a long while and he became terrified that he had overstepped. What had he been thinking? He started to stutter an apology and then halted, knowing it was too late to unmake the choice *she* had allowed him. He hung his head in acceptance.

*She* spoke right at his ear, as if next to him, and he jumped. 'There are questions to which even I do not know the answers, my fond and foolish Faal. Belloraine was ever *capricious,* and that led to her eventual undoing. It could be that the Faction of Origin and all the other factions are correct. It could be that all are wrong. Yet the lines of thinking organise us, just as we have organising intellects in the other realms. More, they keep the likes of Belloraine alive and evolving where her body could not do so. The alternative is chaos and a final ending, is it not? Perhaps it is all a matter of . . . faith.' The last word was so silent it was all but absent. His memory was already telling him he had not heard it. 'Your question matters not then, Faal, and only invites chaos. You will never dwell upon or ask it again. I will know it if you do.'

'As is your will, eternal one!' he whispered, never so petrified as at that moment.


Ba'zel was slammed violently into a stone floor. The air left his body in a whoosh and he felt the walls of his lungs stick together. They refused to reinflate and he began to suffocate. He opened and closed his mouth desperately and his eyes bulged as he thrashed about.

Hands pushed down on his shoulders. 'Welcome to the fourth realm. Do not move. It feels as if you are dying, I know, for the same happened to me once, but you must be still. Loosen your tendons. Use your magic to reposition your internal organs. Concentrate. This is no way for one of our kind to meet his end.'

The hands were removed and the guardian of the Gate stepped away. Ba'zel had been given the minimum help required. Now he would be tested.

Fighting his every instinct, he loosened his limbs, in turn easing the tension in his chest. Then he lined his internal cavity with magic and pushed outwards with it. It was always difficult for an individual to use their own magic on themselves, not to mention dangerous, for a small misjudgement could be disastrous, but he had no choice. Mercifully, the walls of his lungs unpeeled from each other and he was suddenly gasping the heady ethers of the realm.

'Who are you and what is your intended destination?'

Ba'zel at last found his voice. 'In the name of the Eldest, you must destroy the next thing that attempts to come through the Gate. Do not even wait to see what enemy it is that comes against you, for hesitation will be fatal. Strike in the instant. Bring all that can be raised for the confrontation.' His chest heaved. 'And I must be led to the Gate to the fifth. So it is commanded by the Eldest!'

The guardian took a step back, his eyes moving between Ba'zel and the Gate. 'The elders of this realm have heard and hasten to obey. We cannot question the command of the Eldest, but would ask if you know what we face, so that we may be better prepared in weapon and magicks.'

'I . . .' Ba'zel took a shuddering breath, thinking furiously. 'An instability has arisen in the third realm and spreads beyond our ability to control or check it. There is a likely possibility that it will come through the Gate seeking to undo the wider Declension. Just sight or sound of it is dangerous to us. It may take a form you recognise, in order to implant itself among you. It may make claims you find plausible if you but allow it that opportunity. Therefore, you will not do so. Now lead me to the Gate at once. We must not delay.'

The elder had no choice but to obey. His distress was evident for, as he led Ba'zel away, he periodically looked back over his shoulder to see if they were pursued.

The stone floor soon gave way to tunnels of wet mud, the roof held up by thick bundles of reed-like plant matter. White and green slime oozed and dripped down on Ba'zel and his guide, until they were soon having to wipe the orbs of their eyes and their nasal apertures clear. A stinking sludge dragged at their feet, slowing them down. Something slithered past.

'What was that?' Ba'zel asked with a start.

'One of the beings of this realm, of course. They are limbed in our manner. Monopods and serpents mainly, some winged, some finned. Do not be fooled. They are highly intelligent and dwell in vast and complex colonies. They are slippery and cunning, almost impossible to catch if you do not have the technique. You must be in need of sustenance, no, given what we expend to come through a Gate? And one so young does not have significant reserves.'

Another test, even in the midst of flight. Ba'zel had to concede the truth of the guardian's words, but knew better than to give anything more away. 'Indeed.'

'You still have not told me who you are and what your intended destination is. Why do you not stay to hold back the instability with us? What role sees you travel to the fifth realm?'

'You would question the messenger of the Eldest's will?'

'I question the messenger, yes, never the Eldest. It is neither foolishness nor wariness on my part. It is simply my role as a member of the Declension. Our Great Saviour here also questions you.'

Another of the beings of the realm came undulating out of the wall to Ba'zel's left. He snatched at it, but it easily twisted from his grasp. He exerted the power of his presence, but that somehow just slid off the creature as it disappeared back into the muck. The guardian laughed knowingly and moved ahead more quickly. Ba'zel struggled to keep up, the mud sucking at his feet and sapping his strength. Then his weight saw him start to sink in a waterlogged stretch of tunnel. He knew he could lighten himself, but that would require the use of even more vital magic. He waded on but it only pulled him lower.

The guardian returned, walking effortlessly upon the surface, and smiled. Ba'zel was at a complete disadvantage and they both knew it. 'You will answer my questions.'

Without inflection, Ba'zel replied, 'I am Ma'zel, scion of Faal. My destination is the seventh realm. I do not stay here because it is not my role to do so. I am the messenger of *her* will. You will not delay that message or will any further.'

'We obey that will even now.' The guardian nodded, thumping the butt of his trident rhythmically against the wall. 'It is the weakness of the messenger that causes delay. I will quickly have you fed and freed. In the meantime, you will explain why *her* will would use a messenger so weak, particularly when the Eldest can communicate directly with the mind of any in the Declension.'

'The message is more than just thought, concept and instruction. A messenger is required because actions must also be taken and initiated. I was chosen precisely because of my youth and weakness. I do not and cannot understand the meaning of the message. Therefore, I can take no selfish advantage in all this that might jeopardise the message. If I am lost, then reprisal will be taken and a new messenger will be issued with a clearer path before them.'

In answer to the thumping of the trident, small beings wormed out of the area around the guardian. The elder desiccated some of his own hide and sprinkled it as a drying salt on them, causing them to writhe and shrivel. He scooped up a generous handful and offered them to Ba'zel. 'They contain little blood or life energy individually when just this size, Ma'zel, scion of Faal and worthy messenger of the Eldest. But consumed in sufficient volume, they suffice. Come, feed, and we will be on our way.'

Ba'zel quickly ingested the life energy and ejected the husks of the lesser beings. He did not by any means feel invigorated, but was restored enough to rise and move along in the guardian's wake once more. They splashed through the liquid grottoes, past sodden side caves and long free-flowing gutters, until their surroundings finally began to firm up.

'You are fortunate I was here to guide you, messenger, for the route often changes. It is always melting and shifting. I have to travel between our sites constantly to remain familiar with the way and ensure our Watchers are not lost to a collapse.'

The ground trembled.

'What is that?' Ba'zel asked.

And a greater vibration still, which split the roof wide and saw great molten cascades come pouring down on them. The ground suddenly rolled and the guardian lost his balance. He pitched into a wall and was swallowed whole. He emerged within seconds in a spectral form, before solidifying and coming to pull Ba'zel on through the deluge. They skirted a wide sinkhole that appeared before them and forged on.

'You dare?' thundered a voice through the realm, the walls slumping and the whole roof sagging low.

'That voice!' the guardian whined.

'Do not listen to it! It is the instability, nothing more. I warned you of this.'

'All who resist OBEDIENCE will be broken open and worn as my living skin, to be absorbed during millennia of agony.'

'It is the Virtue!' the guardian cried, weeping blood in fear.

Ba'zel pushed him further down the tunnel. Another sinkhole formed and the elder could not halt his momentum. He teetered. Ba'zel nudged him just enough to send him falling with a long and despairing cry.

A wave rushed up behind the scion of Faal and swirled him up and around the walls. He thought he saw light ahead as he was swept forward, but then the roof came tumbling in.

Aspin woke with a jolt, not sure what had brought him out of his dreams. He rolled from his blankets, knife ready. There was nothing left of their campfire and it was still before dawn, so there was precious little light by which to see. Where was Torpeth? A sudden shriek from beyond some rocks answered his question. It sounded like the holy man was being cut open from neck to groin. The hairs on the back of Aspin's neck rose, and it took all his courage to leap past the rocks to face the horror he'd begun to imagine.

Torpeth looked up blindly from where he knelt, tears and snot dripping from his matted beard. He was alone and seemingly un-harmed, although clearly distraught, just as he'd been since they'd left the lower village.

Aspin panted with relief and sat back on a rock. Once he'd caught his breath, he said irritably, 'You scared me half to death, you crazy old goat. Can't you suffer more quietly? Even the hardiest warrior needs a few hours sleep. Otherwise I'll be of no use to Jillan whatsoever, should we ever find him. Things will be hard enough once we enter the Empire without our being exhausted as well!'

'What care I for sleep?' Torpeth wailed at the sky. 'What care I for anything when I will never see my beloved Sal again, when I know I have, in my pride, doomed our people and the very Geas itself? I have even corrupted my only friend, my sweet Praxis, and made him a ravening monster.' He coughed blood onto the ground, so raw and torn was his throat. His own words cut and bled him. 'He can never be made again the innocent he once was. No amends can I ever make. What absolute crimes I have committed! I cannot stand this existence, yet I cannot escape it!'

Aspin knew there could never be any sort of meaningful sympathy for a soul so cursed. He rubbed tiredly at his eyes. 'Look, she said we might delay our doom. Who knows, we might do so for whole lifetimes, hundreds of years maybe. That's better than nothing, eh? So just pull yourself together and we can be on our way. Besides, you're acting like you've never been in love before. Someone your age should know better.'

This only caused Torpeth to cry in yet greater anguish. He yanked handfuls of his ratty hair out of his scalp and wax ran freely from his ears. 'Ignorant youth, who has but recently left his mother's milky teat, whose voice has hardly broken and whose balls have but stirred for the first time! Arrogant youth, who uses a word like love as if in understanding! With age and experience, love can become greater and more powerful than limited and presumptuous youth can ever understand. You do *not* know. You do *not* understand the torment.'

Exasperated, Aspin retorted, 'I understand enough to know that if you can't keep your torment quieter, you'll bring half this mountain down on top of us. Get a grip of yourself. You're meant to be a wise and holy man. Or have you entered your dotage and returned to the tantrums of your early childhood? You've suffered terrible torment before, Torpeth. Your name is a byword for it, by all the gods. Our people use your name to curse others. Just as you say love can become greater, then surely so can torment. You *know* this. It is not new to you. Why then are you so hysterical and unmanned now?'

'That torment was as nothing till now – till she said I would never see or hear her again. How then can my doom be delayed, for it is already upon me!'

The sun dared to peep above the horizon and Aspin now saw what a truly terrible state Torpeth was in. There were deep scratches and rents all over his face and body. His eyes were staring and clouded. And he'd soiled himself so badly that it looked like he'd tried to void himself of his very innards. It was no doubt only the curse of the gods that saw him still alive. 'All right. I will not pretend to understand, even though I may well never see Veena again. Perhaps we would be better not to love at all, Torpeth. We would not suffer half as much, would we? Come along, perhaps you'll feel better after a cup of herbal tea. And I think I might have some pine nuts as well. Looks like being a day of fair weather. At least that beauty is not denied you.'

Torpeth shook his head. His voice became soft. 'Ah, but it is, young warrior, for I will be near blind while we remain in the mountains. Your tea will turn to demon-piss in my mouth and the pine nuts to ash. So the gods declared through Sal. Aye, we might feel less if we did not love, but you may as well advise me not to miss my sight. You may as well tell a fish not to swim or a moth not to fly towards a flame. Or tell a flower to hide from the sun. Or a deer not to flee the hunter. Or a stupid old man never to make another movement his entire life, not even to feed himself.' He whispered, 'There is nothing else. Nothing.'

Aspin decided he liked the holy man's quietness even less than his shouting and railing. He cleared his throat. 'As I recall, the headwoman also declared that you were to do whatever I commanded. So I bid you be that mischievous and meddling old goat of before, that holy man who saw me initiated as an adult, and that naked warrior who so bedevilled the others at Godsend. You will leave off this morose turn of mind, for it renders you useless, and I have no intention of carrying your unwashed carcass out of these mountains for you. I would probably catch something off you.'

'Fleas probably.' Torpeth nodded miserably. 'But you do not know what you ask, young warrior. The creature you speak of was the selfsame one that doomed our people. You cannot let it loose again with a clear conscience.'

'Old goat, I fear I will not be able to find Jillan and help him escape the others' snare without your help, so I have little choice. Besides, if you have already doomed our people and perhaps the Geas itself, there is little you can do to make things worse, is there?' Aspin smiled. 'In fact, you have made things so bad, I suspect anything you do from hereon will only improve things. Beyond all that, if I do not insist on this, I doubt I will ever get any worthwhile sleep again, and that's one of the few things in the world that makes me truly grumpy. So, you will do as I command and whatever you may to help us find Jillan.'

Torpeth sighed. 'Silly ox, silly ox! Do you even know where Jillan is?'

'Er . . . well, I thought we'd start at Godsend. By the way, what does demon-piss taste like?'

'Like your herbal tea, silly ox! Now gather me some casting stones so that I may determine where the lowlander is.'

Aspin was about to tell him to get his own stones, when he remembered Torpeth could not really see. Feeling a bit guilty, he quickly stooped for whatever he could find and held them out to the reeking holy man. 'Here.'

Torpeth fumbled for the stones and sorted through them by touch. He sniffed each of them and threw several of them back at Aspin, just missing his ear with one. 'Silly ox, some of these are just lazy stones. Don't you know anything? Get me some stones that are discoloured and have unique edges. None of these stream-smooth pebbles. And be sure to fix Jillan in your mind as you do so.'

Muttering under his breath, and already wondering if he had made a mistake in reinstituting Torpeth's former self, Aspin collected another half a dozen stones. He passed them to the holy man and retreated to a safer distance than before.

Torpeth mumbled to himself as he fingered the stones and then cast them onto the thin and patchy soil before him. He splayed his fingers wide and used his hands to read how the assortment had landed. The darkest of the stones had fallen onto a small area of bare rock and become lodged in a crack, which made Torpeth curse and frown mightily, and a couple of yellowish stones had landed just beyond the dark one, almost out of reach. The other stones – mainly browns, greens, a red and a purple — had landed loosely clustered near some moss. The holy man removed his hands and wrapped them under their opposite armpits. He got onto his haunches and rocked back and forth as he pondered. 'The young lowlander is almost beyond us. He has left Godsend behind him. He does not travel alone, yet would be safer if he did. He heads towards the west, and if we do not move quickly we will not be able to catch or help him, just as if one of the stones I'd cast had flown that bit further or bounced awkwardly and skittered off down the mountain. You have tarried too long, young warrior. You should not have allowed yourself to become a mooncalf over the girl of the waterfall peak, although I may never criticise another for such a thing. We have not served the lowlander or the gods well, if we ever have.'

'Are you sure?' Aspin asked worriedly. 'Can mere stones really speak so clearly? Could your magic mislead you?'

'Silly ox!' Torpeth brayed. 'It is no magic. Are you so dull? So insensible? Less than one of these stones? All things are connected one to the other or through another. Does not a stone know the will of Gar in its time, the embrace of Akwar, the upbraiding of Wayfar and the regard of Sinisar? Is it not a part of this mountain? Will it not join the lowlands also, when this mountain is worn away or the stone is turned to a grit that travels on the wind? Will it not become mud, nutrition and a part of plants, then sustenance and a part of animals and people? Do not those animals and mortals then die, petrify and become stone once more? Has this stone not been through all this many times over already? It cannot step out of that existence. It is an essential part of it, as are you and your thoughts, silly ox, and as is the young lowlander. All are a part, all are bound together by it. It is all the Geas. What is wrong with your mind, silly ox, that you do not already apprehend this? Maybe it is your mind and selfishness that is in the way, for it should be an essential knowledge and instinct in you. Should I creep upon you during darkest night, trepan your skull while you sleep and steal some of your brains out?'

'You will do no such thing! I command it!' Aspin squeaked. He was properly rattled by both Torpeth's casting and threat. He had to take several steadying breaths before he could trust himself to speak further. 'So. All right. It seems that we will have to take the Broken Path sooner than I'd hoped. The headwoman said only to use it when desperate, and sparingly even then, for it is most dangerous and difficult, and gets more so each time.'

Torpeth made a curious flat tone and strummed on his bottom lip with a finger. He tilted his head. 'Broken Path? Broken Path? What's this? I have not heard of it, have I, and I the eldest of our people?'

Aspin could not resist mimicking the holy man's hectoring style. 'You do not know the Broken Path, old goat, when it likely works upon the same principle as you have already described? What is wrong with you that you do not already apprehend it? Must I sneak up on you at night, trepan your skull and steal some of your brains out, eh?'

Torpeth's head tilted so far that he tumbled over before rolling back up into a crouch. 'If you think it will help, young warrior. A cumbersome approach compared to just telling me though, is it not?'

Aspin shook his head. 'You were there when the headwoman explained it. I was hoping you'd followed what she said, because it involved some sort of conjuring, I think. I don't know anything of such magicks. They're . . . well, they're . . .'

'Frightening? Dark? Always requiring of payment? Perilous? Foolhardy?' Torpeth nodded to himself. 'Yes, they're all of those things. The headwoman is powerful as a shaman, not one to be taken lightly or messed with unnecessarily. Alas, I was lost to personal devastation when she spoke her wisdom to you. What a wonderful creature. Oh dear. Dare we attempt it, hmm? Dare we not? What say you, young warrior? Or should it be silly ox? What hope can there be for an ox and a goat? Precious little. There is precious little to be lost then, eh?'

Aspin took a bone out of his tunic, handling it carefully, and held it up. 'Look. She told me to use this. It's from one of the ancestors of our people.'

'Oo! Who is it? What should we do with it?' Torpeth gaped. He leapt forward and grabbed it. 'Eat it?' And he tried to cram it into his mouth, even though the bone was too long and stretched his cheeks to the point of piercing.

'No, Torpeth!' Aspin yelped. 'Spit it out, I command it!' He slapped the holy man on the back of his head.

'Itsh shtuck! Ack. I'm choking! Help!'

Aspin clouted Torpeth on the top of his back, and the bone shot free. It was only the mountain warrior's quick dart forward that caught the relic before it went spinning away down the mountain. He glared at his older companion.

Torpeth returned a sullen look. 'Tasted of ashes anyway!'

With a shake of his head, Aspin came to sit cross-legged on the ground, facing the rising sun. He signalled for Torpeth to join him. 'All right, old goat, pay attention. The headwoman said we should drip some of our blood onto the bone, fresh blood. We should hold an idea of our ancestor Pessarmon in our minds at the same time and say the words . . . er . . . the words . . . damn! I can't remember them exactly.'

'Don't worry, silly ox. The words are just to help you focus your mind, I imagine. Words rarely carry any innate power, you know. Besides, Pessarmon was never the smartest. As long as you get things roughly right, he's sure to respond. He always liked a bit of attention too, you see.' The wind blew hard at this, whipping Torpeth's hair across his face. 'See!'

Aspin was agog. 'You knew Pessarmon? The rockbreaker himself? Did he really wrestle bears and ogres?'

'Usually when he was drunk on fermented goat's milk. Gave him breath far worse than the mountain ogres. Felt sorry for them really. An ogre takes particular pride in the foulness of its breath, you see. Then the oaf would insist on wrestling them whenever they dared stick their snouts out of their caves. They took it pretty hard, I think. Probably why they stopped showing their faces in our part of the mountain range altogether.'

Aspin couldn't decide whether to believe the holy man or not. Surely ogres didn't exist except in stories? Too often Torpeth would swear some flight of fancy or extravagant metaphor was true, simply because he did not expect any sensible or intelligent listener to take his words at mere face value. It meant most of the mountain people thought Torpeth crazy, although they would still seek him out when the world defied their understanding. 'Never mind. Let's just do this.' Aspin took out his knife and held its tip to his thumb. 'Ready?'

'Your hand's shaking.'

'I know. Shut up and think of Pessarmon.' Aspin pricked his thumb and let his blood fall onto the bone. 'By blood and bone, Pessarmon, we call you to us!' The wind gusted higher, and light speared from the horizon into their eyes, making them flinch. Aspin cut Torpeth's palm and more blood dripped onto the bone. 'Ancestor of my people, by thought and memory we ask you to guide us through your realm.'

The wind moaned and blew up a scattering of rain and grit, forcing Aspin to blink rapidly. Was that a figure coming towards them out of the half-light of the dawn? Chilled, Aspin trembled. Much gloom still clung to the land below them, lingering between trees, shrouding glades, crouching beneath boulders and creeping through defiles. It defeated the eye and tricked the mind.

The shade of Pessarmon stood before them.

The ancestor had a grey and ghastly aspect, his eyes wide and staring, his nose broken and bloody, and his bearded neck torn wide. He wore a bearskin over his shoulders, which made him tall and brooding. He raised an accusing finger and pointed it at Aspin's heart, speaking in a hollow and ragged voice. 'Mine is a place of woe and suffering. It is not for those who are yet quick. Beware, blood of my blood. Should you enter this realm, you will begin to pale. Should you become too weak, you will be trapped here forever.'

Aspin gulped. 'W-We must take the Broken Path to the west, to bring aid as quickly as we can to a friend who fights for our people. Your realm connects to all places, yes, as a casting stone can foretell the whole? We ask that you guide us, Pessarmon.'

The shade's appalling gaze took in Torpeth. '*You* are not welcome, betrayer! No spirit of our people will agree to serve you.'

Torpeth grimaced and shrugged. 'My blood was also used to summon you, precious Pessarmon. You are bound by it, just as you were when you occupied the land of the living.'

'Pessarmon!' Aspin interceded. 'Torpeth serves me in this. You do not serve him by leading us by the Broken Path.'

The ancestor looked balefully at Torpeth for a long moment before finally saying, 'So be it. Gather up your accoutrements and take my hand, being sure not to let it slip at any time. If you become lost, I will not be able to save you from the fell beings that surround you.'

Aspin collected his weapons and approached his ancestor. He haltingly reached for Pessarmon's hand, but Torpeth interposed himself. 'Do not, young warrior. Allow this trial to be mine, for it is long overdue.' So saying, the holy man deliberately grasped the shade's hand in Aspin's stead. Then Torpeth offered his other hand for Aspin to take, so that the three of them formed a chain.

Pessarmon smiled mirthlessly as Torpeth blanched and groaned. 'Yes, it hurts, does it not, betrayer? My cold touch burns you now, just as your cold heart sent so many of our people here.' The shade looked stronger and more solid than it had moments before, where Torpeth now seemed haggard and wan. 'Come then, before the sun rises too high and prevents us from entering that half-place which is the nether realm.'

And so they were led like the condemned into a world of ghosts and shadows. Tremulously, Aspin asked, 'Is this the realm of the dead, then?'

'The hinterlands of that realm,' Pessarmon allowed.

'But how does it exist?' Aspin wondered as mists closed around them. 'How is it that we can even enter such a place?'

'When a creature dies, residual energies will cling to the body for a while, particularly if the one that dies is vivid in the mind and memory of the living,' Torpeth panted. 'I suspect those energies constitute this in-between place of spirits, wraiths and ghouls. But these denizens must always be hungry, for they cannot help but crave the warmth and more vibrant energies of the living, those who remember the dead as they once were. No doubt the denizens haunt people's dreams, lurk in remote places to catch the unwary, and seek to waylay the weary so that they may feed off them by some means. They are always there in the corner of your mind, or in full view when you double-take. How is it that we can even enter such a place, silly ox? Can you not feel it already drains us of our essential energies? It exists because, like a parasite, it feeds off the living. As it drains us, so it is easier for us to enter, because we become more like its other denizens. Do you not feel that your spine has already turned to water?'

Aspin gripped Torpeth's hand ever more tightly. 'We must hurry! Quickly, Pessarmon, quickly!'

The shade nodded sombrely, although his shambling gait did not noticeably alter. 'Aye, before the demons of this place sense your presence and are drawn to you in too great a number to be held back.'

'What demons are there?' Aspin whispered.

'I dare not name them,' Pessarmon answered, a vibration like fear passing through Torpeth and on into Aspin.

Shapes writhed and contorted within the mist and dissipated just as quickly as they had formed. Something rushed at Aspin and he jerked back, almost losing his hold on Torpeth.

'Careful, silly ox, else they spook you from the path before we have even begun. The strength of your grip must be as grim as the place itself.'

There were distant shimmers of light and the rapid blink of shining red eyes. One moment the trio's footsteps would sound loudly, as if they were in a small place, the next they would be as silent as if they walked a vast plain. There was no way to judge distance, time and direction. If they were to lose hold of each other, mere yards could separate them and they would never find each other again. There was the sweet smell of flowers, which sickened to the odour of death, became something poisonous and sulphurous, earthy and damp, and then fertile and flowery again. Aspin feared they were moving in circles.

More red eyes. And then the whispering. An echo. 'Torpeth is here!' Running parallel with them, away from them and close behind them. Then racing ahead of them like wildfire, passed like a vicious rumour from one invisible mouth to another, an increasing sibilance like a rising snake, dragon or basilisk. 'Torpeth is here! Torpeth!'

A far-off roar and an infernal eye burning through darkness. 'Pagansssss!' The ground trembling.

Aspin felt ice in his gut. He knew what searched for them, tried not to think of it, but could not help it. A rabid and hate-filled spectre was out there and coming for them.

'I will have every last one of them and crunch up their bones!' promised the pitiless hunger. 'And is that little Aspin? It is Aspin, isn't it? I had you in my punishment chamber before, didn't I? You remember. As if it was only yesterday, an hour ago, moments ago, as if you were still there now. Well you *are* still there, Aspin. You never escaped. You are in that chamber, chained to the wall, drifting in and out of consciousness. You can see the walls around you and the dirt on the floor.'

Torpeth was pulling on his arm, shouting at him, but Aspin couldn't hear what he was saying.

'You have been hanging there on that wall for such a long time. You must be so tired, no feeling left in your arms and legs. Only heaviness and tiredness.'

Aspin's feet would not obey him any more. 'It's Azual. The mad Saint. There's no escape.'

Torpeth screaming, threatening, pleading. Being shaken. A bite to the cheek. Unfelt. Pessarmon shaking his head sorrowfully.

'Don't worry, little Aspin. It will all soon be over and then you can rest. I'm coming to finish all that terrible torture you've been through.'

A towering Saint Azual came striding towards them, his fiery eye flaring and forcing the mist and shadows back, so that his prey could not hide from him any more. 'Now, my little pagans, we will settle things between us once and for all.'

Panic squirmed inside him like something he'd ingested, something that refused to give up its life and tried to fight its way free. It sank hooks into the lining of his stomach and dragged itself up into his throat. Its hard little limbs levered and jumped it upward, choking him. Claws forced their way past his soft palate and into his mouth, out between his teeth, trying to prise his jaws open.

Ba'zel stopped the soft parts of him that would otherwise undo him with their autonomic functions here in the liquid mud. He stilled his heart and silenced his lungs, surviving on his precious store of life energy instead. He kicked and flailed with his limbs, making painfully slow progress forward. At least the medium would also slow the Virtue in its pursuit of him, or so he hoped.

He was of course blind amid the filth of this realm, so navigated using what life energy and magic he could sense. The Gate was a hundred steps away, but it would take a week to get there travelling like this, and he was sinking. He didn't know how he would be able to climb up to the Gate in this slurry. How long and far would he sink? Until he reached the resting place of the lesser beings of this realm and slowly expired among them? It would be an utterly shameful way for one of his kind to end. And now he sensed the energy of the Gate flickering erratically. It was about to fail and trap him here in this primeval ooze forevermore.

'Brother, I see you there,' resonated the Virtue, further liquefying the mud and making Ba'zel sink that little bit more. 'What is it that you try to do? You know there is no escaping OBEDIENCE, brother, so by what madness do you try? You make an unbecoming exhibition of yourself and our kind. Return here. You will not refuse.'

The panic squirmed inside him again, and this time would not be stilled. The vibration in the mud reached into his core and attempted to trigger him into vomiting himself inside out.

It took his every memory, thought and fibre of being not to give in, not to start thrashing about. How could he refuse? There was no escape or hope. He'd made a promise to the sifters to find meaning and discipline in enduring, to search the realms of the Geas for purpose, to return only at the very end when all became dust. He'd promised. He could not give up. But there was no way forward. The Virtue had him trapped in this bog. He was a lesser being skewered on stone fangs and feebly twisting its last moments of life away.

The lesser beings around him fled the soul-shaking emanations from the direction of the Virtue. Eels and serpents flipped and lashed away, as if in their death throes, but still making greater progress through the mire than he was himself. He was just like them now, of no real value to the Declension. He was nothing but a worm. Sobbing, he wriggled and curved one way and then the other, spiralling and forming S shapes. The Gate stuttered. He strived to reduce himself to the meanest and most primitive of lesser beings, and gradually pulled away.

'Brother, look at you! Stop this display,' the Virtue sneered.

And yet somehow he was at the threshold of the failing Gate. Somehow he was falling through it just as it collapsed. He prayed, like the lesser beings did, to whatever god, animus or greater force might be prepared to listen, if it even existed. He prayed desperately. He prayed fervently. He begged that neither sin nor virtue would be able to follow and condemn him any more.

## CHAPTER 6:

# And order revealed as mere fantasy

atigue from having used his magic against the Unclean washed through Jillan. He gripped the reins of the horse Floss tightly, only just staying in the saddle. Dully he looked down at the hulking rock woman rolling along the road beside them. She had no trouble keeping up. He could not help envying her strength and stamina.

*That's about all you envy though, eh?* the taint whispered, now that the Peculiar was no longer around and blotting it out. *Wouldn't want her looks, would you?*

'Go away!' Jillan mumbled out loud. Freda gave him a sidelong glance.

*Wow. You really must be missing Hella if you're eyeing up a monster who's in league with Miserath.*

*I'm also in league with Miserath, if you hadn't noticed,* Jillan thought back. *Perhaps I'm a monster too.*

Yes, perhaps he was a monster. The townsfolk of Godsend had certainly avoided and whispered about him as much as they ever had about Freda. And hadn't the dying Azual told Jillan he was just like the Saint? *More than that, wouldn't I have killed Tebrus and his people if it weren't for Freda? Perhaps I'm a worse monster than her after all.* Perhaps that was why Hella had chosen Haal over him. He found that he couldn't blame her any more, that he couldn't stay angry with her.

Compared to him, Freda wasn't much of a monster at all. People were just scared of her because of the rock blight more than anything else. Just because she looked ugly to their eyes, they assumed her soul was similarly ugly. Yet look how handsome Miserath could be. Look at how seductive Saint Izat of the west was. And *ugly* wasn't the right word for Freda, not really. She was like a rock, that was all. The words *ugly* and *beautiful* didn't really apply. She was . . . well, she was *natural-*looking. Maybe the pagans even considered her blessed by Gar of the Unmoving Stone, rather than cursed as the People of the Empire saw her. It was funny how truth was so unfixed. What was it Miserath always called it? *A matter of interpretation?*

Was there no truth, then? Or was it what they were actually searching for? If not, what was left? Just Freda rolling along at his side, making Floss shy away every now and then. Freda, with her skin of grey stone, slightly browner at elbows and knees. When she was still, she could look just like a boulder, for it required a keen eye to read the image of a woman amid the tracery of cracks and seams covering her. Yet, with time, an observer would begin to see that some of the texture was superficial while other lines defined powerful limbs, the natural folds of a human body and strongly carved features. And then the observer would notice her dark and glistening eyes and be in no doubt that here was something that *lived*, someone that was full of a hidden and vibrant energy, a force that was stronger than that which possessed any normal being. Here was someone who would endure like the mountains, watching with a slow and quiet wisdom as the world turned. Here was someone who could make a normal person believe in something beyond their own mundane lives, something like the gods, the powers that held their reality together, perhaps even the Geas itself.

'She's no monster. If anyone's the monster it's me, who talks to voices in his head.'

Freda looked across at him. 'Friend Jillan, are you well?'

'Yes. Distracted, that's all.'

'I worry for you, friend Jillan. Would you have killed those people?'

*Maybe not. Your magic is diminished. It would have singed them a bit, no more. Besides, if you hadn't acted, who knows what Miserath would have ended up doing to them?*

'I think so,' Jillan replied unhappily.

'It's not like you, friend Jillan. You're not yourself.'

'No. You're right. The magic is unpredictable. It takes over sometimes. It's like a . . . a rage. A storm in the sky that can't be controlled. It's dangerous. Sometimes, sometimes I wish I didn't have it.' *And maybe I'd still have Hella if I didn't have this magic in me that made me a monster.*

*Now hold on there! You're getting everything confused. Miserath was hell-bent on attacking those people and taking some child. You had no choice. You and Freda actually saved them. This self-recrimination isn't healthy. It'll make you doubt yourself. You'll end up hesitating at some vital moment in the future if you're not careful. Didn't your father once tell you never to hesitate?*

'Don't you dare mention my father!' Jillan replied, and banished the taint from his head, although it would only be a matter of time before it came creeping back.

Freda's brow creased. 'Do not worry, friend Jillan. I will not mention him. I did not know him.'

'I'm sorry. That was something else.' He sighed. 'I tried to save my parents with my magic, but I failed. I made an agreement with Miserath – your friend Anupal – to try and save them. That failed too. I tried to save my friends in Godsend, but many of the townsfolk are already fleeing back to the Empire.' *I tried to build a normal life with Hella, one where I was not a monster.* 'Freda, it's all gone wrong!'

Freda nodded sadly. 'I do not understand this world of the Overlords any better than I do the world of the Underlords, friend Jillan. But I do not think things were right from the beginning. Things did not go wrong really, for they were already wrong. There is something broken somewhere. I think friend Anupal is taking us to find this broken thing. I do not know if it can be fixed, but I think we should try. Otherwise, everything will always be broken and there will always be something broken in us. I had a friend called Norfred once, when I was down in the world of the Underlords.'

Her words were strange to him, but made a sort of sense. There *was* something broken in him, something wrong, whether it was his magic or the taint. Her words calmed him somehow. 'What happened to him?'

'A bad man called Darus broke my poor Norfred's head. But there was something already broken in Darus to make him do that. And there

137

was something already wrong with the world of the Underlords that broke that thing in Darus.'

'I see,' Jillan murmured. 'What did you do? Did you punish Darus?'

'There were too many people. I ran away.'

'So did I, from Godsend.'

'I came up to this world looking for Norfred's son, Jan, whom the Overlords had taken away. Then another bad man tried to kill me. He was going to eat me! Saint Goza. But friend Anupal saved me from him.'

'He *saved* you?' Jillan echoed in surprise.

'Yes. I know you argue a lot with him, and don't like or trust him because he sometimes does bad things, but there's something broken in him like there is in everyone else, and he *is* trying to fix things, I think.'

Jillan frowned. 'Are you sure?'

Freda hesitated. 'Maybe. As I said, I do not understand the world of the Overlords any better than I do the world of the Underlords. I just know both worlds are broken somehow. If I can just put together the symbols I've seen in the temples properly, then maybe that will help fix things.'

'Symbols like these?' Jillan asked, indicating the golden runes on his leather armour. 'Can you read any of these here?'

Freda squinted up at him. 'I've tried reading them before, but not done very well. Some of the pointy shapes feel angry somehow, but that's not very useful, is it?'

Angry? Since the very first time he had donned the armour, Jillan had wondered if the pagan armour influenced his moods, and whether it might increase the sway of his magic and the taint over him. He could not imagine giving it up, though, because he felt so exposed without it. And he suspected it was only because of the armour that he could resist the glamours and bewitchments of the likes of Miserath and the Saints. 'Well, it is armour, after all. If it's used for war, then some of its runes are always going to have anger about them, I suppose. You never know, if Anupal manages to fix what's broken, then I might not need such armour any more, eh?' *And maybe I can fix things with Hella.* 'Until then, I suspect I'll need to keep wearing it for a while, especially if this is the place Anupal said we should be turning off the road. I don't much like the look of it, do you?'

The road had dipped sharply, and tree branches had grown together overhead so that it seemed like they were entering a tunnel down into the ground. As they descended into the hollow, an odour of damp leaves and rotting things assailed them.

Freda gasped. 'The trees are bleeding!'

It took Jillan's eyes a few moments to adjust until he could see where she pointed. Reddish sticky flows were indeed coming down the trunks of the larger and more ancient trees. A few flies and mosquitoes buzzed. 'Don't worry, we're not in any charnel house. It's not blood. It's juice from the beef mushrooms growing on the oaks. See those shelf-like growths? Break some off for me, would you? I'm starving!'

Freda reluctantly did as he asked. 'Ugh! It's raw flesh.'

'No, Freda. It's just how it looks, that's all.' Jillan put a large piece into his mouth, chewed and swallowed. 'Doesn't taste the best, admittedly. Bit muddy. Still, as long as it doesn't kill me, eh? I'll save the rest till later. Hopefully, we can find an onion or some wild herbs to cook it up with. So, off to the left here, did he say?'

Freda looked between the trees, which only seemed to get closer together the further they were from the road. 'There doesn't seem to be much of a path,' she said dubiously.

'Hmm. But those trees over there don't look that old. Maybe they've grown up in the middle of the path. If you can push a way through, then I'll lead Floss on foot.'

The going was slow as they squeezed forward. Frequently, they were forced off a straight line by incredibly dense thickets, and several times they were forced to backtrack.

*At this rate, you'll end up further away from Thorndell than when you started. Wouldn't surprise me if Godsend was just around the corner. And the day's a-wasting. Have you wondered whether these woods are enchanted, specifically bent upon preventing anyone finding Thorndell? It would be just like Miserath to hide some of his worshippers away from the Empire for a rainy day, no? And was it really very wise to go eating mushrooms growing round here? You're crazy enough as it is, without some poison or magic messing with your judgement or sense of direction.*

As much as he hated to admit it, and as hungry as he'd been, Jillan knew the taint was right.

*Of course I am.*

'Freda,' he sighed. 'You're going to have to start flattening things or we'll never make it through. We're far enough from the road now that no one will see the new path you make.'

She gave him a gloomy look but didn't argue. She raised her massive arms and bludgeoned a way forward, sweeping a clear route for them except when they came to a particularly broad tree.

'I will not tackle the larger trees,' she said over her shoulder. 'They scream when they die. The other plants are too young to feel much.'

'Oh, of course,' he said, feeling vaguely guilty, although he wasn't entirely sure why.

Floss shook her head, not liking the undergrowth scratching at her lower legs, but Jillan kept a firm pull on her and she moved after him without further complaint. Their progress still wasn't easy, particularly now the ground was starting to rise, but at least it was quicker than before.

They rose steadily, and an off-key sound of trickling water reached their ears. As they came to some sort of crest, they found a wide black pool filling a shallow bowl ahead of them. The giant trees around it blocked out the sky and stopped anything else growing in or around the pool. Two outlets allowed streams to run off down the far slope, but little more could be seen from where they were. Although the water was certainly not stagnant, there was the sort of sultry gloom in the air that might otherwise be found hanging over a place in mourning. There were no birds in the trees and no evidence that woodland creatures ever came to drink here.

'This is the springhead, then,' Jillan told Freda. He shivered. 'Even if Anupal had not told us not to tarry, I do not think I would be inclined to rest here. Let's keep going. We need to descend between those two streams there.'

They skirted the pool, stepped over one of the streams and made their way onto the ground the Peculiar had told them to follow. Even though they stood at the top of a slope, there was little to be seen between or beyond the thick and tangled mass of briars blocking their way forward. The plants were several feet higher even than Freda. The two streams angled away from them under the dark mass, cutting into the ground and quickly disappearing from sight.

Jillan had never seen briars quite like these. There were nearly black save for the odd trace of green, which made them look sickly. And they had red-tipped thorns that oozed some sort of sap.

*Poison, I shouldn't be surprised. Make sure you don't get scratched.*

'Damn. I wish I had Samnir's sun-metal blade. That would allow us to win through.'

'Don't worry, friend Jillan. It may take a while, but I should be able to take us through. Even if they are too tough to break, I should be able to uproot them.'

Freda gripped the nearest thick and spiny growth, flexed her arms and tore it apart. It could not withstand her strength or penetrate her hide. The rock woman began to work methodically, ripping, crushing and stamping on the writhing briars. Sap sprayed everywhere, but Jillan made sure to stay well back from it with Floss. For a while it seemed that the plants tried to lash Freda or snake around her limbs, but once she had undone the thickest of the tendrils, the rest shrank away from her.

'Okay, Floss, stay close behind me,' Jillan warned the horse, whose eyes were rolling nervously, 'and we should be all right.'

They ventured forward in Freda's wake, Jillan using the end of his bow to flick broken off-shoots out of their path. A thick branch suddenly sprang up and slashed towards his face, but the runes of his armour flared and the briar withered and fell back to the ground.

Jillan gasped with relief and hurried on. 'Freda, tell me we're nearly there!'

'Not far now, friend Jillan.'

Jillan looked back over his shoulder. Was it his imagination or were the briars already closing back over the path they had made? 'Quickly, Freda!'

And then they were through the barrier and looking down upon a sloping meadow of deep purple poppies. They had yellow and black interiors and stood as fragile as a field of butterflies. The flowers stretched all the way to distant ridges either side of the small valley, beyond which the two streams sounded like fast-flowing rivers with rapids at the bottom of chasms. The far-off roar of the water only made the sense of peace in the meadow seem more profound. Somehow, the poppies drew warmth down from the air, refracting light to create a rainbow sunset of the sky.

'Oh, friend Jillan, it's beautiful!' Freda rumbled, breathing deeply. 'Never did I see anything like this in the world of the Underlords, and little did I believe such a thing could exist in the harsh world of the Overlords. Not even my happiest dream ever enthralled me with such a sight.'

'Yes.' Jillan nodded, finding tears coming to the corners of his eyes. He would have loved to bring Hella to this place, to sit with her and tell her all he felt and all he hoped for, to reassure her that the terrible things they had gone through were not all there was in life, that there was a purpose. 'I can see now why Thorndell would want to hide itself away from the world, why it would want to protect itself however it could from the selfish outsiders who would fight to have this place as their own. They would invade and trample it underfoot, destroying its beauty rather than have it exist beyond their own possession.'

'I hardly dare move forward,' Freda agreed, 'lest I damage these blooms. Perhaps I should sink into the earth and travel to the other side that way, yet I also do not wish to leave this place.'

A bee moved drowsily from one poppy to the next. The flowers swayed reassuringly, as an unfelt zephyr caressed them. Jillan felt himself relaxing for the first time in a long while. When had he last properly slept? 'Look there,' he mumbled. 'Thorndell must be beyond those trees at the end. I think I see a drystone wall. Perhaps I smell woodsmoke too.'

He drifted forward, the purple reaching up to his waist. Floss ambled along behind him, her reins loose in his grip. Freda smiled a goodbye and sank down into the ground.

*I don't know why you're getting so carried away. They're just flowers. An ugly suitor would present the same to distract the eye of a fair maiden. Remember, the inhabitants of this place worship Miserath. Jillan, are you listening to me, or am I wasting myself? Jillan!*

He waved away the annoying horsefly of the taint's voice. He would not allow it to ruin this moment as it had so many others. His breathing slowed and a feeling of ease came over him. Gone was the bite of the blister on the sole of his right foot, gone was the burning rub of his armour under his left arm, gone was the soreness from his limbs, and gone were his feverish fears. He welcomed the lassitude and soporific mood which took their place. For once he was comfortable in his own body and mind.

He yawned. Tired, so tired.

Floss's reins tugged free of his hand. The horse wandered off a few paces and came to a lazy halt.

*This isn't good. Wake up!*

He thought he was floating, but his foot snagged on something. Dreamily, he peered down through the waving poppies. Nestled against the toe of his boot, a white skull grinned back up at him.

'Fancy putting that there. Careless place to leave it.'

*Stop breathing in the scent of these cursed flowers! Get up on the horse!*

He frowned. 'But whoever left it here might not be able to find it when they come back for it. We should wait here so that they see us.'

*Jillan, listen to me carefully. They won't be coming back for it. They no longer have any use for it. They're probably waiting for you in Thorndell. Come on – let's not keep them waiting. Let's go. That's it. Over to the horse.*

But as he turned, his foot caught among the ribs of the skeleton. He lurched and fell forward, as if throwing himself bone-wearily onto a bed, his eyes already shut before his shoulder hit the ground.

*No! Jillan, you idiot, get up! Jillan!*

The soil under the meadow had been thinner than expected. Instead of the rich loam she'd imagined and looked forward to, she moved through little more than dust. Rather than it sustaining her as most earth did, she felt drained coming up and out on the far side. Looking back across the field now, the bright colours were all gone; instead, there was only an unhealthy miasma hanging low over the scene. She sniffed and wrinkled her nose in distaste. She hadn't noticed before how sickly sweet the perfume of the flowers was. It reminded her of unpleasant things.

'Friend Jillan!' she called, her weak eyes seeing little in the failing light, and the gentle nodding of the poppies masking any movement she might otherwise have perceived.

Freda mimicked the sort of clicking noise she had heard Jillan make to Floss earlier in their journey. Was that the horse standing there, struggling to lift her head? A quiet whinny and the sound of the animal hitting the ground heavily.

Freda was suddenly scared. She should never have left Jillan! If anything happened to him now, it would be her fault. She'd known back at Godsend friend Anupal had been going to do something bad to get Jillan to go with them, but she hadn't done enough to stop it. And then the Jillan who'd ended up coming along with them just wasn't the same: now, he was unhappy, or angry, or just more wrong than before somehow. He'd been ready to kill innocent people, and it was her fault. He also did strange and perhaps dangerous things, like eating that mushroom. And now she'd led him into some new trouble in this disconcerting place. She could feel the heartbeats of both Jillan and the horse becoming alarmingly slow.

She'd let friend Anupal *manipulate* poor Jillan. She even suspected Anupal had had something to do with the phagus attacking Jillan, for didn't such creatures tend to obey Anupal's commands? And if she recalled, Anupal had told her to remain particularly close to Jillan the day of the attack, to be ready to save him. Friend Anupal had said it was because he cared and worried for Jillan, but Freda now suspected it was friend Anupal's way of getting Jillan to be grateful to them or something like that. Freda didn't always understand friend Anupal's complicated reasons for the things he did, things that often seemed so bad, although when explained were made to seem different. But this time she was sure she should not have simply gone along with what Anupal wanted. Without her, Anupal might not have been able to manipulate Jillan. She was responsible! And now Jillan was in some sort of terrible trouble.

If friend Jillan died, she would not be able to bear it. Friend Anupal would of course be angry with her, but she would hardly notice that compared to the anguish and guilt she would feel at Jillan's loss. Imagine how distraught Jillan's friends in Godsend would be. Hella, whom Jillan seemed to care about more than any other. Samnir. Aspin from the mountains, who had always been polite to her. Even Thomas and Ash. The wolf would growl angrily at her and perhaps hunt her. Why was it she could never keep her friends safe? She should have stopped Norfred fighting with Darus, should have saved him. She should have stood up to Darus far earlier. She should have made sure Jillan's parents were taken safely out of that city, for she had had the ability. She should have come up through the ground and dragged mad

Azual down before he could kill all those people. Otherwise, what use was there to her? What purpose? Why have friends if she only helped cause their deaths? Was this why Anupal had saved her and chosen her to be his companion? So that she could help him cause the chaos for which he was said to be worshipped? If so, she wanted to hide away from everyone and everything. Perhaps she should bury herself so deeply that not even the miners would be able to reach her. Perhaps get all the way down into the bottomless pit where poor Norfred had been sent. But the Underlords waited down there and would eventually find her. And there was nowhere she could go in the world of the Overlords either. Her only choice was to be here. She had to save Jillan, he who had gifted her the coloured rocks she wore round her throat, the only things she'd ever had as her own. She had to make sure friend Anupal fixed everything properly, had to force him if necessary. She had to fix everything. And she had to fix herself in the process.

Freda dived back into the ground and sped in the direction of the gentle vibrations caused by Jillan's heart. She did not care that she tore through the tissue of the flowers' roots, for she now knew the poppies grew off the life of others. They drained soil, animals and people of everything they had. There was more *wrongness* about them than anything she had come across before. They only lived to bring death, and lived off the death they caused. They were a living death. Just as monstrous as they had previously appeared beautiful.

She burst up out of the ground right next to Jillan. He lay with eyes closed and would have looked peaceful were it not for his deathly pallor. His chest hardly rose. She pulled him up and slapped clumsily at his cheek, but there was no response.

'Friend Jillan, wake up, please! Wake up!'

She threw him over her shoulder and stamped over to the horse, crushing the poppies all around. Floss lay on her side, foam bubbling from mouth and nostrils, her breathing very laboured.

'I don't know if I can lift you!' Freda said, close to panic. 'Can't you get up?'

Freda's vision blurred and she became dizzy. She knew she had to act quickly. She put Jillan down. Then she raised her shoulders to make the plane of her back as wide and flat as possible and got under the horse. She heaved with her legs, her knees grinding in protest.

'Gar, help me!' she wheezed, and the stones at her throat flickered fitfully. She tried to plant her feet more strongly in the ground, but the soil was thin and exhausted, and threatened to betray her.

As she slowly rose, she tilted so that she could get a hold on Jillan's tunic. Then she straightened and took a ponderous step forward. Her back creaked ominously. Ignoring it, she took another. Her lungs were already burning. She was forced to inhale more of the poppies' poison. Another step. The other side of the meadow was so far away!

The slight downward slope of the meadow gave her some momentum and cadence, but it also meant she had less time to test and judge the sureness of her footing. The soil shifted like treacherous sand under the huge weight. Ironically, if it had not been for the roots of the flowers, nothing would have held the ground together beneath her.

'Come on!' she panted in time to her steps, the bellow of her lungs and the molten cascade of her heart. 'Come on!'

She was increasingly lightheaded and couldn't quite . . . concentrate . . . on where she wanted to get to. Fatigue set off tremors in her limbs and she knew an earthquake was about to start within her and that it would see her broken apart. She came to a juddering stop and braced herself, fighting with all that remained to her. She just about held herself together, but had now sunk past her ankles into the field.

With a cry of agony she hauled one foot out and then the other, desperate to regain momentum. Her feet sank again. She leaned forward against the ground and became a rock slide, rolling forward, and further, and on, with greater and greater speed. Soon her legs could not keep up and in desperation she threw herself forward full length, holding Jillan up off the ground as best she could. Her chest and stomach hit the ground, but at the same time she merged with its substance so that they would not be slowed.

They shot down the slope, Floss still on Freda's back, Jillan half balanced on her head, tearing a large swathe through the meadow. Freda stayed partly merged with the soil and surfed a wave of it all the way to the drystone wall. Then she was twisting to cushion Floss and Jillan from the inevitable impact. The contact with the blessed hardness of the stone immediately strengthened and bolstered her and she was lifting them all up and over to the other side.

They thumped down onto stony ground and a dusty breath of relief exploded from Freda's lungs. 'Oof!' After a few seconds: 'That would almost have been fun if it hadn't nearly killed us all.'

She eased Floss off her, and was so delighted that the horse was still awake and did not appear to have broken any limbs that she almost cried. But then she did cry, for there was no rousing Jillan. He lay completely still. She searched for the vibration of his heart, but could feel nothing.

'It must be too faint for these thick-skinned paws of mine to sense, that's all!' she hiccuped. 'There must still be time!' she begged of the darkening sky. 'I can still find someone who will know how to save him. Friend Anupal, where are you? If you can hear me, and if you have any power in this place, please help us! Forgive me, horse, but I must leave you here!'

Freda lifted Jillan back up and hurried along a path that led off among shadowy pine trees. She churned forward as quickly as she dared in the near-night of the woods.

'Oh where is Thorndell? It cannot be far!' she called out. 'I do not see any lights. Hellooo!'

A howl sounded somewhere, but she wasn't sure of its direction or distance. She took a path towards where she thought it had come from, hoping it would lead her to some community, as the dogs of Godsend sometimes did. Another howl came from the other half of the woods, this call longer and more haunting than the first. There were answering barks from different places, hungry and savage. Some were very close.

She now knew that whatever these creatures were, they were to be avoided. She went quickly back to the main path and ploughed forward with determination, for once not caring that she damaged the roots of powerful and ancient trees. Even here the earth did little to sustain her, but she was no longer encumbered by the weight of a horse across her back.

There was an excited yip from where she had entered the woods, and a frenzy of snarls and yelps built behind her. They had her scent now and would soon be upon her.

She thundered forward and abruptly the woods gave way to a vast glade of huts and cottages. Yet the sight of what was there turned her blood cold. There were rotting corpses everywhere. Demonic hounds worried at old flesh and sinew or crunched through bones to get at the marrow. Several fought over one of the larger bodies, others circling and watching for an opportunity to dart in and steal some titbit. The reek was so bad it seemed the air itself had become corrupted.

The biggest of the hounds gnawed on the skull of a dead child and growled at Freda as if she were about to attempt to take its prize. Appalled beyond rational thought, she backed away. Red feral eyes all around the clearing turned to watch her. She stopped. Hackles rose. Saliva dripped.

'Flee!' moaned a chorus of voices. 'Flee!'

Heads spiked on wooden posts lined the main path through the clearing. Those still with a vestige of their eyes rolled them at her, engorged and blackened tongues flapping out of mouths. Others had either been picked clean or decayed more quickly, for they were little more than bare bone. There was a ghostly glow clinging to all of the heads, however, as if their tortured souls could not escape their mortal remains.

'What nightmare is this?' Freda cried, not knowing which way to turn.

Then firelight flickered on the higher far side of the clearing. Hope. In the same instant slavering hounds came pouring out of the woods behind her. Madness rose up all around.

Freda charged forward, Jillan in the crook of one arm. She deliberately broke up the ground behind her so that those coming on could not keep their footing. A gaunt beast came racing in from her right and leapt, jaws stretched wide. She hammered it in the throat with the fist of her free arm, instantly killing it and throwing it back. Three incoming hounds changed direction in order to feast upon it. Another came in on her left flank and she bowled it over so that it landed on its spine with a crack. Emaciated creatures wasted no time tearing its guts free.

Teeth broke on the calf of her right leg, as one of the pack tried to hamstring her or get its jaws locked on her. Something heavy landed on her back, razor-sharp claws scrabbling for purchase. She ducked, and the hound's own momentum saw it fall past her. She stamped its head into the ground and stormed ahead.

Several leapt in at once. With a kick, she caved in the chest of one, but the other came inches from tearing Jillan from her grasp. A sharp lift of her knee prevented it at the last moment and she trod the hound underfoot.

The night was alive with bounding, twisting bodies. More and more came out of dark doorways as she passed. They seemed to have no care for themselves, so voracious was their appetite and so intent were they on bringing her down. A tooth snagged in one of the cracks in her arm and the weight of the hound made her lean precariously, threatening to pull her over. She lashed the arm up and down and righted herself.

'Go back!' belched a spiked head before its jaw fell away and it could only goggle at her with maggot-filled eyes.

The way was blocked by a rabid seething mass and she knew there would be no winning through them. Their numbers would overwhelm and pin her. Tooth and claw would find fissures in her stone exterior and pull her skin away from her soft interior. Her eyes would be scratched out. A muzzle would force its way down into her mouth and rip her tongue out.

Pulling herself around Jillan, she dived into the ground. The hounds tried to follow her, digging frantically at the compacted surface, but she moved beyond them. They barked their outrage and gnashed at each other. Their sharp sense of smell followed her even as she began to move through the ground. They constantly circled and started digging whenever she slowed.

Freda burrowed through the earth and across the glade. She exploded up out of the ground, scattering the wild dogs, located the thick-walled cabin that showed a fire through its shutters, and then went back under before any could come close to her. She rushed heedlessly on, angling down slightly for some distance and then coming up steeply, to burst out of the floor inside the dwelling.

A thin and ragged urchin with dirty black hair draped over her face screeched and scuttled back from the fire, where she'd been crouched. 'I knew you would come! *He* sent you, didn't he? I was right to perform the summoning! He will set all to rights.'

Freda ducked the bones of all shapes and sizes that hung by pieces of sinew from the rafters of the roof and placed Jillan gently down. 'Friend Anupal sent us. This is Thorndell, yes? My friend needs your help.'

The gangly urchin capered in excitement among the flickering shadows cast against the wall of the cabin. 'I knew it! I knew it! My lord will come.' She danced closer to Jillan and stopped to sniff him. 'Dead,' she said with a shake of the head.

Jillan stood in the midst of desolation. The land was blackened and cracked. Many of the rocks had a glassy quality, as if they had been subjected to an intense heat, and steam vented from deep below the ground. The sky was an impenetrable ash grey and there was no sign of any sun or moon. It was hard to breathe and it slowed his movements.

There was a hill ahead of him. He recognised its shape from the waking dreams he had experienced when Saint Azual had forced some of his blood on him. On this occasion, however, there was no trace of any green grass or paradisal garden on the hill. It was charred and barren now. The only sign of what had been was a half-buried pile of skulls which had once constituted Azual's throne at the very crown of the hill.

'How am I back here?' Jillan wondered, and then spied the narrow defile at the base of the hill that he'd once entered before.

He went to it and squeezed inside. It was a tighter fit than he recalled. Perhaps he was growing at last. He pushed deeper into the heart of the hill. The earth became soft and then ribbed and fleshy, like the brains of the hunted animals his father used to bring home.

He stepped into the core, a large echoing cavern. There was the curiously lit statue that he remembered, a large and featureless grey skull supported by impossibly thin limbs. It saw him come. He was reflected in the voids of the Saviour's black orbs. It watched him like a conscience. He became painfully aware of his own inadequacy and insignificance in its presence. He became guilty for the very thing he was.

*So you have dared return, pernicious mite, even after all you have wrought!* The voice boomed in his mind, making him feel sick. Then it became softly suggestive: *Perhaps that is why you have returned, to survey the very devastation you have brought about. Does it give you, in your desperation for self-assertion, some satisfaction or affirmation to witness it? For you have become the bane of the Empire. You have become the destroyer of life, have you not? You define yourself by bringing death to others, do you not? You would prefer a world empty of all life rather than one with a form of existence with which you do not agree. Is that not so?*

He could not bear it. The Saviour spoke of secret fears and self-doubts of which not even the taint knew. The Saints and Saviours *always knew*. It was like hearing his own confession, except he lacked the wherewithal to ask for forgiveness, for he knew he was entirely undeserving of it. How dare he ask anything of such a blessed and knowing being? How dare he even venture into its presence?

*Where once cattle grazed upon the slopes of this hill and gentle people reclined in its sleepy orchards, now there is only a blasted and infertile waste. And so it always is with your kind when they are allowed freedom and any sort of power over others. There was one before you – Torpeth the Great – who was just the same. Indeed, you wear his armour. He was the destroyer of his people. We have never understood the desire for self-destruction of your kind, pernicious mite. It is so strong that sometimes it is a challenge to save you from yourselves.*

'I don't want anyone to die,' Jillan replied earnestly. 'It was Azual's men around the top of the hill, with their spears of sun-metal, who were killing the people below. It was terrible!'

*In its imperfection your kind must be presented with challenges and difficulties to overcome. It must have a reason to strive and better itself, or it will never seek to pull itself up out of the mud. It must be allowed to see a better place, and see that a small few have attained it. Then your kind must be denied that place. The very denial is what inspires your kind to seek to be worthy, to seek to be more than it already is. Azual's men simply prevented the majority from reaching the summit. If you recall, pernicious mite, most of those who died actually threw themselves upon the Heroes' spears in the torment and anguish of their selfish desire. Or their fellows pushed them onto the spears, hoping to mire the Heroes temporarily and thereby win a chance for their own progress.*

'Can't everyone be allowed the summit? Can't they just be left alone?'

*Still with the pernicious challenge and questions, eh, mite? Allowed power and free rein, your kind always seeks to acquire more. Individuals fear they will not have enough for themselves and scramble to seize the fruit of the orchards before others can. In the scramble much of the fruit is trodden on and destroyed. Stronger individuals declare particular trees their own and bully others away, not caring if it sees them starve. Oh, you will try to deny it, mite, but you are the same. Allowed power, did you not immediately kill one of your own kind?*

Karl. The Saviour meant Jillan's schoolmate Karl.

*Did you not then flee the consequences of your crime like a coward? Did you not flee so that none could take your powers from you? In your selfishness you did not care that those powers were a plague that would kill so many others. You, pernicious mite, are one of those who push others onto the spears of Heroes for individual gain.*

'I tried to save those with the plague!' Jillan cried, tears hot upon his cheeks. 'I healed people in Godsend. I do not want this magic if it kills people!'

*Tried to save them, did you? In your arrogance you set yourself up as a Saviour, saving people from the selfsame plague you gave them. Your self-serving blasphemy knows no end. If those with the plague did not accept you as their Saviour and join your personal empire in Godsend, then their alternative was death from the plague. An evil choice. Death or join the empire of Jillan that would seek to destroy everything they'd ever believed and held dear. In your envy you have sought to make Godsend your own private summit and orchard, have you not? You have given yourself a throne there, and guarded it with your own Heroes. And yet you stand here and pretend you do not want this selfish power and magic? All of your actions demonstrate the selfish lie behind everything you say and believe. You love the power and thrill of your magic. You love the power it gives you over others. It makes you feel better than them. It gives you everything you want. It forces others to worship and love you against their will, even as it takes their town and lives from them. Or will you persist in telling me, pernicious mite, that you are saving Godsend? Will you insist on telling me that everyone in Godsend has to die so that you can save it from the army of the Empire?*

Had Hella only said she loved him so that he would heal her father Jacob of the plague? Had his magic forced her to lie? Was that part of the same lie of which the Saviour spoke? What had he done to her? How could he ever make it up to her? 'I-I have left Godsend and will not trouble it again. Please, there is no need for anyone to die.'

*No need, pernicious mite, when they have blasphemed against the Empire and you have turned some of their minds with your selfish and corrupting beliefs? No need, when I have already said your kind must be presented with challenges and difficulties to overcome? No need, when you still have not given up your powers, are apparently abroad spreading your corruption and may one day seek to return to Godsend as a safe haven? Pernicious mite, there is every need, unless you recant your misdeeds and can prove your penitence to us. Once before, you swore to reveal the Geas to us. We hold you to that vow.*

'Please believe me: Godsend is already turning back towards the Empire. And I will find the Geas.'

*How will you do so on your own, pernicious mite?*

'Miserath is helping me.'

There was a sharp and angry whistling sound from the Saviour. *Pathetic mite! The Peculiar is not to be trusted. You are all too easily manipulated. Tell us where you are and we will come for you. At once!*

'I-I am not sure. Thorndell. They worship Miserath.'

He'd been about to mention their journey westwards, but the Saviour was already speaking again. *If you dare aid the Peculiar, Hella and all those in Godsend shall suffer a slow execution, do you understand? Yes, through our servant Saint Praxis, we know well of your attachment to this creature Hella. Imagine her dying and cursing you, the strength of her feeling making those words ring on forevermore so that you can never stop hearing them or shut them from your mind. They will drive you mad and you will never know rest, be you alive or dead. Saint Praxis will take her into our power and all will be as I said.*

Praxis! The man who had haunted him all his life. He who had first made Jillan understand fear, guilt and self-loathing. He who had first made him know resentment and anger. Jillan had hoped the Minister had died in the battle at Godsend, but knew no one was ever really free of themselves, their past or their self-torment. Just as the Minister was alive once more, and more terrible as a Saint than ever before, so the old resentment and anger reignited in Jillan and flamed higher than he'd ever known. It was like he'd been asleep and had at last woken up. He was coming back to himself now. He realised he'd been listening to some inhuman description of Hella being tortured to death – and this from some detestable being that claimed to be a blessed Saviour with only humanity's interest at heart! How he despised it. He found it hard even to tolerate it mentioning Hella's name. And he realised the thing had also got him to tell it where he was going and who he was with. *You are too easily manipulated,* isn't that what it had told him? He realised now that it manipulated all his people.

The golden runes on Jillan's armour twinkled in the darkness of the cavern, throwing light on the Saviour. It hissed and retreated a step. Jillan squared his shoulders and stepped forward. 'Where are you going, blessed Saviour?' he asked mildly. 'Come, stay awhile and share more of your wisdom with me.'

*You dare, disgusting mite?* the Saviour screeched in outrage.

'Surely you need not fear one so disgusting and pathetic, blessed one? Surely you need not fear one so imperfect? Where are you going? Surely not to hide? There are no shadows deep and dark enough to conceal you from me. Stay. I would know your name and other thoughts.' Did he hear its mind whistling and whispering? 'D'Shaa, is it?'

*Sacrilege!*

'How close is this army of yours to Godsend? Where is Saint Praxis?' He tried to snatch her thoughts, but this time they skittered away from him like spiders. He leapt towards her and she propelled herself far off into the darkness. 'I will find you!' he shouted after her. 'For I think we are somehow linked by Azual's blood. Tell Praxis that if he harms a hair on anyone's head in Godsend, then I will deliver his blessed Saviours to him in a meat pie! You hear me?'

Saint Praxis raised the crystal goblet to his lips and sipped on the latest tithe exacted from the People of Hyvan's Cross. Ah, but it was as potent as the citizens were decadent, for they knew no self-restraint and denied themselves nothing. Some fortified themselves through the consumption of live animals, some experimented with rare drugs from the sultry Obvarian Islands far to the west, and others performed despicable acts of fornication that involved all manner of imported bodily fluids. It was right that this tithe be taken, for it meant the People would not have as much energy with which to indulge their waywardness. Yes, perhaps he should see to it that the population of the south was bled every year rather than just one time in their lives, when they reached puberty. It mattered not that a more regular tithe would drastically shorten the lifespan of the People, for surely it was better for them to lead a shorter and less wanton life than it was a longer and more sinful one. Yes, better that the People were too drained and listless to be tempted from the right path.

As Saint Praxis swallowed the blood and absorbed its energy, he also found his way inside the thoughts of more and more of the population. The more he learned about their lives and the staggering variety of sins they committed on an all-but-daily basis, the more he abhorred them. These People weren't actually *saved*, were they? How could they be? A good number of them considered the blessed Saviours to be a *story*, or myth at best, their Saints to be power-crazed warlords, and their Ministers to be glorified wet nurses for the children of the rich burghers! The enormity of it had shaken the Saint to his very soul. How cunningly had the Chaos insinuated itself into the minds and thoughts of these city-dwellers! How artfully had it wrought a belief system that was so akin to the true religion of the Empire that the People could hardly tell one from the other, that perhaps even good Saint Azual had not perceived what was going on! With such subtlety had it created a false-but-true-seeming church, a church that was slightly more forgiving than it should be, slightly more indulgent, and therefore greatly more attractive! With what artifice had it introduced forms of penance that involved the personal sacrifice of gold coin to the so-called Minister of this false and evil church! To think of the threadbare and small-portioned existence he'd endured as Minister of Godsend, while all the time these slippered Ministers of the Chaos had dressed in cloth of gold and gorged on the richest and sweetest of meats, and much forbidden fruit and flesh besides.

No wonder Saint Azual had been undermined and toppled within his region. No wonder the Chaos-driven plague had taken hold so easily here. But now he, Saint Praxis, had come, and he had found out the secret and conspiring ways of the Chaos, for it could not hide from the righteousness of his gaze. His keen eye was not to be deceived by any mask, no matter how genuine or flesh-like it might seem to others. He had found out the demons who walked among the population of Hyvan's Cross while deporting themselves as the most pious of individuals so that they might all the better lead others astray. And now he would exorcise them from the midst of the People, so that the People could in turn be purged without interference or negative influence.

'Must he make such a noise?' Saint Praxis demanded of the bloody Hero serving as torturer. 'It makes it hard to think.'

''Scuse, holy one,' the burly man grunted. 'It's the pain, see? Ain't no quiet way to remove the skin from a man's face, unless you wants him unconscious?'

'No. Minister Renish must remain awake so that he suffers for the mask he wears as much as those whose souls have suffered because they were fooled by it. Remove his tongue instead.'

'Pleeease, Praxis!' the prisoner in the stocks sobbed hysterically. The frame was so arranged that the criminal stood facing and quailing before the Saint at all times. 'Have mercy! I will repent anything that you accuse me of. Anything! I have always served the Saint of this region well. I am *loyal*!'

'Well?' Saint Praxis shouted. 'Yes, you served the Saint, and look what happened to him! That served him well, did it? Well, did it? Speak up, Renish, or I will know you have no need of that tongue.'

'Please, Praxis, none grieve more than I for what happened. You must believe me!'

'You dare tell me what I must do?' Saint Praxis asked in quiet astonishment, his pale eyes wild and staring. 'Unbelievable. You address your holy Saint and tell him what he *must* do? Truly, the Chaos possesses you. I have heard enough. Torturer, his tongue!'

The Hero nodded and took up a pair of rusty tongs. He cuffed Minister Renish round the head to encourage him to put his tongue out. Hot urine splashed down the terrified Minister's sumptuous robes.

'Oh, he is putrid!' Saint Praxis complained. 'Does the Chaos seek to flee his body so that it will not have to endure the punishment? Renish, you will unclamp your teeth or my man will have to smash them in. Cooperate with the punishment that is your due and I will see it as an act of repentance. That's it! Good boy.'

The tongue was gripped in the tongs and then the torturer lifted an implement like sheers. He snipped off the offending organ without preamble. Blood poured and the Minister began to choke. His legs were no longer able to support him, and his entire weight hung from just his neck in the stocks. Unhurriedly, the torturer lifted a hot poker from a small brazier and placed it against the stub of the writhing Minister's tongue. There was a brief sizzle, the smell of cooked meat, and a strangled yell. Veins stood out all over the Minister's head as if they would tear it apart. The torturer then considerately lifted the Minister at the waist, so that the man would not die and escape his punishment so easily.

'There, you see, that wasn't so bad,' Saint Praxis observed, sipping from his goblet and licking his lips. 'I just wish you hadn't made such a mess of my floorboards. I bet they'll stain. Ah well, we must all make sacrifices, even me. Renish, you will now eat that trouble-making tongue of yours and we are done. Come now, it is for your own good. It will help you lose that excessive appetite of yours. Torturer, help him along if you please. We are busy.'

The tongue was reinserted into the mouth from which it had come, the jaw held closed and the Minister's throat stroked by the torturer's dirty finger to trigger the swallowing reflex. The Hero then straightened up and nodded it was done.

'Very good. Now have him chained in a public square so that all may see what he has done to himself in allowing the Chaos to suborn him. He has soiled himself. He has chosen to forfeit that part of himself that once praised the Empire but then turned to whispering the temptations and influence of the Chaos to others. And the self-feeding greed of the Chaos has then caused him to begin consuming himself. Have a crier placed in the square with him so that the truth of it might be explained to those not as enlightened as we are. Watch for any in the crowd who hurry away in fear, for they will be in league with the Chaos and will need to be brought before me. Watch for any who regard him with sympathy or even look to help him. And bring in the next.'

The torturer called in two Heroes, and they released the Minister and carried him out. An elderly man in dark robes was led in and put in the stocks in place of the Minister. Old though he was, the facial features beneath his white hair were well defined and his eyes had a sharpness about them that the Saint took for evidence of defiance.

'I have done nothing wrong! This is an outrage!' the prisoner declared in a clear voice, obviously used to his words carrying great weight.

'And yet you already condemn yourself,' Saint Praxis said with satisfaction. 'It is not for your overweening pride to judge your own innocence or guilt. It is for my holy office, instituted by the blessed

Saviours themselves, to make such judgement. Or, in your Chaos-created arrogance, do you not recognise that authority?'

'Holy one, there must have been some mistake. I am a visiting lector from the western region,' the elder replied, working to moderate his tone. 'I am a representative of holy Saint Izat here in Hyvan's Cross. The learning I offer had always been welcome before.'

'Lector you call yourself, eh?' Saint Praxis smiled, riffling through some papers on his desk. 'I hear you have set up a seat of learning here, is that right?' He brandished a page of script. 'Is *this* what you call learning? This is your work, is it not?'

'I . . . yes. A treatise. B-But it is harmless . . . holy one.'

'*Harmless?*' the Saint spat. 'How dare you! Do you think I am so witless?' The Saint's breath came hard for a few moments, and then he regained his composure. 'Come, Lector, you are an intelligent man. Explain to me how there can be anything for the People to learn beyond the Book of Saviours. Tell me how there can be anything they *need* to understand that is not already allowed them by the blessed Saviours. Elucidate for me if you will why they should spend their time reading . . .' here Saint Praxis announced the title of the treatise '. . . *On the falling of apples*, rather than studying the good book and kneeling in prayer. Please, educate me as if I were one of your young and impressionable students.'

'H-Holy one, I-I-I—'

'You splutter like a village idiot, now, O man of letters!' the Saint sneered. 'I will ask you one more time and you will answer clearly, lest you be guilty of wasting my time and keeping me from my holy duties. Come, show yourself the great teacher. How do you justify these apples? Answer me!'

Sweat rolled down the old man's brow and into his eyes, making him blink furiously. Now he spoke fluently, 'Holy one, I have dedicated my life to the pursuit of knowledge, nothing more or less. There is no sedition in that, nothing subversive. Quite the opposite. The acquisition of knowledge, and its contingent self-improvement, raises man above the animals. It helps us better understand the world so that we can work with it rather than be mindless victims of its movement and actions. Two objects of differing weight dropped from the same height will land at the exact same instant!'

The Saint shook his head in disappointment. 'Seek to understand the world better? And you say that is not sedition? Why, I do believe you have argued yourself into a corner. The Chaos is ever so tricky that it ultimately tricks itself. The blessed Saviours have given us to understand the world perfectly, or as simply as they wish it. To attempt any understanding or power beyond that is to seek to place man in a position of authority over the world. That is the worst of blasphemies, for it ultimately seeks to supplant the blessed Saviours. *You*, lector, have done as much as any other to subvert the People of this region. *You* undermined their faith in their own Saint. Torturer, cut off his hands.'

'No, not my hands!' the elder begged in horror.

'Let us see how you write a treatise now.'

A heavy cleaver came down. Once. *Crunch*. A wet thud. A mute cry. A second time. *Crunch*. Another wet thud. A high-pitched gurgle. The spitting sizzle of the poker cauterising the wrists. 'Arrghhh! Saint Izat spare me!'

'Have him escorted out of the region. Seize his books and everything he has ever written. Have it all burned in the square so that the People might finally learn something worthy from the work of this false preacher.'

Saint Praxis took a large mouthful from his goblet. Drinking too much might make him more giddy than he liked, but his was thirsty work. The constant vigilance he needed to maintain, the relentless questioning and the emotional strain of seeing divine retribution visited upon the guilty all saw him drained. But it was becoming easier. Already, the People of Hyvan's Cross were becoming more fearful, and therefore capitulating more easily to his will. The more who succumbed, the more his will was enshrined among the wider population, and the stronger he grew. Their fear made him strong, and the stronger he became, the more they feared him. As quickly as the next prisoner was brought in, he was already impatient to have them cowering in terror before him, confessing to consorting with the Chaos and making a personal sacrifice as an example to others, others who all too often did not have the stomach for such sacrifice themselves, who selfishly feigned squeamishness but did not hesitate to commit heinous acts when they thought no one was watching or knew. Well, he would see to it that every single one of them was coerced, cowed and conscripted into self-sacrifice, so that they remembered the holy words and command of the book: *Sacrifice and duty safeguard the People against the Chaos.* They would remember *the Saint always knows.*

The next one locked into the stocks was a sensitive-looking man in his late twenties. He had milky-white skin and doleful eyes. This one had clearly never done an honest day's work out under the sun. There was something *delicate* about him that revolted the Saint.

His thirst raging, Saint Praxis reached to refill his goblet, or had he only just done that? Never mind. 'Artist!' he condemned the prisoner. 'You mimic nature, the divine bounty of the blessed Saviours, and carve idols for the People to exclaim over. They marvel and wonder at the artistry of man, ignoring the greater miracle of nature that is already around them. You make false idols for worship, I say! Put out his eyes!'

Then came a female actor and the torturer was moved by her soft entreaties. The heavy-browed Hero looked to the Saint in appeal.

'Gentle torturer, do not let her take unfair advantage of your better nature. Remember, she plays a role and is not true. Her poetic solicitations are nothing more than learned lines, not the true testimony of a beautiful heart. She plays you, man! Her pleasing looks are paints applied as a disguise. See, she is all deception! Do not let her distract you from your holy work. Twist her feet so that she may never again strut these streets and divert those who would otherwise be working for the good of the Empire.'

Yet none of them quenched his thirst. He realised that dealing with the People individually never would. He needed to settle the issue with larger numbers of them at a time. Dismissing the torturer, he called for General Thormodius and the angelic Captain Skathis to attend him. As the General entered the room, Saint Praxis watched him carefully, to see if he would betray any disapproval of the righteous inquisition that had been taking place. The General's face did not so much as twitch. Well, he was a soldier, after all, and had no doubt seen much more in his time, or perhaps perpetrated much more.

Saint Praxis signalled for his commanders to be seated. 'General, have all those with the plague been rounded up and separated from the others?'

'Yes, holy one, all as you commanded.'

'How many?'

'One thousand, holy one.'

'Have them taken beyond the city and slaughtered.'

Not a flicker. 'Yes, holy one. In what manner would you want them slaughtered?'

'What?'

'In what manner, holy one?'

Was the man being obtuse? Captain Skathis shifted uncomfortably. 'My angelic Captain, do you have lice? You seem ill at ease.'

'If I may speak freely, holy one?'

'I will indulge you, my angelic Captain.'

'Nearly all of the thousand have relatives and friends among the rest of the population. The slaughter might test the People's . . . loyalty to you. Holy one, they are weak and their faith is all too often lacking, even when our actions but seek to safeguard them.'

Saint Praxis felt for the Captain's thoughts. There was no subterfuge there. 'What would you suggest instead, my sentimental Captain?'

'Rather than slaughter them, perhaps we could . . . perhaps we could send them into a permanent isolation? Like a leper colony? They could build their own community, with a few guards standing by to ensure they do not attempt to return to the general population. Those with plague in the other towns, Saviours' Paradise, Heroes' Brook, and so on, could also be sent to this colony. Otherwise, we will have to slaughter the People wherever we go. It could be that most will die of the illness anyway, but a number might survive and then have some valuable resistance to the plague.'

'And who will provision these people while they build their community? Is it not a waste of our resources?' Saint Praxis asked smoothly.

'Those who are sick have their own means, holy one, and their families will feel some obligation to provide for them. Perhaps there will be some small requirement for charity—'

'*Charity?*' Saint Praxis seethed. 'Captain, I have heard enough. May I remind you that these people are sick because their own sin has corrupted them? None will condone or support that corruption, on pain of death, do you understand? No, I have a better idea. The thousand will be turned into an army and sent into the mountains to hunt down the pagans there. Allow each of them enough food for one week, which is far more that I was provided with when I was sent on my holy mission. Let them do penance by serving the Empire. They will renew their faith in the process and thus be protected by the blessed Saviours. Therefore, those who choose not to renew their faith will naturally bring about their own deaths. Let it be so, my angelic Captain.'

The Captain slowly nodded. 'Yes, holy one. You are wise.'

The Saint's eyes narrowed, but he sensed no mockery in the Captain's thoughts. 'Very well. And how much longer until your men have finished administering the holy communion to the People of Hyvan's Cross? The sooner it can be done, the sooner the Chaos can be forced into retreat and the fewer victims it will have claimed. It will be forced back to Godsend and down the very throat of the Empire's bane!'

'Two more days, holy one,' the Captain promised.

'And then we will move on to Heroes' Brook with all speed. Have your men ready to march, General.'

'As is your wish, holy one. I would propose taking Saviours' Paradise after Heroes' Brook, so that there is no potential of a fallback position for the rebels of Godsend. I would not relish having to lay siege to Godsend if there were any chance of another rebel force coming from Saviours' Paradise. We would risk being caught between a rock and a hard place.'

Saint Praxis looked to the Captain, who nodded his agreement. 'Very well. That is my wish,' Saint Praxis replied, reaching to refill his goblet.

Samnir approached Heroes' Brook with his one hundred mounted men. On the road less than a day before they had encountered a ragtag band of a dozen or so coming the other way. Their leader, Tebrus, had told of meeting Jillan and being promised sanctuary in Godsend. The band intended to return one of Jacob's horses and the stolen supplies, which was good enough for Samnir. What had worried him, however, was Tebrus's description of Jillan's two companions, Freda and what could be Miserath. It had been too much to hope that the god had genuinely been undone in the battle at Godsend. Mischief was never so easily ended. And if Jillan were travelling with the dark brother, then no good could come of it.

'Damn it, I should have looked out for the lad better!'

Tebrus had told Samnir that Jillan had headed in the direction of Heroes' Brook, wished him luck and then been on his way to Godsend with his band. Heroes' Brook as a destination made little sense, but who could fathom the divine madness of Miserath?

Samnir sent a dozen archers into the trees on each side of the road and halted the rest of his men beyond the reach of any bow in Heroes' Brook. The town's gates were closed against them. Dozens of grim-faced Heroes looked down from the town's high and thick stone walls. His heart sank. If Jillan was trapped inside, there would be no chance of getting him out.

Samnir nudged his horse forward a few steps. He tried to keep his tone light and unthreatening, jovial even, but knew he wasn't going to make a very good job of it. 'Hellooo, in the town! We come to parlay. We mean you no trouble. Forgive our rude health. There is no sickness among us. We represent Godsend.'

'There is nothing for you here, Chaos spawn! Turn around and be gone, in the name of all that is holy!'

The voice that had spoken was nasal and peevish, not the sort Samnir would have expected of a soldier. Samnir squinted and picked out the speaker, a Minister by his clothing. Captain Gallen, one of Samnir's officers, moved forward and murmured to his commander, 'Minister Stixis. Fanatical. We would do better with some of the other elders.'

Samnir nodded in acknowledgement and rode forward alone. He risked himself to be sure that all the men on the wall would be able to hear him clearly. 'Good Minister and people of Heroes' Brook, we need not be enemies! Like you, we mourn that a battle took place in Godsend, that Hero fought Hero, brother against brother, child against parent. The Saint came to kill us all because he saw us as the cause of the plague. It was a madness of sorts! All knew of the rages to which he was given.'

'Blasphemy!' whined Minister Stixis, but everyone else on the walls remained silent.

Samnir licked his lips, mouth dry. 'The Saint was just a man! And like every man, he made mistakes. In his haste to undo others, he did not think they would attempt to defend themselves. His inattention brought about his own end!'

'No! Do not listen to him! He contaminates your ears! All know that there is a magician among them. All know that they are in league with the pagans and the Chaos!'

Samnir shook his head and raised empty hands. 'Our Minister did bring pagans with him out of the mountains for reasons I did not understand, but most died and those who survived returned home. There are none left in Godsend. What does remain then? Men. Men just like you. People who want uncomplicated lives and simply wish to get along with their neighbours. People who want food on their tables and ale in their tankards of an evening. People who want to share a yarn and a song in the inn and then have a friend help them home afterwards. Is that wrong? Can you say you do not want the same?' -

'Silence him! He weaves a pagan spell to ensnare your minds! Captain, shoot him, I order you!'

There was the creak of leather. Was that the sound of a bow being drawn? Samnir held his breath, waiting to hear the whistle of an arrow, preparing to throw himself from his saddle and praying that his old body would not break to pieces on the road.

The gates of the town swung inwards a yard or so and a lone horseman came out to meet Samnir. The rider stopped about a horse's length away from the commander of Godsend.

'Well met, Samnir the Sand Devil. Never could stay out of trouble, could you?'

*The Sand Devil.* He had not been called that in longer than he cared to remember. Samnir stared hard at the Hero facing him, looking past the scars and lines of experience, seeing the lean fighter who still existed beneath the portly and balding figure of this old soldier. 'Callinor!' He gaped. 'How did you ever survive the eastern deserts? You always held your bow upside down as I recall.'

Callinor spat over the side of his horse and smiled. 'Once you were removed from our squad, things suddenly became far less dangerous for us. Somehow, we just didn't manage to track down as many groups of pagans, barbarians and giants as when you used to sniff them out like a starving man downwind of the latrines. We ended up in a lot less shit without you, if you take my meaning. Meant a lot more men got to live long enough to earn themselves a comfortable posting back-of-beyond in which to see out their final days. There's food on my table and ale in my tankard, thank you very much. So why do you want to come along stirring everything up again, eh? You've still got that crazy itch of yours, haven't you? Heard you fought the mad Saint himself. Near did for him by all accounts too. But what did it get you, eh? Mind broken and chained in the square of the smallest town at the arse-end of nowhere, ain't that right? Should have taught you a lesson, that. But even then you didn't know when to lie down, did you? Oh no! That would have been far too easy and peaceful-like for the Sand Devil. No, you had to get back up on your feet and start poking at the nest of termites again. Why couldn't you just let it lie, eh? You probably drove the Saint to distraction, beyond even his own holy endurance. No wonder he was so intent on murdering everyone. And you know what you've brought down on us now, don't you, Sand Devil? An army of ten thousand of the buggers! Led by the bloody General himself, just when I thought I'd got over peeing my pants because of memories of him. And they say there's a new Saint in Hyvan's Cross already, one who makes mad Azual seem about as threatening as a virgin maid's fart. Praxis is—'

'*Praxis!*'

'Aye, so I heard. Wasn't that the name of your Minister from before? He'll certainly have it in for you, I imagine. And with what's coming, you'll understand that folks here want less than nothing to do with Godsend. They're not about to let you drag them down along with you.'

Samnir glowered at the man. 'Callinor, you were never a fool. You know that what happened in Godsend was not me looking for trouble, but trouble finding us. We have won ourselves a few moments of freedom for the first time in our lives. Don't tell me you don't feel it too, even beneath all those pounds the good life has put on you. It's like having slept for far too long, with the same dream repeating over and over like a nightmare, but now you're finally awake and free of it. Like being smothered all your life and then they lift the pillow away to see if you're really dead. Or like drinking too long in a stuffy room and then stepping into the clean cool air. Like having a headache for the longest time, for so long that you almost forget you have it, until one day the nagging and the grinding just disappears. Your head becomes clear and you're a different person. Callinor, as old as I am, in many ways I have never felt so young. Do you not feel it too? Tell me you cannot! And are you meekly prepared just to let things go back to the way they were? For things will be even worse if you do, now that you know there is a happier life, now that you will remember these few moments without the pain of a slow asphyxiation and gradual brain death.'

Callinor chewed the inside of his cheek, his bottom lip and then his knuckle. 'Damn you, Sand Devil! What would you have me say? That I know of what you speak? What would that achieve? And what would you have me do? Join you in your madness? I cannot!' Tears came to the corners of his eyes. 'There are ten thousand of them, man!' he whispered. 'Please, flee while you can, if not for your own sake then for the People of Godsend. There is still some time. You might make it to the mountains.'

'And will there be safety in the mountains, dear Callinor? I think not. The cursed Saviours will hunt us wherever we go.'

The Hero lowered his voice. 'Sand Devil, I pray you, do not speak so blasphemously. They are always listening. They always know!'

Samnir returned a humourless smile. 'Yes, old friend, they are always listening. They are always there in your mind, aren't they? Are they crouched and hidden or restless? They eat away at you from the inside, do they not? You do not look well, old friend.'

Callinor scrubbed a hand over his face, trying to smooth his harrowed brow. 'Please, Sand Devil,' he begged, unable to look at the man who had once been his comrade-in-arms.

'Would you have me relent, then? Give in to them? Go willingly to the waking death? I nearly did a few times, you know.'

'Even you?' the Hero asked in hushed horror.

Samnir allowed his years to show for a moment, dropping his shoulders a fraction, loosening the tightness of his jaw, easing the intensity of his eye. He nodded. 'They wear you down, old friend. They never rest. I was restless in my turn, wasn't I? You called it an itch. I now realise that I was fighting back against them, always fighting. But they kept at me, never letting me sleep, until they broke me.' Unexpectedly, his lip trembled and he became hoarse. 'They broke me, Callinor!'

More tears came to the corners of Callinor's tired eyes. 'You always shamed us, Samnir. That's why everyone feared and hated you so much. They respected you too, though, you know.'

Samnir looked rueful. 'As you say, lot of good it did me. I just couldn't stop living. But, in the end, they broke me.'

'How is it you're still here? You're in a real shit-pickle, but somehow you've managed to give them a bloody nose, hen't you?'

'The boy, Callinor. It was all the boy.'

'The bane?' Softer than any breeze. 'Tell me of him.'

'Just a boy, Callinor. Funny, lively of eye, Undrawn. You know what it's like. Your mind might tell you that you've forgotten it, but that's just *them* there in your head. The rest of you doesn't forget. It never forgets. It's the last bit of you, hidden way down deep, where even you struggle to find it. And you dare not find it, in case *they* follow you and take it away from you, leaving you nothing. But *he* found it in me. So easily! And it was like being born again. Washed clean. Innocent again. I would do anything for him, even if it means dying here in a shit-pickle.'

Callinor nodded. He understood, even if he didn't want to. And part of him did want to. 'Damn it!'

'So I cannot flee to the mountains, friend Callinor. I will stand and fight again, as I once did. The boy has given me that. And I will not give it up while I can still draw air, be it the hallowed breath of my being or the final curse upon my lips. You know that if I go to the mountains, our restless enemy will ultimately find us there, just as trouble found me even in the remotest town of the Empire. Godsend has strong walls and some provisions. I hope it will allow us to freshen the Empire's bloody nose a time or two before we die. And I will have a proper soldier's death there. Better that than to run like a coward and be hunted down by a ravening pack upon desolate climes, no?'

Callinor sighed. 'I hear you, Sand Devil, and will not gainsay you, even if those in Heroes' Brook would have you burned as a pagan. I will secretly send what provisions I can to you, but it won't be much, for the Minister and elders here are as watchful of the People as the innkeeper is of his too-beautiful daughter when I'm around. I will also let my men know that if any wish to disappear into the woods in the direction of Godsend, then there will be fewer guards on the gates and walls for the next nights. Beyond that, Sand Devil, I can only wish you the manner of death you most desire.'

'That is kind, friend Callinor. I pray your own is to your liking and that the innkeeper's sight begins to fail long before then.'

Callinor chortled. He spat into the road again and explained, 'So that those who are watching on the walls are sure I am treating you with the contempt they deserve.' Then the Hero turned his horse around and rode away without a backward glance.

Samnir returned to Captain Gallen. 'We are not welcome here, Gallen, for an army will soon be marching from Hyvan's Cross.'

'Excellent,' murmured the impatient and fierce-eyed Captain, a man who remembered and resented having been taken from his family by force when young. 'Commander, might I suggest as many archers as we can spare in the trees along the roads that the army will have little choice but to take?'

'You may, Captain, you may. In fact, have one hundred sent from Godsend with all speed so that they can be in the trees between Hyvan's Cross and Heroes' Brook. Later, have them move to the trees between Heroes' Brook and Godsend. They are never to confront the enemy head on. They must shoot and run, with ambushes laid for any pursuers, just as we have practised with the hunters and woodsmen of Godsend. And ask for volunteers to spy among the enemy host. Our own armour should blend with theirs without trouble.'

The Captain saluted smartly and then grinned savagely. 'Very good, sir!' He wasted no time, turning away to issue orders.

'With luck, Jillan, there'll still be something for you to come back to,' Samnir said to the air. But where had the boy gone? There was no sign of him having announced himself in Heroes' Brook. *Surely he hadn't immediately moved on to Hyvan's Cross to confront the hated Praxis, had he?* Whether Miserath was with him or not, not even Jillan could stand against ten thousand men. Or had the dark god's madness overtaken the boy and led him towards disaster already? 'Just as you said, Callinor, just as you said. A real shit-pickle.'

# CHAPTER 7:

# For vanity and its opposite prey on each other

Ba'zel was slammed violently into the rocky floor. He tried to alter his substance so that he would be able to pass into the rock and have it absorb some of the impact, but the rock proved far denser than he had expected and he only succeeded in making himself less cohesive than he had been before. He ended up splattering himself across the chamber into which he'd been hurled. Parts of him slid and dripped down the walls. The agony was beyond belief, and his mind all but broke apart with his body. His awareness and grip on existence had never been so tenuous. His scattered parts did not have sufficient sentience individually to bring themselves back together. Fortunately, a certain proportion of him, including most of his consciousness, remained as a fine mist in the air, and he just about managed to achieve contact with enough of his disparate but essential parts to command them to become entirely gaseous, draw together and coalesce into a viable body of sorts.

Ba'zel became a soft and amorphous jelly and went around sucking up as much of the rest of his substance as he could find. He then tried to harden himself into something more solid, but found he'd used up too much of his core energy to regain his physical integrity. If he could not find sustenance quickly, then he might never be able to form a thick enough membrane or skin to prevent a constant loss of self to the environment. Already he felt himself leaving slimy residue whenever he moved across the dry bedrock. He was like a slug.

Where was the Guardian to help him? Where? Despite the mental discipline in which Mentor Ho'zen had spent years schooling him, Ba'zel found himself perilously close to panic.

'Calm yourself. You've already survived apparently hopeless situations. So why panic now? What will it gain you? A quicker ending.'

*But what if I have lost some part of my mind in this accident? Maybe it dribbled down into a crack in the rock. Or drifted away down that tunnel there. What if it was the best and controlling part of my intellect? Gone! Nothing to stop the panic. The instability now let loose in my mind, disrupting and corrupting it, causing it to unravel. A constant loss of both body and mind to the environment, then.*

'Oh, be quiet, you idiot. Since when did your intellect have a properly controlling part anyway? If you'd had such a thing, you wouldn't have splattered yourself across this chamber in the first place, now would you? If you'd had such a thing, you wouldn't have ended up having to leave the home-realm. If you'd had such a thing, you wouldn't be here now, would you? The Virtue wouldn't be chasing you, would it? If you didn't lose something of your body and mind to the environment, you wouldn't disrupt and change it, you wouldn't be a threat to the Declension!'

The revelation jolted him, taking all the momentum out of his rising panic. *Am I a threat to the Declension?* he wondered. *Can it really be? Look at me. I can hardly keep myself together. If there had been a Guardian here to witness my ridiculous arrival, he wouldn't have known whether to laugh, cry or destroy me.*

'No being can keep itself together forever. Each of us is nothing but a collection of dust particles oscillating in a harmony of being. We inherit the magic of the First Animation yet are no more than an echo of it. The harmony of our being therefore ultimately fades or becomes a disharmony. Our oscillation sees us constantly shedding exhausted particles of skin and other waste – slime in our current situation. Yes, there is a time in our lives when we seem to grow, but that is no more than the accretion of more and more waste as a skin. Our skin thickens, expands and hardens, as do parts within us, seeking to hold the animated particles within us as best we can. But the closer and more tightly we hold those particles to us, the more limited and less animated they can be. Their oscillation diminishes and we find ourselves slowing down. Our minds atrophy and hear only a disharmony of being. And then we hear nothing at all.'

*We are all* unstable *then. The instability is in all of us, the disharmony comes to all?*

'Eventually. But I fear I am the catalyst that brings it all the sooner. I am the constant loss of self of the Declension, the shedding of exhausted particles, the disharmony of being. That is why I am a threat to them. That is why the Virtue pursues me. I have already caused chaos and destruction in the two realms I have visited. They need to control or eradicate me if their harmony of being is to be preserved at all.'

*Must I bring destruction? Is that my role and destiny? Is there no escaping it? Will genocide and apocalypse always follow in my wake? Surely that is not the purpose the sifters commanded me to seek out, is it? I cannot think it. It is too . . . terrible? Do I even know what terrible is any more? The Virtue seems terrible to me, and yet it is* virtuous *in how it safeguards the Declension. I seem to be set in opposition to it, even though that opposition is not of my own choosing. And what of the Great Voyage? Is that purpose beyond me now that I am set in opposition to the Declension?*

'I do not know if I want this purpose of destruction. I would not wish to see the Declension . . . my father . . . undone. Neither can I undo myself, for I have pledged myself to the sifters. I must find and seize another purpose before it is too late. There must be some other course!'

Ba'zel flowed across the chamber and out through a low doorway. He passed along a corridor of smooth and polished marble, his way illuminated by nuggets of sun-metal set into small evenly spaced niches. He noticed that a lighter-coloured marble was inlaid into the floor, ceiling and walls in places and that the patterns seemed to form a language of sorts. If he had not been in such desperate need of sustenance, he might have lingered long enough to decipher more meaning from his surroundings. Were those figures meant to be depictions of Saviours? And were those lesser beings bowing before them? None of this could be the work of the Declension, for it was far too elaborate and painstaking for the relatively simple themes depicted. Only short-lived lesser beings would need to record such information so that it could last from one generation to the next. By contrast, the

Declension needed to record very little beyond bloodlines and lines of thinking, and much of the latter was kept a closely guarded secret, certainly not displayed on walls for any passer-by to see. Yet why would a corridor so close to the Gate be decorated in the language of lesser beings? Again he wondered why there had been no Guardian in the chamber of the Gate.

Reaching the end of the corridor, he emerged into a vast roofless cavern and almost retreated in fear and confusion at the scene before him. Thousands upon thousands of lesser beings were bowed to the ground before him. They made a moaning sound that he felt more than heard. What it was he could not tell, whether song, prayer or grief. The beings were short bipeds, almost broader than they were tall. They seemed to have heads, but the faces of those who dared to look up were all much the same to Ba'zel. Every being was sheathed in a dull grey metal, but he couldn't tell if that was their natural skin, a sort of self-adornment or some contrivance. They were lit by a fierce radiation coming down from the pure white sky far overhead. Did they wear the metal to protect themselves? Ba'zel felt his eyes running and wondered if he was already being damaged by the strong emanation. He felt warm now, uncomfortably warm.

He stood at the top of a dozen black marble steps, with the congregation of lesser beings below him. He realised the cavern walls made a perfect circle, suggesting that the place had been deliberately carved out of solid rock. Yet the walls were hundreds of feet high! The scale of the work involved was staggering, even to one from the Declension. More, every part of the walls was carved in relief with figures and scenes that seemed alive in the agitating light. Lesser beings were shown warring endlessly with each other, until the Saviours had arrived, apparently bringing peace. Then the lesser beings had begun to work in concert, levelling mountains and delving deep below, remodelling their entire realm just as they had been remade by the arrival of the Saviours. It was a story spanning countless generations, but a story that defined these beings and was their all-consuming work going forward. This cavern was a temple to that story and the Saviours who had determined it. Incredible to think that an entire realm could be so simply captured and controlled by a narrative. No wonder there was no need for a Guardian. It was as awe-inspiring as it was awful. And Ba'zel knew he was powerless against such a force of epic magnitude. Worse, he knew he had already been snared by it and could not escape.

It was already too late to retreat into the corridor from which he'd issued, for two of the lesser beings were approaching him up the stairs and entering into the diminished power of his presence. As he desired existence, so he could not resist trying to Draw from them, but their metal sheathing resisted him in turn. And one of the lesser beings wielded a short sun-metal blade!

The bladecarrier chittered at Ba'zel. Then the blade was pulled across the base of the second lesser being's head and ichor imbued with the magic of being sprayed Ba'zel. Ba'zel fell upon the sacrifice, unable to care that he disgraced himself with such a display of weakness before so many. He sucked like a giant leech until all the ichor was gone, and all the other fluids in the body too. *Ah!* The metallic outer shell of the being clattered on the stairs as Ba'zel discarded it. His own skin became dry, dense and hard, defence at last against the searing white of the air.

The bladecarrier was chittering again, but this time Ba'zel could understand it, for as well as life energy he had apprehended a good deal of knowledge from the sacrifice. 'This one was called the Hundred and Fourteenth Gift, for the purpose of his line was always to serve as offering to any Saviour who came. He was truly blessed to find your acceptance. Many previous Gifts have passed without fulfilling their purpose. The shame was theirs, for they were therefore unworthy of acceptance. The Hundred and Fourteenth Gift will be carved large here in the Round, so that he may serve as inspiration and instruction to all future Gifts. There can be no greater attainment for a Gift. And I, the Hundred and Twentieth Blade, having enabled the acceptance, will also be recorded and made part of the immortal definition of the Selian kind and existence. I exalt and am most humbly satisfied, but my satisfaction is worth less than an unaccepted Gift compared to serving and satisfying you, Saviour. If it pleases you, Saviour, then the Hundred and Fifteenth Gift will be brought to you as further offering, but it is young and has not yet had the chance to bear and raise the Hundred and Sixteenth Gift.'

Clearly certain of the Selios were bred to serve as willing sacrifice to any Saviour that arrived through the Gate. It was a part of their definition, a part of the narrative that described them, but Ba'zel still could not grasp from the knowledge of the Hundred and Fourteenth Gift why they would embrace suicide so eagerly. 'Why are there Gifts?'

The Hundred and Twentieth Blade nodded. 'You are right to test me, Saviour, for we have not been visited since the time of the Fifty-Third Blade. Fear not. Every word spoken by the Saviours to the Selios has been carefully recorded and learned over and over most faithfully. Why, the first word that came from the mouth of the Hundred and Twenty-First Blade as I cradled him in my arms was *Saviour*. There are Gifts because payment is ever due. The Selios owe themselves to the Saviours, for we were on the verge of destroying ourselves before the Saviours came. All that has followed and all that we are is therefore devoted to offering what we owe. We only strive for your acceptance. We will find it. We are very close now. We creep ever closer to the deadly Geas hiding below, that which caused all the evil among the Selios in the beginning. Thousands of Diggers die each cycle just to move us the smallest fraction closer. But the irradiating rays of the Geas are stronger and more quickly lethal the closer we come, no matter how thick our digging armour. Those who are Diggers now have names like One Hundred Million. I know you will wonder why there are so many present here, when they might instead be digging below, but we have to allow a good number to reach maturity so that they can breed before descending. Otherwise, we would run out of Diggers completely and then we would never reach the Geas.'

Yes, it was as awe-inspiring as it was awful. The Selios pursued their own doom with more belief and passion than they did their actual lives. How could any beings so forget themselves? They sickened him. He admired them. They disgusted him. He pitied them. Yet had he not also been trapped in a narrative, his father's narrative of bloodlines and lines of thinking? Had he not been defined by the Declension's Great Voyage and the Eldest's will and intent? Did not that narrative, in the guise of the Virtue Obedience, still pursue him? Could he ever be free of it or was that just a foolish dream? Youthful innocence, inexperience and naivety? Was it possible to create his own narrative, one that would interfere with and disrupt the dominance of the Declension? As long as he lived, then so might his own narrative. Live to escape and escape to live.

'Hundred and Twentieth Blade, where is the Gate to the sixth?'

The Blade hesitated. 'Saviour, I have never heard of such a thing. The sixth what? Blade? Gift? Digger?'

'The sixth realm. Do you not know this is the fifth realm?'

The Blade goggled at him. 'I-I . . . Saviour, I have trained my entire life so that I am able to quell my nerves and fear in even the most pressured and unusual of situations. I am also versed in all that has been said to our kind. All this so that I may answer the questions of any Saviour completely and without delay. But now I struggle for words. I know of no previous reference to different realms or their number. Neither do I know of the Gate you mention. The very ideas are . . . difficult for me.'

'Well, there's a first time for everything. Speculate where the Gate might be.'

The Blade's face crumpled in on itself, presumably a sign of original and taxing thought going on. Then enlightenment. 'Why, it would be behind the sacred seal, Saviour, I would think.'

'Take me to this sacred seal. And tell me of it as we go.'

The Blade bowed. 'This way, Saviour.'

The lesser being led Ba'zel down the steps. The congregation parted so that Blade and Saviour could move forward without impediment. Ba'zel reduced the power of his presence to avoid Drawing unintentionally from any of them. Strangely, now he had communicated with the Selios, he found himself loath to cause them needless harm. They were very different to the lesser beings of the other realms. They were more meaningful somehow, simple though they were. He was even experiencing unusual feelings about the one he had consumed, the Hundred and Fourteenth Gift. It was more than indigestion. It was . . . was there a word? Guilt? No, that term was used for the state of weakness that was contingent on an individual's ambition being thwarted before witnesses of the wider Declension. Or maybe it was anticipated guilt. He had consumed the Gift based upon an ambition for life, an ambition that would ultimately be undone by the Declension.

'The sacred seal, Saviour, is the wondrous shining place where the other Saviours went to undertake their great vigil so many cycles ago.'

*A safe place in which to enter the Waking Dream, presumably.* 'Well out of this debilitating light no doubt.'

The Blade glanced back at the Saviour, clearly unsure whether or how to answer.

Ba'zel took pity on him. 'No, that wasn't really a question. Tell me, Blade, aren't you at all curious?'

'Curious, Saviour? Forgive me, I do not presume to ask a question. I only wish to express how difficult it is for the primitive Selios to answer and serve a Saviour to the Saviour's satisfaction.'

'Blade, do you not wonder where the Gate through which I came leads? Do you not wonder about the other realms I mentioned? Do you not wonder about the Gate to the sixth? Does it not make you wonder about the purpose of the Saviours in all these realms? Does it not make you consider the work of the Selios differently? In short, Blade, aren't you at all curious?'

'Saviour!' the Blade squeaked in apparent distress. 'It was such curiosity, division of purpose and fragmentation of belief that caused the Selios to war among themselves before the coming of the Saviours!' The Blade suddenly relaxed. 'Ah, I see I am tested again, Saviour. That is good. No, the Selios are no longer curious. To be so would be to beg our own destruction once more. We would never find the acceptance of our Saviours. The Selios were saved from their curiosity. They were provided with the words of the Saviours as tools to our future salvation. We were provided with the great work of uncovering the Geas and offering it up to the Saviours so that the Selios might have a unity of purpose, might make the payment that is ever due and might ultimately find the acceptance of the Saviours. We have been given all we need. We have no need to question. We have no need to be curious. And the Selios exalts in that, in the blessing of the Saviours.'

Ba'zel sighed inwardly. If he could not inspire even curiosity, then perhaps there would never be an escape from the all-controlling narrative. Besides, the Selios seemed to exalt in the narrative. They seemed content. They found fulfilment. Did he really want to take that from them? 'Very good, Blade,' he said distractedly. 'Lead on.'

They made further progress across the floor of the cavern. The congregation continued to bow and make their low resonating moan. Did the rock itself vibrate to the power of the conjoined voices of the Selios?

'Why do they make this noise?' Ba'zel shouted to the Blade.

'Unlike me, Saviour, the Diggers have not been trained to quell their nerves and fear in your sacred presence. Quite the opposite. Theirs is a powerful outpouring of emotion. They lose everything they have to it. They are no longer individuals in many ways. This is the Great Entirety. Its strength will allow these Diggers to make better progress towards the Geas than they have in many cycles. Thus, your presence has blessed and inspired them, Saviour. Just your presence leads us towards our future salvation.'

Ba'zel's skin now resonated painfully to the sound. And the surrounding radiation raised blisters and lesions, despite his thickened carapace. 'Let us move more quickly to the sacred seal, Blade. Quickly!'

'Of course, Saviour,' his guide replied, falling to hands and feet to propel himself at greater speed across the floor.

Ba'zel articulated his long limbs and took larger and larger steps until he reached a high and wide arch on the far side of the cavern. He moved after the Blade and found himself on a walkway through the rock. Less of the radiation penetrated here, but enough leaked in to limn a ghostly path ahead. He followed it back and forth and soon realised they were in a labyrinth where they might wander forever.

'The Saviours are not easily approached,' Ba'zel observed.

'Of course not, Saviour. Precious few are worthy enough to learn the way. I myself have never trodden here before, although I have spent my life reciting the route in my mind. I am more blessed and fulfilled to walk it now than I have ever been.'

'Well, you will die happy now, I guess.'

'Yes, Saviour, if that is your command.'

'Not yet, Blade, not yet.'

The path became more and more ghostly in the otherwise pitch-black, until Ba'zel wondered if it was in his mind more than it was real. He closed the orbs of his eyes and there was no difference to what he saw, save perhaps that there was a tinge of gold and red when his orbs were closed. Yet when he opened them again, there was nothing but a haze of gold and red to be seen. Were they still within the rock or had they somehow crossed into another place?

'Blade, where are you?'

'Straight ahead, Saviour. The ground rises here.'

It was like climbing a dark hill, coming over the top and having the sun rise right in your face. A mighty dome of dazzling sun-metal filled his eyes and mind. He assumed there was darkness beyond, but could not see past the bright umbra in which they stood.

'The sacred seal!' the Blade breathed in adoration, shielding his streaming eyes but unable to stop looking upon the confirming beauty and promised truth of the narrative which had formed him.

'The Saviours are inside, Blade? How might I enter? Can I pass up into the dome from below? No, it will be a sphere, will it not, so that the sun-metal can protect the Saviours from the white radiation above and the power of the Geas from below? There is an inverted matching dome beneath the ground, is there not? Ah, it is a perfectly sealed sphere so that the Saviours are totally protected. I see it now. Yes, the real reason that there is no Guardian is not down to the controlling narrative but the fact that a Guardian would not be able to last too long beyond the sphere. It all makes sense to me now. Blade, do you know of any way to enter? Blade, answer me!'

The Blade looked sightlessly at Ba'zel. 'No, Saviour. That has never been made known to the Selios.'

He had to get inside. The Gate to the sixth could not be anywhere else, else the Selios would have known of it. Besides, if he did not find entry, then he would soon die of the radiation in this realm. He could not go back through the Gate to the fourth, after all, because it had collapsed just when he'd escaped that realm. Would that Gate be able to take him elsewhere? In all likelihood he would only be able to navigate back to a realm he already knew anyway, and there was less than no chance of a polite welcome in any of those.

Ba'zel knew that there was no magic that would allow him to pass through sun-metal as he might through rock. Sun-metal was an inert but essential substance of the cosmos which denied the will of all others. It prevented omnipotence and allowed, if not forced, the cosmos to exist as a plurality with free will. Yet Ba'zel also knew sun-metal could be moulded if it was made to absorb sufficient magical energies. He did not have enough strength for that alone, of course.

'Blade, the Selios will help me enter the sacred seal. I command it.'

'I . . . Saviour, we have been told that none are to attempt to breach the seal. Were we to help you, it would be in contradiction of that which we have already been commanded. It would create a schism in us. It would destroy us.'

'Surely there are sun-smiths among the Selios. Send them to me. And I command the Great Entirety be brought here. Their strength will be turned towards the seal as the sun-smiths direct, so that a way through the sacred seal can be created for me.'

The Hundred and Twentieth Blade of the Selios completely lost the composure he'd spent a lifetime working on and started to cry, his face completely caved in. 'Saviour, I cannot!'

'But you have just told me you are more blessed and fulfilled now than you have ever been.'

'It is against everything I know, everything that the Selios are!'

Ba'zel paused. Was this the moment when his own narrative could begin? 'Yes, Blade, it is. Listen well, then, when I tell you that the words of the Saviours are not the tools for your future salvation, but the means of your ultimate doom. The Geas that you seek to tear from its natural place is the beating heart of this realm, from which comes all life. In giving it up to the Saviours, the Selios will be no more. All that will be left are the meaningless carvings on the walls of the Round.'

The Blade cried out terribly, his eyes starting from his head and beginning to shrivel in the light from the dome. The lesser being staggered as if mortally wounded.

Alarmed that his words had been too much for the Blade to take, Ba'zel reached out and steadied him, keeping a firm grip on the lesser being's limb that held the knife of sun-metal.

'No, Saviour, it cannot be. You test me again, I know it. I beg you, tell me that you test me.'

'I do not test you, Blade. You will believe my words, I command it. And share my words with the sun-smiths and Diggers in order to bring them here and have them break open the seal.'

'How can I believe your words, Saviour, when they represent an opposite belief to the words of the other Saviours? Where is belief then? How can I follow your commands when they will lead us back to war, destruction and doom?'

'You are heading for your doom anyway, Blade. My words are the same as the words of the other Saviours in that. Thus, you know my words to be true. Thus you believe and will obey my command. At least with my words there is hope of salvation. It is not a given that war will bring about your doom, Blade. It will probably bring much death, but it can hardly be more than is already being brought about by the Geas defending itself. Go now.'

And so it was begun.

Pessarmon stepped between Azual and Aspin, deliberately breaking the line of sight that had Aspin transfixed. 'Back, enemy of my people, enemy of the Geas, enemy of all living things! You have no claim on them. You cannot touch them. They are impervious to you.'

'That's right!' Torpeth agreed, holding tightly to Pessarmon's back, looking over the spirit's shoulder and sticking his tongue out at the Saint. 'Go back to whatever stinking pit serves as your grave and dream over and over of how you died. Remember the mad vanity that was your undoing and step back from it now. Remember the tears, fear and sadness you felt at the end and let it occupy you now.'

Aspin had slumped to his knees, only Torpeth's iron grip on his hand keeping him halfway upright. 'Torpeth,' he pleaded weakly. 'Do try not to goad him.'

'You cannot resist, can you, arrogant creature?' Azual grinned knowingly, his teeth shining. 'Are you still so proud, *Torpeth the Great*? Still filled with the pride that saw you kill so many of your people and that saw you topple your overweening and overweened gods? Yes, we have watched you for a long time, pagan, and rejoice to see that you are unchanged and have the capacity to learn nothing. We know you will ultimately deliver the last of your people to us, as you did so many others, and thus the Geas itself. Let's face it, the Geas will be far safer in our hands than it ever has been in yours. For what has ever been safe in your treacherous care, hmm?'

Torpeth snorted hard, snot flying through the leering apparition that was the Saint. 'Should I listen to you, exhalation? You who are the dying echo of the Saviours' tired flatulence? And you who breathe their rank wind so that you then have noise of your own to release. Come, bring your arse closer and bend over so that I might better hear you, for surely that is from where you speak. Come, for I am not afeared. I doubt you are capable of matter or issue more substantial than air, eh?'

Aspin coughed. 'Torpeth, don't!'

Pessarmon turned dead eyes towards the holy man. 'This is not wise. You give him too many words and too much energy. We must keep going or risk lingering here too long.'

Torpeth's eyes rolled between Aspin and Pessarmon, a moment of doubt finding him. And Azual seized that moment.

The Saint lashed out with a taloned hand and all but dashed Pessarmon's head from his shoulders. 'Ha! You are as weak as the minds of all your kind!'

The rockbreaker made not a sound, fumbling to find the top of his dangling spine in order to restore it to itself. Azual immediately launched another blow. With a cry of denial, Torpeth kicked high with one of his toughened feet. He connected with the Saint's forearm, pushing it up and away.

Azual staggered back. Torpeth was forced into a backflip by the momentum of his kick, and he nearly dislocated both of his shoulders keeping a grip on his companions. The holy man cried out in anguish, the foot that had come into contact with the Saint collapsing under him. 'Aiee! I cannot feel it. It is dead!'

'Fool,' intoned Pessarmon. 'You have given him more intent and energy than he has had since his death. Would you resurrect the enemy of our people, then, betrayer? Is that your intention, to speed the end of our remaining people? Wretched thing! I reject you as blood of my blood, bone of my bone, people of my people. I abandon you!'

Pessarmon faded out of Torpeth's grasp, leaving him to clutch despairingly at the air. Torpeth drew breath to beg, but a perishing cold filled his lungs and froze the words inside him.

'Pessarmon! Ancestor!' Aspin croaked. 'You are still held in the thoughts and minds of our people. I am one of them. By that, I abjure you not to leave us like this. I must bring aid to one who is friend to our people, one who has helped us in the past, one who is enemy to the mad demon before us here. Our people owe Jillan whatever help might be rendered!'

'The bane!' Azual spat lividly, his bloody eye standing clear of his head. 'You will not mention his name here. Even here, even in my death, he plagues me! I will never be rid of him, I can never rest, until he is dragged to the terrible altar of death and immolated upon it! Only then will I be saved. You pagans will never be permitted to bring the aid of which you speak.'

Pessarmon regarded Aspin bleakly. 'Of my people or not, descendant or not, I will never guide you while you remain attached to the betrayer. But I will hold our enemy here as long as I may. Go quickly, then, for where once I would have easily subdued this mad demon, the actions of the betrayer have made our enemy stronger than I would wish. Come then, demon, and wrestle me,' Pessarmon challenged Azual, offering him his embrace. 'For I am the rockbreaker! I will grind your bones to flour and make soulbread of them.'

Azual laughed maniacally. 'Pagan, your kind is all but done in this realm, just as your people are ending in the land of the living. You cannot stand against me. I will reign in this nether realm, just as the blessed Saviours will Draw all life to them, just as they will finally claim the Geas as their own. I will devour you and all your kind and then be reborn to the blessed Saviours and eternity. Until then I will suck the marrow out of you, drill holes in your bones and make flutes of them, so that all may dance to my merry tune.'

Aspin pushed himself up under Torpeth's armpit and brought them both to their feet. The holy man was the blue of a corpse found buried in mountain snow. And he was so light, far less substantial than Aspin had ever known him. 'Pessarmon! I do not know the way. Please, help us!'

The pagan ancestor dared not look back at him, but called emptily, 'Make a casting stone of yourself, so that you may find your way through the ruins of this place and our people. And remember me, Aspin Longstep, remember me!'

Azual rushed at Pessarmon and the two giants crashed together with such force that the realm shook. They reared back from each other, preparing to smash heads.

'Azual,' came Torpeth's brittle voice, like ice cracking. The mad Saint's evil eye flicked towards the holy man. 'I will be sure to pass your regards to Jillan!'

The centre of Pessarmon's formidable forehead crunched into the bridge of Azual's nose and shattered it. The Saint fell back in a howling rage of injury and disbelief. Pessarmon pursued him closely.

Knowing that there would be no better moment, Aspin pushed

forward with Torpeth into the lifeless mists of the nether realm. He prayed that they would be able to warm up once they were moving, but quickly realised that the more progress they made, the more would be drained from them. It was the payment required of any of the living who used the Broken Path. His teeth were already chattering. How soon before he lost all feeling in his extremities?

He wasn't even sure they were going the right way. What if they wandered out of the hinterlands and into the kingdom proper of the land of the dead? What terrible nullity existed there? What long-buried, half-forgotten and monstrous memories of mortalkind awaited them? What measureless evil or faithless temple? He glimpsed their looming forms ahead of him, immense gargoyles there as guardians, grotesquely seductive succubi calling to him. How sweetly they crooned. 'Aspin! Aspin!' They told him of the empty throne kept for him, that only one of such lively majesty could occupy it, a lively majesty that placed him above all others. Life here was his to gift and deny. He would be the god-king of the dead. He but had to complete his royal progress to the palatial necropolis and empty throne at the dead heart of the nether realm. He but had to hear the pleas and praise of his subjects so that they could bring him to the throne through acclaim. He but had to allow his eye to fall upon and recognise his subjects so that they could show him the way. He but had to favour and raise up those long-buried and half-forgotten memories of mortalkind so that he knew all that went on in his kingdom. He but had to acknowledge them and he would become the immortal god-king of the dead. 'Aspin! Aspin!'

Their lips caressed his ear, nibbled at his mind. Their teeth nipped at his lobe and then peeled the skin back from his skull. They prised apart his cranial plates and exposed his brain. 'Aspin! Aspin!' Their rotten breath filled his nose and mouth, shrivelling his tongue and withering his lungs. Their corruption moved through him and became a cancer to tighten around his heart.

'Aspin! Aspin!' Torpeth screamed in his ear, all but deafening him. 'You must fix your mind elsewhere before it is too late! Aspin! Aspin! Please, silly ox, please! Hear me! Think of Veena! Think of Jillan. Forgive this old goat. Think of those who you love. See them smile at you and welcome you. They are the only ones who have anything to give you, for they are the living. By your life, you belong with them!

You do not belong here among these abattoirs of mind and memory. Take us out of here. Fix your mind. Aspin! Aspin! Please, my strength gives out and there are no words left in me. I will become trapped as the silence of this place.' The holy man's voice faded. 'Aspin! Aspin!'

As Ba'zel had commanded, the sun-smiths of the Selios were brought to him. They were even broader than the rest of their kind, as broad as they were tall, their chests deep and their arms, near reaching the ground, thick with muscle. Yet the thing that truly set them apart from the other Selios was that they did not wear any dull grey armour to block out the realm's radiation. As a result they crackled with energy, an energy they no doubt used to bend sun-metal, but they were also covered with contusions and running sores. There was a wildness to their eyes that spoke of a sickness of both body and mind. The Selian Diggers who waited just beyond the umbra of the sacred seal had let the sun-smiths through with something approaching reverence.

The Blade introduced the four sun-smiths. 'Saviour, here is the Thousand and Ninth Forge Master, the Prime Forge Master. Here is the Thousand and Tenth Forge Master, offspring to the Prime Forge Master. Here is the Thousand and Eleventh, offspring to the Thousand and Tenth, and here is the Thousand and Twelfth, offspring to the Eleventh.'

'Four generations working together?'

'Yes, Saviour. Sun-smiths are short-lived and must look to pass on their craft to the next in line as soon as and wherever they may. It is the price of the craft, a craft that is close to the sacredness of the seal itself. The sacrifice is a small price to pay for the fulfilment it brings.'

'Prime Forge Master, you know what I require of you?'

The largest of the sun-smiths stepped forward and nodded. His face was a constant animation of twitches, winks and blinks. Raggedly, he answered, 'Unless there has been a misunderstanding. Perhaps the Blade failed to glean your proper meaning, Saviour. Words are some-times not as clear as they seem. They are less certain to me than rock, metal and a hammer. They are wayward air until they can be turned by Scribe, Sculptor or some other crafter into a permanent form.'

'Careful, Prime Forge Master,' the Blade interposed. 'None may question the word.'

'It's all right, Blade,' Ba'zel assured him. 'For I might seem to have questioned the word or the Selian understanding of it, no? Prime Forge Master, there is no *mis*understanding, just a *greater* understanding. You and your sun-smiths will create a way for me through the seal, do you understand?'

The Prime Forge Master's face actually ceased its movement for a second. He looked like he had found an instant of peace or death. 'Yes, Saviour, I understand.'

'Good. Blade, the Great Entirety is here?'

'Yes, Saviour, as you commanded. Ten thousand Diggers fill the labyrinth.'

'Then the assembled host must listen and hear me. My word will be passed among you so that all will share in the blessing of greater understanding. The Selios occupy the fifth realm. We Saviours occupy and travel through many realms. It is our Great Voyage. I must travel on to the sixth realm via the Gate that exists beyond the sacred seal. The Great Voyage takes precedence over any concerns governing an individual realm. My onward journey takes precedence over the word of the Saviours previously received by the Selios. It is this precedence that now blesses and inspires the Great Entirety. It is this precedence that guides the sun-smiths of the Selios as they open a way through the seal for me. Through these actions, Prime Forge Master, my words will be more than wayward air.

'And hear me further, you Selios. It is by the precedence of the Great Voyage that you will keep a way open through the seal forevermore, even should the Saviours within seek to prevent it. You will *war* on those Saviours if necessary!'

The Great Entirety moaned.

'Yes, you will war on those Saviours just as you war on the Geas! It is a part of the same work. Fear not that such warring will see you return to your early days of internal schism, division and fragmentation, for in this war you will be united and act in concert. You will be of the same belief and purpose. You will serve me to my satisfaction and you will find fulfilment and acceptance through that!'

The moan became a roar, but a roar that was far more than sound. It came rushing through the labyrinth, smashed into the dome and made the seal ring as if struck upon an anvil. The dome's umbra actually receded slightly before it reverberated with the force of the attack and pushed back out against it.

The eyes of the Selios around Ba'zel had glazed over. They were lost to their conditioning, his narrative and the great work. And the power of that narrative now howled and tore furiously at the dominion and definition of the Declension in this realm.

The four sun-smiths moved into the direct path of the titanic energies generated by the Great Entirety and raised aloft their mighty smithing hammers. Their eyes and hammers blazed as brightly as the sun-metal dome itself. Then they charged into the heat of the dome and smote at it as if wielding weapons against their most hated enemy. The concentration of the cascading energies bent the air as if pulling reality in on itself. A perfect moment of stillness. Exquisite. Awful. Then the impossible violence and explosion of the collision, concatenation, destruction and decimation. Selios blasted and obliterated. Ba'zel hurled backwards and only saved at the last by utterly changing his state to ghost. Hitting the ground moments later, reaching for the nearest Selios and feeding upon it even as he pitied it for what it was. And another.

He looked up. There, silhouetted against the dome, their torsos wreathed in a spectrum of flame, the sun-smiths stood unbowed and undaunted. They seemed gods at the beginning of time forging creation. They were the will of the Great Entirety, the will of the Selios and the Geas itself. Though they could not destroy the substance of the sun-metal, neither could it forever hold all the energies of the realm. It could not hold against them. With a sound akin to the end of the cosmos, the sun-metal morphed, melted and parted, a running rent appearing in the sacred seal.

'The breach is made!' Ba'zel cried. 'The perfect sphere of the Saviours is undone. Their giant shining skull is broken open. See the dark break and the corruption within. Beware the sin that will leak from it. Guard yourselves! Rise up, Selios, and enter, to face the evil waiting there, the evil that has always beset you. End it once and for all!'

Thousands of Diggers formed up behind Ba'zel and he led them towards the dome. The Diggers that were to the fore burned and screamed horribly. Those coming on behind used the bodies of the dead as shields until the grisly shields turned to ash and their carriers became shields in turn. The Diggers died in their hundreds but crept closer to the dome, in the same way that generations of them had always died trying to reach the Geas.

The four sun-smiths flanked Ba'zel and kept the worst of the shimmering energy away from him. He reached the breach, hesitated a moment, and then stepped inside with his guards.

'Torpeth?' Aspin asked in fear. 'Where are we?'

'In a terrible place beyond imagining. It pursues us, it draws us to it. You must block it from your mind, warrior! You must *unsee* it. *Unknow* it! Think of your friends. Fix on them.'

The wreckage and ruin of fallen civilisations. The self-destructive folly and selfish crimes that had brought them to this. The unspeakable horrors perpetrated in their name, in the name of progress, in the name of exploration, in the name of improvement. The genocide of species. The denudation and devastation wrought. The deafening silence. The utter silence, the silence of the dead. Hope not just abandoned but no longer understood. Never understood.

'See the mountains of our people just there, Aspin! We have left their lower slopes and entered the lowlands. You remember, don't you? Tell me you remember that. We spoke with the headwoman, my beloved Sal, and she sent us to find our good friend Jillan. Veena is waiting for you to return. Veena of the waterfall peak. With dark hair and leaf-green eyes. Not just pretty, young warrior. As lovely as life itself. A life you will have with her, with children and the contentment all men seek.

'We have entered the lowlands and now we head for the west. Already we have passed Godsend, where dwell Hella Jacobson, Haal Corinson, your friend Thomas, stern Samnir and Ash the Unclean. Now we venture into new and strange parts of the land, but land that once belonged to our people, Gar of the Unmoving Stone and Akwar of the Wandering Waters. Land that bore the soft feet of our children and the hard march of my armies. Land that was fed and watered with our blood so that it could live and grow even when we left for the mountains. Our blood is still in this land, young warrior, and it is blood of your blood, bone of your bone, people of your people. You are a casting stone of this land, connected through and to it, bound by and to it. It is an essential instinct and knowledge in you, just as you are an essential instinct and knowledge in it. It guides, navigates and takes us where we will. See, we are nearly upon the west now, our difficulties behind and distant from us. Are those trees there? The trees of the west? Aspin, do you think we will arrive just beyond them? Do you think it? What do you do if you do not think it?'

'I . . . think it. I see those trees, old goat. We are almost there,' Aspin affirmed with a frown, sure he'd forgotten something. What had he forgotten? He looked back over his shoulder.

'No, young warrior, that is the wrong way. Look there. The trees are thinning before us. The way is clear now. Sinisar of the Shining Path is fully risen above the horizon and the confusing mists of before are burned away. Feel how Sinisar warms you back to life. The air is fresh here. Feel how Wayfar breathes new life into your lungs. You are renewed and the fugue lifts from your eyes and mind. We have left the nether realm.'

Aspin blinked slowly as if waking, and then more rapidly. Awake! They had walked the Broken Path and were fully alive once more. Back in the land of the living, the gods be praised! He thought back on the land of the dead, but it was indistinct in his mind. He could not form a picture of it, and something told him that was a good thing. He had the definite feeling that some things were best forgotten, best not mentioned. There was a very good reason for the mind's imperfect recall, it seemed.

Yet there were things he did remember. 'Look, you old goat, next time I tell you to stop goading our enemies, then you will do as I say, do you understand? The headwoman said you were to be commanded by me. You will do as I say, or, by the gods, I will toast your testicles and serve them up to your enemies myself!'

Torpeth's bushy eyebrows beetled up his forehead. He seized his dangling balls and proffered them to Aspin. 'If they are of such interest to you, then you may have them, young warrior. I have little use for them, in truth. I am not sure you should be eating them though. That will avail you little. It is unlikely to improve your own endowment, you know. Is that the problem? Are your stones so small? You are young yet.'

Aspin ground his teeth. 'You are missing the point. Deliberately, no doubt. For all your foolery, you still fear being skewered, it seems. No, don't answer that! I command it. I know there is little to be gained bandying words with you, one who has lived so long that he has not only twisted every word ever known but turned the world itself upside down. The problem, old goat, is that you inspire your own enemies far too much.'

Torpeth became blankly innocent. 'Enemies? Me?'

'Yes, you! The last time I checked, just about everybody in the entire world is your enemy. The dead hate and revile you. The gods themselves, even! I am probably your only friend in existence, and still I am tempted to kill you.'

'Well, when you reach my age, you're bound to collect a few enemies,' the holy man groused.

'A *few?*'

'I'd tell you to wait and see for yourself, silly ox, but you probably won't live nearly so long. You're far too self-sacrificing. Anyway, you're not my only friend, so there! There's also my good friend Praxis.'

'Are you insane? Praxis is a servant of the Saviours! He tried to have us slaughtered in Godsend. That's not exactly very *friendly*, now is it? What's the matter with you?'

The naked man lifted his chin haughtily. 'He is as much a victim in all this as anyone else. Perhaps you should pity him rather than seek to judge and condemn him. You never know, you might be grateful of the same from him one day. I take it then, ungenerous youth, you're not going to thank me for saving you back there? No manners, the youth of today.'

'What?' Aspin responded incredulously. 'It was you who nearly got us killed in the first place. Should I thank you for that also?'

'But you must have enjoyed it when Pessarmon broke the mad Saint's nose, eh?'

'Azual was already dead. What difference did it make?'

'But you did enjoy it, silly ox?'

Aspin sighed. 'Yes, all right! I enjoyed it.' He smiled. 'He cried like a baby that had messed itself.'

Torpeth grinned. 'See, better than nothing, is it not?'

Aspin shook his head. 'What's the use? You will forever stubbornly be a mystery to me, holy man. Be quiet for a bit now, as I will probably get more sense from talking to myself.'

'As you command it, young warrior. May I keep my testicles, then?'

'Yes, you may, old goat. For now.'

'Thank you. Although I have no immediate use for them, you never know when they might come in handy. I have grown quite attached to them, you see.'

'Do not make me wish I was dead,' Aspin groaned.

'You didn't really think this would be permitted, did you?' scraped the giant Saviour, the overwhelming power of its presence instantly felling the sun-smiths and pushing Ba'zel so hard onto his knees that their caps buckled.

There was a Null Dragon – the sigil of the Eldest's line – carved into the speaker's chest. It began to Draw Ba'zel's life energy from him.

'Great Saviour!' Ba'zel whined. 'The Eldest commanded that I use any means necessary to reach the Gate to the sixth. She commands that you let me pass!'

'Incredible. It even has the temerity to use *her* name falsely. Unthinkable. Youth, the Eldest speaks directly to the mind of a Great Saviour, not through something as base as yourself. What has happened? Has one of the Declension somehow been contaminated with the verminous blood of a lesser being? What *are* you? An abortion all thought dead that slithered away when none was watching, so that it could grow hidden in shadows? Or a stillbirth somehow possessed and animated by the malign afterlife of one of our enemies? Speak your last, for there can be no escaping us and our command. What did you seek to achieve in turning the Selios against us? It is senseless. Why endanger our progress towards the Geas of this realm? Nothing is achieved by it. There is only loss. All the Selios with whom you have come into contact will be culled, for you have clearly written between the lines of our controlling narrative and had them read of it. Their minds are an evil to us now. Fortunately, we see that there are still enough of the Selios working deep below to breed a new and uncontaminated population. They have not heard or read your undermining words. Speak!'

The Null Dragon opened its maw towards Ba'zel, the all-dimensional vacuum of its void Drawing everything out of its victim – substance, mind, memory, thought, incipient refusal. He could only obey and succumb. It was the Question, and he could only provide whatever inadequate answer of which he was capable. 'Great Saviour, I am *unstable*. I am outcast. I am forbidden the definition of the Declension, for I disrupt it. I can do no other. I sought to free the Selios, even as my actions see the threat of genocide visited upon them. They are my hope and you are my guilt. You cannot cull all with whom I have come into contact, Great Saviour, for the four sun-smiths here are the entire line of the Prime Forge Master. Undo them and the forging of sun-metal will be lost to the Selios. The essential element will deny them. Who then will repair the sacred seal, tell me? How will you rediscover your defence against the radiation of this realm? Will *you* repair it, *Great* Saviour? We both know you cannot, for the sun-metal has always denied you, has it not?'

'Devil!' skittered the Great Saviour, ferociously reining in the Null Dragon and quelling the power of his presence. 'Sun-smiths, you will not end. Rise while you may and leave.'

Only the Prime Forge Master showed any signs of life. His massive frame slowly came up and he shakily got to his feet. Mournfully, he looked down at the bodies of his lost line. Then he turned hate-filled eyes on the Great Saviour and raised his glowing hammer.

The Great Saviour took an unsteady step backwards, the hard crests and crenations of his ancient skull scouring the roof of the high chamber in which their confrontation took place. 'No! I command you! Hear me, Selios! You have always known of the evil of which the Geas is capable. You have always been warned to resist its influence lest you become a very devil to your own kind. So see that this one is the devil among you! It disguises itself as a Saviour all the better to bring strife and destruction to the Selios. Its words have taken the fulfilment and happiness you had from you. Its words have brought you here to this tragedy, where your line lies dead before you. See the consequence of heeding that devil! This is your proper punishment, destiny and doom if you hear its words. Close your ears and mind to it. Strike it down before its subverting speech can cause even greater chaos within you and the Selios. Fear not, for you will recreate your line once he is gone. Fear not that you will be culled. Your tongue will be removed only and you will suffer much isolation, but fulfilment and acceptance can still be yours. You will have your line and your craft, and you will satisfy the Saviours. Strike now!'

The Prime Forge Master stood paralysed between the competing narratives. Slowly, slowly, he turned back towards Ba'zel, with plain murderous intent.

Ba'zel lowered his head in despair and dived through the floor.

'Warriors awake!' demanded the Great Saviour. 'The *unstable* element flees below! You will destroy him! He makes for the Gate. Guard it well and he will never pass.'

Ba'zel tumbled faster and faster, down through chamber after chamber. They flashed past so quickly that he didn't have time to take in what they contained. But he dared not slow himself, because he knew that with every second that passed more and more warriors would be gathering to block his path to the Gate. He sensed his destination not far ahead . . . at the lowest point of the sphere? He was fortunate that the Gate hadn't been placed high up, as he would never have been able to ascend as rapidly as he now fell. Even so, he was terrified that at any moment he would slam into a ward and be scattered in just the same way as he had been when he'd arrived in this realm. If that happened, he would not have enough energy to recover this time.

Faster and faster, hurtling towards oblivion, extending his senses as far ahead of him as he could, but images, sound shifts, substance and decay all rushing through his mind more quickly than he could properly process them. He just couldn't think fast enough. Nothing but a thick roaring and heady blur. Becoming brighter and brighter. Too bright to contain.

He knew he must be reaching the sun-metal perimeter. A crowd of warriors waiting below. He tucked himself into a ball and held his breath. Wait. Into open air and solidifying. Smashing down onto the thick skull of one of the oldest warriors and sliding off it, punching through an elder holding a trident of sun-metal. Please. Momentum dwindling. Fluid leaking from his skull. No! Colliding with the largest of them before the Gate, and then, tangled with each other, tipping into the cosmos. The elder wrestling with him, breaking and crunching through his limbs, sinking its stone fangs into him. Ba'zel no longer had the energy to resist.

The only thing that remained intact was his guilt. Despite his best efforts, he had brought genocide to the Selios, the Selios who had done nothing but help him. If he had not come to the fifth realm, none would have been harmed. The Prime Forge Master would have had his line. The Great Entirety would still have been whole. He had shattered them and ultimately achieved nothing that could harm the Declension. *What have I done? Forgive me.*

# CHAPTER 8:

# Just as those that love too much

*O*h, *my head hurts*, the taint groaned.

'It's not your head! It's my head,' Jillan replied. 'And try to keep your voice down, would you? You're really not telling me anything I don't already know.'

'He's coming awake!' Freda's relieved voice said from somewhere.

A grunt of acknowledgement from closer by. Jillan opened his eyes and nearly swallowed his tongue in terror. Harrowing eyes, eyes which had seen terrible things, looked straight back into his. Eyes that continued to see those things as if they were still happening all around them. Rape, decapitation, heads boiled to make a bloody soup while their owners were still alive.

*Ye gods!* the taint gibbered. *Jillan, go back to sleep. Quickly! So that we may wake up somewhere else. No, don't. She'll eat us while we sleep. Would that be better? I don't know. I've never been eaten alive before!*

'Who's in there?' croaked the witch-urchin, pushing back one of Jillan's eyelids with a dirty fingernail and peering intently. 'Well? Is my lord hiding in there? He should be. Come out, my lord! I have summoned you. How else would the boy know of this head otherwise? It is *my* head, but I will share it with you, lord, if you will but come forth. Otherwise, I will be forced to peel the flesh of this vessel off until you are revealed to me.'

Beneath a fall of black and greasy hair, the witch-urchin had a face that was youthfully pretty but still repulsive to behold. Her looks attempted some perverse seduction. There was only *wrongness* about her. Behind and above her there were bones, so many bones. Bones with cuts and teeth marks on them.

'Freda!' Jillan wailed.

'I'm here, friend Jillan,' answered the rock woman, coming past the witch-urchin's shoulder so that the other was forced to move back a little. 'Do not be alarmed. All is well. This is our friend. She brought you back.'

Back? Back from where? He'd been with the Saviour called D'Shaa, hadn't he? How had he got here, then? And where had he been before that? Hadn't there been a beautiful field of poppies? Or had that been a dream?

*Don't listen to her. She's hardly a judge if she calls Miserath a friend, now is she? We have to get out of here.*

For once, Jillan was inclined to agree with the taint. 'Freda, we have to leave as soon as we can. There's already an army of Heroes on its way to Godsend.'

*There is? Hang on. What have I missed?*

'And Praxis is made Saint. There's no time to waste.'

*What? That dog a Saint? Oh, this is bad.*

The witch-urchin surreptitiously moved over to a hessian sack that held something bulky and began to whisper to it, stopping every now and then as if listening to a reply.

'Should we return to Godsend then?' Freda worried.

*Yes.*

'No! Even if we can hold back this particular army or help everyone escape, I now know the Empire will never stop. There will always be another army, the next one bigger than the last. And more and more Saints. People will die. We will grow old. And the Empire will still be there. It will grind us under unless we can find the means to be rid of it once and for all. We must find Haven. And the Saviours fear Anupal. They *fear* him, Freda!'

*Jillan,* the taint said gently. *What of Hella? Godsend will not be able to stand without you. Surely this army will be there sooner than you can find Haven. Do not underestimate Hella's importance.*

'None can leave until the Dewar Lord appears to me!' the witch-urchin declared vehemently. 'I have made the necessary sacrifice to complete the summoning. Then I have returned life to one of his servants to balance the cost of the summoning. I have done all that is required of me. I summon him!'

*Jillan, listen to me—*'

The thick door of the cabin burst inwards, tearing off its top hinge. Daylight from outside flooded in around a large shadow. It had the outline of an ogre dressed in the skins of its kills. It came inside, its rank and meaty breath preceding it.

'By the gods, it gets better!' Jillan muttered to himself, searching for magic but finding none. 'Another of your friends, Freda?' he asked hopefully.

'What have you done?' the tusked ogre roared at the witch-urchin, before shifting into the more familiar form of the handsome Anupal-in-toga, his circlet of sun-metal now fully revealed.

'Friend Anupal!' Freda rumbled happily.

'Welcome, my lord!' the witch-urchin cried, crawling on her thin belly. 'I knew you would come.'

'Where is the shaman, you murderous magog? They're all dead! *All* of them!'

The witch-urchin's eyes narrowed. 'He is *mine!*'

'Where is he? I will not ask again. And I am not asking you now. I am commanding you!'

'Hi, Miserath!' Jillan called from where he lay on a blanket. 'Where have you been then? Anywhere nice? And what took you so long?'

The witch-urchin had slithered backwards and placed herself between her sack and the Peculiar. 'Mine!'

The Peculiar curled his lip. 'Disgusting creature!'

'Friend Anupal, she saved Jillan,' Freda volunteered uncertainly.

The Peculiar at last acknowledged the rock woman. 'Not through any noble sentiment. Her reasons will have been entirely selfish, simple Freda. Honestly, must you be so stubbornly trusting *all of the time?*'

'Well, it sounds like I for one should be glad of those selfish reasons,' Jillan put in. 'Miserath, you seem a bit overwrought. Maybe some tea will help you calm your nerves. Do gods drink tea? They should, you know. Otherwise, they're missing out. I take it your recent adventures elsewhere did not go well?'

'Listen, you *child*! She has killed every last soul in Thorndell. *Every single one of my followers!*'

Freda nodded. 'Thorndell is not a good place.'

Jillan sighed. 'Well, I would say she must have had a bad day, but I doubt that even begins to cover what she's been through. Years of abuse and horror, I would hazard. Where were you then, Miserath, eh? Were you watching? You probably get pleasure from watching, don't you? Does it make you feel powerful to watch the suffering of us mortals?'

'You know nothing of which you speak!' The Peculiar sniffed.

'Oh, really? Since when have you been the slightest bit bothered by the death of mortals? Your real concern is that they follow you, isn't it? Otherwise, you just wouldn't care. Tell me, are you made less powerful by this?'

The Peculiar pouted in mock sadness and shook his head. 'Poor Jillan! He thinks this is all about his parents. He still wants to blame everyone else that they're dead.'

Freda moaned in distress and put her hands over her ears.

'I killed him!' the witch-urchin said softly. 'The shaman. I had shown magic when I was very young, so my parents made me share his roof and fire, to learn from him. They wanted me to be the next shaman, so that our family could be the most powerful in Thorndell. In return, I kept house for the shaman, brought him food, made sure that he wanted for nothing. Yet the more I did for him, the more he wanted. He was never satisfied. In the end, he wanted that which I would not share with anyone, for it would have taken much of my magic from me. He took it anyway, without care for my tears. None in Thorndell would help me, for the shaman was more important to them than I was. I went to my parents and they slapped me for being ungrateful and telling lies. When I tried to run away, the people sent the hounds after me. I prayed to the Dewar Lord that he would help me, show me how I might win free of the shaman's will and tell me how I might find my revenge.'

Freda and Jillan looked at the Peculiar disapprovingly, but he simply shrugged and gestured for the witch-urchin to continue.

'I warned and threatened the shaman, but he just hurt me more,' the witch-urchin said to the fire. 'And then I began to read the book of the Dewar Lord. It told me what to do. I cut the shaman's head from his body, using my magic to keep the head alive. The head chanted spells against me, so I removed his tongue. But the people of Thorndell turned against me, even though I showed them the living head so that they could see they would still have the shaman's magic as before. They trapped me here and were about to burn the place. In my fear, I called out to the Dewar Lord and realised he was waiting for me to cast a summoning.'

The witch-urchin fell silent and they all listened to the hiss of the fire for long moments. Jillan became conscious of how loud his own breathing sounded.

'What happened next? How did you escape the people of Thorndell?' Freda's voice asked like a ground tremor.

The witch-urchin's head tilted, but her face was hidden by her hair. 'The people had moved away from their proper worship of the Dewar Lord, as they would not listen to she who was now the shaman. And they needed to be punished for what they had done to me before. But I knew the Dewar Lord would not come while so many of his followers spoke against me. I knew the people needed to be silenced and retaught the meaning of sacrifice. I would be the only follower left and then the Dewar Lord would have no choice but to answer me. It was so easily done too, for the shaman had collected items, fingernails and hair from all the people in Thorndell over the years, so that he could have a better power over them. I used those items to bind the people and have them sacrifice themselves. Just as they had lost their heads in life, so they would lose them in death.'

'All of them, though?' Jillan asked sickly. 'Even the children?'

'Of course. They felt no unnecessary pain. I had to become the only follower. The Dewar Lord was testing me. He would have come before otherwise. I had to show myself worthy, and show that the shaman and the people were wrong to do what they did. The Dewar Lord had given me the means to punish them all in his name. How else could I prove myself his worthy servant and truly become the next shaman? A ritual of becoming had to be completed. If I truly believed they had transgressed against his servant, and thus the Dewar Lord himself, I would not hesitate to punish that transgression. If I truly believed in the power of the Dewar Lord himself, as others clearly did not, then I would not hesitate to enact that faith. So the ritual was completed, the faith enacted and the Dewar Lord successfully summoned, to free me of this evil place and its bedevilling hounds.' They heard her joy, which almost sounded innocent: 'He is here to free me!'

'So,' Jillan said to the Peculiar. 'If you had come here sooner, when first called upon, the people of Thorndell might not be dead now.'

'A god can't come running every time someone trips over or bumps their head on a low beam,' the Peculiar rejoined. 'I'm pretty busy, you know. And I couldn't really hear her over the voices of the others.'

'But she hadn't just tripped over or bumped her head, friend Anupal,' Freda amended.

'I have been out trying to save this miserable world, unless you hadn't noticed!' the Peculiar said in a raised voice. 'Would you have me throw that over just to wipe the tears of some homicidal hag? Just to sit and listen to her twisted logic and fantasies? We have other places we need to be. We're falling behind time!'

'Well, don't complain when you find all your followers dead then!' Jillan shouted.

The Peculiar pursed his lips for a second. 'All right. I shall try not to be upset. All right?'

'All right.'

'Let's get going then.'

'We're taking her with us. She saved us, so it's the least we can do.'

'What? You can't be serious! She's a liability. And will you sleep soundly at night with her on the other side of the campfire? I don't think so. You'll wake up decapitated, and if you dare complain she'll have your tongue out.'

'She's our friend,' Freda said. 'And your follower, friend Anupal.'

'For the last time, she is *not* your friend, Freda! You can't be friends with everyone.'

The rock woman frowned. 'Why not?'

'Look, let's not get into that.' The Peculiar sighed. 'Have it your own way. Just don't come crying to me when you're rolling around minus a body. Now, can we please get going? The hounds aren't so fond of the daylight, and I don't fancy being stuck here for the night with the door hanging off its hinges.'

'That's your fault for wanting to make such a dramatic entrance in the first place.'

'Yes, sorry about that. Old habits die hard. But I do it so well, you have to admit.'

*

They moved in silence through the grisly town, Jillan holding his nose and not knowing where to look. Every time they left a staked head behind them, he would feel the hairs rise on the back of his neck as if they were being watched. They only came across one hound, and at a gesture from the Peculiar it slunk away.

They passed through the wood. Not a single bird sang. Miraculously, they found Floss unharmed near the wall at the edge of the field of poppies. Jillan checked her over, climbed into the saddle and offered his hand down to the witch-urchin. She came up behind him as if she weighed nothing. Beneath her rags, she was skin and bone, and all she carried was her hessian sack. He hardly felt her arms around him.

'Let's skirt around Thorndell on the way back,' Freda suggested.

The Peculiar nodded and leapt ahead, waving for them to follow. Jillan kicked his heels into Floss's flanks and they went racing after him, Freda not far behind. They were all keen to leave the cursed town far behind them, and knew that if they didn't hurry, the places they needed to get to wouldn't be there any more.

After an hour, Jillan slowed Floss to a walk. 'We may as well lead her on foot for a way. The floor of this small gorge is all awkward stones and it will be easier for Floss to pick a safe path for herself without us on her back.'

The witch-urchin clambered down without speaking and wandered off a distance. She clutched her sack close to her side.

Jillan shrugged and called ahead to the Peculiar, who stood watching impatiently. 'What I don't get is the coincidence of our heading west through Thorndell just when she'd cast a summoning. Surely our need to travel occurred before her spell, no? Yet how is that possible? It's backwards. And there's no way it was her spell that made us want to find Haven just so that we would pass through here. Our fight against the Saviours is what drives us. Perhaps you knew of the summoning before you suggested taking the route through Thorndell then?'

'No. I didn't know of the summoning,' the Peculiar replied uncomfortably.

'So is it just coincidence? Surely not!'

'It's complicated,' the Peculiar havered, flaring improvised wings so that he could make an unnaturally long leap to the top of a boulder. 'You're thinking of cause and effect as separate things rather than a continuum. They're often part of the same thing, you know. If you think about it, an effect can sometimes occur before a cause. Not all the time, obviously, but every now and then.'

'How?'

'Well, let's see. Sometimes you will smell a fragrance and only then turn your head to notice the flower from which it came. Or you might see the flower and only then realise you can smell it. Or animals will flee long before an earthquake hits. I guess it's like forecasting weather. When the weather arrives it should make you wet, except that you've already seen the outcome and have taken steps to avoid it, creating a new cause for the new outcome. If you see? Our deciding to come to Thorndell helped cause her to cast the summons, and her summons helped us decide to take that particular route towards the west. They're the same thing really.'

Jillan wasn't sure he liked the idea. Surely they made decisions of their own free will, not because someone they'd never met had cast a spell somewhere. And the reverse relationship was even worse. How could his decision to journey somewhere help cause someone he'd never met to kill loads of people in a place he'd never been? And what did it have to do with flowers and smells?

It made no sense to him . . . or not complete sense, anyway. Besides, he knew better than to trust the Peculiar. He tried again. Was it Hella kissing Haal that had made him want to leave, or was it his wanting to leave that had made Hella kiss Haal? Or were they the same thing? Yes, maybe it did make a sense of sorts. So, had that kiss been caused by the sacrifice of the people in Thorndell, or could the sacrifice have been caused by the kiss? No, that was silly. The events were completely unconnected, weren't they? They had no one in common, no one except himself . . . and Freda and the Peculiar. He looked towards the Peculiar suspiciously, but the god chose that moment to flit far ahead.

They pushed on into the evening, climbing into misty uplands. The soil was dark but shallow, meaning the grass grew in patches and tufts. Where rainwater had found courses to run down the slopes the soil had been washed away, so that the grey rock below was exposed as a set of natural interwoven paths. They followed one of the wider paths now, which ran uncannily straight and true, as if cut by builders and merchants.

'I do not know this place. Does anyone live up here?' Jillan asked, his voice echoing strangely in the mist as if someone was already whispering a reply.

The Peculiar adjusted the bent sword of sun-metal around his brow. 'I'm not sure. I haven't been here in a long time. If I recall, thousands of years ago a primitive ancestor of yours might have been found in the caves hereabouts. Troglodytes, trolls, trilopses, or some such. The stupid creatures had a tendency to eat each other, which kept their numbers low. The last one probably ate itself. And they smelt awful, so bad in fact that they might have suffocated themselves. Or was that in the uplands to the north? Hmm. Maybe this is where the local Saint – Sylvan of the Endless Reach, I think his name was – got fed up with travelling so far to collect the Empire's tithe every half-year. Or was that Saint Zoriah? No, she was that island weather witch. Anyway, the blood of the locals didn't give up its magic too easily, and they were difficult to control, or something. The long and the short of it was that they were too much bother and were wiped out.'

The witch-urchin nodded. 'The book of the Dewar Lord says men who commanded the sun brought their power to fight against those who lived in the high places, but that the Dewar Lord helped some escape to find refuge in Thorndell.'

The Peculiar smiled smugly at Jillan. 'There you are, you see! I'm not as heartless as you might think. Well done, follower.'

'I'm sure you were happy to increase your following,' Jillan replied. 'Still, they're all dead now, aren't they? And if there are any left round here, then they're not going to welcome the sight of that blade of sun-metal on your head.'

The Peculiar's face fell somewhat and he watched the shadowy mists around them warily. 'I sense nothing out there. I would hear the whisper of their minds otherwise.'

'Are you sure? The locals were always a bit different, remember. You said so yourself. And that sun-metal is like a beacon, even in this mist. It'll draw them from miles around. And let's not forget the vengeful spirits of the dead. I'm sure their ghosts will be plentiful round here.'

The Peculiar hastily produced a thick hood and smothered the light of his brow. 'Be careful how you speak of the dead, fool! You risk attracting their attention. There's a good reason the living never speak ill of the dead.'

It was as Jillan had suspected. Miserath was not his usual self. Since they'd been in Thorndell, the god had seemed anything but the self-loving poser Jillan had come to know and loathe. Instead Miserath was uncomfortable, uncertain, jittery and, in response to Jillan's latest testing comment, downright lacking in confidence. To his surprise, he found it quite disconcerting, and realised he had always taken a certain reassurance from the god's apparent ability never to be fazed. It was more worrying still if a weakening Miserath also meant a weakening of the Geas. Was this all because Miserath was reduced to just one follower? 'I thought you were the god of such things,' he said without any hint of accusation. 'You know, corruption, darkness, death and all that. Are the dead not followers of yours? They must be beyond counting.'

The Peculiar kept his face hidden in his hood. 'Yes and no. The dead are as nothing, a nothing that seeks to consume whatever it may, forever hungry, impossible to satisfy. They do not give me strength. No, they drain even me, for I am a god of the living.' The last sounded almost desperate.

'You should not antagonise the Dewar Lord, Jillan,' the witch-urchin warned in his ear, making him jump, for he had all but forgotten she sat behind him on Floss.

'Oh, don't worry. He causes me trouble whether I'm antagonising him or not. I may as well get something out of it, eh?' he replied with a forced grin, trying to keep his tone light. 'What's your name, by the way? I'd prefer not to call you *witch* or *follower*.'

'It is dangerous to let others have your name,' she answered.

'Do you mind if I make one up for you?'

A hesitation. 'If you must, but I will not be bound by it.'

'Very well. What about Anara?'

She made no response to the name but said, 'My lord, it is dark. Will we continue through the night or stop soon?'

The Peculiar's head came up. 'Stop, I suppose. Invariably, you mortals will be cold, tired and hungry. If I don't let you recover now, you will be useless when we descend into the west tomorrow, where we will need our wits about us. And we don't want the horse stumbling and going lame in the dark.'

'Are there caves around here?' Jillan asked, unable to see more than a yard or two ahead.

'Er . . . I'm not sure,' the Peculiar confessed. 'Freda! Are you out there, dear one?'

The ground rumbled behind them as the rock woman broke through the surface. Floss cantered forward a few steps before Jillan could rein her in. 'I am here, friend Anupal. There is a cave over there. It is empty.'

Freda led them through the dark and down into a sheltered hollow. The Peculiar allowed his crown to light up the place, and a low cave entrance was revealed.

'Perfect. We should be able to get a fire going,' Jillan told his companions. It wasn't that he needed heat himself, for his armour kept the damp and cold away from much of him, but he had felt Anara shiver against him. 'It is out of the wind, and the light will be hidden from view down here. I have kindling and other pieces of wood in my pack, thanks to Freda for retrieving it. You must tell me what happened in that field, Freda. Let's get settled first though.'

Jillan organised the quiet group, chivvying them along and giving each of them tasks. Jillan unsaddled Floss, wiped her down and provided her with grass and water. Freda searched the cave for any dry grass, bracken or wood. Anara collected edible moss to go with the dried meat she'd brought from Thorndell. And the Peculiar attempted to get the fire started, although he didn't have much success. In the end Jillan took over from him.

'The task is beneath me!' the god declared, refusing to be embarrassed.

'Of course, divine one.' Jillan smiled as he used flint and metal to set tinder smouldering. 'It is of no consequence. Let us talk of other things instead. Anara has already shared her story with us and we should do the same. Miserath, what of the time you spent away from us? Then Freda and I will tell you a tale of our derring-do, of how we bravely fought our way through a haunted forest, past evil vines and across a field of lethal beauty, where so many had previously fallen, finally to free the damsel Anara. Is it not a tale suited to the greatest of . . . what did Old Samuel call them? Knights? Is it not a tale suited to the best of company? Is it not what a campfire is truly for? Its heat is only for Anara, so why do we others gather round unless it is to hear tales of wonder and humbling heroism? We all know that the tales we tell within the light of our fire can hold back the darkness from our spirits and minds.'

The Peculiar seemed more like himself as he hunched forward, his eyes shining brighter as the fire caught. Freda and Anara sat on each side of him and Jillan completed the circle. 'Jillan is right that there may be an old and simple magic in such telling. Perhaps it will keep the restless spirits of the uplands at bay and see us safely through the night. Listen closely then, for the tale I will tell is of a god stalked by a terrible evil, just as this world has been cast into shadow by the presence of the elseworlders. Of a god who turned to confront that evil and sought to discover its true nature so that it could then be defeated. Of that evil fleeing the light of the god's divine brow and hiding in the deeper shadows created by that very light, shadows that might well be the same as the darkness around us now, a hungry darkness that crouches and waits hungrily just beyond the light of our fire. Of a god who fell into confusion because none should be able to avoid his power to detect and find them, none should be able to avoid he who could hear all things that existed, past, present and future. Of a god who thus realised that the terrible evil that stalked him could only be his own doom, the doom of the world and a doom of his own making. Of a god who tried to flee the terrible evil that stalked him, only to find the evil had already been ahead of him and killed all his followers but one. Of a god who cowers now upon ravaged uplands and is beset on all sides. Of a god who fears he will not see his way safely through the night. Of a god who fears!'

'Of a god who got carried away. Basically, you couldn't find who's been following us. Right?'

The Peculiar pulled a face. 'Who's the storyteller here, you or me? It shouldn't have been possible for anyone to avoid my looking for them, Jillan. There is no one more sly and tricky than me.'

'Friend Jillan, don't ruin everything!' Freda insisted.

'All right! Let's try again. Your turn then, Freda.'

*

Later on, when Jillan had retired for the night and the Peculiar had taken himself off somewhere, the witch-urchin leaned close to Freda and asked, 'What is a damsel?'

Freda was quiet as she searched her memory. 'I'm not sure, but I think it is a type of fruit, friend Anara.'

Anara stared meditatively into the fire. 'I have not been described as such a thing before. It is good, I think.'

Freda nodded, unconvinced that she would want to be described as a fruit herself. They were full of acid and as often bitter as they could be sweet. She much preferred getting her nutrients straight from soil. Still, it was perhaps a matter of taste, and she knew better than to try and completely understand the thinking of others. She remained impassive and unmoving, keeping her vigil through the darkness. Anara stayed with her for a while, content to share the companionable silence, before finally going to lie down.

'How dare they attack my holy army!' Saint Praxis shrieked from where he crouched among his personal retinue of two dozen guards. 'How dare they! They damn themselves over and over. It is an attack on my very person! Sacrilege against the holy Empire and the blessed Saviours.'

With Saint Praxis, General Thormodius and Captain Skathis riding at the front, the army of ten thousand Heroes had left Hyvan's Cross and begun the two-day march along the forest road to Heroes' Brook. The weather had been warm and clear. Warm enough for the men to remove helmets and much of their armour. And clear enough for the bowmen hidden in the trees each to pick an easy target for themselves.

The second flight of arrows was already in the air before any in the Saint's army realised what was happening. Near two hundred men went down screaming before officers bellowed for shields to be raised and the men to move into defensive formations. Arrows came from both sides of the road and groups that were slow to pull together quickly found themselves with higher casualties.

General Thormodius had ordered units of infantry to charge into the trees on both sides, and his men had responded without hesitation, for they knew they were trapped out on the road and that their main strength was in their numbers, numbers designed to overwhelm any force that stood before them. Unfortunately for the holy army, they soon discovered they were dealing with a force that had no intention of standing to face overwhelming numbers.

Swords blazing, hundreds of Heroes ran into the half-light at the edges of the forest. They slowed momentarily to allow their eyes to adjust, their bright weapons not helping in the least. Every other man fell with a flight through eye, throat, chest, limb or groin. Those still on their feet rallied, roared their battle cries and ran forward again, at last able to see, but to their consternation found only empty forest before them. Eerily, it seemed the arrows had come out of nowhere. Their enemy was invisible. Spooked, they retreated to the road and the rest of the army, an army in chaos.

A handful of minutes later and another barrage of arrows hit the holy army, although this time the effect was not quite so devastating, as these were disciplined men and not about to be caught with their guard down so easily a second time.

'Get our bowmen into the trees!' the General had thundered. 'Line of sight as distance between each man. Get us a safe perimeter. Move if you value your stinking hides!'

It was then that the crouching Saint Praxis had begun to shriek his righteous outrage and demanded that his general and angelic captain serve as his audience. 'I hold you responsible for this, General! Where was your vigilance? It is my holy duty to safeguard the morals of the faithful, it is yours to protect their physical persons. What has happened, General? Has the Chaos found you out and dulled your mind?'

General Thormodius blinked slowly and replied carefully, 'Holy one, my men and I have been campaigning in the deserts of the east for the last twenty years. Warfare is somewhat different there. But we have held off this attack and won't be caught in this way again. It should be safe to stand up now, holy one. I am surprised that the enemy was prepared for us so close to Hyvan's Cross. Undoubtedly, they have had some sort of advance information. I had been led to believe that our enemy would keep itself safely behind the walls of Godsend. Clearly, their leader is not so predictable and is happy to bring the fight to us. I need to know more of him . . . or her.'

'Advance information!' the Saint repeated, his eyes going wide. 'There are traitors among us!'

Captain Skathis interceded. 'It cannot be ruled out, holy one, but I do not believe any here could escape your own holy vigilance. It is more likely that word was spread by gossips in Hyvan's Cross or those plague victims that have been sent out of the city before us, whose bodies we are already starting to see buried at the wayside.'

'Yes, my angelic Captain, that is possible.'

The General cleared his throat. 'And are you able to tell me more of our enemy, holy one?'

'The Chaos is our enemy, General! It must never be underestimated. Why do I need to explain this to you? Are you being obtuse? I fear for your soul.'

The General bowed his head slightly. 'Forgive me, holy one, but I specifically seek to learn more of those who serve the Chaos in Godsend. I would have advance information of my own.'

'It is the bane!' Saint Praxis said, his eyes becoming distant. 'Child of the Chaos. Its incestuous lover. Its whore!'

'And militarily, the boy Jillan will be guided by one Samnir, an old Hero,' Captain Skathis advised the General.

The General's thick eyebrows came down. 'Samnir? I knew a Samnir. He was the very devil himself. Sand Devil, they called him. Could it be the same?'

Captain Skathis took an even breath. 'I know he spent time in the east during his fighting days. He was later sent out from the Great Temple in disgrace. He commanded in Hyvan's Cross for a while, but did not, let us say, get on with Saint Azual.'

'Blasphemer! Heretic!' Saint Praxis declared to the sky.

The Captain glanced at the Saint, to be sure it was safe to continue. 'Samnir ended up in Godsend, as far away from anything of consequence as possible, or so we thought. With Jillan's rise, Saint Azual was brought to Godsend. Samnir fought the holy one to a standstill. I have never seen such a thing.'

'Unholy demon!' Saint Praxis cried.

'And he was a conspicuous figure in the battle at Godsend,' the Captain finished.

'This changes everything,' the General decided. 'If it is the devil who sets himself against us, then he will second-guess our every move, harass us when we most need rest, and come for us when we can no longer resist sleep. Holy one, once we are past Heroes' Brook I would advise striking at Godsend as soon as we may. Let us leave off Saviours' Paradise, as otherwise it will only give the devil more time to eat away at our body.'

'The sooner that the devil can be exorcised from this body, the sooner the voices of all can be raised in praise of our blessed Saviours,' Saint Praxis pronounced.

'And I must take steps to see if this can be ended even before we arrive at Godsend. I see now that I should have killed you all that time ago, Sand Devil!' the General muttered as one of his officers approached and waited to be noticed. 'Report!'

'Around five hundred dead or injured, General.'

'And the enemy?'

The officer licked his lips nervously. 'Has not been sighted, General. I have overheard some speculation about ghosts and elves.'

'Creatures of the Chaos!' the Saint shouted. 'They can only have power against you if you are sinful or weak of faith!'

'Lieutenant!' the General snapped, drawing the officer's attention back. 'Ghosts do not use real arrows. And the fey are a children's story. They do not concern themselves with the affairs of men. If you hear any soldier saying otherwise, then he is to be flogged. Do you understand?'

The lieutenant came to attention and saluted. 'Yes, General.'

'Dismissed! Holy one, we must make for Heroes' Brook with all haste. A forced march, through the night if necessary. This enemy will not desist until we are safely behind the walls of Heroes' Brook. And I fear how many we might lose before then, for my archers have little woodcraft. Captain Skathis, what of your men?'

'They are my personal guard!' Saint Praxis all but squawked. 'Would you have me undefended? I knew it! You conspire against me on behalf of your own Saint, do you not?' Saint Praxis's retinue tensed, most of them visibly anxious. As Heroes who had always been based in Hyvan's Cross under the command of Captain Skathis, they had received the holy communion so that they were joined to their Saint. Loyal as they were, however, they knew that if they were called upon to seize the General, they would then have to face down an angry army of ten thousand Heroes from the eastern region, an army that needed its General's leadership more now than at any other time since it had entered the southern region. Saint Praxis seemed to glean something of these thoughts, his eyes flicking round his retinue, and he snarled, 'Be careful, General, for neither Saint Dionan nor your rank can save you if you damn yourself. All men are equal, for they are as nothing before the Saviours. You would do well to remember that.'

Saint Praxis turned away and moved for his horse. The powerfully built General studied him for a second and took a step forward, causing the Saint's guards to scrabble for their weapons in alarm. 'Holy one, I would suggest that you march with the men rather than make an inviting target of yourself upon your horse. You will thus be a most holy example to us that all men truly are equal.'

Captain Skathis remained expressionless. He wiped sudden beads of sweat from his brow with the back of his hand.

Saint Praxis turned back to the General and smiled tightly. 'I am glad that my lesson to you has been of such value. Trust me, then, that I will teach you another overdue lesson very soon.'

'As is your will, holy one. I look forward to it.'


They rose as soon as it was light and started across the uplands. The mist was gone and the heather and gorse lay before them all the way to where a leaden sky weighed upon the horizon.

'It looks ordinary now,' Jillan observed to no one in particular.

'Well, Gar and Akwar often lack imagination,' the Peculiar replied, leaving off a strange tune that he'd been humming.

'I think it looks bleak, sad and beautiful,' Anara said from behind Jillan. 'And there are all sorts of interesting bones and ruins beneath the surface, just as there are with people.'

'But you witches are obsessed with bones, eh?' The Peculiar smiled. 'No, as landscapes go, it's pretty dull, just like Gar and Akwar. They only tend to make an effort in places where there are potential followers, you see, where their work will be the subject of much wonder, where witless mortals will constantly be inspired to praise the glory and majesty of the gods. It's all a bit desperate, really. Still, perhaps the flat and boring bits make the other bits seem all the more amazing and exciting.'

'I like it,' Anara insisted.

'At least there's no one trying to kill or undo us here,' Jillan agreed.

'Always an advantage, I suppose,' the Peculiar conceded. 'Still, if you stayed here for long, you'd soon start to miss everything and everyone else. And if you didn't, they'd start to miss you and would come for you instead.'

'You know, I wish the Empire and the gods would just leave us alone.' Jillan sighed. 'Why don't they, Miserath? What is it they really want from us? It can't just be prayers and praise, can it? Are they so vain or inadequate that they really need to hear such things all the time? Are they lonely, Miserath?'

The Peculiar laughed neutrally. 'Ah, it is nothing so innocent, young Jillan. Yet you ask me to reveal something powerful, something dangerous. If I were to tell you what a god truly wants of mortals, then you could not help trying to aid or prevent the realisation of that want. You would take a side and would end up warring for or against the gods. Other mortals would do the same and there would only be division, destruction and doom for us all. It has happened before, when Torpeth the Great sought to rally mortalkind in the name of the gods. He did as much to hand this world to the elseworlders as any other.'

'What if I promise to remain neutral, to reserve judgement?'

The Peculiar shook his head. 'Nope. Wouldn't work. You would come to an important decision point and refuse to act, in the name of neutrality. Unfortunately, not acting would probably be disastrous. By contrast, if you had never known what the gods wanted, you would have made the decision without hesitation and acted. So, you see, the knowledge you ask for is too powerful and dangerous. It is insidious, infectious and completely beyond your control. You would not possess the knowledge, it would possess you. Trust me, young Jillan, in certain matters ignorance is bliss. Besides, if I were to share this secret with you, it would see mortalkind begin to lose their free will as they fought for or against the gods, or tried to remain neutral. With mortalkind losing their free will, the gods would start to become omnipotent and then, perversely, I would be undone as a god by the Geas so that its reality could continue and reassert itself. It is what caused the gods to fall before. Jillan, the gods *cannot* be allowed omnipotence and omniscience, as it would undo all but themselves, and thereby undo them anyway. So be careful of the questions you ask. Be happy that I work in mysterious ways, ways that will seem marvellous and malevolent to you by equal turns. After all, things are far more fun this way, no?

Think how dull it would be if you knew everything and there were no surprises. Even bad surprises can be good for you in some measure. Smart mortals know better than to complain and bemoan their lot. Smart humans know to rejoice in the presence of a god. Smart humans know to be worshipful and to pray. Smart humans are polite—'

'All right, all right, you're desperate for new followers. If I want a sermon, I'll find a temple or something. You can't really expect to convert me after everything we've been through, can you? Really? Speaking of temples, where precisely is the next one? Please tell me that is at least a question to which you're allowed to give a straight answer, because otherwise I think I'll end up crazy long before we get there.'

'Anara, did I sound desperate to you?' The Peculiar frowned.

'Er . . . no, Dewar Lord,' the witch-urchin replied thoughtfully. 'Everything you said had a divine logic. It would be a new chapter for the book.'

'A new chapter. Yes, I like that. Start work on it when you can. You can write, I take it? Make sure you leave out the bit about Jillan saying I sounded desperate.'

'Yes, Dewar Lord. I am . . . am happy.'

'Excellent! See the benefit of being one of my followers, Jillan? Anara is *happy*. Can you say the same? No. You've been a complete misery since we left Godsend. Why, I've known trolls who are less grumpy and snippy than you.'

Jillan took a deep breath and let it out slowly. 'The temple?'

'Oh! Yes. The temple. The temple of Akwar is beneath Saint Izat's palace in the centre of the bejewelled city of Shangrin, the main city of the west.'

Jillan blew out his cheeks. 'It won't be easy getting to it then. There'll be some of those bad surprises you mentioned along the way no doubt.'

'Maybe, maybe not. Izat doesn't know we're coming, so we should have an advantage there. With luck, and let's not forget that in my time I have been worshipped as the fickle god of fortune, we can be in and out of Shangrin in the same day. We'll find Sinisar's temple just as quickly, get to Haven, defeat the elseworlders and be back in Godsend before anyone's even realised you're missing, you'll see.'

'If I'd known overturning an eternal Empire would be that quick and easy, I'd have done it far sooner and on a good number of occasions, even making a hobby of it, I'm sure. Miserath, just what is it the Saviours want of us? You can't tell us why the gods won't leave us alone, I understand that, but what of the Empire? I cannot believe that it seeks to *save* the People, so just what does it want?'

The Peculiar's head suddenly spun a full half-circle, and he scanned the horizon behind them. 'Nothing. No matter how quickly I turn, I just can't catch it. And yet I *know* it's there.'

'Like with mirroring water when you try and catch your reflection doing something different to you. You watch it out of the corner of your eye, waiting for it to make a mistake. Or casually turn away and start doing something else so that you can then try and surprise it,' Anara hazarded.

The Peculiar frowned. 'No, that's paranoia, dear one. But you're close. What do the elseworlders want of you mortals? Why, that's easy. Everything, of course. Your blood, your bones, your dreams and fears, your children and old people, your demons and gods, your beauty and foulness, your magic and dullness, your warts and all. They wish to possess and control, divest and dissect, drain and consume you. Every single last one of you. Until you are no more and never were.'

'But why?' Jillan asked in a horrified hush, the world around them stilling as if to listen.

The Peculiar alighted on a rock, crouched and grinned like a gargoyle. 'Why, for the power it gives them. Not for the simple sort of power you might think of, of kings, queens and gods giving commands and being obeyed. No, for far more than that. For the power to *transcend*. To reach far beyond this trivial world and take the cosmos in their hand. The magic of the People and the power of the Geas will ultimately be theirs, and this world will be nothing, less than a memory even. You live on borrowed time, you mortals. The elseworlders only permit some of you to live so that they may collect a regular tithe of magic to sustain their presence and control here while they search for the Geas. And many of the People actually help the elseworlders search for the Geas! Incredible, is it not, the folly and selfishness of man? Having said that, the gods have behaved little better, succumbing far too easily to the elseworlders. Perhaps it was inevitable, for Gar, Akwar, Sinisar and Wayfar are entirely tied and limited to this world and its

People. As the People fell to the elseworlders, so did the gods, and vice versa.'

'What of you? Are you not entirely tied to this world? I remember during the battle at Godsend Torpeth was accused of betraying this world. How can you be entirely tied to this world if you would sell it out to the Saviours to avoid your own fall? How could you do such a thing? I think it has won you very little, after all. Just one follower left. And a battered old sword bent around your head. Perhaps you have also fallen. Your act of betrayal was your fall, no? Perhaps the Saviours drain and consume you just as they do the rest of us. Perhaps you also live on borrowed time. Or have you ensured that you are not tied and limited to this trivial world, so that you may also seek to reach beyond it? Have you chosen to become just like the Saviours, to be as bad as them? Have you used them as your model to avoid a fall at any cost?'

The Peculiar stretched and cracked his neck back into place. 'Ah, that's better. What were you saying? Oh, yes. There were a lot of perhapses in there, young Jillan. Perhaps I should have left you in Godsend, to be brought to your knees by the Empire? Perhaps you're right. Perhaps we should all just give up. Perhaps we should stop loving and living and instead go find graves for ourselves. Perhaps I should kill you here and now and we can all be done with it! Or . . . we can carry on loving and living, no matter what pain it brings us, and play the *other* to the Saviours. The other that lets one god remain at large, saves a rock woman from being boiled alive by Saint Goza, provides a young boy with a helmet of sun-metal to undo Saint Azual, and risks their last follower in seeking to throw off the enemies of this world. I know which one I think is more fun. What about you, Anara?'

'You speak for me also, Dewar Lord,' the witch-urchin replied from where she sat on Floss. She tightened her grip slightly on Jillan as she spoke, pushing the air out of him at just the right moment so that he did not have the breath to argue any further. He pulled his chin down, to refill his lungs, and looked as if he was nodding a reluctant agreement.

'Then the vote is carried unanimously!' the Peculiar gaily cried. 'I am gladdened that our hearts are in accord as we head into the difficult lands once ruled by brother Akwar, for blood was ever thicker than water. Anara, make a note of that. It sounds apocryphal.'

A blinding headache overtook her, as if a soldier were bashing in the back of her skull. Hella wobbled to the desk where she usually updated the stock records and slumped into the chair. She closed her eyes and rested her forehead on her arms. *Just for a second.* It was her own fault. She'd gone too long without sleep, pushing herself too hard. When had she last eaten? *Lot of good you'll be to anyone if you never wake up again.*

Everything had suddenly changed. Where there'd been a steady stream of people leaving Godsend before, now there were new arrivals on nearly a daily basis, arrivals who needed shelter, food and sometimes the physicker, arrivals who needed close questioning in case they were enemy spies, arrivals who constantly needed to be directed to the right people and places. It all needed organisation, and for some reason they all looked to her in Samnir's absence. It wasn't that they couldn't organise themselves when she wasn't around, but everything seemed to run more smoothly when she was the one giving the instructions. There was no backchat, resentment, second-guessing, alternative suggestions or improvisation when she asked someone to do something. They would just smile and do precisely what she asked. They would then tell her when they'd done as she asked, as if her approval meant everything. It was rapidly wearing her down. 'It's a way you have about you. Not everyone has it,' her father had said proudly. But it still exhausted her. She'd tried getting an assistant and delegating tasks, but that had caused unexpected confusion, a fight somewhere and a near-fatal accident. She was trapped. And it was wearing her thin. She felt like a ghost sometimes, just as she had seen Jillan look when he had used too much of his magic. She certainly didn't feel young any more.

Jillan. It was all his fault. Why wasn't he here to help her? When she next saw him, she'd smother him in kisses, hold him tight and then wring his stupid neck. Fancy leaving her like this, just when she needed him most. Or did she need him most precisely because he wasn't there? She was too tired to be confused. It was enough that she knew she needed him.

At least she'd had some word of him. Incredibly, the group of robbers who had attacked her father had turned up at the gates of Godsend with her wagon, the horse Tilly and most of their supplies intact. Their leader, Tebrus, had offered his apologies, and she'd seen how thin and desperate his group was. He'd admitted they were Unclean exiles from Heroes' Brook, and said that Jillan had offered them Godsend's protection.

'You saw Jillan?' she had demanded.

'Yes, milady.' Tebrus had nodded.

'Where? Tell me everything.'

'On the road to Heroes' Brook. With a sufferer of rock blight and, though you may doubt it, the god Miserath.'

No, she did not doubt it. Not for an instant. Freda and that cursed pagan god. They'd taken Jillan from her. Whatever hold they had on him, he'd still managed to see to it that Godsend had its supplies back and her father had his wagon returned. It was hard to stay angry at Jillan at such moments, but at other times it was all too easy.

'Where is he now? Did he not return to Godsend with you?'

'No, milady. He went the other way.'

A perfect example! The handsome tousle-haired idiot had gone off looking for more trouble, as if there wasn't already enough coming to their doorstep. His appetite for it seemed insatiable. There never seemed to be enough. It gnawed at him. It made him restless, withdrawn and sometimes absent. She'd even caught him talking to himself once or twice. He would take on the entire world for those he loved, to make it a safe and happy place for them. He would take on the whole world *for her*. It was what made her love him, but also what made her despair. It would never end. They would never be together. It was what made her so angry with him, so angry that her heart bled and made her constantly pale, so angry that she couldn't bear to think of him. Yet he had no choice in what he did. And she had no choice either. None of them did, as long as the Empire decided the lives of everyone. Well, if it meant she never woke up again one day, then so be it. At least she'd got to kiss him and make him smile a few times in their short lives.

A day after the group of robbers a handful of soldiers from Heroes' Brook had come to Godsend with a useful amount of supplies. And a few days after that hundreds of staggering plague victims from Hyvan's Cross! Many had lost hair and teeth, and all showed black spreading bruises and an unusual amount of bleeding. Each had been made to swear that they were prepared to fight against the Empire before they were allowed admittance, although few looked like they were strong enough to lift a weapon. They had little more with them than the clothes upon their backs. Hella would have become frantic about there being sufficient foodstuffs for the swelling population, but few of the plague sufferers seemed to have much of an appetite. But more than that, the soldiers of Heroes' Brook had brought news with them that meant the rationing of foodstuffs was no longer her overriding concern. For a Saint-led army of ten thousand Heroes was now less than a week away from Godsend.

*Just for a second.* She drifted away. To find another place, a timeless place, that was what she needed. But this world wouldn't let her go. It was like a constant presence, a weight on her shoulder. A presence.

Hella's eyes snapped open and she found an old woman leaning over her, touching her shoulder. The creases of the woman's face would have seemed kindly, but the irises of her eyes were disconcertingly dark.

Hella leaned away with a gasp. 'What do you want?'

'I did not mean to startle you, child,' said the grandmother with a voice more powerful than her twisted frame should have allowed.

'I didn't hear you approach.' Hella noted the walking stick the crone leaned on. It should have made a great deal of noise on the warehouse floor. Had she really been so deeply asleep?

'You carry a burden and I do not mean to add to it.'

'What do you mean? I do not know you, do I?' she asked uncomfortably, sliding sideways off her seat and putting the chair between them.

The woman showed brown and uneven teeth. Her breath smelt of carrion. 'We have always been here, child, you know that. Watching over you as we watch over all the People.'

The hairs rose on the back of Hella's neck. 'Stay back!'

The old woman took an awkward step forward, her face turning grey. 'Your care is our only concern, child. Yet you have been taken away from us. We fear for you and pray for your return. Do not give up hope, for it is not too late for you to find your way back. But time is so short. Our army approaches and all will turn to chaos.'

Hella shook her head, searching for words. 'You . . . you are behind all this! Saviour!' She spat the last word like an insult.

Her white hair falling from her shrivelling scalp and her wrinkles deepening, the possessed intruder shuffled forwards another step. 'Do not turn against us, child,' she begged tragically. 'It is all for nothing! They have not told you?'

'T-Told me what?'

'That he is dead!' came the cracked whisper. 'That a stray arrow took him as he sought entrance to Heroes' Brook.'

'No!'

'He is gone, child. He will never come back to you. Look at me. If you try to wait for him, you will end up like me. Alone. Withered. A lifetime of emptiness.' The skin across her arthritic knuckles, along her jaw and at her temples split open and she hunched lower. 'Please, child! We grieve for you. Leave all this. Do not resist us, for it will only see more die needlessly. You are killing them! You are hurting us. You cause death all around before you have ever been properly allowed to love. You have even been denied our love when there is no need. Come to us before it is too late and none in Godsend will ever feel anger or pain. They will know only happiness as they welcome our army with open arms.' The crone tried to stretch her arms wide, but the effort was too much for her and it clearly broke her chest. She rattled and then sagged to the floor, becoming dust before Hella's very eyes.

Hella tried to hold back a sob, but she had to release it or choke. How could he be dead? No! She would instruct him to be alive. Everyone obeyed her instructions. So stupid. A stray arrow. No. 'You idiot, Jillan! My poor boy!'

She fell into the chair again as the sobbing overtook her, her head on her arms. What had it all been for if he was dead? What was there to fight for? She didn't know any more. She needed to find another place, a timeless place. She closed her eyes and prayed she would never wake up again.

They stood at the end of the uplands, looking down into the west. Freda had surfaced and joined them.

'It's so bright!' The rock woman squinted. 'It's a place of light.'

'Reflections from all the water, I suspect,' Jillan replied. 'I can't see much, though.'

They descended into light woodland, and after an hour or two the Peculiar called a halt. 'Just beyond those trees is Vizimouth. It's the town where the main routes from the north and south meet the river

Vizis. Here, nearly all trading goods are loaded onto barges and boats and moved to the markets in Shangrin. They're used to all sorts of people from outside the region, but even so I fear we will stick out a bit.'

'That's why you've changed your appearance,' Jillan observed to the middle-aged, moustachioed and strong-jawed man wearing rich blue and yellow velvets. 'We should be all right, shouldn't we? No one here is likely to know us.'

'Think!'

'Oh yes.' Jillan blushed. 'The Saint of the region will see through the eyes of her People. We don't want her to know we're coming, but she might well recognise us. My armour . . . and Freda . . . We could wear hooded cloaks?'

'Better. But it's sunny, isn't it? Cloaks with hoods up would make you just as conspicuous as anything else.'

'Oh.'

'Look, you two will wear cloaks with hoods down and we'll just cross our fingers that we get to Shangrin without being spotted. One face with rock blight is much like another, and you're so plain that the Saint might not remember you anyway, Jillan. Anara will be staying here in these woods.'

'What? Why?' Jillan and Freda chorused in protest.

'Because I'm her god and I say so. Our journey from here will present all sorts of dangers, and I will not have my only follower risked unnecessarily. Besides, if we get into any real trouble, we'll need a rescue party. Anara will hear me if I call her. She will also keep a close watch on the town and let me know of anything untoward that happens. We'll leave the horse with her too, rather than cart it back and forth on boats. Added to that, Anara can be writing a new chapter for the holy book of the Dewar Lord. And that's an end to the matter.'

'It is a good plan,' Anara stated, taking the wind out of Jillan and Freda's sails.

'Do you think I'm that plain?' Jillan asked Freda in a quiet voice.

'You *are* next to me,' the Peculiar interrupted, striking a pose and twiddling the end of his moustache between thumb and first finger. 'Every eye will be drawn to my fine figure and bearing, so that you may pass by all but unnoticed. I am a man in his prime, while you are but a boy without any stubble on his chin. I have the instant respect of other men and the immediate interest of all women, no matter their age. Just the sight of me will have grandmothers remembering what it is to feel young. You will find that these things are of particular importance in this region, if you know anything of the tastes and appetites of Saint Izat. They will think of the two of you as my ugly servants and completely ignore you, if we are lucky.'

Jillan remembered back to the time he'd met the female Saint in Godsend. She'd had a strange effect on Samnir, apparently far more seductive than her normal beauty should have allowed. It seemed that she was his Saint and therefore had a considerable power over him, a power that manifested itself through the interplay of attraction, pleasure and denial. He didn't fully understand it and it made him more than a little uneasy.

'I have heard it said it is all in the eye of the beholder, friend Jillan,' Freda rumbled uncertainly. 'But do not mind friend Anupal. From what I know, the gods and Saints are much alike in their vanity. They like to think that they have their places based upon being somehow better than others. Gangleader Darus was the same. I really didn't like him.'

'Well, what else would it be based on, you lumpen heretic?' the Peculiar bridled.

'Just tricks,' Freda answered mildly.

'Tricks? Tricks? What do you mean tricks? Anara, don't write down any of this. What tricks, Freda?'

'Well, the trick you use to change your form so that you look so . . . so nice, friend Anupal. You're still the same person, though, no matter how you've made yourself look. I'm sure I could pick you out of a crowd no matter how you were disguised. A mask, do they call it? And the Saints are Saints because of a different trick, aren't they, a trick that other people don't know?'

Jillan laughed and nodded.

The ends of the Peculiar's moustache began to smoulder and the hair on his head curled up tightly. 'Honestly, Freda, I thought you had more sensitivity than that. I thought you were my friend! If you're going to be like this, then I just wish you'd stay under the ground. You clearly don't understand things above the ground properly. They're just too . . .'

'Tricky?' Jillan grinned.

'I didn't mean to upset you, friend Anupal,' Freda offered in her least gruff tone.

'I am *not* upset! Argh! What's the use? I'm off to get two cloaks, and you two can reflect upon your poor behaviour while I'm away. In this region they set great store by good manners, so it's about time you yokels started learning some. Believe me, your rough country ways will not go down at all well in a sophisticated city like Shangrin. Obviously, I am going to have to give you two some lessons on the boat before we get there. To think that a god must stoop so low as to have to deal with two such obtuse individuals!' And with that the Peculiar stalked stiffly away.

'He seemed upset to me,' Jillan confided to Freda. 'What do you think, Anara?'

The witch-urchin nodded. 'Yes. Upset. It is difficult being a god, I think.'

The Peculiar returned just a few minutes later and threw ragged cloaks at Jillan and Freda. The garments were poorly patched, dirty grey and smelt of old sweat and more.

Jillan held his up by fingertips and at arm's length. 'The latest fashion in the west?'

'It's all I could get quickly,' the Peculiar replied smugly. 'It'll stop people wanting to get too close to you. Come on!'

'I don't want to get too close to me in this,' Jillan grumbled.

They made their farewells to Anara and moved away through the trees. They emerged at the side of a wide well-maintained road and stood, taking in Vizimouth.

'It's enormous. Bigger than Hyvan's Cross even!' Jillan exclaimed.

'What? Did you think the southern region was the centre of the world and all that went on in it?' the Peculiar replied archly. 'As far as westerners are concerned, Hyvan's Cross is a miserable little hamlet. You won't even find it on some maps. Godsend certainly doesn't exist. And yet Vizimouth is little more than a staging post compared to the magnificence of Shangrin.'

'So many people,' Freda commented uncomfortably. 'So much noise.'

'Admittedly, the place has grown since the last time I was here. You

222

mortals always breed with such urgent frequency and speed. Every time I turn around, there are more of you getting under my feet. I often think it's a good thing the elseworlders limit your population by taking so many Heroes to die in the east, as otherwise you mortals would gobble up the world. Of course, things are a bit different here in the west. Here, your kind breeds with . . . what's the right word . . . *industriousness*? The Saint understands that her People are a natural resource that should be allowed to multiply like a herd of cattle or a financial investment. Look how busy they all are, scurrying about their business, striving to build and organise, constantly looking for advantage and more efficient ways of doing things. Even that beggar there is more hard-working than those in the south. See how he laments for one passer-by, japes for another and dances for the children. A true artist and professional.'

Jillan did not understand many of the phrases the Peculiar used. Besides, he was only listening with one ear, because he was so distracted and fascinated by all the activity going on before him. The place teemed with life, and yet no two people ever collided with each other, as cramped and crowded as it was. It was almost like a big dance in which everyone knew where they should be and what they should be doing at any given moment. And the din of their shouted voices was the music that kept their movements in time. *Oh, how exciting it must be to be a part of such a thing, in harmony with so many others.* He wanted to be the ship's captain directing the loading of his vessel, or the brawny docker pulling on the rope that swung the crates over the ship, or the wiry sailor guiding the cargo down onto the deck. He wanted to be the strolling man selling hot pies for pieces of copper. He wanted to be one of the quick children stalking the pieman. He wanted to be the man in the fur-trimmed coat walking with the pale-skinned but brightly dressed woman on his arm, she disdaining every hawker's wares and occasionally holding a handkerchief to her nose. He wanted to be the ironsmith making amazing things appear, or the street conjuror making coins disappear. He wanted to be shouting proudly from behind the vegetable stall, he wanted to be driving the cow along the cobbled street, he wanted to be juggling eggs, he wanted to be one of the squad of Heroes marching in well-polished armour. He wanted . . . The squad was led by a tidy man in undecorated black silk. The man had keen eyes and seemed to be able to watch everything and everyone at once. Every now and then he would bring out a small book and make a note in it. Jillan wondered how he hadn't noticed the curious figure sooner, and then realised that all the inhabitants of Vizimouth subtly kept their attention away from the fellow. Up till that point Jillan had only been following the things to which everyone paid attention. The black silk remained invisible unless you made a deliberate effort to focus on it. And nobody wanted to do that. Apparently it was dangerous to do so.

And apparently it was already too late. The man in black silk met Jillan's gaze with glittering intense eyes.

'Er . . . Miserath?'

'Yes, he has seen you,' the Peculiar said out of the corner of his mouth. 'Look down at the ground. Drop your shoulders. Look humble. We should have left your bow with Anara. Jillan! Do as I say! There's still time to appear an innocent and wide-eyed outsider. A second longer and you will be impudent and challenging. Break free of it! Blink! Now!'

By force of will and the sheer good luck of a wagon passing in front of them, Jillan managed to wrench his gaze away. In his mind's eye he could still see the man staring at him. He kept his thoughts still and his head ducked.

By the time the wagon had rattled past, the Peculiar was loudly regaling his retainers so that all might know of his considerable education, experience and importance. 'Attend me then, my dear lackwits, for few of my words and little of my time should be wasted upon such as you. I will not have you importuning me when I am about my business for the benefit of all in my estate! You must be silent. You must not stand within my sight, for you will spoil the scenery . . .'

The black silk watched for a few moments more and then turned away, followed by the squad of Heroes. The crowd opened up and then closed behind them, as if they had never been there.

Jillan realised he'd been holding his breath. He released it now and puffed out his cheeks. 'Who was that?'

'Back, you dogs!' the Peculiar cried at the streetsellers who had suddenly descended upon them to pull them deeper into Vizimouth. 'I have not become so wealthy by giving away my coin to charlatans, hacks and ne'er-do-wells such as you. You would poison me, rifle my pockets and leave me dead in the thoroughfare, I know it. Back, I say, or I will bring the town guards a-running and see the punishment chambers full. Guards! Guards!'

The hawkers scattered like seagulls. The other people in the street waited to see if there would be any further disturbance to entertain them, realised it was not forthcoming, shrugged disappointedly and went about their business. The noise of the crowd picked up again.

'One of the Saint's priests.'

'Priests?'

'Like your Ministers, I suppose. Certainly just as bad. But there are a lot more of the priests around. They particularly watch and listen out for those from outside the region. They are her eyes, ears and voice. Now keep quiet before you get us into even more trouble. You never know who might be listening or reading our lips. Freda, you're doing very well.'

'Thank you, friend Anupal. I do not like it here. Can I go back into the ground?'

'I'm afraid not, dear one. If anyone were to see you do so, you'd cause all sorts of consternation. And all know there are three in our party now. It would cause comment and speculation if we were suddenly two. And I must ask you to be brave, dear Freda, for we will need to board a ship or barge to Shangrin. It is the quickest way there. You will be separated from the ground for a while. Will you be brave for us?'

'Here, Freda,' Jillan said, offering the rock woman a reddish stone from his pack. 'I hold this when I'm feeling scared. You can keep it if you like.'

The Peculiar rolled his eyes and shook his head. 'The superstitions of you mortals. Still, whatever works. Who am I to quibble with the power of belief?'

Freda looked at the small pebble Jillan had dropped into her giant hand. She grinned shyly up at him. 'It is beautiful, friend Jillan, and precious. But won't you need it?'

'It's all right. He can pick up another one anytime he wants. There are lots of stones just lying around.'

Jillan pointedly ignored the deity. 'I still haven't properly thanked you for saving me from that field, Freda. Or the phagus, come to that. It would please me if you had the stone.'

'Well that's nice! No thanks or present for me, though,' the Peculiar grouched to himself as he led them over to a fairly humble-looking boat. 'This will do us. Ahoy there!'

'Why this one?' Jillan asked, expecting the Peculiar to have chosen something of a higher status or more flamboyant.

'It looks sound, seems fitted for passengers more than goods and is small enough to be able to overtake larger and more heavily laden vessels on the river. Oh, and the Captain's female.' A large woman with a weathered no-nonsense face turned to look them up and down. 'And fine-looking she is too!' the Peculiar called more loudly. 'Would you have room for me, Captain?'

Jillan detected a vibration in the god's voice and knew he was seeking to bewitch the woman.

The Captain spat tobacco juice over the side of her boat and wiped her chin. 'You look like too much trouble to me, milord.'

Jillan couldn't help smirking. The Peculiar gave him a wicked look.

'Captain, I assure you—'

'You're a man, ain't'ee? Then you're trouble. You can assure me this and assure me that all you want with your airs and graces, but none of that's speaking straight, now is it? No. It speaks of trickery and trouble, that's what it does. Or would you be telling me I ain't Captain of this ship and ain't no judge of nothing?'

'I . . .' the Peculiar broke off and muttered something to himself about mortals getting above themselves. He took a deep breath and drew himself up again. 'I will pay good gold if you can get me and my companions to Shangrin as quickly as you can.'

'That's better. Far more straight-talking now, ain't'ee? I could quite get to like you like this. It'll be expensive, mind, if you're asking me to pull up my plank before I have another half-dozen passengers. And there won't be no bunk for your finely scented head, milord. And no sharing neither.'

The Peculiar's temper got the better of him. 'There are other ships—'

'See! I knew you was faking it. You're trouble and no mistaking. Off you go then, milord. Go see that all the berths are owned by traders

226

waiting for new shipments to arrive, and that they won't be having no room for lolly-gagging posh-frocks nowhere. Go see, and then buy yourself some old nags and a wagon to git you where you're going. Go breathe the dust of the road, for you'll never be setting foot on my ship!'

The Peculiar looked crestfallen one moment and incendiary the next. Terrified at what might be about to happen, Jillan nudged Freda. 'Go on. Say something. Anything!'

Freda took a crunching step forwards. 'Captain, this is my friend. You don't need to call him lord. None of us do. He's ordinary like us. He makes himself look nice and speaks nice because he thinks people will like it. He didn't mean to make you angry. He was trying to be nice. He needs more practice, maybe. Anyway, the thing is, we need to get to Shangrin as quickly as we can. Bad things might happen otherwise. We just want to help people, not cause you any trouble. And we will give you as much gold as you want. I can find more if you need it. I'm good at finding sun-metal and other things like that. And we will say sorry for not saying the right things before. Do you know anyone called Jan, by the way? I've been looking for him for another friend.'

'Men can thank the Saviours that there are women to sort out the messes they make for themselves, ain't that right, milady?' the Captain softened, holding Freda's eyes. 'You'd best bring yourselves aboard then, or I'll be known as difficult for no good reason. Sorry to say, I don't know of any Jan, milady, but I'll listen out for word of him 'case you ever come back this way.' Freda nervously shuffled across the gangplank, which bent and creaked alarmingly under her weight, then came Jillan and finally a nonplussed Peculiar. 'That'll be six golds, milord.'

The Peculiar fished out a dozen and told the Captain to keep them with his blessing.

'That I will, milord, but will let you have free passage the next time you have need of it, and no mistake, providing you don't think to make free with anything else. Now move towards the bow if you would. Cast off there! Raise the plank! Move, you doxies, if you hope to see your men in Shangrin while they still remember who you are and you still remember what they're good for!'

'In the name of Her Majesty, you will hold that order until we are aboard!' a harsh voice cut through the air. The priest and his squad of

Heroes stood at the edge of the dock. The man in black silk kept his eyes on Jillan.

'Come aboard then. My ship is of course Her Majesty's ship,' the Captain said without sounding too grudging.

The priest quickly brought his men onto the boat.

'Cast off!' the Captain shouted again. As she passed the Peculiar, she quietly grumbled, 'I knew you'd be trouble!'

'Minister Stixis.' Saint Praxis nodded, having dismounted from his mount. 'Elders.' He surveyed the crowd of thousands bowed before him. 'You may all rise.'

'Holy one, we rejoice that you are here, for now we will be delivered from evil,' the Minister gabbled.

Saint Praxis turned cold eyes towards him. 'The word of the holy book and your proper faith are all you need to keep you from evil. You are the appointed Minister of this town. If I find that it is in the grip of evil, then you will be held responsible. I have already had to punish aberrant Ministers in Hyvan's Cross. They are in no condition ever to sin again.'

To the Minister's credit, he did not flinch before the inquisitor's gaze. 'As is your will, holy one. We have been beset by evil on all sides, but have held firm and been sustained by our faith. Unlike the other towns of the region, we have had no plague. We have not suffered the Unclean to remain among us. Devils from Godsend came to our door and we turned them away. Still we rejoice that you are here, holy one, for you are the word made flesh and will drive the devils out of this region entirely. We beg your blessing, if you judge us worthy.'

One of the town council crept forward. 'Forgive me, holy one, but we have prepared a holy feast to celebrate your coming. Or we can show you to a sanctified place where you might rest.'

'You will host my men, who have been hard-pressed by devils all the way from Hyvan's Cross and whose spirits will need to be fortified by the sacrament of the holy feast. Here is General Thormodius, who will take all you have. I myself stand within the grace of the blessed Saviours and want nothing but to attend to my holy duties. I must not be kept or distracted from the task of seeing the holy communion administered to all the People of Heroes' Brook. Captain Skathis, go with the Minister and see that all is prepared as I require. Have the Heroes of this town receive the communion first, for a goodly number of them will then fall under your charge, my angelic Captain, and march with us onto Godsend. Go quickly, Captain!'

'As is your will, holy one,' Captain Skathis replied, gesturing for Minister Stixis to lead the way.

His hands shaking violently, Saint Praxis raised the goblet containing the tithe to his lips and gulped down the contents, not caring that some spilled down his white shirt in his haste. He waited and waited, holding back panic. Why was it taking so long? Was the blood of these People so thin? Or tainted? New strength slowly spread through him, restoring him, sharpening his mind and senses and then taking him to a place of ecstasy and revelation. Ah! The rapture!

He saw them all, saw through their eyes, saw into their minds. He removed their memories of the bloody communion, for it only confused them and caused them to doubt. There must be no doubt, only the conviction of true faith. Only those with doubt were tempted by the Chaos and needed to fear the divine retribution he would enact against them in the name of the blessed Saviours.

It was always difficult to separate the People's fantasies from their real memories, what they thought from what had actually happened. Some seemed to exist in a total fantasy as well, meaning there was little to be gleaned from them. Some lived only in the past and some just in the present, their minds, consciously or otherwise, staying away from things that disturbed them too much. Most of it was an unreadable jumble, and he knew that the Chaos used this to hide itself among the People. It made itself flesh through them. They must be exorcised!

As in Hyvan's Cross, he would find the Chaos here. His keen eye would not be deceived. It was those who showed the greatest doubt and fear who had been most tempted. Yes, he saw them now. Ah, but look how they had transgressed! He now understood why, when he had first entered the town, he'd experienced the urge to rip the Minister's head from his shoulders and drink his blood there and then. It was because his saintly sensibility had immediately detected the corruption in the man. He could see it, smell it, hear it. Now to draw it out and consume it. *I am become a holy sin-eater!*

'Captain, are you there? Attend me!'

Captain Skathis was there at once. 'Command me, holy one.'

'Bring the torturer. I have work for him. Round up Minister Stixis and Captain Callinor. I will hear their confessions so that their souls might be cleansed.'

'As is your will, holy one.'

'And see that you collect a greater tithe from the People of Heroes' Brook, as we've yet to bring the best out of them.'

As soon as the boat had cast off, Jillan had become nauseous. The priest still watched him. Jillan wiped sweat from his brow. The black silk moved towards him. Jillan's stomach heaved and he splattered the priest's shiny shoes. Jillan opened his mouth to apologise, but that proved to be another mistake. The priest hurriedly retreated to the far end of the ship.

'Well that's one way to keep our enemies at a distance.' The Peculiar smiled. 'How long do you think you can keep it up, eh? All day? All the way to Shangrin, ideally.'

Jillan held onto the side of the boat for dear life. 'Never been on a boat before,' he coughed.

'You don't say? And there was me thinking you'd spent half your days on the high seas.'

'High seas?'

'Yes, large bodies of water where the swell is far greater, where ships are tossed by waves and storms, where the deck rolls u-u-up and down, u-u-up and down, u-u-up—' Jillan was noisily sick again. 'Who would have thought you had so much in you?'

'Friend Anupal, what's wrong with him? Is it bad magic? Poison? His face is not the right colour,' Freda worried. 'We should never have come on this . . . this boat! Can't you make it stop, friend Anupal?'

'Some call it Akwar's Curse, but it's quite normal really. His stomach isn't used to the ship's motion. See how he tries to keep still by gripping rigidly to the sides? That means his stomach sloshes back and forth every time the ship moves. What he should actually do is stand with knees slightly bent so that his legs absorb a lot of the rise and fall. I think you'd better help him up.'

Freda set Jillan on his feet so that he could try to do as the Peculiar advised. He became light-headed and put his head over the side again.

'It doesn't seem to be working, friend Anupal!'

'He hasn't got his proper balance yet, that's why. Standing up makes him dizzy, I imagine. Make sure he doesn't fall overboard, would you? He'll keep at it till he's empty. But if you see the priest make another move towards us, get loads of water into Jillan so that he can start throwing up again. I think you and I will be much safer standing prow-side of him as well, Freda.'

The Captain having promised to get them to Shangrin as quickly as she could, and with the moon large and the lanterns lit, they'd sailed through the night. Jillan saw none of the beautiful firefly displays over the water and heard nothing of nature's night-time chorus, as he'd become delirious with exhaustion and been allowed to pass out in a hammock long before dusk. His mind was a fluttering moth and his thoughts the whisper of black silk.

He was nothing till the shout of 'Shangrin ahoy!' Then he heard the creaking of the boat around him. The sound of the water had changed.

'Jillan! Come see. It's beautiful!' Freda said in squinting wonder.

He tried to open his eyes to the world. A flare of white. His eyes watering. 'I can't see!'

A shadow fell over him. 'Is that better?' Freda asked breathlessly. 'Everything is gold and silver. I have difficulty looking upon the city as well. It is blinding. Jewels everywhere!'

The river they had been following had opened into a wide, wide lake. A thin line of purple hills on the horizon marked the furthest shore, but the view was dominated by a towering island of shining walls, domes sheathed in sun-metal, slender spires and flighted bridges. With the sun rising behind them, the water became a mirror to the city, amplifying its majesty and brightness even further.

'Shangrin. Crowning glory of our kingdom,' the Captain said near them, wiping at the corner of her eye. 'As many times as I have seen it, it is still almost too much to look upon, seat of our holy Queen, she who has loved us and seen us saved. Is it not beautiful beyond words? To look away is to know grief and loss. To look away is to find ugliness and despair.'

Jillan came unsteadily to his feet, his sickness all but forgotten in the spell-binding moment. He was truly awed. The only thing marring the scene ahead of them was the shadow of their boat, as if they were unworthy even to approach this perfect place. And then an encroaching darkness at the edge of his vision. The black silk had suddenly come close.

Jillan glanced to the side, but the priest's rapt gaze of devotion and worship remained fixed on the scene ahead of him. 'The holy isle!' the priest rhapsodised. 'The holy city! A refraction of the blessed Saviours' heaven, a glimpse allowed the People of this region and all pilgrims so that they will remain inspired and faithful, so that they will not heed the lesser temptations of the Chaos. A gift to the People as sign that they are loved, but a gift to overwhelm them so that they always know of their unworthiness and so that they will constantly strive to love their holy Queen, faith, Empire and blessed Saviours all the more!'

The Peculiar wandered across the view, stretching lavishly as he yawned. He farted. 'What's for breakfast? Sorry to interrupt, Father, but the boy will collapse if he's kept gawking for too long. The vision of Shangrin in the morning light may feed his soul, but it does precious little to feed his body, and he has been very ill. Even pilgrims need to eat, or risk never completing their journey, eh? I am sure that the faith can see that. Even the silk-clad faith must agree that the poor and lowly need to eat.'

The priest smiled ambiguously. 'There are no poor in this region. All are provided for by Her Majesty's mercy.'

'There are poor elsewhere in the Empire, and we are all one People and all one faith. All must share the responsibility.'

Keeping up his smile, the priest inclined his head, but his gaze was now penetrating. 'And we welcome those poor should they make pilgrimage here. We recognise them, just as we recognise you. Fear not, we know precisely *who* and *what* you are.'

Freda stilled and Jillan held his breath. The Peculiar cocked his head. 'And how is that, good Father?'

'Why, our Queen *always* knows. None are strangers to her, and all are welcome when they are of good faith.'

'Which is as it should be.' The Peculiar nodded. 'Come, my retainers, let us find somewhere we may break our fast.'

Once they were safely out of earshot, Jillan said weakly, 'They weren't meant to know we were coming. What are we going to do?'

The Peculiar tried not to look ruffled. 'He might have been bluffing. Other than remaining calm, however, I haven't got the faintest idea what we're going to do.'

It was only as their boat came closer to Shangrin that Jillan realised how truly enormous the island city was. It filled his entire vision. Dozens of ships were moored at the various docks. His heart sank as he saw fully fifty Heroes waiting on the quayside.

'I don't think I have the strength to draw magic,' he quietly admitted to his companions.

'Don't worry,' the Peculiar said. 'It would be foolish to try and fight them anyway. It would raise the entire city against us, and what would we do then?'

The Captain saw the ship safely guided in and secured. She gave Jillan's group an apologetic look and ordered the gangplank lowered. The priest and his squad disembarked first and then stood waiting for them. The Peculiar stepped forward proudly and led Jillan and Freda onto the island. As his foot touched solid ground, he met the priest's eye fearlessly.

'Welcome to Shangrin,' the priest said smoothly, performing a short bow. 'This honour guard will see you to the palace, for you are to be Her Majesty's honoured guests.'

'Oh, there's no need for any fuss.' The Peculiar waved him away.

'Her Majesty insists. Besides, the People will want to see and welcome the noble liberators of the south as we go.'

'They will?' Jillan asked in amazement, already feeling better now that he was off the ship.

'Why of course, brave warrior,' the priest replied, bowing again. 'All know how the plague in the south tragically caused the mania of holy Saint Azual. All know that in his confusion he turned on his own People, blaming an entire town for causing the plague. The story of the defence of Godsend is an inspiration to us all. Such sacrifice! It is an example worthy of the Book of Saviours itself. And to think you even fought off pagans from the mountains, who thought to take cruel advantage of the People's travails.

'All are proud and give thanks for the aid our Queen brought to you in your hour of need, for by it she showed her love for all the People of the Empire, and demonstrated how through love, faith and unity all are saved from the Chaos. The south and the west stood together and should always remain so married, so that from their happy union there can be continued joy and glorious issue. Truly Her Majesty is the holy Queen of hearts, and of the sacred heart itself. And now you have at last come to consummate the sacrament performed in Godsend.

'I am so humbled to be in the presence of the Saviours-inspired Jillan Hunterson, the indomitable Freda and the uncomplaining servitor Anupal. And yet even in that humility I am ashamed, for I have made much of my office while you travelled anonymously and without any selfish desire for recognition or praise.'

'Well, your story isn't exactly how—' Jillan began.

'How we would want ourselves known,' the Peculiar cut in. 'We are not vainglorious heroes. We are not shining knights. It is the People who finally triumphed in all this, not ourselves as individuals. We are but simple pilgrims come to give thanks to Her Majesty for the kindness she rendered unto us.'

'Oh, sweet souls and surrender! Never have any been so loving and loved!' The priest wept. 'I now understand I had not known beauty till now. My heart trembles and swells.'

The Peculiar cleared his throat. 'Very good. Well, we are eager to pay our respects to Her Majesty, so we should probably be moving along, eh?'

'Say no more!' the priest declared, all a-flutter. 'You there, begin the procession and we will progress to the palace.'

The honour guard of Heroes marched away smartly, their armour and helmets gleaming virtuously, leading Jillan and his companions through a giant arch in the city's walls. As they entered Shangrin, a roar of adulation rose from the crowds lining the streets and echoed off the sky.

'Hear how even the heavens cheer as those we so love arrive in the holy city!' the priest sang with fervour, his eyes glistening. 'Oh, praise be!'

'Jillan, I love you!' cried a comely maiden. 'He is so handsome.'

'I thought you said I was plain,' Jillan shouted to the Peculiar above the din.

'There's no accounting for taste. She's probably carried away with the moment. She can't have smelt you, for your recent illness really hasn't increased your appeal to any but a warthog.'

'He looked at me!' screamed a matronly woman who fainted on the spot.

'Freda, everything I have is yours!' yelled a giant of a man.

'He looks about your size too.' The Peculiar nudged the rock woman.

Freda became bashful and pushed the Peculiar away, sending him reeling into the delighted crowd, causing all sorts of giddy mayhem.

'I touched Anupal!'

'Yikes! Get off! Help!' yelped the Peculiar, and he had to be rescued by a number of burly Heroes.

'Jillan, bless my child! He is named after you!'

'Just wave your hand about. A bit of mummery will suffice,' the Peculiar counselled.

Jillan did as suggested and the crowd became even more enthusiastic.

'And me, Jillan!'

'Here! Here!'

Jillan grinned from ear to ear. It felt like the first time he'd smiled in ages, since leaving Godsend. Perhaps since his parents had died. It was the first time in his life that he actually felt like a hero, without any embarrassment, anxiety, grief, self-doubt or guilt. Tears of happiness came to his eyes.

Even Freda seemed to be overcoming her usual shyness. The crowd had begged her to put down her hood and she'd done as they asked. The People of Shangrin had poured out their compassion and love for her and she'd laughed aloud with pleasure – the first time Jillan had heard her laugh anywhere but deep in her chest. She stood straighter and taller than he'd ever noticed before too, almost as tall as the many-storeyed buildings on either side of them, almost as high as the sky itself.

And the Peculiar was suddenly charged with more energy than Jillan had known before. The deity danced, spun, leapt and soared. He was everywhere at once, making the People laugh riotously, dance dizzily and sing madly. He even seized a young girl in his arms and flew the length of a street and back with her. Then, placing her gently back on her feet, he kissed her hand and returned her to the care of her grateful mother once more. He was a god of the People once more, and they loved him for it.

'Truly, this place is heaven!' Jillan breathed.

'Truly this region has become a hell,' Saint Praxis admonished Minister Stixis, 'because of what you have done. I see now it was you all along. You did more than any other to bring about the undoing of the holy Saint who was counsellor, careful farmer, tender gardener, mother and father of the south. Where he had given well-judged advice, you then followed with smiling subversion. Where he sowed the seeds for a rich harvest, you would come and gorge those seeds down before they could grow. Where he had cattle safely penned, you would throw the gates open at night. Where he showed the People the love of a parent, you would whisper to your siblings that you had been shown a greater love by the Saint, and thus cause jealousy and division. *You* have been a main agent of the Chaos in this region! No wonder the Chaos-driven plague had not touched Heroes' Brook, for this town was already in the thrall of evil! No wonder that the bane of the Empire manifested in this region, for you had done so much to create the conditions for it. It was *you* who aided wily Izat when she entered this region in order to keep the bane out of Azual's righteous grasp. But for such meddling, Azual might have had the boy far sooner. It was *you* who allowed her to take innocent children of Heroes' Brook as her own. Do not deny your calumny, for though your mind is hers, I see enough to apprehend the truth! She has always sought to undermine this region, has she not? Tell me!'

Although he sweated profusely, and although he'd been stretched on the restraining frame so as to cause him extreme pain, the Minister's expression remained one of unnatural calm. 'Will I deny my devotion to her? Will I recant my love and allegiance? Never! She is purity and love, where you are ugly hate, pathetic Praxis!'

The torturer fidgeted, expecting and hoping to be called forward, but Saint Praxis gestured for him to stay where he was. 'You will confess what you know of her designs, false Minister. I will not permit you to conspire and hide any more. I shall strip away the lies, ideas and images that you hid behind when manipulating the People. Without the circlet of sun-metal with which you hid yourself from fair Azual when conniving with Izat, you cannot deny me. I will push here, like this, pull there and tear everything away.'

Things broke in the Minister's mind and he screamed as blood poured from nose, eyes and ears. He screamed until his throat was gone and he could only gurgle.

But the Saint was not about to relent. 'I will constrict the blood here, so that obstinate part of you starves and whithers. Increase the blood here to create an unbearable pressure. Why do you protest, Minister? This is precisely what you did to the mind and soul of this region. Did you not ignore the protests of the innocent when you created a perversion of the holy Empire? You created a monster of this region! And passionate Azual became distracted with grief beyond endurance, for what parent can remain sane when they know they must put down their own murderous child? I will ease the pressure now, not as respite, but so that you do not lose consciousness and escape facing your responsibility as your own crimes are visited upon you. Come now, confess her designs!'

'She . . .' The Minister shuddered, the whites of his eyes scarlet, his voice ruined.

'Yes?'

'. . . is . . . love.'

'Very good, but we're going over old ground here. Let me pinch that off for you. There! Now, what things have you told her? You have told her of Samnir's visit to Heroes' Brook, yes?'

'Yes.'

'Good. Does she plot against Samnir too?'

'No.'

'Why not?'

'Samnir is also one of her children.'

'What?' the Saint hissed. 'I see it all now! Samnir has always been her pawn. On her behalf, it was he who nurtured Jillan and then helped him escape Godsend when his magic killed Karl. Now I think on it, Samnir was the only guard on the south wall right next to the home of Jillan's parents. And Maria and Jedadiah were originally from the unholy town of New Sanctuary! Blessed Saviours preserve us! Did not some of the original inhabitants of New Sanctuary come out of the west also? What vast and evil scheme is here? Oh, but it seeks to become as large as the Empire itself! Only holy war can save us. Every man, woman and child in Godsend must be put to the sword, for I know that under Samnir she will have also made them hers. Stixis, what others are hers in this region? Quickly!'

'She is here,' the Minister whispered happily, black tears of joy coursing down his pale cheeks. 'Thank you, Mistress.' He began to choke.

'No!' shouted Saint Praxis, grabbing the Minister's chin and looking into his eyes. 'You will not take him from me! I see you in there, Izat, do you hear me? I accuse you of the murder of holy Azual, do you hear? Saviours damn your soul!' He turned his vengeful gaze on the shaking Captain Callinor strapped to the other restraining frame in the punishment chamber.

'H-H-Holy one!' the Captain squealed, his eyes shut. 'I am yours, as the blessed Saviours are my witness! Be merciful, I beg you. As a Hero, I have sworn my loyalty to the Empire on the holy book.'

'Loyalty to the Empire!' the Saint spat. 'The word is sullied by your foul mouth. Torturer, remove his teeth and then cut off his lips and tongue. If he makes any sound after that, remove his lower jaw and throw it to the dogs outside.'

'As is your will, holy one!' the torturer replied with childlike glee, selecting large pincers from among his other implements.

'I will tell you anything, confess anything!' the Captain gibbered. 'Please, holy one, I beg you! Blessed Saviours protect me!'

'You will not mention them again, you foresworn knave! You have consorted with the enemies of the Empire and will never know salvation. The goods of the Empire which you have already smuggled to Godsend will allow the enemy to withstand any siege for longer, and that will cost my good General yet more lives. The lives of innocent brave souls who have never done you wrong. The lives of men to whom you should have been a brother but are instead a back-stabbing murderer. How is it you can ask me to be merciful, rogue? Should I allow good men to die and bad to live? Should I name the sun as the moon? Should I name the Saviours as devils? Should I remove my own tongue rather than your own? Would that satisfy you and the Chaos creatures with whom you consort? Torturer, do not delay!'

'Noo!'

The torturer came forward and grabbed the Captain's jaw. The struggling officer kept his mouth tightly shut, beseeching with his eyes. The torturer grunted in irritation. 'Holy one, may I cut off his lips first? It will make it easier.'

'What?' Saint Praxis answered, bringing his eyes away from the dark corners of the room, where he'd been searching for more enemies. They were everywhere! All around him. Who knew if she still had other spies in the region? Who knew if there were assassins stalking him even now? 'Oh. Yes. Of course. Don't bother me with details. You know your business. I will see you invested as a holy administrator of divine retribution. You must be given a certain licence to operate, for there is far more work to be done than I had previously imagined. You must oversee the recruitment of more torturers and see this region turned into a holy charnel house. I will see you anointed High Torturer of the Empire. Carry on.'

There was a *thump* at the door and Saint Praxis jumped. He moved round the room so that the torturer was between him and the entryway. 'I said I was not to be disturbed, guard! Through you I can see others there. Is that the General? What does he want now?'

The General's voice came back through the door. 'Holy one, does Captain Callinor still live? I believe he can still be of use to us. May I enter and explain, lest we are overheard?'

The General came inside the small chamber. Four of Captain Skathis's men watched him closely from outside. The General spoke quickly.

'It is fitting,' the Saint said slowly. 'Very well, but you will take personal responsibility for the success or failure of this plan, General.'

'Gladly, holy one. The morale of the men is already low enough without their having to hear of the Captain of Heroes' Brook being tortured nigh unto death. This way, the Captain will have a soldier's death and our struggle may be greatly foreshortened.'

'He will need his tongue, lips and jaw for this, yes?' the torturer asked disappointedly.

'I fear so.' The General nodded.

'What about his teeth?'

'Those too.'

The room into which Jillan was shown was bigger than his parents' entire house. There was a bed as big as his kitchen! The floor was of gold-flecked marble and there was a sunken bathing pool in one corner bigger than Godsend's duck pond. There were rich tapestries on the wall, which depicted scenes of scantily clad youths chasing through forests and around small hillocks. Jillan blushed to see them and turned away, only to find the pretty chambermaid standing right behind him.

'I am to prepare milord for Her Majesty's feast.' The girl Keren curtseyed, her eyes cast down demurely but with a pronounced cleavage on display as she lowered herself before him. 'Milord has travelled a long way, yes?'

Jillan found himself uncomfortably warm. 'Yes,' he managed.

Keren rose and looked with some concern at what he was wearing, biting her bottom lip. Her eyes were the colour of light oak, nothing like the sky blue of Hella's own. 'The road was dusty, yes?'

He became very self-conscious. He knew he must appear a filthy village oaf to her. 'And I smell of horses, right? The cloak isn't mine by the way. And, no, I didn't steal it off a beggar. We came playing the part of humble beggars, you see.'

'Quite convincingly, milord.' She dimpled. 'If it please you, milord, the palace tailor has made up a suit of clothes so that you may present yourself without shame or apology to Her Majesty.' She stepped even closer to him and started to undo one of the buckles on his armour. He felt her gentle breath on his cheek.

'What are you doing?' he squeaked.

'Why, helping milord out of his armour so that he might bathe. The water in the pool is quite warm.'

'It's all right! I can undress myself.'

Flushed, he stepped away and finished removing his armour on his own. He stripped down to his small clothes, relieved that Keren kept her eyes averted, and then quickly stepped down into the pool before he could feel too exposed. He gasped involuntarily as the heat of the gently steaming water penetrated his muscles. It was a blissful feeling.

'I didn't realise how sore I was!' he called out.

There was a light touch on his back and he leapt upwards with a panicky shout. Keren was there in the water with him, entirely naked.

He couldn't help noticing it because she was now right there in front of him. She was quite clearly naked. Her breasts were round and pert, her nipples a dark pink.

'What are you doing?'

She looked confused. 'I thought to help milord bathe. That is one of the tasks of the chambermaid. Does it not please you?'

'I-I am not used to anyone helping me bathe.' He moved his hands down to cover his embarrassment.

'This is how the lords and ladies of Her Majesty's court always bathe. Is this not the practice in the south?'

He shook his head.

Keren moved towards him. He retreated.

She stopped. Her eyes became tearful. 'If I am not to milord's liking, another maid can be brought to milord. Or a boy?'

'No! No. There's no need. Why are you crying? You . . . you are to my liking, honestly!'

'If I do not please milord, then Her Majesty will be angry. I will be punished! How else can we worship the blessed Saviours except by the ardent expression of our love for the holy Empire, its most courtly People and Her Majesty?'

*Where are we?* the taint suddenly shouted in Jillan's head, making him wince. *How did we get here, Jillan? What's happening? And why has she got no clothes on? What are you doing? What about Hella?*

Jillan ground his teeth together. 'Shut up! Go away!'

Keren sobbed and put her hands to her mouth.

'No, not you! I was talking to someone else.'

'It's all right, milord. I understand.' Keren turned away. She showed him her back, her slender, beautiful back. Her shoulders were shaking, he realised.

'Keren, come back!'

*Let her go.*

'Leave me be, damn you! I don't owe *her* anything!'

Alarmed now, Keren hurried out of the pool and slipped back into her dress. 'Milord is clearly overwrought from his long journey and needs rest. I will leave him and return when Her Majesty is ready to receive him, and when he is calmer.'

*Forget this chit of a thing. She's clearly meant to distract you from* whatever else is going on. Jillan, you've got Hella and Godsend to save. You shouldn't be here cavorting with some innocent sex-slave of the Saint. What are you thinking? And since when did Saints start styling themselves as kings and queens? It all stinks, stinks as badly as you do right now. Come on, get yourself washed and then we can find out what's really going on.

'Just for once!' Jillan groaned as he watched Keren leave the room. 'Just for once I didn't want to have to be constantly thinking of others. Why couldn't you just have let me have those few moments? She was willing, compliant.'

*You know she wasn't.*

'Damn, damn, damn! One kiss wouldn't have hurt. And Hella certainly kissed that bastard Haal. Perhaps they even—'

*Don't. I've already told you I don't believe what went on, even though we saw it. There was something that just wasn't right about it. It didn't fit. It was wrong.*

'Too bloody right it was wrong! And *I* was wrong, wrong to think she was different, wrong to think Samnir and the others were any less selfish than anyone else, and wrong to think there was any point to any of this. And why should the People of Godsend have to risk everything? They need to live, just like everyone else. I hope they have the sense simply to surrender to the Empire's army.'

*See! Look what a simple scene with a silly girl has done to you! She's got you forgetting yourself and giving up. Do not underestimate this Saint! She will have been watching you through the girl's eyes, remember. She probably got some voyeuristic pleasure out of it. What have you done with Freda? She wouldn't approve of this. And I never thought I'd care enough to ask, but where's Miserath?*

'Freda will rest once she's seen the royal gardens. There's some rock garden that they're keen to show her or something, although I don't understand how you can grow rocks. As to Miserath, who knows? I bet he hasn't frightened off any chambermaid. I bet he's got more than one as well.'

*Doubt it. Heard a story that he had a thing for goats.*

'What? That's . . . Is that possible? I—'

*Stop trying to picture it. Oh, that's sick. Look, think of the chambermaid again if you must.*

*

'What have I done? Let me out!' Freda pleaded. 'Have I upset Her Majesty?'

A spear tipped with sun-metal came through the bars set into the tiny chamber's door and jabbed her in the arm. She cried out in pain and fear.

'Quiet! That's as warning to you not to cause me any trouble. Try and escape and I'll use nails of sun-metal to pin you to the wall. I've been told all about you, demon. Don't be trying to pass through the walls or floor, because it's a waste of time. Ironwood, see! They tell me you won't be getting through it no ways.'

Freda had punched at the door and walls a few times when they'd first tricked her into the confined space, but done little more than scratch the surface of the densely grained wood. It had a metallic smell to it that got in the back of her throat and made her feel sick and weak.

'I don't like it in here!' she wailed. 'I haven't done anything wrong! There must be a mistake. We are guests of the Queen.'

'I said quiet! Any more and I'll have your tongue taken out, hear? I ain't gonna let any demon get its snake-twisty words into my head.'

'Friend Anupal! Friend Jillan! Help me!'

The spear came back, laying her open and searing her all at once. 'Scream if you want then. See if I care! No one can hear you down here. See how you like this! And this!'

Freda cried. Why were they doing this? She didn't understand. It made being alive the worst thing she'd ever known.

'Better make yourself comfortable, demon, as you're going to be rotting in this oubliette for a long, long time, and I'm going to make sure I get all the enjoyment I can out of it!'


'Sweet Majesty! Radiant Queen!'

'Darling Cassanon, it has been too long! Forgive me, but I could not wait to see you. Your companions need their rest, I know, but as I recall you were always quite tireless. And it has been so long!' Saint Izat declared, offering the Peculiar her hand.

The Peculiar, dressed in cloth of gold valuable enough to ransom a kingdom, climbed the few stairs up to the throne, knelt and chastely kissed Izat's finger ring. The attendant crowd of courtiers sighed as one to see this perfectly appointed, exquisitely mannered and breath-stoppingly handsome suitor present himself to their beloved Queen. A number of ladies had to be supported and fanned, so overwhelmed were they by the romantic beauty of the scene.

With perfect poise, the Peculiar retreated to the audience floor before any could think him too forward or presumptuous. 'Your Majesty, each moment out of your presence was a new death to me more dreadful than the last. I could only endure it because it was so commanded by the blessed Saviours, who in their divine mercy willed that I see you again. And here I am returned to heaven and its Queen.'

'Ah, that tongue of yours so pleasures me, darling Cassanon.'

Courtiers tittered in amusement, but none were shocked, for they were at ease with the love of their Queen. Where there was such great love, there was no room for outrage or embarrassment.

'To pleasure you is the only reason for my coming.'

'Cassanon, it is naughty of you to tease and taunt me, though it quite quickens me.' Izat pouted. 'There must also be a reason for you bringing your two companions, the young prince and the woman of such hard looks every lord here cries to be punished by her?'

'Ma'am, your beauty is such that its fame has spread as far as the unworthy south. My companions would not let me rest until I had escorted them safely here. They are unseemingly eager to know Your Majesty.'

'We will allow it, procurer though it make you, my generous Cassanon. And in return you must have some other gift of me. Tell me what you would have. Name it and it is yours.'

The Peculiar delicately licked his lips. 'Your Majesty, my selfish interest lies in that which is below.'

The Saint put her hands into her lap and smiled. Her velvet and diamond-studded dress comprised a many-layered skirt and a high-necked fitted bodice. Although the ensemble gave the initial impression of being constraining and forbidding, careful examination revealed artfully placed slits in the fabric that allowed her to breathe freely, and allowed those who looked upon her tantalising glimpses of her creamy skin beneath. Her cheeks were rouged to a healthy glow and her lips were ripe and full, but few noticed this as they were caught in the power of her gaze. It was a gaze that knew every thought, feeling and emotion of man. It was a gaze that knew you intimately. It caressed you, massaged you and hurt you. It devoured you. Even the Peculiar struggled to remain immune to it. He was reminded vividly of the primitive lust and commingling carnality he'd shared with her aeons before, the closest he'd come to a genuine and pure union with any mortal, although she was perhaps more than that now. Izat knew the fact and thrilled in it, loving that he twitched at that moment. She trembled with excitement. 'Then what I have below is yours, my magnificent Cassanon. Come, let us go together, so that you may have a private viewing.'

She rose and her court bowed and curtseyed to the floor, where they remained until she had led the Peculiar out of the oversized and extravagantly painted throne room. She took them along corridors decorated with friezes and mosaics depicting scenes from the Book of Saviours. Even the battles contained unusually high numbers of nudes, each in some compromising position or other.

'Surely that wouldn't fit there. And is that meant to be a picture of me?' the Peculiar asked, his eyes and mouth wide.

'Oh, it would fit. It just takes practice. Yes, I think the artist got carried away. I don't remember it ever being that large.'

'Well, if you'd like—'

'Later. After you have seen the temple. That is why you've come here, is it not? I know that you use the boy to search for Haven. The fact that you are here and wish to go below tells me that the temples of the Geas can somehow help you with that. Afterwards, we can discuss what you will do for me in return.'

'In return?' the Peculiar asked, his eyes becoming hooded.

She didn't bother to look back at him. 'Yes. It would seem I am free of the blessed Saviours for now. I don't know how, but soon after the battle at Godsend I was simply . . . released. Perhaps reprisals took place within the Great Temple, who can say? Anyway, I am free. I had almost forgotten what it felt like. I feel young again. Alive. Giddy, almost. I have the boy to thank for it, do I not? And you, perhaps? But you will help me remain this way once I have given you what you want, will you not, Cassanon, Miserath, Peculiar, or whatever your name is? Otherwise, I may be forced to hand you back into the gentle care of the Empire.'

Now she stopped and stared into his eyes. He considered for a moment and, with some reluctance, nodded. 'I see now why you are a queen . . . Your Majesty. You may consider it a bargain struck.'

Satisfied, she led him deeper into the island, through small iron gates, down narrow sloping stairs, along culverts and across hidden courtyards where water cascaded, trickled, spouted and splashed. There was a musical quality to the fountains and falls, and the Peculiar thought he almost heard the strains of his brother Akwar's voice. He paid close attention to it all so that he would be able to direct or lead Freda and Jillan after the evening's feast.

Saint Izat took him through grottoes and caves, until they moved from stepping stone to stepping stone across an endless underground lake. The water carried a soft light and seemed bottomless. And the water was every conceivable colour, every possibility of life and form drifting, swirling, shifting and tumbling around them.

'These stones have no base or anchor. They should not be possible,' the Peculiar mused.

'This is holy water.' The Saint shrugged. 'In the past it melted or drowned all those who were not faithful to Akwar. He *allowed* the stones, one of his faithful once told me, so that those seeking baptism or his blessing for the first time would be able to approach the temple in the centre. It was said that those who were already his servants could walk through or on the water.'

The Peculiar snorted. 'All a bit dramatic, but it tends to impress the mortals. Lot of good it eventually did him, though. He was always too wet to get very far with the elseworlders.'

'I suppose. Shame, though, because they say this place used to be far prettier and more wonderful. It would rain upside down here. There were ice sculptures that walked and talked. Water nymphs would make love to you in the depths.' She shivered. 'Delicious! And worth drowning for, I imagine, although the faithful could breathe the water as easily as the followers of Wayfar could ride the wind.'

'All very useful, I'm sure. That light there. The temple?'

Izat nodded. 'The central island is a floating piece of clear ice. The walls of the temple are clear too, so clear it almost isn't there. The light is from the giant bowl of sun-metal placed inside.'

'And that bowl is my brother's prison?'

The Saint glanced at the Peculiar. 'It is. You will not make me regret showing you this place.'

'No. Akwar got what he deserved. I tried to warn him, but he refused to listen. He must bear the consequences of his divinely stupid choice. And I am bound by the compact I made with the elseworlders. For all that, his is a cruel fate. I hear the bowl ringing, but it is his constant scream. The sun-metal heats him and boils him dry. He condenses on the frozen ceiling above and grows as an icicle that drips back down into the bowl and is heated and boiled again, over and over without end. An agony of forever.'

'It is the price.' Izat nodded sadly, a single tear sitting upon her cheek like a jewel. She was beautiful.

They reached the invisible island and set foot on it. The Saint invited the Peculiar to enter through the gold-lined gap in the thick wall, which served as the entrance. 'You will want to pay your respects to your brother since you are here, darling Cassanon.' Her voice thrummed like a rapid heartbeat, pushing him forward.

He stepped into the gap and stopped. He whirled back round, but she was already moving. A gold section of wall slid down between them. Another section slid down behind him, trapping him inside the temple wall. There was a faint hiss as the seal became complete. He stood in a semi-opaque box of gold, a box that had an eerie familiarity.

Her laughter tinkled and she clapped her hands. 'Why, my darling Cassanon, I have caught you! I did not think it could be so easily done. Are you quite yourself, my love, or has naughty little me turned your pretty little head?'

He shook his head and assumed his spectral form, ready to step free even if it cost him the sun-metal around his brow. 'But, my dear, you know there is no prison of mortal design that can hold me. I am *otherness*. I am the darkness to Sinisar's light. I am the inferno to Akwar's ice. I am the vacuum to Wayfar's air. I am the instability and fracture to Gar's diamond and stone. I am the exteriority to their interiority. A prison must be constructed of at least one of the aspects of my four brothers, but I am *other* to those aspects, to prevent their omnipotence. I am the shadow that passes through every barrier. I am the unheard scream that wakes people in the night. No prison can hold me. Surely you know this.' He prepared to escape to demonstrate the point.

'Ah, ah, ah! I wouldn't do that if I were you. You are encased in sun-metal, my darling, and will get quite a nasty surprise if you try to escape.'

'There will be joins in the sun-metal. There always are. I will escape through those.'

She stuck out her bottom lip. 'Ahhh! My poor darling still hasn't worked it out. He still hasn't realised the genius and wonder of his prison. You see, trapped between the magical layers of Akwar's ice, there is a layer of gas. A very special gas. My clever little sun-smith is the first to succeed in making a gas from sun-metal.'

'A gas?' The Peculiar repeated in consternation. He became uncertain for one of the first times in his existence. *A gas!* He worked through the implications at furious speed.

'Allow me to instruct you, my darling. The gas is lethal to anything that lives. If you try to pass through it as you are now, it will fatally disrupt your being. If you try to break the ice, the gas will be absorbed through your outer surface, no matter how hard you make it, for not even you can create an outer surface of absolute inertness, now can you? Isn't it simply marvellous? I do believe that I have set you a problem that could keep you entertained for years, for millennia, forever! Not that you will be allowed so long, obviously.'

'What do you want, Izat? And do make it amusing, for my patience wears thin.'

'You will tell me precisely how to use the boy and the temples to find Haven. You will tell me how I can keep the Saviours at bay. You will tell me your secrets, my darling. You will do these things or I will deliver you as part of a bargain I make with the Saviours.'

'I am their representative, you foolish mortal. You know I am bound to them.'

'Oh, do not seek to trick me so simply, my darling. You are forgetting how well I know you. You are bound and *not* bound. I'm sure the Saviours are quite angry with you for what you got up to in Godsend, even if Azual was a frightful bore. So, you see, I think I have been foolish only in my feelings for you. Truly, it hurts that you think so little of me. And during all the centuries you didn't once send me a message or any other token of love. Really, I am very cross with you, you know. No sign of affection. Nothing! I thought I meant something to you. You know how finely attuned, how sensitive, my feelings are, and yet you took not the slightest care of them.' She dabbed at her eyes with a lace handkerchief. 'You have been simply beastly. I am not sure I will ever be able to forgive you for this, darling Cassanon.'

'I was busy,' he said a little guiltily. 'Look, you know every time I help the sun rise, it is my token of love so that all may see your beauty better. How can you do this to me if you love me as much as you say?'

'And see! You've made my face paint run. Oh dear, this is terrible. Still, all is fair in love and war, is it not, my darling? You have taught me that. I must be cruel to be kind, both to myself and to you.'

He took a steadying breath, but found himself vastly irritated nonetheless. 'Listen carefully then, and understand what it is you do. You have imprisoned an undying god and inspired his divine and infinite ire. Whether it be a day or a millennia from now, I will somehow be free of this childish box of yours. If you deliver me to the elseworlders, they will eventually release me to do their bidding. And then, my dear, I will come for you. There will be nowhere you can hide, no disguise I cannot penetrate. Destroy your looks as you will, and still I will find you through the wind, earth, water and light of this world. Leave this world for another, if you can, and I will still find you wherever you go in the wide cosmos. With every gust of wind, you will feel my angry breath coming up behind you. The burning sun will be my cruel eye looking down upon you. Every crack in the earth will be there waiting for you to tread upon it, so it can open up and swallow you. Every falling star will be me descending out of the sky to destroy you. You will be unable to sleep again, as you watch and wait. You will be too afraid to move lest the world around you becomes aware of you and turns on you. This is the curse you bring upon yourself, *foolish mortal*!'

She met his eye with cold hard hatred. 'Broken thing. Fallen vanity. Empty being. Ugly unreason. Aggressive goblin. Masturbating malevolence. Molested male. You have brought this on yourself. I was left with little choice in all this. It cannot be coincidence that I now have two of the pagan gods in my collection. Perhaps I will have them all before I am done. I shall leave you to reflect on and hate yourself. I have more worthy subjects who require my attention. When I return, you will give me a clear answer one way or the other. And I know what that answer will be. It will be a new sort of bargain between us, one where I dictate the terms, one where you will never again be able to go and leave me all alone.'

The Peculiar folded his legs under him and sank down onto the cold floor in order to think. He had already underestimated her once and was not about to rush into doing so a second time. There would be a way out. There was always a way out. It would just take time, although he was not sure just how much he had, or any of them had.

Jillan tugged at his stiff collar and, slightly overwhelmed, followed Keren along the sumptuously decorated corridors of Shangrin's palace. They passed a goodly number of people standing in conversation, promenading in pairs or hurrying by on some errand. All bowed or curtseyed to Jillan as soon as they saw him. At first he'd returned the courtesy with a clumsy bow of his own, but this only seemed to cause consternation or nervous laughter.

'The Queen has named you a prince. You outrank them. Don't bow so deeply to them,' Keren explained. 'Just nod your head.'

'Oh. Sorry. Should I bow to the Queen?'

'Just when you first meet her.

*Idiot! She's a Saint. A servant of the Empire. Don't you dare bow to her.*

*I'm still her guest,* Jillan thought back. *It doesn't hurt to be polite.*

They came to a pair of golden doors. Keren opened one of them and ushered Jillan through. 'Good luck. Try not to be nervous!' And then she closed the door and was gone.

He turned slowly to face the room. His mouth was dry all of a sudden and his palms were clammy. He swallowed, his Adam's apple rubbing on the high collar of his white shirt. He'd never worn anything so costly and uncomfortable in all his life. He'd felt like a thief when he'd first put it on, and like a fraud now he was wearing it. And he'd never seen such a brilliant white. He was constantly worried he would make it dirty.

'Ah, my prince!' she purred as she came across the room towards him. 'I have so looked forward to seeing you again. Imagine my joy when Samnir informed me that you might be coming to visit me. I am so glad you chose to accept the invitation of our last meeting. I was worried we'd got off on the wrong foot and you'd got a poor impression of me. Samnir can be a little possessive and jealous sometimes, and it makes him say things he wouldn't ordinarily.'

Queen Izat wore a robe of scarlet silk that was open to her waist and only protected her modesty when she wasn't moving. She was coming towards him and he wasn't sure where to look. Blushing, he remembered to bow and set his eyes on his feet for a few seconds in order to try and regain his composure. As he came back up, he breathed her heady scent and looked into her large inviting eyes. 'S-Samnir told you we were coming?'

She took his hand and led him over to a low table with cushions arranged around it on the thickly carpeted floor. 'I thought we could dine here, rather than deal with the formality and fuss of a court banquet. We can talk more freely like this and properly get to know each other, yes? Be a dear and pour the wine for us, would you?' Izat reclined on the cushions and watched him.

His hand shaking, he raised the precious bottle of glass off the table and poured the red into the two waiting crystal goblets. He carefully lifted one with both hands and offered it to her. Her fingers brushed his as she accepted it. His skin tingled.

'To us!' she toasted and sipped, giving him an encouraging smile.

He raised his own goblet and gulped at its contents.

*Us? How can there be any us? What are we even doing here, Jillan?*

'Y-Your Majesty,' he said thickly. 'You have a very nice palace.'

She laughed attractively. 'How sweet of you to say so, my dear prince! It is at your disposal, as am I and my armies. It is the least I can do for the prince who liberated us.'

'Liberated?' His thoughts were muzzy. What did she mean?

'Why, of course! In bravely striking back against the Empire's tyranny, you freed me. Perhaps it was as a consequence of some of the unnoticed help I gave Godsend at the time. Jillan, you freed me and made me yours. I am yours to command. Together, we can save Godsend! Why, your glass is empty. Allow me.'

She leaned over to serve him, her silks falling open. She was the most beautiful woman he'd ever seen.

'Yes.' He nodded. 'We must save Godsend. Please save Godsend before it is too late.'

'Of course. They have made Praxis a Saint, you know? He is a maniac. Do you know he has tortured and expelled my representative in Hyvan's Cross? And killed others. It is unthinkable! He hates Samnir because of Samnir's love for me. I must save my beloved soldier.'

'Yes, save Samnir,' he slurred.

'Anything for you, my prince! I am so glad you are here. It is so lonely being a queen. So long have I waited for one who was my equal and could be my husband. And here you are, here to claim your prize. Say you will be mine, my prince!'

She was suddenly right before him, her lips open and seductive, her breath hot.

*It's the wine! It's got something in it. Her blood! Jillan, fight it! Jillan! Can you hear me?*

He fumbled for his magic but could not get a proper grip on it. He fell back from her, flailing among the cushions. She pounced on him, pinning him down with her weight, straddling him with her thighs. Her smile was predatory now as she pulled a thin tube of sun-metal from her hair and plunged it into his neck.

# CHAPTER 9:

# Pray for each other

They came through the Gate high above the ground of the sixth realm and were hurled down. Ba'zel had no idea how far they fell before they impacted, for there was no frame of reference. The violent collision came suddenly, the elder beneath him having to cushion much of the shock. Ba'zel made his forelimb as dense, hard and sharp as he could and neatly separated the other's head from his shoulders. As sand rained back down on them in their crater, threatening to bury them, bright jewels of blood and life energy were scattered before Ba'zel, yet they just as quickly dulled and sank from view. He frantically scooped up and ingested what he could, but took in more of the absorbing sand than anything else. He hardly knew who he was and realised the stuff must be leeching him from the inside! He seized the elder's head, which blinked once at him, pulled open its cranial plates and sank his stone fangs into the revealed gore.

It was only as he was licking the last of the elder's mind and essence from around his mouth that he realised he had just committed the most fundamental of crimes – cannibalism. Only an insane being would consume its own kind, and it was said such consumption only caused greater insanity. Already the memories of the elder were crowding in on him, far more than his own limited experience could digest and contain. They threatened to overwhelm him. He heard another's voice in his mind. He was invaded. It was too much! Ba'zel vomited the gore back out, only holding onto enough to see him able to repair his own being, but not so much that it would drown him.

He wasted no time disinterring himself from the sucking sand and looked around. He knew he would need to find somewhere to replenish himself again very soon, or end up dried out by the insatiable desert.

He looked up at the kaleidoscopic sky. Colourful sheets of plasma chased across it, constantly clashing, merging, stretching or fracturing. At one moment there were patterns, at the next none. The sand shimmered almost as a reflection of the display above. There were scintillations of energy in the air too. It fed him, sustained him! He sighed in relief, for the first time since he'd left the home-realm not under any immediate pressure to race, deceive, frenziedly feed or fight in order to stay alive. Despite first impressions, this realm was the most hospitable he'd visited so far. He *liked* it. If he wanted, he could just stand or sit down here for millennia, thinking and contemplating. That would be closer to contentment than he'd known. No tutor Ho'zen telling him he didn't know enough, no father telling him to kill himself, no elders testing him, no Virtue . . . but that was where it all went wrong. The Virtue was coming for him. There would be no standing or sitting for millennia as long as the Virtue sought him. And the Declension in this realm would perhaps find the Geas sooner rather than later. There would be nothing in the air to sustain him, only a black sky above and killing sands all around. He could not stay here. It would be foolish to remain so close to a Gate. And it would be foolish to remain in this realm, unless he could discover some way of preventing the Declension from finding the Geas here.

He sighed and slowly turned full circle, scanning for any sign of difference among the rolling dunes. Was that something on the horizon, or was it just some trick of the shimmering air? For want of any other direction offering anything, he set off towards the something that might be nothing.

He found he quite enjoyed the walk. It was as good as just standing or sitting. He started to hope that the something would indeed turn out to be nothing, so that he could then spot another something that might be nothing and walk towards that.

But the feeling in his stomach told him the something could not be nothing. The Declension would not have placed the Gate so far from everything else that there would be no sign or obvious direction for any new arrival to pursue. An arrival would need to find the Saviours and lesser beings of this realm with all speed, so as not to delay the business of locating and seizing the Geas.

Sure enough, the something soon showed itself as a mountain of sorts. The closer he got, the closer it reached to the sky. The mountain was too uniform to be natural. It resolved itself into an enormous stepped pyramid larger than any construction he'd ever seen. It was well over a hundred levels high. The very top level was cast in sun-metal and so bright it could only be viewed askance. What giants could have constructed such a thing? There wasn't anything like it even on the home-realm. What purpose could it have? The beings who had created it had to be vast. Had they been a challenge to the Declension itself? He felt so small, so insignificant. What was he doing here? What could he possibly hope to achieve in the face of such a towering power?

He walked for a long time before he could make out more detail of what was ahead. Around the base of the pyramid were thousands of small brown huts and, beyond them, wide fields of dirty yellow crops. How could anything grow in this empty sand? The ground beneath him soon became firmer and darker. It stank badly and tiny black things buzzed and hovered in clouds. Some landed on Ba'zel's skull and tried to spike through his exterior, but he used the power of his presence to turn them to dust.

The ground was black with old blood in large areas, and brown and sticky where waste was still rotting down in others. Bleached bones poked out of the surface everywhere. He walked through fields of death, he knew. The lesser beings of this realm had to be desperate if they relied upon such fields for sustenance. Presumably they did not eat the flesh spread upon the ground because it was the meat of their own kind and would make them insane. But that meant they had to die in regular numbers to keep the ground properly manured. They would be short-lived and have to breed very young to keep their population up. And the crops did not strike him as particularly nutritious. If anything, they were likely to be weakening or poisoning because they came out of corruption and contamination. Surely such beings could not have built the pyramid, could they?

Ba'zel came to the edge of one of the outer fields, a mean plot of land where the crops were stunted and thin. A single lesser being crawled around, scraping in the sludge. Was it trying to make a furrow for a light brown sludge to ooze across the slightly darker sludge of the field? Irrigation. Was the light brown sludge the closest they had to water?

Ba'zel picked his way across the field, using the power of his presence to dry out and harden the ground beneath him so that he could make better progress. The lesser being did not look like it could be any sort of threat. Indeed, it cried out and fell onto its back – a submissive posture – upon seeing Ba'zel. It trembled as it beheld what Ba'zel's feet had done to the field. Its thoughts were easily read and understood.

'Devil!' the child-thing wailed. 'I know that I am sent to the outer field as punishment, but will you not spare me?'

'Why do you call me devil rather than Saviour?' Ba'zel asked curiously.

'B-Because you have come out of the desert, where only the devil can survive. Your feet permanently mark the earth. You have horns like a sharis. Because the prophecy says the devil will come and ask why it is not called Saviour. It will seek to ascend to the holy of holies that is meant only for the Saviours. It will seek to supplant them and they will hurl him down in their wrath. It will . . . it will bring about the end of the People, but that will also be an end to our suffering.'

Ba'zel saw that the child-thing had aged just while he'd been speaking to it and quickly dampened down the power of his presence. The child-thing was already proving to be extremely useful, so it wouldn't do to exhaust it too soon. At the same time Ba'zel smoothed away the pronounced ridges that had recently formed on his skull, so that he would not so easily be named the devil by other lesser beings.

'What is this prophecy of which you speak? Prophecy is notoriously self-referencing, child-thing. Or it only foretells something that is extremely likely to happen anyway. When enough time has passed, it is all but inevitable that the events described by the prophecy will have occurred. Think about it, child-thing, if that is not beyond you. It is all but inevitable that someone different will eventually come out of the desert. It is inevitable that they might protest at being named the devil. It is inevitable that they will ask about ascending, is it not, when this pyramid is so dominating?'

The child-thing's eyes went wide, then narrow, then wide again. 'The prophecy said the devil would challenge the nature of prophecy.'

Ba'zel sighed. 'It's a clever prophecy then. It doesn't matter what I say, does it? No! Before you interrupt, child-thing, let me guess. The prophecy said I would say that.'

The child-thing nodded, its mouth hanging open.

'And what does this prophecy say you and I will do now?'

'It . . . it says I will bring clothing to disguise you and take you to my home.'

'And then?'

'I will help you to ascend, and in return you will take me with you, at least for a few levels. You will use magic to age me so that I am old enough to be permitted ascension.'

'That seems suitable. Go then, child-thing. Bring this clothing of which you speak.'

The child-thing hesitated.

'What?'

'You are meant to say that you will eat me if I do not obey you.'

'Eat you? Oh yes, that's right. I will eat you if you do not bring this clothing. And tell no one you have seen me. Do you understand?'

The child-thing seemed more reassured, happier even, now that it had been threatened. It scampered away across the field. Ba'zel watched it go, wondering if such a small and puny thing could ever grow into the sort of giant that could build the pyramid. For he'd seen in its mind the belief that its people had built that pyramid. Generation upon generation had been sacrificed. Incredible. And yet so mundane.

In the name of belief, the People had been gathered from all across the desert, for previously they had lived in nomadic groups that had moved herds of sharis from one place of water to another. Before building the pyramid for their new gods, the People had dug down into the waterways deep beneath the desert and brought all the water together in one large reservoir and placed a holy seal upon it, for all knew water was life and power, and should only rest in the hands of the gods. Then the pyramid had been built over the reservoir. Now, all the People could have water whenever they needed it, but only as it came down from the gods at the top of the pyramid.

The People occupied the levels of the pyramid and were allowed to ascend one level each year, bringing them closer to their gods, salvation and the source of purity. For the water was cleanest when it emerged from the highest level. It then came down through the levels and was used over and over. By the time it reached the lowest levels, it was so thick that it hardly ran at all. Simple filters and squeezers had to be used to release any moisture whatsoever, and it still wasn't drinkable. The People at the very lowest levels mostly survived by using the liquid they extracted from the sludge to make a mash with some of their crops; and that mash was then fermented and strained to make a clean, light beer. And then there was the trading that went on between levels. In return for cleaner water, those at the lower levels would provide food and livestock to those above. It was an entire economy based on water. Water was life.

When a child was born, it would naturally have to start its life at the bottom of the pyramid, unless its parents had somehow accumulated sufficient resources to allow it to remain with them. Most parents gave up their children, however, allowing them to be raised by the criminals or Unclean who had been thrown down the pyramid. The children would have to work for a number of years before they were ready to be Drawn to the Saviours and allowed to ascend to the first step of the pyramid. Very occasionally, some parents would choose to give up their places on the pyramid so that they could descend with the child and raise it themselves – such parents were known to be selfish and morally compromised, for their own actions took them further away from their gods and salvation. Just as occasionally, there would be a request from on high for a child to ascend to the very highest levels. Such a child was blessed indeed, and considered too pure for the struggle of this world. Its urine would be clean and its blood pristine when it was tested – for next to water, urine and blood were the most valuable substances traded up and down the pyramid. Blood, particularly, was collected as an annual tithe by the all-powerful Levellers and their guards.

A desperate people. Desperate to live. Desperate to be clean. Desperate to ascend. Desperate to be pure. Desperate for salvation. Desperate not to fall. Desperate in so many ways. And he suspected the Geas of this realm would also be desperate. He suspected the water was running out. Water was life. Soon, there would only be the People left. They would be the Geas entire, their blood more puissant than ever. And then the Great Cull would come. Yet he was the prophesied devil of this People. It was inevitable he would come and seek to supplant their Saviours. It was predictable that the People would rise up just before the end, as the final revelation came upon them and they truly came to know their Saviours.

Content in his role, and knowing he could not escape it even if he wanted to, Ba'zel walked across the field. One of the few things he didn't like was the strong suspicion that someone knew he was coming. Damnable prophecy! Was it possible that time worked differently between the realms and that knowledge of him had arrived here long before he had? Foreknowledge? Was the Declension already waiting for him? And he really didn't like the bit in the prophecy that said they would hurl him down in their wrath. Not one bit. Was that fore-knowledge too? Had it already happened? Was that not what had already happened in the fifth realm? Had he not fallen there? And in the fourth and third realms before that? Why did the devil never win? How could he break free of the predestination of that character? How could he break free of that character even? He wanted no part of any obedience to it. He knew he must fight the Virtue Obedience. He knew prophecy said he must lose.

The devil will come and ask why it is not called Saviour.

'We'll need to get you some clothes, Torpeth,' Aspin decided as they watched the people come and go in the bustling town of Vizimouth.

'It's not that cold. My man part hasn't shrivelled at all. See?'

'I'm not talking about the cold. Stop it! I don't need to look. I'm talking about us not attracting too much attention. We're in the Empire now, surrounded by enemies. We need to pass unnoticed if we're to have any hope of finding Jillan.'

'Oh, this lot look fairly harmless. You worry too much. I know the Saint of this region. Izat. Let's just ask her where Jillan is. It'll be far quicker and far less fuss.'

'Are you mad? We'll be telling her that Jillan's in the region if she doesn't already know.'

'Do mad people know they're mad? Azual didn't, did he?'

'What? Forget that. You know what I mean. We can't let the Empire know he's here.'

'Silly ox. Everyone already knows he's here. Can't you tell? You're meant to be a reader.'

Disconcerted, Aspin looked more closely at the townsfolk. 'I don't . . . What are you talking about?'

'See how happy they all are, as if they know a secret? So it isn't a secret, see? Except to you maybe, because you're a silly ox. And the Saint always knows what's going on. She'll have seen through her People, won't she? Wouldn't be much of a Saint if she hadn't. You really shouldn't underestimate her, you know. Too many people do that. So we'll just ask.' Torpeth gurned and winked. 'She was always very accommodating when we knew each other in our younger days.' He thrust his hips suggestively.

'Eugh! Please! Just stop it, would you? Look, we can't just go prancing up to her home, knocking on the door and asking if she can come out to play.'

Torpeth looked mystified. 'Why not? Oh, do you think she might be out visiting friends? Besides, I can't put on any clothes, as I'm the naked warrior. I wouldn't be much of a naked warrior if I had clothes on, now would I, just as Izat wouldn't be much of a Saint if she didn't know what was going on? And the gods have said I'm to walk the earth naked. I don't want to go getting them all upset again, now do I?'

'Perish the thought!' Aspin muttered. 'Look, if we start parading around willy-nilly, it won't be long before they realise we're from outside the Empire. We'll be lynched before we get to ask anyone about Jillan. And you can still be the naked warrior while wearing clothes – you'll be in disguise, that's all. You wore a loincloth at the request of Praxis, as I recall.'

'Ah, well, Praxis had me caught in two conflicting oaths, you see, so I could legitimately break one oath. He's clever like that. As for this disguise idea of yours, I'm not at all sure about it. Seems a bit like cheating to me. It's more trouble than it's worth usually. You know as well as I do they won't lynch us. You can read that the worst that'll happen is they'll arrest us. And then . . . what will happen then? Let me see . . .'

'Then we'll be carted off to some punishment chamber, probably under the palace, you idiot! The Saint herself will question us and we'll be at her mercy.'

'Ah, just like the old days! It's got me quite excited, I must confess. See?'

'Listen, you're clearly more interested in seeing your old girlfriends than finding Jillan. Don't you care that he's probably in serious trouble? I've half a mind just to leave y—'

'And who will be in the cell next to ours if we end up under the palace, eh, silly ox? Can you read that at all or are you too busy huffing and snorting?'

Aspin glared at the holy man. 'I am not huffing and snorting!' he said tightly. 'I can't see what the person in the next cell has to do with anything, even if they're . . . oh . . . Jillan himself. Damn!'

Torpeth gave his companion an insufferable smile. 'So I don't need to put any clothes on?'

'No, you don't need to put any clothes on.'

'Oh, really? You should have said so before. Honestly, Aspin, you really need to take all this a bit more seriously, you know. Jillan is probably in some serious trouble, and we just don't have time for your larking about. You seem far more interested in your vulgar little fantasies about my past acquaintances than anything else. I put it down to your youth. It's all the young think about, or so I'm told. Alternatively, you might have some obsession stemming from madness.'

Aspin rubbed at his temples. 'Finished?'

'You're right. I don't have time to stand here talking to you all day. Come on. This way!'

Torpeth strutted out into the street and immediately started a commotion. People stopped to point and stare. A few jeers and shouts of encouragement went up. A large woman called out crudely and there was laughter. Torpeth's demeanour did not change. He continued on at a steady and unhurried pace. Then the strangest thing happened. People began to step aside, clearing the way for him. Now they murmured to each other and bowed respectfully. Dumbfounded, Aspin hurried to keep up.

A man fell to his knees in the muddy street. 'Holy pilgrim! Your blessing, I beg you!'

Torpeth reached out and touched the top of the bowed man's head. 'Your sins are seen and forgiven. Be a better man, so that you may love better and be more worthy of love in return.'

Men in black silk and Heroes appeared, but the People congregated in such numbers to line Torpeth's path that the priests and Heroes could not find a way through the crowds.

'All are born naked,' Torpeth said, and his words were repeated back through the crowd, like a ripple on a still pond.

Ba'zel crouched in the child-thing's brown mud hut. He kept his nasal aperture tightly closed, meaning his voice came out more resonant than usual. He didn't want to scare the child-thing, so tried loosening his vocal cords, but that only made his voice deeper. In the end he opened his nasal aperture again and kept his breathing shallow. 'You have never been Drawn, have you, child-thing?' He could tell from its prompted thoughts that it had not. Good, none of the Declension in this realm should yet be aware of his arrival. 'What is your name, child-thing?'

The child-thing shifted nervously. 'Vay,' it lied.

Incredible, that it would dare lie to a Saviour. *But I am not a Saviour as far as it is concerned, am I? Rather than my being far above it, it sees me as a lesser being. That is why I find it novel to speak to such a being, simple though it is. It is refreshing. I like it. I will be . . . . disappointed to see it die.* 'No, it is not. Your name is Suray. But you were wise to try to keep your name from me. I am the devil, after all.'

For a moment Suray was scared. He – for the child-thing was male – opened his mouth.

'How did I know? I can read your thoughts without much difficulty. I can see you live here alone. You are . . . pleased to have my company.'

'I have other friends!' Suray replied defiantly.

'Yes. The girl Sala. She is a different type of friend to me. You secretly hope she will be your life mate one day, if you reach the right level together. Oh, and you often talk to one called Basri, but he is not your friend now, because you argued.'

'Aha!' Suray said triumphantly. 'Basri told you about me, didn't he? That sneak! And you have been watching me while you were skulking out there in the desert and I was sent to the outer field for . . .'

'For stealing.'

'I did not! You take that back! Besides, if I did steal then it was because the devil told me to do it. It's your fault! You got me in trouble and sent out there deliberately, so that you could then make me disguise you and bring you among the People without anyone knowing.' Suray horrified himself with his own thoughts. He often did. He rarely slept well.

*Why do I feel sympathy for it? It is far less than me. I should not be able to identify with it in any way. Is it because I feel luckier than this Suray in having had a father to raise me? Or was I less lucky? That amused him. Was I luckier to be born a member of the Declension than a lesser being? I certainly don't feel lucky. And Suray is relatively happy with his lot. Stop! You will not envy a lesser being. You are weakening yourself and your resolve. It is the lesser being who is your devil. You are a Saviour! You will think nothing of this lesser being or it will cause you to undo yourself.* 'You stole because you were hungry, Suray. You did not need me to tell you to steal to stay alive, did you? But if you wish to blame me, if you wish me to play your devil, then I am . . . pleased to do so in return for your help. Your Saviours may blame and punish you for wishing to stay alive, but I will not. Far from it. Only beings who do what they must to survive *deserve* to survive. It is obvious, no? So, is that another bargain struck between us? I will play your devil, and you can blame me for things, if you help me in return?'

For some reason Suray looked unhappy, perhaps guilty. His voice was small as he said, 'Yes. A bargain.'

Strange. It seemed Suray did not want his devil any more. Ah, it was because he now realised the devil was of his own making. 'Ha! Tricked you!' Ba'zel said with an attempt at merriment, in order to cheer Suray up and keep him dynamic and useful.

'Oo! You dreadful creature! I knew it!' Suray said animatedly. 'How long must I stay trapped with you in here? They will eventually notice I am gone from the outer fields.'

'Only until it is dark. We will have a better chance of scaling the pyramid unobserved when it is dark. Don't worry. If anyone comes looking for you here before then, I will eat them.'

'Not Sala though!'

'Has she ever been Drawn? No. Not Sala then. We will have to take her with us, though, if she comes here.'

'Really? Would we? Can I go and get her?'

'Yes. But speak to no one. Do not even seek to explain anything to her until she is here. Trust me in this. And, remember, I will be watching you. Any false moves or secret signals to others and I will have to eat you and then disappear back into the desert. There I will vomit your twitching soul into the sand, where it will suffer forever. After, I will choose another friend and scale the pyramid with him instead. Do you understand, Suray? You have no choice in this. It is the prophecy. You cannot escape it. Therefore, you cannot be blamed for it. Play your role as I do mine. We have a bargain.'

'I don't want to obey, but I must!' Suray replied excitedly and went to the doorway. He peeped out to check the coast was clear and then ran off in a half-crouch.

Ba'zel repeated his earlier thoughts over and over while he waited. *It is the lesser being who is your devil. You are a Saviour! You will think nothing of this lesser being or it will cause you to undo yourself.*

Suray soon returned with the girl Sala. She looked much like the boy, but then all lesser beings looked much the same to Ba'zel. '. . . told you it's a surprise!' Suray was saying. 'Sala, this is the—'

'Saviour,' Ba'zel interrupted, 'who has come to take the two of you up the pyramid. I have adjudged the two of you to be too pure for this base level, and so you will ascend.'

Sala burst into tears. 'It cannot be true! I am not worthy.'

'Your humility makes you worthy, Sala. You and Suray will be happy together, with my blessing.'

Ba'zel winked at Suray. Suray beamed proudly and put his arm round Sala. She hugged him with a ferocious joy, as if her life depended upon it.

Suray and Sala led Ba'zel through the flickering darkness towards the bottom level of the pyramid. Its first step was twenty feet high. There was a flaming torch every fifty paces or so along its length. There were a few guards, but they were mainly near a staircase leading up to the next level. Ba'zel saw from Suray's thoughts that the Leveller was to be found at the head of each staircase.

'Tell me about the Levellers,' Ba'zel commanded his companions. He saw images of tall lesser beings who engendered fear in Suray and Sala. The Levellers had powers, some known but many not. It seemed that the Levellers became more powerful with each step up. It was said that those on high were close to being gods themselves, and so power-ful that they could control the weather of the realm and the amount of crops that grew from the ground. Clearly, lesser beings could not have such powers . . . could they? In any event, they should not represent any threat to a Saviour. However, Ba'zel knew that it might take him a good while to make or fight his way through all of them, by which time the Declension would have been fully alerted to his presence and have had ample time to awaken and prepare its warriors. The Levellers were therefore best avoided for as long as possible. Perhaps he could make it all the way to the Gate to the seventh without the Declension even knowing he'd been here? Suray's prophecy would then simply wait for the next Saviour that came out of the desert. Would that be possible? Could he ghost his way through? Could he be an unknown ghost, even to prophecy? Could he escape his character and predestination?

'The Levellers are to be obey—' Suray began.

'Never mind. You've already told me enough. We will climb up just there, where it is dark and there are no guards.' They ran to the wall. 'Get onto my back. See, it is broad enough for you waifs. And so we ascend.'

Ba'zel grew tiny hooks all over his limbs and moved effortlessly upwards. Within a handful of seconds, they were peering over the top of the wall. All was quiet, but the floor was covered in sleepers bundled up in blankets. Ba'zel rose. In five long steps he was at the next wall. They went up again. The next floor was so crowded that there was hardly room to move. One of the lesser beings next to the edge rolled over in its sleep and fell down onto the step below with a thud.

Sala gasped in dismay.

'Shh!' Suray said gently. 'You know the weak ones have to go on the outside. They don't die when they fall, though, not really. Their bodies are traded and used as fertiliser, so that they come back as plants. Then, when the plants are eaten, they become babies in girls' tummies and get born again, so they get another chance to ascend.'

'That's not how it happens!' Sala giggled.

''Tis too. Basri told me.'

'Basri doesn't know anything. He's never even kissed a girl.'

A curious form of reproduction if it was true, Ba'zel decided. Suray certainly believed it. Sala didn't, but had no certain knowledge of— *Enough of this.* 'Quiet. Hold tight.' They climbed to the third level. 'This level has fewer people on it.'

'Sometimes there's a fight and lots of people fall,' Suray told him. 'The guards come to stop the argument and people get jostled over the edge. Or the Leveller will decide that one of the rooms inside needs to be cleared for some reason. People lose their places then too. Displaced.'

'It's to remind us that we can always fall from grace. We must be vigilant about where we are and whom we have chosen as a neighbour. We must not become complacent. We must not think we have a right to ascend just because we have lived another year. We must constantly strive to improve ourselves and our position in order to ascend. And we must guard against our neighbours becoming complacent also, for if they get involved in a fight or jostling, they might drag us down with them,' Sala said by eager rote. 'Isn't that right, Saviour?'

'And how exactly would you guard against your neighbours becoming complacent?' Ba'zel absently wondered.

'By warning them and then, if necessary, displacing them so that I have a different neighbour. Yes, Saviour?'

'Murder, then. You would push them over the edge.'

'It is not murder,' Suray said, coming to Sala's defence. 'By falling, an individual has judged themselves. They have failed to guard against complacency, they have allowed themselves to be displaced. They are responsible for their own fall.'

'And would you guard against a complacent life mate in the same way, Suray?'

There was an uncomfortable silence. Sala held her breath.

'Well, Suray?' Ba'zel prompted.

'Never,' Suray said honestly.

'He speaks the truth, Sala.'

'Thank you, Saviour!' she whispered hoarsely. 'I would never do such a thing either.'

'She speaks the truth, Suray.'

'Thank you . . . Saviour!'

The higher they went, the fewer sleepers there were outside. Around the forty-fifth level, the step was empty, all the People instead in their own rooms inside the pyramid. There weren't even any guards to be seen in the distance. Clearly not so many People reached the age usually required by this level. Those who did would have far easier lives than those below, and would not need such close watching. There was a well-maintained watercourse with sluice gates around the step, rather than the open sewers of the lower levels.

'It's so clean!' Sala breathed.

'And the air! It's heavenly. It makes me feel wonderful, Sala!' Suray exclaimed.

'Look at the water there. It's so clear. And . . . I don't believe it! Each room has a garden outside. They have their own plants. Things I've never seen. The colours! Such green! What are those orange and yellow balls? Oh, Suray! It is the garden of paradise we have heard of from the Levellers. I am dreaming.'

'Such a beautiful dream!'

'And this is where I will leave you,' Ba'zel said. *For you are of no more use to me.* 'Find yourself an empty room and occupy it. If your presence here is challenged, tell them a Saviour brought you. I think they will welcome children here and will want to look after you, yes?'

'Must you go?' Sala asked quietly. 'Can't you stay here with us?'

*It is the lesser being who is the devil. You are a Saviour. You will think nothing of this lesser being or it will cause you to undo yourself.* A part of him wanted to stay, to sit looking down upon the realm and talking of all manner of things. *Why talk to them? You know what they think before they do. They are detestably limited. There is nothing to be learned or gained from them. Nothing.* Why did a part of him want to stay, then, if there was nothing to be gained? *You have been weakened by them and become caught in a fantasy or dream where you can sit as long as you like with them, where there is no Virtue coming for you. See! They are the devil. They are only a drain on you. They are already wasting your time, your precious time. Do not answer the lesser being Sala. Just turn away and climb. If she speaks again, kill her.*

Suray had approached and looked up into Ba'zel's eyes. 'I do not think you are the devil. You cannot be. You have saved us.'

'Perhaps. Or perhaps the Leveller for this step will find you to-morrow and hurl you down the pyramid in his wrath.'

Suray did not blink. He just continued looking up. 'It will have been worth it just to see this place, just to know it is real. And to share it with

Sala for a short while. Even if it is just for tonight, Saviour, you have saved us.'

'Or damned you. I know you will taste the forbidden fruit of those plants tonight. There will be no going back, Suray. There are no outer fields here to work off the debt of your sin. There is only the fall. Perhaps you would have been better off if I'd never spoken to you at all. Our mistake was seeing and acknowledging each other right at the beginning. Better if we had remained unknown ghosts.'

Suray shrugged. 'Then we will be cast out of heaven. I prefer to go through that than remain the rest of my life fighting on the lower levels of the pyramid. I had never dreamed I could ascend as high as this.'

'It is time for me to go, Suray.'

'I know. If you *are* the devil, I hope you manage to supplant the Saviours up there.'

'Thank you, Suray . . . for your help. I hope that you do not die too soon. Goodbye.'

Ba'zel turned away and went to the wall of the next step. As he passed through one of the gardens, he plucked a ripe apple and threw it back to Suray. Then he slithered away.

He hurried up, trusting his instinct that he had very little time left. When he reached the eighty-first level, he sensed only a single lesser being inside the pyramid. It lived alone, its strength nearly exhausted. It had to enjoy its solitary existence, as otherwise it could have used the extensive resources it had amassed during its lifetime to procure companions for itself. It enjoyed being alone, free of the devil. Did it live in a fantasy or dream of its life past most of the time? Was that all it needed? Curious as he was, Ba'zel knew he could not go and ask such questions of the lesser being, for that would end its self-defining existence. He would be death or the devil come to collect its soul. And through its eyes, the Saviours of this realm would see Ba'zel and prepare for his arrival at the top of the pyramid.

He raced up through the empty levels and sensed powerful beings turning their attention towards him. Levellers. They detected him. They were moving to intercept him. They could not be sure what he was, so the Declension would also be unsure. Might they think he was simply a rogue or overambitious Leveller? He should avoid them as long as possible. If he presented himself to them as a Saviour, they would surely stand aside, but then the Declension would know he was here. Would the elders who were guardians simply lead him to the Gate at his request or his insistence that it was the Eldest's will? He could not believe that. Prophecy was the dominant force in this realm, just as the Declension had established a controlling narrative in the fifth realm. They knew precisely who he was: the devil. They knew why he was coming: to supplant them. They *knew*. The Levellers would not stand aside. They would fight him by command of the Declension. They would hurl him down in their wrath. Damnable prophecy! It was a clever device, he had to admit, for it meant it was inevitable the Geas would fall to the Declension here. Ah, that was why there was no need for others of his kind to come to this realm. Others were not required and therefore not welcome. They came at their own peril, and the home-realm must know better than to send any here. Any who did come were rogue or the devil by definition. That was why the other Gate had been left in the air, deep in the desert, without a guardian and with little obvious sign or direction. It would be impossible to find it again to use as an exit. Instead, it was the way into one vast trap of prophecy. And he was right in the middle of that trap. He'd simply walked into it. He'd snared himself, done it to himself. He was a victim of himself. He should have listened more closely to Suray when the boy had explained one of the key principles of this place. *By falling, an individual has judged themselves. They have failed to guard against complacency, they have allowed themselves to be displaced. They are responsible for their own fall.*

He realised he'd stopped climbing. Was there any point? He should not have come through the Gate. He should not have come out of the desert. He should not have approached and spoken to Suray. He should not have climbed these levels. But he'd never had a choice, had he? It was prophecy. Could this have been inevitable all along? Could it have been inevitable even before he'd entered this realm? Inevitable as soon as he'd left his father's chambers on the home-realm? Inevitable as soon as he was born? Was his existence one vast trap? A trap of character and predestination. How did one escape one's own existence? Was it inevitable even before he'd been born? Inevitable when he was nothing but an unknown ghost or another's desire, intent and imagination? Who was

269

that other who had created this trap? It could only be the Declension, as it grew and overwhelmed the cosmos, remaking it in its own image. Now he understood what the sifters had asked of him so long ago. To return. Return to where it had begun, to where the trap had first been formed, to where the desire, intent and imagination resided. He must return there and undo it if he was ever to be free of the Declension, its narratives and prophecies, if he was ever to have an existence to call his own. Return to where he had been an unknown ghost still fighting for its freedom and still free of the devil.

The unknown ghost. Could he be that now? None of the Levellers or Declension had seen him in this realm yet. They thought they sensed something, but they did not know for sure he was here. They did *not* know. They did not know he had come through the Gate and out of the desert. Despite all they had done to create predestination, prophecy and foreknowledge, they still did not *know*. Their prophecy and fore-knowledge had not yet become manifest. If he could be the unknown ghost and stay clear of them, they would *never* know. He would never have been here, would never have come out of the desert and would never have come through the Gate. He could never have done. He would ghost through their trap. All would be as if it had never occurred, just as with prophecy all was as if it had already occurred.

In the blink of an eye he assumed his spectral form and passed inside the nearest wall just as a rangy Leveller came careering around the corner of the step. The Leveller raced to the section of wall where Ba'zel had concealed himself. The being's nostrils flared. 'I smell you. Where are you? Come to me.'

Ba'zel silently drifted up to the next level. A more powerful Leveller was already prowling there above him. He sensed the sharpness of its vision. It might be able to see him if he went any closer. Instead of rising, Ba'zel moved inwards, entering an internal room of the pyramid. He passed up through the ceiling and entered another empty room. The Leveller sensed the move and sped for the room. The door was hurled open just as Ba'zel disappeared into the ceiling.

'I have missed it!' the Leveller broadcast. 'It passes up to the ninety-second. I do not know what it is. It cannot be one of our kind!'

'Boastful creature! You are not the strongest of us. You do not know if it is our kind or not,' sneered back the Leveller of the ninety-second from where it stood on the piece of floor in which Ba'zel was secreted. The Leveller hammered its fist into the floor, smashing a hole, but Ba'zel had moved under the Leveller's feet. The Leveller jumped as if its feet were burning and Ba'zel shot horizontally through the floor, angled up through the wall and into the next level.

The ninety-third Leveller's fist was already flying. It wrecked the wall where Ba'zel hid, bringing it down and forcing him to crouch in the resulting pile of rubble. The ninety-second Leveller was right below him, waiting.

'Now we have you.' The ninety-third smiled.

But then the roof fell in, crushing and burying him. The ninety-fourth Leveller had been waiting directly above and was unceremoniously brought crashing down as well. Behind its back, Ba'zel leapt free and coursed up to the ninety-fourth level. Now knowing what to do, he solidified his forelimbs and battered down supporting wall after supporting wall. He displaced a full dozen Levellers this way before he finally stood above them all.

He moved up through one more ceiling and to the very surface edge of the floor of the last level of the pyramid. Everything was sheathed in sun-metal and utterly still, the air dead. Nothing had disturbed this place in aeons. Ironic that this shining home of the gods should be so lifeless, so devoid. He could not sense anything. Was that due to the sun-metal? Here was the end of prophecy, then. The silent tomb.

He did not enter, he did not breathe, for otherwise they would immediately know where he was. They waited for him to betray himself by some sign. They listened intently. They would not move themselves, else that masked his entry. While they did not move, he did not dare enter. They knew he had risen above all the Levellers. They suspected he was Saviour and devil. He was a potential threat, but they also knew he could not enter while their stillness guarded them. The threat would not materialise, it would not become real. If it did, then the trap of prophecy would be sprung.

Here was his only escape. To lie forever at the interface of life and death without moving or breathing. To lie at the interface between prophecy and freedom, as an always paralysed but always self-aware character. To lie like an endlessly dreaming stone. Was that an escape or an even worse trap than prophecy?

He waited.

They waited.

He could not bear the thought of having life but not being allowed to live it, of being able to move but always having to remain still, of having character but never being allowed to assert it, of seeing freedom right before him but always resisting any reach for it, of experiencing thoughts and feelings but never allowing them to have consequence.

They waited.

Better to face their wrath and the apocalypse than to exist eternally in a life of unbeing. Why be the devil if you were not permitted the occasional bit of devilry and bedevilment? What could be worse for one hell-bent on such purpose? Why be a Saviour if you could not save anything? Well, he would bedevil and save himself come what may.

Ba'zel gathered himself and burst up into the vault of the Declension. Up, up! He sensed nothing stir in response. Would they be slow to come out of their Waking Dream and to animate? Would they need blood? Where was their wrath, their warriors, their guardians? He did not slow for an instant. If they had not expected him to cross the interface, if he had caught them out, if the trap of prophecy had become stiff or rusty with age, or there was some fundamental flaw in it, then he was not going to wait around while they worked out what they were going to do about it.

The Gate had to be at the very top. There was precious little to see or navigate by, so he judged his direction solely by moving against the pull of gravity and heading for where the nothingness seemed to be at its most complete.

Don't think about stopping. Don't think about finding the dusty vessels of this realm's Saviours and destroying them before they can rouse themselves. There will be wards and traps. The Null Dragon may be waiting. Fly, Ba'zel, fly!

Do not think you can liberate this realm. It is a fantasy, nothing more. Do not think you can make the realm safe for Suray and Sala. You cannot. You've tried such a thing in other realms and failed. It is a trap. It is *the* trap. It will see you achieve the opposite of your intent. It will hand the Geas to the Declension all the sooner. Do not think you can shut the Declension out of this realm. Knowledge of the Saviours is too strong in the minds of the People – they will always allow the

Declension to find a way into this realm through the Waking Dream. Faster, Ba'zel, faster!

Do not start to fear if all will only be repeated in the seventh realm just as it has been in the others before it. Do not hesitate. Do not doubt yourself. Do not fear all is futile. Assert yourself! Be quicker than thought, Ba'zel, quicker than thought!

He shot up through the final level, solidified and smashed into the slanting stone roof. Better that than passing through the stone and coming into fatal contact as a ghost with the covering of sun-metal on the outside of the apex. He crashed back down to the floor in a broken tangle of limbs and woozily raised his head. Twenty yards away was the shining Gate to the seventh. He'd made it. Against all the odds, he'd made it. He'd escaped prophecy! It should not have been possible, but he'd made it all the same. Somehow he'd reached the highest place in the home of this realm's gods. He was not the devil, it seemed. He was the holy ghost.

Don't think about it. Don't! Get up. Move, Ba'zel, move. Forget your hurt. You'll find something to replenish you in the seventh. His lower limbs splintering and buckling, he tottered closer to the Gate. It was right there. A bit more momentum and he'd topple through. Its light bathed him and set shadows chasing around the chamber.

Quickly! The shadows are dark ghosts to your holy ghost. Move. The shadows flickered past him and began to coalesce in the Gate. The Gate darkened. No. A huge figure of nightmare stepped into the room. The Virtue had found him!

'OBEDIENCE is come! All will kneel before the Virtue of the Declension!'

The power of the being's presence forced Ba'zel to his knees, those joints splitting open. The membranes of his skull buzzed and screamed so that he could not think.

'Why, brother! You did not think you could escape, did you? Surely you know there is no escaping OBEDIENCE. Did I not tell you it was madness to try? Did I not promise that you would be broken open, worn as my living skin and absorbed over millennia of agony?' spoke the hideous voice through a sickening chorus of yawning mouths.

The giant was a terror to look upon, threatening to unhinge Ba'zel's mind. Rows of heads embedded in the Virtue's surface stared back at

Ba'zel, pleading, warning and hating him for being still free. Jaws stretched wide in rictus cries, gnashed hungrily or hung slack in defeat. The tops of torsos and lost limbs writhed and undulated, fighting for space, separation and survival. And above it all was the Virtue's true head, its features in a permanently unyielding expression. Its gaze was infinitely uncompromising. There was no reasoning with it, no asking for mercy or compassion, no explaining. There was only absolute punishment and submission.

The constant moan of torment, sighs of despair and the keening of anguish were all around. Ba'zel would have clapped his hands over his ears to block it out, but knew there was no escaping it. It was an abjection experienced by all the senses: the reek of the foulest fears, the trembling of a petrifying panic, the vision of himself dissected and dissolved, the echo of his own insanity, and the gagging taste of dreams turned to dust.

'What? Will you not struggle, brother? Will you not make an exhibition of yourself by fleeing? Surely there is some ridiculous trick you will attempt to amuse me. Perhaps you might distract me and make a desperate dash for safety, delaying the moment of your doom insignificantly. Or bribe me with an empty promise of power. What, nothing? You disappoint, brother. But all do ultimately before the Virtue of the Declension. All are found lacking. And do not think any are left with their dignity. None remain stoic. None who are chosen find honour in the punishment I bring. There is no martyrdom. No. Everything will be taken from you: every secret, every joyful memory, every guilty pleasure, every self-interest and every shred of self-respect. Your name will end and all record of you will be destroyed. If you had offspring, that bloodline would be ended. Everything the Declension had previously permitted you, your existence entire, is now rescinded. But you will not be allowed the simple escape of death, no, never that.'

It was then that Ba'zel truly understood there were things and punishments far worse than death, far, far worse. He raised claws to his throat and ripped it out, sluicing his blood across the floor. He expelled all life energy that he could, becoming an unsustainable cloud of being that would fade to nothing. He committed suicide right there, even as his mind realised the actual desire.

The Virtue brayed its laughter. 'Pitiful, brother! I have already told you that there is no escape permitted. Can you not see it? Surely even your simple mind has now realised this realm was a trap for you, and how existence defined by the Declension is a trap for all.' The giant shook its head. Affronted, it thundered in its legion voice, 'WE ARE THE DECLENSION! WE ARE THE VIRTUE OF OBEDIENCE!'

The giant deliberately stepped into the cloud of Ba'zel's being, its many mouths inhaling and devouring. Ba'zel was absorbed and forced into a small skull on the Virtue's chest. The skulls around him turned and started to gnaw on him without surcease. He screamed and screamed, but was completely drowned out by the harrowing host.

*All is prepared as I commanded,* the Eldest spoke across the cosmos. It was a statement rather than a question.

'As is your will, most holy,' the Great Saviour in the seventh realm whimpered.

The Eldest wondered how genuine the Great Saviour's awe of her absolute authority truly was. He was of her own bloodline and therefore never to be underestimated. More than that, he was one of the most cunning of her line, which was precisely why she had consigned him to the seventh, as far from the seat of the Declension's power as possible. Had he clumsily overdone the whimpering or was he trying to communicate a certain contrition for his own cleverness? Maybe a bit of both, which only further demonstrated how dangerous he was. She waited, but he knew better than to so much as twitch with presumptuous curiosity. The twitch would have betrayed him and rightfully angered her. At the same time she would have been happier to have him twitch rather than not . . . unless the twitch turned out to be a calculated bluff. How she hated him, but he was the only overseer who might succeed in the troublesome seventh. The cursed seventh realm! The Chi'a had found a way beyond it, and so would the Declension! The Great Voyage could not be allowed to founder because of such an ugly and inconsequential realm. Apparently, it had a number of lesser beings whose blood was near unpalatable! It was outrageous.

*How long before the Geas in the seventh is ours?*

Did he hesitate? 'All progresses as per our will. We now possess the means to find Haven, most holy.'

*Tell me of those means.*

'Instabilities that we have allowed and contrived have seen the Geas tie itself to a particular lesser being, a young and inexperienced lesser being who is easily steered.'

*Should these means fail – and lesser beings are notoriously fragile – you will open the trap of sun-metal, but only then. Inform our Saviours in the seventh that it is our will that the trap remain closed until they are commanded otherwise.*

'As is your will, most holy.'

*What sign of an eighth realm?*

'None. We suspect that sign exists either with a partial being called the Peculiar or in Haven itself. I have begun a convergence to ensure the revelation will be ours.'

She did not tell him that she had done the same in order to negate any need for him once and for all. There was no doubt he would try to discover the contents of the sun-metal box, but there was no chance of him succeeding.


The more they struggled to escape the Virtue, the more tightly they were bound by it. They twisted and turned, becoming more tangled and ensnared than ever, throttling themselves, causing themselves worse and worse suffering.

Ba'zel knew there was no fighting it. Unlike any of the others, he submerged and effaced himself, passing deep into the Virtue. He let go of himself, not rejecting everything he'd ever been, but no longer insisting that it defined him. Yet somehow he still existed.

'What are you doing, brother?' the Virtue's voice wormed. 'Do you search for your own hell? For that is all you will find.'

Ba'zel moved into the Virtue's core.

'No! Stop. GET OUT!'

But the Virtue could not get a grip on Ba'zel, for Ba'zel had given up all self-assertion and form. He had become part of the essential Virtue.

'You will obey me, brotharrrgh!'

Now the essential Virtue was different. It was more than just Obedience. There was something *other* now, something that changed and disrupted its core definition. Obedience commanded itself to obey

Obedience, turning on itself and demanding submission and punishment. The punishment saw the Virtue absorb itself while tearing itself from its previous form and self. It began to unravel. It was *unstable*.

The movements of the beings embedded in its surface became exaggerated. A head and half a torso heaved itself up and fell flailing to the ground. A skull came loose and bounced heavily, once, twice and then broke open. Bloody limbs slithered apart like a disintegrating nest of vipers.

The core of the Virtue was only *instability* now, it was only Ba'zel. He stepped free, greater than he had been before. He moved round and past the half-beings that had wrestled and flowed out of the Virtue. They weakly reached for him, but there was nothing he could do for them. There was nothing he could give them. They were the miscarriages and stillbirths of the Declension. One of them dragged itself over to a helplessly floundering thing and bit at it.

'I'm sorry,' Ba'zel whispered, horrified.

He exerted the power of his presence and finally brought rest to their tortured souls. As he did so, he turned away and stepped through the Gate.

The Eldest sensed the Virtue of her bloodline being extinguished, as she had always intended it would be. She watched through the dying eyes of one of the pathetic creatures on the floor of the Gate's chamber in the sixth realm as Ba'zel stepped through the Gate to the seventh. He stood tall now, the most powerful weapon the Declension had yet created. All occurred as she had decreed it. Ba'zel had already given the Declension the Geas in the third and fourth realms, by bringing instability, exposing change, desperation and a new way of things. The Great Cull had followed in each of those realms and all had been fed to the Geas of the home-realm. It was stronger and more hungry now than she had ever known it. The Geas of the fifth realm was close to falling, the sixth would soon follow. And now Ba'zel entered the seventh. The cosmos would be hers for the taking! Its secrets would be hers. It could deny her nothing.

Ba'zel was hurled against the impossibly hard and bright floor of the seventh realm. The Gate snuffed out behind him. His skin smouldered then burned. He was inside a box of sun-metal. Trapped! Tears of blood trickled down his cheeks and evaporated. There had never been any escape after all.

CHAPTER 10:

# Even as they transgress

Confident that Captain Gallen could coordinate the attacks on the Empire's army along the forest road between Heroes' Brook and Godsend, Samnir rode back to Godsend to oversee preparations there. He nodded approvingly when he saw that the trees had been cleared to a distance of at least fifty yards from the walls of the small town, and that a deep ditch had been dug just outside the walls to make any approach more difficult. A lot of labour would have been involved in augmenting the fortifications – ideal for distracting Godsend's soldiery from the wait and for releasing tensions. Better they take out their anxieties on uncomplaining wood and stubborn ground than each other. He wondered who he had to thank for seeing to it that the work was done. Hella, more than likely.

Men stopped what they were doing and saluted enthusiastically as they saw him come to the north gates. Then their eyes took in the empty road behind him.

Preventing any rumour before it could begin, he called to those nearest him, 'We have not lost a single man! The Empire has lost untold numbers. I would not be surprised if their army doesn't get this far.'

There were cheers as men went back to their work with renewed energy or turned to a neighbour who had not heard properly. Samnir entered the town and saw squads of men practising with their bows or drilling with sword, shield and heavy spear in close formation. There were civilians placing polearms, stabbing spears, bundles of arrows and even piles of stones at regular intervals along the walls. Others brought buckets of water, carried foodstuffs or ran past with intent expressions. Everyone seemed to know what they were about. No one had approached him yet and he was already halfway to the stables. Could it be that he would get to see his horse properly settled and that he would be allowed an hour's sleep for the first time in days? The girl was a miracle. If Godsend survived the coming fight, it would be down to her more than anyone.

He knew he should go to see how she was bearing up, but he was so tired it was all he could do to stay on his horse. As it was, it was a good job the animal seemed to know the way to the stables, as Samnir himself was doing very little to get them there.

'Horse, you're in charge. Could you see me settled in a stall and then go and see how Hella's doing? I promise not to eat all your hay and oats.'

He felt an itch in his left shoulder blade. Someone was watching or shadowing him. He turned in his saddle. It took him a moment to make out just who was hovering there.

'Well, I'll be! Callinor, you old rogue! What? The innkeeper's daughter would have none of you and sent you packing after all?'

Callinor smiled weakly from where he stood on the shadowed side of the street. He was clearly ill at ease. His cheeks were a yellowish red and he had dark rings around his eyes. 'No, she would have none of me. And she was the last thing of loveliness left in Heroes' Brook.' He shook visibly. 'Sand Devil, the Empire is torturing them all. Even the innocent. Saviours forgive me, but I am a coward. I couldn't bear it. I fled!'

Samnir was down from his horse and clasping the Captain of Heroes' Brook by the tops of his arms. Callinor could not look at him. 'No man who has fought in the east can be called a coward, you know that! The enemy we fought was a terrible thing, blacker than night itself, blacker than a man's own fears. The very ground of that region is corrupted, opening up to devour a man of good faith, or spawning unimaginable terrors in our midst to swarm us under. A man fears every shadow and step he takes in that forsaken wasteland, where nothing of worth or beauty can survive. You have been through it, facing demons within and without. I know you for a brave soul and a true comrade, Callinor.

If you could not face Heroes' Brook any more, then it is not because you are a coward! It is because you are a man who cannot stand idly by while the innocent and young are punished by those who hate them for what they are. You cannot stand idly by without hating yourself for it. You cannot stand idly by!'

Callinor was sobbing and nodding. Snot dribbled down to his chin.

'Come,' Samnir commanded him, releasing his arms. 'Raise up your chin, for you should be proud of what you are. That is an order, soldier! That's better. Now we will order some wine and retire to my command post, where you will tell what you have seen and how the enemy is disposed. I need to hear what we face in this Saint. Praxis was ever cruel to the People of Godsend.'

A tremor passed through the portly Captain. Samnir thought for a moment that Callinor would collapse, but the man caught himself at the last. 'Aye, Sand Devil, I could do with a drink at that.'

Samnir passed his horse to a nearby soldier and asked for wine to be brought to his room near the barracks. Then he led his old comrade along the wood-chipped streets of the town's northern quarter.

'I've never seen the town so crowded,' Samnir commented, noting that refugees had erected makeshift shelters in many of the less-used side streets. 'Yet many more have died on the road from Hyvan's Cross. You must have seen them, yes? Callinor?'

The Captain jumped, trying to take in what was around him. Samnir knew the man's mind was probably seeing other things over and over, horrifying things. He'd known other veterans who had ended up like this. With time some recovered, but many did not. He imagined it was like when he'd been trapped in his own body and chained in the Gathering Place. He'd prayed for death, and would have died were it not for the girl Hella. He hoped that Callinor did not pray for death, but feared the Empire would never allow him the time he needed.

They went inside the stone and timber command post and into the small room Samnir used as his own. He sat in his hard-backed chair with a groan, laid his arms on its rests, put his head back and closed his eyes for a second. 'Have a seat, old friend. Take the reports off that seat over there and put them on the desk . . . or the floor. Doesn't matter. I don't find reports, they find me.'

Callinor's breath rasped in the stillness of the room, but there was no sound of the soldier moving. There was a knock at the open door and Samnir raised his head and opened his eyes. A young soldier brought in a jug of wine and two goblets. He placed them on the desk.

'Good to have you back, commander. Shall I pour?'

'No, lad, but thank you. Dismissed.'

The young soldier saluted and left. Samnir poured two goblets, took one for himself and pushed the other towards Callinor. The Captain gazed sightlessly at it and did not reach out. Samnir drank a mouthful from his own and sighed. 'Ah, that's good. Needed that. It's a bit watered, I'm afraid. Not as good as what your innkeeper's daughter used to serve you, eh?'

Callinor's gaze found Samnir. There was only defeat and dejection in the Captain. 'I'm sorry. You must believe that, Sand Devil.'

'You do not need to apologise to me or any man here, Callinor.'

The Captain trembled. 'I should have listened to you. About how things couldn't just go back to how they were. I was scared, Sand Devil, so scared. It is like a slow asphyxiation, just as you said. A gradual brain death. And now it is too late. I am so sorry.' Without blinking or any betraying sign, he drew his blade of sun-metal.

'Callinor! You do not need to do this. We can still fight them, still beat them. We will save your innkeeper's daughter.'

The shadows in Callinor's face deepened, until he looked like someone else altogether. 'Oh, but there is every need, traitor!' he sneered. 'The People need to see that there is no fighting the Empire and no hope. They need to see their evil commander killed, when all believed themselves safe within Godsend's walls. Thus they will all know fear, for fear is knowledge of the truth, the truth of the blessed Saviours, the truth that the Chaos cannot hide or stand against the righteous power of this region's Saint. In seeing you killed, they will see you revealed as a traitor, inveigling agent of Izat and corruption agent of the Chaos. The People of Godsend will have this lesson. I was ever their Minister and teacher. They must be taught for their own good, and punished if they do not learn it well.'

'Callinor, this is not you! Do not let yourself be used. Force him out!'

'I cannot!' the Captain cried and brought his sword crashing down, sheering the desk in two, the wood unable to resist the power of the sun-metal.

Samnir tipped his chair onto its back legs and then as far as it would go. The top of his back smacked the wall behind him and the back legs of the chair slid forward, bringing him crashing to the floor. He was in all sorts of agony, but just out of reach of the oncoming Captain's sword.

Samnir brought his knees up towards his chest, planted both feet on the chair's seat, and shoved the piece of furniture into his attacker's lower legs. Callinor stumbled, then cleaved the chair in two with a single motion of his blade. Now he hacked straight at Samnir's lower half, but the chair had given Samnir the vital second he needed to free his own weapon. It came up at the last instant and deflected Callinor's blade into the floor. The sword went straight through the floorboards as if they weren't there, and all the way to the hilt due to the momentum and force the Captain had put into the blow.

Callinor laughed, his face just short of Samnir's own. 'Look at that. Putting my balance too far forward like an eager greenhorn. Any soldier worth their salt knows sun-metal shouldn't be forced. Miss your target and you end up running yourself onto the other's blade.'

'It's not your fault, old friend,' Samnir said with a sad shake of his head. 'That idiot in your head is responsible. Believe me, I will see you revenged on him every which way.'

Blood boiled and bubbled out of Callinor front and back, for Samnir's blade had gone right through him. 'I'm not frightened any more,' the Captain coughed. 'Glad it's over in truth. Shame about that innkeeper's daughter.' His eyes closed and his voice faded. 'I'm so sorry. You must believe that, Sand Devil.'

'I know, old friend, I know.'

The Captain slumped on top of Samnir. The commander held onto his oldest comrade, whom the Empire had forced him to kill. He knew that brother would be forced to kill brother, parents and children would be forced to kill each other, and neighbour would be forced to kill neighbour before all was done. And the Empire said there was a lesson in that. The only lesson as far as Samnir could see was that he wasn't going to be allowed any decent rest until the Empire had been undone once and for all. Perhaps Jillan had understood that all along, and that was part of the reason why he had left Godsend. 'Stay safe, lad, wherever you are!' And the other thing Samnir had learned was that a rare and proper punishment for Praxis was long overdue.

Saint Izat tried to swallow, but gagged on the blood and had to spit it out. 'Gah! You're Unclean! I should have known.'

Jillan looked blearily at her from where he lay on the cushions. 'Had a bath before, honest. Keren saw.'

'Quiet, idiot! I'm trying to think.'

*She's right, you know. You are an idiot. Didn't I tell you she wasn't to be trusted? But would you listen? Ooooh, no! It doesn't hurt to be polite, you said. But her sticking a tapping tube in your neck did hurt, didn't it? And it wasn't exactly polite either, now was it? She overawed and trapped you with meaningless etiquette, vanity, costume, theatre and sex. She may smile sweetly and have a more comely shape, but she's the same as Azual. And you would never have got amorous with him, would you? No. So get it through your village idiot head once and for all. She . . . is . . . a . . . Saint. Maybe I should go over that again for you, as you do insist on being so slow on the uptake. For want of a kiss and the promise of flesh, you have put yourself in the Saviours' power and doomed this world. Well done, you! I bet she's not even as good a kisser as Hella, either. I bet Izat tastes like a dirty old corpse.*

*What shall I do?* Jillan moaned.

*I have no idea. I really hadn't anticipated that any individual could be quite as stupid as you, you see. And even if I did know what you should do, there'd be no point telling you, because you wouldn't listen anyway. You never do. You think I'm a taint, remember, some evil and manipulative thingy trying to thwart you at every turn? Or I'm some dark influence encouraging you to sell out everything and everyone, including yourself. Or I'm some demented version of yourself that you daren't trust. Or the voice of your magic that you want at your beck and call only when it suits you. Or the Chaos itself. Remember? How quickly you have forgotten the revelation of needing me when we fought Azual. How quickly you have forgotten we were once the same, you and I. And how slow you insist on being to remember it again.*

Saint Izat frowned prettily.

*You're right to be upset,* Jillan conceded. *You're right to feel sorry for yourself—*

*I am* not *feeling sorry for myself! This is not some childish tantrum. The end of the world is no—*

*All right! It's true. You're not being overly dramatic. It's just that—*

*Overly dramatic? How dare you!*

With the beautifully crafted fingernail of her first finger the Saint thoughtfully tapped one of her perfect teeth. *Tick! Tick! Tick!*

*I didn't mean . . . Look, I promise to listen. You're right. I don't think we've got long, so if you have any sort of idea—*

*Tick!*

*Well, normally, I'd tell you to scream for Freda . . . or even the Peculiar. They're forever saving you, aren't they? With suspicious frequency, in fact. Remind me to have a word with you about that some time. Anyway, I'd advise shouting for them, but you've allowed yourself to get hopelessly separated, haven't you, so there's little point. She's no doubt got them stowed somewhere nice and safe, though how she's managed to detain a slippery customer like the Peculiar I really—*

*Tick!*

*What? She's got them prisoner somewhere? We have to help them!*

*You think? How exactly? We* need *their* help, *remember?*

*Tick!*

The Saint stopped. Her eyes became distant. There was the clash of metal from somewhere deep in the palace. Shouted orders. Awful cries. She drew in a deep breath.

'What is it?' Jillan dared ask.

*There's something bad coming, something very bad. I thought we were in trouble before, but this is a whole new category of bad. Look, even she's afraid. That should tell you all you need to know. Hide!*

*Hide?*

*Yes, just for once listen and do as I tell you. Stop gawping like a yokel and hide. Honestly, why the Geas had to pick a simpleton from the bogs of the south is quite beyond me sometimes.*

Jillan rolled awkwardly off the cushions and got to unsteady feet. He dully looked for somewhere he could hide.

*I'd move quicker than that if I were you.*

There was a lewd tapestry on one wall. A man in a state of undress was riding—

*Forget the detail! Move.*

Jillan stepped towards the tapestry, but the Saint grabbed at his sleeve. She held onto him desperately.

'My prince, you have to help me! Husband, call your magic and defend me. What would you not do for the woman you love?'

'I'm not . . . That wine. I can't call my magic.'

*Get rid of her! Do or say whatever you have to. Punch her. Knock her out cold!*

The Saint's eyes became wild. 'When it gets here, we will tell it you had just asked to marry me so that south and west could be joined. You wished to rejoin the Empire and to show us where Haven was.'

Of course. It was all about Haven. It always had been. Her talk of marriage was simply to ensnare him, to add his power to hers. What else could it have been? It wasn't as if she knew him or was smitten by his clumsy manners. It was like waking up from a dream. His head was becoming clearer, the effects of the wine wearing off. She was the same as Azual. The taint was right. He should lash out at her. He clenched his right hand into a fist. Would he hit her pretty chin, her button nose, her doleful eye?

*Too late.*

There was a crash. One of the golden doors was thrown right off its hinges and halfway across the room. The other immediately followed it. Filling the doorway was a glorious suit of armour, against which Jillan was forced to shield his eyes.

*What is it?*

*A Disciple of the Great Saviour! If you get a chance to get past it, do not hesitate. Fly like Wayfar himself. Don't get any stupid ideas about trying to help Izat either. She is theirs. There is nothing you can do for her. Nothing whatsoever.*

With a wail, Saint Izat threw herself down before the Disciple. Its feet thumped into the room, burning the priceless rugs on the floor as it came. It planted its boots just short of the Saint's head. Her lustrous hair began to singe and shrivel. She squealed. A bright gauntlet reached down, grabbed her by the scruff of the neck and held her off the floor. The other gauntlet came across and smashed a phial of blood into her teeth and mouth. Her lips split open and she made a horrible noise in her throat.

*Run.*

Jillan darted forward, keeping low. There was a gap between the Disciple and the doorway. The armour was distracted and Jillan moved quickly. He'd timed his move well, terrified though he was. He was going to make it!

The Disciple stamped down hard, shattering flagstones, shaking the floor and unbalancing Jillan as he went past. Jillan's left shoulder collided hard with the door post and he was spun off his feet. A shining hand clamped around his ankle, dragged him back into the room and then lifted him upside down. Saint Izat had been thrown a dozen yards across the floor.

'What do you want?' Jillan cried. He felt the bones of his ankle coming apart. He stared into the eye slits of the helmet, but there was only emptiness there.

'An end to the instability,' a hollow voice echoed.

The armour made a massive fist of its other hand . . .

*This is going to hurt!*

. . . and hammered it into Jillan's head.

The Disciple dropped the bane of the Empire and turned its head back to Saint Izat. She was struggling to her knees.

'Holiness . . .' she lisped through the wreckage of her mouth.

'Silence. Nothing you say is required. It is known before you speak it. The Saviour D'Syr is now the organising intellect of this region. You will only be permitted existence as it serves her. We would remove you for how you have erred, but that would only increase the instability you have started. It is not coincidence that we find the bane here – nor the rock woman and the Peculiar – for one instability always seeks to cause another and is thereby attracted to all those with the potential for instability. The bane and his companions have found you out. They had you caught a long time ago, for you tied your region far too closely to the *unstable* south even before Azual. You have made this moment inevitable. You defined and trapped yourself with selfish ambitions that worked to destabilise the Empire. You are simple and foolish, like all your kind, and live within delusions of your own making. You are vain. And you will punish yourself by your vanity, just as you trapped yourself. You will tear your face off so that you will never again seek to have this region as a mirror to your own wants and desires. From now on, whatever you behold of yourself reflected in others will appal you.'

Her hands shaking in fear, eagerness to obey and temptation to resist, Saint Izat used her beautiful nails to rend the flesh from her beautiful face. 'Thank you, blessed Saviours!' she burbled, losing all reason with her sense of self. 'Thank you!'

Enemies everywhere. Callinor had failed. Of course he had. He had all but committed suicide, as if to frustrate Praxis in his fight against the Chaos. The Chaos thought nothing of sacrificing lives to achieve its evil ends. It was the General who had allowed Callinor the opportunity for that suicide. Praxis was sure the General was another enemy. The man was loyal to Saint Dionan of the east, after all.

By rights, Callinor should have assassinated the devious Samnir, who was both a proven agent of the Chaos and loyal to Saint Izat of the west. So, the agent of the east had taken Callinor from Praxis's grasp, and Callinor had deliberately failed in striking against the agent of the west. It said but one thing to the brilliant and Saviours-guided mind of Saint Praxis: east and west were in league against him. *Dionan and Izat must be jealous that I have the bane and the pagans within my grasp. They must want them for themselves. But to what end? What power do they seek by it? They seek the Geas for themselves, so that they can rule the Empire! I must uncover the full extent of their conspiracy before it is too late.*

He would have the angelic Captain Skathis watch the General even more closely. Yet how was it the Captain had been unable to report anything damning against the General so far? Surely there was no doubt concerning the Captain's loyalty, was there? *I can see everything in his mind, although there is little enough to see.* That was strange in itself, for Praxis knew the Captain to be an intelligent man. *By the Saviours, what if he is able to keep some of his thoughts from me?* It was an alarming idea. *How can we doubt the Captain when it was he who saw us safely to the Great Temple?* Yet what better way for a traitor to stay close to the new Saint in order to share the Empire's plans immediately with the Chaos? Surely it was no coincidence that the Godsenders had been ready and waiting with an ambush on the road between Hyvan's Cross and Heroes' Brook. And the Captain had always been close to the perhaps too trusting Saint Azual! The famously virtuous Saint could not have failed unless he had been betrayed by those close to him. The Captain had led such an overwhelming size of force against Godsend that defeat should have been impossible, and yet he had managed to bring about defeat all the same. Under cover of darkness, he must have stolen the Empire's child of glorious and righteous triumph and replaced it with the ugly changeling of the Chaos.

Enemies everywhere! Not one could be trusted. Praxis looked up. The torturer, who had been standing and staring like some dribbling lackwit, took a step back from the table where Praxis was seated. 'Well? Why have you not siphoned off a measure of the prisoner's blood and brought it here?'

'M-More, holy one?'

What was the dolt talking about? Was the idiot going to pretend that he'd already brought him a goblet? He couldn't be trusted. Was he hoping to keep the blood for himself? The prisoner had already confessed all, but through his blood and the magic of the Saviours the Godsender's answers could be verified. *Is the torturer trying to keep the truth from me? After all, he killed the last enemy soldier we captured before I could finish questioning him. At the time I put it down to carelessness and overenthusiasm, and he claimed the prisoner had become weakened through blood loss, but what if it was more than simple incompetence?*

Saint Praxis stared into the torturer's eyes, into his mind and then into his soul. He found the sacred heart of the man's experiences and beliefs, those things that gave him identity, passion, appetite and self. He found the secrets there. He saw how, as a boy, the torturer had come to understand physical suffering as his mother's loving care for him. *I must be cruel to be kind*, the woman explained calmly as she used a leather strap to raise weals on her child's back. *The world is a hard place. I must toughen you so that it can never break you. Good boy. No tears now. Be brave for Mama.* Saint Praxis began to subvert the defining image. The mother's blows did more than cause weals now. They laid open the boy's back so that the white bones of his spine were there to see. Cartilage and nerves were ruined, paralysing the torturer so that there was no escape. The mother whispered in her son's ear, *And now the final truth to toughen you. What if I did not beat you because I was being kind? What if I were to tell you I did not do it because I loved you? What if I did it because I secretly hated you for how you'd ruined me? Should I speak those words? Should I?*

Such terror that it threatened to extinguish the man's eternal soul.

The very seat of his being about to fall away from beneath him. There would be nothing left. No redemption. 'No! I will give you everything, Mother! Holy one! See me! I am yours. There is only you. Your word. You are truth. You!'

There was no lying. There could not be. Saint Praxis held the man's sacred heart in his hand and mind. He had the man's entire reason. The unreasoning fear that possessed the man instead – fear of his mother's words – prevented any rationale of deception. There was no hiding. The man's being was exposed, just as was his spine and brainstem.

Holy fear gripped the torturer, squeezing his sacred heart. Fear was knowledge of the blessed Saviours' truth. And Praxis was that holy fear incarnate. He would bring that fear to Godsend and take the bane's sacred heart in his hand. He would find the boy's secrets, including the hiding place of the Geas, expose his being and then extinguish his eternal soul. In the process, surely the corruption of the east and west would be exposed. He, Saint Praxis, would see the entire Empire cleansed, restored and transformed into the paradise it was always meant to be. He would walk with the Saviours and cast no shadow upon the ground.

The torturer had not lied. The fellow genuinely believed that he had already brought him a goblet of the prisoner's blood. Extraordinary how the simple-minded mistook their own intentions for actual memories. Never mind. Saint Praxis realised that his holiness and righteous power were now growing beyond the need for the distasteful and potentially contaminating exchange of blood. He was on the verge of being able to instil fear and possess the soul of a sinner without having to come into any sort of physical contact with them. Their own sin undid them when they beheld his saintly being and nature. In his presence, they could only see themselves for what they were, and that unravelled them. It prostrated their minds before him.

Saint Praxis turned his punishing gaze on the prisoner strapped to the restraining frame. He seized the enemy's sacred heart and exorcised the soldier's mind. He discarded the minutiae of his enemy's self-obsessed life and looked into Godsend, searching for the true source of the Chaos.

The bane was not to be found! The bane had fled. Of course, the bane would flee in holy fear, terrified that the saintly nature of Saint Praxis would cause the boy's sin to lay himself low.

*Praxis, hear me*, D'Shaa of the southern region intoned.

'Blessed Saviour!' Saint Praxis gasped. 'Command me!'

*The bane is in the west.*

'He seeks sanctuary with the enemies of the Empire, blessed Saviour. I believe that the west and perhaps the east conspire against us!'

*Fear not. All is known to me before it occurs. It was always my will that he should flee, eventually to lead us to the Geas.*

'I am but a child, blessed Saviour,' Saint Praxis sobbed. 'Is he not beyond our grasp?'

*Think further on the revelation I have permitted you, faithful Praxis. You do not need physical contact with him to instil the necessary fear that will possess his soul. The sacred heart is not so easily escaped. You move ever closer to taking it in your hand. Why was it that Jillan fought so hard to keep Godsend from Azual? What was it that Jillan had hidden here that caused him to risk all? From what does he now seek to distract your attention by fleeing to the west? What lies in Godsend?*

'His sacred heart is here!' Saint Praxis grinned in wild-eyed epiphany. 'His experiences, beliefs and appetite all hinge on his passion for the girl! It was always about her.'

*Yes. Jillan could withstand anything we might perpetrate upon his own person, but he could not deny us if we were about to visit the same upon the girl, she who is his sacred heart. He will never be beyond our grasp if you take her in your hand. Should he ever command the full power of the Geas, he will never use it against us. No, he will gift it to us instead, becoming servant to our divine Empire. You will break open Godsend, decimating it as you will, seize her and bring her to the Great Temple.*

'As is your will, blessed Saviour.'


'I cannot bear it, Thomas,' Hella whispered to the oblivious blacksmith, who continued clanging with his huge hammer against red-hot metal and anvil. 'The crone claimed he was dead. I have not slept since, but my waking hours have become as bad as any nightmare. Worse. It's like my mind is not my own any more. I fear it. I want to hide, but there's nowhere left to go. Only here.'

The blacksmith hammered on, his eyes seeing only the glowing shape that he fought to bend to his will. Sweat rolled down his body and he shivered with effort. For Thomas there was only the unending struggle of his existence, the struggle against the fiery dragon of his grief.

'Only here, where none can hear themselves think, the heat is stifling and there is only darkness beyond the fire. It keeps everything else out. Is that why you do it, Thomas? So that you will not have to think about anything else? So that your mind remains your own? Is that your life you are trying to forge just so? Is it never finished? Never quite right?'

His lungs were bellows, his eye the furnace, and his hard muscles his will. He tempered reality with his effort and being. Hella was caught up in the rhythm of his work, the flare of the metal as it was struck and the ringing bell of substance against substance. It was hypnotic and had her in its spell. It was a trance, everything contracted to this place, fire and labouring monster. Where was she in all this? Where was Jillan? How could they ever survive the forces of this world? How could there be anything recognisable left of them?

'The substance remains. Its shape might be changed, but the substance remains.' She blinked and came back to herself, as if he had just quenched her in the barrel of water nearby rather than the blade he'd been working on.

'Wh-What did you say, Thomas?'

'I said nothing, lass,' the blacksmith replied, watching her. 'The hiss and steam of the water must have spoken to you. It's not unknown. You asked questions of the world, yes? I trust you got the answers you wanted? The gods still have not seen fit to speak to me.'

She thought she had heard an answer, but what question had she truly asked? Had she asked about Jillan, whether he was dead? It felt like he was not, even though he might be much changed. She clung to that belief and found herself relieved, grateful and more at peace with herself than she had been since Jillan had left Godsend. 'But why would they not speak to you, Thomas? You are a good man. I know it.'

He shook his head sorrowfully. 'I have erred many a time, wilfully ignoring all warning. To my shame, lass, I have acted against the will of the gods. I do not deserve to hear them. It was Jillan who showed me how I might find some penitence by fighting in their name. I wanted to sacrifice my life to them in the battle, but they did not let me die. I realised then that I must continue to live without their forgiveness as yet further penitence. And I will not flinch from that punishment, or the work given me.'

'Perhaps . . . perhaps the gods speak to you through other people.'

He gave her a crooked smile, his teeth white against his soot-stained skin. 'Aye, it is a good thought, lass. Speak, then. What task do you have for me? Or have you already had what you came here for?'

What more could she need of him? He'd already given her back Jillan and her reason to fight. 'Thomas, you have forged weapons enough for everyone in Godsend. There is only one weapon left to make. You will make me a blade.'

'Lady, it will be my life's honour.'

'It will not be some giant two-handed thing, Thomas.' She smiled. 'And whatever it is, you will need to show me how to use it.'

Thomas trembled with some emotion. 'It will be my greatest work, milady. It will be a blade worthy enough to have graced the hand of one of my precious daughters.'

'Might it have runes on it, like on Jillan's armour? Do you remember those?'

'The blade will speak and move with them. The blade will live! I know now that I must at last attempt to work with sun-metal, although I have always feared it.'

'And then, sweet Thomas, we will go to fight the Empire, you and I, to see if the gods will let us die.'

He knelt before her – still as tall as her – with a tear washing down his cheek. 'It will be my greatest joy, milady, but I swear no enemy will come near you while I live.'

Torpeth and Aspin passed through the palace's outer gates, which had been mangled and destroyed. A woman knelt crying over the crushed body of a guard. Squads of Heroes and black silks ran past, weapons drawn. Servants wailed or stood watching numbly, at a loss as to what to do.

'What has happened here?' Aspin asked with some trepidation. 'Surely it isn't safe.'

Torpeth snorted. 'Silly ox! You are a reader. Do any of these people intend to stop us?'

Aspin hesitated. 'No.'

293

'That makes things safe then, doesn't it? Come along. Things have clearly started happening without us, so we're probably behind time. Very tricky when you're behind time. Means that you're not a defining force. Means that you won't be there at the concatenation or nexus. Means your hopes and desires will have failed even before they are conceived. Quickly, silly ox, or we'll end up just bystanders. This world will then end up an irrelevant bystander to the will of the others.'

'You think you're making some sense, don't you?' Aspin sighed and picked up his feet to get after the holy man.

Torpeth suddenly stopped, words tumbling out of him. 'Perhaps you're right. Maybe we should give up on that concatenation and wait here, to get ahead. Odds aren't good though. The next concatenation would find it even easier to get round us. Double-quickly then!'

And Torpeth was off again. Aspin had to change direction once more, now even further behind the holy man. Grumbling, he sprinted to catch up. They ran through the smashed doors of the palace into a large entrance hall, staircases and corridors leading off in all directions.

'I can make no sense of it!' Aspin wondered as he looked around, not sure whether he was overawed, unimpressed or just plain confused. 'Who are they? Pagans? That one is naked like you.' He gasped and brought up his spear. 'Shape-shifters!' The shifter who resembled him did the same.

'It's a mirror, silly ox. Like water, but made of shiny metal. A reflection. Forget it.'

Torpeth somehow had half a dozen stones in his hands, although where the holy man had been carrying them about his person, Aspin had no idea. Torpeth cast them on the floor, his eyes flicking as they scattered hither and thither. They'd hardly come to rest before he was instructing Aspin. 'You take the stairs down. I will go up.'

'What should I do down there?'

Torpeth looked left and right, as if to check they were not being overheard, and brought his face close to Aspin's own. 'Now listen carefully, silly ox, for this is very important. You must not get yourself killed.'

Aspin waited. 'Is that it?'

Torpeth nodded solemnly. 'Yes. You understand? Move quickly, but not so quickly that the concatenation will have to see you ended. If you get yourself killed, it will make it very difficult for us to help your friend Jillan, perhaps impossible.'

'Right. Good to know. Old goat, where shall I meet you again?'

'Don't ask stupid questions. We don't have time for them.' Torpeth frowned, turning his back on the mountain warrior and climbing the wide sweeping staircase ahead of him. He slapped the bare cheeks of his behind as he went. 'Go, silly ox! Go!'

Jillan squeezed through the jagged crack, inevitably tearing his pretty white shirt as he went, and pushed deeper into the heart of the hill. At last he reached the echoing cavern of the core and crept forward. He heard booming and whistling voices ahead of him. There was more than one Saviour here. If he'd been wearing his armour, he might have confronted them. As it was, all he dared do was crouch in the shadows and eavesdrop on them.

The one he knew as D'Shaa was the most solid-looking of the Saviours present. There were three misty figures of a similar size to her, the four of them arranged in a circle of cardinal points, looking in at a horned and dominating shadow in the centre.

'The Disciple has the boy,' the indistinct Saviour to D'Shaa's left said.

'And the child of the rock god?' the gloom in their midst demanded. 'She seems the necessary guide to the Empire's bane.'

'She will be claimed momentarily. My Saint has her fixed in place.'

'Good, D'Syr.'

'Enlightened one, how will the bane's cooperation be secured?' asked another Saviour faintly.

'D'Shaa, have you not told D'Zel, he who Declared for you, of our organising in the south? I am surprised. Or do you share more with the east now?'

D'Shaa did not move a fraction or hesitate in her answer, but Jillan felt her discomfort. 'No need has arisen before now, enlightened one. D'Zel, we use D'Jarn's army of the east to bring proper stability to the south. In so doing, my Saint and that army claim the girl who is the bane's sacred heart.'

Jillan felt sick to his soul. They were talking about Hella. What had he done? Because of him, the entire Empire and its Saviours had turned its intent towards taking Hella. There was nothing that could prevent or deflect such a power once it had determined its course. Surely he had doomed her. Nothing she had done could ever justify such punishment. How could he have done this to her? How could he have abandoned her so? He realised now that he did not care if she had or hadn't kissed Haal. It was just as Saint Izat had said. What would he not do for the woman he loved? And now it was too late. His selfishness had condemned them both.

D'Zel had allowed a second to pass. 'Yet the boy is an *unstable* element and has only caused *instability* in the Empire, even more so once the Peculiar was let loose, enlightened one.'

Jillan could not fathom what D'Zel was hinting at. Was he disagreeing somehow? Was the Peculiar a genuine threat to the Empire? If so, why had the Empire let him loose? And why had they even imprisoned the Peculiar, when it was the Peculiar who had betrayed the old gods to the Empire in the first place?

All looked to the giant Saviour in the middle, him they called *enlightened one*. 'It is the paradox of convergence, as our will in this realm becomes manifest and we move ever closer to seizing the Geas. As the Empire's all-defining order comes closer to triumph, so paradoxically the power of the *instability* will grow. Should the bane somehow elude our attempts to secure him and if he has assumed the full power of the Geas, then only a trap of sun-metal can end matters. The Great Saviour himself has overseen the building of a box of sun-metal around the Gate in D'Jarn's region. The box may only be opened by express command of the Great Saviour, and only then if the bane has already assumed the full power of the Geas and managed to deny both us and his own sacred heart. Yet it is impossible for any to deny their sacred heart, as it would create a state of unbeing. By that, we know our triumph is inevitable now the convergence is begun. As is our will. The Geas will be ours.'

'As is your will, enlightened one.' The four bowed.

Every hair on Jillan's body stood on end. His fists were clenched so tightly that his fingernails had drawn blood from his palms. He realised that he had also put one of his fists to his mouth and bitten down hard on it, to keep from swallowing his tongue. They said it was inevitable he would betray the world. And in his heart of hearts he knew it was true. What would he not do for the woman he loved, she who was his sacred heart?

Torpeth sprang up the stairs, deliberately breaking the rules by taking six at a time. Well, what was the point of being a follower of Wayfar if you couldn't get to cheat a little every now and then? He knew he would pay for it later, but dared not let the concatenation escape him. Once one slipped away, it was rarely recaptured. He took the entire length of a corridor in two flighted bounds and landed lightly at the side of a young fast-moving maidservant just as she was about to take a corner and disappear into the labyrinth of the palace. Her face twitched with anxiety, but she was remarkably self-possessed, given what was probably going on in the palace. He immediately knew she would have the wherewithal to help him.

'Hello.'

She yelped in surprise. 'Where did you come from?' She took in his nakedness. 'Did you lock yourself out of your room . . . milord?' She did not miss his begrimed and unkempt condition, but apparently that did not preclude him from being nobility.

'I am a close friend of your Saint. My name is Torpeth. Perhaps you have heard of me. No? Probably for the best. What is your name then?'

'Keren, if it please milord.' She bobbed a curtsey.

'Aha! Keren. Yes, I have heard of you. They mentioned your dimples. Jillan would like them.'

'What else did they say? The others are terrible gossips, and I really don't have ti—'

'No, I don't have time for it either, my dear. Nor does Jillan. Now, I need to talk to Izat. She wants to talk to me, you see. But I haven't been to the palace in a while, since before you were born actually. All the corridors look the same to me. And I need to look in on Jillan on the way, unless he's already with Izat. So thank you for offering to help me, Keren. You're a good girl. I shall mention you favourably to Izat. They said you were the right person, a person who knew things. Lead on then, before too many people see me naked with you and even more gossip starts circulating.'

Keren bit her bottom lip, unable to sort through exactly who had said what. 'Well, I don't know if Jillan is back in his room—'

'Fine. Let's go and see. Quickly, Keren. I hear someone coming.'

They hurried along several corridors and Keren stopped at a pair of doors. There was the slow thump of footsteps coming towards them from an adjoining corridor. Torpeth dragged Keren inside the room and closed the door.

'Milord—'

'Shh!'

'Her Majesty's guest is not here. Jillan must still be with Her Majesty.'

'If he had any sense, he'd be hiding in here. But if he had any sense, he'd also be wearing his armour.' Torpeth gave the maidservant a sidelong glance. 'Young lady, why is it that Jillan is not wearing his armour, hmm? Exactly how did you get him out of it, may I ask?'

Keren's cheeks coloured.

Torpeth nodded. 'I thought so. Still, I've fallen for it myself in my time. With the same armour, as it happens. Dare I put it on now? Or would the old insanity return? The mad desire to right the world? If I am to see Izat, it might be wise to wear it. See how its golden runes wink at me. It knows.' Torpeth whirled round. 'Keren, what do you think?'

Keren, who was backing away towards the door, jumped. 'I . . . er . . . yes, milord. The armour would suit you.'

The thumping footsteps sounded right outside the door. She turned her head in fright, staring at the wood panelling. When she glanced back into the room, Torpeth had vanished. Someone tapped her on the shoulder. She screamed. Somehow Torpeth was right behind her, wearing the armour.

'Shh!' he opened the door a few inches.

'Don't!'

A massive knight of sun-metal crashed past them, an unconscious Jillan slung over its shoulder. A wave of heat came through the door and Keren had to step back. Jillan had been wrapped in a tapestry of metal thread, and that appeared the only thing saving him from being burned.

Torpeth closed the door and hopped from foot to foot. 'Oh dear. A Disciple. Too difficult, too difficult. If I freed Jillan now, where would it lead? Nowhere good. An angry Disciple and the Saint's People all around us. The silly ox and the rock woman would be all mixed up in it. Then where would we be? Too dangerous to free him.' He froze, one foot up in the air. 'Perhaps I should kill Jillan then, to stop the others using him against the Geas. It's a thought. It would be easy for me to kill him too. I will just step up behind the Disciple and gently break the boy's neck. Bet the others wouldn't have seen that coming. It might be the kindest thing.'

'Please don't. You're frightening me!' Keren warbled. 'I was wrong. The armour doesn't suit you! With your dirty little member and hairy arse hanging out, you look like one of those monkeys they use in the mock battles for Her Majesty's entertainment.' She realised what she'd just said and clamped her hand over her mouth in fright.

Torpeth went into a low crouch and winced as his testicles hit the floor. 'Let me think again. If he were dead, what then? All the trouble here would disappear. The others would have no reason to keep any in Godsend alive. The Empire would be made stronger than ever. All eyes would turn towards the mountains and my friend Praxis would become guide to the others. Aspin would be upset about losing his friend, do something stupid like attacking me, and be killed. His father, overtaken by unreasoning grief, would become an angry tyrant to the mountain people. He would seek revenge against me, the Empire, his own people and the gods themselves. He would hurry the end of the mountain people. Only the east and Haven would remain. The entire Empire will descend upon it and all will be lost. Too dangerous to free him, too dangerous to kill him then. Best to do nothing for a bit. Keren, my dear, let us go and see your Saint. Maybe she has some ideas. Otherwise, I will entertain her like one of those monkeys she likes so much while we wait. Lead on.'

Her blood had flowed like lava from the countless wounds the guard had inflicted upon her with his spear of sun-metal. He had never seemed to tire of hearing her shriek and cry for mercy. And so she had fallen silent, and the guard had become frustrated and bored. Finally he stopped.

'Who said you can't get blood from a stone, eh?'

She knew better than to answer him. He spat on her through the bars.

'End of my shift, Saviours be praised. I'll be getting some grub. Don't go anywhere, you hear?' He chuckled. 'Mind yourself, demon, cos it's Raggar's shift now. He's not as nice as me. Give him any trouble, and he'll have your innards out so he can wrap 'em round your neck and strangle you with 'em. On account of how his baby son died as it was being born, see? Strangled by all its mother's gubbins as it tried to win free of her, it was. All know that she must have promised the life of her firstborn to a demon in return for the love of a good man like Raggar, or some such. Killed many firstborn in your time, have ye, demon?'

Freda huddled against the far wall, trying to stop her ears. And then he was gone. Blessed moments of being left alone. If only she could be alone all the time. Maybe she should never have gone to help Norfred during that cave-in so long ago. She could have stayed where she was in the thickness, safe from people like Darus, Saint Azual, the Overlords and this guard. But no, the miners of the Underlords would have found her eventually. There was no hiding place. Jillan had told her something similar once. There was no hiding from the Empire. He had to fight against it, so that Hella and his friends might be safe. He had to wear his armour to stay strong, and use his magic to hurt people, even if he didn't really want to.

Her blood stopped flowing and crusted over, becoming as hard as the rest of her skin. She waited for Raggar. If she got the chance, she would hurt him, even if she didn't want to, and even if she felt sorry for him because of what had happened to his son. She wondered what had happened to the child's mother. Maybe she would ask Raggar, or would that make him angry? It might be better to keep quiet, but if he became angry he might make a mistake and she would get the chance to hurt him and escape. She was pleased with her plan and thought that even friend Anupal might nod and smile to hear it. *Very good, dear one. It's good if I don't have to do everything for you. It's time you understood the world, even if you lose much of your endearing innocence at the same time. Time to escape!*

The vibration of feet approaching. For some reason she expected Raggar to be as large as herself, perhaps larger, but the guard who looked in at her was of normal build. And his face was not harsh like the other guard's. Instead, it was . . . She squinted up at him. He waved at her and smiled. He looked kind. Was it some trick? Friend Anupal could make his face seem gentle, even when he was killing someone.

'Hello there. What have they got you in here for? Not pretty enough for the courtiers up above? That's why I ended up down here, you know. When I was younger, they couldn't get enough of me. But there's always someone younger who comes along. And I got caught with a noble's courtesan. Not a great career move. Are you thirsty?'

He was trying to get her to speak. It had to be a trick. But she nodded her head.

He held a beaker of water through the bars to her. It might be poison. Or he would deliberately drop it as she reached for it. This was the moment. She would break his wrist without any effort at all. She would haul his arm between the bars, slamming his head against the door in the process. Again and again. He would give her the keys at her demand. Or he would black out and she would be free to hammer at the door without interference. Surely its hinges could not hold against her determination. This was the moment when she would escape.

'Thank you,' she said before she'd realised it. Freda flinched, expecting a blazing spear to stab her. Then took the water, sniffed it and sipped. His face had not changed. 'Are you not Raggar?'

The guard laughed. Despite the strangely flat echoes of this place, it was still a joyful sound. 'I should say not. I neither look nor smell anything like him. Stomach trouble, apparently, so I got his shift. But between you and me, I suspect he's been at the worm liquor again. Worst drink in the world, but guaranteed to get even a god drunk, and make them ill too.'

'Do you know Jan?'

The guard paused. 'I am Jan.'

'You are? Really?' Was there something about his features she recognised? 'And you know Norfred?' Dear Norfred.

Jan's face lost all trace of humour, but he couldn't hide his curiosity. 'Who are you? Did one of the others put you up to this? If so, it isn't funny. Or are you a demon after all?' Now he feared it was her tricking him.

'Look.' Freda gestured at her size and skin. 'I was born in the mine in the north. I helped Norfred when he was trapped. He . . . he taught me things. Told me about the world. Told me about you. He was like my father too, but I have never thought of it like that before.'

Suspicion. 'What do you want?' Anger. Fear. 'Why do you say he *was* like your father? What happened?'

There was a lump in her throat. Why couldn't she see properly? It was called crying, she remembered. 'It-it was Darus. I tried to save him, honestly I did. And Mistress Widders tried too, but there were too many of them.'

'Darus,' Jan moaned, resting his forehead against the bars of the door. 'I should have been there. But it was so long ago. The mine, like a dream.' He didn't draw another breath for a long time. 'Father insisted I should leave for the world of the Overlords. He was so proud, so proud.' He looked at her. 'And you came to tell me this? Is that why you are here . . . because you are my sister?'

She struggled to speak. 'Before Norfred went to join the Underlords, he asked me to leave the mine, to find you. He said if I ever saw you, I should simply tell you that he loved you more than anything. I looked everywhere for you. North, south and now in the west.'

He nodded his understanding. 'That was . . . kind. What is your name then, sister? And why are you in this cell?'

'Norfred called me Freda. Everyone calls me that now. I don't know why they put me in here. They said they were going to show me a rock garden. Jan, I haven't done anything wrong. My friends and I are meant to be guests of Saint Izat. They said we were heroes for saving the south. One man said he loved me. But it was a trick, I think. I had never met him before. I do not think he was telling the truth.'

Jan shook his head sympathetically. 'Not many people in Shangrin do. And the things they used to tell us in the mine about the Over-lords . . . I don't think they were true either.'

'I try to tell the truth, Jan.'

'And that's probably why you've ended up in here, Freda. Perhaps I should release you, but I'm not sure if it will do any good. The Saint will know. She always knows. There would be guards everywhere before you could get very far.'

'And you'll get in trouble. I wouldn't want that. Unless you could come with us?'

He sighed. 'If only I could, sister. But the Saint owns me. I was

Drawn by her, you see. I cannot disobey her even if I want to. And in a way I love her. And she loves me too. She loves all her People. It doesn't make much sense, does it? I know it doesn't. Freda, I'm as trapped and locked up as you are, in truth, and so's the Saint. Sometimes I just wish it would all end. Perhaps one day we'll wake up and it will all be different. Maybe tomorrow they'll decide to let us all go.'

Jan closed his eyes and fell to the floor.

'Sorry, we can't wait till tomorrow,' Aspin said and resheathed his knife, having used its handle to knock the guard cold. 'For that day never arrives.'

'Friend Aspin!' Freda rumbled. 'How are you here? What did you do to Jan?'

'At your service, milady. I read that he wasn't going to release you. And Torpeth said we should hurry. Knocking him out seemed the quickest thing to do. And the Saint won't have seen me through his eyes this way. If we're lucky and she hasn't been paying close attention, she'll assume her guard has fallen asleep at his post.'

'He's not hurt, is he?'

'No, no. Nothing to worry about.' He took the keys from Jan's belt. 'Let's get you out of there. Where's Jillan?'

*Down below, dear one!* the Peculiar spoke to her. *The temple of Akwar is here.*

'I-I'm not sure. I think we need to go deeper though. Goodbye, Jan. I hope we can talk again another time. Tomorrow perhaps. I hope you feel better soon. I will let you out of your prison if I can.'


He did not approach her as he would a mountain deer. He was not so slow and careful that he could lift a salmon out of the water, hold it in his arms like a child and kiss it before it realised what was happening. He did not approach as he would a resting butterfly he wanted to observe more closely. Nor a songbird that filled him with wonder. Nor a dew-jewelled cobweb that was so delicate he dared not breathe. He approached as if he did not want to, as if he should not be there at all.

He sat near her and did not speak.

'Do not look at me. You must not look at me. I command it.' She giggled. Her head was bent forward, her long dark hair hiding her face.

'Since when did I ever do anything you told me, my Queen?'

A fat drop of blood landed wetly on the rug beneath her. There was a sticky pool there, the ends of her hair brushing into it like it was face paint about to be applied.

'Torpeth?' she piped. 'Can it be you? You *are* naughty. I told you that if you left you were never to return.'

'You did? Perhaps they were words spoken in the heat of the moment,' he offered. 'It was so long ago I hardly remember it, my Queen.'

'Why are my old lovers returning all at the same time? And why do they bring pain and torture with them? It cannot be coincidence.'

'We are too old to believe in coincidence.'

'We are too old.'

'I think that's why I smell bad.'

'That's because you don't wash. You always smelled of goats.'

Torpeth bleated. 'So it is said. Torpeth the Great Goat.'

'I do not want you here.'

'I know, my Queen. I do not want to be here. These things are not of our own making though.'

'Yes, they are of our own making. We have lived long enough to make that the case. I wish it were not so. I wish . . . so many things, Torpeth. And now it is all ruined. I have ruined it, and ruined myself. I was so close. It was almost all mine! Now I am nothing. There is nothing for you here. Can't you just leave me be? You only add to my torment. Do you come to mock me now that I am so ugly?'

'My Queen, we excited each other so much when we first met precisely because neither could control the other. I had ruled the gods and you ruled the largest of the new regions. Each of us was used to being surrounded by those who submitted wholly to our demands and whims. Mirrors all around. It was like being trapped in our own minds, and we were insane with it. We were natural enemies but, as soon as we met, we loved each other as much as we hated each other. We needed and wanted each other. It ended the constant reflection of self. It made us sane for a while. And in that sanity I saw it was good that my tyrannous reign of self-reflection was ended. I saw I had killed so many just because they were not me. And those that had not died had had their selves erased. I saw that I had fatally lessened the gods by making them nothing but reflections of myself. I saw that my desire for an end to the constant reflection of self, my desire to have the sanity of being with another I could not control, was me allowing the others to enter and topple the weakened gods and my rule. Through you and them, I was set free! So yes, my Queen, you came close and it was nearly all yours, but perhaps it is better like this. You were so beautiful before that I felt ugly next to you, and hated you for it as much as I loved you. Now, I do not feel ugly and only love you. And the love of your People for you will not lessen. They will see you now as they have always seen you. You have the power over them to make sure that happens. Apart from me, then, the only person who will see you any differently is yourself, and perhaps that is a form of sanity after all.'

A few tears fell with her blood onto the rug. 'Why do you tell me this, Torpeth? What is it you want? Your interest is in my prince and the Disciple more than it is me. I know it. You fought at Jillan's side in Godsend, did you not? What is it you would ask of me?'

'It is this. Let go of your designs on Jillan. Do not think of him as yours or as any prince you might win. Should I free him of the Disciple, do not seek to reclaim him. Even as I leave your palace to free him, do not seek to prevent me. See what you do to yourself in trying to hold him to you. The closer and more tightly you hold him, the more he will hurt you. You try to hold nettles, you grasp at thorns, you embrace fire, my Queen. Leave him be and find another peace for yourself.'

Saint Izat's reply was a hysterical laugh. 'Peace? What do you know of peace, pagan? Who are you to use such a word? You are doomed to walk the world naked and alone. Do not pretend you know what peace is. You ask things of me that would only increase my pain and torture. A Saviour listens to my thoughts and words even now. Should I accede to your request, I will be most severely punished indeed. I must serve their will. I *must*. You ask the impossible.' She raised her ravaged face and looked straight at him. 'Do not say more.'

He considered the glistening tendons laid bare where her cheeks had been. They stretched and contracted as she spoke. That the sawing and yawing of tendons could describe so much meaning when combined with the wet sack of her lungs inflating and deflating fascinated him. How could such a fragile and tender physicality speak and conjure ideas to knit an empire together and then control it? How could it decide the fate of an entire world? It should not be possible. By what magic was it done? Always he had sought an answer and never had he found it. He tilted his head at the bloody skull, wondering whether it would be better to lick it or speak back to it. What might the taste of it tell him? Would it give him his answer at last or just make him sick? Pine nuts seemed to be the only food he could stomach any more. Why was that?

And how did it make the Empire real? How did it give it a body and animate it? Somehow, it was through the sawing and yawing of tendons. And there it was. He realised that the Empire was no more than the weak and vulnerable physicality before him. It struggled to live, little more than glistening tendons, a wet sack and a bloody skull. Its struggle was a constant pain and torture. It suffered to an almost fatal degree in attempting to continue its existence and to create a living Empire. It sought power to create life. It attempted to reconstruct the mechanics of it, looking to mimic and supplant the natural power of the Geas. It was in constant pain and torture because, although it had mastered much of the mechanics, it could not fully discover the true secret of the power – all it could produce were deformed half-beings, miserable grotesques and the rotting and infertile undead, monstrous parodies of those who were truly living.

Would it ever give up looking to discover the secret and power of creation? Could it be persuaded? Could it stop striving to continue its existence forever? Probably not. It did not want to die. Torpeth understood that, precisely because he wanted to die more than anything else and was perversely denied it. He'd tried to end it, of course, many times and in many ways. He'd only succeeded in making himself extremely ill or seriously injuring himself – and he always recovered. He'd realised that he was causing himself great suffering to no avail, apart from amusing the gods immensely. He'd then had a vision that stopped him trying to force his own death. He saw himself throwing himself off a mountain and down to the plain far below. He lay broken and unable to move, but always aware. Drifting sands and silt buried him so that none could find him. The silt hardened and he was encased in rock, unable to move. He saw nothing, heard nothing and could not speak, but was always aware. He felt only pain. And he stayed this way forever.

He shuddered now to think of it. Better not to seek death unnaturally or cheat it unnaturally than to end up buried alive forever, be it in the Great Temple or a broken body. He considered the glistening tendons of the creature that insisted on cheating death. 'My Queen, I do not need to show you a mirror for you to know pain and torture are already yours. Should you obey your Saviour and hold Jillan to you, pain and torture will be yours. Should you disobey your Saviour, pain and torture will be yours. That is of your own making. It is inevitable. The result for you will be the same, but the result for the world will be very different, depending upon your action. I will go now, to discover what you decide. Goodbye, my Queen.'

'Stay with me, Torpeth! I cannot bear to be alone!'

'One day, perhaps, as long as you do not try to have me wash, my Queen.'

She smiled raggedly. 'Even if I tried, since when did you ever do anything I told you?'

He inclined his head. 'I will send in the girl Keren. She will tend to you. Treat her well, for she loves her Queen and will be distraught at what the Empire has done to you, if you let her see your true face.'

Runes drifted past her eyes, light, dark, translucent and ghostly. They were a shifting liquid text that told the living tale of Akwar, his followers and the world. They were the water. Every swell of blue and rippling rainbow was a new page before her, being turned so that her eye travelled on. Freda looked into the depths and saw older tales there, some terrifying, some exquisite and some half-forgotten, but all part of a greater whole.

'There's something coming!' Aspin called urgently. She saw the air shimmer with the chiming runes of sound. She gazed about her in wonder.

She looked down at her hand. It was inscribed with layer upon layer of chiselled runes. No, they were more than inscribed. They *were* her. They were more than a language. They were the description and being of will. They had a logic. Whose logic was it? Just as the runes were her, so the logic was her intent. All was embodied and embodiment. Rock was not separate from water, water was not—

*Here, dear one!* Anupal demanded, interrupting and waving away her thoughts as if they were smoke. *Quickly. Across the lake. Use the stones. Act now! Hear and see nothing else. I command you as you are bound to me.*

Her gaze was fractured and smashed. Runes spidered out of the corners of her eyes. Beauty and narrative became fleeting and random, meaningless. He disrupted her sight and mind, just as it was his purpose to disrupt the world, to prevent the perfect ordering of the other four gods, so that they could be neither omnipotence nor absolute destruction. He was their necessary anti-will, just as sun-metal was the necessary thwarting of all things. Gaps and voids grew between the runes, unbinding and twisting them until they were a senseless chaos. A bloody purple pool. A bruise and plague spreading through and across Akwar's clear body.

Freda looked to the stones leading out across the lake. They floated impossibly. She could not discern even the runes of Gar. She did not understand what she saw. Surely they could not support her. They would tip her into the bottomless depths of Akwar's holy lake and she would sink forever, sink like the stone she was. Her fear of them was absolute. How could it be that she feared stone itself when she was a child of the rock god? Anupal. He had done this to her. He had made her scared of her own shadow, scared of herself. He'd trapped and bound her with his dark and confusing words, anti-runes, binding agreements and commands. She realised that from the first moment she'd stepped into the waking world of the Underlords and Overlords she'd been owned, trapped and commanded. Darus, then Goza, then Anupal. Even Norfred had laid the aegis on her of finding Jan, Jan who had stood guard over her prison. None of them had freed her from the other – they'd simply passed her from one form of captivity to the next, and each one was worse and tighter than the last.

'Freda, it's here! Ye gods, it has Jillan. Help me, Freda!' Aspin cried.

*Your cursed limb rises and is planted on the first stone. Do it, you lumpen shrew! You will free me!*

Part of her sought to obey, just as she was bound. Yet it was his own power that defeated him now. Was it that his command could not operate in the temple of another god? Or, in disrupting the incarnate runes of the other gods, had his power unbound the stones before her and made them impossible to attempt?

And Aspin needed her. He who had freed her, where so many sought to do the opposite. And Jillan was here. He who had sought to free them all. He who had lost so much in trying to do so. He whom the

Empire and Anupal wanted trapped and owned more than any other. Anupal's hold on her had slipped for a moment, and a new determination and self had at last come to awareness in her. She was stone. Terrible crushing rock. Obdurate will. She turned her back on Anupal.

*No! Graceless wretch!*

Aspin stood balanced on the balls of his two feet, one spear held ready below his waist, one ready above his shoulder. His people did not adopt such a stance lightly, she knew. It signalled challenge and intent. To fight. And his people did not fight unless they were ready to kill. To be otherwise was to cede a potentially fatal advantage to any opponent.

Yet he was naught but a thin silhouette to Freda, for a dozen feet beyond him was the blazing sun as a suit of armour. Its light was so fierce she could only squint at it. There was a band of dark over its shoulder. Jillan.

'Release him!' Aspin demanded. 'Freda, are you there?'

'I am here, friend Aspin.'

'You are as futile as you are mortal! There can be no defiance before the indivisible, indissoluble and irresistible will of your Saviours!' scraped and echoed the armour. 'We are their will made manifest as the most essential substance of the cosmos. We are here for the rock woman. She will be chained by us or she will see Jillan die. She will bow before us.'

Freda glimpsed a thin chain of sun-metal dangling from one of the Disciple's gauntlets. This being was the next in line of those who would own, trap and command her. And each was worse than the last. Her new determination and self seethed with anger and rebellion. 'If you wanted Jillan dead, you would have killed him already,' she growled back at the thing she hated most in the world. 'Aspin, enough of these words!'

The mountain warrior was in the air in an instant, his upper spear driving through the dark slot in the armour's visor. As Aspin landed right before the Disciple, the end of the first spear snapped off inside the armour and made clanging noises as it fell down into one of its boots. His lower spear came up and stabbed into his adversary's groin area. The second spear shattered on impact.

The Disciple stepped forward, making no effort to bat Aspin aside, apparently intending just to walk through or over him as if he were not there, or was of no consequence. As its first leg moved, Aspin stepped against the inside of its knee joint, so that the armour would fall and he could push off and away from it, to get beyond its immediate reach.

But the armour did not fall. It did not even wobble. It remained solid and came forward without interruption. It stayed right on top of Aspin. The warrior only avoided being trodden down at the last instant by throwing himself awkwardly aside, all balance lost. If the deathblow came now, he would never be able to avoid it.

The Disciple ignored the pagan warrior and kept coming for Freda, its chain winding and lisping through the air as if it were alive. It flicked and snapped out towards her. It would have wrapped itself around her neck if she hadn't already started to sink forward into the ground.

Aspin was immediately up and coming at the Disciple from the side. He rammed the end of one of his broken spears between the plates of its bent knee joint and heaved. At the same moment Freda dived, came up beneath the shining servant of the Saviours and hauled on the foot of the same leg. The Disciple's leg dragged; it teetered, and its own momentum pitched it forward onto its front, flinging Jillan's wrapped form forward and off its shoulder. The armour clattered awfully on the rock.

Aspin was instantly on its back and jamming the last broken half of spear up under the back of the Disciple's helmet, trying with all his might to lever it off. Freda rose out of the ground and turned.

'Aspin, no! Leave it. We must get Jillan away from here while we can.' She came round the Disciple as quickly as she could, knowing she had only moments to act.

With a roar, the Disciple pushed itself up off the ground. The inhuman strength of its arms threw it back into the air and straight onto its feet. Unprepared for the sudden and violent movement, Aspin flew backwards and landed badly on his back, winded.

The Disciple's fine but infinitely strong chain lashed out and licked around one of Freda's arms. It pulled on her hard and she was spun and bowled away from Jillan even as the chain unwound from her arm.

The Disciple advanced, reaching for Jillan. Freda flung herself forward, half below and half above the ground. Her paw closed on nothing as the Disciple lifted Jillan away from her. Then it moved with speed to grab her with its other hand. She went under the surface, but the hand punched through the ground and clawed at her. Lumps of her skin were torn away by its merciless fingers and she cried out. She tumbled away, hoping that she could find refuge deeper down. She feared to go too deep though, in case she broke through into the lake somewhere. *You're not thinking straight!* she told herself. *Back up!* She realised with horror that the vibrations of the Disciple were moving away from her . . . and straight towards Aspin.

Too late, she burst back above the ground. Jillan was draped across the armour's shoulder once more. The Disciple had wrapped one of its giant hands around the mountain warrior's head and face and was holding him off the ground. Aspin was trying to beat off the grip, but had to remain half holding on so that his neck would not have to bear his entire body's weight. Even as she took in what was happening, Aspin's struggles and muffled screams were becoming weaker.

'You *will* bow before our inevitable and irrevocable will, rock woman. We do not need this pagan alive. You will bow to us or see it die. Decide quickly, before its face melts from its skull. It is already being burned so badly by our touch that it is unlikely to survive. We are the light and its pagan soul is the darkness.'

The smell of Aspin's sizzling skin and hair assailing her nostrils, Freda fell to her knees and glared up at the Disciple. 'Release him!'

Aspin was dropped and the Disciple's chain whipped out, looping a turn and a half around her neck and its loose end returning to the Disciple's same hand. She grimaced as the sun-metal heated her skin.

'Resist and you will end up pulling the chain tight yourself. Resist too much and you will cause the chain to separate your head from your body. You will carry Jillan as we go.'

And the Disciple led Freda on a chain from the palace of Saint Izat.

'Are you still alive, silly ox?'

'No!' coughed the charred and smoking mountain warrior.

Torpeth tutted. 'You have been careless, silly ox. Did I not warn you to stay alive?'

'I still blame you for getting me into this, old goat. Where were you? Romancing some old girlfriend? What if the headwoman were to find out? Meanwhile, you left me to burn alive. I feel like I have looked directly into the eyes of Sinisar himself. Bury me in the deep here, where Akwar's holy waters might at least bring me some relief.'

'Ah! That is a good thought.' Torpeth left for a few seconds. 'Ready?'

'No.'

Water was thrown onto Aspin's face and he screamed. Hot coals were pushed into his eyes, through his cheeks and down his throat.

'It will subside. It is healing!' Torpeth yelled back, putting his fingers in his ears. 'I will be back soon. There is someone I must go and laugh at first.'

The holy man left Aspin writhing near the edge of Akwar's mystical lake and went sure-footedly across the stepping stones that led into the distant darkness. He went on for some time until a light grew ahead of him, the light at the centre, the light of the sun-metal bowl that was Akwar's prison.

Torpeth leapt lightly onto the invisible island of ice and walked up to the sparkling box in which the Peculiar sat in cross-legged con-templation, eyes closed.

'Well, well.' Torpeth grinned. 'Trapped by a mortal. Humiliating, eh? Fair enough, it's only humiliating because you now have an audience in me. Sorry about that. Out-thought by a mortal too. What do you think it means then, troublesome imp? Or were you too clever for your own good? Did you set one trap too many, so that not even you had an escape? Trapped yourself?'

The Peculiar opened unreadable eyes. 'I am free in here. You are trapped out there.'

Torpeth stretched lavishly and whirled his arms around. 'Funny, it doesn't feel that way to me.'

'Release me.' An even tone.

'No.' Even more even.

'You know none can survive without me. The elseworlders will bring all under their control if there is no random element to thwart their planning.'

'We were surviving very well until you betrayed us to the others. The survival we've had since has hardly been worthy of the name.'

'Still you will not accept your own responsibility for the fall, Torpeth the Great? Still you have not learned? Your doom still rests heavy upon you, I see. Outcast of your own people. Yes, I was the means of the betrayal. I do not deny it, for that was ever my nature. Yet yours was the intent that allowed the betrayal, was it not? You cannot deny it, even though you try.'

Torpeth yanked handfuls of his beard out and threw them at the clear wall between them. 'You seduced me with your whispering wiles!' he spat.

The Peculiar gave a mild shrug. 'Yet there are laws of my own nature even I cannot break. I did not and could not supplant your own will. Do you accept responsibility?'

Foam gathered at the corners of Torpeth's mouth. '*All* must accept responsibility!'

'Release me.'

'What, Trythaniogg the Tempter? No promises of power, sweet seducements or exotic inducements this time? Is it because I am divested of all selfish needs and desires? Is it because there is *nothing* you can offer the naked warrior? Is it because you are rendered power-less by me and so shown to *be* nothing?'

Slyness came stealing up. The dark god put a finger to his lips and beckoned Torpeth closer.

Torpeth's eyes widened in fear. He put his ear to the side of the box. He wanted to pull away, before any words could be spoken, but he had challenged the god – to refuse to hear his words now would be to admit error, defeat and guilt. And the logic of that defeat would mean the need to release the god. He could not still his trembling.

The ghost of the god's words came through the glitter. 'I will gift her to you, Torpeth. Old Sal will be yours. The headwoman. She will forgive you. She will l—' his tongue lingered in delectation as he formed the letter '—ove you again.'

'No!' the holy man howled, his mind teetering on the brink. He had fallen off the mountain before, in his vision. He knew what awaited him. He frantically wiped the thick drool from his mouth into his beard. He staggered back from the madness. He pointed a shaking finger. 'I do not deserve her, damn the evil hydra that is your tongue! Never will I release you into the world again.'

The Peculiar transformed into the deformed and raving loon of his hideous nightmare form. 'RELEASE ME!' he roared, shaking the box and causing cracks to jump crazily through the ice. His eyes flared in fear and he was suddenly a demure youth again. He watched the creeping and creaking cracks in terror. 'What have you done?' he whimpered.

'I'd be silent if I were you,' Torpeth hissed, turning away. 'One more word might be all it takes. I would not even move.'

The Peculiar froze.

Torpeth ran as if rabid dogs were snapping at his heels and flailing testicles. He skipped across air, water, stone and light, anything that could take him more quickly from this place. Aspin was in his arms and then they were out of the palace. They were on a horse, racing along the track at the side of the river that meandered away from Shangrin and beyond the west.

'I know this horse,' a much healed Aspin noted as he bounced behind Torpeth in the saddle. 'Floss. Belonged to a trader. Jacob, was it? Of Godsend? How is it here? Surely it is not coincidence.'

'We are too old to believe in coincidence,' Torpeth intoned. 'These things are of our own making.'

The witch-urchin, a sack over her shoulder, sprang from stone to stone and came up to the starred ice that imprisoned the Peculiar. 'I am here, my lord.'

*I was not sure you would hear my call.*

'I am yours, Dewar Lord. I have always been yours. Did you not heed me when I summoned you to Thorndell? How then could I not answer your call when it came? Did your book and guidance not free me from the cruel people of Thorndell? Did you not then appear to me yourself, free me of the terrible hounds and lead me out of that place? I have come to release you in turn.'

The Peculiar stared at her, the first and only tear he had ever shed upon his beautiful cheek. *I cannot force you to release me. Nor do I have the courage to ask it of you. For it will be your death, and you are my last remaining follower. Trapped between the two layers of ice is a sun-metal gas. If you break the layer on your side, the gas will be released and you will need to breathe it all in if I am to escape. You will not survive it.*

'While you are not free, Dewar Lord, neither am I. I realise I have never been free really, but in helping you I might be. Besides, who else is there to help you? No one. And when there was no one left to help me, you were there.'

*Dearest one, you humble me. I have not known true grief before. It is the most terrible thing, and the sum of all the horrors with which I have plagued mortalkind since the beginning of time. And you have gifted it to me, sweetest heart. Is there nothing I can offer you in return? But ask it of me and it is yours.* What was he saying? Never before had he been so foolish as to make an open-ended promise to another.

She looked tragically at him and he tried to recoil from the heaving and slick serpents that forced their way into his mind's eye and set about trying to penetrate and devour his being. 'My lord, I do not do this for myself, but can you promise me I will forget all that happened to me in Thorndell when I am dead? Dewar Lord, take these memories from me, I beg you. Please, Dewar Lord, please. I cannot bear it.'

*I will find you in the nether realm, darling Anara, and see to it that you are troubled no more. And I will maintain the shaman's head you have there in the sack, so that his torment will continue even once you are gone. I swear it.*

'My Dewar Lord is kind. The only kindness shown me by any-one . . . except Jillan.' She hesitated to speak further.

*Go on.*

'Will you betray him, my lord? No, I know you must do as you will. Must you kill him, though, my lord? Perhaps there is another way.'

What was it with this wretched boy, that those who had known him for mere moments would plead for him more than themselves, even as they were about to die? How he hated the miserable mortal for his unseemly influence. Gently he said, *There are worse things than death, Anara. You know this.*

The witch-urchin looked down and nodded. She bent to where the ice had deep and intersecting cracks and knocked three times with her knuckle. A piece fell out with a serpent hiss and she sucked and swallowed all the poison into herself, until there was no more.

She fell from a crouch into a seated position, lifted pretty golden eyes towards her lord, whispered her love and did not move again.

His heart broke. He told himself it was because he had lost his last follower more than because he'd cared in any genuine way for her soul. He told himself that it was because he was now much diminished and

315

therefore more like the mortals than ever before. It was not because of anything else. He would not allow it to be. Besides, he still had the rotten head of the shaman as a repository of the last of the witch's power. As distasteful, disgusting and humiliating as the head was to him, it was just about enough to sustain his godly status. It had to be.

Angrily, the Peculiar smashed his way out of the back of his prison and stalked over to the giant bowl of sun-metal. For a few moments he enjoyed watching the rising steam and melting icicle that were the suffering god Akwar. 'Ah! Brother! There you are. Not looking your best, I must say. Where are your followers? Why have they not freed you? What's that you say? They think you are too much of a drip? Dear me. You've clearly been too soft on them. Spoilt them, I'd say. Fortunately, your ever loving brother is here to give you a hand. But I will need something in return, I'm afraid. A binding promise that you will act precisely as I command it, the first time I command it, at any time of my choice in the future. Are we agreed? I thought so.'

# CHAPTER 11:

# Unravelling all

Dread had settled over Godsend. Grown men started at any sudden noise, as if the enemy were among them and creeping up from behind with blades bared. Citizens stayed in their homes, doors and shutters tightly closed, not daring to peep out. Refugees cringed in the shadows at the sides of the streets or in alleyways, as if fearing the light. Even cats and dogs slunk about close to the ground whenever they were seen. The atmosphere was suffocating. The fear was like an infection.

'It's like I'm going crazy,' Jacob explained, his hand at his brow. 'Surely you feel it too, commander?' Frowning with concern, Hella put a hand on her father's arm.

Samnir nodded. He was not insensible to what was going on, although he was not as affected as the majority seemed to be. 'Such tension always comes the night before a battle. All know that Captain Gallen and his men returned this morning. The Saint's army should arrive tomorrow. The people are saying their prayers and clinging to their loved ones this night, as they know this might be their last. Others will be drinking to give themselves courage. Or sharing a last meal with friends, as we are here. It is a type of grief that comes *before* loss. Although the pain of it is understandable, good Jacob, you should try to fight it. Otherwise, it will constrict your chest and stop your breathing. I have seen it happen even to veterans.'

Jacob shook his head. 'No. It is more than that, I think. I am no coward, commander, fearing what tomorrow will bring. It is . . . is something else. It feels like when we were still within the Empire, when there was some sort of watching presence in here, in our heads. Except the presence now is not the false joy of holding to the delusional faith of the Empire, but something far more terrible.'

Thomas the blacksmith spoke up, his plate and goblet already empty where the others had barely begun to eat. Jacob smiled and piled more meat and vegetables before him. 'Samnir, I think this Praxis is already reaching out for the minds of the Godsenders. Who knows what powers the Saviours have allowed him? The Saviours will not easily give up their claim upon the souls of this region's People. The God-senders will resist him, of course, but they were Drawn to the Saviours by blood when children. Perhaps that Drawing can never really be undone. Hella and I have never been Drawn, you know, so are not as troubled as the rest.'

'And I was Drawn in the west,' Samnir murmured. He looked at Jacob again. 'I am sorry, goodman Jacob. Say on. Do you have any visions?'

'Not while I am awake. But when I sleep, I am plagued by awful dreams. I wake up exhausted and sweating. The things I see being done, and that I see myself doing, are . . . are . . . unspeakable.' He tried to look at his daughter but clearly could not bear it. 'I avoid sleep altogether now, as do many in Godsend, I suspect. As much as I want the enemy never to arrive, there's a part of me that can't wait for them to be at our gates so that it will finally be over. I just want it all to stop, before I completely lose my mind!'

Jacob buried his face in his hands, and with a small cry Hella hugged her father.

Thomas squeezed his goblet until its wood creaked and threatened to break. 'Samnir, if all the townsfolk and our soldiery are going through this sort of torture, we will not be able to survive a siege of any sort of length. We will not be able to trust them with weapons in their hands. Who knows what they will do to themselves? They will begin to see death as a respite from their suffering. What are we to do?'

Samnir ground his teeth and pulled a face. 'I hear you, Thomas, I hear you. We cannot take the fight to their great army, for it will see us slaughtered, but we may be able to draw them onto us. We must provoke them into attacking us as soon as we may. Hella, bring us more wine, for none of us will be sleeping. We have a long night of preparation ahead of us.'

Saint Praxis showed the minds of the People the hell that they had made for themselves in forsaking Saint Azual. They had taken the region out of the protection and grace of the holy Empire. The south had become a place of corruption and decay, both moral and physical. It had become the dominion of the Chaos, as had each individual's heart, mind and soul. He led the holy crusade into this dark and rotting land. He must purge them all and exorcise the demons from among them. Where reason could not prevail, they must be forced to confess and recant. Those who still resisted must be executed, lest their evil influence flourish.

He showed them the hell they had made. Handsome and beautiful faces now disfigured with the oozing sores and bleeding wounds of the plague of sin started by the bane of the Empire. Where there had been social order, peace and a happy People, now there was only perversion, desperation and wilfulness. The People were now denied Salvation. Children were no longer Drawn to the blessed Saviours, as their self-loving parents raped their souls instead. Where there had once been the rule of law organised through Saint Azual guiding the Minister of Godsend, and that Minister in turn guiding the town elders and its Heroes, now the towns and the People competed against each other, and only the most cunning and conniving survived.

He showed them what they had done. Children brutalised. Fields burned. The land a smoking ruin. The People led in chains of sin to demonic torturers. Men nailed to trees, their tongues cut out, and their genitals torn away and stuffed down their throats so that they choked. Women tied to tables and butchered until there was nothing left that identified their gender or individuality. Ravening dogs then set upon the barely breathing bodies, to eat or fornicate or both.

All this he showed to the minds of the People, and the People knew fear, fear for their souls and their loved ones. The People wailed for what they had done. They begged for forgiveness. They begged for punishment. They begged for death. They begged for Salvation. They begged for their Saint. They begged for *him*! They were abject. They subjected themselves entirely to his will, for they knew it was only through him that they could live and find redemption. Their minds became his, and the power of his vision and projected will became greater still. He would restore the holy Empire to this region and make it greater than it had ever been before, for he would also make it a holy Empire of the mind and spirit, a paradise enshrined by his own mind, where there was no evil, discontent or dissent.

'They will throw open the gates to us,' Saint Praxis informed General Thormodius and Captain Skathis with unshakeable certainty as they rode through the predawn.

'As is your will, holy one,' Captain Skathis replied haggardly.

'I pray it is so, holy one,' General Thormodius responded, no trace of sarcasm or deception evident in his voice or broad weathered features. 'We have paid a heavy toll to come this far – five hundred good men – and would not want to lose many more. If I cannot return to the east with the larger part of this host intact, the Empire risks being at the mercy of the desert tribes and barbarians.'

'You would do better to keep your faith in the power of the Saviours than to count the lives of men, General. All men are tested,' Saint Praxis advised him. 'Those who died were lacking and undeserving. They succumbed to the forces of Chaos. Their own sin found them out, and was their undoing.'

'Their holy Saint Dionan never had complaint of them,' the General said neutrally.

'Then your men had not been properly tested before now.' Saint Praxis smiled. If it were not for the fact that he needed the man until the attack on Godsend had begun, he would have ordered Captain Skathis to kill the General on the spot. 'I compliment you on your loyalty to your men, General. That loyalty is misplaced, however. Is it not true that plague is now rife among the men? Did you really think to conceal it from me?'

The General licked his lips. 'I did not wish to trouble your holiness unnecessarily.'

'Is it for you to make such judgement, General? The plague is the Saviours' punishment for sinners. *All* sinners are of concern to me! Would you seek to hide them from my gaze?' Saint Praxis pushed at the General's mind, but the veteran's defences were a fortress.

'Yes, holy one . . . I mean, *no*, holy one! I apologise if I have overstepped my position.' There was a sheen of perspiration on the older man's forehead, despite the coolness of the day.

'General, those with plague will be separated from the rest of the men and will launch an assault alone against Godsend. It may go some way towards redeeming them in the eyes of the Empire. And it will afford them . . . Now, what did you call it? Ah yes. *A soldier's death*. It is the best they might hope for, is it not, General, sacrificing themselves in the name of the Empire? After all, they would not live long enough to see out a siege, would they? What say you, General?'

'It is a good plan, holy one,' the General said, the lines of his face etching deeply. 'It is . . . merciful.'

'And General?'

'Yes, holy one?'

'You will lead the assault of the sinners against Godsend, do you understand?'

'Yes, holy one. It will be my pleasure. And with every throat I cut, and every heart I pierce, I will think of you, holy one.'

The sun would not rise, as if it too feared what the day would bring. Samnir and the few thousand defenders stood waiting silently upon the ramparts of Godsend, watching the forest beyond the town darken with more and more of the enemy. The sky above the dark green of the fir trees was a purple bruise running into black. Unusually, the wind came from the south, out of the far-off mountain home to Wayfar's last followers, across the graveyard and midden pits outside Godsend's most southerly wall, and then to the defenders on the northern wall. It pushed at them, as if it was thinking it would be a kindness to send them to a quick death below. The smell of damp earth and mouldering death filled Samnir's nostrils, an odour with which he'd become very familiar during the long years of lonely vigil as Hero at the end of town closest to Jillan's home. It was somehow comforting to him now.

Yet those who stood with him were anything but comforted. Every face looked pale and drawn, with hollows for eyes. Goose pimples on their arms and breath held, they watched the trees, knowing that the doppelgängers, demons and monsters that they'd always been told dwelt in the deepest parts of the forest were about to emerge. Their nightmares were about to come forth. The thing of which each of them was most scared had them trapped and was coming for them now. There was no hiding this time. It had found them. A few of the younger soldiers whined with an animal terror.

'Enough of that!' Samnir shouted, but his voice sounded small against the sky. 'You are free men and women, beholden to no one! Your lives are your own. You will not apologise or quail before any enemy, be it ghost or corporeal. You will stand proud! Here, see the fierceness of my blade!' He cut his forearm with his sword of sun-metal and dripped blood on it before holding it aloft. 'None can stand against it, whether they call themselves Hero, Saint or Saviour. I have beaten Saints before and will do it again. We will all beat them!'

'Aye!' Thomas bellowed from the corner of the north and west walls. Hella echoed him.

'Aye!' called Haal from north and east.

'Aye!' called an officer, lifting his own blade of sun-metal.

There were more shouts and the semblance of a cheer. But then came a high-pitched cry, 'Look! There! The enemy advances! Gods, preserve us!'

A group of mounted men came out from under the trees and positioned themselves on the road from the north gate. Armed men could now be seen along the entire treeline of the north wall.

'They face us along the western approach too!'

'And the east! We are surrounded!'

Yet all eyes were drawn to the horsemen on the road to the north, to one particular figure in a long black coat who sat taller than any other. His pale eyes met the gaze of every single one of the defenders at once. He saw each of them as if they stood alone, just as they saw him. The straight lines of his face were right before them. They watched like nervous schoolchildren who wanted to please their teacher but feared they had displeased him. His rigid posture told them they had erred, and erred badly, but he smiled, and they clung to that with hope. Every one of them heard when he spoke.

'My children, do not be afraid, for I have returned. Godsend need not be alone any more. *You* need not be alone. You will have both Saint and Minister again, and all will be well, for I am one of you. We are all one People. Simply open the gates and all will be forgiven. You *know* the disharmony and unhappiness you have caused by stepping away from the Empire, but even so you will be forgiven. How can I blame you for what has happened when I was not there to guide you during your hour of need? My People, I blame myself! Will you not forgive me as the blessed Saviours forgive you? Will you not open the gates and embrace me as the Empire wishes to embrace you once more? Will you not let communion replace division? Will you not let peace replace suffering? Open the gates to Godsend, to your hearts and Salvation!'

Thomas was shouting, railing back against the words. Samnir shook himself and looked around. A number of the men below had moved to lift the bar from the northern gates. 'You men, halt!' he barked in his best parade-ground voice. Trained to obey his commands, they came to a stiff stop.

'Nothing will be asked of you if you but do this. There will be no punishment or guilt,' the voice of Saint Praxis continued around them. 'There will only be celebration. Open the gates to Godsend, your souls and paradise!'

The soldiers at the gate started to unbar it again. Samnir grabbed a bow and arrow from the slack grasp of an archer near him and loosed at one of the guards below. The angle was difficult, the light of the dawn was still weak and he had never been the greatest of shots. He cursed as he took the man in the neck and a horrible gurgling cry broke the Saint's spell. 'Restrain those men!' Samnir shouted. 'By Wayfar, Gar, Sinisar, Akwar and even Miserath, restrain those men or may the devilish Saviours take you!'

The defenders of Godsend blinked and struggled back to themselves. Jaws became firmer, the grip on weapons tighter and the set of shoulders more determined.

'Praxis, you are a snivelling worm!' Samnir called from where he stood above the northern gates. 'Though I do not wish to sully the good name of other worms.' Thomas laughed loudly and the men jeered the enemy. 'Every person here knows how you betrayed this town to Azual and how you sought to see us all slaughtered. *That* is how you and the Empire seek to deal with free thinkers, is it not? Why are you even here? What is it you want of us? We owe you nothing except payback for your crimes. And I will not negotiate with the sort of unprincipled creature who would send my old comrade Callinor, Captain of Heroes' Brook, here in the guise of friend but actually compelled to attempt assassination!' The defenders shouted in outrage. Samnir noted a good number of the soldiers among the enemy ranks muttering to each other. 'That is not the act of an honest preacher! You speak of communion, peace and embrace, but you would hold us close all the better to use a concealed weapon.' The sun began to show above the distant horizon, its first rays fully illuminating Samnir atop the battlements and glinting off his polished breastplate. 'If you were an honest man, if you truly cared for any of the People, you would face me in single combat so that the lives of both the townsfolk and the eastern army would be spared. Well, are you honest enough, preacher? Are you man enough to meet me in single combat, preacher? Or will you attempt to wriggle out of that challenge like the worm we already know you are?'

Saint Praxis gave a humourless and brittle laugh. 'You would call me childish names as if the immortal souls of these townsfolk were some laughing matter. You have betrayed them to the Chaos and eternal damnation and now stand there pleased with your handiwork, posturing and arrogant demon! Well, the blessed Saviours will not allow you to perpetrate such a calumny unpunished. It is precisely because we care for the People that this army has come to reclaim their souls, at risk to their own lives. Only a Chaos creature would stand in the way of their redemption. You say you owe nothing, but you have stolen their souls from the protection and grace of the blessed Saviours. You accuse others of betrayal, yet was it not you who first defied good Saint Azual and helped bring about all that has come to pass? *You* brought about all the death and suffering that this town has already seen, and it is *you* who seeks to bring about more, all so that you can feed your master the Chaos, all so that it can gorge on the souls and misery of humanity! Any deaths that occur today are on your hands. You seek single combat as if the Empire might cede all these souls to the Chaos on the single toss of a coin or over a single hand of cards. *Never* will the Empire cede those souls to the Chaos, demon, do you hear me? *Never!* Step aside, demon, and none of the townsfolk shall be harmed, as the blessed Saviours are my witness! You and the Chaos creature Hella will put yourselves into our care and release the People of Godsend, none of whom will be harmed. Refuse, and you will bring the divine wrath of the blessed Saviours down upon you. People of Godsend, hear me! Throw down the Chaos creatures called Hella and Samnir and you will be forgiven! Throw them out or the divine retribution of the blessed Saviours will see you all punished. You know the punishment that awaits you. You have all seen it in your dreams!' The Saint's voice gathered force, as if it were the heavens themselves now speaking. 'You *fear* it! As you *fear* the damnation of your own souls! As you fear being abandoned by the divine! As you cower and know your own frailty and failings! As you know your own imperfection! As you know your innate sinfulness, even as you try to be better and self-sacrificing.' The depths of hell called out to them.

The battlements of Godsend descended into panic and tumult, all discipline lost. A few stood lost and unknowing. Others clasped their hands over their sacred hearts and choked out sobbing prayers. But the majority were petrified, clinging to the battlements for dear life or grabbing anyone near them and wailing for rescue. One individual became unhinged and hacked with his sword at any who came near him. Men to either side of Samnir turned accusing eyes on him and looked as if they would lay hands on him, but he snarled at them and they retreated in terror. The whole town cried out, overtaken by a writhing mania and suffering. The din was overwhelming. Samnir could not block it out. He had done this. The guilt would always be his. He vomited onto his boots, staggered and fell to hands and knees. In despair and biting himself cruelly, a sergeant threw himself off the walls to his death. Another followed him, and then another. More hurled themselves to their deaths, first handfuls, then dozens at a time, then a mad rush. The first that landed were killed outright, but those coming after had their falls broken by the dead and only earned themselves shattered limbs and crippling impact injuries, until those coming on after buried them and slowly crushed the life out of them. Their groans and whimpers alone were a torture to hear.

He knew the battle was about to be over before a blow had even been struck against the enemy. 'Get ahold of yourself!' Samnir shuddered, reeling back to his feet and pushing back against those who threatened to carry him over the wall in their haste to end it all. 'There is nothing to fear!' he yelled, as much to convince himself as those around him. 'The fear comes from him, from the enemy! He exhorts you to your deaths! You want no part of such sickness. Fight it! You are soldiers and that is what you are here for. To fight! Where is your courage? You will obey me and stand firm! You will obey the voice of sanity within you.

You will hold to the gods if nothing else, and they will protect you! You have been given life for a reason, and that is to live it! Live! Shout it proudly! Live!'

Mercifully, those who could not get to the edge of the wall because of the crush before them heard his words. They turned their faces back towards him, hardly daring to hope. He slapped the one nearest to him hard across the cheek. 'Live! Shout it, damn you!'

'Live!' the soldier croaked in wonder at his own voice.

'Live! Pull them back from the edge, man!'

First one man, and then small groups, worked to obey him, holding close to each other so that they could not be dragged back into the sea of madness. But it was like trying to hold back the tide. 'Live!' they begged their comrades, but too many could not be reached in time. 'Live!'

Saint Praxis held his arms aloft, chanting mayhem and directing the murderous maelstrom of negative emotion. 'Redemption through death!' His eyes had become wild with power, his face a livid and leering mask. 'Die, you sinners! Unburden your souls of your undeserving corpses!'

The air over the town was a black storm of fear that sucked away everything that might sustain life, all light, all hope. The miasma built and thickened, lightning striking and forking down at those thinking to resist. A thickset soldier right next to Samnir was blasted. His eyes were liquefied and sent running down his cheeks. He opened his mouth to scream and his tongue blackened and smoked. The murk pressed down on Godsend, increasing the pressure until even the sane were holding the temples at the sides of their heads and raving.

Samnir gave an inhuman cry. He couldn't save them. It was hopeless. How did man in his arrogance ever think he could stand against the incalculable forces of the cosmos? How did this pitiful species dare feign any sort of comprehension of eternity and the divine? Such things were entirely beyond its self-obsessed knowledge, reach and worth. Man was a spoilt and petulant child that aped experience and wisdom. It was a grasping animal that called its base habits *character* and *reason*. In truth, it was as thoughtless and unknowing as it was undeserving. Its presumption was contemptible. It demanded its own destruction.

'I cannot save them,' the old soldier wept. 'Jillan, I am sorry!' The darkness around him deepened. The sound of the dying faded. He knew that this was when it all slipped away from him and his own fight ended. At last he would be able to rest. The irrational defiance that had driven him, even as a young man, would finally be taken from him and he would know peace. His wayward and bloody years of fighting in the desert, the disgrace of his service in the Great Temple, the crimes of his time as a Hero upon the walls of Godsend – that guilt would be stripped from his conscience just as his life would be taken from his body. At last. He welcomed it, wanted it more than he'd ever wanted anything in his life, more than he'd wanted to be free of the— *No, do not think of such things*, he told himself, even though he was not sure why he should not think of them. He'd done his best, after all. He just hoped Ji— *No, do not think of him. It is enough.* He frowned, not sure why he should not think of *Jillan*. Samnir forced his eyes back open.

Without being aware of it, he'd been on the brink of throwing himself off the wall! He pulled back behind the safety of the battlements, cut his arm with his sword and used his blood to make the sun-metal flare and drive back the filthy occlusion that mired him. For a few seconds he breathed cleanly, and then the Saint's will came crowding back in. How many cuts and how much blood before he was too drained to hold it back any more?

'Rally to me!' he called, not knowing how many still survived.

He poured his life out onto his sword and held it high, clearing twenty yards in all directions. Dozens of soldiers and young messengers were curled up in foetal positions or hunkered down around him. They squinted up at him.

Suddenly there was an answering flare of light further down the wall, red eldritch energy crackling through the nightmare that the dawn had become. It cut straight into the black heart of the doom and dissipated much of it. Pagan runes wrote themselves across the sky, flaming like an angry sun. Hella strode along the wall, the blade Thomas had forged for her sweeping away the evil clouds of influence. She directed the blade straight at the distant Saint Praxis and slashed the burning runes into his eyes. He fell back in his saddle with a cry of rage and covered his face with his arms, his hold over Godsend undone. 'The Empire did not give us life. It is not for the Empire to take it away!' she declared. 'You did not create us! And you will not succeed in making us in your own image, pretender! The Geas will not permit you. Rise up, people of Godsend! There is nothing to fear.'

'See the Chaos witch revealed!' Saint Praxis retaliated, his bloody gaze seizing his army. 'So be it. General, lead your penitent sinners against the last of these heathens. Not one life will you spare save the witch's. She is to be brought to me in chains so that she will know the worst torture of all. The Chaos will be driven out of Godsend, General. The glory of Godsend will be restored and all your sins will be forgiven. Any of your men with plague who survive will receive my own healing touch and blessing. They will be raised and have their names recorded in the Book of Saviours. They will be put forward for beatification. Their souls will know an eternity of peace and ecstasy.'

The General turned his bleak eyes towards Godsend. A muscle twitched at his jaw and his neck corded for a moment, then stilled. 'Thy will be done, holy one,' he replied pitilessly. 'Captain Skathis, have our archers step forward and rain down vengeance upon the walls. Have them use arrows of sun-metal, for nothing will prevent their course. Provide cover for the advance and concentrate your aim as necessary so that we will establish a foothold.'

The Captain shouted the orders, and all too quickly the archers of the Empire were spreading disarray among the beleaguered defenders of Godsend.

'Upon my command, brave soldiers of the east!' the General said to his body of a thousand sick men. 'Ladders and shields to the fore! Advance!'


His head screaming, Jillan came awake. The taint's gibbering was wild and incoherent, all but drowning out his own thoughts.

'Friend Jillan?' came a voice near his ear. Was that Freda?

'Shut up, can't you?'

'Sorry,' she said quietly.

'No, not you, Freda. Give me a second.' *Taint, I can't function like this. I'm going to shut you away.* 'There, that's better,' he mumbled, realising his lips were swollen, his nose felt broken and he was having trouble opening one eye fully. The endless sky above him swooned, and he would have fallen if it were not for the fact the rock woman was carrying him. 'Where are we?'

'On the edge of the western region, I think. About to enter the central region. Can you stand? You should escape before it realises you are awake.'

He tried to make out his surroundings, but nothing would remain still. The ground seemed an awfully long way away, as did his feet. He experienced nausea, vertigo and agoraphobia all at once and shut his eyes tightly. What was wrong with him?

*Concussion*, the taint's muffled voice came back. *It's all right. You can let me out now. Sorry. I was having a hysterical few moments. What's happening? Look, the Disciple's got us. It has Freda by some sort of chain.*

'If you say so,' Jillan replied, keeping his eyes firmly closed.

Freda dropped him.

'Argh! What did you do that for?'

'But you said—'

'I didn't mean . . .' *Look out, mister shiny buttons is turning round!* 'Where am I going to go on my own? I can't even get up, let alone walk.'

*Maybe we could roll away then?*

Freda wrung her hands in distress. 'I don't know, friend Jillan. And I don't know the way to the nether realm either. The runes told me that there is a temple there we didn't know about before. A fifth temple.'

*She means there's a temple that Miserath didn't tell us about, a temple dedicated to himself, I suspect. That two-faced two-timing double-dealing devil was going to keep all knowledge of it to himself. He was going to wait until Freda had shared the revelation of the other four temples and then, using the missing information only he had, go off and find Haven on his own. Makes you sick! No wonder he's depicted variously as hyena, weasel and jackal. Still, you have to admire him in a way. You could probably learn a thing—*

'And you still think Anupal is your friend?' Jillan demanded, slapping the ground and trying to muster some strength.

'It's all my fault!' Freda moaned.

*Technically, it's more your fault, Jillan. You went and made a deal with the Peculiar when I'd warned you against it. We wouldn't be in this mess now if it weren't for that. And then you wouldn't listen when . . . Anyway, same old, same old. Better start rolling away as best you can, cos twinkletoes is about to grab you.*

'I've just about had enough of this,' Jillan decided, opening his swollen eyes and drawing power up from his core. It sputtered fitfully, but he managed to unleash a blast straight at the Disciple as it came bearing down on him. It was rocked back on its heels and stopped in its tracks. It slapped the flat of its palm against its helmet, ringing it like a bell, and gave a shake of its head. Deciding all was well, it growled and came on again, apparently completely unscathed.

*Oops. Try again? Or are we going to start rolling away?*

But he was now so drained he did not even have the energy to roll away. 'Help?' he asked the world.

'Did someone call?' came a loud hail from behind the Disciple, followed by an animal's deep and guttural warning.

'Ash?' Jillan grinned in disbelief. 'Where have you been? You took your time, didn't you? I thought you'd never get here.'

The woodsman raised innocent hands. 'Well, you know how it is. Timing is everything, my young friend. I wasn't about to go rushing in like some bravo, now was I? It would have been the surest way to earn myself an early grave. No, I had to wait until I had the Empire precisely where I wanted it. Besides, there was this lovely inn we passed a way back, with a most solicitous and lonely widow as owner. Someone had to help the poor woman in her distress and, well, it would have been very ungallant of me not to oblige. And she'd got all her beer barrels mixed up and could no longer tell good from bad, but was lacking an experienced taster to reorganise her cellar, so . . . Anyway, you can work out the rest. After all, I had the time to spare, since I have perfect timing, do I not? I hope you don't mind me bringing my friend the wolf along. He needed the exercise, you see. Roll away to your left.'

Jillan rolled at the exact moment required to take him out of reach of the lunging Disciple, whose weight and balance was all to its right side. Ash strolled forward, raking his hands through his unkempt hair and beard as if he'd only just got out of bed. He yawned and stretched his lean frame. His eyes twinkled and he winked at Jillan. 'And roll to the left again. Wolf, when you're ready. Why, Freda, hello there! How are you? Long time no see. Your friends don't exactly take you to the best places, do they? That's a pretty enough necklace you're wearing, but it's not really you, is it? Your boyfriend insists you wear it, right? He must be a crashing bore. No offence.'

'He is not my boyfriend, friend Ash. It is a Disciple of the Saviours.'

'I see. Forcing his attentions upon you, eh? Needs a lesson in manners, it would seem.'

The Disciple, having at first gone to the right, now turned and reached with its right arm round to the left. It kept reaching after the rolling Jillan, opening itself up to the giant black wolf that came leaping in from the rear. The suit of armour crashed onto its back, its helmet gripped in the massive jaws of the wolf. There was the smell of singeing fur, but the helmet began to lever away with the painful screech of metal on metal.

'Go on!' Jillan cried.

When the Disciple had fallen, Freda had been dragged down to the ground by the neck. The chain had cinched tight and bitten deeply into her throat. She tried to yank the chain from the Disciple's left hand, but there was no give at all. She was being strangled. With agonising slowness, she crawled towards the Disciple to slacken the chain. Yet it had cut and burned so deeply into her neck that it would not come free or loosen. Her thick stone fingers could not get any purchase on the buried links. Her vision blurred and she fell onto her back. What of the temples? What of the rock god? And the Geas? And friend Jillan?

'Allow me.' Ash smiled down at her, finding where the chain met her neck and beginning to pull it out of her cracked flesh. 'Wolf, drag the knight to the left a bit. That's it. Now release and retreat, for it is about to lash out.'

The Disciple's right arm came smashing up and across its body, hammering into the ground above its left shoulder – where the wolf had been but an instant before – and raising its torso half off the floor. It was all the time Ash needed to finish prising the chain out of Freda's neck, draw its loop wide and slip it from around her head.

'Into the ground, my dear,' Ash advised her and she gratefully sank from view. He took a long step away from the Disciple and over to Jillan. 'Hmm. I suppose I'll have to carry you. I don't think we could outpace it though. Unless you might carry him, wolf?'

The black beast snarled savagely in response, saliva dripping from its curved teeth. Its orange eyes flashed with feral fury. 'Maybe not. All right, all right, keep your fur on! It was just a suggestion. Honestly, you can be so temperamental, you know that?'

With a roar, the Disciple surged to its feet and slammed its loosened helmet back into place. 'Prattling and futile mortals!' it boomed. 'Sunmetal cannot be resisted, just as the Saviours' will that I embody cannot. You cannot outdistance it, for it is indefatigable where you always weary and fail. It is unbending where your bodies are weak and fragile. It is eternal where you are limited and finite. Resist and you only bring suffering upon yourself, suffering of your own making. Obey and please us and you will glimpse the divine.'

'And I can get a pair of those boots? They're self-cleaning, right?' Ash said with a thoughtful finger to his lips. 'Bit flashy though. Maybe not.'

'These boots will come down upon your spine and grind it to dust,' the Disciple promised. 'They will crack your skull open and smear your mind into the mud. You guarantee yourself the worst of endings, and an inescapable one. The will of sun-metal is absolute.'

'Now, now, bright underling, that cannot be entirely true,' Torpeth brayed, leaping down from a fast-arriving and lathered Floss. 'Sunmetal cannot be used as a weapon if it enables omnipotence. You know that. It always thwarts the will that seeks to own it absolutely. Sorry to be so late. The silly ox set us behind the concatenation in Shangrin and we have been missing since. See, silly ox?'

Aspin rolled his eyes and wrestled to keep Floss under control as her flaring nostrils caught the scent of the wolf.

'Silence your sorry and self-serving sayings, mortal! The convergence is begun. All is within our sway, and you have helped bring that about.'

'Really? Oh dear.' Torpeth blanched.

'Jillan, you will give yourself to us so that you may be saved,' the Disciple commanded. 'If you do not, Hella will die, for she is within our power and of no importance to us.'

Jillan's face fell. The ember of hope that he'd kept burning and banked within him was suddenly snuffed out. His magic was gone and the taint was such an absence it was as if it had never existed. He looked to Aspin, his soul bare. 'Is it true, Aspin?'

Floss had stilled. 'I-I do not know! The sun-metal – there's nothing there to read. It may be lying. I don't know, Jillan!'

The Disciple had already begun to move with intent for Jillan. Ash stepped adroitly into its path, but his trips and nudges only earned him burns and bruises. He rode with the armour's movement, avoiding any serious injury, but could do nothing to deflect it from its determined path. 'Well, don't just sit there, Jillan! You'll have to work with me on this.'

Yet Jillan didn't hear him. He didn't see the shining will of the Saviours filling his vision. His mind searched in vain for Hella. He could not find her!

The wolf circled and leapt at the Disciple's back, but its scrabbling claws slid off and its teeth found no hold. It fell on its flank but immediately came back up. It tried to close its jaws around one of the Disciple's thighs, but a clenched fist came down and cracked it on the muzzle. It yelped and fell away, its tail between its legs.

'Wayfar, lift my steps so that I may run across the sky!' Torpeth called, jumping high. He loosed an ululating cry. 'W-a-a-a-y–!'

As the holy man sprang over and past the Disciple, its hand came out in a flat chopping motion and cut the air out from under him. Torpeth tumbled to the unforgiving ground, cracking kneecaps and elbows. A buckle had torn loose from his leather armour and part of his midriff was exposed. The Disciple's flat hand speared down and into Torpeth's stomach, tearing him open, seizing his intestines and dragging them out of him. His insides wriggled, flopped and writhed like a nest of serpents as they sizzled and cooked.

'Argh!' the ancient pagan shrieked. 'That stings!'

'Torpeth!' Aspin gasped, trying to get the shying Floss to face the right way. He vaulted from the saddle, bow raised and ready.

'Do not come closer, silly ox! You must not get yourself killed. The headwoman would never forgive me.' Torpeth thrashed. His back arched, he doubled up and moved no more.

'What have you done, old goat?' Aspin frowned ferociously, tears in his eyes. He did not know where to shoot the Disciple. It was useless. There was nothing he could do.

'All right, I will obey you!' Ash was promising. 'Just back up and explain this glimpsing the divine thing again.' He ducked and the Disciple's arm whooshed overhead. 'Or not. Tell me what you're going to do to my spine again.' Ash turned side on and did a backwards head over heels as the armour rushed the spot where he had been standing. And now its shadow fell across Jillan.

'Bane of the Empire, you cannot escape us now. And you never could have done. The first moment you rebelled against us, the Geas became ours, just as we had always known it would.' The Disciple leaned forwards to claim him . . .

. . . but somehow did not come any closer. Its feet had sunk into the soft ground as it had brought its weight to bear. It leaned further forward, but only sank more quickly. The earth made a loud and thirsty gulping noise and the Disciple abruptly dropped, only one arm left above the ground. The arm flung itself out, seeking to latch onto Jillan's foot, but Ash dragged him back by vital inches at the last moment. And then it was gone. There was a sudden and shocking stillness.

Floss snorted. Deep below, the ground rumbled.

The wolf whined.

'Didn't even say goodbye. No manners, some people,' Ash murmured, kicking at the ground where the Disciple had disappeared.

Aspin went and sat cross-legged by Torpeth's body. The young mountain warrior shook his head tearfully and laid a hand upon the holy man's shoulder.

The earth trembled and Ash stepped out of the way as Freda came up out of the ground. 'There. It will soon fight its way free, but we will have some time to find the nether realm now,' the rock woman managed through her raw throat.

'The nether realm?' Ash asked curiously. 'Never heard of it. Doesn't sound particularly inviting.'

'It isn't,' Aspin answered despondently. 'Foothills of the land of the dead.'

'Nice,' Ash said, pulling a face. 'Do we really have to go there?'

'You should pray not.'

'There's a temple there we have to find, don't we, Jillan? Friend Jillan?'

'What? Yes, I suppose,' Jillan agreed. 'How . . . is your throat?'

'It will mend, friend Jillan. Are you well, friend Jillan?'

'The Disciple claimed the others have Hella,' Aspin explained as he rose and came to crouch before Jillan. 'Jillan, what happened to your face? I hardly recognise you. It's good to see you again though.'

'What? Oh, it's nothing. Thank you for coming all this way, Aspin. What are we going to do? Why did I leave her? It was selfish of me. Now they're going to kill her.'

'Oh, I doubt that.' Torpeth convulsed. 'It's not how they tend to do things.'

Aspin's head whipped round. 'You're dead!'

'No. It's just a scratch. This damned armour's always been so unreliable. Fancy it letting that oafish Disciple do that to me. Made me look completely stupid. I shouldn't have put it on in the first place, you know. You can have it back, Jillan. You're more than welcome to it. More trouble than it's wo—'

'What do you mean it's not how they do things?' Jillan interrupted. 'Who?'

'The Saviours! The others! The elseworlders! Pay attention, Torpeth, would you? This is important. And no roundabout answers.'

Torpeth sniffed. 'All right, but only if you promise to take this armour from now on. Look, even if they were telling the truth about having Hella, they'd keep her alive so that they could use her against you another time. As long as you stay out of their clutches, they'll keep her alive. You nearly blew it there with the Disciple, you ninny. You're almost as silly as the silly ox here. No wonder you're friends. And they'll want to use her against you as long as you have or are about to have something they want. You'd better make sure you get something like that, eh? In the meantime, you might get the chance to free your love and play kissy-kissy, if you keep ahead of the convergence, eh? Good kisser, is she? Good thighs, I thought, when I saw her in Godsend. Probably good at climbing trees and things like that. Useful skill if you need someone to get bee honey that's high up.'

'Stop talking about Hella's thighs, would you? Thank you. We have places to get to if we're to be ahead of this . . . What is it?'

'What's what?'

'The thing you said.'

'Hella's thighs?'

'I told you not to talk ab—'

'Convergence!' Ash shouted, startling them all.

'No need to shout,' Torpeth huffed.

'How do we get to this nether realm?' Jillan asked, looking around at his companions.

'Well, we used the Broken Path before,' Aspin volunteered. 'But

335

Torpeth isn't on the best of terms with our ancestral guide any more. I don't think Pessarmon would help us again.'

All eyes turned to Torpeth. For once he looked both apologetic and guilty.

'Perhaps I can be of some help,' a new voice interposed. A diaphanous youth appeared among them and gifted them with a transporting smile.

The wolf's hackles rose. It gnashed and snapped its jaws.

'Nice to see you too,' the Peculiar sneered. 'Or should I say nice to see you at last. It was you and this Unclean woodsman following us all the way from Godsend, was it not? It is only the woodsman's deceitful use of timing that could have allowed any to skulk beyond my immediate knowledge and gaze.'

'Well, he followed and skulked with good reason. You're hardly known for being the most trustworthy of individuals, are you?' Jillan pointed out. 'And it would seem that you have been keeping the matter of your temple a secret from us.'

'I would have told you of the temple at the right time. There are certain things that I cannot disclose.'

'What's in the sack?' Torpeth asked.

'I don't want to talk about it.'

'Oh, come on. I promise not to laugh.'

The Peculiar pursed his lips. 'It's the last of my followers.'

Torpeth guffawed, holding his side that had recently split. Tears ran down his cheeks.

'You said you wouldn't laugh,' the Peculiar said sourly.

'I lied,' the holy man hiccuped and descended into more gales of laughter.

'Where is Anara?' Freda asked with obvious concern.

'Don't worry, we'll see her again in the nether realm if you want.' There was a tremor beneath their feet. 'Now, if we've all finished laughing about the considerable sacrifices I've made for you ungrateful mortals, we need to be moving along. You'll need to link hands. The wolf and the horse will have to stay.'

The wolf licked its lips.

'Don't you dare!' Ash admonished it.

*

The young Hero leapt from the top of the ladder onto the rampart. His eyes were wide and wild, fear and adrenaline driving him as he laid about him in a furious panic. He was strong and quick. Samnir held back just beyond his reach, out of the corner of his eye noting another of the enemy reaching the top of the ladder. He waited . . . The Hero hacked around him blindly, working himself up into a berserker rage and finding a strength that was near superhuman. And waited . . . The Hero sheered through a defender's side and spine with his blade of sunmetal and kept turning with his swing, bringing the sword straight through the dull metal of another defender's weapon and burying it in his shocked face. He took a shuddering breath, his starved lungs slowing him for an instant. Samnir stepped forward, punching his blade out straight and opening the young Hero's throat with its tip. No sound. The instant lasting forever. A hand going up and trying impossibly to stem the flow.

Samnir took another step, bending deeply at the knee and, with his shoulder, shoved the Hero back into the next man. Another step and he was tipping the dying man back through the crenellations and down, taking three other men to their deaths with him.

It was like killing a younger version of himself. He'd fought in the same mad whirling style and had been called the Sand Devil because of it. He fought like the spiralling desert winds of the same name that came up from nowhere and could be so devastating. His comrades had always wanted him to lead them into battle, but they made sure never to get too close to him. And when they returned to camp later they still made sure not to get too close to him. If they saw him, they looked away slightly too quickly. When forced to meet his eyes, they would smile slightly too widely. They had seen the sand devil within him and feared it would rise at any time, no matter how deeply he might seem to have buried it. By some unspoken agreement, they had all started to avoid him. He was too dangerous. He didn't obey the orders of his officers properly in battle. He was considered as much a liability as an asset. None wanted to be associated with him. He sought out battle even when ordered not to. Had he struck an officer? Probably.

He'd been punished and punished, but the Sand Devil had hardly noticed, although it had learned to keep to the shadows more, learned to choose its moments better. Learned to wait. And wait. It knew its time would come, as it always did, no matter how old Samnir became. A man who is marginalised must be seen to suffer.

And so they had come, and dragged the Sand Devil out of him. The ever-thirsting, dry and dusty Sand Devil. A force that animated the dust of the desert and the countless generations of the dead, a force that so desperately wanted the wetness and life of blood. No matter how much blood it took, it was never enough. It would never be enough to turn the desert into an eternal oasis of life.

It was better like this, though, now that the letting had begun. No more thinking, fearing and worrying. No more waiting and wondering. No more concern for how many of the defenders had been lost to the unnatural pall of the Saint. No more concern about the gaps left among his soldiers on the north wall. Should men be pulled from the east and west walls to restore the full complement of the north? Why did the enemy only send around a thousand against the north wall? Why did they not attack the other walls? Was it some ploy? Did they wait for him to draw numbers away from those walls before they attacked? It hardly mattered, for the defenders were so outnumbered it was only a matter of time. It was better like this, now that the letting had begun.

Samnir pushed the ladder away and looked up and down the battlements of his wall. The enemy had gained the walkway in at least two places, one to his left and one to his right. He went to his right, where flashes of a shield with a bright sun-metal covering told him a champion of the Empire had gained the walls of Godsend. Samnir's men were being rapidly thinned, allowing more and more of the enemy to swarm up onto the wall.

Samnir skipped past groups of men frantically pushing away ladders with pole-arms, hefting rocks over the parapet and stabbing over the edge with spears. One of his men fell and Samnir stepped over him into the gap. The commander of Godsend knew the ragged wall of his men would not be able to hold against the sun-metal weapon that the Empire's champion was bound to be wielding.

'Fall back!' Samnir shouted. 'None of you have sun-metal. I have the blade to settle this.'

The men around him shuffled back, giving him a moment and the

338

room to use his weapon more freely. He took down two of the enemy with quick and efficient slashes and then faced the champion.

'You.'

'General Thormodius.'

'I should have killed you all those years ago, Sand Devil. You were always trouble, but never did I think you would turn traitor.'

'Search your soul, general, and you will know why you did not have me murdered. Because you were once honourable, and a better man than this,' Samnir panted.

'And I fight for the honour of the Empire still, for I would not break my oath as you have done.'

'It is the Empire that has broken its oath to us, and you know it. What sort of general is it who leads an attack on enemy walls himself? Only a suicidal one who has given up hope.'

'And what sort of man is it who would lead so few against the eastern army of the Empire? Only a suicidal one who has false and heretical hope.'

'Perhaps we are not so different, General.'

'We are nothing alike! I am a man of good faith. You are one of the damned, Sand Devil, and always have been. This ends here and now!' So saying, the General skewered forward with his long thin blade. Samnir only just battered it aside with his short blade in time. Samnir swung his shield out on the flat, but the General was an experienced warrior and knew better than to come following in after his first thrust. He swayed back, avoiding the shield by a comfortable distance. His blade had the longer reach. He could afford to bide his time until a clear opportunity inevitably presented itself.

'Clumsy, Sand Devil.'

Samnir swung his shield out extravagantly again as he came back the other way, leaving himself wide open, but the move was so amateurish for one of his reputation that the knowing General refused to take advantage of it. Which was his mistake. Samnir let go of the shield at the top of its flat arc and it flew straight into the General's face, its rim cracking the top of his nose.

The large man staggered back, flailing with his weapon to keep Samnir at bay, but was bumped by the crush of men behind him and thrown sprawling forward again. His sword hand hit the stone walkway. He just about held onto his blade and brought his arm quickly up to the guard position before him, completely severing his hand in the process. As the General had come on, Samnir had side-stepped and held out his short blade so that the General would disarm himself on it. The hand fell to the walkway and the men of both sides stared.

'Finish it,' the General commanded, waving the stump of his arm, which had been as neatly sealed as it had been cut.

'No.'

'Curse you!' the General snarled, bringing up his sun-bright shield and charging Samnir.

Although Samnir was the taller of the two, the General was by far the broader and heavier. Thormodius slammed his shield into Samnir's torso and drove him backwards across the walkway to the crenellations. His sword trapped between shield and body, there was nothing Samnir could do to halt the enraged man. His chin burned horribly on the edge of the General's shield. The commander of Godsend screamed, but deliberately let go of his legs and allowed his face to drag down the full length of the incandescent surface. His hair went up in flames and he felt his nose and the end of his chin disappear as he fell under the General of the Empire, who pitched over the wall and down to the dead below.

The arrows of sun-metal had raked the battlements and taken a terrible toll. For some reason, the only section of wall that remained unscathed was the one which Hella occupied at the corner of the north and west walls. Then the charge with ladders had come and it had been a desperate effort keeping the enemy back. She'd been shaking with exhaustion within ten minutes, and they were coming in greater and greater numbers. Only Thomas seemed untroubled by it, flinging rocks with one hand that she would have been unable to lift with two.

If the defenders of Godsend had not lost so many to the Saint's evil magic and then the onslaught of the sun-metal arrows, they would have turned back the attack successfully, Hella thought. As it was, as the sun cleared the horizon, the relentless push of the enemy inevitably secured a toehold at several places along the north wall.

Taking his mighty blacksmith's hammer in hand, Thomas wasted no time moving along the walkway to the nearest incursion, yelling, 'For Godsend, you miserable dogs! Will you go meekly or roaring your passion for life?' His comrades shouted in answer and redoubled their efforts. He pushed his own men aside so that he could better get at the enemy. His hammer smashed through two heads in one swing. And another. Swing, *squelch*, swing, *crack*, swing, *crunch*. He worked with the same tireless rhythm and ferocious intent as he did in his forge. The battlements of Godsend were his anvil and the enemy were the material that he bent to his will. Single-handedly, he undid the entire group of the enemy that had established the bridgehead.

More Heroes made it onto the wall between where Hella stood and where Thomas had moved to. A scarred and grim-faced Hero at the top of a ladder threw some liquid from a bottle into the eyes of the knot of defenders trying to repel him. The Godsenders screamed, fell back and wiped furiously at their eyes. Their faces reddened and blistered. The wind carried a whiff of the acid and burning to her nostrils and she felt sick to her stomach. Grimface sprang onto the walkway and dispatched the six blinded Godsenders with unhesitating and practised efficiency. One fell clutching his throat, blood gouting between his fingers. One went down trying to hold the mess of his loins where the blade had come up from low. One with thin armour despairingly tried to hold his guts in. Two fell silently, their faces missing. And the last lost his legs, fell on his back and had his throat crushed beneath a stamping heel. Then the scarred Hero turned his eyes towards Hella.

'Thomas!' she cried, no idea if he would hear her over the terrible clash and the sound of death, cursing and suffering. What right did she have to be heard over the urine-soaked youth who wept in paralysed fear, or the old man who coughed his final prayer as bloody foam? 'Thomas!'

The blacksmith's head came round sharply, saw Grimface and understood the threat immediately. 'Face me, whoreson of the Saviours!'

Grimface ignored the challenge and methodically carved his way towards Hella. This was no ordinary soldier. This was a man who'd dedicated his entire life to killing. He was a master of the art, a priest of its worship. Although his sword was of normal steel, his other hand left an after-image whenever it moved, and she realised he had a tiny sliver of sun-metal as a second weapon. He used it to deadly effect.

The huge blacksmith sprang after him, but more of the enemy were gaining the wall and getting in his way all the time. Thomas swung his gore-covered hammer again. A spear tipped with sun-metal separated the head of the hammer from its handle. The flying metal head crunched through the chest plate of one of the Heroes and threw him down to the cobblestones of Godsend. Thomas staved in the spearman's face with the handle of his hammer and wrested the spear from his dying grasp. Now the blacksmith swung with one weapon and stabbed with the other, none able to avoid his reach, resist his strength or halt their own deaths. Yet they slowed his progress, and Grimface moved ever closer to Hella.

'Protect Hella!' Thomas bellowed, but the Godsenders were sorely pressed and barely able to protect their own lives. The few that managed to pull away were effortlessly cut down by Grimface.

Hella brought up her sword, knowing she would now have to face the Hero. Her blade was perfectly balanced and felt like an extension of her arm, but she did not have the hard muscle or training of a fighter. Thomas had taught her the rudiments, but there had been no time for more than that. Her sword hand felt sweaty and she gripped the hilt hard, even though Thomas had told her never to grip too tightly. But what else could she do? The blade would slip from her fingers otherwise. She held the sword up and out, trying not to let it waver and betray her fear. *Let the blade do the work for you*, Thomas had said. *Its sun-metal is deadlier than you will ever be, lady. Just make sure you keep it on the centre line connecting you and your opponent. Always push and defend along the centre line.*

Grimface approached warily, probably more out of respect for the blade than for her, she realised. Its runes glowed threateningly at him and she unexpectedly felt hope. She steadied herself and took a stance with her weight balanced on the balls of her feet as Thomas had shown her.

'Witch!' Grimface sneered, his voice itself the whisper of a blade. His eyes locked unblinkingly on hers.

'Murderer!' she squeaked.

He smirked. 'Put that down before you hurt yourself.'

'I will put you down, you rabid animal!'

Too late she realised that his fixing gaze and words had been meant to distract her as he drifted forward within her reach. She twitched her sword left and right. She tried to keep the movement of her hand slight – Thomas had shown her that a small hand movement could move the tip of the weapon a comparatively big distance, and that it was important not to move it too far – but even so she took it too far from the central line between them. With his sliver of sun-metal Grimface pushed the blade wider still and gave himself all the room he needed to step in close to her and club the side of her head with the hilt of his sword.

She lost all ability to coordinate, dropped her precious sword and flopped down to the walkway. The world and the sky spun and tilted. She felt sure she was sliding off the walkway. Was that Jillan shouting for her, looking for her? She tried to reply but her tongue was too big for her mouth. Or was it Thomas shouting?

Grimface slipped his sliver of sun-metal into a special sheath at his belt and reached for her sword. It skittered and clattered away from him. 'Unholy thing!' He cursed and kicked it off the walkway and down into the town. He took hold of her and hauled her up.

'Let go of me!' she said thickly.

He blinked in confusion and his hand fell away from her. He frowned and grabbed her again, pinching her throat so that she would not be able to speak again. He turned just as Thomas was about to reach them. 'Back or she dies!'

'Release her or so help me—'

'One twitch of my hand and her throat will be torn out,' Grimface said softly. 'If you cause me to make any sudden movement, *you* will be responsible for her death. Ease up.' The Hero moved towards a ladder protected by four of his comrades, lifting Hella and forcing Thomas back.

'No!' came a shout from those fighting behind Grimface. A figure broke free and drove an old short sword into Grimface's back. The Hero arched and let go of Hella. He turned, wrenching the blade stuck in the ruin of his backplate out of his assailant's hand. The sliver of sun-metal came up into the dying Hero's hand and he cut his killer open from sternum to crotch before falling dead. The Godsender, dressed in a hotchpotch of mismatched and ill-fitting armour, fell on top of him.

The four Heroes went for Hella, but Thomas was on them before any could touch her. He drove his spear up under the chin of one and out through the back of skull and helmet. He pulped the face of another at all but the same moment with a backhanded swing of his metal hammer handle. He brought the spear horizontal, despite the weight of the Hero impaled halfway down its length, and lanced forward with it through the third's chest. The blacksmith crashed into the fourth Hero's shield and felt heat slicing through his side. The enemy had stayed on his feet and his sword came up for a finishing blow.

'Drop your sword!' Hella said with as much authority as she could muster, pointing at the Hero.

The man froze. Thomas swung his long handle and near-decapitated him. Blood sprayed everywhere. It coated them, was in their mouths and filled their lungs. Hella retched. She couldn't clear herself of it. It filled the air. The sun itself seemed to burn red.

Thomas looked down at the wound in his side. Grimacing, he used the sun-metal of the spear to sear himself and slow the bleeding. He would live, but only just.

Hella crawled over to the Godsender who had saved her. 'Gods, no. Haal!' she wailed. 'You shouldn't be here. Not like this!'

'I wouldn't want to be anywhere else,' he said faintly. 'Tell Jillan I'm sorry.'

'Don't go! I order you not to die!'

His eyes tried to focus on her but could not. 'Hella, tell me it was you I kissed. Tell me I did not imagine it. Even if –' he coughed blood down his chin '– it's a lie!' The last word came out as a slow exhalation.

'It was me!' she lied for him.

A ghost of a smile touched his lips and he heard and saw no more.

'It's cold, so cold!' Ash chattered at one end of their line, holding tightly to Aspin's hand. The woodsman looked as wan as any phantom, and ice had formed in his beard and eyebrows.

Jillan certainly couldn't ignore the temperature, but it did not seem to affect him as badly as it did Ash. He suspected his armour, which he had donned once more, was protecting him with its magic. 'Hold on, Ash. We're nearly there. We're reaching the end of these mountains at last.'

'Mountains?' Ash echoed. 'I see only forests in winter.'

'Each of us sees in the mist whatever we imagine this place and death to be,' Torpeth said next to Aspin, who was keeping his eyes deliberately fixed on the ground. 'Here, imagination, will, body, life and death come together. Ash, if you keep telling yourself how cold you are, then you only speed how quickly this place drains you. You weaken your own will. You will yourself towards death. Jillan, if you see yourself walking along icy crags and precipices and fear to fall, then you are only a small step from doing so. You put yourself at risk. You must discipline yourselves like Aspin and always see the ground before you. He knows that those who walk the Broken Path are only victims of themselves.'

'That's not exactly true, but it's close enough,' the Peculiar replied, the band of sun-metal around his brow burning away the mist directly before them. He held Torpeth by one hand. Jillan and then Freda were on his other side. 'The mists here will fashion what you imagine, know and fear, yes. Yet there are also things within the mist that pre-exist you. Ancestral memories, shared stories and prayers, ancient tribal images on cave walls, spirits, monsters and locations that many have seen through the ages or believed in.'

'Are they real?' Ash asked with head lowered, now mimicking Aspin.

'To all intents and purposes, yes.' The Peculiar nodded. 'They are certainly dangerous. That is one of the reasons that we must hurry. The longer we are here, the greater their chance of finding us.'

'But they're not dangerous to you, surely,' Jillan objected. 'You are the god of this place. We're going to your temple.'

The Peculiar did not answer at once. The mist swirled in among them, dimming the Peculiar's crown for a moment. The silence stretched. Jillan thought he felt tension building, as if something out there waited hungrily for the Peculiar's answer.

'It is best if we do not speak of such things,' the Peculiar at last said with some care. 'Our words and thoughts expend too much energy, an energy that can all too easily attract the wrong sort of attention.'

Ash jumped and shakily made to look back over his shoulder. 'There's something following us.'

'No, there is not,' the Peculiar insisted. 'Do not look back. There is no need. There is nothing there. You are too suggestible, mortal. We descend now into the valley where we will find my temple.'

They moved down a steep rocky path and onto a field of moss-covered rocks and low tumuli. Jillan trod on a rock and it broke beneath his foot. He realised it had been a large skull instead of what he had assumed. What he had taken to be the branches of denuded bushes now resolved themselves into bones sticking up out of mouldering piles of the dead.

'It's a graveyard,' Ash moaned.

'But what creatures were they?' Torpeth asked with keen interest. 'I do not recognise the skeletons. See, that humanoid skull has horns. And that one claws. They are enormous. Look, that one still holds . . . is it a weapon? It's too curved, isn't it? Was it used for cutting, throwing, both?'

'I don't want to see it, Torpeth. Enough!' Aspin warned.

'The warrior is right. Do not look too closely,' the Peculiar said. 'These here sought to seize the temple for themselves long ago, but were not strong enough. Pay them no heed or they will become resurrected around us. Focus on the temple ahead. That is our only concern. You should not see anything else. It is too dangerous. Close your eyes, all of you, and I will lead you. You must trust me. Even inside the temple, there will be depictions you must not see.'

All except Torpeth obeyed the Peculiar as he pulled them forward. 'I see the temple ahead. Some sort of stony barrow, is it? A wide low entrance. How far does it go beneath the ground? I do not recognise the style of construction or the carvings I see there. It was not built by people like us, was it? There were mortal beings that came before us, weren't there? What were they like? Like the mountain trolls, who have their own gods?'

'Please, don't!' Ash whined.

'Torpeth, shut up!' Aspin demanded with his eyes shut, but crushing the holy man's hand for emphasis. 'The headwoman said you were to obey me. You almost got us killed with your nonsense last time we were in this realm.'

'Ah, but I did not kill us, did I, silly ox? Surely that is the more important thing.'

'Listen to your tribesman, Torpeth the Great,' the Peculiar advised, his face becoming ugly. 'This is not wise.'

Torpeth shrugged. 'How can I be wise if I do not know and experience more? I do not claim to be wise, but I would be foolish to listen to you again, dark brother.'

'You must trust me.'

'You are the god of mistrust. I cannot trust you. I will not trust you. What is it you seek to keep a secret from us? This temple was not always dedicated to you, was it? You usurped it. You stole its secrets for yourself. It was built by those who came before Man. They worshipped another god, didn't they? An older god. One that you still fear.'

'Are you mad?' the Peculiar asked, his ugliness replaced by the face of a young boy who has lost his parents in a crowd and is now being led away by precisely the sort of stranger he has always been warned against. He tried to let go of the horrid man's hand, the leering old man, but he was held tight.

Jillan felt the air gust faster around his feet, and bones being disturbed. 'Torpeth, stop it! This is not the time or place!'

Freda tried to sink into the ground, but the bones somehow prevented her and she only served to trammel them up. One skeleton looked as if it was about to climb free.

'No, dear one!' the Peculiar called out. 'You must keep hold of Jillan's hand or you will become lost to us. This place will claim you for its own.'

The rock woman was close to hysterical.

'Freda, remember the rocks I gave you for a necklace. They shine so prettily, so bravely in this fog. It's all right. Your friends are here with you. We will not leave you.'

'What was the god's name?' Torpeth pushed. 'Don't you hear them whispering it? Chanting it? Singing it? Don't you hear it?'

'You stinking pagan!' Ash whimpered.

'Old goat, don't!' Aspin shouted fearfully.

'You'll kill us all!' the Peculiar gibbered.

'Kathuula!'

The sky thundered and the ground bucked beneath them. Ribcages and skulls rose before them.

'Run!' the Peculiar yelled, dissolving his hand out of Torpeth's grasp and dragging Jillan and Freda on towards the temple.

'Don't leave us!' Ash cried, but his voice was lost in the tumult. 'Where are you?'

The Peculiar, Jillan and Freda were scrambling up into the barrow of stone and earth, and then suddenly falling down into its dark and echoing underground chamber. Jillan had been forced to open his eyes during their flight so that he didn't trip. He looked around now by the light of the Peculiar's crown. Quickly, he took in the large and intricately carved block of stone in the centre. It was hideous and made his stomach squirm. He looked away, and prodded at the soft and sticky blackness of the floor. It had saved them from injury but stank worse than anything he'd ever known. It overwhelmed him and made him dizzy with appalling images. It was the putrid ichor of death, the sludge of the decomposition of the countless generations and species sacrificed upon the altar of death at the centre of the chamber. He realised he had only seen the very top of the altar and that it went down and down into the pestilential well of filth. How deep did it go? Did it go down forever? And yet it was almost full. Were they so close to the end of mortalkind, so close to the end of all life in their world?

'We have to go back for them! We can't just leave Ash and Aspin out there.'

The sky thundered again, for all the world an angry voice, the voice of Kathuula.

'It's coming closer. We don't have long. Jillan, they will have to find their own way,' the Peculiar told them. 'Freda, have you found the runes?'

'I'm sinking!' the rock woman shouted from near one of the chamber's earth walls. The ichor had quickened in answer to the will of Kathuula and she was already up to her knees. She grabbed at the roots of the plants that had grown through the walls, but they were long since dead. They snapped and crumbled in her hands.

*Jillan, the runes are down here,* a voice bubbled up out of the sucking rot.

'Mother?' he mouthed.

'Dear one, you must get to the altar of death,' the Peculiar urged

348

Freda, thrashing over to the block and waving her to come and join him. 'The runes will be there. Be brave!'

*I am here too, son. We are so happy to be with you again. Join us.* It was his father, Jed.

'I thought I'd lost you.'

Freda flung herself as far towards the altar as she could. She waded and fought against the liquid death. It was at her waist.

She lurched sideways towards Jillan, who was trying to worm his way down into the muck. She hauled him out, slapping away his efforts to fight her, and determinedly breasted her way towards the altar.

'Here, Freda! Can you read this side? Now move round to the next side. Go on!'

'Who dares invade the temple of Kathuula?' boomed the chamber. The bones of the dead pushed out of the walls, splashed down into the ichor and took on black, dripping forms.

The pool of death was up to her neck and rising all around her. She heard Norfred calling to her from below, dear Norfred.

'Swim, Freda! Let go of him. It's too late for him!' the Peculiar exhorted her.

'YOU!' thundered the chamber, bringing down a section of the roof right above where the Peculiar crouched on top of the altar. 'Desecrating thief!'

The Peculiar leapt clear of the altar at the last instant and dived into the inky substance next to Freda. They were all pulled under.

Jillan breathed death down into his lungs and core. He swallowed it until he could swallow no more. He looked for his mother and father but they weren't there. No one was there. This was the grave absolute.

An innocent face begged him for mercy. He hacked it in two straight down the middle. His sword caught in the skull for a second, so he put his boot to one cheek of the dying soldier and shoved the man away. A demon reared up before him, menacing and wily. It swayed, flicking out a strange sinuous sword. Samnir trapped the weapon under his arm and struck the demon's head from its shoulders. Then he took up the demon's sword and charged the creatures backing away from him as if to taunt him.

He knew he was dying. He had fought all his life, in one way or another, so it seemed right that this would be the manner of his death. He was not sure exactly when he had started to die, or how it had happened, but it didn't really matter. Perhaps it was the world around him that was dying and taking him with it, for Godsend had become a veritable hell.

'Face me!' he roared through his ruined face at the last of the enemy. His nose was a hole through which air whistled and snorted. His cheeks were gone. He wondered if they saw his exposed skull.

His sight gradually dimmed as he came closer to death. He needed to finish it before all became totally dark. He chopped forward with his short blade, its sun-metal slicing through armour. He used the sinuous blade to deflect his enemy's defensive blow and hewed and bludgeoned with his short blade. Bludgeoned and bludgeoned. Blood and gristle splattered him as he followed the so-called Hero down. A shadow loomed, and he scythed out low along the parapet with the demon's blade. There was an eerie cry and the last of the enemy slipped onto the stumps of its ankles and then fell from the walkway.

At last. He waited for the eternal night of death to take him. He had done everything asked of him. 'Where are you?' he forced through the raw agony of his throat.

A grunting behemoth approached him. The unholy avatar of the War Demon.

'Where will you take me, demon? Is there a place for me in the ranks of your army of the dead?'

'Not yet, Samnir, my friend. Not yet.'

He recognised the voice. It was from a lifetime ago. He strained to remember its owner. 'T-Thomas? Is that you?'

'Aye, or what's left of him anyway.'

A slight and bedraggled woman came out from behind the blacksmith. She held up her long runic sword and lit the night red. It made her look more ghastly and harder of feature than a moment before. 'Hello, Samnir. The Empire soldiers are all dead.'

'Hello, Hella. I'm glad to see you,' he replied, looking around him with effort. The enemy were piled several deep on the walkway and on the cobblestones below. Godsenders lay among them, holding them close like old friends or lovers. Some defenders still survived, standing at a loss or sitting slumped against the parapet. A young boy moved with a bucket, offering ladles of water. A few accepted. Others failed to see or hear him.

'Some few hundred of our men survive. If we get the physickers up here quickly, we might save a few dozen more. A total of four hundred at most. If the Empire assaults more than one wall tomorrow, or even tonight, then there can be no hope,' Thomas said flatly.

'If there are any inhabitants still prepared to flee,' Samnir mumbled, so dizzy with tiredness that it was a struggle to think, 'they should leave under cover of darkness by the south gate. Those who remain must be asked to line the walls.' He hesitated. 'Unless we now choose to surrender, to end this madness and spare them.'

'No,' Hella replied firmly. 'If we surrender, he will kill them all unopposed. Or, worse, he will Draw them back to the Saviours and condemn them to the living death of the Empire once more. It is better to die free than surrender. Jillan knew that. It was his example to us. We cannot surrender to the evil outside our walls. Ever!'

Samnir nodded. He knew she was right. Her words reaffirmed his resolve. He would defy and resist the Empire to the end. He would not let those who had sacrificed their lives die in vain. 'Yet you must not be allowed to fall into their hands, Hella. I know they will not hesitate to use you against Jillan somehow. There is still time for you and Thomas to leave. Perhaps you will be safe in the mountains.'

'Nowhere is safe, Samnir, you know that. They will be watching for us. They will hunt us down. We are all too weary to stay ahead of them. Even if we were to make it to the mountains, I would not want to be responsible for bringing the Empire to the last of the pagans. No, I will stay and face that monster Praxis, and pray that I have the chance to meet him here upon the walls, so that I may wet my blade with his blood. I will fight, Samnir. We will all fight. And if I should die, then I will be content, for then they will not be able to use me against my beloved Jillan.'

She humbled and inspired him. Yet he had faced the demon many more times than she had. He knew and understood it in ways she never could. He had fought it his entire life, waking, sleeping, on walls, in the desert, from without, inside himself and as the Sand Devil. It was the most subtle and cunning of enemies. It hid when challenged, raised a fog of confusion when pursued, waited with infinite patience until it was near forgotten, and then stalked and struck from among the shadows. It would never dare meet her upon the walls. It knew better than to give her that chance. It would find another way, seeing her betrayed or sacrificed at the last.

*I will not allow it,* he swore to himself. The rage built in Samnir anew and he threw off his exhaustion. He went to the edge of the north wall, waved his star-bright sword and shouted into the waiting darkness where the demon sat unmoving and watching from his horse. 'You have failed, Praxis, do you hear? They are all dead! The General is dead! You know, he thanked me as he died. He hated you for a craven incubus. He died cursing you, as all with you curse how you have bound them to you with your soul-consuming magicks! Why do you and your elusive Saviours need to use such ill-gotten powers? What of loyalty, comradeship and open-hearted belief? None of those things are yours! Do you fear them, Praxis? You should, for they will find you out and unravel your desperate attempts at control and rule. Those around you will turn on you and free themselves. You should fear, Praxis, for I will come for you this night! *All* will come for you! Nothing will be able to protect you.'

Samnir turned back to Hella and Thomas. He smiled and nodded to them and they watched him leave with tears in their eyes. They knew nothing could prevent him. He went through Godsend, the town he had defended for so long, and finally came to the south gate, where he had spent half his life in lonely vigil. It was by this gate that Jillan had first left Godsend to flee the Empire. Samnir had let him through that night, and had always wondered if he should have gone with the boy. Now at last he would. He stepped into the graveyard beyond the gate, his blade of sun-metal sheathed and shrouded so that all was darkness.

'I want to die!' Jillan groaned. Something evil bubbled inside him. He tried to force it out, but it refused to be dislodged.

'He's choking!'

Something was pushed down into his throat, triggering his gag reflex, and he violently spewed up the contents of his stomach. It poured out of him and threatened to take his life with it.

'Oh, that's horrible!'

'Friend Jillan, you must be sick more quietly,' Freda rumbled with concern, 'or they'll hear us. There are lots of soldiers here.'

'I'll never get the smell off me,' the Peculiar complained. 'How could he have taken in so much? There's more coming out than should have been able to go in in the first place. He can't be bigger on the inside than the outside.'

'I want to die.'

'Well, you pretty much did, as it happens. How was it, by the way? I've always wondered. It's something that's always been denied the gods, of course. Every spirit I've asked tells it differently. Not so usual for one of the living to have experienced it. How would you describe it? Don't just say it was dark and empty. That's too dull an answer. Only the shades of the sorts of people you're secretly glad are dead give that sort of answer. Did you end up in your own personal hell?'

'Yes,' Jillan said stickily.

'You did? Really? Amazing! What was it?'

'It was feeling terrible, vomiting and then being harassed by questions from you.'

Laughter rumbled in Freda's chest.

'That's not funny, thank you very much, especially after all I did to save you, you miserable pair.'

'I wish you hadn't.'

'Well next time I won't! You can be sure of that,' the Peculiar harrumphed.

'All right. There was no hell.'

'No? That's a relief. What then?'

'Just –' Jillan shaded his eyes '– light. So bright! I can't see. Where are we?'

'Welcome to the Fortress of the Sun, seat of Saint Dionan's power, formerly the temple of my brother Sinisar of the Shining Path.' The Peculiar smiled, moving his head so that he blocked the sun from Jillan's eyes, although the sun-metal on his head was just as blinding.

'It's so hot! I'm boiling in this armour.' Jillan smacked his lips. 'Some water?'

'Well of course it's hot. These are the deserts of the east. Haven't you got any water, Freda?'

'No. I am sorry, friend Jillan. Deep in the ground, I think there is some. But very deep.'

'Well, we'll get some later,' the Peculiar said. 'We need to get moving.'

'I really don't feel so good. Like I'm burning up. So thirsty.' There was heat from the sun above, of course, but just as much coming off the ground. It felt like he was in a furnace. Perhaps this was his own personal hell after all, and the Peculiar and Freda were two demons in disguise set there to taunt him.

'Maybe he's poisoned, friend Anupal,' Freda fretted. 'Look, he's shaking. What are we going to do?'

The Peculiar sighed in irritation. 'He'll be fine. Even if he's not, there'll be a cure in Haven, I'm sure.'

'What if friend Jillan can't wait till we get to Haven?'

'We'll just have to hurry up, won't we? You'd better carry him. The remains of Sinisar's temple are beneath us. The Empire uses it as a workshop for all its sun-metal. You go through the ground and I'll take the main route down.'

'Yes, friend Anupal. We must be quick.'

Freda disappeared down with Jillan clutched in her arms. The Peculiar gave himself the form of a battered Hero of the east and stepped out from behind the low wall where they'd been hiding. As one, fifty men trained their bows on him, ready to release gleaming arrows of sun-metal. In front of them was a small unassuming officer and a giant Disciple.

'Oh, hello. Sorry if I kept you all waiting. Army food, eh? The toilet is free now, but I wouldn't want to be the next one in there, if you know what I mean.'

'You are the one called the Peculiar,' called the officer in a clicking voice that made all who heard it itch. 'The sun-metal at your brow betrays you. We have been expecting you.'

'You have? I'm not meant to be that predictable. It's worrying the way things are going. And you are Dionan, I take it. I must say, I was expecting someone a little more . . . remarkable. Still, it explains why the Empire has never been able to take the east.'

'Now, now. There's no need to be rude,' the officer said in reproof, his words buzzing and stinging at the Peculiar's temples.

'Well, it's not you who's got several dozen bows trained on them, is it? Is that really any way to treat an ally of your stuffy old Saviours?'

'Where are the bane and the rock woman?' the Disciple boomed. 'You are bound by our agreement to deliver them to us.'

'Yes, that's true. I didn't, however, say *when* I would deliver them, did I? It just so happens I still have need of them, so you're going to have to be a little more patient. Maybe take up a game or hobby to help you pass the time or something. What is it Disciples like to do on their days off? You do get days off, don't you? No? That might explain why you're sometimes a bit irascible and uptight. Oh, come on, don't tell me I'm the first one to have mentioned it.' A few of the Saint's men smirked.

'You will deliver them to us now. Where are they?' the Disciple demanded.

'None may hide from the sight of the divine Saviours,' the officer resonated at a high pitch, his words swarming around them. 'The termites, beetles, locusts, spiders, lizards, snakes and scorpions of the desert all see them moving below us.'

'Don't tell me you have Drawn such creatures!' The Peculiar grimaced. 'That's . . . well, it's disgusting. They deserve what you've done to them even less than the People of the Empire.'

'Combined, they see and know things you could never even begin to imagine,' the officer vibrated, his edges now less distinct as he became a cloud of whirring, chittering and scuttling insects and predators.

The drone that filled the air rattled the membranes of all in the fort, and caused such pain to a good number of the men that they dropped their weapons and clutched at the sides of their heads. The Disciple was apparently unaffected and lumbered across the wide courtyard of ochre and yellow compacted earth in the direction of a large set of stairs leading under the fort.

The Peculiar moved to intercept the bright armour. 'Now just hang on a minute. I'm not about to let you cheat me out of my finder's fee after all I've done for you. I've had no end of trouble corralling that stubborn rock woman and wayward boy so that we have them just where we want them. I pretty much ended the plague in the south, as we agreed. You know very well that the south would have been entirely lost to you if it weren't for my actions and interventions. If it weren't for me binding and forcing Jillan out of Godsend, none of your armies would have any hope of prevailing in the south, and you know it. If it weren't for me bringing him under control, you'd never have any hope of finding Haven. I'm giving it all to you, but you're now jeopardising that, you imbeciles!'

'None may prevent the will of the divine Saviours,' Saint Dionan seethed and rushed, darkening much of the sky.

'Just run along and play, will you, saintling? Your elders and betters are trying to have a grown-up conversation. We don't want to listen right now to your childish whining and sycophancy. Disciple, I will not let you take them until I am paid what you owe me. And if you cannot pay me right now, then you will instead let me keep hold of them a little while longer.'

The Disciple ignored the Peculiar, not breaking step, and brushed him aside.

'None may deny their will. Stand aside, Peculiar, for you are alone and outnumbered. Ally you may once have been, but we will use force against you if necessary.'

The Peculiar looked up at the massing and devouring plague. 'You know, you are really beginning to annoy me. Besides, I didn't come alone. Behold! My last follower!'

He pulled the rotting remains of the shaman out of the sack he had tied to his waist and held it aloft. Its eyes rolled and dribbled a milky substance, maggots falling out of the bottom of its neck. Several flying scarabs landed on it and began to cut at its carrion flesh.

'It is a dismembered head,' Saint Dionan swirled and sneered.

'It can give you a very nasty nip. Hmm. Perhaps you're right.' The Peculiar widened his mouth enormously, popped the head inside and bit down on it. He chewed it around and swallowed. 'Mainly tastes of ammonia, as you'd expect. Still, it's all I will need to see you packed off to bed without any supper. You've been a very naughty Saint. And you can't say you weren't warned. Now, GO TO YOUR ROOM!' The Peculiar's voice was released with such immense power that it obliterated half of the swarm against the walls of the fort, and blew the rest out into the desert beyond. He turned towards the Disciple. 'Now, where were we?'

*

Saint Praxis wouldn't have put it past General Thormodius to have deliberately failed in the attack on Godsend, even to have deliberately got himself killed. *Saint Dionan could have ordered the suicide of the General in order to sabotage my efforts. Yes, I still have eight thousand men, but they are no doubt loyal to the memory of that turncoat General. For all I know, they are all sitting outside my tent even now plotting my assassination. And that bitch of the west, Saint Izat, is bound to have spies among them fomenting trouble. Perhaps her spies relayed information through her to her servant Samnir, all the better for him to rebuff the assault. Of course! It makes complete sense. I should have anticipated it before. Saviours, preserve me! I can't trust any of them.*

Even his angelic Captain Skathis was not above suspicion. Saint Praxis could not forget that back in Hyvan's Cross the man had been reluctant to be Drawn back to the Saviours. Imagine resisting the holy blessing of the Saviours and salvation! What right-thinking man would do such a thing? No right-thinking man, that was who. The man had clearly been under some sort of malign influence . . . and perhaps still was. The Captain's mind seemed blank too much of the time when the Saint tried to read his thoughts. And when it wasn't blank, it was full of blades! Naked uncomfortable blades which constantly cut back and forth. They were like an inward memory or echo of the criss-crossing scars that disfigured the Captain's face and made his scalp a patchwork. Praxis knew that, with sufficient time and effort, he could break down the Captain's defences, but it might kill the man who was realistically the only one who might continue to determine the right tactics for the army to use.

*I need him for now. But he can't be trusted!* As night had fallen and Praxis had left the field of battle, eight thousand pairs of eyes had watched him making his way to his tent. He'd ordered the lamps turned up as bright as they would go, to be sure there was no assassin lurking in the shadows, and then dismissed the Heroes of Hyvan's Cross detailed to be his guard. He wanted them nowhere near him. Who knew how well they could veil their thoughts from him?

He'd sat in his tent alone, alert to every sound without. The muttered observations and profanities of men around campfires. The whicker of tethered horses. The sudden screech of a hunting owl. The distant moans and cries from the physickers' tent. And he saw through the eyes of the men of Hyvan's Cross. The unlucky roll of dice. A thoughtful gaze up at the moon and stars. A stick being whittled with a knife. A sword being whetted to a killing keenness. A surreptitious glance at the Saint's tent, where he was silhouetted as an easy target by the bright lamps!

Saint Praxis hurriedly dowsed all the lamps in his tent, plunging himself into total darkness. He prayed they would not be able to find him in the dark. He prayed that he would hear their stealthy footfalls long before they got near him, so that he could use his saintly power to bring them to their knees, burst their hearts, have them cut their own throats and unravel their minds. He prayed that their evil souls would be washed away in their own venom. He prayed that if Samnir did come for him that night, the Saviours would deliver their faithful servant from evil, so that he could continue to do their holy work.

He saw Samnir before him now. How ugly was the true face of evil. It had been plain for all to see there on the battlements. How ugly were its words. All had heard its foul threats. It had been revealed in all its monstrosity. That was but the first aspect of the holy power of the Saviours: to expose evil where it had previously been hidden, so that all might see it and know to turn away and refuse to consort with it. The next aspect was the bringing of fear to that evil, as it saw it was exposed and friendless. And the last was to have that evil undone by despair and self-loathing when it saw it was denied and unworthy of any life or presence within the holy kingdom.

Surely the army of Heroes could see it. Had it not been as obvious as the sun in the sky? Did they not know it as well as they knew their blades would cut flesh? Did they not feel it as deeply as they did the love of their lives? Ah, but their enemies blinded them, interrupted their thoughts and numbed all natural inclinations in them. That was why the world needed the likes of Saint Praxis to lead the fight against the Chaos, to remind the weak of their duty and to castigate the wrong-doers. Why, he could imagine that even if Samnir were spotted by guards making his way through the shadows of the camp, the Chaos would tell them it was a trick of the light, some wild animal or their overtired minds imagining things. The commander of Godsend would not dare to come here. Saint Dionan might then whisper to those of greater fortitude to let it pass anyway. What did it matter to them what passed through the camp this night? Godsend would still fall the next day anyway. Let it go. Have nothing to do with the Sand Devil. It is better and safer that way.

Yes, Saint Praxis could see Samnir ghosting through the dark, staying well away from the fires and silently slitting the throats of those who inadvertently got in his way. His eyes glinted with a merciless intent and evil determination. The commander spied the dark tent that could only be the Saint's because of its size and position. He crept ever closer.

Gulping and praying fervently, Saint Praxis watched the entrance flap to his tent with wide staring eyes. He waited for a telltale movement, for fingers to come clawing around the edge. The canvas fluttered and his breath caught. *It's the wind, it's the wind. Please be the wind!* No enemy could walk into the middle of an army of almost ten thousand Heroes and find him out. It was not possible. He was beloved of the blessed Saviours. This could not be happening to him. He had proved himself time and again.

The darkness of the tent deepened. Had the entrance flap opened? Had the evil come inside? He couldn't see properly any more. He desperately wanted to relight the lamps and send the Chaos fleeing back to its dark lair, but he dared not betray where he knelt. His heart was in his throat, blocking his airway. His lungs were starving. His jaw hung slack: he couldn't close it because that would be to bite down on his heart. His eyes had dried out and felt like they were about to fall from his head.

A silent whisper. *I see you, Praxis.*

Quiet! He was here. Sweet Saviours, the devil was here! Hair fell from Praxis's head in clumps.

'Stay back!' Saint Praxis squeaked.

'Stay back? Did you listen when we begged your thousand men to stay back from Godsend, you murdering dog? Will you commit genocide and then ask for mercy yourself?'

A shimmering blade of sun-metal slowly revealed itself, scraping and laughing as it came free of its scabbard. The Sand Devil's face was lit from below, a red and bloody mask of vengeance.

'You are the devil!'

'Yes, I am. And it was you and your fornicating Saviours that made me the devil. I have come to repay you for that now, Praxis, and all your other crimes. All the deaths. So many innocent people. I have come to drag you to hell, Praxis.'

'No!' The Saint backed away from the bloody warrior.

'Oh, but I insist. You know there is no escaping it, for what we have done and what has brought us here makes us what we are now. You should have let the boy be. But no, you had to take his childhood and parents from him, didn't you, turning his life into one long moment of grief? He was innocent, you monster, full of hope and joy. Is that why you hated him? You couldn't bear that there was something essential in him, while you only had an empty faith and a dusty old book. Is that why you were obsessed with destroying him?'

'He is the bane!' Saint Praxis screeched, coming to his feet. 'You will not speak so of him. All this death is because of him! What hold is it he has over you, Hero? Tell me! How did he have you break your sacred vow to the Empire?'

Saint Praxis stared into Samnir's eyes, into his mind and then into his soul. *I will not fear evil, no matter how it may test me, for the power of the blessed Saviours protects me.* He found the sacred heart of Samnir's experiences and beliefs, those things that gave him identity, passion, appetite and self. He found the secrets there, the very seat of Samnir's being.

Saint Praxis saw Samnir as a youth being torn from the loving embrace of some dowdy woman, presumably his mother, by a hard-faced Hero. The woman protested and received a heavy blow to the face that dislocated her jaw and sent her reeling away. Samnir fought against the Hero with tooth and nail, almost overcoming him, but was finally knocked cold by another Hero coming to the aid of his comrade. It was in that moment of struggle that Samnir had come to hate everything about the Empire.

Saint Praxis subtly subverted the defining image. The woman's embrace was no longer quite so loving, her protest no longer so forth-right. She looked hungry. She all but pushed Samnir into the Hero's hands.

'Damn you!' Samnir said through gritted teeth, squeezing his eyes shut but unable to block the image from his mind. He strained to take a step forward and raise his sword, but was paralysed by the internal struggle.

*Go along, Samnir. Be brave. You're a big boy now*, the woman said.

As the Hero gestured the woman away, he passed her a small bag of coins behind Samnir's back. She smiled gratefully.

'No!' Samnir moaned, his arms falling to his sides.

*Thank the Saviours we're rid of him*, the woman later confided to her husband. *He was eating us out of house and home. And all he ever did was whine and complain that he wanted more. Well, the Empire can deal with him now. Hopefully, he'll get his ruddy little neck cut somewhere out east.*

'Stop!' The blade of sun-metal fell to the carpeted floor of the tent.

Yet Praxis wasn't finished with him. He showed him a picture of Jillan making his parents' life a misery, tormenting his classmates and railing against the care of his Minister. Jillan trying to force himself on his mother, and then upon Hella.

'See what he is!' the Saint spat. 'See! *This* is what you fight for. This filth!'

Samnir weakly tried to fight back with other images. Jillan having long talks with him on the south wall. Jillan and Hella smiling and holding hands. Jillan carried in Jedadiah's arms. Then the images became stronger. Jillan healing those with plague. Jillan fighting at Samnir's side against the inhabitants of Godsend who had been possessed by the will of their Saint. And, finally, Jillan standing against the monstrous and terrible Saint Azual.

Once more rage burned in Samnir, the emotion that defined him more than any other. It always came back to the Saints of the Empire. The selfish seduction of Izat, the insatiable voracity of Azual and now the fearful mendacity of Praxis! Saint Praxis clawed at Samnir's sacred heart, trying to reassert the image of Samnir's abusive mother, trying to reawaken the fear that would paralyse the soldier. The rage became ferocious, burning away everything else.

Samnir's eyes came open and beheld Praxis. 'Perversion,' he whispered balefully. 'The things she did to me! The Saints are nothing but a gross perversion. Blood-drinkers. Parasites.' The sword came back into Samnir's hand and he stepped forwards purposefully. 'No more. This is your end. Say a final prayer if you wish, but it will do you no good.'

'Please!' the Saint wheedled. His heels caught a fold in the carpet and he fell.

'Beg if you wish, but it will do you no good.'

The sword came up, trailing fire.

'You don't understand!'

'Speak if you wish –' it came down, slicing through one of the Saint's cheeks and out through the other '– but it will do you no good.'

Praxis raised his arms before him.

'Lift beseeching hands if you wish—'

'Hold, Sand Devil!' roared a voice on top of them, and the darkness suddenly came to life around them.

Samnir was caught mid-stroke and clubbed from behind. Even as he went down, he tried to stab his sword through Saint Praxis's gut, but the movement was now a mix of sweep and thrust and went wide.

A lamp was lit and a formidable figure came forward, although it had but one hand.

'Sweet General!' Saint Praxis whined deep in his throat. 'It is a m-m-miracle. I have been delivered from evil, my prayers and good faith answered.'

'Holy one, it must have been for this moment that the Saviours allowed me to survive the fall from the benighted walls of Godsend. Restrain this pagan, you men! Quickly!' the General ordered with a gesture towards Samnir. He knelt to help the Saint up himself. 'Holy one, you are hurt?'

Saint Praxis, his wounds already magically healing, goggled at the General. 'He attacked my very person. Me, the representative of the blessed Saviours. Can you believe it?'

'He should be executed at once, holy one. He is a spirit of vengeance. If he is not laid to rest this moment, all will come to regret it.' He made no effort to hide the stump where his sword hand had once been. 'How I wish I had seen it done years ago, holy one. He is the Sand Devil!'

The Saint patted the burly General on the chest, as if to be sure he was really there. 'All in good time, good General, all in good time. He has not yet suffered anywhere near enough. He must know a fear in his soul that will undo him. It must torture him eternally. He will be an example to every living thing in the Empire and creation.'

Down and down they went through the layers of earth, back into the past when the gods ruled the world and the lives of mortals. He did not recognise all the types of rock that they passed. Shards of crystal thicker than a man appeared with increasing frequency, refracting light from an unknown source, perhaps within themselves. The brightness, heat and pressure intensified the further they went. It was unbearable.

Freda ground her teeth noisily, clearly in discomfort despite her hardened skin and affinity for the substance through which they travelled. Jillan knew that if it were not for his armour and the rock woman protecting him, he would have succumbed to the extreme forces around them long before.

'Friend Jillan, there is much sun-metal below us, more than I have ever known in one place. I do not know how much further I can take us.'

'Shall we go back up?'

'We dare not. I sense much trouble above. I do not know what to do, friend Jillan!'

*Where the hell are we? Why do I feel so sick? What's happened, Jillan?* the taint screamed faintly.

He couldn't think clearly – their surroundings, the poison spreading through his body and mind, the screaming. He wanted to sleep but knew he wouldn't wake up again if he did. There was some sort of vital decision to be made. Once they entered this temple, the location of Haven would be revealed to them. There would be no going back. All hung on this – the Geas, the Saviours, the People, Godsend, Hella, his friends, everything. He didn't want to make the decision, but refusing to make it would be a decision in itself, and one that would probably see him and Freda killed or, even worse, captured.

*Answer me, you dope! Where are we?*

'The Temple of Sinisar of the Shining Path,' Jillan mumbled.

Freda started moving down again, shaking with the effort.

*The mad one? Oh, great. I feel even weaker than when you let the phagus take chunks out of us.*

'It's because of the visit to the temple of Kathuula in the nether realm. The stuff I swallowed there. No choice now. Got to follow it to the end. Death or a cure and life. Haven is the cure, I hope.'

*The nether realm? Are you serious? I'm half glad I missed that. You didn't do anything stupid like disturbing Kathuula, did you?*

'Torpeth's fault.'

*Oh, sweet excrement of an overfed devil! Whether we can frustrate the Saviours or not, he's doomed us all.*

'Knew what he was doing, I think.'

*That would be a first!*

'Probably paid with his life.'

*Well at least there's that, although we're never that lucky.*

They moved through pure crystal now. Intersecting planes and fractures threatened to shatter Freda at any moment. They channelled so much light that it seemed they fell or floated through a white radiance. The heat and pressure assailed Freda mercilessly and her body began to melt and morph.

'Look, Freda. Your skin. It's changing, becoming a sort of crystal. Hard like diamond. It's so beautiful!'

She smiled shyly and then grinned dazzlingly. She laughed, and it was bright, tinkling and chiming, rather than the usual laboured rumble. 'Friend Jillan, it's amazing! Do you see the runes of light?'

But there was a darkness in Jillan that dimmed his sight. He could not see what her shining eyes and being saw. He could not share in the wondrous revelation. He did not envy her, though. He rejoiced for his friend. It was right, in a way. It was like falling into a sun, where light, matter, ether, energy and being were all brought together in a single articulation of cosmic power. Yet where Freda was one with it, his was a different sort of existence. He was the eclipse, a black hole and the void. Where she might be immortal, he was entirely mortal. There was no ascendance or transcendence for his kind. No all-defining answer. There was only rending struggle, poisoning pain and grief as the corollary to free will, self-determination and individual meaning and consequence.

Together, they crashed down into the heart of the place, a pulsing, beating heart. At the centre a deformed man with the distinct glow of magic about him pounded away on an anvil of sun-metal. Around him were stacked the shining arrows and blades that he had forged. There were other strange objects that Jillan did not recognise, although they reminded him of Ash's carvings. The muscles of the arm that wielded the man's hammer were so large and heavy that he couldn't stand straight, for his other arm was all but withered by comparison. Where his torso was bent, his hip seemed to have fused with his chest. His permanently contorted frame meant that he had to hop in order to swing his overgrown arm over and down. Jillan instinctively felt sorry for the man.

Weeping blood-red eyes turned towards them. 'You're not my lunch, are you? Good Dionan usually sends a rat or two down here for me to catch. I think I'd get indigestion from the likes of you two. Are you sure you're meant to be here?'

'I have already seen and read the runes. We have found what we wanted, friend Jillan,' Freda said. 'We should leave at once. I feel the Disciple approaching.'

'Wait. I need to ask this man some things. I am Jillan and this is Freda. Whom do we have the honour of addressing?'

The man ceased his hammering, although his panting continued the rhythm of his work, the colourful columns of crystal that were the walls of the temple flashing in time to his breathing. 'I am the sun-smith. I have no name, not one that I remember anyway. It was never of much use to me. I only need the sun-metal. Its beauty sings to me and there is no need of a name to mar the art of our being.'

'It sings to you? Is it alive?'

'It is and it is not. It is all the company I need, however. You should go. I will return to my work. I want nothing but the freedom to be with my life's companion, to exist within the constant magic of creation and its substance.' The sun-smith turned his crooked back on them and took up the crashing insistence of his work once more.

'Friend Jillan, there is no time. We must leave now.'

'Sun-smith, you fashioned a box, did you not? A perfectly sealed box?' A box the shadowy Saviours had mentioned when Jillan had eavesdropped on them.

The man froze mid-swing. The bellows of his lungs kept time and echoed round the chamber. 'We do not wish to speak of it. We are not happy they insisted we make it.'

'Why not, sun-smith?'

He would not face Jillan. 'Two such boxes we have made in our time. Terrible things. Wrong things. We did not want to do it, but they said they would take our work away from us forever if we did not obey. No one would ever know, they said. Yet you are here. They lied.' He hung his head.

'How are the boxes wrong, sun-smith? Tell me.'

Tears of blood running down his cheeks, the sun-smith turned and shouted, 'Because none should be allowed to commit such a crime against nature! None! No will should be allowed a perfect seal. Sun-metal should not be used to form such a dread and unthinkable prison. Never! Sun-metal will not ultimately permit it. All will be punished for it, including me. Especially me! What have I done?'

'There is a box somewhere here, isn't there, sun-smith? You will open it for me. It must be opened.'

'It was inevitable that you would come here. It is meant to be, I see that. Yes, I will open it and suffer my punishment at last. It is below us, a beautiful and dreadful coffin.'

They went down and came to a blinding wall. The sun-smith struck it with magic and hammer, and it came open. A black crystal that absorbed light lay within.

'What is it, friend Jillan?' Freda asked, much of her voice also taken by the crystal.

'I am not sure. I think it is something called the *unstable* element. Will you take it?'

The temple above them shook with the rapid approach of the Disciple of the Saviours. Hurriedly, Freda's diamond hand reached for the dark object. 'It is impossibly heavy for something of such a size! It will slow us down, friend Jillan. We do not have time for it. Your sickness will overtake you. Let us leave it.'

'It doesn't matter what happens to me. We must free it of its prison or all will be lost. I just know it. Trust me, Freda, please!'

The woman of purest diamond heaved with all her being and raised the dark crystal to her chest. The walls of the temple flashed and flickered out of rhythm and made a discordant clashing sound.

'The punishment descends upon me,' the sun-smith smiled and cried. 'Leave quickly!'

'You said you made two such boxes,' Jillan pressed.

'Do not make me speak of it.'

'Quickly! Now!'

Freda gasped. 'I have heard his screaming. The mad one buried beneath the Great Temple!'

'Who is it?' Jillan demanded of the sun-smith.

'Bane of the Empire,' the temple rang out angrily. 'Godsend is falling. Your sacred heart is now in our grasp. Kneel before us!'

'Forgive me!' the sun-smith sobbed. 'It is sweet Sinisar, my beloved father, who is imprisoned within. My own father! Oh, what have I done?'

That morning the broken commander of Godsend was paraded in chains before its walls. Saint Praxis of the Empire commanded the People to know their sins, to fear the divine retribution that was rightfully theirs, and to repent before it was too late. Then the army of Heroes advanced on Godsend from east, north and west. They were a glorious sight, their armour and weapons polished to a sheen, so that each man moved within a halo of light, and trumpets and drums proclaimed the mass enactment of the blessed Saviours' will. Arrows of sun-metal traced rainbows through the sky. Ladders were raised along with voices of praise for the deliverance at hand. A battering ram with the General's shield strapped to the front was launched at the northern gates. The gates rang like a bell summoning the People to prayer, and then fell open before the holy host of Heroes. In less than an hour the town of Godsend was saved.

The miraculously resurrected General Thormodius and the angelic Captain Skathis approached their Saint and knelt before him. 'The town is ours, holy one, praise be to the blessed Saviours,' the General reported.

'And the witch?' the gentle-browed Saint Praxis asked.

'Is our captive, holy one,' Captain Skathis confirmed. 'Here is her sword.'

'I will not touch that repugnant thing. She has been gagged so that she cannot visit her unholy magicks and depravity upon the innocent?'

'Yes, holy one.'

'And the pagan blacksmith?'

'The fight went out of him once we had taken the witch and she was no longer there to command him.'

'He is her familiar, clearly. Hand him over to our holy torturer. I suspect the blacksmith knows the whereabouts of small groups of pagans hidden in the deep woods.'

'And the other inhabitants of Godsend, holy one?' the General asked with reverence.

'Those with any sign of the plague are marked as sinners beyond redemption. They are to be shown the mercy of a quick death. The rest are to be offered the holy blessing of being Drawn to the blessed Saviours. Any who resist are to be executed as an example to the rest. Then we will undertake the pilgrimage of our return to the Great Temple, to offer up prayers of thanksgiving for the deliverance of the southern region and the restoration of harmony and peace in the holy and eternal Empire of the blessed Saviours. So it has been commanded.'

'As is your will, holy one.'

# CHAPTER 12:

# Sparing none

The effort of confronting the sun-smith only saw the poison spread through Jillan's system all the faster. Darkness had swirled through his vision as the Disciple reached for him. It had only been Freda's timely action that had saved him at the last, carrying him through the earth, along with the black crystal held tight against him.

The ground was thunder. The sky was a crushing weight on his chest. All was delirium. Desert sand filled his nose and throat. The sun pushed spikes into his eyes.

'Hold on, Jillan,' the woman of diamond kept repeating. 'It's not far. It's not far.'

*It feels like forever. We're so deep into this wasteland that there aren't even flies out here. Just dust. This is no place of the Geas. Perhaps the Peculiar tricked us after all.*

Ba'zel awoke in his small bedchamber in his parents' house in Godsend. He frowned. He saw his collection of stones in the niches of the wall. His father – Jed? – brought him a new addition to the collection every time the hunters of Godsend failed to catch something for their cooking pots. The stones were an unusual colour and caught the light strangely, or was there some energy about them? He reached for a red one and, as he touched it, felt better somehow, more grounded.

He heard movement in the kitchen. His mother would be making breakfast. Ba'zel had never known his mother, so was not sure how he knew she was there making tea and laying out bread and honey, his favourite. He did not even know what honey was, did he? What did the Declension know of honey? How did he know his mother's name was Maria?

He dressed quickly and emerged from the bedchamber. He watched the small woman as she bustled backwards and forwards.

'There you are, sleepy head.' She kissed him on the cheek as she passed. 'Come along, Jillan, or you'll be late for school.'

Jed looked up from the table and smiled at him. 'Hurry up or there'll be none left for you. A hunter needs to keep up his strength, you know. He's got to eat when he can.'

Ba'zel went to the chair that was clearly meant for him and sat. Curiously he looked down at what was laid out on the table.

'No appetite, dear? Jed, his forehead's warm too. Maybe he's ill. He should stay at home with me today.' There was a mixture of maternal concern and, oddly, hope in her voice.

Jed lowered his brows disapprovingly. 'You're just slow to wake up, that's all, isn't it, lad? Bad dreams. Do you really want to stay with your mother?'

The two humans watched him, waiting. They expected him to speak.

Ba'zel thought for a second. 'I think there is something I need to do. I cannot stay.'

Jed nodded, but Maria was upset. 'It's too dangerous!' she said. 'You can go another day.'

'Maria,' Jed gently chided her, his eyes full of understanding.

'No, Jedadiah!' she choked. 'You know we should have let him stay at home with us that day. He tried to tell us he didn't want to go. Why did you have to force him? He was just a boy, far too young to face such monsters, such horrors!'

Jed sighed and looked down at his hands, as if pondering how useless was their strength. Through his beard he said in his deep bear-like voice, 'Woman, you love him too much. You cannot protect him all his life. He cannot stay here at this breakfast table with us forever. Keep him here and the Empire has won. It will remain unchallenged, and its capture of the Geas will be certain. You know this.'

Ba'zel wondered at their word *love*. It seemed both a good and bad thing, certainly dangerous. It caused people to make mistakes and misjudgements. It was the taste of honey, sweet and golden. But taken in excess, it was sickly. Perhaps he'd be better off not having any of this breakfast of which they spoke. Yet it was his favourite, he recalled. 'I will take something with me and eat it on the way.'

'Aye, lad, that would probably be best. Besides, the fresh air will do you some good. You don't want to stay in this stuffy little house. You should get out and stretch your limbs. See your friends. You shouldn't mope around with your parents.' Jed leaned forward. 'After all, we're dead, you know.'

Maria began to sob quietly.

'Go on, lad. Your mother and I will be fine. We'll still be here when you come back.'

Ba'zel awkwardly lifted a piece of bread and applied honey to it, although the honey seemed to want to adhere to his fingers more than the bread. Holding the mess in one hand, he shunted his chair back, went to the door, looked back once at the kindly humans and stepped out into the bright morning of Godsend.

He negotiated his way through the labyrinth that was the southern quarter of town. Something moved across the top of his vision, a bird winging its way across the sky. He found his feet following it back to the southern wall and the long stairs up and around to the Hero keeping a solitary lookout over the south gate. Samnir nodded to him in welcome and turned his grey eyes back to the wilds.

'Anything moving?' Ba'zel enquired.

Samnir continued to scan the landscape. After a second or two, he replied gruffly, 'Thought I saw one of the mountains move to the left earlier.'

Ba'zel considered this. 'Perhaps you should report it to someone.'

The Hero smiled bleakly. 'Don't be witless, boy. No one would believe me. They'd say old Samnir was getting spooked out here on his own. Or pagan spell-casters deep in the woods were exerting their dark influence over his mind. Your Minister would accuse me of being susceptible to the powers and temptations of the Chaos. I'd be seen as a weakness in Godsend's defences. This post would be taken away from me and it would be the end for me, for this is the last post in the last town of the Empire. There is nothing beyond that, nothing except damnation. So you and me will keep the movement of that mountain our special secret, right, boy? Now run along. I don't want the Minister saying I've been keeping you from your studies.'

Ba'zel hesitated. 'Are you a weakness in Godsend's defences, then? Is the last post in the last town a weakness in the whole Empire's defences? Could all fall because of an individual human?'

Samnir spun round, breathing hard with emotion, his expression as defiant as it was ravaged and burned. 'Damn you, boy! What is it you want from me? Don't you know I tried my damnedest? But it wasn't enough. I faced him in his own tent. Cut his leering face open for him! And it still wasn't enough. It's never been enough, no matter how hard I've fought and how many I've killed.'

Ba'zel took a terrified step back, but held out the dripping piece of bread and honey. 'Here, you should have this.'

He almost dropped it, but the Hero moved quickly and caught it. Ba'zel fled, leaving the Hero to sorrow over the mess in his hands.

Ba'zel ran all the way to school. He was desperate to see the familiar faces of his few friends, to be reassured they were still there. Surely nothing bad had happened to them. All would be well. He wanted things to be as they had always been, didn't he?

The other children of Godsend stood waiting outside the large oak door to the school. They kept together for shelter from the wind that whistled across the expanse of the Gathering Place at the centre of the town. None looked pleased to see him, however.

None except Hella. 'I was worried you'd be late!' she said with a dimpling smile.

'What's that smell? Middens are strong today!' Haal, Elder Corin's son, said loudly. His friends Karl and Silus sniggered.

Normally Ba'zel would have ignored Haal's comment, for he'd been saying such things for years, but Ba'zel wasn't feeling normal today. He knew now that today was not a normal day. Today was a day when parents argued, Heroes faltered and friends became angry. Today was a day when Ba'zel began the fight that would last the rest of his life.

He squared his shoulders and faced Haal, intent on destroying the creature. Why was there no fear or uncertainty in the other's eyes? Something was wrong.

'Don't do this,' Hella breathed.

'Because we're already dead, and it's your fault!' Haal sneered. 'Hen't so tough now, eh? Brave and defiant Jillan gets everyone killed.'

The school's door swung open, showing only darkness beyond. Ba'zel instinctively backed away.

A cold breath issued from the portal. It was a cavernous mouth, yawning wide.

'Hella, don't go in there!' he cried.

But the others had grabbed her and were dragging her inside. He reached out despairingly.

'Come in, children!' creaked Minister Praxis's voice. 'Quickly now, for we should spend whatever time we may learning of the blessed Saviours for our own improvement. Are you out there, Jillan Hunterson? There's a seat for you too.'

'Jillan, leave me! It's too late for me,' Hella shouted.

The dark mouth grew and Ba'zel knew a sort of vertigo, as if he were falling into it. He understood now that the love these simple beings spoke of was the exact opposite of this horrible loss.

'Run, Jillan! As fast as you can.'

'But where, Hella? Where is it taking you?'

'The Great Temple! Forget us, Jillan. It's a trap. It's too late for us.'

Ba'zel turned and fled. The mouth roared after him, swallowing Godsend whole.


As strong as the seals on his father's chambers were, the dust of the realm still found its way inside and covered everything. It was in the air, invisible but still there, like so many things. It coated the inside of Jillan's throat and made his eyes run constantly. There was no escaping the dust, for it was pretty much all that was left of his realm.

Jillan picked up the broom and swept the floor and other surfaces of his father's chambers. Why he bothered, he was not entirely sure, for there would only be more dust to remove as soon as he had finished this round. His father said the chambers would become uninhabitable if they were not constantly cleaned, but Jillan suspected his father actually just wanted to keep his *unstable* son occupied and out of trouble. The repetitive nature of the work also reminded Jillan of the sort of drill Mentor Ho'zen put him through each day in order to discipline his *unstable* mind and fitful magicks.

'The Great Voyage of the Declension requires an infinite patience, one that outlasts the list of individuals and even countless generations of rebirth through our Geas. It is the challenge of eternity and immortality, a challenge that our kind embraces. As we progress further on the Great Voyage through the different realms, we rise above the beings of all those realms, becoming more than we ever were, becoming greater,' Mentor Ho'zen would lecture him.

'You must therefore learn patience, young Ba'zel. You must learn discipline and mastery of self and form. Such magicks will see you leave your father's chambers and become a full member of the Declension. It is such magicks that allow us to establish the Gate of the Waking Dream, move to the other realms, master those realms and discover the energies we need to sustain our onward journey.'

Yet time was running out, Jillan knew. Time for both him and this realm. If he did not display the required discipline any time soon, his father would see him fed back to the ever-hungry but failing Geas. To do otherwise would be a waste of the Declension's precious resources.

Jillan instinctively looked up at the sand clock in one corner of the chamber. Mentor Ho'zen should have already arrived for their daily lesson. He had never been late before. Jillan put the broom down, knowing that his teacher wouldn't be coming at all that day or any other day. Time had just run out. Time to leave.

He noticed a creature from a lesser realm sitting quietly in a cage in another corner of the chamber. Did he and his father drink of its blood? He felt nauseous thinking about it, and unlatched the door of its prison. Then Jillan went to the thick stone seal of the chamber. There were magical wards here that he didn't understand. Yet he used magic from his core and successfully disposed of the wards all the same. He put his weight against the seal and it slowly swung open. He knew a moment's dizziness because of using his magic, and his mind hungrily pictured the lesser being in the cage. Disgusted at himself, he banished the image and moved away down the crumbling corridor beyond. He had to get away before his absence was discovered.

Out of the gloom came a large prowling elder. The elder's nasal aperture widened, either in hunger or in order to identify the approaching stranger. Unable to control his response, Jillan found a growl issuing from his throat and magic flaring around him. Displaying such indiscipline and power in front of another was shameful, but it succeeded in intimidating the elder, and they passed each other holding close to opposite walls of the corridor.

More dizziness. The thirst and hunger even greater now. His feet took him in the direction of the feeding pools. Both the blood and the Geas called to him. It was all he could do not to break into a run, but to do so would be such a loss of control that it could not be tolerated in the presence of others. He would be attacked en masse by every elder in the area and torn apart so that not one scrap of him remained. The closer he came to the pools, the more elders he sensed around him, some standing like statues, some secreted in the walls and others lurking in the shadows. How he feared and hated them.

Minds probed at him. His nerves jangled. They would find cracks in him and force them wide, exposing the soft and vulnerable being below.

Jillan dragged his feet to make long trenches in the dust, and kicked the stuff up into the air. He turned his thoughts to dust and crouched lower. They were already coming for him, long limbs slashing through the air.

He kicked more and more up, tumbling to stay within the clouds and away from the extending scything forearms and legs. He escaped into a small side tunnel and scrambled away.

His body shook with exhaustion and a self-consuming hunger. He crawled up the narrowing and collapsing tunnel towards the surface. Foreign thoughts of surprise, shock, betrayal and outrage came seeking him out. His father had discovered his absence from their chambers.

*Ba'zel!* thundered the thoughts. *Where are you? Return, my son, and all will be well. You are one of us.*

'No! I am different to others. My skin is too soft. I know no discipline. You will feed me back to the Geas,' Jillan cried.

*By the hunger you feel, you know yourself truly one of us. It is the hunger of our Geas. It is our need to make progress on the Great Voyage. It is all one. You cannot deny it.*

'You will feed all the realms to our Geas. It is monstrous!'

*No, Ba'zel. It is* you *who will feed all the realms to our Geas. It is inevitable. It is the will of the Geas that rules you. It is the will of the Eldest, she who rules our blood. Look within yourself and you will also see it is your own will.*

'It cannot be!' Jillan wept, and fled up the tunnel.

How he feared and hated them. He could not be one of them! He *would* not be one of them. Panting and coughing, he kept his head down as he pushed on. The top of his head and hands began to burn and he knew he must be close. He couldn't see anything but a blinding whiteness. He pulled the hood of his robe over his head and wrapped his hands in its voluminous sleeves. It helped a little, but he could feel his skin start to bubble and crack.

With a final surge, he came through an avalanche of sliding sand and suffocating dust and out onto the barren surface of the realm. He knew better than to open his eyes immediately. Winds tore at his robes, seeking to pull back the material and sacrifice him to the ailing and angry eye of the heavens. Jillan wrapped himself as tightly as he could and tottered away from where he had emerged.

Where was he going? There was nowhere. There was no escaping himself. It would always be there inside him. Like his bloodline. Like the hunger. Like a poison. Like the storm of his magic, which left him weakened and slumped on sinking knees. He would be pulled down and covered over soon, for he did not have the strength to rise again. This desert would be his dusty grave. As the last of the energy and moisture was whisked from him, the dry husk of his body would collapse. It would be blown to the winds with the last of his essence.

*We have taken you up in the fold of our wings. You will be protected for a while, perhaps replenished. The poison within you might be slowed, but never stopped. We will take you to the Gate.*

A sifter had found him at the last. 'The Gate? Why? What would you have of me?'

*You will find the Haven of the seventh realm and reveal the Geas.*

'You want that?'

*Yes and no. It is now inevitable, but it grieves us. Look at what has become of we sifters, as you call us, the Declension, and the other realms. It is enough for us that the Declension once rejected you and now seeks to bind you – because of that, we shall spare you and allow you a few moments more. You will return one day, for all the cosmos comes to us as dust eventually.*

376

'I will not betray the Geas of the seventh realm.'

*It may be unavoidable, like the hunger of your kind and the poison we have slowed within you. It consumes us all eventually. You will leave now, for Haven awaits.*

Jillan was gently lowered back to the ground. He stood shielding his eyes as he watched the sifter lever itself away in the wake of the endless storm of the home-realm. Then he ascended a short slope and looked down into the gaping mouth of a wide tunnel. He wasted no time moving below, out of the savage light.

He went down through long well-maintained corridors, peering anxiously in all directions and intersections, expecting to see the flicker of rapid movement at any moment. He knew that it was through these corridors that the lesser races were marched from the Gate of the Waking Dream to the feeding pools, where their blood was let and they were sacrificed. He felt like one of them now, his doom laid upon him.

He dared not stay here, and so he ran for the Gate's chamber. There would be elders after him, and they could move with frightening speed. Yes, he sensed them now! They'd entered these corridors and were swarming after him in huge numbers.

Panicking, he flew round the next corner and saw the doors to the chamber ahead. As he raced on, an enormous guard stepped out of the shadow of an alcove beside the doors and levelled a trident of blazing sun-metal at him.

'So small?' the elder sneered.

Jillan called magic from within his core, seized the Saviour with it and used him to smash in the doors to the chamber. Then he dashed the guard against the floor and clumsily trod on him to get past.

He hurried to the Gate, which waited for him like a dark mouth. A cold breath issued from it. He hesitated, fearing to enter. To step through was to find Haven. Would he be leading the enemies of the Geas straight to it? Would he be betraying the Geas despite all his best promises? Dizziness assailed him again, the inevitable price for having used his magic, and he teetered on the edge of the darkness. The hunger urged him to give in to it. It felt like the poison. It sounded like the taint.

And into the chamber stepped his father. 'Ba'zel, my son, will you not join us? If you must leave, then I will look forward to your return one day.'

They had found him! 'Can the Declension not simply forget I ever existed? Can they not just leave me be?'

'Fool!' his father replied with what sounded like affection. 'You will always be a part of the Geas of this realm. Attempt to act otherwise and it would be better if you killed yourself here and now.'

'Father, spare me, please!'

'You have the temerity to ask yet more of me? You are shameless and despicable in every way.' His father bared stone fangs and raised clawed hands.

Jillan closed his eyes and fell into the darkness of the Gate. 'Hella, I will find you!'

There were stars in the darkness. Jillan realised he was looking up at the night sky. He was lying on his back between two sand dunes. Freda sat not far away, her lines and facets winking and glowing with starlight. The sand was warm from the heat of the day, but there was a chill wind ghosting back and forth across the desert.

He stirred and tried to sit up. She came and helped him, propping him against a rock that jutted out of the sand.

'It is good to see you awake, friend Jillan. The fever has broken, yes?'

He nodded. 'Water?'

She grinned and carefully brought a hollowed out stone to him. 'I had to go a long way down, but I found some. There are caves far below, where there are deep pools.'

He gulped greedily and it was gone too quickly, but it was the finest elixir he'd ever tasted. 'Thank you, Freda. I was so dry that I felt like I'd swallowed half the desert.' He remembered the surface of the home-realm momentarily. Had he really been there? It had been so vivid. He looked around for the black crystal and saw it next to where he'd been lying. The crystal seemed different somehow, more alive, reflecting the stars above where previously it might have absorbed their image.

'Sorry, friend Jillan. It is likely because we travel beneath the ground much of the day. I can travel faster that way, and it is slightly cooler for you. Yet your mouth hangs open much of the time, as much as I try to keep it closed. You breathe and swallow a lot of dust, I fear. Then at night we come to the surface, where it is cooler. Are you better now?'

'Some would say I was never that well, Freda.' He smiled crookedly.

*I hope you're not going to blame me for that. You do for just about everything else.*

'Oh, you're all I need.'

Freda frowned in confusion.

*She thinks you're funny in the head. Unlike me, however, she's just too polite to say so.*

'Sorry, Freda. I was distracted for a moment. How long have we been travelling?'

'This is our second night.'

'And are we nearly there?' How long could Hella and his friends wait? Did Samnir still live? And Thomas? He could not bear to think they did not. And what had happened to Ash and Aspin?

Freda paused. She shifted uncomfortably. 'I-I'm not sure. The runes said Haven should be here, but I do not sense anything.'

'Freda, we will not give up. We *cannot*! There are too many lives at stake. Too many have died or been consumed by the Empire.' Was Hella being drained even as he spoke? 'Their thoughts are invaded and watched. It's like having something living in your head. It makes people crazy, like they don't know themselves.'

*Well, it's not that much fun for me either, you know. Your mind isn't a great place to be at the best of times.*

Freda shivered, appalled. 'Friend Jillan, it is so wrong. These Saviours are the same as the Overlords, I think. I know they keep people captive in the dark, like the mine where I was with dear Norfred. These people do not own their lives. They are slaves and are killed by others like Darus and your Saint Azual.'

'I have seen that the Saviours intend to kill us all, Freda. They will feed us to their own Geas, and our entire world will die.'

'But what can we do, friend Jillan?'

'We must find Haven and a way to destroy them, Freda. It's the only way we will ever be safe. Ever.'

'But where is it, friend Jillan? Where? Maybe we should have waited for Anupal.'

'Freda, he has manipulated us from the beginning, surely you know that. We cannot trust him. He tries to control us, just like the Saviours do. He abandoned Torpeth, Aspin and Ash in the nether realm precisely because they wouldn't be controlled by him. They will find their own way, he said. Well, we're going to abandon him now, and find our own way to Haven.'

Freda was quiet. She wouldn't meet his eyes. She dragged a finger through the sand, tracing runes.

'What is it, Freda? If there's something bothering you, you can tell me. I won't be angry.'

She put one of her diamond hands to the coloured stones he'd given her and which she wore at her neck. She met his eyes and said guiltily, 'Friend Jillan, I have been meaning to tell you something for a long time, but I have never found the proper moment. Anupal has always been there or we were running somewhere—'

*Or were being attacked by a phagus, death poppies, demon hounds, a cannibal witch, a sex-mad Saint, a demented Disciple, or the ancient god Kathuula himself, lest we forget.*

'—but it is about how you talked of being manipulated from the beginning. Friend Jillan, it was never my intention to manipulate you. You must believe that.

'Freda, I—'

'You must, friend Jillan! Please. When I saved you from the phagus and you went back to Godsend to see Hella, she whom you cared about above all others, well, Anupal changed his form. He put on a blue cape. I tried to stop him, but he said to me, *Offer a man dying of thirst a poison chalice, and will he not drink?* Friend Jillan, he looked just like Hella when he went after you. Jillan?'

But he no longer heard her. He was seeing the northern gates of Godsend again. The large youth there in a clinch with a young maid. The onlooking guards making wolfwhistles and catcalls. Realising it was Haal, and smiling for a moment because his friend had at last found someone to share his heart with. The smile freezing on his lips and burning like ice as he saw that the maid in the blue cape also had blonde hair and Hella's face. Turning his back on them all as the rain lashed down and abandoning all those in Godsend to the Empire.

Why had he been so willing to believe it of her? He had known Hella better than that. He should never have given into that fear, the fear that the Empire and the Peculiar used alike against the People. He should have known! And the taint had warned him, had told him that something wasn't right.

From the very beginning he had let them down. He had turned his back on them. He had not had the faith he should have in his friends or the woman he loved above all others. He had not had faith. In fearing and rejecting the faith of the Empire, he'd come to fear and reject even the faith an individual must have in their friends and love. He realised now he had walked about empty and numb in Godsend, waiting for the doom of the future instead of rejoicing in the life of the present. Numb. His character had been forced down into a deep and dark place within him, just as Freda had been enslaved by the Overlords in her mine. His character had become an insidious and whining taint that he feared and rejected as much as anything else.

*Praise be! I thought he'd never get there!*

Where together they might have been able to hold out against the Empire and perhaps even win the freedom of the south, he'd divided them and sped the demise of Godsend. What had he done? How could he have betrayed them so? How many had died? How many? Had he also condemned Hella to death? He would never forgive himself. Nor the Empire. How he hated them.

*Offer a man dying of thirst a poison chalice, and will he not drink? I did tell you not to make any agreement with the Peculiar, but there was probably never any chance of you listening back then. He would have seen to that.*

Well, he had drunk from the poison chalice, hadn't he? It was only a matter of time now. It would soon be over, but he would do his utmost to free Hella and destroy the Empire before he died. The rage grew within him; just as the black stuff he'd swallowed – his death – spread throughout his body; just as the storm of his magic built as strong as ever and demanded release; just as the taint laughed and laughed.

Freda was cowering back from him. The stones at her neck shone and set off rainbow hues within her. She stilled in wonder.

'Anupal will know which way we are heading, won't he, because we are somehow bound to him?'

'Yes, friend Jillan, I think so.'

'Good, for I would not want him to miss this. Yet, knowing him, he has probably overtaken us during the night and is already ahead of us. There is little time. We must hurry.'

'I blame you for this, you know,' Aspin grumbled at Torpeth.

'Me too,' piped up Ash as the three of them stumbled hand in hand along a misty mountain pass.

'I wonder if we're going the right way. Hard to tell, isn't it, silly ox? Are we heading down into the land of the dead proper, or are we heading back to the land of the living?'

'Aspin, by all that's holy, can't you keep him quiet? Every time he opens his mouth, we seem to get into even more trouble. He raises the skeletons of dragons, disturbs an insane god we are far better off not knowing, and then goes and calls old red eye to join the party.'

'Azual, you mean, strange forest man?' Torpeth asked.

'You see, you didn't have to go and say his name, now did you?' Ash whined. 'You're just doing it to cause trouble and upset me. Please be quiet, pretty please?'

'I had to call the Saint, strange forest man,' Torpeth huffed through his beard. 'How else could I save you from Kathuula?'

Ash winced violently. 'Aspin, he's doing it again! He's using names.'

'I gave up trying to reason with him long ago,' Aspin sighed.

'You wouldn't have had to call the mad Saint at all if you hadn't disturbed the god in the first place, would you, you nude lunatic?'

'I had to call the god, strange forest man. How else could I save you from Miserath?'

Ash twitched and looked around nervously. 'We didn't need saving from him!' he hissed. 'But don't say his name too loudly, or it'll bring all his enemies running at once. Look, we were doing just fine before you opened your mouth. So the way I see it, about the only person we need saving from is *you*. Besides, weren't you the one who caused the gods to fall way back when or something? Didn't you sell us out to the Saviours, or some such? If it weren't for you, we'd have probably helped Jillan sort out his latest misunderstanding with the Empire by now and I could be safely in Godsend's inn with an ale or three right before me.'

Torpeth put the end of his dirty beard in his mouth and chewed on it meditatively. With something of a full mouth, he said, 'They do shay we all need shaving.'

'Shaving? What's he talking about now? Aspin, what's he talking about? I can't make head nor tail of him. Aspin, please!'

'I think he means *saving*,' the mountain warrior said resignedly.

'Yesh, shaving! Shaving, shtrange forest man! We all need shaving from ourshelves.'

'What shelves? Shavings from our shelves? You're not making any shense. Sense! Look, he's got me doing it now. Ye gods, I can't cope any more. I'm going to let go.'

'No!' Aspin and Torpeth squawked together, Aspin holding even tighter to Ash's left hand and Torpeth suddenly grabbing Ash's right.

They stood in a closed circle. Torpeth spat his beard out and pulled an extraordinary face for a few seconds. 'Sorry, a hair stuck at the back of my throat.' Then he fixed a boggling eye on Ash. 'See, strange forest man, we all need saving from ourselves, that is all. None with any sense looks to hold onto Miserath the Traitor God, Morlah the Untrustworthy, Anupal the Lord of Mayhem. We could not follow his lead, or all would have been lost.'

'But we *are* lost!' Ash wailed.

'No, strange forest man, we simply have not arrived at the right place yet. I called on the god of infinite eyes and limbs so that we might have some chance against Miserath. When Miserath escaped, I was forced to call on the mad Saint and the other fallen Saints of the Empire so that they might hold back the insane and vengeful god. They will still be fighting now. None will prevail until matters are settled back in the land of the living. And I fear matters will be settled, for the convergence has begun. We will arrive at the next concatenation all too soon. I just pray it is not the last.'

'Better?' Aspin asked Ash brightly.

'No,' Ash complained. 'That sounds even scarier. I preferred it the way he was speaking before.'

'Made shense to me!' Aspin smirked.

'Don't you start,' Ash whimpered. 'Not both of you.'

Sand was replaced by rock, and Jillan asked Freda to go back up to the surface so that he could look around. They emerged into the light of the day, both of them squinting even though the sun was a good few hours from its zenith yet. They stood on an uneven hard surface of dusty pink and orange rock which was stepped with shelves and strata. It was a giant stone staircase that wasn't sure which direction it was going and prevented them from seeing too far. Jillan made for what he thought was the highest point in the area, to get a better view, but had to step down and around several layers and edges to get closer, ended up losing sight of where he was trying to get to and then got completely disorientated, despite knowing where the sun had been a moment before. He tried retracing his path, but didn't recognise any of the lips of rock or surfaces he sweated up, over and across. It was only then that he realised he no longer knew where Freda was. Exasperated, he shouted her name, and she presently came out of the ground near him.

'This is impossible. Do you sense anything, Freda? The sky seems a lighter blue over there, but that could be a trick of the light. Haven could be a dozen yards from us and we wouldn't know it. I suppose the Peculiar would just fly up high and see where he was going, wouldn't he?'

'I'm not sure, friend Jillan. There is no wind here, and Anupal needs that to go higher, I think. Yet I do sense something. Strange echoes and vibrations in the rock, as if . . . as if it were alive.'

'Alive?'

'I think so.'

'Hellooo!' Jillan shouted, turning a full circle. His voice echoed at one moment and fell like a rattling stone the next. 'We need to find Haven! We ask that you help us. Without the power of the Geas to aid us, we will never be able to throw off the Saviours. Their grip on our lives and world becomes ever tighter. They choke and squeeze the life from us. It is only a matter of time before they find the Geas if we cannot.'

There was a moment of silence and then came the response. The earth shook, knocking Jillan from his feet. Huge golems rose up or separated themselves from the rock around them. They stomped closer and Jillan thought he would be crushed. They were surrounded by a dozen of them, even Freda dwarfed by their size.

The largest of the stone golems, his face a set of deep seams and shadowed hollows, loomed over them. 'We knew you would come. The arrival of the one of gold, he whom we could not prevent, told us that the long-foretold convergence had at last begun. And see, here is our sister of diamond, who has brought you to this place. Our time as the guardians of Haven is fast coming to an end.'

Freda looked up at the golem in wonder. 'Do I know you? I feel that I do.'

'You have always known us. We are the children of rock god. We are one. Welcome home, sister. I am Freom.'

Freda's eyes shone with tears of light. 'Freom,' she repeated. 'Can it be true? You are my people?'

The golem nodded slowly. 'Yes, my beautiful sister. All rejoice that you are come to us, even though it heralds the realisation of terrible prophecies.' The boulder that was Freom's head swung to regard Jillan. 'Can such a soft and vulnerable creature truly offer us any hope, sister? See, it cannot even keep its feet. And there is something wrong within it, something that twists, insinuates and strangles, something that should not be allowed anywhere near Haven, we think. Perhaps you have erred in bringing it here. Should it win the power of the Geas for itself, surely it will twist and strangle our entire world. Perhaps it would be better to kill it rather than allow it any opportunity to destroy us.' The shadow of Freom's giant hand hung over Jillan.

Freda quickly moved to protect her friend. 'Freom, no! This creature may seem outwardly soft, but I have seen it make harder sacrifices than any of us could brave. The humans are creatures belonging to all the gods, and have suffered in the name of each of them, even the dark god, from whom their wrongness surely comes. And they have suffered yet more at the hands of their so-called Saviours, to whom their dark god betrayed them, I think. How could they not rail against the world, twisting and insinuating themselves where they may? They are short-lived, Freom, not enduring like . . . us. Each short day is a precious wonder to them, where it is but a moment of little consequence to those who last as long as stone. Even so, I have seen them give up their span of days so selflessly while slaves to uncaring powers. Would you end this one and see the one of gold seize the Geas unopposed? Who is this gold one of whom you speak, Freom? What fate does it offer that you would consider allowing it to take the power of the Geas unopposed? What words did it insinuate into your mind, my brother? How did it twist you to its purpose and seek to strangle all opposition?'

The other golems rumbled in discontent and anger to hear the largest among them so challenged. They sounded like a cataclysm beginning just beyond the horizon. 'You speak like a human!' Freom cracked at Freda contemptuously.

'Proud rock people!' Jillan called out as he made an effort to stand, his knees quaking. 'Freda is the best of all the people I have ever known, and because of her I can bear only love for your kind. I trust her better than I trust myself. If she tells me I am wrong, then I am wrong. If she tells me the sky will fall, then I am in no doubt that it will fall. If she tells me that I go too far in how I use my power and that I must be ended, then ended I must be. If she tells me I must destroy you in order to reach Haven, then I *will* seek to destroy you, for, be in no doubt, I *will* save my beloved Hella and any of my kind that I may. The wrongness within me was understood and exploited by my enemies so that I would betray my people. The blame is mine, though, for I did nothing sooner to try and understand and pre-empt that wrongness. I but ask you to allow me to find Haven so that I might right that wrong. Freda will be your surety. Should I err in the future, then she will finish me and I will do nothing to prevent her.'

'Jillan, no! Never ask such a thing of me,' Freda pleaded.

'It is acceptable to us,' Freom intoned. 'Will you be so bound, sister?'

All looked to Freda.

'Freda, you must do this. It is the only way. Please. I cannot leave Hella in their hands. Or Samnir and all the others. I cannot.'

The woman of diamond searched her young friend's eyes and then hung her head in misery. 'Take us to Haven then, brother, before the one of gold can outdistance us. Does he have such a great lead?'

'No, sister, not once we have trammelled through the earth as only the rock people may. The progress of the one of gold is as slow as it is irresistible.'

Freda took Jillan up in her arms and he took the black crystal from her. Immense though its weight was, it was somehow manageable once he had lodged it inside his armour.

*

386

'Does it hurt, sweet Hella?' Saint Praxis crooned in her ear. 'I imagine so, but it's hard for me to tell when we have you gagged like this. We cannot allow your perfidious and bewitching words to twist and tempt the mind of my gentle torturer, you see.' He shook his head ruefully. 'You are such a disappointment to me. Hella, where did it all go wrong? To think one of my own students should be guilty of such crimes against the Empire! Was I to blame somehow? Was I too indulgent when your teacher? Hella, look what your wilfulness has done. Instead of giving you detention, I have had to bring war to the south. All because you wantonly refused to learn the divine lessons of the holy book and the blessed Saviours. It is *their* word that is holy, not yours!' Colour came into the Saint's cheeks and his voice rose. 'You are some whoring Minister of the Chaos! Do you deny it?' he screamed in her face, his long pointed nose stabbing into her cheek.

She tried to turn away, but her head was strapped against the restraining frame. She squeezed her eyes shut, tears running down her face.

'In your shame, you cannot bear to meet my eyes. By this you display your guilt, Hella Jacobsdotter. How you *disgust* me! How could you give succour to the bane of the Empire? How dare you fight in his unholy name!' She flinched as the spittle of each accusation hit her. 'It is the flowering of his seed within your body and mind, you slut!' Saint Praxis punched her low in her abdomen and she shrieked. 'Do not squirm there as if you might seduce me also, you succubus! You are a perversion of the holy role of Minister and the miscarriage of child-hood. I will not allow anything more to be born of your foul fornica-tion with the Chaos. I will see your womb torn out of you so that nothing may ever quicken in your belly. Torturer, are your righteous irons yet burning red within the fire?'

'Yes, holy one,' came the grunted reply.

She could not pull away from his hot breath. He cruelly penetrated her with his power of fear. She lost all control and evacuated herself, hot urine flooding down her legs. Making a revolted sound, Saint Praxis took a step back to avoid being splashed. The torturer now had room to work.

*Not yet, Praxis*, divine D'Shaa commanded him. He quickly put a hand out to stay the torturer. *Remember, the girl must live. She is the bane's sacred heart. She will give us an advantage over him. Afterwards, you can do with her as you wish.*

Eyes starting from his head, a vein pulsing in his neck, Saint Praxis fought against his own righteous desire to see the sin eviscerated from Hella. 'Yes, you are right to fear your teacher, Hella Jacobsdotter, just as all Chaos creatures fear the holy Saints and blessed Saviours of the Empire. And the bane too fears us. Why else would he run from Godsend? Why else would he abandon you?' The grip of his power forced her eyes back open and she could not hide her misery from him. 'Yes, that is the truth of it, is it not? He has used and abandoned you, leaving you to face the consequences alone. He tricked you with talk of love and faith. Where is his love and faith if he would leave so many to die meaninglessly? You see now, Hella, that the Chaos is not capable of love and faith, for the Chaos is the very opposite of such things. Only the Empire represents love and faith. The Empire would *never* abandon Godsend in such a way. The Empire cares for every single soul of the People, even when they have gone astray. Not one soul will the Empire willingly cede to the Chaos. Even you, Hella, might share in the love and faith of the Empire again, should you but recant your dedication to the bane. You will be allowed to see your father again, whom we also have in our care. He worries so much for you, Hella. He has begged to be Drawn back towards the blessed Saviours, praying for their divine mercy. Will you not join him, Hella, so that you might be a family once again? I can see that is what you want. Renounce the devil, Hella, so that your immortal soul might be saved! Ask for the Empire's forgiveness. That is all. A few simple words. Be not proud, dear child. The blacksmith and Samnir have already pleaded for such forgiveness, sobbing like children, for are we not all children of the Empire? Come, Hella, be that innocent child once more and join your father and friends, so that all might rejoice and Godsend can know days of joy and celebration again. All will go back to how it was before, when all were happy and secure in the care of the Empire. Do you not want those days of happiness once more?'

She did not want to believe it, but Jillan *had* abandoned her. How could he have done such a thing? *Why* would he do such a thing? She didn't know any more. She couldn't remember. She wanted things to go back to how they were before, so that she might say and do things differently, so that Jillan might never have had to leave, so that Haal might never have had to die. It was all confused in her head – the love, the fear, the disappointment. There seemed no way out of the nightmare of death, loneliness and misery. No way out. But Saint Praxis promised it *could* all go back to how it was before. She saw it so clearly in her mind: her father's forgiving smile as he told her that it was not giving birth that had killed Hella's mother, but a surfeit of happiness bursting her heart; her Minister's forgiving smile as he re-assured her that she was the ablest of students and more than worthy to be Drawn during the Saint's next visit to the town; Haal's forgiving smile as he told her that he was fully recovered and always there for her. All was forgiveness. It was surely all she could want. She only had to ask.

The torturer had removed her gag. Saint Praxis watched her with understanding and expectant compassion. 'Yes, Hella, what is it, child?'

'Kill yourself!' she choked, fumbling to direct her power of command against him.

The Saint gave her a sickly smile. 'But of course, my dear. Why didn't you say so before?' He hesitated and frowned. 'Are you sure that's what you want?'

She put her entire will into the instruction: 'Do it!'

And in that moment he had her. He seized both her mind and magic. Gloatingly, he said, 'We allowed you to speak freely. In our mercy we allowed you the chance to repent. Yet, knowing the dupli-citous nature of the Chaos, we also took the precaution of mixing our sacred blood with the water you were given when you were first captured. Now your own evil has ensnared you. Your duplicity and allegiance to the Chaos have seen you ruin yourself, harlot! You have robbed yourself of your last chance at salvation and damned yourself forever! There will never be forgiveness for one such as you.' With that he invaded her consciousness and annihilated her love for the bane of the Empire.

'Jillan, forgive me!' she cried, her heart breaking, just as the gates of Godsend had broken.

It started as a crack in the parched earth and widened out all the way to the horizon: a green valley laid out before and beneath them. Jillan stood with the rock people, looking down through wisps of cloud at a hidden world, slopes rolling down into rich depths of life. Behind him was arid desert, ahead and below was an abundant and verdant environment. He saw trees laden with all sorts of fruit, birds floating on rising air currents or swooping down for insects, and bees humming as they went about their business pollinating flowers. He heard the complex song of these creatures, some that were unseen adding a rustle from thickets here or a skittered stone there. It flowed through and around him, a gentle stream building to a noisy cascade. He opened his mouth as if to catch its refreshing spray. It energised him like nothing else before, making his fingers, hands, limbs and whole body tingle. He experienced a true sense of wonder, as if rediscovering a most precious possession that had been thought lost forever. If only Hella were here to share it with him. It overwhelmed him as much as it drew him towards it. He felt he could fly, and might well have launched himself out over the edge if Freda hadn't spoke at that precise moment.

'Haven, friend Jillan! At last.'

He nodded mutely and realised he was crying.

'We knew it was here, but did not dare hope it would be. I see it with my own eyes but still do not believe it. My brother, is it real?'

The massive Freom nodded. 'It is, sister. It is said that the soil is so rich that it brings dead plants and animals back to life. And that the water is so clean and clear that you can breathe it. And that the fruit and plants taste so powerful that you will never taste anything again. It is the power of the Geas.'

'I fear to enter,' Jillan said softly. 'Will I not spoil it?'

Freom sighed. 'Perhaps, friend to the rock people. Yet we also believe that something of this place is already within each of us. The hard ground of the desert is like our skin. Beneath that exterior, though, is this great power and beauty. Do you not feel it within you, or is it spoilt somehow, you whom we know carries something that twists, insinuates and strangles within you?'

The sun was past its zenith and moving towards the horizon. As shadows filled the deepest and furthest parts of the valley, something glinted up at them.

'There! Did you see it?' Freda gasped. 'It was sun-metal, friend Jillan!'

'We must go, before it is too late!' Jillan said urgently.

'Freda must remain here with us, friend of the rock people. Freda is one of us and will stand as a guardian like us. This is a test for you alone.'

'Hurry, friend Jillan!'

Jillan wasted no time throwing himself over the edge and into the glorious Haven of the Geas. Near the top the sides of the valley were perilously steep, but he jumped and slid down without any regard for his own safety. If he fell and cracked open his head, then perhaps the soil would bring him back from the dead as Freom had said. As it was, the softness of the soil betrayed him first, for it gave under one of his feet and his momentum saw him overbalance. It was only catching the thin branch of a sapling at the last moment – and the fact that the sapling was sturdier than it looked – that saved him from plunging a hundred feet or so.

He charged on, grimacing as ankles and spine jarred with each great leaping step down. Inevitably, he landed awkwardly on a loose stone, his foot turned over and he went rolling and tumbling. He tucked his head in and covered it with his arms as the world spun around him. He feared the moment when it would stop, when his back broke against a rock, a branch punched through his torso or he smashed against a rockface or tree trunk. He was going too fast! He unwrapped himself and spread himself wide, just as he bounced into a hollow filled with briars and stinging nettles.

He dragged himself free, waited for a second to allow his head to catch up with the rest of him and then bounded on once more. His lungs spiked with pain, as if he had inhaled the barbs of the plants that had just cushioned his fall. Fortunately, the slopes of the valley were becoming less pronounced. Surely the bottom couldn't be that far away, could it? He hadn't seen it yet, though.

Where was the other? His vision sawing like his breathing, he struggled to make sense of what he saw and heard. There! No, it was light carried down from above by a rivulet that sounded like it would soon become a waterfall, or was that roaring the sound of his own blood in his ears? He could not separate what was inside from what was outside.

He realised that the dark poison the sifters had temporarily calmed was quickening inside him. It marbled his skin. It seemed the closer and more quickly he came to the Geas, the greater it punished him. To arrive would kill him, but to stop now would see the poison do its work without any possibility of a cure. He giggled at the madness of it.

And there ahead was the golden figure, moving with slow inevitability. He recognised the armour of a Disciple. How could it be here? How could it have known the location of Haven?

He staggered after it, gaining ground even though he weaved wildly. They were on a shallow path still heading downwards. The route disappeared around low bluffs and humps, beyond which smoke and steam rose in plumes and columns. He steadied himself against an outcrop and snatched back his scalded hand. Superheated air rose from a vent in the ground near his feet. What was beneath them? Some dragon? The Disciple was wreathed in shifting ghosts of white. It moved on relentlessly.

'Wait!' Jillan coughed.

The Disciple looked back over its shoulder, tilted its head strangely and kept moving without any break in its stride. Its steps echoed and boomed as if there were caverns below them. It was like a bell tolling.

Jillan wiped sweat out of his eyes and ran, veering left and right. He managed to draw near.

'Ah, Jillan! I was wondering if you'd turn up,' the armour said in hollow but familiar tones.

'Anupal.'

'Of course. Who else would it be? I'll be glad of your company as we go.'

Jillan matched the armour's pace, but made sure to stay out of its reach. 'Why didn't you join us in the desert? You want the Geas for yourself, don't you?'

'Why, Jillan, whatever do you think of me? I'm quite hurt, really I am. After all we've been through together. We are comrades-in-arms, you and I. I did not join you in the desert because I could not. I only had a general idea of where you were. It's a big old place, you know.'

Jillan didn't believe him. *Well of course he's lying! He's the god of such things. I wouldn't even bother trying to catch him out. Waste of time.* 'Why haven't you asked about Freda then? Because you don't need her any more?'

'I haven't had a chance to get a word in edgeways, that's why, my suspicious friend. And I imagined you would have told me immediately if there was anything amiss.'

*Think, Jillan. What would have happened if you hadn't caught up with him?* He opened his mouth and nausea almost saw him retch upon the ground. The armour marched on. 'All this,' he managed after a second. 'You've manipulated everything from the beginning, haven't you? Using Freda and me to show you the way here. And using me and Godsend to force the Empire to send out these Disciples. You need the armour of sun-metal, don't you? That's what all this has been about from the beginning. The armour will allow you to overcome any defence the Geas attempts. That's it, isn't it? All so that you could have its power. You want to be the god over all things! You want everything.'

The head turned towards him. 'I could tell you that you are lost to paranoia, Jillan. You are ill, aren't you? Whatever you swallowed in the nether realm is killing you. You don't look like you've got long left. You'll do well even to make it as far as the Geas. I could tell you that the poison has turned your mind in on itself. I could tell you that you have created a conspiracy theory that can never be disproved, for in order to survive it insists on becoming more complex than any potential explanation. I could tell you such things, and you would be left without a sensible response, but there is no need, for you are dying. You are a weak mortal. There is nothing you can do, so as some form of payment for what you have gone through on my behalf, I will at least tell you *why* you are here dying. Be grateful, for it's more than most mortals get. And besides, I'm quite impressed that you've worked much of it out. I didn't think you had it in you.

'So here it is. I have been planning this for millennia, poor Jillan, perhaps longer than that. Even as the other gods fell and the else-worlders arrived, I was putting things in place just to achieve this moment. I helped see my brothers brought down and formed an alliance with the elseworlders precisely so that I would have freedom enough to orchestrate – most subtly – the generations and lives of all the mortals of the Empire. Unseen, I was there in Downy Gorge, inflaming the sexual perversion of Daimon's father, so that the boy would be traumatised, and then I was there to free him and set him on the path towards becoming Saint Azual and seeking murderous vengeance. I was there helping Azual conquer the south, while making sure sufficient numbers of pagans escaped to the mountains, so that the elseworlders would not seize control of the Geas so simply. I was there whispering to Azual in New Sanctuary, so that his madness overtook him and your parents fled to Godsend, where they never quite fitted in. I was there in the eastern deserts keeping Samnir alive while I encouraged him onto such horrific slaughter that he began to hate himself and the Empire, ultimately seeing him exiled to Godsend and his post watching the gate near your home. I was there in the deep northern mine, causing a cave-in to trap Norfred, bring Freda to his help, have her distraught when I arranged for Darus to kill him, help her break free and then see her set out on the path of the temples and runes. I knew Gar would allow one of his own children to understand the runes where he would not allow any other. And yes, Jillan, I was there and invisible in the classroom of Godsend, ensuring that the Minister hated you, your classmates would attack you and that you would flee Godsend. I saw to it that the Geas would inevitably choose you as one of its own, so that you might defeat Azual and finally see the Disciples sent forth from the Great Temple. Think hard, Jillan. Was I not also there in your dreams, as the small voice inspiring the questions with which you so antagonised the Minister?

'I was there. I have always been there. Always. Do you think I would simply allow these elseworlders to come here and take my world from me? *My* world! *My* power! I was ancient long before the Geas of this world ever developed awareness, but I was trapped here, imprisoned. I enabled the life of this world far more than the simple-minded Geas ever did. And now I will see my aeons of labour return to me what is rightfully mine! The power of the cosmos!'

It brought Jillan to his knees. His guts felt torn out. 'It is *you*! You are the Chaos! The devil. Evil walking. Minister Praxis was right all along. I thought its existence was a story of the Empire used to control the People. But it was not! It was you all along.'

'Correct.'

'No. It cannot be so. You have not done all this. We have free will.'

'Yes and no. You have the freedom to choose from a very limited number of options. I started the convergence a long time ago. This late in the day, there is very little choice or free will left to mortalkind. And that is how it should be. Mortals exist to serve the gods.'

'No. You did not create me! But I see now you plotted things so that my parents died in Hyvan's Cross. It may not have been your hand that held the blade, but you were the one who killed them. Was that so that I would always blame and hate the Saviours so much that I would never negotiate with them? Was that to force the battle that saw Azual defeated? I will never forgive you.'

'It doesn't really matter any more, does it? It's time for you to lie down and die, Jillan. I really must be going.'

'And you took Hella's shape outside Godsend so that I would see her kiss Haal.'

For an instant the Peculiar's foot froze at the top of his next step, and then he carried on. 'So Freda told you. No matter.' And the next step.

Jillan pushed himself back up, feeling something tear inside him. He tasted blood in the back of his throat. 'Torpeth was right not to do anything that you asked. You did the same thing to him long ago that you have done to me. You will turn this world into a hell. I will see this through to the end, although it will be the end of me. I will not let the Chaos take the power of the Geas unopposed. I will never forgive you for what you have done.'

'As you wish, but don't expect me to wait for you.' The Peculiar shrugged. 'It is of no consequence. You will not be able to enter the presence of the Geas in any event. See there? Jillan, focus, for it will be the last thing you see.'

He looked up blearily. The path had opened up before them. A wide channel flowing with lava blocked them from going any further and filled the bottom of the valley cauldron. It apparently encircled an island, but the heat shimmer rising off the river of molten rock was so intense that it warped the air, creating a kaleidoscope past which nothing could be seen, not even the sky. What lay beyond?

'At last it will be mine,' the Peculiar's voice droned. 'It will no longer be able to deny me. Do you see it, Jillan? Nothing of the Geas's creation can go past this point. The lava would undo even the rock people. Any being attempting to fly across will meet gales and be forced down to their destruction. Any beings of light – for they do exist, be they scintillations, spectrals, lustres, lumines or visifers – will be refracted and caught forever in that sheering of their element, that starring miasma you behold. But I am more than a mere creation of the Geas. It will not be able to keep me from what is rightfully mine. It will not prevent this armour. Goodbye, Jillan, for you will be dead by the time I return.'

So saying, the Peculiar stepped down into the lava and waded out. His progress was tortuously slow, for he moved through rock, but progress he made all the same. He sank to his knees, then his waist, and Jillan hoped he would go completely under, but the lava was dense enough to support him, and its flow inched the Peculiar further across the barrier.

Jillan's breath was thick and laboured. His chest burned as if his lungs themselves were full of the lava.

*There is no more time. It must be now*, Ba'zel implored.

Jillan fumbled the brick of black crystal out of his armour and let it drop from his palsied fingers into the channel. It slapped down, throwing sparks into the air, and immediately began to absorb the bright energy around it. The lava darkened outwards from the crystal, forming a crust across the channel. The matrix of the crystal grew until a bridge led from Jillan's feet right to the island.

*Across, Jillan of the seventh realm!*

Jillan stumbled onto the bridge. Ink wormed across his vision, turning the world into a place of shadows. Heat assailed him from both sides, singeing his hair and eyebrows. He knew that if it weren't for his armour, he would have gone up in flames there and then.

*Beware. Move away to your left!* Ba'zel warned.

Jillan adjusted his course, just avoiding a drop into the deadly river. He was starting to lose much of the feeling in his body. He was not even sure he was putting one foot in front of another any more.

'What is this?' shrieked the outraged Peculiar from Jillan's right, slightly behind him. 'What compact have you made with powers outside this realm? Answer me, wretch! You are *my* creature. You will deliver the Geas to me!' Then the deity's voice suddenly changed, disconcertingly reasonable in the instant. 'That's right, Jillan, remember our agreement. I will save all those of Godsend in return for the efforts you have made in bringing me here. Think of Hella, Jillan. I can guarantee she will be taken out of their clutches and returned to you. Simply bring the Geas to me. I will pledge to share its power with the other gods and mortalkind. None of your fears will be realised, Jillan. Do not allow yourself to be ruled by fear, for that is the weapon of the Empire. You know that. Nothing you and I have done together has been wrong. It has brought freedom to the People. Freedom to us all. Terrible sacrifices have been made, which you should not allow to become meaningless, especially now success is within our grasp. Do not throw it all away. Do not let your selfishness turn you into the all-powerful tyrant Torpeth once was, an all-powerful god who turned this world into a hell. Remember, it is his armour that you wear. Do not become what he was. I had to betray Torpeth all that time ago, or all life would have eventually ceased under his unremitting appetite for perfection and his obsession with seeing his singular vision realised. Do not take the Geas for yourself, or you will become a worse monster than the Saviours have ever been, and I will be forced to confront you in the name of the People. We are friends, you and I, remember that!'

The Peculiar's voice drummed in time with Jillan's heartbeat. The words sounded as if his own mind and self were speaking them. They were seductively logical. They matched the rhythm, pattern and sentiment of his own thoughts. He was losing his separation from the Peculiar. The fifth god, who brought unexpected dreams, insights, temptations and questions to humankind, had Jillan in his thrall, bewitching and compelling him.

*One more step, Jillan of the seventh realm. Just one more.*

Jillan fell through the kaleidoscope, and the Peculiar's hold on him slipped, affording him a vital moment of lucidity and self-possession. He was on a circular flat-topped pillar of rock about fifty paces across. The air was close and dim, the dome of colours surrounding the island somehow muted. He tottered forward. There was nothing here! He reached the centre and collapsed to the ground, defeated. All for nothing. One last great trick of the Peculiar and existence. His hopes and dreams dissipated. There was a final image of Hella, her face loving, melancholy and then closed. She was beautiful to him, no matter how it ended; she was the most beautiful thing he'd ever known, particularly because everything was ending. His thirst for her, for life, was beyond his endurance. He realised he was glad he had taken in the poison of life, for at least he had known the sweetness of its moisture for a fleeting moment. He saw a small dirty puddle by his knee. He scooped some of its foul water into his palm and slurped it down, not caring how rank it tasted. The rest evaporated from the rock before his eyes. That was how life ended – there one moment, gone the next.

Fractures of gold appeared at the bottom of the dome as the Peculiar rose onto the island and forced his way into the space. A gauntlet came up, angry and demanding. 'Give it to me!'

Jillan laughed forlornly. 'There is nothing here.'

'You lie! Do not think I do not know. I am the god of lies!'

With the last of his strength, Jillan shook his head. 'Nothing.' His chin fell onto his chest.

'I cannot be fooled or gulled. You will give me the Geas, or I will take everything from you that you hold dear. Hella will die in indescribable agony. Samnir will curse you as he swallows his own sword. I will seek out the spirits of your parents and make them playthings of Azual forever. You are bound to me.'

'You will not mention her name again,' Jillan croaked, sounding a death rattle.

'Pathetic human,' the Peculiar sneered. 'Then know in your final moment that I will see every torture known to mortalkind, the gods and the Saviours visited upon Hella.'

And in that final moment of love for Hella, hatred for the god who would threaten her, and despair that he would not know life any more, Jillan released everything that he was, letting go of the sustaining energies of his core, unleashing the magic that had fought for true freedom all his life, pouring out the terrible rage of mortal existence. All was directed down on the Peculiar, blood-red energies deluging the god. Lightning forked down from around the dome and detonated against the armour. All creation fell upon the sun-metal; the air around it combusted; light lanced through the gaps in its visor; water condensed upon it, crept into its joints and then froze and expanded, trying to burst it apart; the ground became adamantine teeth and tried to crush it. The world railed against the Peculiar, smiting him with forces so titanic that it seemed it would undo itself.

As Jillan's power drained away and the air cleared, the Peculiar was revealed, laughing. His head was thrown back and his arms lifted on high as he gloried in the halo of the futile assault against him. He was unyielding and unbending. All would fail thus before him. Still laughing through his words, the Peculiar mocked Jillan. 'Self-defeating from the very start. For all their tantrums, mortalkind and the Geas itself are but the waste and by-product of the true forces of the cosmos. A random or incidental emission. An exhalation of used breath. You cannot stand against *me*. I am a god and you a mere mortal. Even the other gods and the Geas are but part of the transient nature of this world. The convergence is complete. Your body and the Geas are exhausted, your resistance a joke. Give me the Geas or I will take it: both serve me the same. All now suits my whim.' And the deity's laughter rolled around and around the dome, building as it went.

With nothing left to fight against the poison, Jillan was lost. Darkness seeped from his every pore, covering and drowning him. He was the ichor of the nether realm. He was absence, absorbing the light and sound, just as Ba'zel had before him. The laughter of the Peculiar drained into him and became a deafening silence. Now black flames rolled from Jillan and tortured the Peculiar. Black lightning spat from Jillan's raised hand and tore rents in the very fabric of the Geas's reality, threatening to tip the Peculiar into the void, removing him from the world entirely.

'No, it is not possible! You are nothing!' the Peculiar stormed, beating at the flames running up and down his armour, vainly trying to smother them before they could smother him. He stamped across to the empty figure standing at the centre of creation and brought his mighty fists of sun-metal down to obliterate its head. The gauntlets winked out as they disappeared inside the figure – and the anti-energy began to draw the rest of the Peculiar into it.

'Nooo!' the Peculiar wailed, his beauteous face and eyes suddenly clear behind his visor. Mournful tears rolled down his cheeks. 'Jillan, please! Forgive me. I beg you.'

The figure of uncompromising darkness leaned forwards. 'Kathuula sends his regards.'

'Argh! Avatar of madness, spare me! I give you this Disciple as sacrifice, as payment!'

Inside the armour, the Peculiar shifted into a swirling gas and attempted to extract himself through its visor. Yet the sun-metal had begun to run, so much magic had been channelled against it and engulfed it. The helmet lost its edges and shape, melting down into a lump, trapping the Peculiar inside.

The Peculiar whimpered and screamed within the armour as it became his white-hot and molten coffin. The antimatter that was Jillan picked up the armour and hurled it out through the wall of broken light and down into the lava.

Jillan came on after it and, as he passed through the wall, saw the darkness filtered, dragged and torn out of him. He stood restored to his normal self on one end of the bridge and watched as the remains of the Disciple seared down through the lava and disappeared. He felt nothing – no sense of relief, satisfaction or grief.

He crossed the bridge, stepped onto the edge of the channel and turned around. 'Hello.'

'Hello, Jillan.'

'You are Ba'zel?'

'Yes.'

'Are you a Saviour?'

'No. The Declension rejects me as *unstable*. Despite my best efforts otherwise, I have destroyed whole worlds.'

'And I fear I will destroy this one. I am an outcast of the Empire. I am called pagan or Unclean. I am called the bane. I do not want people to die, yet no matter what I do, my magic cannot seem to stop it. My magic only makes things worse.'

'One way or another, Jillan, it will end. Let us go together and see if we can make sure it is the Declension and the home-realm that ends rather than this place.'

'All right.'

'Did you claim the power of this realm's Geas?'

'I-I'm not sure. I would know if I had, wouldn't I? I feel the same.'

'I do not know. I do not think every Geas is the same. I do not think they are all one, despite what Mentor Ho'zen taught me.'

400

'Perhaps your kind is controlled by false stories and beliefs, just like the People of the Empire.'

'That is . . . interesting. Yes. What if the Great Voyage itself were a fantasy presented as a truth so that we might be manipulated? It is almost unthinkable, Jillan, almost unthinkable.'

# CHAPTER 13:

# And pre-empting hope

As they came up through Haven, Jillan was entranced by the place all over again. Every movement of leaf in the warm breeze, every shine of light, ever blur of wing and every drift of cloud worked together to hypnotise the eye. The way he was staring at everything, he felt witless or drugged, intoxicated or overawed, or all of those things at once. There was splendour even in the simplest detail, and that was some sort of great wisdom or revelation.

Even Ba'zel was not immune to it. 'Your realm is so full of life,' he said, inspecting a lacy red and orange butterfly that had settled momentarily on one of his upper limbs. 'At first I thought the life here was just a fungus growing over the rock. That is how my kind tends to think of the life of most realms: as parasitic and transient. Yet here even the ground seems alive.' He spoke to the butterfly: 'Hello, creature, can you talk?'

Jillan smiled. 'No, it can't, at least not in a way I can understand.' He wanted to feel lulled and calmed by the place, but the urgent plight of Hella and the People worried at him. He knew he must not let the soporific nature of Haven overcome him. There was something dangerous about it, or at least he wasn't ready for it yet, and never could be until the affairs of the outside world had been properly settled. *But are they ever settled?* 'Ba'zel, we should go.'

'Of course,' the being from another realm replied, not missing the urgency in Jillan's voice. Ba'zel shook himself and extended his limbs further than before.

Jillan ran in order to keep up, not tiring in any degree despite the fact that the valley through which they travelled seemed more extensive than when he had first passed through it. He noticed shaded pools, grottoes and enticing glades that he had no memory of seeing previously. He was relieved when at last they arrived at slopes he recognised.

They moved steadily up and came to the edge of the desert to find Torpeth, Ash, Aspin and the dark wolf in a tense stand-off with Freom and the rock people. Freda stood between the two factions, apparently just about keeping them from coming to blows. Floss the horse was off to one side, looking bored.

'I have already told you we are the Guardians of Haven and will not permit you to enter!' Freom directed at Torpeth.

'There is more sense in you guarding this,' Torpeth fumed, showing the golem his naked behind.

'Torpeth, you're not helping,' Aspin said through gritted teeth.

'Jillan!' Ash interrupted. 'There you are!'

All eyes turned towards Jillan and Ba'zel. Aspin skipped around one of the distracted rock people and came to embrace his friend.

'It is good you returned when you did,' the mountain warrior said with relief. 'Are you all right?'

'Friend Jillan, did you find the one of gold? Was it Anupal? Where is he?' Freda asked, coming forward.

'Sorry to interrupt, but did you find anything to drink down there? I'm parched. There isn't an inn at all?' Ash enquired as he tricked his way past two of the rock people, who contrived somehow to bump each other out of the woodsman's path.

'Who is that?' Torpeth and Freom said together, their voices cutting through everyone else's as they pointed at the member of the Declension.

'Oh, this is Ba'zel,' Jillan replied.

'He is one of the others, is he not?' Torpeth said accusingly, his eyes full of hatred.

'He is not like the others. He will help us.'

'No! He will seem to help us, then ultimately be proven to serve *them*.'

'There is no place for this elseworlder among us!' Freom rumbled.

'We need him if we are to move against the Great Temple,' Jillan insisted, glaring at Torpeth and Freom. 'He helped me against the Peculiar. If he hadn't, this world would have become a hell of the dark god's design. I *trust* Ba'zel. He was there when none of the rest of you were, because you were too busy arguing about your embarrassingly naked arse, who gets to play Guardian and whether there's any sort of inn round here. Well, I've had enough! Ba'zel and I will try to save Hella and the People, with or without your help!'

All were silent. He'd been screaming at them. Ash looked scared. Jillan realised the glow of magic had come to his fingertips without his being aware of it. He refused to feel shocked or guilty about it. Damn them, didn't they understand what was happening? That Godsend had fallen and the whole world was about to follow, that the Saviours were about to take it all?

Torpeth licked dry lips and pulled at the hair above his temples. 'Jillan, you cannot do this alone. Do not make the same mistake I did, I beg you, for all our sakes. We are here because all share a similar goal and enemy. I know that you feel you have done so much alone, but we have all made sacrifices, believe me. It is the nature of all beings to see themselves as the main character of every drama, and others as less important, supporting characters who do not feel as much, do not contribute as much, do not sacrifice as much and do not matter as much. When we are disappointed or angry, we tell ourselves that we do not need them. We tell ourselves that we're the only ones with the power, vision and will to make the important things matter anyway. Yet we are wrong in that, for it is only in our relationship to others that our lives have meaning, unless we're all going to become hermits, in which case mortalkind would die out entirely. So do not think you have no need of us, not after Aspin has given up Veena, I have given up my goats and Ash has given up his inn to be here. Do not hoard the power you have taken because you trust no other to wield it. Do not keep the power that rightfully belongs to the gods for yourself. I did that and caused their fall. Without them, you will never defeat the others. The others will exploit your self-obsession otherwise, strip you of everything and leave you to argue about your embarrassingly naked arse.'

'I have been the main character in Ba'zel's drama, and he in mine,' Jillan replied intently. 'It is hard to explain, but we swapped early parts of our lives for a while. You'll just have to take my word for it. You say that our lives only have meaning in our relationship to others. Well, I include Ba'zel among those others.'

'Do not err,' Freom warned Jillan. 'Remember our agreement and surety. Listen to the naked one, Jillan, and return the power of the gods to them.'

'Ash, what do you think?' Jillan asked. 'Should we allow the return of these gods who have always been more trouble than they are worth?'

The woodsman frowned. 'Do I take it from all this that there isn't any sort of inn down there? I thought Haven was meant to be some sort of paradise. It all sounds very dull and worthy to me. Let 'em have it if they want it so bad, that's what I say.'

'Thank you . . . I think. Aspin?'

Aspin stuck his spear into the ground and leaned against it. 'You've got to expect Freom to advocate the return of the rock god, I suppose. My own people would probably want me to plead for the return of Wayfar. After all, he helped us in Hyvan's Cross, after a fashion, and my people played no small part in the battle against Azual at Godsend. Personally, though, I would stand by you no matter what your decision, and no matter whether you were guided by Ba'zel here or not. Also, I have to say, Ash has got a point. If there's no inn, they're welcome to it.'

Jillan nodded. 'Freda?'

'I cannot bear the thought of Sinisar in that prison. I have heard his screams, remember, and they will haunt me forevermore if I do not try to help him, friend Jillan. I would want to find the sun-smith again and take him to open the box.'

'Ba'zel?'

Torpeth and Freom looked as if they were about to protest, but Jillan raised a forbidding finger at them.

'Ba'zel?'

'Jillan of the seventh realm, these gods sound as if they would increase the uncertainty of any outcome. That would be in your interest during this time of convergence, as it might confound the plans of the Declension. Also, there is a pleasing circularity or pattern in raising them now, is there not, if it was the naked one who saw them fall in the first place? Of course, there is one god whom you will not be able to raise. Your fifth god? The Peculiar? Correct?'

'Yes,' Jillan affirmed, to the evident perturbation of all assembled there. 'It seems Ba'zel is in accord with you, my friends. Will no one speak for the raising of Akwar though?'

'Akwar is already here!' a voice bubbled up from below. The ground became damp and a spring burst from the ground, raining up a slender figure.

The rock people, Freda, Ash and Aspin bowed respectfully. Torpeth shrugged. Ba'zel moved his hard skull backwards and forwards as if trying to see better. And Jillan intercepted Floss, who had clearly decided she was thirsty.

'Welcome to Haven, holy Akwar!' Freom declared.

'Well met, child of the rock god,' the deity said mellifluously, sparkling in the desert sun. He looked around the group, taking in Freda, Ash and Aspin, and then stopping at Torpeth. 'So, you are at last seeking to make amends, ancient mortal?'

'All water under the bridge, eh?' the holy man cackled.

Akwar turned sharply to Ba'zel. 'Elseworlder,' he gurgled unpleasantly.

'Now let's not go getting teary,' Torpeth interceded. 'Besides, in a straight contest, I suspect Ba'zel would make short work of you. You're really not looking your best, old Akwar, you know. More like an elemental rather than the god of floods and tides.'

'No thanks to you, cursed mortal!'

'Now it's just that sort of attitude, when a person's trying to help, that gets you into trouble in the first place.'

'Jillan, maybe you can shut him up?' Ash begged. 'He just can't help himself. Whenever there's a god around he starts getting all shouty and antagonistic. How any of us survived the nether realm, I still have no idea.'

'Torpeth,' said a straight-faced Jillan, 'if you do not remain silent, I shall invest Akwar with the power to see to it that it burns like fire whenever you pee, that you become incontinent, and that then you become impotent. Not even your goats will want your company. And that's just for starters!'

The holy man glowered at Jillan, but thought better of saying anything.

'It's a miracle!' Ash all but wept.

'I didn't think it was possible,' Aspin agreed.

407

Jillan glared at the see-through water god, whose face was constantly washed away by the plume of water that issued from the top of his head and came down as clear, liquid hair. It was impossible to read the deity's expression for more than an instant. 'The gods failed us before. What reason can there be to reinvest them?'

'Blasphemy!' Freom ground out, and his people echoed him.

Jillan ignored the interruption. 'You gods have ever treated us mortals as servants or playthings to be dispensed with at whim. If we were to reinvest you in order to overturn the Saviours, we would simply be replacing one lot of oppressors with another.'

'I cannot let this pass!' the incensed leader of the rock people bellowed, the sand of the desert jumping as he came clumping forward.

The hackles of the dark wolf rose and it came to stand at Jillan's shoulder, its growl as deep as the golem's own. Jillan brought magic up from his core and his eyes burned red with intent.

'Wait!' Akwar commanded, pouring towards Freom and forcing the rock man back, before turning to answer Jillan. 'Our failure last time was based on how we are inextricably linked with mortalkind, just as all life is connected through the Geas. If we are to succeed now, it will only be through that self-same connection. Just as you can raise the gods back up, Jillan, so the gods can raise the People against the elseworlders. You will need the People if you are to confront the Great Temple. Or do you think the People will rise in *your* name, Jillan? Jillan of Godsend commands it, so it must be done? I think not!'

'How can you raise them? They are in the thrall of the Saviours.'

'Are the bodies of the People not made of water and clay? Along with my brother Gar, I will command them. I will drive them before me.'

'You will force them, you mean,' said Jillan. 'They will be forced to sacrifice themselves, whether they are willing or not. You are *worse* than the Saviours. I will not have the People used so.'

'You think there is a choice, foolish child? The convergence has begun! The elseworlders have arranged all so that you will find Haven, claim the power of the Geas and deliver it to them at the Great Temple. They know you are coming to them and have prepared all their armies and power accordingly. They are waiting for you! It is a trap, and perhaps already inescapable. Do you think the gods will permit you simply to go there and exchange the power of the Geas for the meaningless life of a girl? Never! Will we permit you to place all existence within the power of the elseworlders simply to satisfy an immature infatuation for some wench? Never! Will we allow you to end the lives of the gods and the People, without the People even having the opportunity to fight for their world? Never! Would we see untold numbers of mortals ended so that the world might have some chance of living on? *Always!* And the lives that we would see ended above all others are yours and Hella's, for the two of you have done more than any other mortal to bring about this convergence. You have brought us to the brink of apocalypse, mortal! HOW DARE YOU! Are you now proud of yourself? Or do you now see why no mortal should be allowed such power? Do you now see why the gods must exist, and why they exist above mortals? Do you now see why mortals *must* be ruled by the gods? It is the *natural order* of things, without which there would be *nothing*!'

Jillan's eyes blazed red hot, and his ferocious gaze turned Akwar's edges to steam. He was so angry he had to work to unlock his jaw. 'Ruled by the gods?' he hissed. 'As Miserath ruled over us and saw to it that we lost everything and everyone we cared about, just so that we'd lead him to Haven in our desperation? Just so that he could claim the power of the Geas and create a hell of our world? He saw thousands of pagans slaughtered when they farmed the southern region. He brought about the terrible events of New Sanctuary. He killed Karl. He killed my parents! He ruined Samnir's life. He brought about the plague. He killed so many of the people of Godsend! And he didn't bloody care for a second. He *never* cared. And now you stand there and tell me you fully intend to see the person I love above all others ended, the person without whom life is meaningless to me! After all, we're *just mortals*, eh, holy Akwar?' Jillan spat sizzling blood over Akwar. 'Just the sight of you gods makes me sick to my very soul.' The rage within him wouldn't be contained. He fractured – and it was the voice of the taint that thundered out of him at the last. '*I have already slain one god today, and will delight in destroying another!*'

The wolf howled savagely. Ash tried to run, tripped over his own feet, and only narrowly avoided being trampled in the rock slide of Freom and his people rushing forward.

Tears ran down Torpeth's cheeks. 'Jillan!' he sobbed. 'Do not become like me. It's my fault. I should never have disturbed Kathuula, but there was no other way!'

Freda wailed and hammered her fists against the sides of her head. She threw herself into the centre of the struggle even so, thinking somehow to use her bulk to keep those she cared about away from each other. Aspin flanked Jillan on the opposite shoulder to the wolf and readied his spears, reading precisely where Freom would be in the next instant, and where the tip of his weapon would find the golem's eye.

Foam bubbled from Akwar's mouth and he rose as the whole body of an ocean. Up and up, higher and higher, he went, casting a shadow over all those below him as he gathered an unstoppable force. He reached for the moment when he would be suspended and teetering above them, when they would see the terror and majesty of his godhead, and realise the true error of their mortality, before he came crashing down upon them.

Yet the maelstrom of Jillan's wrath had already built beyond all belief, in that very instant outstripping Akwar. Skeins of red energy and searing orbs of power electrified the air and tore apart sky and earth. Where the heavens had been a clear and infinite blue a moment before, now devastating tempests warred and consumed each other, growing beyond compass. Jillan's fair hair streaked out like lightning. His features bled one into another and bleached out in sheering light.

And into the epicentre of the conflict stepped Ba'zel. He moved faster than any other, as if he had long ago foreseen all that would come to pass. His taloned foot came down and the power of his presence detonated among them. There was a dull *crump* and everything collapsed. Slowly at first, and then faster and faster, energy vanished into the dead zone of his making and insistence. As a vacuum snuffs out a flame or the void swallows life, so he suppressed and depressed the ardent combatants of the seventh realm.

The rock people crumbled to the ground, the vital force knitting them together stripped away. The shine of Freda's substance and the wolf's eyes dulled to the point of being extinguished.

'What have you done, elseworlder?' Akwar trickled through the ringing shock of the moment, reduced to such a thin course that he was little more than a collection of individual drops.

Ash lay unmoving. Torpeth was caught in a slow and stiff agony, as if at last he felt his true age. Aspin sat with head hung, jaw slack and eyes vacant.

'Why, I have saved you,' Ba'zel replied. 'In the manner of my kind, those you call Saviours.'

Jillan was on his back, smoke curling from his hair, his skin burned as if he had been out in the sun too long. He was paler than one of the dead. Yet he stirred.

'The schism among you would have ultimately destroyed you. Jillan may have won out here, but would have been divided, just as the Declension have ensured the division of the powers of this world. He would have been riven by guilt and grief for what he had done to his potential allies. He would have gone to the Great Temple greatly lessened and sought only expiation and suicide. If by some manner he had resisted that urge, the Declension would have killed Hella, inspiring an insane act of vengeance in him. If he had resisted that, he would only have wandered this world lost and tortured, and would have been taken by the Declension at their leisure. The convergence of the Declension with the power of the Geas is now inescapable. And the Declension have brought everything about so that no other possibility can exist or occur. The moment you may have desired – of the forces of this realm and Geas coming together and finding a unity with which to resist the Declension successfully – was always impossible. There could never have been agreement among you, for the schism was created the moment we entered this realm and its gods fell. A new order, accord and nature of existence based solely on your Geas cannot come about here, for the schism that the Declension represents will run its course. If it were not for my presence, if I were not the *unstable* element, and if Jillan had not let me loose in the first place, all of you would now be undone.'

'Now he tells us.' Torpeth chuckled madly, the weight of his years unhinging him.

Ash suddenly started breathing, his chest heaving as he struggled to take in the air his body so desperately needed. The rock people began to rebuild themselves.

The black wolf went and licked Jillan's face assiduously. At last Jillan had the strength to push the massive beast away and sit up. 'Can there be no hope?' he rasped.

'There is only the convergence.'

Jillan crawled over to Torpeth and laid hands upon him, healing him as best he could, just as he had healed those with the plague what seemed a lifetime ago. 'Go reinvest Wayfar, he who is so dear to the mountain people. Bring him to the Great Temple. He should be there to witness the end.' He moved to Akwar and bathed his hands in the holy water, repairing its energy and flow. 'Raise up the People as you will. They have the right to be there.' And to Freom. 'Here is the strength to free Gar. Do not thank me for it, for it is likely a curse more than a blessing.' And Freda. 'Dear friend, whose heart is bigger than any I've ever known, find the sun-smith and release crazed Sinisar if you must.'

Jillan looked to Ba'zel. 'And we will take these others as our companions through the desert. The wolf knows the paths of the Geas.'

'I have one condition,' Ash coughed.

'And what is that?'

'If we're on our way to see the end of the world, then I sure as hell want to stop at an inn along the way.'

Aspin blinked. 'And I get to ride the horse.'

Jillan smiled, only now fully appreciating just how much he'd missed his two friends.


Humming a simple rhythm over and over, the torturer used a rag to pull the red-hot knife out of the brazier and carry it to his prisoner's bared torso.

'Do yourself a favour and kill me while you can!' Samnir snarled from where he hung in the restraining frame. 'Every moment I'm alive is another in which I can plot to free myself. And once I get free, I'll have your guts out and you strangled with them so fast that you won't even have a chance to cry for your mummy!'

The torturer slowed. A frown came to his face. The end of his tongue stuck out as he thought through Samnir's words. His eyebrows rose slightly and he looked a little worried. 'Holy one says Horath shouldn't kill you. Just make you scream till you say sorry.'

Samnir laughed evilly. 'You shouldn't have told me that.'

The large man's brow furrowed and sweat trickled down his wide face. 'What do you mean? Horath can say what he likes. Horath is not the prisoner, stupid man. You are!'

'If I know you're not allowed to kill me, then I don't need to say sorry, do I? Sure, you can torture me a bit, but it won't be too much, will it, because you daren't kill me? And if I don't say sorry, then you're going to get in a whole lot of trouble with the Saint, aren't you? What happens to people who make the Saint angry, eh?'

The torturer's eyes became distant. 'He hurts them,' he whispered. 'Not like Horath does. Not just making them bleed. He gets into their heads. Does things that makes them remember, then hurts their memories.' He shuddered.

'He's going to do that to Horath. Like before, yes? But worse this time. Much worse!'

'Don't say that!' the torturer roared, caught between anger and fear. 'Horath will yank your wormy tongue out, cook it here on the fire and eat it!'

'That will make the holy one angry too.'

The torturer blinked. 'No, it won't. How?'

'Well, I need my tongue to say sorry, don't I? If you yank it out, I can't say sorry.'

The torturer licked his thick fleshy lips. He tried an endearing smile. 'Heh, heh! Horath was just joking with the stu— Not stupid! The clever man. Horath won't yank the clever man's tongue out. Please, say sorry. Horath doesn't want to hurt the clever man. Horath likes the clever man.'

'And the clever man likes Horath, but if Horath isn't allowed to hurt the clever man too much, then the clever man doesn't need to say sorry.'

Horath chewed so ferociously on his bottom lip as he concentrated on his predicament that blood trickled down his chin. A cunning look came into his small eyes. 'The clever man can say sorry but not really mean it, to stop Horath hurting him, and to help Horath. The clever man likes Horath and wants to help Horath.'

'But the holy one is in Horath's head, isn't he? The holy one will know Horath has told the clever man to lie. The holy one is going to be very angry now, very angry indeed.'

Panic took hold of the brute. 'No! The clever man has tricked

Horath! It is not Horath's fault. Yes! The holy one will know the clever man tricked Horath. The holy one will forgive Horath. He *must* forgive Horath!'

Samnir tutted. 'He will only forgive Horath if Horath can make the clever man say sorry. If Horath cannot do that, then Horath is a *bad* torturer and no more use to the holy one. The holy one will not want or need Horath.'

'No!'

'But Horath cannot make the clever man say sorry. Horath is a *bad* torturer!'

The torturer moaned like a gored beast. 'What will Horath do?'

'Horath will be punished by the holy one, for being bad and stupid.'

'Horath is sorry!' the big man blubbered, snot running from his nose.

'Unless . . .'

Horath stifled his sobbing. 'What? The clever man knows clever things. Tell Horath!'

'Oh, there's no point. Horath will be too scared.'

Horath sniffed hard and stuck out his chest. 'Horath is brave. Tell Horath!'

'There is a place you could go where the holy one would never find you. It is a beautiful place, a safe place. There is everything you can imagine to make you happy there. You will have lots of friends and everything you want. But Horath won't run away to this place, because he is too afraid of the holy one.'

'Where is this place? The clever man can tell Horath. The clever man likes Horath,' the torturer said softly, as if sharing a confidence.

'I wish I could, Horath, but if I told you the holy one would also know where the place is. The holy one is in Horath's head, isn't he? No, the only way for you to get there is if I lead you blindfolded. But you would need to free me, Horath. Don't worry, I understand if you're too afraid to do it. It can just remain our dream. And the clever man still likes Horath.'

His hands trembling, Horath put down his knife and commenced unstrapping Samnir. 'Are there nice animals in this place, clever man? Will they come and sit in Horath's lap? Horath had a rabbit he used to feed, but he hugged it too tightly and the rabbit stopped moving forever. Are there rabbits in this place, clever man?'

'Yes, of course, lots of them.' Samnir smiled, rolling his head to loosen his neck now that the strap around his forehead had been undone. 'You can play with rabbits all day. And there are children who know the best games. Even the adults like to play and run and laugh. They play hide and seek whenever you want. Quickly, Horath, before the holy one sees through your eyes and realises you are setting me free. Undo my wrists. That's it. Now, close your eyes and I will take you to the secret place at once. Do not worry if it hurts a bit. Horath is brave, yes?'

Horath complied without hesitation. 'Horath is brave. Horath does not mind if it hurts. Horath's mother always hurt Horath because she loved him. The only thing Horath is afraid of is when the holy one does things to his memories.'

Samnir took up the cooling knife, slammed it up to the hilt in Horath's gut and dragged the blade sideways. The torturer's intestines came spilling out.

'Oo, clever man! Horath does not feel good.'

'I know, Horath, I know. Keep your eyes closed. It is better that way. Picture the place in your mind. Can you do that? Can you see the place?'

'Yes, clever man, I see it. I see it!' Horath said faintly.

Samnir held the large man and lowered him gently. 'Do you see the rabbits and the children? Maybe your mother is there?'

'It is beautiful, just like the clever man promised. And the holy one won't find Horath?'

'No, Horath. You're free of the holy one now.'

Horath stopped moving, a wide and innocent grin on his face.

Samnir straightened up and breathed deeply. He knew he had to be quick, for guards would already be on their way. He took a cleaver and a rod of iron from Horath's grisly rack of tools and mounted the stairs out of the horror chamber. He remembered the layout of the complex above from his days serving in the Great Temple. He had a good idea of where they would be keeping Thomas. There was very little chance of their being able to escape the Great Temple, but escape was the last thing on his mind, for he had far too many scores to settle.

*

Even in the desert the wolf knew the paths of the Geas, and led them with its nose close to the ground and its ears constantly pricked. Floss had apparently lost her fear of the predator during the time Jillan and his companions had been away in the nether realm and followed closely, meaning Aspin did not have to do any work steering a course. They took a circuitous and counter-intuitive route, entering wadis that seemingly went nowhere, rounding promontories on their far side and occasionally going back on themselves, but the speed with which the sun crossed the sky told them either time had speeded up or they were covering extremely large distances. Only twice was their passage interrupted: once when an unusually big and stubborn scorpion would not let them descend a particular dune until the wolf had circled it anticlockwise three times, and once when the wolf bared its teeth and pulled them up short approaching an oasis. Six giants came lumbering towards them, hungrily sniffing the air.

'Ye gods!' Ash had shrieked and crouched behind Jillan.

The giants had reeked of carrion and their faces were distorted by bulging foreheads, bone-crushing jaws and protruding teeth. They were loosely clothed in skins and undersized pieces of armour, most of which looked like it had previously belonged to humans. Jillan stepped forward and made a display of his power, charging the air to make everyone's hair stand on end. The giants took it as a challenge and the largest of them thumped the ground with a rock-breaking fist that sent tremors up into their skulls.

Fighting to keep the terrified Floss under control, Aspin shouted, 'Beware! They have a primitive magic of sorts. They intend to attack.'

Ba'zel appeared as if from nowhere, took a long and menacing step to the fore and made the air buzz with pressure. The giants yelped, whined and threw themselves on the ground in submission.

'They are not as primitive as you might think,' Ba'zel said. 'They think entirely in abstraction. They are very different to the other beings of this realm that I have so far encountered. I must wonder if they hold some clue to the eighth, but we do not have the time to explore that. They hate your kind, Jillan, and with good reason it would seem. And they mistrust me, sensing something of what the Declension must be and how it seeks to rule this realm. I have explained our purpose, but do not think they apprehend it in our terms. They want us gone. We should oblige them, I think.'

They hurried away, the wolf, Floss and Ba'zel moving well ahead of Jillan and the flagging Ash. Jillan looked back over his shoulder. 'Come on, then.'

'What's the hurry? I'm in no rush to get to the end of the world. It's going to happen whether I exhaust myself or not, isn't it? Besides, it's not as if we'll be late. I have perfect timing, remember.'

Jillan reluctantly slowed to match the woodsman's pace. 'I've been meaning to say thank you for following me all the way from Godsend. It can't have been easy to . . . well, to . . .'

'To leave the inn?' He laughed. 'No, it wasn't. The problem with when you stop drinking is the hangover, and I'd been putting mine off for months. It lasted for weeks! I'm still not sure I've got rid of it. So, yes, you should thank me! Traipsing around after you has been the least fun I've ever had. I had flaming Miserath come after me at one point, and he's a tricky and sneaky bugger at the best of times. Do you know, he set traps for me and the wolf? Awful fiendish contraptions. Divine machines to snare and torture us. I still have nightmares about some of them.'

Jillan looked Ash with a mixture of wonder and horror. 'How did you escape them?'

The woodsman shrugged. 'Oh, you know, by hook and by crook. Perfect timing means you can just stumble along through things and come out none the worse for wear. That's how it's always been for me. In fact, my life is one big divine trap through which I have to stumble.'

'What made you do it? Leave Godsend to follow me, I mean?'

'It's that bloody wolf. He's worse than a nagging wife, or a conscience maybe. Just wouldn't leave me alone until I'd put down my drink and come out of the inn. I happened to need a visit to the jakes at the time, so finally agreed. Once I was out of there, he told me he'd found a spare barrel of ale off a ways. My judgement was a bit slurred and blurred at the time, so I followed him, and the next thing I knew the sneaky bugger had led me down paths that took me a long way from Godsend. I fall asleep and wake up the next day to a grinning wolf and that horrendous hangover I told you about. Wolf says he's going to take me back to Godsend, but just leads me further after you.'

'Oh. I see.'

'So, yes, you should be thanking me! I nearly wet myself when we had to go through that place full of rabid hounds and heads on spikes.'

'Thorndell. It's where Miserath's followers lived.'

'I don't give two hoots what it's called. Then several miserable nights on some uplands, surrounded by unquiet ghosts, a fight with some nut in shiny armour, a visit to the nether realm – thanks very much for that, by the way – a scary argument with the god Akwar – always good to have gods as enemies, eh? And now I'm nearly eaten alive by stinking desert giants on my way to watch the end of the world – a fun-filled time all round, I'd say. So, yes, you should thank me, Jillan. What I wouldn't give to be back in the inn at Godsend right now.'

'Godsend has fallen to Saint Praxis and the Empire. If you were in the inn right now, you'd probably be dead. The wolf may have saved your life taking you out of there.'

'What I wouldn't give to be back in my hut in the forest then, nice and quiet like.'

'Really?'

Ash sighed and was quiet for a moment. 'No, not really,' he said, looking down at his tunic and picking at a seam. 'Something you said to me once got inside my head and has stayed there ever since, curse you! My hut and isolation were a prison the Empire had built for me. Their pronouncement that I was Unclean was them passing a life sentence on me. Is there no escaping it, Jillan?'

'I'm Unclean too.'

Aspin had dropped back unnoticed to join them. 'Well, I'm a pagan. That's much worse than just being Unclean. I'm not even allowed in the lowlands, let alone anywhere near an inn.'

Ash barked out a laugh. 'You don't know the half of it. You get to swan about in your mountains, free as you like, while we're penned in by Heroes and most of us have Saints guzzling our blood every five minutes.'

'Well I'm Unclean *and* a pagan!' Jillan declared. 'Oo, and I'm the bane of the Empire.'

'Yeah, but you get to have fancy magicks and fireworks,' Ash reminded him.

'You've got perfect timing, though,' Aspin rejoined.

'Says the soulreader!' Jillan snorted.

'I have to put up with Torpeth spouting nonsense, causing no end of grief and waving his unwashed bits in my face,' Aspin complained.

Ash nodded sympathetically. 'There is that, I suppose, but it's probably all you deserve for being a pagan.'

'Come on. No one deserves *that*!'

'Better than the end of the world?' Jillan hazarded.

'I'm not so sure about that,' Ash said with a shake of his head. 'Torpeth would probably still find some way to haunt us afterwards.'

'Ye gods, you think? Actually, it sounds like him. Imagine having him bleating at you for the rest of eternity. It doesn't bear thinking about. Jillan, I think we're going to have to try and save the world after all. And I'm beginning to doubt I'll ever get that drink otherwise. That wolf is such a sneaky bugger that he's probably going to lead us away from every inn between here and the Great Temple.'

Thomas slapped the meat of his hand against one of the bars of his cell and listened to it resonate. He hit it again, at the precise moment required to amplify its resonance further. Its pitch rose. And again, and again, until it sang.

'Hey, stop that!' the guard shouted.

Hairline cracks appeared in the mortar around the top and the base of the bar. The metal found more movement for itself, and a higher frequency.

'Sonofabitch!' the guard shouted and pounded down the short corridor to the cell. 'How many times do I have to stick you with this spear before you get it through your thick villager's skull that I'm not messing around here? Let's see how many bars you're banging on with a great hole right through you.'

The guard jabbed through the bars with his weapon. On the last half-dozen occasions the guard had had cause to spear his troublesome prisoner, Thomas had acted dully, offered no resistance and taken the punishing flesh wounds. This time, though, his hands clapped together around the thrusting spearhead and yanked the weapon into the cell. The guard clanged against the bars as he was pulled forward. Thomas reached for him, intent on getting the keys from the man's belt.

Yet this was no ordinary guard. This was a Hero who had been selected to serve in the Great Temple based upon his presence of mind as much as his strength of arm. Even as he was pulled forward, he had the wherewithal to let go of his weapon. He dipped his head, and it was the front edge of his helmet that took the blow against the bars rather than the bridge of his nose. His hands were immediately up and shoving him back, beyond the blacksmith's reach.

The guard hit the ground in ungainly fashion, but safe in the knowledge he had done enough to escape being grabbed by the massively built prisoner. Thomas pulled the spear all the way into his cell and flipped it round. He pulled it back in order to cast it.

'Help!' the guard roared, already crabbing back and to the side to avoid Thomas's throw.

As Thomas brought the spear back, its butt caught the wall and jarred, taking it off its line. There was no time for adjustment. Thomas was already committed and knew he would have no other opportunity. He hurled the weapon through the bars, praying it would be enough. It flew towards the guard, but the last inch of the weapon's tail deflected off a bar, causing it to wobble and taking it a fraction wide of the flinching Hero.

There was a pause. Then the Hero blinked and smiled with relief. 'You'll pay for that.'

Thomas ignored him and slapped the meat of his hand against one of the bars. He hit it again and again, to set it singing.

'I don't think so,' the guard sneered. 'The lads will have heard my call and will be here in a second. Then we'll see just how tough you are.'

The guard rose to his feet and turned straight into Samnir's cleaver. The heavy edge chopped through the corner of his jaw and deep into his neck. The Hero's breath caught. His blood sprayed up into his face, filling his mouth and blinding him.

'Sorry,' Samnir grunted, pulling the cleaver free. 'Not the cleanest strike.' He hacked again. The Hero's head rolled free. The body keeled over sideways.

'About time!' Thomas groused.

'There are Heroes everywhere, from all across the Empire. It is a holy war, Thomas. It took me a while to get past them, not to mention the guardroom just down there. Besides, I shouldn't have had to come and save your sorry hide.'

'You didn't have to. I'd just got him where I wanted him. Seeing as you're here now, and seeing as you've taken my guard from me, you may as well do the honours, I suppose. Just don't expect a round of applause.'

Samnir retrieved the keys from the decapitated guard and opened the cell. 'The armies of the Empire are camped outside the temple. The Saints have gathered. Praxis will be holding Hella out there, I suspect.'

Thomas nodded. 'All to bring Jillan here, so that he may be defeated by overwhelming numbers. My friend, is this the end?'

'While we have breath in us it is not, Thomas.'

'Aye, well said, my friend. And if this is the last I will breathe, then I will take at least one of these cursed Saviours with me. Never did I think I would win my way into the Great Temple. Maybe the Geas intended this all along. Maybe the fall of Godsend was meant to be.'

'You were ever a man of faith, Thomas. One way or another, I sense the sacrifice of the People will soon be at an end.'

'I understand now why I was not allowed death before. It was for this moment. I understand why I have struggled and fought in a smithy all my life. It was to give me the strength of arm necessary to take this chance. Find me a hammer and I will bring my joy to these Saviours!'

'This way, then, good Thomas, for a warhammer stands waiting for you in the guardroom there.'

'And do you not see why you were made the Sand Devil, friend Samnir? Do you not see it was to have these Saviours regret forcing a cruel Empire and punishing existence upon the People?'

Samnir gave a savage grin. 'Perhaps, my friend, perhaps. All I truly know is that I would not want to be any Hero, Saint or Saviour if you and I can find but a moment to visit our fury and vengeance upon them.'

The wolf led them out of the east and into the central region. A tumult of sound rose ahead of them, although they were still many leagues from the Great Temple. Jillan and his companions had to raise their voices just to hear each other. Clouds raced ahead of them, and the rays of the sun that broke through struck at the horizon towards which they headed. The ground shook as if with the movement of all the feet in the world, and mighty rock slides travelled in the same direction as they did. Rivers rushed with such power that they overcame slopes and carved new channels for themselves. They saw countless groups of animals and people running, flying, slithering or dragging themselves. All the forces of the world were converging.

'We should not go any further!' Ash yelled in terror.

Yet time and the world swept them along. Their steps were suddenly vast. Ba'zel extended his limbs all the way to the horizon. The wolf took a small path that corkscrewed left, and then right, and they found themselves at Ba'zel's side, looking down from on high across a vast plain, with the Great Temple dominating the opposite horizon.

The sight all but overwhelmed Jillan there and then, and Aspin had to catch him, to save him from falling. There were more people than he'd ever imagined in one place, filling the third of the plain closest to him – a chaos of humanity, crying, singing, squabbling, jostling, cowering and raving. The centre of the plain was a half-mile stretch of open and blasted ground, and then the ordered ranks of the Empire's huge armies filled the rest of the plain, drawn up before and below the dark crags of the Great Temple.

He could not take it in. He could not make sense of it. Jumbled images, the cacophony, the stench, the impossibly thick air, the barrage of rebelling and pleading minds – all assailed him at once.

'Ye gods!' Ash cried.

And from out of the madness emerged the gods, approaching Jillan and his companions. From among the golems of the desert and the hard-faced people of the northern region came chiselled Gar, his skin gold-veined white marble, his eyes sapphires and his brow encrusted with every conceivable gem. From among the phagus and naiads of the deep, and the winsome and wet-eyed people of the west, flowed Akwar, a beard of foam, his eyes drowning wells and his brow wreathed in coral. From among a constellation of ethereal beings and the fiery-eyed tribal people of the east shone dazzling Sinisar, who blinded as much as he caught the eye. And from among the wyverns and birds of the sky, and the mountain warriors of the south, gusted smoky Wayfar, his eyes playful, his chest impossibly large and his brow windswept and bare.

'This soft thing undid our brother?' Gar asked in ponderous but uncompromising tones. 'I cannot think it. How is it he is the bane of the Empire? How is it that he claimed the power of the Geas? It can only be because of the aid of our child Freda.'

'And the occasional god, of course,' Wayfar breathed.

'And the elseworlder there, whispering in his ear,' Akwar sneered.

'Still, it has served a purpose, and that purpose has served us, no?' Sinisar opined overbrightly. 'He has freed us! We should not be so greatly ungrateful.'

'Not ungrateful, brother? When he presumes to bring us here and risk all for no good end?' Akwar spat. 'He would see the gods serve a mortal! What madness is this? It turns the world upside down, unmakes it even. If we must fight this war, then it will be for our own ends, not the passing concerns of mortals!'

'Madness, brother?' Sinisar giggled. 'It has been my only companion since the last time this issue was fought. And yet madness sometimes makes more sense than not. All is madness, therefore, and it has illuminated me. Look you, then, upon the enemy, for I will show you how they are arrayed.'

The god of the Shining Path twisted the light of the air and all saw the armies of the Empire as if they were right before them. 'See the army of the north to the far left. Prodigious Saint Goza stands over them, his vast hammer of sun-metal seemingly a child's toy in his hand.'

'I will take my mortals and face them,' Gar of the Unmoving Stone cracked, 'for that is the self-same hammer that saw me nailed deep beneath the earth of my own kingdom! My divine retribution will see a mountain pushed through his chest and his bones powdered to manure the ground.'

'See there on the far right the numerous and well-turned-out bodies of the Empire's western army. Masked Saint Izat poses among them, just the tales of her beauty enough to still mortal hearts.'

'She is mine!' Akwar seethed. 'I will lead my mortals against her, for she incarcerated me in a bowl of sun-metal to make a mirror for herself. She stole my face and throne.'

'And the eastern army is one of the two central ones,' Sinisar simpered. 'That shall be my own. Well do my followers know and long have they fought Saint Dionan and his General Thormodius. The beautiful prism that is Freda has agreed to stand by me, as has my not-so-sunny son, he who is the sun-smith. Leaving only that tiny army as the other one in the centre. Are you able to handle it, brother Wayfar? Beware, it is more than it seems. See the different colours and banners among that host? There are Saints of various enclaves, islands and far reaches there, along with the fearful Saint Praxis.'

'Praxis is ours!' Aspin asserted forcefully, drawing all eyes towards him and ignoring Ash's desperate attempts to hush him. Gar frowned in disapproval, Akwar looked outraged and Sinisar looked amused, but Wayfar nodded proudly.

'What mortal is this now? Will every one of them dare to speak uninvited in our presence?' Akwar demanded. 'Wayfar, now is not the time for your fickleness. Control your follower!'

Torpeth came tripping in among them, treading on Akwar's foot as he came. 'Oops, I think I've wet myself. He is Aspin and he commands me, just as I once commanded you.'

'You!' Gar thundered. 'I will bury you.'

'Nice to see you too. Your temper hasn't improved, I assume.'

'And he is my son!' snow-haired Slavin declared, reaching the heights where they stood.

Akwar threw his hands in the air in disgust. 'Will all the millions have their say?'

Aspin bowed low. 'Father, you honour me.'

Slavin returned the bow, bending just as deeply as the younger warrior. 'It is you who has carried the honour of our people, Aspin Longstep. You have made sacrifices while we remained distracted by more selfish concerns.'

Wayfar shifted restlessly. 'My people of the mountains are formidable and much proven in battle, but precious few. Why should they risk themselves here, when the plain below teems with others? Should the mountain people find their doom, then most assuredly so will the Geas.'

Slavin bowed even lower to his god. 'Holy Wayfar, we will not stand on ceremony when our god goes into battle, even should he command it otherwise. We cannot stand by when the people of the Geas fight for the freedom of all. We are not separate from them. Our over-proud isolation must end, even if it means our doom, and even if I must bear the guilt and burden of leading them to that doom. And last, we would serve as honour guard to Jillan, he who has been friend to our people when all others sought our end.'

'It is time!' Sinisar sang out, looking to the sky. 'Before the world turns and my powers wane. Come, my brothers and you mortals, for the heat becomes unbearable.' The sun flared in answer. 'Do you not feel it beating down? Do you not feel your hearts beating in time to it, like the drums of war? It consumes and fires our blood! It is the white-hot rage of our existence!'

The hundreds of thousands who were Sinisar's followers screamed their insane anger at the heavens and the Great Temple. Sinisar of the Shining Path was the light that led them and they blazed a trail across the plain.

'Wait!' Jillan cried, unready for the apocalyptic scale of what they faced.

*You can never be ready,* the taint whispered.

'There is no more waiting, even for Gar of the Unmoving Stone,' the rock god boomed. 'My people pass like the sands of time. They ripen like fields of wheat. They must have their harvest and a time of burning, or all will rot and the ground will become a dust-blown waste. Nothing but dust blown to the heavens, until there is no more! Are you not deafened to all else by the sands of time roaring through your mind? Do you not feel the growth of life stretching you as if on a rack? It is the all-consuming agony and hunger of our existence!'

The people of the north cried out in their pain, even as they endured it. They thundered across the plain of dust towards the Great Temple that had wasted their lives and land.

*There is no stopping it.*

'Things will never be settled between us, mortal, know that!' Akwar warned as he cascaded down to the plain. 'Mortals are but drops of rain or waves in the sea. In sufficient numbers you may have significance, but as individuals you are nothing, unable to alter the flow and tide of existence. Do you not feel it pulling you on? Do you not feel it swell within you, impossible to dam? It is the surge and essence of our being!'

The people of the west were a mindless flood pouring across the plain, finding an increasing momentum as they rose to challenge the rocks of the Great Temple. They wailed as they went, drowning in a personal despair even as they swamped any that sought to resist them.

*It will take you.*

'Come then,' Wayfar trumpeted, 'and we will be the furious tempest that scours all clean! Do you not feel the lightning igniting in your chest? Do you not feel the breath of life filling you and giving you voice? Rise then, my people, and fly upon the storm and issue of gods, mortals and the Geas. Descend upon our enemies, harass and tear at them. Strike them down and blow apart the overbearing philosophy they have dared to build!'

Wayfar sprang up and alighted upon the back of a mighty wyvern. The serpent let loose a shriek that echoed across the plain and wound its way up into the sky. It unfurled limitless wings to eclipse the heavens and cast all below into shadow. The people of the south raced forward, their voices lifted in a battle hymn of devotion to their god and all they held dear.

*It is the intent and will of your kind, Jillan.*

He leapt down to the plain, much as he had tumbled down into Haven. With the flighted mountain warriors all around him, and the god of storms above, Jillan sailed in among the charging people of the south and found himself carried at frightening speed towards the waiting ranks of the Empire's armies.

Sinisar and his shining host had taken the attack forward first, and were upon the enemy almost as soon as they were seen. They captured and defeated the vision of all who looked upon them. Colours danced to the fore one moment, then separated, blurred and reformed at a sudden distance. In a blink they were spearing into the eastern army of Heroes, as the rays of the morning sun dispel the darkness. And they brought with them heat – the divine spark of life, but also the terrible heat of the inferno. Flames poured from Sinisar's eyes and mouth and arced and spiralled into the Heroes. Heroes and attackers alike cried out as they burned like votive candles to the god, or were thrown as offerings on the waiting brazier. The divine rage engulfed them all, boiling blood in veins, shrivelling eyes in sockets, setting light to hair, blackening skin and melting flesh from bones. Black smoke roiled upwards and the desert people of the east and Saint Dionan's army burned together.

Her eyes streaming, Freda could see nothing through the pall, not even the Holy Lord of the Shining Path himself. She struggled to breathe, and the searing air almost overwhelmed her. She knew she would have combusted already if she were not made of diamond. She pushed forward desperately, as much to escape the crucible in which she found herself as to reach any enemy. How many had already died? *Don't think about it*, she told herself. Yet in her worst nightmares she hadn't thought it could be like this. Radiant Sinisar, the elementals of light and the people of the east had been a beautiful rainbow cast across the plain, but now they were smothered by thick billowing death.

She came out of the murk, expecting to see only devastation and twisted remains ahead of her, but the lines of the enemy still stood firm. A giant shield of sun-metal had been raised to bear the brunt of the assault, a massive soldier in the armour of a general standing to the fore of his men.

Sinisar and his most powerful elementals sheeted and detonated power against the immovable shield. Their magic rebounded and staggered them. A thin spectral became fragmented and winked out of existence. A lumine, appearing as a tall column of light, became drained and simply faded away. Hovering visifers hurled fireballs deliberately wide of the shield, looking to scorify those beyond the protection of the disc of sun-metal, but the air buzzed and thickened around the cast energy so that it discharged before it could do any damage to the pitiless Heroes of the Empire.

'How is the air so occluded?' Sinisar demanded.

Even as he spoke, dark clouds swarmed around several of his visifers at once and snuffed them out. Insects filled Freda's eyes, flies crawling up her nose and beetles trying to burrow into her mouth. She crunched on them and spat them out, but that only allowed more in.

Sinisar exploded with light and power, his violent umbra incinerating the winged and chittering creatures that filled the air in all directions, allowing the sky above to show once more. Yet the divine demonstration left him exhausted, and he was dulled in the moments that immediately followed. It was now that the forces of the Empire advanced.

'Archers, release!' General Thormodius boomed. 'Front rank, ready pikes! Forward!'

The thousands and thousands of desert people who had been towards the back of the initial charge, and who had thereby escaped the con-flagration of the two sides coming together, were now catching up to their god. They emerged from the smoke, only to be shredded by the Empire's arrows of sun-metal, arrows that penetrated through several attackers each before losing momentum. Freda watched as the quickest of the desert warriors ducked left, then right, and raised a shield to a quarrel he could not dodge. The flight went through the shield's boss, through the arm that held it up, through the man's stomach and then out through his spine and back. The man gaped, slowed and came to a standstill. His body refused to topple, but he was dead. She watched him for long moments, failing to register the awful cries of warning and ending that went up all around her.

She was trapped by the moment and by the sight. Darkness was closing back in around them, at the corner of her eye at first and then crawling towards the centre of her vision. The thousands fell away under the deadly barrage, and all that was left in the encroaching night was the standing corpse, the dwindling star of the god and the advancing line of the Empire's pikes tipped with sun-metal. She hardly saw herself any more, realising that a diamond without an immediate source of light was as nothing. And the void laughed and laughed, as Saint Dionan of the Empire extinguished the bright hope of those who dared stand against the blessed Saviours.

Gar and his rock people ploughed across the plain towards Saint Goza and his northern army. The force of their progress only increased as they went, until they were an unstoppable earthquake. They would bring down the crags of the Great Temple upon the mortals who dared stand against them, and bury them so deep they would never be found again.

The rock god smote the ground and cracks raced ahead of the attackers, becoming clefts and then chasms that would swallow the opposing army whole. Yet giant Saint Goza lumbered forward and smashed down his mighty hammer of sun-metal. The concussion waves that resulted saw his own men thrown from their feet, but also saw the walls of the chasms broken apart, so that every trench was filled in and their energy dissipated.

Gar roared his anger and the ground shook in response, deadfalls, rents and hell mouths opening up all over the plain. Thousands of Heroes fell into the depths, limbs and necks breaking or bodies ground up. Even more people of the north and towering golems who followed in their god's wake were also lost, however. Lava bubbled up over the ground, dissolving feet and spraying to set the living burning. The earth was a mass of running sores and open wounds.

Gurgling anguish and shrill death filled the air. The impetus of the attackers was completely lost. They cried out for their god to help them, but the deity was unmoved. He was heedless obdurate stone. The weakness and plight of mortals was not his concern.

Freom did not know where to turn, how to act. Mortals died everywhere, crushed, mangled and aflame. There was no helping them all, and any he did save would be unable to find either a safe escape or an approach to the enemy. His first loyalty was to Gar, whose divine example surely he had to follow. Yet there was something in the impassioned pleading of the humans that moved him greatly.

Then Freom saw one of his own kind – Fallor the Slow, whose sister Freom loved – ruined by exploding lava and caught in the grinding teeth of the earth. How could a being as old as the mountains be undone so easily and without the rock god showing the scantest regard? How? This was not how it was meant to be. The rock people had dedicated their entire existence to protecting the source of all life, and remaining true in their faith and devotion to the rock god, so how could this be their end? In dedicating their existence, had they in fact sacrificed it? Had their millennia of tireless and careful vigilance all been for naught? Had they been deluded or tricked somehow? Were they simply fools? It could not be that their faith was misplaced, could it? Or was all this the inevitable trap of the convergence? Was there simply no escape?

He ran in the footsteps of his god, praying it would lead to salvation, even though it took him straight towards the enemy. He would stand with Gar, but what help could he truly offer a god?

Gar pulled chunks of rock up out of the ground and hurled them at Goza. The Saint's hammer met the missiles unerringly and saw them disintegrate before they could do any real harm. The giant human was soon bathed in sweat and panting, but he derisorily waved Gar on.

'Come closer, little god, and my hammer will do the same to you as it does to these pebbles you toss. Come closer, little god, and I will eat you whole, for I am working up an appetite.'

The rock god hauled up bigger and bigger boulders. Freom added to the barrage. Saint Goza could not move quickly enough, and dozens of Heroes were crushed and smeared against the ground at a time. The army's leader shrugged, lifted the soldier nearest him, bit off his head, chewed and swallowed.

'Ah, that is better! I am fortified anew. Bring the cart forward!'

The unnaturally disciplined ranks of the northern army allowed a cart that stood taller than a man to be dragged to the front. Secured in the back of the heavy and apparently reinforced vehicle was an elongated dome of sun-metal, sitting on its side, its open end turned towards Gar and Freom. Saint Goza struck it with his hammer. He struck the huge bell again and again.

Heroes all around dropped their weapons and pressed their hands to their ears, blood trickling between their fingers as their eardrums ruptured. Their screams were drowned out by the doom tolling around them.

Gar and Freom were caught in the full force of the bell. Hairline fractures became visible across the divine marble of Gar's body and gems fell down his face like tears. Freom tried to advance, but as he brought his main weight down on one leg, his knee crumbled and the top half of his lower limb slipped off the bottom and crunched into the ground. The rock god and the greatest of his rock people went to their knees before the Great Temple of the Empire's Saviours.

As a torrent, then a deluge, Akwar, his naiads and the people of the west rushed upon Saint Izat and her army. The ground beneath the feet of the Heroes became sodden and then like quicksand. Soldiers quickly sank up to their ankles and then their knees in their heavy armour. Wave after wave of the people of the west hit them, and held or trod them under so that they drowned. The ground water turned red.

Like their god, the people of the west foamed at the mouth. Their eyes rolled like the sea. They were an oblivious uncontrollable flood, churning each other underneath as much as they did the enemy. The Heroes of the western army had more presence of mind, however, and many worked towards high points in the ground, using the bloated bodies of the dead as stepping stones. They gathered to their beloved Saint, who sat in a palanquin sheathed in sun-metal. Naiads had come up from under her rugged palanquin-bearers in order to drag them down, but the sun-metal had burned the watery attackers to steam.

Akwar and his sea of followers now swept towards Saint Izat. She stepped out to meet them. Through an exquisite mask of sun-metal, she called out to them, 'Ah, my god of bitter tears, and so you are come to me in your pain, a pain so terrible that your tears blind you to your self and what you do. I hear your anger, sigh and moan, a poetry of grief. Desperate for consolation, you rush towards my arms.'

The people wailed and Akwar momentarily seemed to flounder. 'No! I am the ocean! I am more than the mere tears of a mortal. I will . . . I will—'

'You will swamp me with all that you are!' Saint Izat shuddered, her bosom rising and falling with emotion. 'I know your vastness . . . and your loneliness. That is why you come to me, small as I am. As much as you hate what I represent, I am all that you want. As much as you hate me, so you love me. As much as you rail against me, so you entreat me. See, you still hurry towards my embrace.'

'I will kill you,' the god averred, but he seemed to have lost much of his direction.

'I know you will,' the Saint said with gentle and infinite compassion, 'and in so doing you will save me, and these our children. To kill is to love. To know pain is to love. To know rage is to love. To know beauty and horror is to love. And I am both beauty and horror, my love.' Saint Izat removed her mask for all to see, and all present were aghast, revolted and heartbroken. She cried for them, and they for her. She covered herself again. 'I am the object of all things, cruel and kind Akwar. Come then, for you are nearly here, my love, so nearly here. How I yearn for you, and how I hold the agony of that yearning as my very heart, even as it kills me with the grief of separation.'

And at the last Akwar of the Wandering Waters washed up to the feet of Saint Izat and rose to kiss her deadly mask of sun-metal before the Great Temple of the Saviours.

Wayfar of the Warring Winds stormed across the plain, his wyvern spitting down lightning to cause disarray among the enemy and to scorch and scar the earth. He would bring the entire sky down on their heads and mortalkind would learn abject terror of even the most distant

431

thunder once more. His voice was the clash of the cataclysm, the shaking of the firmament and the unsleeping nightmare of the tempest.

He watched the dying mortals below. It was largely meaningless to him. Should he care about leaves caught in the wind? Should he give a moment's thought to the dust and detritus the maelstrom of existence blew up?

He flew down towards the relatively small army of the south and its hangers-on. He sneered. What could a mere twenty thousand or so mortals do before the rage of a god? He could dispense with them on his own, with no need of his mountain warriors or the upstart youth Jillan. He threw a tornado down upon the Heroes, deadly lightning of different hues and character flashing and leaping at those positioned beyond the funnel's direct path.

Incredibly, a dot moved to intercept his power. What was this? A single human entered the eye of the storm and drew it down and down. It was the cursed Saint who manipulated the divine spark and electricity innate to every mortal and living thing. Yes, that witch from the island in the Bitter Sea, she they called Saint Zoriah. She had long frustrated the ancient storms he'd sent to ravage the rock to which a handful of mortals clung. She had allowed things to grow there, and ships to come and go, where previously all had lived and died at his whim and been suitably ardent in their worship of him. Witch!

The tornado unwound, there was a lull and then Saint Zoriah discharged the energy she'd gathered straight back up at him. The wyvern was thrown back, tumbling over and over. Its wings went up in flames and, screeching, it plunged towards the ground like a falling star.

Wayfar had abandoned his mount just before they'd been struck. Protected by tightly circling winds, he floated down towards the ground layers of fire and punishing turbulence. He smiled. So be it then. He would steal the breath from these mortals one by one if necessary. Besides, it was always more satisfying to see an enemy's face as they died. Now, where was the witch? Wayfar blew towards the ranks of the Empire's southern army.

'Archers, fire at will!' commanded a scar-faced officer.

The air was immediately full of the mortals' primitive missiles. Yawning, Wayfar waved his hand and winds sent the arrows clattering to the ground.

'Arrows of sun-metal!' barked the unruffled officer.

Wicked light speared through Wayfar's protective perimeter and he had to use the full extent of his power to part the new attack by just enough to give him a safe, if narrow, passage forward. As it was, one shaft scored along the top of his shoulder and caused him a deal of annoyance.

'Spear—' the officer began to call.

Having heard more than enough from him, Wayfar took the air out of the man and battered the front ranks of the enemy with something approaching a gale, so that they could not steady themselves sufficiently to launch another attack. The god leapt forward and closed with his foe. And now, their ululating battle cries announcing them, the mountain warriors arrived.

The Heroes of the south locked their shields together and braced themselves in anticipation of the enemy trying to crash through, but such an attack was not the way of the mountain men. Instead, they darted forward with their long willowy spears to pierce exposed throats, skewer eyeballs and spike bared calf muscles with murderous accuracy. The Heroes sought to return the attack with their shorter spears thrusting over the top of shields or swords hacking downwards, yet they found only air as their attackers sprang back as soon as they had hit a vulnerable spot.

The mountain men had the longer reach, the greater speed and the better freedom of movement. As much as the Heroes were desperate to break ranks and take the fight to their enemy, instinct and training insisted it would be suicide to expose themselves in such a way. So the Heroes stood and allowed themselves to be picked off one by one. Within a minute the five hundred mountain warriors worrying at the Empire's army had taken down several of the enemy each, without suffering a single loss themselves.

The most devastating damage was done to the Heroes by the tall and far-wielding Slavin and the naked and terrifying Torpeth. Where Slavin moved with eye-defeating fluidity and uncanny poise, Torpeth tumbled, knocked and bumped the enemy so that they did not know which way they were facing or whether they even held their weapons the right way up. One man tried to back away from the harassing Torpeth, only to find his smalls had somehow been loosened and fallen around his ankles. He tripped, fell back and undid himself on the sword of the man behind.

The snow-haired leader of the mountain people swished his striking spear slightly so it bowed as he pushed it forward, allowing it to curve around the edge of a shield and pass into the surprised owner's gorge. His other spear came across his first strike – a move forbidden to younger exponents of the mountain warriors' fighting style – and found the armpit of a second Hero, who had raised his sword in anticipation of coming to the aid of the first victim.

Lithe Slavin spread his legs wide and bowed deeply at the waist, so that his chin brushed the ground. The strikes of the Heroes trying to force him back so that they could move into the gap in the front rank left by their falling comrades swished a good foot or more above his head. He thrust low and up with his two spears, catching one Hero precisely in the groin and the other in the thigh where the main artery ran. He released his weapons and did a backward roll to avoid the slashes of the dying men. He stepped forward again, parrying deftly with palm and forearm, retrieved his spears and continued the dance of death as before, not allowing the enemy even a moment to reform any sort of united front.

Torpeth fell histrionically to the ground, and then rolled on his side under the shield wall of the enemy. He bit through an ankle, hamstrung a leg with his dirty nails and then hammered a heel into someone's crotch. There were filthy curses and mentions of his long-forgotten pagan mother as men struggled in the press to twist their blades so that they pointed downwards. Someone lifted a foot to stamp on him, but Torpeth had been waiting for the attempt and took out the Hero's other leg. The soldier fell and Torpeth's hard foot smashed into the man's throat, crushing it instantly. Men coming on from behind tripped on their fallen comrade or were brought down by a judicious elbow from Torpeth to the side of the knee. Half a dozen Heroes went down, and the holy man sprang on top of them. He ran up a shield and was moving across heads and shoulders before any realised it. As he landed and pushed off, he made sure to exert enough pressure to snap a neck or collarbone with every leap and bound.

Meanwhile, Wayfar flung men from his path and made straight for the diminutive form of the witch. She had long black hair standing out from her head, so electrified was it. Her eyes sparkled and her face seemed young and innocent, but he knew she was anything but. He would see her torn apart and then he would move straight for the vile Saint Praxis, who stood watching from a hillock beyond the army as if all went on solely for his personal entertainment, or as if he were about to give a sermon to all gathered below.

Wayfar gusted on, intent on raising a hurricane to obliterate Zoriah. She raised her arms, trying to make herself a lightning rod to draw all the energy out of him. Wayfar's howling winds threw Heroes back into her, knocking her down. His swirling power gathered up a handful of fallen blades and he prepared to cut the witch to pieces.

He cast the weapons forward, but there were rushes and flashes before him faster than he could follow. The blades were knocked off line or against the wind, and they fell like dropped cutlery. He sought to raise a commanding hand, but something knocked it sideways. Wayfar lashed out ferociously, but his blow was intercepted before it could gather any momentum. He tried to draw breath into his divine chest so that he could blow away all opposition. He was struck hard in the solar plexus and he spluttered. The holy hurricane of his will lost its impetus. Heroes managed to push themselves back to their feet.

'None is faster than Saint Sylvan of the Endless Reach!' swished past the god's ears.

The witch rose again. *No, I will not permit it.* She floated towards Wayfar, whose every move continued to be pre-empted by Sylvan, so that the god was kept still and impotent. The witch's hands reached out. *It cannot be! Cursed mortal!* And she laid her hands on the god and took the divine spark from him.

His lungs burning, Jillan just about managed to cross the plain ahead of the chaos of the charging southern people. The dark wolf and Aspin had stayed with him, but the rest of mountain men had raced ahead with their god. Jillan and Aspin arrived now, just in time to witness Wayfar fall before two beings of power who could only be Saints.

'It is not possible!' Aspin gasped.

They saw snow-haired Slavin spearing and stepping his way through the enemy with savage focus and intent, the leader of the mountain people seeking to come to the aid of the deity. Ancient Torpeth tumbled and twirled, his purpose making a wreckage of all men as he too went to help.

The male Saint disappeared. Something unseen caught Torpeth's beard as he was mid-leap and yanked it down hard. The holy man's chin hit the ground first, forcing his head back to a spine-snapping angle. Heroes closed in on him and he was lost from view. The female Saint calmly moved to face Slavin, cast a net of power wide around him and drew it tight. Slavin's body was shocked, he lost all coordination and fell to the ground, where he twitched and spasmed.

'Noo!' Aspin moaned in disbelief. His jaw tightened and he threw himself into the fray, his entire determination and self bent on killing the despised lowlanders of the Empire. He saw and read the intent of every opponent before the intent was acted upon. He parried thrusts before they could gain meaningful force, he blocked blows before they were launched and he opened throats before any could beg for mercy. None could touch him as he moved deeper into the press.

'Your god is dead!' came a hideous drone from the mouths of the Heroes.

'Close ranks and prepare to advance!' yelled an officer of the Empire. Jillan saw it was the hated Skathis.

The people of the south came staggering up, the wild passion that had been stirred in them by Wayfar now gone. They were disorientated and confused. Many were without weapons. They were so numerous that they jostled the pagan warriors of the mountains and pushed them towards the re-forming army of the south. As Captain Skathis called the advance, Aspin's people were suddenly without the space for man-oeuvre they'd enjoyed when battle had first been joined. The mountain warriors now began to fall, first singly, then in small groups. Even Aspin was forced back towards Jillan as a shield wall advanced on him in perfect unison, without chink or flaw, as if directed by a single mind.

The people of the south offered no resistance as the Heroes hacked into them. The people did not seem aware of what was happening. Their eyes had taken on the same dullness they'd always possessed when under the Saint's control. 'Wayfar is dead!' they chorused as if in prayer or praise. 'Sacrifice and duty safeguard the People against the Chaos.'

The wolf snarled and howled in anger and distress. One second it would snap and tear at the people of the south coming up behind it; the next it would face the Heroes and plant its feet with hackles raised.

Tears came to the corners of Aspin's eyes as he saw his people being hewn down. Barely half now remained, and they clustered towards Jillan. 'What can we do? The southerners won't fight. They have betrayed us! Damn them!'

'They are being Drawn back to the Empire.'

'We are surrounded!'

The people of the south began to tear at the mountain warriors, catching dozens unawares. 'Pagans!' they hissed and snarled. Jillan, Aspin and their warriors were a mere handful amid thousands pressing in on them.

'I will not let it end like this!' Jillan cried, calling up all the magic he had. How had it all gone so wrong so quickly?

'All the gods have fallen!' the People leered at him. 'You have done this, Jillan!'

He did not want to hear them, but he knew they were right. He had brought them all here. Even as he watched them pulling down more of the brave mountain warriors, he could not hate them. His magic sputtered out.

'So many dead! Their blood is on your hands.'

The words battered at his mind and he put his hands to his ears. He squeezed his eyes shut, just wanting it to be finally over.

'Jillan!' Aspin screamed, slapping his friend hard across the face. 'What's wrong with you? You can't just let us die like this. Please, Jillan! What about my father? And Torpeth?'

His misery was absolute. All strength went out of him, and he went to his knees in the mud. The gods were gone. Slavin was gone, and Torpeth. He had killed them all. And in so realising, he saw that, as much as any other, he was responsible for his own parents' death. It was the fundamental truth he'd sought to deny ever since the awful events of Hyvan's Cross. It was a truth from which he'd always run. Yet now there was nowhere else to run, there was no escaping. He'd feared and hidden from it, but it had found him out at last. He was appalled at what he had done. He had brought about the end of the world. He loathed himself and everything he had represented. There could be no forgiveness. He had magic but would not allow himself to use it. How

437

could he? He would only bring more death and suffering. He must give up his magic, give it into the safe hands of the Empire, so at least some few people might live on.

'No!' Aspin howled, reading the torment Jillan was suffering. Or was that the wolf howling? 'It is Praxis doing this to you! I see it even if you cannot!' The mountain warrior's words bit at him like the wolf's lacerating teeth. Jillan's blood welled up, and with it his magic once more. 'Fight it, Jillan! Think of Hella. You owe her freedom. Think of all those who have fought for you. You owe them their freedom. You are *not* afraid, Jillan! I will not let you be! Open your eyes, Jillan. See Praxis there, the insane preacher who would give the whole world and the Geas to the parasitic others. If there is anything you love in this world, *anything*, you must help us! Anything. Anyone. Hella!' The wolf bit into Jillan's hand and shook it, exposing bone and then crunching into it.

Even without opening his eyes, Jillan could see Praxis. The servant of the Saviours stood above the ferment, directing the Heroes and People against the mountain warriors, but all the while keeping his existence-sucking eyes fixed firmly on Jillan. Praxis. It had always been him. Praxis had always been there, looking to punish Jillan just for existing. From the youngest age Jillan had feared the Minister's accusation of *dark* and *sneaking* thoughts. He had always feared the Minister could read his mind. Jillan had come to fear his own mind as a consequence. He had feared himself, feared his own magic. Fear had done all this to him. Fear had done all this to the People. It was the Saviours' most powerful and subtle weapon. Fear and threat had brought this world to its knees. They'd allowed fear for their immortal souls, rather than love of their own lives, to define them entirely. Fear would kill them all. They would all die of fright, Jillan now saw.

Praxis sucked at Jillan's existence, sucking the magic and marrow from his bones. *They want my magic from me. They urge me not to resist, to sacrifice myself. They fear what might happen if I resist them. It is they who fear! Well, now, I will give them something to fear. I will make them fear me so badly that even those in the Declension's home-realm will wonder if they would be better off dead, for there are things in the cosmos far worse than death, far, far worse. I will make them rue the day they ever thought of the Great Voyage.*

Jillan rose to his feet and brought the storm of his magic up with him. He became wreathed in power —and sky, earth, water and light all awaited his will.

Saint Praxis screeched in righteous outrage, all the People echoing him. 'Child of the Chaos! Evil entity! You are proud in patricide and monstrous in matricide! You are a living blasphemy. It will not be allowed! The People will not permit it. The blessed Saviours will see you punished for all eternity. All hate you as you hate them!'

Yes. He hated them. He hated everything about them: every word, every name, every idea, every thought, every judging look, every action, every Saint, every Hero, every follower and their every moment. Oh, how he hated them! The storm of Jillan's hatred and rage fought him for control and demanded its freedom. He'd feared it before, but never again. He would let it rampage across the plain unchecked. Let it destroy them all!

'Saint Sylvan, fly at our nemesis in the name of the blessed Saviours! Saint Zoriah, quell the sin and corruption of the Chaos before it can touch these innocents! The Saviours have spoken!'

The holy Saint of the Endless Reach vanished from where he'd been a second before. Jillan sensed the being approaching. Aspin read their enemy's intent and movement, stepped in front of Jillan and almost lazily extended his spear so that it skewered straight through Sylvan's eye.

'Didn't see that coming?' the mountain warrior asked. 'That's what Torpeth would have asked if he'd been here. That was for our holy man.'

The gyre of Jillan's power built higher, overshadowing all who stood on the plain. Saint Zoriah rose off the ground and hungrily Drew Jillan's power towards herself. 'The power of life is mine to command!' She laughed.

Jillan smiled faintly. 'Then there is one thing you will never command, vainglorious Saint!' He insinuated a shadow into the glittering waves and lines she took from him.

Her eyes went wide with horror. She tried to stop Drawing his power, but he would not let her dismiss it. She tried to shrug it off, then wrestle free, but it entangled her. She screamed horribly as the shadow reached her and entered into her. Her youth fell away, her hair became white and brittle and her skin sagged so badly that it all but sloughed off her frame. Her scream became a croak and then her internal organs collapsed with age. The ravages of time finally caught up with her. The bag of bones fell to the ground.

The dark power Jillan commanded now expanded exponentially. It spiralled wide over the plain. It found Saint Goza and forced its way into his holy mouth, making itself a deadly meal for the gourmand. 'What, no appetite all of a sudden? Such a waste,' belched the shadow. It ate the tyrant of the north from the inside out, leaving him a tottering and naked spine in his final moment. The force snatched up Saint Dionan and visited a death of a thousand stings, bites and cuts upon him.

The black hatred engulfed all the People, and their every craven and selfish thought only fed it further as its thick tentacles set about crushing, suffocating, leeching, bludgeoning, ripping, throttling, penetrating and invading them. The more death that was visited upon the plain, the more powerful it became. The beast that was Kathuula coalesced and none could escape its being. 'I am the Dark Geas!' screamed the leviathan of the People as its unnatural birth took place.

And its demonic eyes were turned wholly on Praxis. 'We have waited so long,' it crooned and burbled. 'So long!' It licked at the Saint's ear. 'Always you have loved us. Rutting at our every puckered orifice when none other would have us. Forcing your panting and desperate seed upon us. Performing every concupiscence upon our altar even as you screamed your orgasm of prayer, entreaty and rape. You are our father and mother. And now we will have eternal incest of you. The People will hold you close and you will never leave our embrace.'

Although his face already seemed to wear the pale lividity of death, Saint Praxis managed to curl his lips. 'And so at last the Chaos is Drawn out of hiding and revealed. At last its foul corruption is there for all to see. The faith of the Empire is made and manifest. The stinking evil that has always sought to steal the People from the Empire has crawled from out the pit. In your self-harming lust, self-consuming jealousy and wanton appetite, you have ultimately been Drawn towards the blessed Saviours. It could never have been otherwise. And now you will be Drawn by them, in their infinite and divine mercy, and you will be ended forever, so that this world will be their eternal paradise and succour. Girl, step forward and command the Chaos of your making!'

Hella stepped from a small tent to the side of Saint Praxis. Her hair was drab and her eyes sunken. She moved unsteadily, as if a mannequin. Yet there was power in her voice, the power of grief, bitter experience and the sort of suffering that unseated the soul. 'Jillan!' she breathed. 'Where are you? Will you not answer me?'

The tiny part of Kathuula that had been Jillan could not deny her. His memories stirred and he remembered himself.

'Jillan, my love, you must stop this. Don't you see? You are killing them all. This was never what you wanted. They are innocent!'

Kathuula writhed and shook with internal division. Saint Praxis smiled and nodded, mouthing the words the instant before they were spoken by the enslaved Hella.

'Jillan, will you not come to me?' She held out her arms. 'We can never be together if you are like this. Give up this power that perverts you. Let the Saint Draw it from you. Be cleansed and come back to me, Jillan!'

He could not refuse her, she who was his sacred heart. He started to fight his way free of the midnight horror he'd become.

*No! I am a part of you!* the taint, his magic and Kathuula said together. *We are one. No other can stand when we are together, you know that. You dare not let Praxis claim any part of the Geas's power. He will see this world ended because he does not judge it perfect. His judgement is terrible and absolute. Strike down Praxis and his conniving mouthpiece before they can utter more lies to undermine us. Strike them down!*

The taint was exhorting him to kill Hella. He could not do it. He could more easily kill himself than her. And the killing would not end with Praxis and Hella. It would be just the beginning. In his grief and in his hatred of the Empire and the People for bringing about the death of his sacred heart, he would see them all undone. He would bring death to every living thing on the plain, and then every thing that lived in the world. He would squash the Geas in his hand like an over-ripe piece of fruit and guzzle down its sweet and rotting flesh. And the Saviours would be welcome to the emptiness that followed.

'I could never do such a thing to her,' Jillan avowed. 'Now, taint, I see, hear and know you for what you are. For a time I believed you were

441

the Peculiar's voice manipulating me. For a time I thought you were my magic or some other part of me. Now I understand that you are Kathuula, speaking to me from the nether realm, whispering forbidden secrets, things unknown by all others and knowledge not meant for the living. More than any other you have used and exploited me, all so that I would bring the land of the living to this point. You are death. You would rule all realms absolutely!'

*No, Jillan,* the taint said in hurt tones. *Do not let them turn you against me like this, not after all I have done for you. Think of all the times I have saved you. Think of all the times I have been there for you when others shunned and turned their backs on you. When you were lost and vulnerable, I found and protected you. Think, Jillan. I am the voice of your parents. I am Haal, I am Slavin, I am every Godsender who sacrificed themselves for you. I am everyone who has ever loved and cared for you. If I seek to rule, then it is only so that we can have the power, you and I, to drive back the Saviours, drive them back through all the realms to their home-realm, to pursue them to a final resting place and bury them forever, so that the cosmos can be safe and free once more.*

Yet the taint was also Azual, Bion, the Peculiar and every enemy who had fallen against Jillan. It spoke of saving him and this world – the cosmos even – in exactly the same way as the Empire always had. All his life Jillan had been tormented, harassed, caged, hunted, threatened and blackmailed by them, just so that he could be saved. But saved from what? Saved from himself, they said. He must not be himself. He must not have dreams, ambitions, hopes, love or magic, for they were selfish things, they said, things that might cause and allow him to act in ways they did not want, ways that might challenge their own ambitions and determination. Any hope, love or magic on his part was a crime against them, for which he must be punished. His existence was a crime. The existence of the People was a crime. Their liberty and everything else therefore had to be taken from them and they had to be punished unto death.

How could he choose between allowing the death that was Kathuula to sweep through the cosmos and allowing the Declension the power they needed to end this realm in order to continue on their Great Voyage? How? Why? He did not want to make such a choice. They said there was always a choice, but this was no choice the world could want.

It tore him in two even as he fought it, fought it with every fibre of his being. He brought every last vestige of his magic up out of his core, and his very soul with it. He brought the full power of the Geas to his fingertips. He drew all of Kathuula's power away and added it to the vast vortex about to annihilate the plain.

*Yes!* the taint cried in ecstasy. *Bring them Armageddon!*

'Yes!' Praxis rejoiced. 'Give it all to me!'

And let it all go. He let go of himself. No will, no direction, no intent. Just release.

Magic spilled, shocked and sparkled, suffusing everything. It spun, cascaded and drifted through the plain in every conceivable colour and pattern. All that had been taken from the People was returned to them. Even the gods rediscovered something of themselves. The power of the Geas was restored to the world, and all were left standing in wonder.

Dark Kathuula was a distant memory. Freed of the control of the Saints and the Saviours, the Heroes and the untold thousands they'd been fighting stood looking at each other in awe and numb delight, no longer harbouring any desire to harm each other. Jillan saw Hella and she smiled radiantly at him, returned to herself and love for him. Some shouted with the joy of being alive. Others blinked as if understanding what they saw for the first time. Yet others cheered.

'What have you done?' Praxis whimpered, his hands clutching at himself as if he'd lost something. 'You have destroyed us all!'

'My long-legged friend Praxis!' a grinning Torpeth called. 'Come, let me take you to my bosom.'

'I would rather have died, vile imp. Surely this is hell!'

'Come now, you're just overwrought. It's quite understandable.'

'Blessed Saviours, preserve your faithful servant!' the wild-eyed Praxis echoed up to the Great Temple.

In answer to his prayer, onto the lower crags came four cowled and looming figures, a golden Disciple accompanying each. Every person on the plain could not help but feel the dread of their presence.

'See, the blessed Saviours come among us!' Praxis heralded. 'On your knees, my People, and give thanks for your deliverance. On your knees, I say! You are in the presence of the divine. Bow your heads so that you may be saved.'

In their innocence, many of the People humbled themselves.

Conditioned to obedience their entire lives, yet more joined them. Some stood unsure for a moment, and then followed the lead of the majority.

'General Thormodius!' Praxis sang. 'Organise your men. Any of the People not kneeling are to be forced into submission for their own good, the blessed Saviours be praised! If any think to fight you, do not hesitate to make an example of them. Obey the holy Saint of the Empire. Remember the vow you took and do your duty!'

Although the General did not move immediately, unease and fear spread through the crowds of people. More fell to their knees and took up the chanted prayers they knew by rote. As each new person abased themselves, the fear grew stronger and Saint Praxis visibly became taller and straighter.

'Praxis, my friend, do not lose us this chance!' Torpeth shouted, but none heard him.

Jillan could not believe what was happening. 'Get up! I order you! Don't do this, please! Not after everything we've done. Not after so many have died. What's the matter with all of you?' None heeded him. Tears came to his eyes, as they did to Hella's.

'Filthy, miserable lowlanders!' Aspin spat, he and his few dozen warriors raising their spears once more.

'Captain Skathis!' Saint Praxis smiled malevolently. 'The bane's power is spent. Advance your men and—'

The scarred face of Captain Skathis remained impassive as he stepped out from behind Saint Praxis. The soldier's sword was thick with blood. 'I should have done it long ago, holy one. See, you bleed just like the rest of us. Do you not believe it? Come now, you are a man of faith, are you not?'

'But my angelic Captain!' Praxis coughed, blood pouring down his chin. He staggered and clung to his killer. 'It was you who led me out of Godsend to the Great Temple all that time ago.'

'The mistake was mine, holy one. Forgive me,' the Captain said. The Saint's eyes closed for the last time and he was gently lowered to the ground. As the Hero straightened back up, he looked across the field to General Thormodius, who gave a nod of acknowledgement.

*So be it!* the Saviours spoke to every mind on the plain. *We will attend to your deaths ourselves. Let the Great Cull begin.*

The sun-bright suits of armour that were the Disciples leapt down from the low crags and set about laying waste to swathes of Heroes. Heads were dashed from shoulders, corpses lifted to club the living, bodies crushed under burning feet of sun-metal. The Heroes had no defence against the merciless avatars of the Great Saviour himself. They tried to get away, knocking down comrades and trampling them.

'Brother!' Freda cried to Freom. 'We must drag the Disciples back down into the earth, from where the sun-metal originally came. Quickly, before all is lost.'

'Fear not, for holy Gar is with you, glorious Freda!' declared the rock god, clapping his hands and stamping his feet to create tremors that toppled the Disciples. Wide cracks opened beneath the armour and hands of stone pulled them inexorably down. 'And now Gar will bring down the Great Temple that so defiles our world! He will bring it down on the elseworlders with such force that they will never raise their heads again.'

The gods of the Geas rose together to challenge the Great Temple, but the four organising intellects of the Empire exerted the combined power of their presence and laid them low. The power extended outwards and all humankind was dragged down to writhe and moan in the muck. The Saviours began to Draw the life energy of the People towards them.

*None can stand before the Declension.*

Yet there was one who did not fall. He extended long limbs across the plain and stood over the beings of the seventh realm. He protected them with the power of his own presence. 'You may not take them.'

D'Shaa, D'Jarn, D'Syr and D'Zel reared back, letting loose an alien cry of outrage. *They are lesser. You have no right to keep them from us.*

'They freed me from the Declension. Payment must be made. I am Ba'zel, destroyer of the Virtue Obedience. I am the *unstable* element.'

*You are no member of the Declension and are without meaning. You cannot undo us.*

'I cannot undo you, but I can prevent your progress. I can hold you here. While you defend against me with all your being, you will not have the power required to escape.'

*Fool. Why would we wish to escape when all is about to be ours?*

445

'That's our cue!' bellowed a human voice. 'Come on. Keep up, old man!'

'Less of the old,' Samnir panted back at Thomas, 'unless you want me to paddle your overlarge behind.'

Together, the blacksmith and warrior leapt down onto the lower crags of the Great Temple. Weapons of sun-metal held high, they threw themselves at the Saviours.

'Surprise!' Thomas roared. 'Yeesh! They're uglier than you, Samnir.'

'We're looking to slay them, not marry them! Or are you that desperate these days?'

*Impertinent beings! You say nothing. You think nothing of consequence. You are nothing. You would dare attack us?*

*Squash them, D'Jarn. End this aberration.*

*Their lives are unworthy of the term. They are but transient flashes of base elements reacting one with the other.*

*Aiee! One has pricked me with his sun-metal. I will drink every human dry for that. Ba'zel, you will release us.*

Samnir swung a powerful two-handed stroke straight at the abdomen of one of the Saviours. With a few feints, the veteran soldier had quickly ascertained the balance of weight and centre of gravity of the being he faced, so that he could unleash a blow that was impossible for his adversary to avoid. And he committed to the blow with all his belief and self. The Saviour saw its doom coming and tried to shift the nature of its substance, but Ba'zel prevented it. The convergence of the blade of sun-metal and the Saviour was inevitable. Faster than should have been possible, the Saviour brought forelimbs of adamantium into the path of the blade. The weapon of sun-metal bit deep and slowly pressed through. It was as if time and the world stilled to watch.

One forelimb fell to the ground, then the other. The sun-metal would not be blocked or denied. It was the unstoppable force of the cosmos. And the Sand Devil of the seventh realm brought his deadly attack home against his immortal Saviour. The tip of the sword pierced and pinned the ancient being. Samnir drew the blade up and opened his enemy from abdomen to skull. Ichor oozed and gouted, then caught fire.

The hideous cry of the dying Saviour shattered sky and earth. Something fundamental changed.

*D'Jarn is ended! It is not possible that a lesser being should triumph over one of our kind.*

'They are not lesser, then. Or you are not greater,' Ba'zel replied.

*Only the Declension are worthy in nature of the Great Voyage.*

Purest and inhuman rage rose from deep within the Great Temple. Just the sound of it would have seen mortalkind descend into madness were it not for Ba'zel. The form of a massive black dragon rose up out of the Great Temple, its teeth the rending pain of futility, its breath the bitter poison of failed aspiration, its wings overarching despair, its claws sharp and puncturing moments of horror and its eyes the infinite void. The dragon's jaws stretched wide to swallow them all.

*The eternal Null Dragon of the Declension's will encompasses all.*

All knew dread and were overwhelmingly daunted, all except Thomas the blacksmith. Thomas laughed with such delight, and it was at such odds with everything else, that every ear heard it and felt uplifted. He laughed as if his daughters were still alive and he were catching them up in his arms. He laughed as if his wife were still with him and he knew the love of a good woman. He laughed as if his loss and grief were ended. He was unbowed, overflowing with strength and unashamedly brave. 'Dragon, there you are! At last, my reason is here. We have tested ourselves against each other in the forge all my life, you and I. My entire existence has but been preparation for this day. O Dragon, I am so happy that this moment has arrived, that you have come forth and we may settle our issue once and for all. Come then, Dragon, and we will fight each other as never before. Set to!'

As the Null Dragon descended, Thomas enthusiastically scaled the crag to meet it. It swept down for him and the blacksmith sprang high, bringing his mighty hammer down straight between the beast's eyes.

'Thomas, no!' Samnir shouted. 'Wait for me!'

Without looking back, the blacksmith cried, 'You will only slow me down, old friend. Your knees are not up to the climb. Besides, you must deal with those Saviours there. Come now, there are only three of them left, surely no match for the Sand Devil!'

The Dragon was shaken to its core and rolled backwards in the air, tendrils of smoky substance fraying from its edges. It tried to rise above the blacksmith for advantage, but Thomas leapt after it.

'Thomas, do not leave us!' Hella begged, tears in her eyes.

He nearly looked back then, but set his jaw even more firmly. 'Dearest lady, I must do this if you or I are ever to know peace. Jillan has come back to you, as I always knew he would, and all will now be well. Do not mourn me, milady, for I made Jillan promise me this moment long ago.'

The Dragon drew its breath to unleash a torrent of bile, acid and venom at its tormentor, but Thomas let fly with his hammer to punch the serpent in the middle of its chest. It choked on the death it had been about to release. Tortured, it tumbled back from the blacksmith, shedding more of itself as it did so.

The Saviours moved for Samnir as one, but the Sand Devil had known they would. They moved precisely as he would have done were he not the Sand Devil. They were his lesser self, the self they had made him when he was their servant. He knew them as well as he knew himself. And he would never let them make him that lesser person again. They would not touch him. He pirouetted, ducked and leapt, his blade leaving deadly traces in the air that forced them to veer violently or be sliced apart.

Thomas hauled himself higher, pursuing his dragon into the heights of the crags. 'Do not flee, Dragon! Do not hide! I might still slip or fall. Come back! That's it!'

The trinity of Saviours slashed and whirled around Samnir, the Sand Devil always at their centre. Theirs was a dance and pattern of impossible complexity. It was a harmony of impulse, instinct and inspiration all in perfect balance. It was the movement of atoms, the chase of storms, the turning of the world and, for an infinitesimal instant, the unknowable course of the cosmos.

The Dragon plunged down at Thomas in one last effort. Its tongue lashed the air and the blacksmith jumped to catch hold of it. He was lifted skywards, but clung on and pulled his way into the creature's foul maw. He bit into the root of the Dragon's tongue and proceeded to chew through it. In a paroxysm of open-mouthed anguish the Dragon fell beyond the highest crags, Thomas still struggling within the awful mouth, and darkness exploded within the Great Temple, shaking it to its very foundations. Huge boulders and slabs of rock slid and crashed down upon the sacred heart of the Empire.

One of the Saviours glanced up in fear, and with perfect timing the woodsman Ash stepped in from nearby to trip it, so that it decapitated itself on Samnir's restless and relentless sword. 'Oops, sorry. Clumsy of me.' The pattern fell apart in the instant and the other two Saviours were dead before Ash had even finished speaking. The gods of the Geas were no longer held back, and the powers of the world descended upon the Great Temple, pulverising the dark complex until it was as if it had never existed.

'I knew that would happen,' Torpeth confided to Aspin. 'Those four will try and claim all the glory now, just you see.'

Aspin did not hear his tribe's naked holy man. He was busy looking for Slavin, whom he found sprawled in the filth of the plain. The young warrior knelt at the side of his father's body and wept for the man he had not known well enough, but had still loved and honoured more than any other.

'Ash the woodsman. Ash the coward,' Samnir grunted. 'Good to see you.'

Ash smiled uncomfortably. 'Sorry I couldn't get here sooner.'

'Better late than never.'

'I suppose.'

'Timing is everything, eh?'

The woodsman shrugged apologetically. 'Just as well, I guess.'

'So where were you?'

'Well . . . you see . . . there's this inn . . . No, the thing is . . .' He brightened. 'I knew you would immediately need a drink after all this, so I had to find you a bottle.' He pulled a flask from his tunic and held it out with a shameless grin.

Samnir licked his dry and cracked lips. He was so parched he felt like he'd eaten the whole eastern desert. He took the flask and did not stop drinking until it was empty, to Ash's clear disappointment. Samnir closed his eyes for a moment, savouring the aftertaste, and then smacked his lips loudly. 'Ah. That was good. Woodsman, I have half a mind to forgive you . . . if there's another bottle just like that soon to be found.'

Ash bobbed his head. 'Of course. The inn's just over there, more of a barracks of some sort, but the details aren't important. This way!'

Jillan approached Hella. Already he could feel his tongue tying up. How could he explain? 'Will you forgive me?' he asked.

She smiled. 'Only if you'll be mine forever.'

He nodded, incapable of words.

'And no running off this time!' she warned, putting magic into her words.

He gulped just as she made him laugh and ended up spluttering painfully.

'Idiot,' she said with a shake of her head and threw her arms around him to kiss him, although she had to wait until he'd got over his coughing.

Watching from afar, the wolf stretched and yawned, wondering if anyone would notice a few horses going missing. The blood and commotion had given him an unusually large appetite. None seemed to see him. Surely no one would mind.

# CHAPTER 14:

# To bring the truest test

'You understand something of my kind, Jillan of the seventh realm. You know I must leave now.'

'Not until you've told us something of these other realms,' Akwar insisted. 'How do we find our way into them?'

'You should not!' Ba'zel buzzed in warning.

'Quite so, quite so,' the god of the Wandering Waters accepted pacifically. 'Yet we need to know as much as you can tell us so that we might better defend ourselves from future threats. Brothers, am I not right?'

*Beware these gods of yours,* Ba'zel spoke to Jillan's mind. *They will make themselves in the manner of the Declension if they cannot be constrained. Too much has already been revealed to them. I had not anticipated this. The Declension might still succeed in this realm through vicarious means. I will not speak to them again, Jillan, and I will depart before the powers of this realm can turn against me. I must enter the remains of the Great Temple interred before us and discover if any Watchers still survive. They will be slow to come out of the Waking Dream and will not be able to prevent their destruction at my hands. Then I will enter the Gate and close it from inside. I return to the home-realm, as we always promised the sifters I would.*

*But, Ba'zel, you cannot face the Declension alone. Seal the Gate from this side and stay here!*

*Your gods will hunt me, just as the Declension once hunted the Geas of this realm. It cannot be. I will seek to persuade the Declension that the*

*Great Voyage is a false narrative constructed to limit and control them. Remember, my father is head of the Faction of Origin. That may see me win some support. In any event, I will bring a competing principle into the very heart of the Declension, for am I not the* unstable *element?*

Jillan sighed and nodded. 'Goodbye, my friend. When will I see you again?'

*Hope that you do not, for it will betoken nothing good for your realm. Try not to think of me. Particularly try to forget my memories of the home-realm, those that you shared, for they risk allowing the Declension to open another Gate into this realm. And be well, Jillan of the seventh realm . . . my friend, and the only being in the cosmos named such.*

Ba'zel's limbs, body and then head faded like a dream. He drifted away towards where the Great Temple had stood. Akwar made to go after him.

'Stay here, Akwar,' Jillan said tiredly.

The god ignored him and waved for Gar, Sinisar and Wayfar to follow him.

'You heard Jillan. Stay here!' Hella snapped.

Her words made Akwar slip to the floor. Sinisar giggled.

The deity boiled back up. 'Wretched mortal! You dare interrupt the steps of a god?'

'Hold your peace, silver tongue!' Hella replied fiercely, her hands going to her hips. 'Look about you!'

The power of her command forced Akwar to obey. His gaze washed around the plain.

'All you gods, look! All of you! See what has happened here. Truly see it. For probably the first time in your existence, understand the full agony of human life. Do not be oblivious to the heaps of the dead and the lake of blood amid which we stand. *You* have caused this! *You* are responsible. You *will* feel some sense of shame and guilt, damn you! You have made this world an abattoir for humanity. In your arrogance, you fell and condemned us to serve as slaves to the Empire. Then you compelled thousands to lay down their lives in your name, so that their bodies could serve as steps to raise you up to a new throne, a throne made of the bones of the dead.'

Sinisar still smiled, but it was a sad and affectionate smile. Gar's heavy brows and shoulders came down as if he bore the weight of the world. Akwar's look was turbulent, but there was some reflection of what Hella had said there. And Wayfar sighed mournfully.

'We hear you, Hella of Godsend,' the god of the Warring Winds breathed. 'Yet you mortals were intent upon your freedom, and there was ever a price to be paid.'

'Well we will not pay it on your behalf any more!' Hella asserted, her message capturing and spreading through the multitude who wandered about the plain looking for loved ones, comrades and anything of value. 'Do you not hear the wounded crying out for help? If you had concern for any but yourselves, you would go to them in their time of need and offer them cure, solace or comfort. If you cannot even do that, then what use can mortals ever have for you gods? None whatsoever! We do not want you, do you hear?'

'Why you ungrateful and ignor—' Akwar began.

'Enough!' Jillan shouted. 'Do not make me regret ever having raised you back up, or so help me I will reclaim the power of the Geas to see you consigned to the place of toilet slaves for Kathuula's evil effluence. I swear I will do it!'

Sinisar smirked, Gar frowned and Wayfar's eyebrows rose, while Akwar sneered. Yet the water god held his tongue.

'I will have holy vows from you,' Jillan continued. 'None of you will compel any mortal to be your follower. You will not interfere in mortal concerns unless prayers have been offered up. Should you answer a prayer, it cannot be to the detriment of any other mortal. Agree, and you will be able to lead those who wish to follow you back to their regions. Agree, and your followers will quickly restore your temples. But know this: none will follow you if you cannot help those here who are so sorely afflicted.'

'He would make us the impotent servants of mortals! It is monstrous!' Akwar spat.

Sinisar looked up at the sky. 'I only truly came to understand freedom once I was imprisoned,' he murmured. 'It is the same for these mortals, perhaps. Perhaps it is worse, for their lives are so short. Very well, Sinisar of the Shining Path agrees.'

'Brother, no! We must be of one voice in this,' Akwar remonstrated.

Gar looked down at the ground. 'Gar only truly came to understand strength once he was made weak,' he rumbled. 'The mortals have perhaps understood better than Gar, for they are so very weak. Gar of the Unmoving Stone agrees.'

'Brother, has your brain turned to dust?'

Wayfar puffed out his cheeks. 'And I was never so lost as when none could hear my torment. Wayfar agrees.'

'It is all empty wind and bluster. I will not be blackmailed. I will not have my course dictated to me. There are none to hold us to this nonsensical vow!'

'Come, brother.' Sinisar blinked. 'You said we must be of one voice in this. Will you not add your voice to the rest?'

'Torpeth!' Jillan called to the naked holy man, who wasted no time springing in among them and treading on holy Akwar's foot. 'The gods will no longer interfere in mortal affairs. It will be your task to hold them to that.'

The old man ruminated for a second. 'I have to get back to my goats in the mountains. They will be missing me. Still, I could treat these four silly goats here as part of my herd, a part that wanders far and wide. Very well, friend Jillan, but they must promise not to go stealing any of my pine nuts. Greedy goats!'

'Promise him,' Hella instructed.

'I swear not to steal Torpeth's pine nuts,' Sinisar said in all seriousness.

'But Gar does not like pine nuts. Oh, never mind. Gar promises.'

'I promise!' Wayfar said gaily.

All looked to the simmering Akwar. 'This is ridiculous. I will not make any sort of promise about his mouldy old pine nuts. It's undignified. Brothers, be reasonable. Gah! There is no talking to you. Akwar agrees then, but do not think matters are settled between us, mortal!' The god glowered at Jillan.

'Now, don't be such a wet blanket!' Torpeth chided.

Sinisar chortled, Gar looked confused, Wayfar breathed a cleansing breath and Akwar closed his eyes in a supreme act of restraint.

As soon as the Disciples and Null Dragon had been sent out onto the plain, Elder Thraal had raced through the labyrinth of the Great Temple to the resting place of the Great Saviour. At last, the will of his schemes and plans was made manifest. It had been his genius to destabilise the regions and release the Peculiar, all so that the Geas would be revealed, and now it was. It had been his genius to wage war on the south using the eastern army and to send the Disciples from the Great Temple, all so that the bane would be forced to seek the power of the Geas as a means of defence. It had been his genius that had revealed the bane's sacred heart and brought it to the Great Temple in order to force the convergence. In the singularity of the convergence, he, Elder Thraal, had brought about the revelation of the Geas and the inevitable release of the Null Dragon. The will was his, the events of this realm were determined by him, and the reward of its reality would now be his, for the Null Dragon no longer prevented his path to ascendancy.

Elder Thraal came to the unguarded door of the Great Saviour's tomb and passed straight through it, the web of wards and triggers that had been in place all around it in tatters now that the central power of the Null Dragon had been removed. Without hesitation he moved through the low vault, ignoring the bright weapons of sun-metal and phials of magically imbued blood that the Great Saviour would conceivably need upon waking. There was no time to lose, for the formidable being of the Eldest's line would already have sensed the intrusion and be stirring himself.

Elder Thraal flipped the huge lid off the stone sarcophagus just as the orbs of the Great Saviour's eyes were beginning to open. The being was fighting free of its debilitating torpor. Elder Thraal bared his stone fangs and sank them deep into his enemy's skull. His claws raked down the sides of the giant head, found purchase in the joins between bony plates and tore them open with his long-stored and carefully built strength. The Great Saviour's form flickered as he tried to shift his substance, but Elder Thraal was already gulping down the sweet innards that he'd exposed and Drawing the essence of the Eldest's line into himself. Even before he'd come to this miserable and lowly realm, Elder Thraal had been planning for this moment. As he had willed it, so it had come about.

Even the Eldest would see that the Great Saviour had been unworthy. The Great Saviour's own weakness had brought about its own demise. Elder Thraal ascended by right. Elder Thraal was now the will entire of the Declension in this realm. He was the one who would lead his kind on the Great Voyage. The Geas of the seventh realm was revealed, and so surely would the path to the eighth realm also be there for the Declension's taking. Great Thraal would lead the Declension as it moved inexorably across the entire cosmos, claiming all as theirs. As he willed it, so it would come about. It was the inevitable consequence of the convergence within this realm, the convergence that his supreme will had brought about.

Through the organising intellects fighting out on the plain, Great Thraal watched the lesser beings uniting to challenge the Great Temple. Who would have thought they had it in them? Incredibly, D'Jarn had been laid low, and his slayer held off D'Shaa, D'Syr and D'Zel even though they moved in concert. And one of the lesser beings thwarted the Null Dragon single-handedly! Of course, the beast had been weakened by the undoing of the Great Saviour, and the traitorous *unstable* element aided the lesser beings, so the outcome was clear.

The all-seeing Great Thraal knew that the Great Temple would fall and so he moved deep into the earth, down and down. The Great Temple was of no consequence. It did not even matter if the rest of his kind in this realm failed to survive. All would still converge and happen as Great Thraal willed it. It was inescapable and inevitable.

He reached the wide seam of sun-metal he had discovered when first coming to this realm, and settled himself beneath it. None would be able to sense or find him as he rested. Here he would wait in safety as the convergence he had started cascaded through this realm into the other realms and even back into the home-realm. The entire Declension would soon converge with the seventh realm, and Great Thraal would be the sole means of that convergence, for he would be able to open the Gate when the inevitable moment arrived. Then the Declension would move on to the rest of the cosmos, and Great Thraal would be the one to lead and define all things.

Once the gods had gone among the people to bring them hope and reassurance, Captain Skathis and General Thormodius approached Jillan and Hella. A man a full head shorter and easily half as wide as the burly soldiers followed in their wake.

'Father!' Hella cried, throwing herself into Jacob's embrace.

Jillan nodded his thanks to the two Heroes.

'Praxis had him held prisoner to be sure of Hella's compliance,' Captain Skathis said in a stilted fashion.

Jillan realised the two men were watching him with apprehension. Clearly, they wondered what would become of them now that the Saviours and Saints no longer ruled. Did they expect him to pass some sort of judgement on them? It wasn't his place to do so, was it? And he no longer had the magic with which to punish them even if he'd wanted to. He frowned, unsure what they wanted of him. If Samnir hadn't sneaked off with Ash somewhere then the commander of Godsend could have dealt with them. 'What of the other Godsenders?' he finally asked, sounding more demanding than he'd intended.

Captain Skathis stood straighter, immediately adopting the role of an officer reporting to his superior. 'Some few hundred survive, holy—' He choked off, and for the first time that Jillan had ever seen looked repentant. His scars were stretched white, while the old burns on one half of his face mottled red.

'You were going to call me *holy one*, weren't you? I am no Saint, Skathis. None of us are. We all do the best we can. That's all. That's why I always fought Praxis when he was a Minister, and that's why you killed him in the end.'

'Yes,' the soldier whispered.

'How is it you managed to surprise him? I thought the Saint always knew the minds of the People.'

The man shrugged uncomfortably. 'It was as if it wasn't me doing all those terrible things. I was trapped inside myself, watching it all happen. I was a monster who knew he was a monster. I repeated it to myself over and over through all the years. Somehow it let me keep a sense of myself that neither Azual nor Praxis could touch. It kept me sane, somehow, and finally allowed me to act. Yet it is no excuse. I will willingly submit myself to any punishment for my crimes. If you decide I should be executed—'

'No!' Jillan hastily interrupted. 'Neither of you can be held responsible for all the things that you did. You had no control of your own lives. Besides, a far worse punishment than death for you will be to *live* with the knowledge of the things you were forced to do. I could never add to such punishment. So do not speak thus, Captain. Instead, tell me of the Godsenders.'

Captain Skathis dared a small smile. 'A few hundred of them. They wait there, you see? They stand separately from the other southerners, but then perhaps they always did. Wayfar will lead the pag— mountain people and the other southerners home, but the Godsenders wait for *you* to lead them, Jillan.'

A terrible sense of premonition crept over Jillan. Were he to return to Godsend, things would revert to how they'd always been. The People would take up their lives precisely where they'd left off. Wayfar would occupy the temple in Hyvan's Cross instead of Azual, but there would still be a powerful being at the heart of the region defining its lives. Only Godsend would resist that definition. Strife would eventually follow. The same pattern played out again and again. Would it never end? Was there no escape? 'If it must be me to lead them, then they will follow me into the eastern desert. There is a beautiful place there that I mean to share with Hella and any others who are willing to make the journey.'

'Haven, Jillan?' Hella asked in wonder.

He nodded. 'Will you go with me?'

'What? Give up my tally book and counting all the boxes stacked in Godsend's musty old warehouse? Give up all that for you? In a trice and forever! Father, you will come with us, won't you?'

Jacob smiled gently. 'I could never deny you anything, my sweetest daughter, especially when you use the magical tones you inherited from your mother.'

General Thormodius gave a short bow. 'Then the eastern People, the army of the east and holy Sinisar and his lieutenants will accompany the Godsenders along the way.'

'And I should give you this before we part,' Captain Skathis said solemnly, unstrapping a scabbard from behind him. 'It is the rune blade we wrested from you in Godsend.'

Hella accepted the sword and pulled a length of it free. Although its inlaid patterns of sun-metal lit her face and hair with an otherworldly glow, her expression remained clouded. 'I will take it with me, for it is all I have left of dear Thomas. Yet I hope I will never have cause to use it again.' She looked to Captain Skathis and General Thormodius. 'We will not need soldiers in our future, will we? You speak of the eastern army, General, but the army has nothing to fight for any more, does it? Will it not simply disband?'

The General's eyes misted. 'Milady, it is my most fervent hope that we will never have need of an army again. I am so tired. I want to remove my armour, but it has become fused to my skin with all the years of its wearing. I want to lay down my weapon, but it has grown to be a part of my arm with all the years of its carrying. Any in the army who remembers their home and wishes to leave will do so with my blessing. Yet, for many, soldiering is all they know. Were I to abandon them now, so that they must find their own way in the world, they would soon form into desperate bandit groups, with none left to gainsay them. It is the way of men, it shames me to say, milady.'

Captain Skathis spoke in agreement. 'Though it grieves me, men will still commit crimes. The regions will continue to need their Heroes, to see recalcitrants brought to justice and the innocent protected. I know that already Chief Trader John of Saviours' Paradise will be seeking to gain unfair advantage in the south. For a while there will be shortages, and he will be looking to organise monopolies for the Guild of Traders, so that profits are maximised no matter what the cost in terms of the People's suffering. By the time we return, looters will have ransacked the richer properties. The properties of the dead will have been entirely appropriated by the unscrupulous, disinheriting those with more legitimate claim. And that is just for starters, milady.'

'He speaks truly, daughter,' Jacob confirmed.

'Ye gods,' Hella breathed, causing Akwar, Sinisar, Gar and Wayfar to twitch wherever they were on the plain. 'Jillan, perhaps it was not all the Saviours. Much of it we do to ourselves. It is a sort of madness or sickness.'

'Do not be too hard on them, milady,' Captain Skathis countered. 'They've simply picked up a few bad habits along the way. For some of them, it was probably the only way to survive at one time. I should know, for I have done many things of which I am not proud. It is enough to say that we Heroes will be needed for a while longer, until the People have learned that they need not behave as they did previously. Give them time, milady.'

'Besides, there's no need of Heroes in Haven, not with you around to lay down the law, eh, Hella?' Jillan grinned.

Jacob winced and shook his head. Captain Skathis and General Thormodius prudently stepped away.

Hella rounded on Jillan. 'What do you mean by that? Don't go thinking I've completely forgiven you yet, Jillan Hunterson! Just you wait till I get you alone.'

'Er . . . I only meant you were good at telling everybody what to do.'

Jacob winced again, shaking his head even more frantically.

'What did you say?' Hella asked dangerously.

'No, I mean using your magic to order people about. You know how you do. It's a good thing. Really! Even the gods jump when you tell them to jump. I wasn't calling you a bossyboots or anything.'

'You're making it worse. Just keep quiet!' Jacob squeaked.

'*Bossyboots?*'

The ground shook and Freda came up between them. 'Freda! Thank goodness! How are you? Where have you been? We're returning to Haven. You coming along?'

The woman of diamond became suffused with a pink blush. 'Sinisar has asked me to stay with him in his temple, friend Jillan.'

'Really? And you said yes? You're not going with Gar?'

Freda nodded and shook her head at the same time, shining with joy. 'My brother Freom was not happy to hear I would go east, but he will go with Gar and has promised to see the people freed from the mines in the north.'

Hella beamed. 'I'm so happy for you, Freda. You will be near us then. That's wonderful! And Sinisar is so colourful . . . and hot!'

Freda and Hella giggled. Jillan suddenly felt awkward, and was relieved when Hella shooed him and her father away so that she could talk privately with the woman of diamond.

'Maybe we should go and rescue Samnir from whatever inn Ash has dragged him into. You and I can have a little chat, Jillan.'

'Yes, that might be a good idea,' Jillan conceded. 'I must talk to Aspin Longstep first though.'

Jillan approached his friend, who was working with his warriors to shroud their dead. The battle had seen the mountain people pay a heavy price indeed.

Aspin looked up and gave a wan smile of greeting. 'Holy Wayfar said he will help us carry all the bodies home so that they can be properly mourned by their loved ones before finally being laid to rest.'

'Aspin, I don't have the proper words. I am so sorry about your father. He was a brave and noble warrior.'

'Yes. Yes, he was.'

'Like all of your people.'

'Yes.'

'You know, they do not need to remain in the mountains any more. It must be a hard life for them there. The people of Godsend will be heading for Haven now. Their good friends the mountain people are more than welcome to join them.'

'Perhaps one day. The mountains are our home, though. The warriors that fell here will want to see their spirits remembered and released in the mountains. The mountains are sacred to us and holy Wayfar. They are a part of us. I always thought of my father as being like the mountains. Noble, unassailable, immovable, terrible and sometimes . . . sometimes cold. Yet I would not have had him any other way. Without his fortitude, we could never have triumphed in Godsend or here. It was prophesied he would lead our people to their doom, and that lay heavily upon him, but he ultimately defeated the prophecy to give us life, didn't he? Do you know any other who could defeat prophecy with their own determination?'

'No, my friend. Only the rarest of individuals among your people could do so much to defeat the Empire and its Saviours.'

'And there's another reason Aspin Longstep hurries back to his mountains, isn't there, eh?' Torpeth interrupted impishly. 'That reason has raven-black hair, skin of snow and leaf-green eyes, does she not? Have you not told your friend Jillan of Veena, Chief Aspin?'

'I've told you not to call me that.' Aspin frowned at the holy man, although it was clear the warrior knew he was wasting his words.

'Veena?' Jillan asked with a curious grin.

Aspin nodded, unable to suppress a sheepish grin of his own. 'I hope you will be able to meet her one day. Torpeth is happy for me only because he was worried I would steal the affections of the headwoman away from him.'

'None is worthy of her!' Torpeth warned. 'Do not dare think otherwise!'

'What's this headwoman like?' Jillan asked.

'Tell him nothing, silly ox! He will be consumed with envy and lust.'

'Well, she has eyes the colour of the sky. Hers is the beauty of age, wisdom and the deepest love for our people.'

'Chief Aspin, I beg you, not another word!' Torpeth was frantic, hopping from foot to foot. 'You know what these lowlanders are like. They have always been jealous of our people. They have always sought to steal from us!'

'I think Hella would understand if she was thrown over for such a one,' Jillan adjudged.

'Argh! Good Jillan, remember you are *friend* to the mountain people, not enemy!' There were tears in the old man's eyes.

Jillan relented at last. 'Very well, Torpeth, but I only do this because of the sacrifices already made by your people. In return, you will obey Aspin's instructions better than before, even if he commands you to bathe every now and then and put some clothes on.'

'I will try, good Jillan, I will try.'

'Very well. As to what we lowlanders have stolen from you, perhaps it would be right for your people to use Godsend from time to time, now that it is empty. It could be a place where you trade with invited lowlanders, an occasional site for a market.'

'I will put it to our people,' Aspin replied thoughtfully. 'Perhaps there can be a true peace between the mountain people and the low-landers.'

'I hope so. Just have him bathed and in clothes on market days, or he'll scare all the lowlanders away.'

Izat made her way up through the subterranean passages and galleries that led into her palace. She crossed forgotten courtyards, forced open rusted gates, pushed through overgrown secret gardens and crept through broken and crumbling walls. She was not far from her rooms now and the item that would restore her power.

The Saint congratulated herself on having left the battlefield precisely when she had. It had been a relatively simple matter of taking off her mask of sun-metal, so that none could easily pick her out in the throng, and commanding her personal guard to spirit her away.

She still could not believe that the Empire had lost. It was inconceivable. To think that she'd had the boy in her clutches and been so close to successfully seducing him. So close! If it hadn't been for the untimely entrance of the blunt and clumsy instrument that was the Disciple, she would have glamoured the boy and made him her slave, and thus a slave to the Empire. The Saviours only had themselves to blame.

She did not mourn the Empire's passing. How could she? The Disciple had taken her face and freedom from her, and ultimately allowed the boy to take the power and love of her People from her. Fortunately, Izat was a woman who was not easily inconvenienced or deterred from her own fulfilment. Was she not the eldest and most knowing of the holy Saints? Was she not a queen to the drooling and simpering People, who were so very ordinary? The last thing she was was a common fool. After the uncourtly Disciple had smashed the phial of blood into her mouth, taken her beau and left the palace, she'd wiped some of the holy blood from her mouth and stored it away, anticipating that it might one day come to serve her needs. And in her prescient wisdom, she was proven right. Her being was validated, divinely validated.

Now she would willingly swallow the Saviours' gift, for it would give her the renewed power she needed to Draw the People back to her, without there being any Saviours left to make rude demands of her in turn. She would restore herself, rebuild the kingdom and all would be even more glorious than it had been before. She would be the queen of heaven.

'Well, well, well,' a voice mocked her. 'Here we are again, as I promised you we would be.'

Her heart in her throat, Saint Izat spun to face the figure dressed in motley who crouched atop an ivy-thick pedestal. 'No!'

The Peculiar tutted. 'I gave you your chance, did I not, beloved? I believe I described to you quite clearly what would happen if you sought to take my freedom from me.'

'Cassanon, my love. I—'

'No protestations, my dear. I will not be swayed. Were I to be swayed, I would be made a liar and lackwill. You would not want to add such insult to my injury, now would you? I have my reputation to think of, you know. I am a god, after all. So let us pretend you were not about to beg, promise, cajole, blackmail, seduce and threaten me. Such behaviours are quite unseemly in any case, don't you agree, my dear?'

Izat desperately licked at her ruined lips. 'Cassanon, I will be your follower. I will do anything you command. Anything! I have powers. They are yours to do with as you see fit.'

The Peculiar smiled. 'Hush, dear Izat, hush. That is enough. Do you not know what happens to all my followers? They die, dear Izat, they die. That is what you will now do, for it is the end, dear Izat, it is most definitely the end.'

'But I was so close!' She screamed until the Peculiar's hands choked her off and strangled her.

'Is it real, Jillan?' Hella murmured from where she lay in the crook of his arm. 'Can such a beautiful and peaceful place truly exist?'

They rested in one of Haven's warm meadows. Floss munched contentedly on grass, and the wolf snoozed not far away. There was the drone of bees and the slightest of breezes to prevent the day's heat from becoming uncomfortable.

'For a long time I did not believe this moment and place could ever exist. I haven't told you, have I? Freda told me that Miserath took your form and it was him I saw kissing Haal outside Godsend all that time ago.'

She tilted her head to look up at him. 'So that's why you left. Silly! You should have known I wouldn't do that to you . . . or Haal. Poor Haal. He died defending the walls of Godsend. He asked me to tell you he was sorry.'

'Haal had nothing to be sorry for. Not him, not you, not me, none of us. If I could bring Praxis back, I would do it just so that we could all be properly revenged on him!'

She put her finger to his lips. 'Do not spoil this moment with talk of him, dearest Jillan. Let us have this time in the sun, free of all clouds and dark resentment.'

'You're right. I'm sorry.' He sighed. 'I pray this moment will last forever.'

'They will find us eventually, you know. Ash has everyone organised building his inn. *It wouldn't be paradise without one*, he keeps telling me. I've never seen him so industrious. He already has my father negotiating with desert tribes for ales or whatever to stock the inn, only the tribes don't seem to have any. All they've got is some fermented goat's milk concoction, and that reeks! They're reluctant to part with it too, because they only imbibe it on ceremonial occasions. They seem to think drinking alcohol under the desert sun is not a good idea, no matter Ash's extravagant claims otherwise and his enthusiastic offers to prove them wrong. Ash is becoming so desperate that he's threatening to join the General's army just so that he can get a regular ration of rum. Samnir has said that he can't in all conscience let a reprobate like Ash become a Hero. It would be some sort of stain on Samnir's personal honour or something.' Hella giggled. 'Ash said that if Samnir had any sort of honour then Samnir would have come to an under-standing with the General already, in order to help meet the needs of Haven's inn and people. Well, Samnir wasn't going to have anyone casting doubt on his honour, was he? He threw Ash in a pond and told him to drink that.'

Jillan cried with laughter. He laughed so hard it hurt, and yet he never wanted the pain to stop. Hella held him down and kissed him. He realised he'd been wrong. It was this that he never wanted to stop.

All had transpired as she had intended. After millennia of searching, the Geas of the seventh realm had been revealed. Through the eyes of Ba'zel, her offspring, she had seen the precise location of Haven. Was there not a confirming irony in the fact that it had been the bane himself who had taken Ba'zel there?

As much as the Eldest had determined the events in the seventh realm, and seen them play out as per her wishes, far more had been revealed than even she had expected. Some sort of *nether realm* could be accessed from the seventh realm! Was there an equivalent for each of the realms that the Declension had already conquered? Or for the home-realm itself? What was the nature of this nether realm? What power defined it? It bore further investigation, as did the desert giants of the seventh realm, whom Ba'zel suspected would know something of the eighth realm. And she was fascinated by the slayer who had brought down the organising intellects.

It brought her a perfect sense of satisfaction. All would be revealed to her, for the seventh realm was now entirely at the Declension's mercy.

Ba'zel was returning, and would soon be the weapon she needed to see all fall before her will. Amazing that the simple delusion that he was *unstable* had made so much of him and done so much to aid the cause of the Declension's Great Voyage. Another confirming irony that was the imprint of her will upon the cosmos. And Thraal had acted precisely as she'd instructed his simple and unconscious mind. Nothing could now stop the Declension's progress.

'Faal, do you hear me?' the Eldest called through the home-realm.

*I hear you, eternal one. Command me.*

'Hasten to the Gate, for your son returns and you must welcome him. The Declension entire will praise him, for he has delivered to us the Geas of each of five known realms. He will be known throughout the cosmos as Ba'zel the Destroyer, and he will be the leading Virtue of the Declension.'

*As is your will, most holy.*

Here ends the second of three
*Chronicles of a Cosmic Warlord*

Jillan's struggle continues in the third chronicle:

## TITHE OF THE SAVIOURS